CRIMINAL
RECORDS

Also edited by Otto Penzler

Murder for Love

Murder for Revenge

CRIMINAL RECORDS

edited by Otto Penzler

ORION

First published in Great Britain in 2000 by
Orion
An imprint of Orion Books Ltd
Orion House, 5 Upper St Martin's Lane,
London WC2H 9EA

A CIP catalogue record for this book is available
from the British Library

Typeset in Great Britain by Selwood Systems Ltd, Midsomer Norton

Printed and bound by Butler & Tanner Ltd, Frome and London

Contents

Introduction

The novella is a strangely appealing literary hybrid. It is not as long and textured as a novel, of course, and doesn't have room for complex sub-plots or a large cast of characters. It cannot waste pages, or even paragraphs, on inessential musings that do not directly pertain to the situation in hand.

But the novella is longer than a short story, allowing it enough space to develop characters with far greater depth than is possible in the very short form. And being so much longer than a short story, it can unfold a richer plot that does not need to be quite as linear as its shorter cousin.

Some of the favourite works of frequently more verbose authors are novellas: *The Turn of the Screw* by the normally long-winded Henry James is one of his most widely read works. *The Red Pony* and *The Pearl* by John Steinbeck linger in the memory longer than some of his more ambitious books. And Ernest Hemingway moved on to the fast track for a Nobel Prize for Literature after the publication of his perfect gem, *The Old Man and the Sea*.

The difficulty with the novella nowadays is that there is little opportunity for them to be published. Magazines will seldom publish a piece of fiction of such great length, as *Life*, for example, did with *The Old Man and the Sea*. Crime writers too have an especially difficult task in producing a work of novella length and finding a publisher for it. Too short for a book, too long for a magazine, the obvious solution is simply not to write them.

Orion, however, have commissioned some of the finest crime writers of our time to write original works in this unusual length for the massive omnibus you hold in your hands. Many of these authors have admitted it was a daunting task, as they found themselves working in a length which was entirely new to them. There were stops and starts for some, as they tried to expand a short story into 15,000 words, learning that it couldn't be done without making it seem like so much padded fluff. These were chucked and begun anew with a re-thought storyline.

Other writers tried to condense a novel idea into merely 15,000 words, learning that it couldn't be done without making it seem like a truncated concept, written in telegraphic prose, without adequate character development, as they tried to squeeze too much into the limited number of pages. These, too, were tossed away and re-thought.

Now, each of these stories is the right length for what it is. The tales were begun, then they were told, and when they were finished being told, the writer stopped, as it should be for all good prose. In small bites, though large enough to be satisfying, here are samples of such wonderful authors as Ed McBain, whose story unfolds a bit at a time, like the taking apart of an artichoke; H. R. F. Keating, whose Ganesh Ghote solves one of his most intriguing mysteries in an unusual setting; Susan Moody, whose meticulously plotted crime has a stunning surprise ending, as does Peter Lovesey's edge-of-the seat thriller; S. J. Rozan, who provides a look at a lifestyle that is unknown to most of us, wrapped around a lovely bit of detective work; and Peter Straub, whose poetic suspense story evokes a time and place and a jazz musician that will haunt the memory for a long time to come.

Come to the buffet table and indulge yourself with several old favourites, and try the new flavours as well. This isn't a meal – it's a banquet.

Otto Penzler

THE LOST BOY

Robert Barnard

The young man in jeans and chunky pullover walked out of the sportswear shop into the broad upper walk of the shopping precinct, his little boy riding high on his shoulders.

'Where to now, Captain?' he asked. 'What's the menu – Coke, ice cream or lemonade?'

The child's eyes sparkled, but he thought long and seriously, and when at last he said 'Lemonade, Daddy', the man wondered whether he said it because it was the last option mentioned. Often his apparent pondering was really the sign of his general thoughtfulness.

'OK, well, we'll go to the ice-cream stall downstairs, shall we? They have drinks as well so you can make up your mind finally when you get there.'

'Yes!' said the little boy enthusiastically.

They made an attractive sight as they took the escalator down to the lower floor of the precinct, the little boy glorying in his wondrous elevation above really grown-up people, crowing down on them and drawing their attention. The man was about twenty-five, casual altogether, but his jeans were clean and above the neck of the pullover could be seen the bright check of his shirt. The face would not have attracted a second look, but when it did the passer-by would have noted light brown hair cut short around a long, thoughtful face.

'Here we are, Captain,' he said as they arrived at the ice-cream stall on the ground level. 'Now take a good look and tell me what it is you'd like.'

'What a lovely little boy,' said a middle-aged woman, joining the queue behind them.

'Malcolm?' responded the man softly, his hand ruffling the hair of the boy, now on the ground and staring through the side glass of the stall. 'He's a cracker. But we don't tell him.'

They looked at him. He was oblivious to their conversation, single-mindedly surveying the range of desirables on offer.

'Take your time, Captain,' the man said.

'He's got a good father, that's for sure,' said the woman, half in love with the man's youth and healthy look. 'These days men pretend they're shouldering half the burden, but really they leave most of it to the mother, as they always did.'

'He's everything to me,' said the young man simply. 'He's what makes life worth living. We'll be phoning his mother in a while, to tell her we're both all right.'

'Oh – don't you come from here?'

'No, we're not from these parts.'

'I want the red one,' said the little boy, pointing to a bright pink bowl of ice cream.

'The red one, right. I think that's cherry, not strawberry.'

'Sherry. I want the sherry one.'

So the cherry one it was. The man paid for a double scoop of ice cream, refused one for himself, and when he'd paid over the money he nodded to the woman and led the boy by the left hand out of St James's Mall and into early spring

3

sunlight. The boy walked confidently, one hand in his father's while the other held the cornet which he was licking enthusiastically.

'Don't they make a lovely picture?' said the middle-aged woman wistfully to the girl behind the counter of the stall. The girl looked as if she had seen enough children in her job to last her a lifetime.

'Now then, Captain,' said the man, his little boy's hand still warmly in his as they waited on the pavement, then crossed the Headrow and started down towards Boar Lane, 'we'll go to the station and phone your mother to tell her we're all right, and then we'll go to the car and find a bed for the night.'

Malcolm nodded wisely, and went on licking his ice cream with intense concentration. It lasted him most of the way to Boar Lane, and when it was done he needed to have his fingers and chin wiped with a handkerchief.

'Want to ride on my shoulders again?'

'*Yes!*' It was said with the intensity Malcolm reserved for everything he felt most deeply or enthusiastically about. The man took him under the armpits and swung him up. They crossed Boar Lane towards the Yates Wine Bar, then took the side road to the station.

'Now then, Malcolm,' the man said, 'I think the telephones are through there near the ticket office.'

The boy was taking in the large square concourse and the train departure board, his eyes wide. After a second he nodded. They went through to the booking hall, the man bending his knees to get through the door, the child on his shoulders crowing triumphantly. They found a telephone, and the man brought Malcolm down from his point of vantage to sit in the crook of his arm beside the telephone.

'Now, we put some money in ... That's it. Let's see – 01325. Then 274658 ... Here we are. It's ringing. Now then, Captain, your call to Mummy.'

The phone had been picked up the other end.

'Hello, 274658.' The voice sounded strained.

'Mummy!'

'Malcolm! Where are you? What—?'

But already the man's strong forefinger had come down on the telephone's cradle.

'There we are, Captain. Mustn't take up too much of Mummy's time.'

'I'm getting desperate,' said Selena Randall.

Her solicitor, Derek Mitcham, looked at her hands, tugging and tearing at a tiny handkerchief, and could only agree. He had found, though, with desperate clients that the best thing to do was to keep the tone low and level.

'Everyone's doing everything they can,' he said.

The woman's voice rose dangerously. 'Are they? *Are* they? It doesn't look like that to me, I can tell you. The police, for example. What are they doing, actually *doing*? I can't see that they're doing anything.'

'You can be quite sure that police forces all over the country have a description of your husband, and of Malcolm. They'll all be on the lookout for them.'

In this case the measured tone did not seem to be working.

'But what about publicity? If there was a hue and cry, a proper campaign with publicity in the media, everyone in the country would be looking for them. Carol Parker is everywhere, appealing to people who see her little boy and his father – in all the tabloids, and on daytime television too. I saw the picture of the little boy, the fair hair and the confident smile, and I want to hold him in my arms – he so reminds me of Malcolm, and I feel so *mad*. Why isn't my little boy getting that sort of coverage?'

Mr Mitcham sighed. He knew Mrs Randall was not avid for publicity, only anxious to do everything needed to get her son back. But she must give people who knew her less well a very poor impression, and though he had tried to get the message across to her, this still came up at every meeting they had. He tried again.

'Mrs Parker's husband is German, and he has a history of mental instability. The police are afraid he may take the little boy out of the country, or even harm him wittingly or unwittingly. You must see that your husband is a quite different matter. Children are taken quite frequently by the parent who does not have custody. Usually there is no question of them being in any danger.'

He spoke quietly and distinctly, and now it seemed to work. Selena nodded, taking in, at least for the moment, his argument.

'Oh, I know Dick wouldn't harm Malcolm. He loves him to bits ... But the fact that he's English doesn't mean he won't take him out of the country.'

'You can be sure the police at ports and airports will be especially on the alert.'

'These days you can drive through the channel tunnel and no one gives you a second glance.'

'That's not true, Mrs Randall.'

She looked down at the ruin of her handkerchief.

'I don't think anybody cares. They just think, "The little boy is bound to be all right," and don't give it another thought.'

'Well, that is something that must be a comfort for you.'

'But what about me? I had custody of him, and I haven't seen him for nearly ten weeks.' Her eyes filled with tears and she began dabbing them with the ragged bits of hankie. 'Do you know what I fear? I *am* afraid he'll forget me, as a young child like Malcolm is bound to do quite soon. But most of all I'm afraid I'll forget him. What he sounds like, how he laughs, what it feels like to touch him, have him in my arms.' She looked up at Mr Mitcham, wild-eyed. 'I'm afraid if I get him back he'll be a stranger.'

'I'm sure you won't forget a thing about him. No mother would.'

'Don't be so bloody sentimental! How would you know? ... Sorry.' She resumed tugging at the handkerchief. 'You said everyone would be on the lookout for Dick and Malcolm, but what is there to be on the lookout *for*? Dick is nice enough looking, but there's nothing to distinguish him from thousands of other quite nice-looking young men. Hair colour – that's about the only thing to mark him out: light brown, so that rules out people with black or blond hair. Not much, is it? There's still less with Malcolm.'

'They have a photograph.'

'I wish it was a better photograph ...' She returned obsessively to her theme. 'Dick has quite an arrogant look sometimes. Raises his chin and looks out at the world as if he thinks he's a lot better than other people. I don't suppose ...? No. It's just impression, isn't it, not fact? It's fact you need. Little Anton Parker has a mole on his hip. Malcolm has nothing. She can just pull his pants down and check, whereas I'll have nothing, if I ever see him again. Can you believe it? *Nothing* to distinguish him from thousands and thousands of other boys of his age ... Sometimes I think it's hopeless. Sometimes I think I might just as well give up.'

'I know you're not serious about that, Mrs Randall.'

'No ... It's just a mood. I'll never give up.'

'Nor should you.'

'I sometimes wonder whether Dick won't come back of his own accord and we can all three be together like we used to be.'

'I don't think you should bank on that. But there is going to come a crunch point, and it might come soon. He can't go on running for ever. Where did he ring you from?'

'From Leeds. I can't believe Dick would be so cruel. Just one word ...'

'The last sighting we had of them that was pretty firm was North Wales. Eventually he's going to run out of money.'

There was a pause. Then Mr Mitcham saw Selena Randall's shoulders stiffen as she made a decision.

'I don't think he will.'

'Why not? What do you mean?' He saw the shoulders slacken slightly and he said urgently, 'Tell me.'

Then it all came out. When she had told her tale he asked her, already knowing the answer, 'Have you told the police this?'

'No. I thought it might get Dick into trouble.'

This time Mr Mitcham's sigh was audible. Sometimes he despaired of fathoming the mysteries of people's hearts.

At the cash desk of the Merry Cook, Dick Randall asked if they had a room vacant. The chain of roadside eateries had at some of their establishments a few overnight rooms – inexpensive, simple, anonymous. It was their anonymity that appealed, because it seemed to spread to the rooms' users. He had a name thought up if he had been asked for one: Tony Wilmslow. He enjoyed thinking up names while he was driving, and sometimes thought he could people a whole novel with the characters he'd invented – though, of course, it would be an all-male novel, and the idea of that didn't appeal to him. The girl behind the counter nodded, rang up £32.50 on the till, and handed over a key when he paid in cash. Dick's credit card had been unused since he had snatched Malcolm from the front garden of the house he had once shared with his wife.

'Number three,' said the girl, then turned her eyes to the next customer in the line, totting up the price of the plates and polystyrene cup on her tray.

I'm not even thought worthy of a second glance, thought Dick wryly, but with underlying satisfaction. He went out to the car where Malcolm was still strapped in, and parked it outside number three.

'Home for the night,' he said. 'Come along, Captain.'

They'd eaten at midday, so they had no use of the cheap and cheerful meals at the Merry Cook. Dick took from the back seat a slice of cold pizza in a plastic bag, something left over from Malcolm's lunch, and a carton of milk. For himself he had bought a sandwich. He never ate much when he had something on, though he was one of those people who burned up calories and never was other than slim. Still, eating made him *feel* bulkier.

They ate companionably on the bed, then played the cat's cradle game Dick had himself always loved when a child and had taught his son. Malcolm could undress himself for bed, and loved to do it, his face always rapt with concentration. Dick sat him on the lavatory, then chose one of the five or six stories Malcolm always insisted on when he was being read to sleep.

'Remember,' Dick said, as he always did, 'if you wake in the night and I'm not here, I won't be far away, and I'll soon be back. Just turn over and go to sleep again.'

Malcolm nodded, and lay there waiting for Postman Pat. Dick wished he could wean him on a wider choice of stories, but thought that familiarity was settling to a child's mind at a time when so much of what he was experiencing was unfamiliar. After a page or so the little head nodded. Dick turned off the light, then lay on the bed beside him, fully clothed.

Dick had marked out the bungalow as they'd driven through the March darkness on the approaches to the Merry Cook. Old, substantial, without alarm, and with token lights, obviously switched on by a neighbour. At shortly before midnight, Malcolm sleeping soundly, Dick got carefully off the bed, took the gloves and torch from the little bedside table where he'd left them, collected his old canvas bag from the spindly armchair, and then slipped out of the motel room.

There was no need to take the car. Dick was only interested in portable property. He had a nose for houses inhabited by the sort of people who would have accumulated it. He had a wonderful sense, too, of street geography, acquired during his teenage years: he always knew the best approach to a place and, still better, the whole range of possible escape routes. There was no point in subtlety in the approach to number 41 Sheepscar Road, but as he padded along he renewed in the darkness the possible ways of making a quick exit from the area. The lights in the bungalow had been switched off by the obliging neighbour. All the adjacent house lights were off. Once inside the garden he waited in the darkness at the side of the house to make sure he had not been heard or observed. When no lights went on or sounds were heard he let himself in through the front door with the ease of practice. Where you could use a credit card to do it you knew you were dealing with very unwordly owners.

Which everything in the house pointed to. The jewel box was by the dressing-room table in the main bedroom, and yielded modest to good pickings. The inevitable stash of notes under the mattress amounted, his experienced grasp of the bundle told him, to something in the region of two hundred pounds. The sideboard drawer revealed silver cutlery of good quality and an antique candle-snuffer which he suspected was something special. All went into the overnight bag after a torchlight inspection, as did an art deco vase in the centre of the dining table. He was out of the house in ten minutes. The rooms he left were to all intents and purposes so similar to their state when he'd come in that the neighbour would probably not notice that there had been an intruder.

He was back in the little bedroom with Malcolm half an hour after he had left him. As he undressed the boy stirred in his sleep. Dick got in beside him and cuddled him close. Their future seemed assured for the next week or so.

Inspector Purley looked at Selena Randall with a mixture of sympathy and exasperation. He had always had the feeling that she was holding out on him, either deliberately or unconsciously. In fact, he'd pressed her on this in previous talks they'd had, and she had denied it, but in a way that never quite did away with his suspicion. Now it was going to come out.

'You say there's something about your husband that you've been keeping from us?' he said.

He flustered her further.

'Well, not keeping from you. Just not telling you because I didn't think it was relevant. And I didn't want to hurt Dick, because I always thought – or hoped, anyway – that one day he'd come back and everything would be as it used to be. That's what I really wanted . . . You see, this could really harm him . . .'

'Yes. Go on.'

'He . . . When I met him, six years ago, he was an accomplished thief. A house burglar.'

Inspector Purley bit back any annoyance.

'But he's got no record. We checked.'

'No. I said he was very accomplished. He was never caught. You do see why I didn't tell you, don't you? I mean, if he was to be caught with Malcolm, it wouldn't be just the abduction, would it?'

She looked at him, tearfully appealing. Inspector Purley sighed. The story had changed in seconds from not thinking it relevant to not wanting to land her husband with an even longer prison sentence than he'd get anyway.

'Do you know, Mrs Randall, I think it's time you made up your mind.'

'I don't understand you.'

'You really have to sort out your priorities. Is your first priority getting your little boy back?'

'*Yes*. Of course it is.'

'Then you've got to tell us everything that might be relevant to finding him and your husband. Everything.'

'Yes . . . It's just that I've never felt bitter towards Dick. I loved him when I married him, and I still love him. I can't believe he'd be so cruel as to let me hear Malcolm's voice on the phone and then cut us off after only a single word. It's like he's become another person.'

Inspector Purley thought that might be because he was afraid Malcolm would let slip something that could be of use to the police, but he was not in the business of trying to make her think more kindly of her husband. That was the whole problem.

'That's really cruel,' he agreed. 'Now, about these burglaries – what kind of detail can you give me about them? Your husband isn't on our computer, but the burglaries will be.'

She looked at him, wide-eyed.

'I don't know any details. I only know he was doing them. That's how he dressed so well, ran a car, did the clubs and ate at good restaurants. When I found out, of course, I made him stop. That was a condition of our getting engaged. My father got him a job with a business associate. For a time he did very well. He learned quickly, and Dick always had charm. People warmed to him, looked on him as a friend. He was Under-Manager of the Garrick Hotel in Darlington when the group merged with a larger one, and there were redundancies . . . That was when things started to go wrong.'

'Did he go back to his old ways?'

'No! But he hated being so hard up, and when I got a job he hated being dependent on me.'

Inspector Purley considered the matter.

'So how long ago were these burglaries he did?'

'About five years ago – that's when he stopped. But he'd been doing them for years, since he left school.'

'And he's how old now?'

'Twenty-six.'

'What can you tell us about the burglaries? Surely there must be something about them that sticks in your mind, or one particular job he told you about that stood out?'

'No, there's not. I never knew anything about them. I refused to listen.'

She was pulling back, Inspector Purley thought. She needed to be given a further push to remind her what was at stake.

'He must have been good,' he said admiringly, 'never to have been caught. Didn't he ever boast? Say what it was that made him so good?'

'Well ...' She was reluctant, but was being borne along by the tide. 'He always said the secret wasn't the technical things, how to break and enter – though he was good at that too. He said that what mattered was a good eye.'

The Inspector digested this.

'For what? For stuff that would fetch a tidy sum? Or for an easy target, a likely victim?'

'The last. He always said the best target was a retired couple or a widowed person, someone who had built up a bit of property and was now pottering along.' She was putting it more politely than Richard usually had, but suddenly she put aside her protectiveness again. "Someone who had done quite nicely for himself and was now coasting towards his dotage" – that's how he described it once. He only said things like that when he was trying to get my goat.'

'I see,' commented the inspector dryly. 'He has a nice way with words, your husband. Or a nasty one.'

But privately he was pleased to have had contact with the man through his own words. They sounded very adolescent, and he wondered how much of the daredevil boy was in the man still. But most of all he hoped that her willingness to quote her husband's words and show him in an unfavourable light meant that Selena Randall had turned a corner.

'Dick would never hurt Malcolm,' said Selena, dashing his hopes. 'I've got to believe that. He loves him more than anyone in the world. That's why I don't want to hurt him.'

Inspector Purley reserved judgment. He hoped for her sake and the little boy's that what she said about her husband was true.

Dick Randall came out of the little back-street jeweller's with a spring in his step. The man had not hidden his appreciation of the brooch's value, had commented on the workmanship and the quality of the stones and had offered Dick a very fair price. He was an honest man, and it had been a pleasure to do business with such a person.

Malcolm was still strapped into his seat in the little car park round the corner. It always gave Dick a lift of the heart to see him again. He was solemnly watching a Dalmatian in the next car, which was in its turn watching a lazy car-park cat. It struck Dick how lucky he was that Malcolm was the sort of child who could be left on his own for fifteen or twenty minutes without danger of panic fits or grizzling. He was solemn, watchful and even, in his childish way, self-confident. Perhaps it was because he had had to be.

'Here I am, Captain,' he said, opening his car door and sliding himself into the driving seat. 'A nice little bit of business, very satisfactorily concluded.'

He was talking to himself rather than the child, but as usual Malcolm took him up.

'What's bizniz?'

'Business?' he said, starting the car and thinking how he could explain business to a three-year-old. 'Well, let's see. Business can be something you've got that someone wants and is willing to pay for. Or it may be some skill or ability that you have that the other man hasn't got, and he'll pay you to use that skill for him. Or it may be a sort of swap – do this for me, and I'll do that for you.'

He'd tried hard to make it simple, but he knew he was still talking as much to himself as to the child. He often did this, having no one but a child to talk to. Malcolm is going to grow up too quickly, he thought, unless I can settle him down somewhere where he can make friends and lead a normal child's life.

'So, did you have something that the man you went to see wanted?' Malcolm asked, after digesting his words.

'That's right, I did. And it means we can eat for a fortnight,' said Dick.

'What would we do if we didn't have the money to buy food?'

'Oh, but we always will. That I can promise you, Malcolm. It's what daddies are for – getting money so that you can have food and clothes and a bed for the night.'

After a moment Malcolm nodded, seemingly satisfied, and then went off into a light doze. Dick drove on southwards, at a moderate speed.

They stopped for lunch in Grantham. Dick tried to give the little boy a balanced diet, but today, buoyed by the notes bursting the seams of his wallet, he said, 'Today you can have just anything you want, Captain.'

They found a side-street café that looked cosy. Malcolm chose chicken nuggets and chips, and Dick had the day's special: roast beef and Yorkshire pudding. The café's owner cooed over Malcolm, but knew better than to ask where his mummy was: all too often you got a sad tale of marriage break-up. Men alone with children these days usually meant they were using quality time graciously allowed them by the Child Support Agency. Malcolm had a slice of chocolate gâteau for afters, and Dick cleaned him up in the lavatories before going up to the counter, buying some sandwiches and buns for their evening meal and settling up for everything. When they emerged into the bright afternoon sunlight he felt like a million dollars.

The little jeweller's shop was nearly opposite the café.

'Do you know, Malcolm, I feel it's my lucky day,' said Dick.

He led the child by the hand the hundred or so yards down the street to where his car was parked. He opened the boot and began to rummage in the canvas bag. Malcolm, standing beside him on the pavement, regarded him with wide eyes. The bag, for him, was beginning to assume the mystic standing of a cornucopia, source of endless goodies.

'Have you got something the man will want?' he asked.

'I think so,' said Dick, finally selecting a rather showy diamond ring. 'Now, I'll only be five minutes or so, Captain, and then we can be on our way. So you can just sit in your car seat and watch the world go by.'

He strapped him in and walked, whistling, back down the street, the ring wrapped in tissue paper in his trouser pocket. The door of the jeweller's shop opened with an old-fashioned ring.

'Yes, sir. What can I do for you?'

The words were old-fashioned and welcoming, the face less so. There was a suspicion of midnight shadow over the jowls, the eyes were calculating, the mouth mean. Dick nearly turned round there and then, but he had no desire to draw attention to himself needlessly. There seemed to be no alternative but to plunge in.

'I wondered whether you'd be interested in this.'

He drew from his pocket the little package and unwrapped it. The central diamond sparkled dangerously, and the rubies of the surround smouldered. The ring was already beginning to seem ill-omened in his eyes. The man behind the counter took it noncommittally.

'Hmm. A rather assertive piece. Not really Grantham. However, I do have one customer who might ... and there's a dealer I do business with who sometimes takes this sort of thing ...' The tone seemed to Dick professionally disparaging. 'I'll just take it in to the back, sir, with your permission, and get a better look at the stones.'

Dick nodded. The man disappeared through the glass door behind the counter and Dick saw him go behind a little booth in the back room, where he imagined a microscope was set up. He waited, glancing nonchalantly at the rings and pendants on the trays under the counter and the jewelled clocks and ornaments on the glassed-in shelves behind it.

Suddenly the jeweller's head appeared above the walls of the booth. Dick forced himself to seem to be looking at something else. The man had a telephone at his ear, and he was looking at Dick. When his head disappeared down into the booth again, Dick turned and wrenched open the door.

The shopbell rang.

He began running. In seconds he was flinging open the driver's door, had his key in the ignition and was scorching off down the street. In his mirror he could see the jeweller in the door of his shop. This was probably the most exciting thing to happen in his mean little life for years, Dick thought. Not too fast. Don't draw attention. Get on to the motorway and then open up.

'Didn't he want what you had for him?' Malcolm asked.

'Oh, he wanted it,' said Dick. 'I'm driving fast because I'm excited and pleased.'

That night they spent one of their rare nights in the car. Dick had put about a hundred and fifty miles between him and the Grantham police, then had gone off the motorway and cruised around some little southern English towns and villages. Somehow he felt all shaken up, and he blamed himself bitterly. He would never indulge in childish superstition again. My lucky day, my foot! Like some toothless old granny reading her horoscope! He hadn't had a worse one since the day he'd snatched Malcolm. He just couldn't face the lies and the performance he always put on at bed and breakfast places, or going back on to the motorway to find a Merry Cook with rooms attached. There was also the matter of organising new number-plates for the car. He didn't think the man could have seen his – themselves acquired from an abandoned car in Gateshead – but he wasn't taking any risks.

'Do you mind, Captain?' he asked Malcolm. 'I don't think there's any places round here that take in guests.'

'No, I don't mind. I like it,' said Malcolm stoutly, 'but I'll need to go to the toilet.'

He needed more than that. They found a little coppice just outside a village called Birley, and Dick drove up the lane that bisected the trees and found a little open area between it and a field. They ate the sandwiches and the buns they'd bought at midday, and Malcolm drank a bottle of pop. That did it. He had to leave the car quickly and be sick under a tree.

'Not *very* sick,' he said, accurately enough.

Then he was ready to sleep.

Dick dozed. He found it difficult to get proper sleep on the rare occasions that they slept in the car. In the middle of the night he slipped out and acquired new number-plates in Birley – he couldn't find an abandoned car, but he took the plates off the oldest car he could find parked in the road. When he got back to his own car he spread himself over the two front seats and tried to sleep again. Sleep was very slow in coming, but when it did it brought The Dream again. The Nightmare.

He dreamt he was driving away from a small town, out on to the wider road, Malcolm beside him, excited and chattering. All was well, wonderfully well, and they were laughing together, making silly jokes, and full of joy in each other's company, as ever.

Then in his mirror he saw at a distance a police car. It *couldn't* ... No, of course it couldn't. Why should he assume they were after him? But he increased his speed a little. Then, with the special tempo of a dream, things began to take on the excitement of a car chase in a film. The police car increased its speed too – not by very much, but enough to make sure they would catch up with him before long. Dick in his dream was much less cool than the Dick in real life. He could think of nothing else to do but increase his speed again. The police car did the same. 'I've got to do something,' Dick said to himself. 'I've got to do something that shakes them off.'

The road stretched straight ahead, but there was an intersection approaching. Dick swerved off on to a winding country road. On the left, though, was a wood, and seeing a lane into it Dick swerved aside again and turned into it. Please, God, the police would go on. The road had been dry and there were no tyre marks. But he kept up a good speed. The lane was rutted, the car jolting as it coped with the new conditions. In the seat beside him Malcolm was crowing with delight and jumping up and down. As the car ploughed ahead down the lane as fast as Dick could push it Malcolm released his seat belt and strained forward to see.

'Malcolm, belt yourself in again!' he called.

Suddenly, ahead were trees. The end of the lane, the reassertion of thick woodland. There was space enough between two of the trees, but as he aimed at it the car no longer did what he wanted, diverted by the roughness of the terrain and the thick undergrowth. The left-hand wing bashed with a shattering shock into one of the trees, and the boy in the seat beside him hurtled forward and hit the windscreen with a thud that—

Dick woke, sweating and shuddering. He was conscious that his half-waking mind had exerted some kind of control over his sleeping one, and had prevented him from screaming or trying to reach the boy in the back seat. Stiffly he got out of the car. Trees – that was what had set it off, and the little path winding through them. He fumbled in his pocket and lit a rare cigarette. Then soberly he went about his early morning business, fetching a screwdriver and drill and starting to change the plates. He memorised the numbers as a precaution for if he was stopped. The old plates he buried.

He shivered in the cold of the morning. In the car Malcolm was stirring. They could be on their way.

'We can treat ourselves tonight,' he said to the little boy, who was still rubbing his eyes. 'Look at the money we've saved.'

'Can we have breakfast soon?' said Malcolm, whose mind focussed on immediate rather than long-term prospects.

When Selena Randall had left the police station, Inspector Purley looked at DC Lackland, who had sat in on the interview.

'What did you think?'

'Still hung up on publicity, using the tabloids, getting on television, that kind of thing.'

'Yes. I don't think I got through to her.'

'You got through while she was sitting here, but it won't last five minutes once she gets home and is sick with worry. She's bound to clutch at straws.'

'I know. But the case of Carol Parker *is* different. While there was a chance her son was in the country there was a point to the television appeals. Frankly, the appearance Mrs Randall saw yesterday on daytime television was useless. The woman should be in Germany, not here. That's where the child will be by now.'

'And they're not inviting her.'

'No. And the police there are doing bugger-all. The boy was born in Germany and as far as they're concerned he's a German citizen. The father doesn't have him now, but he's a Catholic with family ramifications from one end of the country to another. The boy could be with any of them, and even if they found him he wouldn't be sent back to his mother. That's German law, and the Common Market hasn't changed that.'

'So, really, Mrs Randall is in a more hopeful position?'

'Yes. But try telling that to her. The main thing is, we're pretty sure the child is still in the country. She had one of these tormenting phone calls only three days ago, from Romford. Once we get hold of the child, returning him to her will be a mere formality. If he was abroad, she'd be bogged down in the local judicial system for years.'

'On the other hand, we don't seem to be any nearer to discovering where the two of them might be.'

'No, and that's because they're *not* anywhere. They're everywhere, zigzagging hither and yon to create confusion. Nevertheless, the indications are that Dick Randall is a good father. I just hope she's not fooling herself about that. If he is, he must be considering the future, facing the fact that the boy needs to be settled, have friends, go to nursery school, live in a house he recognises and relates to. If he finds somewhere and goes on with his burglaries, the local police are going to start seeing a pattern, because he's not going to be able to go very far afield.'

DC Lackland screwed up his face sceptically.

'The police up here apparently didn't discover a pattern when he was a teenage Raffles,' he said.

'Good point. We need to alert them to the pattern. The other thing is, the balance of sightings and traces seems to be shifting. There's still some zigzagging – Romford with a piece of cheek, to suggest they'd gone to ground in London, but it was a rogue report. The balance is shifting southwards. Nothing in the North for over three weeks. It's been Midlands, South, shifting westwards. I'm going to concentrate on alerting police in Devon, Dorset, Cornwall – that's where he's going to be found.'

'The West Country does attract a lot of drifters and oddballs,' conceded Lackland.

'Maybe. Though no more than places like Brighton and Tunbridge Wells. The West at this time of year is a good place to be anonymous in.'

'So, no television appearances for Selena Randall?'

'No ... Even if other things were equal, and even if we could persuade them to slot her in, I'd be doubtful about putting her on the Esther Rantzen programme, or the Richard and Judy show.'

'Oh? Why?'

'Mrs Parker is effective because she's blazingly angry with her ex-husband. She hates him. It comes across white-hot to the listener.'

'Whereas Selena Randall is still half in love with hers?'

'Yes. More than half. And not only that – she still thinks of him as a good man.'

'In spite of those phone calls.'

'Yes, in spite of them. The message coming from her would be very blurred, or no message at all.' He mused, with the wisdom of the police force over the years, unalloyed by feminism or any other -ism, 'Funny things, women.'

This was a sentiment Sergeant Lackland could agree with.

The woman who opened the door of Lane's End, in the village of Briscow, was comfortable, attractive and brightly dressed: a woman in her late forties, neither well-off nor on her uppers but at ease with life and still full of it.

'Yes?' Good, broad, open smile.

'I wondered if you have a room for the night,' said Dick.

She looked at the open face, the lean figure, the little boy on his shoulders. The smile of welcome became still more warming.

'I do, that,' she said. 'Come on in and have a look at it.'

She led the way upstairs and pushed open a door. Two single beds pushed together, chintz as a bed covering, chintz at the windows, and the sun streaming through on the gleaming wooden furniture. It looked like heaven.

'This is wonderful,' said Dick. 'Isn't it, Malcolm?'

'*Yes!*' said Malcolm, already a connoisseur.

'Are there just the two of you? Is his m—?' She stopped, on seeing Dick give a tiny shake of the head. 'Well, if you take it that will be seventeen pounds fifty a night, and I can do a proper evening meal for six pounds extra – three for the little boy.'

They closed the deal at once, there in the sunlight. Already there was a warmth between the three of them which had, in the case of the two adults, a little to do with sex but more to do with aesthetic appreciation, likeness of spirit, a feeling of some kind of reawakening. Dick had consciously begun shaping his story accordingly.

Later in the evening, after a good dinner where his own preferences had been consulted and Malcolm's still more, Dick put the boy to bed, read him to sleep, then by invitation went downstairs to the living room for coffee.

'Will it be coffee, or would you prefer a beer?'

'Coffee, please. I can never get used to beer in cans.'

She came forward, her hand held out rather shyly.

'I've been silly, and haven't told you my name. I'm Margaret Cowley – Peggy to my friends.'

'And I'm Colin Morton,' said Dick, shaking the hand warmly. 'I'm sorry I had to stop you, Peggy, when you were going to ask about his mother. It's something I've been trying to stop him thinking about. If he was a little older it would be different.'

They were talking in the doorway of the kitchen now, and the percolator was making baritone noises.

'It was silly of me to even think of asking. It's not my business, and these days, with everyone's marriage breaking down, it's much the best plan not to ask.'

Dick shook his head. 'Oh, it's nothing like that. Malcolm's mother died in childbirth. We were expecting a little girl, and we knew there were complications, but somehow...'

'Oh, I *am* sorry.' She turned to face him. His eyes were full. 'So it was a tragedy clean out of the blue?'

'If the doctors suspected anything serious, they kept it from us.'

'Poor little boy. And poor you both, of course.'

'I'm trying to put it behind us, make a fresh start.'

'New place, new life?'

'Very much so.' He had blinked his eyes free of the tears, and now smiled bravely. 'Everything in the old house reminded me ... and though with a little boy memories fade, still, I do try to keep his mind on other things. He's got to look to the future, even if I find it difficult, and keep ... well, rambling in my mind back to the past. Stop me if I do that.'

'Isn't life a bitch?' Peggy Cowley's voice held genuine bitterness. 'I lost my husband a couple of years ago. Massive heart attack. He was in his late sixties, but these days that seems no age.'

'It doesn't.' He thought to himself that she must have married a man fifteen or twenty years older than herself, and his thought showed on his face.

'Yes, he was quite a bit older,' Peggy said. 'Second marriage for him. But it was a very happy one.'

'No children?'

'No. Perhaps that was why it was a happy marriage.' They both laughed, but Peggy immediately kicked herself for her tactlessness. 'I don't mean it. We'd have loved to have had kiddies, but it just didn't happen. I'd have liked to have one to lean on when he died. It would have made all the difference. And even little Malcolm – you'll have found he keeps your mind occupied and stops you grieving too much, I'll be bound.'

Dick nodded. He had thought himself into the situation.

'Yes, he does. But sometimes I look at him and ...' Again there were tears in his eyes and he took out a handkerchief. He shook himself. 'That's what I said to stop me crying.'

'Not when you're on your own. It will do you good.'

'And what about you? Do you have a job? Or can you make ends meet with the bed and breakfast trade?'

'Oh, I make ends meet and a bit better than that. I've got the cottage as well.'

Peggy's intention had been to drop this information casually into the conversation, but both immediately knew what was at issue.

'You have a cottage?' Dick's voice had an equally bogus neutrality. They didn't look at each other, but they were intensely aware of each other.

'Yes, just a tiny place at the bottom of the garden and across the lane. It doesn't take more than two or three unless they squeeze themselves in. Actually, the last of the Easter tenants leave in a couple of days' time. I've got no bookings then until the school holidays start in July.'

Dick drained his coffee, and she filled his cup. Then she sat back peaceably and watched him sipping. They needed no words. Dick had half made the decision when he saw her at the door. That was why he had given her the name which was on the false papers he had got from an old contact when he was first contemplating snatching his son. The whole of the last couple of hours had felt like a coming to rest, the thing that all the last few weeks had been leading up to.

'I'd need a job,' he said. 'That's not easy in the West Country, is it?'

'It's possible, if you'll take the jobs that nobody else wants,' said Peggy. Dick was doing sums.

'How much do you charge for the cottage?'

'Oh, we can work something out as far as that goes.'

'No, I don't want you to lose out,' said Dick emphatically. 'There's no earthly reason why you should lose out financially by allowing a stranger to sponge off you.'

Though they both knew perfectly well that there was one possible reason. Sex had edged its way more explicitly to the forefront of both their minds.

'I'd give the place at a reasonable rent to anyone who'd take it and look after it in the low season,' said Peggy stoutly. 'Stands to reason. It's always better to have a place occupied, with a bit coming in for it. Empty you're just asking for squatters and burglars.'

'I suppose that's true,' said Dick, who knew better than most. 'Where is the nearest job centre?'

'Oh, that's way away, in Truro. You ought to look for something more local first. They're wanting a relief barman at the Cornishman, just down the road.'

'Oh? I've never done bar work, but I've worked in hotels so I know what's involved and I'm pretty sure I could get the hang of it. What's the catch?'

'It's just lunchtime. Eleven to three. That doesn't suit most people. Oh, and there'd be a bit of cellar work in addition.'

'I might be able to supplement it with income support. Keep on the lookout for other things.' Other sources of income flashed through his mind, but he resolved to use those skills only very sparingly, if he used them at all.

'Anyway,' said Peggy, getting up to clear away the cups, 'I'll just leave the thought with you. We can go and have a look at the cottage tomorrow, if you're interested.'

'And maybe go on to the Cornishman for a pub lunch. They do food at lunchtime?'

'Of course. That would be a big part of your work. Could well be a help with feeding the two of you. A lot of food goes to waste in a place like that.'

As she washed up the cups and the dinner things in the kitchen Peggy felt a glow of satisfaction. She has gambled, and she felt pretty sure she had won. If she had not told Colin about the cottage, she might have had him and Malcolm in the house for a few days, maybe for a week. But by mentioning it she might not have them *with* her, but she would have them *near* her for much longer than that. She'd had no doubt since clapping eyes on the pair of them that that was what she wanted.

That night, as he went up to bed, Dick said, 'Better go. Malcolm may be needing me. First night in a strange place.'

Unspoken because it did not need to be voiced was the thought that there would be other nights.

Selena Randall pulled a piece of paper towards her. For days she had felt she was going mad, so completely without event had her life become. No news from the police, nothing except attempts at reassurance. No sightings, no media interest, total absence even of those terrible, tantalising phone calls, which did at least tell her where they were at the moment they were made. She had to do something. It had been nagging at her mind for some days that perhaps she should appeal to him though the press, send an open letter to him through the *Daily Mail*, the paper they had always taken.

'Dear Dick,' she began. 'I'm writing to tell you how much I miss you both, and how I long to have you back. It's now nearly four months since I saw Malcolm—' Longer than Carol Parker had been without her boy, she thought resentfully, but everyone knows about her loss, and nobody knows about mine. '—and I can't bear the thought that when I see him again he will hardly know me. I will see him again, won't I? Please, Dick, you couldn't be so cruel as to keep him from me for ever, could you? I know you love him and will look after him. Please remember that I love him too. There is not a day goes past, not a minute of the day, when I don't think of him. Remember how happy we were when he was born, you and me and him. I think you loved me then – loved me too much to want me to be so unhappy now. I know I loved you.'

She paused. She wanted to add, I love you still. Was that wise? The policeman would say no. Was it true? She wanted to write nothing but the truth. *Did* she still love him, after what he had done to her? *Could* she?

Seized by a sense of muddle and futility, not in her situation but in herself, her own mind, her own emotions, she laid her head down on the paper and sobbed her heart out.

They went to look at the cottage next morning, after the sort of breakfast dieticians throw up their hands at.

'I never put on weight,' said Dick, munching away at his fried bread. 'I expect Malcolm will be the same, after he's got over his chubbiness.'

They looked at the boy, already tucking in messily to the toast and marmalade.

'Nothing wrong with chubbiness in a child,' said Peggy.

When they'd washed up, Peggy only allowing Dick to help under protest, they set off down the back garden, then across the lane to the tiny cottage. The tenants were just driving off when they got there, and they shouted that they were going to have a last look at Penzance.

'I wondered whether to go on to Penzance,' said Dick, 'when I was driving around looking for somewhere to stay. Somehow it seemed like the end of the road.'

'You've got to give up thoughts like that, Colin,' said Peggy urgently. 'There's a great wide road ahead of you.'

She didn't notice Malcolm looking up at her. He had never heard his father called Colin before.

The cottage was tiny – 'bijou' the estate agents would probably have called it – and there was an ever-present danger of tumbling over the furniture. But it was bright and cheerful, with everything done in the same sort of taste as Peggy's own cottage. Malcolm thought it was wonderful, particularly the strip of lawn at the back with the apple tree. It was warm enough for him to play in just his shorts, and they watched him as he tried to make friends with a very spry grey squirrel.

'It's ideal,' said Dick to Peggy, both of them watching him protectively to see he didn't stray from the garden down towards the river bank. 'Sort of like a refuge.'

'Don't think like that,' urged Peggy again.

'All right. It's what I've been dreaming about since – you know. Is that positive enough for you? Now, will you let me take us all to the – what was it? – the Cornishman, and we'll have a good pub lunch.'

They looked at each other meaningfully.

All the lunchtime regulars in the pub made them welcome for Peggy's sake. She had herself been a regular there when her husband was alive, but had been less frequently since. She was of the generation of women that didn't much like going into a pub on their own. They got themselves a table and settled in. Selecting the food was a big thing, because it was a good menu with plenty to appeal to a child. By the time they had made their decisions they seemed to have spoken to, or had advice from, half the customers in the saloon bar.

When Jack, the landlord, brought the three piled-high plates to their table, Peggy said, 'You still looking for help at lunchtime, Jack?'

'I am. There's folk that are willing, but not folk that are suitable.'

Peggy looked in Dick's direction and winked.

'Oh, aye?' said the landlord, interested. 'Maybe we could have a chat later, young man, after your meal.'

And so it was arranged. The talk was businesslike and decisive: Dick would come down the next couple of nights to learn the business, get into the routine, then he'd start work proper at the weekend. Peggy would look after Malcolm in the middle of the day – 'It'll be a pleasure,' she said, though she did wonder how she'd cope with the unaccustomed situation. The money was far from wonderful, but it would be welcome. Dick only worried about how much he seemed to be putting on Peggy.

'When we're well settled in we'll start looking for a play group for Malcolm,' he said.

'If it goes well I might even start one myself,' said Peggy.

It certainly went well at the Cornishman. Dick was a good worker and a good listener, and the pub's routines went like clockwork when he was on duty. He never mentioned his hotel training, but it showed. Jack thought he was manna from heaven and tried to press him into doing longer hours, but Dick was unwilling. The boy came first, he said, and he did. Nobody asked too much about his background. Everyone in the West Country is used to people passing through, casual temporary residents who come from heaven-knows-where and soon pass on. People knew that Dick had lost his wife, because Peggy had revealed that in conversation with a friend and it had got around. Nobody displayed curiosity beyond that.

Dick slept with Peggy the night he got the job. The mutual agreement was silent, and Peggy knew she had to go along with any conditions Dick attached to the affair. She knew already that Malcolm would always come first with Dick – and second and third as well. Dick stayed in her room for an hour or so, then went as usual to sleep beside the little boy in the two twin beds put together under the window.

The routine continued when he and Malcolm went to live and fend for themselves in the tiny cottage the other side of the back lane. The boy was used to finding himself alone at night, and didn't worry about it. He knew it wouldn't be for long. Dick and Peggy developed a code between themselves. When he collected Malcolm, or when he met Peggy casually on his days off, he would say, 'See you soon,' as they parted. That meant that he'd be up that night.

Perhaps Peggy should have felt that she was being used, but she didn't. She was happy to have her hours with Malcolm, which were working out better than she could have believed possible with her lack of experience of children. She found him an enchanting child, and she was happy to have the all-too-brief time with Dick at night. She had expected little of her widowhood, and Dick was a wonderful and unexpected bonus.

By the middle of June they were a settled thing, or felt like it. Peggy was refusing all potential summer tenants for the cottage, and had managed to transfer the first bookings she had already accepted to another landlord in the area. Her friends knew what the situation was, and accepted it. Summer would be a lovely time, she knew. It was the time of year she had always enjoyed most, especially as Briscow was that bit off the tourist map. Colin would be working, of course, but he was still resisting the offer of extra hours because he didn't want to leave his son for most of the day. Malcolm was regaining his equilibrium, she felt, though it gave her a start one day when he said, 'I haven't spoken to Mummy for *ages*.' It wouldn't be long before he forgot her, she thought.

Dick was happy too. He knew he had landed on his feet. But always in Eden there lurked the serpent, in wait to spread his poison. Dick knew he was using Peggy – not sexually, because if anything she was using him that way. But he knew he was getting a free childminder, lots of free meals, and he knew Peggy would be charging a lot more for the cottage if she was letting it on a weekly basis to her usual casual tourist clientele.

It irked him to be dependent – because that was what it was. It had been that which had started the rot between him and Selena. He was old-fashioned, he knew, but that was something he would never apologise for. He'd known when he'd planned to snatch Malcolm that his feelings for the boy were old-fashioned. And it was the same for his sense that he was becoming too dependent on Peggy.

The truth was, he could do with more money.

'It follows the pattern,' said Inspector Purley. 'Retired people, away from home, poor security, a nice little haul of jewellery, cash and small household things – nothing spectacular, but worth having. *And* it's West Country.'

'What if the next one's John o' Groats?' asked Lackland. 'That's been the pattern so far – zigzagging all over the country.'

'Ah, but it won't be from now on, you of little faith.'

'Seems to me you're looking at it arse up,' countered Lackland. '*You* decided he was headed for the West Country, and now we've got a possible case there you take it as confirmation, even though we've had other possible cases all over the country. Dick Randall's not the only crook to target respectable retired people.'

He did not dent his superior officer's complacent view of things.

'You mark my words,' Purley said. 'He's come to rest in the West Country, like all sorts of other people – artists, *retired people*, ageing hippies, travelling people and all manner of rag-tag and bobtail. And having come to rest, he can't leave little Malcolm alone for long. The cases we think he was involved in were all over the country because so were they. Now the cases will all be in the West.' He walked over and looked at a map on the wall. 'This one was in a small village called Monpellon. The area includes Launceston, Bodmin, Padstow – places like that. That's where we'll be looking to, because that's where the two of them will have slung their hook.'

'Well, I admire your confidence,' said Lackland, who secretly, or not so secretly, did not.

'I'm so certain I'm right that I'll risk ridicule if he does turn up in John o' Groats and I'll alert the local police down there that I think that's where he is. One more strike and he may have given himself away.'

Dick was his usual efficient and sympathetic self at lunchtime in the Cornishman, pulling pints now with the sure hand of an expert, bringing three or four laden plates at once from the kitchen into the bar and remembering who had ordered what. But at the back of his mind there was a niggling worry.

Peggy had not been quite her normal self when he had delivered Malcolm that morning, not quite the same in her manner. There hadn't been anything that you could pin down: you couldn't say she'd got the huff; decided she'd gone off him; was feeling she was being exploited. She was minding three or four other toddlers now – children whose mothers had got summer jobs when the holiday season had come upon them. The arrival of one of them at the door had covered over any awkwardness, but also prevented any attempt to sort things out. Dick was sure there was *something* – an alteration in her manner, a slight access of remoteness, even coldness.

'One chicken and chips, one roast pork, one steak and kidney pie and one vegetable bake.' He had a cheerful air as he served one of the families who had once been regulars of Peggy's but had been found an alternative cottage this season. They were a fleshy, forceful family, and they took up their knives and forks with enthusiasm.

'Can hear you're from the North, too,' said the wife, smiling at him in a friendly fashion.

'Me father was,' said Dick. 'Or should I say "wor"? I can do the accent, and a bit of it has rubbed off on to me. But I come from Cambridge – and all round. I'm a bit of a rolling stone.'

'Can't be too much of a rolling stone, now you've got little Malcolm to consider,' said the husband. 'Champion little lad, that. We saw him when we dropped by to say hello to Peggy.'

'Champion's the word for him,' said Dick. 'I call him Captain. Can't remember how that started, but I certainly have to jump when he gives me orders!'

'Colin – two hamburgers and chips on the bar,' called Jack, and Dick resumed his service of the crowded and cheerful bar. He didn't like it when people commented on his very slight Northern accent. He'd told Peggy early on that he came from Cambridge, and that was a lie he was now stuck with.

He got away from the Cornishman shortly after three, and went straight to pick Malcolm up. Peggy had got her manner under control now, and was friendly and pleasant as always. She looked him in the eye, but was somehow – was he imagining it? – quite keen for an excuse to look away again. Yes, I am imagining it, said Dick to himself, settling Malcolm on to his shoulders to ride him piggyback to the cottage.

'See you soon, Peggy,' he called. She looked up from the floor where she was playing with one of the other children.

'Oh – yes. Good,' she said.

There is something wrong, thought Dick.

'I think this is a call you should take,' said DC Lackland, and handed the receiver over to Purley.

'DI Purley speaking.'

'Ah, now are you the man who's in charge of the disappearance of that little boy – the one who was snatched by his father in the Darlington area?'

The voice was pure County Durham.

'Yes, I am.'

'Well, I'm speaking from Briscow in Cornwall.'

'Oh, yes?' The heightened interest in his voice was evident.

'That's right, but we're from Stockton, so we read about the case in the local newspapers. There wasn't a great deal in the national papers, was there?'

'No, there wasn't.' It seemed as if he was being accused of not pressing for more, so he said, 'The North is another country.'

'Aye, you're right. Londoners aren't interested in what queer folk like us get up to. They'd rather not know. Any road, we've been coming to Cornwall for four years on the trot up to now, but this year our cottage was taken, let to a young man and a boy.'

'Oh, yes?' Purley was well trained in police neutrality but he couldn't keep a surge of interest out of his voice.

'Nice enough looking fellow, and a lovely little boy. I'm probably way out of order and on the wrong lines altogether, but the little boy is called Malcolm. That was the name of the little boy who was snatched, wasn't it?'

'That's right. The father is Richard Randall.'

'This man is calling himself Colin Something-or-other. But the boy is Malcolm. I suppose he thought changing it would cause more problems than it would solve. If it *is* them.'

'This man is not a local, I take it.'

'No, no, of course not. He's been here since early spring, I believe. And he has a slight Northern accent.'

'Really?'

'Yes. Says he got it from his father. But if you were brought up in Cambridge, like he says he was, you wouldn't have your father's accent, would you?'

'It sounds unlikely.'

'The story is that the little boy's mother died in childbirth. We had that from Peggy, his landlady, the woman who minds the nipper while he works at the pub.'

'Right. And Peggy's name and address are?'

'Peggy Cowley, Lane's End Cottage, Deacon Street, Briscow, Cornwall.'

'I'm grateful to you, very grateful.'

When he had got the man's name and address and also his Stockton address, Purley banged down the telephone in triumph.

'Got him!'

'You haven't got him at all yet,' said Lackland, who enjoyed playing the spoil-sport. 'And Malcolm's a common enough name.'

'I feel a pricking of my thumb,' said Purley, refusing to be dampened. 'Get me Launceston police.'

'So, how was your day, Captain?' asked Dick, watching Malcolm get his hands very sticky from a jam sandwich. Malcolm, as always, considered at length.

'Jemima was very naughty,' he announced.

'Well, I'm sorry to hear that.' Jemima was one of the other children Peggy minded, and in Malcolm's opinion she was a Bad Lot.

'She spilt her lemonade and broke the little wooden horse.'

'Good Lord, fancy poor old Peggy having to cope with a naughty little girl like that.'

'She should have smacked her but she didn't.'

After tea, when Malcolm was absorbed in a jigsaw puzzle of Postman Pat with large but bewildering pieces, Dick said, 'I'm just popping over to Peggy's, I think we left your pully there.'

'My pully's in the—' Malcolm began. But his father was already out of the door.

I want this thing sorted out, thought Dick as he crossed the lane and ran up the bank and on to Peggy's long back lawn. It can't wait till tonight. This sort of thing can fester. And if I can't tell her the truth, I'll tell her a lie. It won't be the first time. Dick had as great a confidence in his ability to fabricate plausible stories as he had in his eye for a robbable house.

He was about to round the side of Peggy's cottage when he heard voices from outside the front door.

'And when did you say this man and his son took the cottage?'

'Back in March,' came Peggy's voice, reassuringly normal. 'I'd have the precise dates in my records. They stayed a couple of nights bed and breakfast, then took the cottage.'

'Are they still there?'

'Yes.'

'What name is the man using?'

'The man's name is Colin Morton,' came Peggy's voice emphatically.

'And does he say he's divorced?' asked the young sergeant, his hard-looking face intimidating, his eyes like deep, cold lakes.

'Colin is a widower,' said Peggy firmly.

'Oh, yes? And what does he say his wife died of?'

'His wife died in childbirth. Look, it's not me you should be asking these questions, it's him. He'll have all the papers and things.' Thinking she heard movement from the back garden, she went on talking brightly. 'But, really, I *know* that's true. I've seen a picture of the poor girl. Such a nice face she had, pretty but loving, too. Colin keeps that in his wallet because he doesn't want the little lad to be reminded of his mother – says that if he'd been a little older when his mother died it would be different, but—'

'And this "Colin", he's working locally, is he?' the sergeant interrupted.

'Yes, he's working lunchtimes at the Cornishman. They think the world of—'

'That can't bring in much. He is paying you rent for the cottage, is he?'

The implication was brutally obvious. Peggy chattered on, seeming to take no notice, but really she was speaking from the front of her mind only. The back of her mind was remembering the night before. The electricity had fused just as she was making her late-night drink. She had no overnighters in the second bedroom, but something – she was reluctant to analyse precisely what – made her want it fixed that night. Dick had done it before, and had made light of it. Surely he wouldn't mind. It would be the first time ... She rummaged in the dark to find her torch in the kitchen drawer, and then set off across the lawn towards the cottage.

The car was not there. The cottage was in darkness and the little dirt square to the side where Dick kept the car was empty. Malcolm was sleeping in the cottage on his own. The moment she thought this she realised how silly she was being, and what a hypocrite: Malcolm was there on his own asleep all the hours Dick spent in her bed. But that thought raised new fears and doubts. Where was Dick now? In someone's bed? He met all sorts of women while he was serving in the pub. He could have made a date with one of them. The thought that she was nothing more than his piece on the side, and that he'd gone on to more desirable pieces, tormented her. It felt like treachery. It felt like the end of her good life.

She retreated to her garden, and stood in the darkness behind a bushy rhododendron. Eventually she heard Dick's car. Well over half an hour had passed since she'd begun waiting. The car came up the lane and was parked in the usual place beside the cottage. She saw Dick's profile before he switched the car lights off, saw him get out of the car. He was wearing a drab jerkin and was carrying that old bag of his. Somehow he didn't look as if he was returning from a sexual assignation.

When he had disappeared into the cottage she turned and trudged back to her darkened house, somewhat relieved in her mind but still doubtful. What *did* one look like when one returned from a sexual assignation? she asked herself. And even if he was not, where *had* he been? What *had* he been doing?

'Now, if you'll take us to the cottage ...' said the sergeant.

'I can get the key if you like, then you can look over it if they're not in,' said Peggy.

She was not betraying them, merely giving Dick time to get them both away. She pottered inside to take as long as possible to find the key. In her heart she knew he was the man they were looking for. In her heart she knew she had lost them both.

'Come on, Captain, we're going for a drive,' shouted Dick, as he ran through the tiny living room, tripping over a coffee-table, then righting himself and dashing up the stairs. When he came down, clutching the bag, heavy from last night, Malcolm was still on the floor with his jigsaw.

'Why are we going for a drive, Daddy? It's nearly my bedtime.'

Dick grabbed his jacket then picked up the little boy and ran out with him.

'It's a lovely evening for a drive,' he said, shoving him in the car but taking care to click the belt in place around him. He ran round to the driver's door, and the key was in the ignition and the car being backed into the lane before Malcolm could make further protest.

He knew he shouldn't drive fast through the village. He tried to moderate his speed, but he was possessed by the urgency of the situation. As he scorched past the Cornishman he saw that one of the local policemen was having an off-duty pint at a little rustic table the landlord had set out for good summer days. In his mirror he saw him getting out his mobile phone.

He knew the roads around Briscow now like a connoisseur. He took a short cut, and another, then was out, not on to the motorway but on the old main road to Bristol. Now he could really open up. If only he had had a new car, or any really powerful one. With a bit of luck the police vehicle wouldn't be much better than his. He put five miles between him and Briscow, six, seven.

Then he saw the police car in the mirror. Moments later he heard its siren.

The police car wasn't an old banger, or even a sedate family model Ford. It was gaining on him. He pushed the accelerator down to the floor. He was seized momentarily with exhilaration, but at the back of his mind something outside him seemed to be shouting, The Dream. The Nightmare. And then he began to sweat, and a quieter voice whispered to him, The dead child. He tried to continue, tried to squeeze more speed out of the car, but his heart was not in it. In the mirror he saw the police car gaining on him, its siren gathering in intensity.

He took his foot off the accelerator. The car dropped speed, began coasting. He changed lanes, let the car slow down, then let it chug to the side of the road and stop. As he pulled on the handbrake the police car came to a halt in front of him. Two policemen jumped out and ran over to lean in his window. One had a hard face and piercing cruel eyes. The younger one had unformed features but compassionate eyes.

'Are you Richard Randall, going by the name of Colin Morton?' the sergeant asked, flicking his ID in Dick's face.

Dick considered, then nodded. 'You know it all, I expect,' he said. 'Yes, I am.'

'And this is your son, Malcolm Randall?'

'Yes, it is.'

'Richard Randall I am arresting you . . .'

The policemen agreed to drop Malcolm off at Peggy's as a temporary measure. Dick knew Hard-Eyes wouldn't want the embarrassment of a child around him cramping his style. 'You must be nice to Mummy when you go home,' he said to the boy as Peggy came out to collect him, not looking him in the face. 'She must have missed you all this time.'

When he was alone with the policemen, driving to the station in Launceston, he suddenly broke down. It was the end of his dream, the very end. Somehow it felt like the end of his life.

He looked up, red-eyed, at the young constable handcuffed to him in the back seat of the car.

'Will you tell his mother I would never have done anything to harm him? That's why I stopped. I love that boy. Tell Selena it's all up to her now. Will you tell her that exactly?'

'Of course I will. What if she asks what you mean?'

He didn't answer directly.

'Tell her I don't want to see her, or the boy. She'll understand. Tell her it's all up to her.'

Then they drew into Launceston police station and began the long business of interviews and charging.

Having Malcolm back was like a dream for Selena. Inspector Purley had flown down to Bristol the night of Dick's arrest, hired a car, then participated in interviews the next day. He had phoned Selena to say they were sure it was Malcolm and he'd bring him back up North the next day. No point in her coming down.

It was late afternoon when his car drove up the street and parked outside her Darlington home. She rushed to the front door, just in time to hear the Inspector say, 'Run to Mummy.' She picked the little bundle up, to hug him, kiss him. Out of the corner of her eye she saw the inspector raise a hand then get back into his car and drive off.

When she put Malcolm down and had a good look at him she could hardly believe her eyes. He had grown out of all recognition, and was assured beyond belief. It bowled her over. As she took him round the house and he gravely inspected his old toys she thought to herself that the mop of fair hair was the only thing that spoke to her of the old Malcolm. He talked with such wonderful, adult confidence, telling her what he wanted for tea before running out into the garden when she told him Finny the cat was out there. All his talk and memories were of Daddy, and he'd tell her quite disjointedly of things they'd done on the road, how Daddy had taken him away, how Jemima at Peggy's was always naughty. When he asked her, 'Are you my mummy now?' she almost choked, and took him in her arms and said they'd never be apart again.

Later in the evening she had a phone call from the young constable in Launceston. She was almost incoherent in her joy and thanks, and she was really grateful to get Dick's message to her.

'I suppose they'll be bringing him back up North for trial,' she said wistfully. 'I could go and see him then.'

'He doesn't want that. He doesn't ... feel he should see you or Malcolm.' Being a kind-hearted young man, he added, 'Yet. I don't think he feels the time is ripe.'

Selena was sad, but she didn't have time to stay sad. Soon it was time for bed, but first she had to wash away the grime and mustiness of travel from the little boy. She ran the bath, just lukewarm as he liked it, and Malcolm insisted on undressing himself, a new departure for Selena who had always done it in the past. She felt oddly uncertain with the naked Malcolm, wondering at his chubbiness, feeling it was like looking at a new child. What had Dick been feeding him on? It wasn't like him to be so irresponsible as to let him gorge himself on junk food. On the other hand, he had made him into such a competent and confident little man – so serious in all the little things he did for himself, things he had previously let her do for him.

He climbed into the bath himself, slowly, seriously, but once in he was more interested in his old rubber duck than in washing himself. Still a child in some things, Selena thought. She worked up a soapy lather on his flannel and began washing him herself. It was pure pleasure, and it felt as if she were washing off all those months when only his father had had him, seen him grow. She leaned over the bath to wash the far side of him, and it was then that she saw it.

The birthmark on his hip.

The oval-shaped birthmark, like a rugby ball, on the left hip. Just as she had seen it described in television interviews, in newspaper articles, by Carol Parker. This wasn't Malcolm. This was Anton Parker, born Anton Weissner, when his mother was married to his German father. She let the flannel fall, felt faint, and sank back on to the chair by the wall. Anton played on, oblivious, dipping the duck's head under the water as he had seen ducks do at Briscow.

It was Dick who had snatched Anton. That had been six days after he had snatched Malcolm. In that time Malcolm must have died. She felt tears come into her eyes for her lost child, but she suppressed them. She had to think, to be practical. How had he died? Naturally? In a car chase, perhaps? There had been various sightings and police pursuits. Dick had taken this little boy as a substitute, called him Malcolm, taught him to call himself Malcolm. That's why he had not let him say more than a word or two on the phone, in case she had recognised or suspected this was not her boy. She thought of Carol Parker, desperate and dispirited, appealing on British television, convinced that her husband had taken their son to Germany for ever.

Then she remembered her husband's words: 'It's all up to her now.' Suddenly they had quite a new meaning. From the bath came splashings and chuckles of pleasure. She drew her head up straight and opened her eyes.

'Come along, Malcolm – out of the bath now and let Mummy dry you.'

DANCING WITH BILLY

K. C. Constantine

As Jefferson Township Police Chief Mike Latusek drove up to the trailer at the end of Molly Quarry Road, he was certain only that a family named Kadylak had lived there until this morning and now all that was left of the family were two boys, one eighteen, the other thirteen. The boys' mother had died seventeen days ago of kidney failure in Clay Memorial Hospital, and this morning, just before noon, the father had been brought to the same hospital by Molly Quarry Rescue Squad Two, shot in both legs, DOA from the loss of blood.

Ten days ago, the father had also been a patient in the same hospital for some kind of urinary infection; Latusek wasn't able to decipher the jargon. Before that, the father had apparently been in and out of the state mental hospital in Franklinburg for the last six years, the last four of them in – until he'd been brought to Clay's ER with his infection. Nobody in the ER would speculate about the father's mental problems, the general impression being that, whatever his problems, he seemed not at all hostile or aggressive. The two descriptions Latusek heard most often were that Martin John Kadylak Sr wouldn't look at anyone and that he talked so softly everybody had to ask him to repeat himself.

As for the two boys, Latusek didn't get a coherent answer out of either one when he'd asked what had happened. The younger one, Martin John Jr, wouldn't say anything except that he wanted his mother, and he kept asking for her in a sniffling whisper. The elder, Daniel James, talking in a listless monotone and gazing dully over Latusek's shoulder, rambled on about how he wouldn't go live with his Aunt Mary, he'd join the Air Force instead, but his brother probably would have to go live with her, even though of the two she liked Martin John Jr least, and, 'She doesn't like me very much either.'

No matter how Latusek asked Daniel James to describe what had happened, the boy would say nothing, just shook his head no, his lips parted slightly, his breathing slow and shallow, his gaze pathetic and vacant. Latusek thought the boy didn't look anywhere near eighteen, more like twelve or thirteen. He was very pale, his lips were full and pink like a baby's, and he had the wispy beginnings of a moustache. He was tall, almost six feet, but he was thin and soft, with little muscle definition.

Latusek had been chief for exactly four days. Three of those he'd spent trying to get the township mechanic to repair the automatic transmission in the Ford Galaxy the townshop supervisors had just bought at the state police auction of worn-out cruisers. The problem was that the machanic quit working on the Galaxy every time a potentially better-paying job wheeled into his garage. Latusek didn't push the mechanic because he didn't know where either of them stood in the township just yet, so he spent a lot of time reading greasy back issues of *Road and Track* when he wasn't chatting with other customers.

Until he'd been hired by the Jefferson Township Supervisors, Latusek had been a patrol officer with the Franklinburg Police Department for six years. Before that, he'd been with Allied Security at Mount Calvary College for Women for four years, and before that, after completing boot camp and advanced infantry training, he'd been assigned to guard companies first at Camp Lejeune Base, North Carolina, and then at Headquarters Marine Corps in Quantico, Virginia, for a total of three years and eight months. He'd been studying criminal justice through the Armed Forces Institute and at various community colleges ever since he'd graduated from high school, but this was the first death he'd ever investigated that wasn't the result of a traffic accident. He was surprised by how well he'd been controlling his nerves – until he pulled up to the trailer just short of the crest of Molly Quarry Road and saw how much blood a man of no great size loses before he dies of that loss.

It had dripped down the two metal steps leading to the front door and was coagulating in the dust in the bright summer sunshine. Latusek could see that much before he got out of the Galaxy. He'd had no trouble finding the trailer; the rescue squad had told him there wasn't another house within a hundred yards on either side of the road on the southern side of Molly Quarry mountain just short of the crest.

The single-wide trailer, crusty with dust from the quarry, sat on pillars of concrete blocks. At one time it might have been white, but now, like everything on the leeward side of the mountain, it was the color of sandstone, except for the black streaks that ran down under each window. There wasn't a flower or shrub to be seen in front of the trailer, just dirt and rocks, as though the road ran up to the front door. Surrounding the trailer on three sides were spindly conifers dusted with sandstone, like dry, tan snow.

Inside, Latusek took three careful steps into the combination living-dining room, stopped, got out his notebook and ballpoint pen, and started his case file, using an arbitrary number because he had no idea what incident report number his predecessor had been working on when he'd begun his retirement.

The blood pool began in the middle of the living room, spread toward the west wall, the wall nearest the road, then south toward the front door, and finally west again, out and down the steps. He counted six different shoeprints in the blood, and thought that if he had a camera he'd have no trouble matching them with the shoes worn by the three members of the rescue squad, the two boys, and the DOA. But because he had no camera, all he was able to do was make notes and crude drawings of what he was seeing. The first note he made was to remind the supervisors that they'd promised him decent cameras. He'd emphasized during his final interview that he shouldn't be expected to work without them. But here I am, he thought, doing what no cop should be expected to do.

He stood very still and just looked around, pausing every so often to make a note of what he was observing, trying to recall every text he'd ever read about crime scene investigation. He'd been through this scene a thousand times in his imagination, so he wasn't surprised that he was fairly calm – until the smell of the blood began to get to him. It wasn't the blood exactly; it was the faint mixture of urine and feces. Latusek surmised that the man had been dead before he'd left the trailer, otherwise his bowels and bladder would not have relaxed. That was not exactly true; it was the muscles controlling those organs which had relaxed upon death – forget about that, he told himself. The nomenclature of the physiology is not what's important here.

He stepped carefully over the narrowest stream of blood to move to a more nearly central location in the room. Once there he started looking at the floor, his gaze going around the room in ever widening circles, while he turned on just that point on the floor until he was sure that he wasn't going to be stepping on anything obvious when he made his next move.

On his third visual sweep of the floor he saw two empty shotgun shells near the couch. He carefully made his way to them and squatted to look at them. Remington 12-gauge. While he was peering closely at them, he caught sight of the buttplate of a shoulder gun sticking out from under the flap of cloth hanging down in front of the couch. He lifted the cloth with his pen, and leaned forward so far his cap nearly fell off. He caught it with a jerk, pushed it down tight on his head, leaned forward again, and, using his pen as a lever in the trigger guard, slid the gun out. It was a 12-gauge Mossberg pump shotgun. The stock was nicked and dented, dull from frequent handling. Had the shooter put it there to hide it? Or had the rescue squad, to get it out of the way? Wasn't the rescue squad – they would've said something; one of them would.

Latusek made a note, underlining it, that he had no way to transport evidence, neither boxes nor bags of any kind, paper or plastic. He wasn't even sure he had crime scene tape to warn off the easily intimidated. He didn't know how he was going to preserve the scene.

Fact was, he didn't know what was in the Galaxy's trunk, if anything. Three days trying not to antagonize the township mechanic, three days reading magazines, chatting and daydreaming, and he'd never once thought to open the damn trunk. Nothing like starting the job in a coma. But, he thought sourly, that's what happens when you allow yourself to get excited and irritated, excited to start a new job, irritated because you let yourself believe somebody else is keeping you from starting it. That's exactly what happens when you allow your emotions to make you forget to do what you know very well you should have done. There's no excuse not to have gone over every piece of equipment in the department with the previous chief before he took off. None. But that's exactly what I did.

He forced himself back to the present, to think what to do next, what to observe, what looked obvious, what looked obviously out of place. He was feeling not nervous exactly, but inadequate. Here he was, at a scene he'd thought about for years, six at Franklinburg, four at Mount Calvary College, during thousands of hours of uneventful patrol, through dozens of hours of lecture courses about crime scene preservation and investigation, through hundreds of hours of reading for all those classes, and he found himself thinking of so many things, so many possibilities, that he was starting to feel incapable of making a move, any move at all. He berated himself further for what he had not done during the last three days.

Here and now, he said, come back to right here, right now. There are two empty shells, and the man was shot once in each leg, a neat, even equation. Latusek stood up and began to turn slowly, letting his gaze go around all the walls. No holes anywhere. He paced the distance, heel to toe, from the shells to the northernmost edge of the blood. It was less than ten feet, so clearly the man's legs had taken the full charge of BBs from both shots. He made a note of that, and another to get a twenty-five-foot tape measure.

Then, looking at the floor before he put his foot down for each step, he went through the rest of the trailer – two bedrooms, two bathrooms, the kitchen, and the utility room where the washer, dryer, hot-water tank, and oil furnace were. Nothing. No holes in any of the walls, and no blood either, neither spatter nor drops, and no sign of a struggle. Only in the living-dining room was there sign of a struggle: opposite the end of the couch where the shotgun was, an end table was overturned and a lamp lay on the floor, the shade dented and the bulb broken, but otherwise intact.

Latusek went back to where the empty shells lay near the couch. He imagined himself standing about where the shooter must have stood, imagined holding the shotgun, firing, working the pump, ejecting the empty to the right and putting a fresh shell in the chamber, firing again, pumping another out and another in, getting ready to fire a third time. He visualized the empties bouncing into the front of the couch and then falling to the floor.

Latusek felt his tongue slipping out the corner of his mouth and jerked it back in. His mother used to tell him, 'I always know when you're thinking, Michael, 'cause you always have your tongue out. I believe you're part snake. What kind of child did I raise who's part snake?' It was always said with loving humor, no mistaking that, along with the smile and the nudge with the knuckle in the bend of his neck. But he wasn't sure he wanted to be part anything else, especially part snake. She danced with Billy the boa, and when she joked about raising a child who was part snake it confused him.

'Why don't you almost not have any clothes on?'

'Because that's what the men pay to see.'

'Wouldn't they pay you if you had clothes on?'

'No. They won't pay to watch me dance with Billy if I have clothes on.'

'Why?'

'Because some men are funny that way.'

'Am I gonna grow up to be a man?'

'Nothin' and nobody's gonna stop you. I won't let 'em.'

'Am I gonna be funny that way?'

'Maybe. I don't think so, but I don't know. I just think any time somebody tries to talk you into watching a lady dance without her clothes on, you'll think about me. Maybe you'll watch, maybe you won't. I think probably you will. But I think you'll have just a little bit different perspective.'

'What's perspective?'

'It's where you look from.'

Done with examining the walls, he started on the ceiling, but when he tilted his head back, the hole in the ceiling was almost directly overhead. There were obvious powder burns all around the hole, a third shot, no doubt. A warning shot? Fired during a struggle? Was there a struggle? Was it over the gun? Or had the gun come into it after the struggle had started about something else? Who had the gun? Who wanted the gun? Where was the gun before it came into this room? How did he know the one in the ceiling was even fired there today? He didn't. Didn't have any way of knowing.

Latusek went back through every room again, this time looking under and behind every piece of movable furniture and in every closet, looking for other guns, boxes of ammo, cleaning kits, anything to show that the gun was from there and had not been brought in from somewhere else. He started in the north bedroom, obviously the boys' room from the disarray of clothing, paperbacks, magazines, comic books, balls, model cars and trucks, tablets, pencils, crayons, and so forth. In the closet, which took up the entire north wall, he found a single-shot .22 Remington rifle leaning in the corner behind the clothing on hangers and the shoes, boots, and sneakers jumbled on the floor.

In the last closet he looked in, in the southernmost bedroom, among shoes, boots, and sneakers jumbled on the floor, he found an upended box of Remington 12-gauge shells, number four shot. There were only four shells in the box, two more among the shoes, another in the heel of a dirty sneaker with a brand name Latusek associated with discount stores. So, more than likely, the shotgun arrived in the living-dining room from this bedroom.

So what? However it got there, the man didn't shoot himself, not in both legs he didn't; that's ridiculous. So it's one of the kids. Should've had them tested for chemical or metal residue – hell, how was I supposed to do that? Don't even know exactly when the shots were fired, don't know whether the shooter's washed his hands since then – or how many times. Not even real sure how long afterward those tests can still be done. I know the sooner you get a suspect tested the better chance you have, but I can't remember what the time limit is. And, anyway, how was I supposed to do everything else and get them to the state police lab to have them tested? God, it's sixty miles to that lab.

He shook his head and sighed. Could make a big production, get a can of hair spray or ant-killer and spray them and tell them if nothing changes color that means they've fired a gun. Would they fall for that? How dumb are they? Aw, forget about that. Look for a bruise, 'cause if one of them did it he's going to have a bruise on him somewhere. The recoil from that 12-gauge would've left at least one red mark on one of them, shoulder, thigh, wherever he propped the butt. Had to.

So it has to be the older one. The younger one, hell, he might've fired once, but not twice. The recoil would've put him on his ass. That boy didn't weigh a hundred pounds. Supposed to be thirteen, looks about seven or eight. Fired once? No way twice. It's the older one. Has to be. Oh, cut it out, man, stop speculating.

But he couldn't stop. Why was the father in Franklinburg? Six years, in and out, the last four in, almost the whole time I was a patrolman in that town. As many times as we got called out there, I don't remember that name, Martin John Kadylak Sr. Did he go back there after he was discharged from the hospital? Why was he here? Had he been discharged? Or was he on some kind of leave because his wife had just died? Man, Latusek thought, this is complicated. Wait, are you complaining? This is what you've been waiting for, what you've been studying for, thinking about, daydreaming about, getting ready for – for how many years now? Yeah, but this is going to take a ton of questions, a ton of calls, interviews and, most of all, a ton of patience. And the first thing I do is go to sleep about what's in the trunk of the damn Galaxy. Jesus . . .

Latusek looked around the living-dining room again, this time at the flat surfaces. On the dining-room table there were two cereal boxes, Wheaties standing, Cheerios on its side, both approximately in the middle of three spoons and three bowls, all with soggy crumbs in milk on the bottom, one bowl precariously near the edge of the table. The table itself was slightly askew. Had somebody bumped it during the struggle? Or had the EMTs pushed it aside to get the litter in? The wheel marks from the litter were the first things he'd noticed in the blood, before he'd started to identify and draw all the shoe prints.

So how soon after breakfast did this happen? How did he know it was breakfast? Just because it was cereal? Maybe they were having cereal for lunch. Maybe cereal was what had started everything. Stop guessing and keep looking.

Opening the refrigerator, he saw two nearly empty plastic half-gallon jugs of milk, one skim, the other two percent fat. Beside them were two bottles of generic diet cola, one unopened, the other less than a third full. On a lower shelf, a jar of generic grape jelly, with only scrapings left; half of a quarter-pound stick of margarine; an empty plastic tub of margarine with no lid; squeeze bottles of generic mustard and ketchup; a jar of sweet pickle chips, with only two chips left; three shriveled carrots in one of the bottom drawers and two oranges greenish white with mold in the other, and a matchbook-size portion of processed cheese wrapped in aluminum foil on the shelf above the drawer where the carrots were.

Latusek closed the refrigerator, opened the freezer above. Nothing but frost and empty ice-cube trays. He closed the freezer and turned to the cabinets above, beside, and below the sink. The only food he found in any of them was cereal: seven boxes of Wheaties, six of Cheerios. One cupboard contained many tins and jars of spices and seasonings. Another had cannisters of sugar and flour, with only residues of each in them. A third cannister contained only one cardboard tag and string from a Lipton teabag. A cabinet beneath the sink contained sponges, raggedy dish towels hung over the pipes, liquid soaps, soap pads, cans of powder cleansers, and two plastic garbage bags stuffed full of empty plastic grocery bags. But nowhere was there a can of vegetables, fruit, fish or beans, or a box or bag of rice or pasta, or a bag of dried beans, or so much as a potato or onion. There was no dishwasher and no dishes in the sink, just the bowls and spoons on the table. These people had apparently been living on milk, cereal, and generic diet cola.

Latusek closed the cupboards, started observing again. There were many photographs of the boys, school portraits in cardboard frames on the walls and curling snapshots fixed to the refrigerator with tiny magnets. But there were no pictures of either parent, not with the boys, not together as a couple, not as individuals. Also on the freezer door were schedules of appointments in Clay Memorial Hospital for dialysis for Mrs Maureen G. Kadylak, schedules for medicine, phone numbers for three different doctors and a pharmacy, schedules for after-school activity busses for the Franklinburg Joint School District, a class schedule for Martin John Kadylak Jr, but none for Daniel James Kadylak. Was the older boy still in school? Had he graduated? Or quit? There was no obvious indication anywhere that he was still in school, or employed, or neither.

Crowding into Latusek's mind was the unnerving realization that he didn't know where the boys were. He'd left them in the hospital, in the care of emergency-room staffers, but they could be anywhere now. God, there was so much to do, so many people to talk to. He took off his cap and massaged his scalp hard with the fingers of his left hand, trying to remind himself that nobody can be in two places at once. It didn't help. Then think this, he coached himself. Do one thing at a time, even if it isn't in the best possible order, and don't get ahead of yourself.

Go see what's in the trunk of the Galaxy. Maybe there's a roll of crime scene tape, at least get a plastic cordon around the place. God, that wasn't much. The rescue squad didn't mention a key for the trailer, and he quit looking after a futile search in obvious places. So all he could do was shut the door and hope he had some tape and hope the tape was enough to scare off the timid. Certainly wouldn't scare off anybody else.

Except for the spare tire, a jack, and a tool kit, the trunk was empty. He thought of himself in the garage's waiting room, flipping through *Road and Track* and playing Mr Chamber of Commerce, and he called himself several names. He closed the trunk and went and slipped behind the wheel, leaning forward until the bill of his cap touched the wheel. He slumped there for a long moment, indulging his anger at himself for his lazy dumbness while the mechanic got around to the Galaxy. He straightened up, picked up the microphone and tried to call the state police barracks in Mechlinboro. He thought he heard them acknowledge his call, but he couldn't be sure because their transmission kept breaking up. He gave his location and requested a trooper with the essentials to collect evidence and preserve the scene, even though he wasn't sure if they'd understood his message, or even received it. All he heard back was a garbled voice behind the static.

This is not the way it's supposed to be, he thought; this is impossible, this is ridiculous, this is – no! Wrong. Stop thinking that crap right now! Everything is exactly the way it's supposed to be. You just have to look at it, observe it, make good notes, stop bitching about what you don't have, and do your best to understand what you do have.

'Momma, is the rat gonna die when Billy eats him?'

'It's already dead, Michael.'

'You said it was frozen.'

'Yes, I did. The people who raised it, they killed it and froze it. I just let it get warm for Billy.'

'Did it hurt?'

'Did what hurt?'

'When they killed the rat? Did it hurt?'

'Only for a little while, sugar pie.'

'Are we all gonna die? Like the rat?'

'No, Michael, not like the rat. But, yes, we're all gonna die. Sooner or later.'

'Is it gonna hurt?'

'I don't know, Michael. All I know is, you ask so many questions I'm gonna start callin' you the question man. I think you're always thinkin', and I think you're always thinkin' up questions. Every time your tongue goes out, I think you're thinkin' up questions.'

'Momma?'

'What?'

'Why do you dance with Billy?'

'Told you, question man. 'Cause I get paid to dance with him, that's why. And we need money. Do you want to be like those people all they have to eat is cereal and ketchup sandwiches?'

'I like ketchup. I like Rice Krispies.'

'I know you do, but you can't grow up if all you eat is just two things. People just eat two things? Or three? You don't wanna be like them. They don't grow up right.'

Latusek rubbed his chin with the back of his hand. How long should he wait to see if the state police got his message? What should he do in the meantime? He read over his notes again, adding details, elaborating on his first impressions. He got out of the Galaxy and walked around the trailer. Nothing caught his eye, nothing was obviously broken or out of place or trampled, nothing indicated that any part of what had happened inside had somehow leaked outside – except for the blood. The only door on the rear side of the trailer was locked. He made a note of that when he reached the front door again, and then went back inside, careful not to step in the blood, looking, always looking, looking so hard he wondered if it was possible to get a headache from concentrating that much.

This time he went into each room, stood in one place, and systematically looked around the floor, the walls, the ceilings, the flat surfaces, and finally in every closet, in every drawer, on every shelf, and in every corner. When he'd finished, all he was sure of was that the Kadylak family was living on food stamps and Mrs Kadylak's Social Security Disability check. He found documents attesting to their financial circumstances in the top drawer of a chest in the bedroom on the southern end of the trailer, the one with the double bed in it.

What struck him about that bed was that it looked like it had been slept in by someone who was afraid to turn over. The covers were turned back on only half the bed and the bottom sheet looked barely wrinkled. It looked like whoever used it not only didn't sleep but also didn't toss or turn. Now, who does that? Somebody who's not making many moves, obviously. Why? Cause they're listening? On guard? Against what?

By the time he went back to the combination living-dining room, the only other thing about which he had no doubt was that what had happened had ended where it had begun.

He got down on his hands and knees in front of the couch, inching along, lifting the flap of cloth as he went, making sure there had been nothing else under the couch but the shotgun until he'd pulled it out.

He sighed, shook his head, chewed his lower lip, and thought he had to get the gun and shells out of there. But how? Then he remembered the plastic grocery bags stuffed into the plastic garbage bags under the sink. He went to the sink and got a dark brown garbage bag off a roll and one plastic grocery bag out of the mass of bags, took them back to the couch, picked up the empties by slipping his pen into them, and dropped them into the white grocery bag. Then he pulled the dark brown bag over the butt of the shotgun and jiggled it up and around the gun until only a foot or so of the barrel was sticking out. He straightened up, grabbed both bags in his right hand, and, holding them chest high, went out to the Galaxy and put them on the back seat. Then he went back in, got the shotshells and box out of the closet in the south bedroom into another grocery bag, put the .22 rifle from the boy's bedroom into another brown bag, and carried them out to the Galaxy as well. Try as he might, he couldn't find any ammo for the .22.

He made notes of what he did and when, and made another note reminding himself to get the shotgun, the empties, the loaded shells, and the box to the state police crime lab as soon as possible. God, he'd have to call somebody at the lab to tell him how to improvise packing. He didn't want to screw that up.

Then he'd have to get somebody from the state police to fingerprint the three members of the rescue squad as well as the two boys and their father. He'd fingerprinted lots of people, mostly drivers under the influence, but he'd never fingerprinted a corpse before, and he wasn't even sure where the kit for taking fingerprints was. It wasn't in the previous chief's desk, that much he knew. But this was just one more thing he hadn't had a chance to fix in his mind because of all the time he'd spent trying to get the damn mechanic to work on the damn Galaxy. Too many things should have been done yesterday. Or the day before. Or the day before that. Now those days were gone and he was standing around hoping that everything he'd ever learned had prepared him to improvise. I'd better be prepared, he thought, there isn't anybody else but me. Later on there will be, when I get the state police involved, but right now there's just me.

'Are we always gonna live in a trailer?'

'I thought you liked livin' in a trailer. You don't like it now?'

'Trailer's all right. I would maybe just like to go to the same school for a while, 'stead of just gettin' there and then leavin' all the time.'

'You think if we didn't live in a trailer you would?'

'Maybe. I don't know.'

'Michael, we live in this trailer because we have to, not because I think it's so wonderful.'

'Well why do we have to?'

'Why're you askin' me this, Michael? You know why. We stayed in the same place too long, people would get bored with us. With me. They'd quit comin'. And I wouldn't make any money.'

'What's "bored with us" mean?'

'You know how you get tired of travelin' all the time?'

'Yes.'

'Bored's another word for tired.'

'You get bored with Billy? You look real tired every time you come back.'

'No. That's a different kind of tired. I don't ever get bored with Billy. Do I get bored with you?'

'I don't know. Do you?'

'Don't be silly. You're not silly. You're my question man.'

Latusek tried calling the state police at Mecklinboro again, but got no better result than his first try. He sat in the Galaxy for almost a half-hour, hoping they'd heard his calls and were on their way, thinking about what he'd observed, planning what to do next, but no state trooper showed up. Finally he just went and closed the front door of the trailer, got back in the Galaxy, shrugged, and said aloud, 'Can't wait for ever. Gotta talk to people. God, so many people – where do I start?'

It took twelve minutes to get off the mountain, the first ten on the same crumbling macadam he'd come up on, the road making fifteen miles an hour seem reckless. The next two minutes were on a state highway and then city streets to Clay Memorial Hospital, where he parked in the lot outside the emergency room. He went in and asked if anybody knew where the two Kadylak boys were. A clerk and two nurses had indeed heard about the boys' father, but knew nothing about the boys' whereabouts.

When he asked for the person in charge, he was directed to Dr Bergenwirth, his nameplate said, a bearded, balding man in a shirt, tie, khaki pants, and running shoes. He wasn't much older than Latusek. Bergenwirth said he was guessing, but he imagined that the boys had been sent to the top floor of the YMCA.

'The top floor? Oh, yeah, right, the detention center for non-violent juveniles – almost forgot. I didn't handle juveniles. How'd they get there, you know? Any idea? Or when?'

Bergenwirth shrugged and shook his head. 'I'm just guessing they're there. That's where I'd start looking if I were you, that's all. I don't know for a fact that they're there.'

'Uh-huh. The name Kadylak mean anything to you? You happen to treat Martin John Sr in the last couple weeks?'

'No, I personally didn't treat him. But I know he was being treated for infections in numerous self-inflicted wounds, including one in his urethra. Pretty hard not to remember that.'

'Uh, self-inflicted? In the where now?'

'Yeah, there, you got it. The tube through which urine passes.'

'Self-inflicted? How'd he do that?'

'Tried to jam a pencil up there is what I heard. But I don't know whether that's true. It's certainly true that he tried to jam something up there.'

'Oh. Okay. Well, now I guess I know what the nurses were trying to tell me when I was askin' about him earlier. Kept talkin' about a urinary tract infection.'

'Well, it was. Just resulted from a self-inflicted wound, that's all.'

'Uh, you happen to know why he did that? Or would do that?'

'You'll have to talk to the people at Franklinburg. I'm not qualified to answer that and I'm not gonna speculate.'

'Okay. One more thing, then I'll let you go.' Latusek asked for the names of the doctors and nurses who had worked on Martin Kadylak Sr and if they'd be on the same shift tomorrow. He made a note of Bergenwirth's response and his name and title, then thanked him and went looking for a pay phone. Before he spotted the phone in the corridor outside the ER waiting room, he found only three quarters in his pocket and made a note to get a roll of quarters. Then he looked up the YMCA's number in the book and got the switchboard on the fifth ring.

He identified himself and asked if there was a guard or a counselor, someone on the top floor he could talk to. The operator put him on hold, and it was then that it occurred to him he hadn't found another empty in the trailer. One shot in each leg, one in the ceiling, but only two empties. Why was that? Damn! He hadn't even thought to look in the garbage. Oh, man, he groaned mentally, what the hell was I thinking about? Just found the damn empties and assumed that was where the shooter was standing. I don't even know if he was shot in the front of the legs or the back. What difference—? 'Yes, hello? Yes. This is Michael Latusek. I'm the new chief of police? Jefferson Township? I was just hired a couple days ago? Who am I talking to, please?'

'I'm John Beaumeyer. I'm officer in charge on this shift. What can I do for you, Chief?'

'Uh, pleased to meet you, John. You have two boys up there, Kadylak, Martin John Jr, age thirteen, and, uh, Daniel James, age eighteen?'

'Yes, we do.'

Latusek learned that the only interview room in that facility was Beaumeyer's office, that nobody had been in to talk to the boys, that they'd been brought in at eighteen hundred hours in the custody of licensed practical nurse Ralph Stemkow-ski on a verbal order from a district, justice named Welcroft. The boys were being held on a custodial detainer, but could not leave without a release from the judge. Latusek also learned that Beaumeyer was on duty till twenty-three hundred hours.

'Okay, good. Hope to get in there, everything else goes reasonably well. After-noon, John, pleased to meet you.'

'Yeah, sure. Me too, Chief.'

Chief. God, if that doesn't sound strange. Well. Chief. Here we go. Chief.

He hung up, thinking about his two remaining quarters. He dropped one into the slot, pressed for the operator, and let out a long sigh. When the operator answered, he identified himself and where he was calling from, and said he had only two quarters left, didn't have a phone card, needed to talk to the state police in Mechlinboro, and knew it was a toll call. He asked her to connect him with them and charge the call to the Jefferson Township Police Department.

The operator said she would do that, and in moments he was talking first to the Mechlinboro dispatcher and then to the watch commander. Latusek apologized for not having been able to introduce himself before now, then explained the situation, and asked for assistance.

'First available body, I'll have him out there, Chief, but, uh, I'm not promisin' anybody tonight.'

'You're not? You serious? Why not?'

'Oh, I'm serious. All these politicians, they're quick as hell about wantin' to lock everybody up, but when it comes to the wherewithal to do that, well, let's just say they're a couple steps slower.'

'You really can't have anybody out there tonight?'

'Thin is thin, Chief, and if we were any thinner we'd be anorexic. Barracks commander's been promisin' me personnel since he transferred in here two years ago, but I haven't seen anybody yet I don't already know. Understand me now, I'm not sayin' I won't get somebody out there, I'm just not gonna promise. It'll depend when they get back from doin' what they're doin'.'

'Man. Well, hell, can you at least spare me a roll of crime-scene tape? And some evidence bags? And boxes? And a padlock? I need to mail a shotgun and shells to Troop A crime lab, and I need to get that scene taped off, I need to get a lock on the front door, hell, I don't have anything – how about a camera? You spare one of those – that's what I really need – and a tape recorder, man, I really need one of those—'

'Well, if you can get yourself here, I'm sure we can get you equipped. Supplies we got. It's bodies we don't, that's all. You comin' anytime soon? Like now?'

'Just as soon as I hang up.'

'Why can't I have a microscope?'

' 'Cause you know why. Not that one you want.'

'Doesn't cost that much.'

'It does if you don't have what it costs.'

'If you'd let me get a job, I could make enough myself. Josie said he'd give me a job anytime I want it.'

'You can't afford to work for Josie.'

'I can't afford to get the 'scope if I don't. And how am I supposed to see what I wanna see?'

'I told you, question man. Take whatever you wanna look at to school and use one of theirs.'

'If I had my own I could use it any time I wanted.'

'Well, you don't and you can't and that's that. And you can forget about Josie, you're not workin' for him – not as long as I'm breathin'.'

'Why's it all right for you to work for him, but not me? What's wrong with me workin' for him?'

' 'Cause I do, and that's exactly what you're not goin' to.'

'Well, where else am I supposed to get a job? We never stay any place long enough for me to get a job.'

'Some things, question man, you're just gonna have to stop askin' me about. And Josie's one of those things. So whatever you wanna see so bad, take it to school. Use theirs. That's what people pay taxes for.'

'Thought you said we don't pay school taxes. Thought you said that was one of the good things about movin' around. And, anyway, that guy treats me like I'm...'

'Like you're what?'

'Like the first thing I'm gonna do is steal somethin' ... like I'm what I am. Carny people.'

'Listen, question man, I've been carny people since right after you were born, and I never stole anything in my life. But the way you've been lookin' at me for the last year or so, it's pretty obvious you think I stole somethin' from you.'

'I never said that. Never said anything like that.'

'You don't have to. It's all over your face. May as well be neon. You been listenin' to somebody don't like carny people. I told you, you can't do that. Why're you doin' that?'

'Haven't been listenin' to anybody. Just been talkin' to some people, that's all.'

'No, you haven't, you haven't just been talkin' to 'em. You been listenin' to 'em, and I told you all along, you can't listen to people who think where they stand is higher than where you stand. Perspective, remember? Where you look from? Don't look at me that way, don't tell me I haven't told you that, you know I have.'

'Yeah? Well, what Josie says is the only people who like us is other people like us. And there's not too many of them.'

'And I told you before, Josie is the best reason in the world why people like him have to believe that. It's the only way he knows how to be. The only way he can do, the only way he can keep on – it's him against them, him against everybody. But Josie's not who you been listenin' to. You been listenin' to somebody else. And you better stop and figure it out, what they're sayin', whoever they are. 'Cause it's obvious to me you're lookin' up at 'em. And that's a mistake.'

'Soon as I can, I'm gonna join the Marines.'

'Not till you graduate you're not. Not till you're eighteen you're not.'

'You can't stop me.'

'Oh, yes, I can. I know how old you have to be to enlist. And if you do, I'll call whoever recruited you and I'll tell 'em how old you are and they'll send you right back to me till you're eighteen. I know more about this than you do—'

'All you know how to do is dance with Billy.'

'Wrong, question man. I know why I get paid to dance with Billy. You might think you know, but you don't. You used to ask me about it, and you used to think about it, but you haven't asked me about it for a long time, especially not since you started lookin' at me like I'm a thief. I didn't steal anything from you, despite what you think.'

'Yeah? What'd you do with my father? Where's he?'

'What did I do with him? Do? I didn't do anything with him, Michael. What, you think I took him from you? And what? Hid him someplace? Jesus Christ, Michael, who put this stuff in your head? What did I do with your father? Honest to God—'

'Yeah, right. Where is he? How come I've never seen him? How come I don't even have a picture of him?'

'Oh, Michael, who have you been listenin' to? I mean it, who?'

'What difference does it make who? Why don't you just answer the question – where's my father?'

It was dark, twenty-one hundred hours, when Latusek got back from the trailer on Quarry Road and parked in the alley behind the YMCA. He'd been to Mechlinboro and gotten everything he needed from the state police – evidence envelopes, boxes and bags, a camera and film, and a tape recorder and five blank tapes. He'd taken thirty-six exposures inside the trailer, correlating each shot with a note in his book about the time and where he was standing. Then he'd collected all the garbage in the trailer, put the contents of each can into three separate brown plastic bags, and carried them out to the trunk of the Galaxy.

The padlock he'd gotten was useless because there was no way to fix it to the front door, so the tape was all he had, and he wrapped the trailer in a single strand, making it taut over the front door as though that might do more than scare off the humans. He knew it wouldn't do a damn thing for all the illiterate creatures that came out at night, once they smelled the blood.

Driving back to his station, comfortable at least with the thought that he'd soon have thirty-six pictures of what the place looked like after Mr Kadylak had been placed on the litter, Latusek tried to put thoughts of nocturnal creatures out of his mind. And the more he thought about what he wanted to ask the Kadylak boys, the easier it was to forget about raccoons, possums, and bears, and all the other carnivores and scavengers that patrolled at night.

In his station, all the while he was boxing, bagging, and tagging everything he'd collected at the trailer, he was feeling more and more adequate and less and less ashamed of how single-mindedly inefficient he'd been while the Galaxy was being repaired. This was starting to feel like a righteous investigation, if he had to say so himself. Stop that, Goddammit. Start thinking about how the work feels instead of how you do it; you're just asking to screw up. Because that's exactly how you screw up. You start thinking about the result of the work, the reward, the praise, the commendation, how the work is gonna feel after you've done it, instead of doing it – hell, that's how you screwed up and didn't know what you didn't have while you were standing around waiting for some mechanic to finish doing his work. Jesus, get to work, do the work, God knows, there's enough to do . . .

On the top floor of the Y, he got off the elevator and nearly bumped into a burly man with bristly white hair. 'You John Beaumeyer?'

'Yes. Chief Latusek, is it?'

'Yeah. Nice to meet you. Need to use your office now. Wanna send those kinds in? Kadylaks? The young one first, okay?'

'I don't think so. He's pretty much glued to his big brother.'

'Then we're gonna have to unglue 'em. Some things you can't separate, some things you have to separate. I'll help you, c'mon. I'm not gonna talk to both of them at the same time. That goes against everything I've ever learned.'

'I don't know why you always get so mad every time I talk about Josie. Josie treats me better'n almost anybody.'

'That's 'cause Josie's real good at hidin'. He's been practicin' all his life.'

'He's not hidin' – what do you mean, hidin'? He's right there. Every day, everybody can see him – he's right there.'

'That's not the kind of hidin' I'm talkin' about. Josie carries his own spotlights with him everywhere he goes. His own stage, too.'

'Aw, he does not. What're you talkin' about? All he does is sell tickets – he doesn't have an act.'

'Oh, Michael, listen to yourself. Josie carries his own lights, he sets up where he wants to set up, he puts the spot where it shows him off the best – that's what I'm talkin' about. Josie's way better than most at hidin' whatever he doesn't want anybody else to see.'

'He treats me all right, that's all I care about.'

'I know you do. It's nice to think we just have to be the way other people are with us. But sometimes you have to think about how people are with other people, not just you. Sometimes you have to put yourself out for other people. Sometimes you have to do what's not always good for just you.'

Latusek followed Beaumeyer to the last double-bunk bed on the right in the dormitory. The Kadylak boys were sitting on the edge of the bottom bunk, facing the wall, the older one holding the younger, rocking him, neither saying anything.

'Daniel?'

'Yes?'

'I'm Chief Latusek. Remember me? We met in the emergency room, remember? This afternoon?'

'Yes.'

'I need to talk to you, both of you. But one at a time. Your brother first, okay? So tell him he has to come with me. I'm just goin' up to the office there—'

'Uh-uh. He won't talk to you, he's too scared.'

'I'm sure he's scared, Daniel, but I still have to talk to him.'

'No. He thinks everybody's gonna die ... or go away ... he's way too scared to talk to anybody. Won't even talk to me much. Only thing he wants to know is if I'm gonna leave him too.'

Latusek bent over and put his hands on his knees. 'Listen to me, Martin. You listenin' to me? I'm sure you're scared. But I'm also sure I have to talk to you. Now, whatever way you think we can do this, I'll give it a listen. But, one way or another, you're gonna talk to me, you understand me, Martin?'

'Want my mom,' Martin sniffled.

'So do I, son,' Latusek said. 'My mom was taken from me same as your mom was taken. Maybe not the same way exactly. She had a different thing wrong with her, but she was taken, Martin, just the way yours was. I mean one day she was there, and the next day she wasn't. I was a lot older than you are when this happened. I was twenty. How old are you?'

'Thirteen,' Daniel said. 'He just turned thirteen.'

'See, Daniel, this is why I wanna talk to you separately. You're answerin' for him, and I don't want that, understand? I ask him something, I want to hear what he's got to say, I don't wanna hear what you have to say for him, understand? Now, I'm gonna go away for a couple minutes, me and Mister Beaumeyer here, we're gonna walk away so you two can talk to each other, decide how you wanna do this. But here's the thing, Daniel. You listenin'? Martin? This will happen. I am gonna talk to you separately. How you two decide which one's gonna go first and what the other one's gonna do while you're waitin', I'm gonna let that up to you, both of you. Just know that it's gonna happen and it's gonna happen in the next couple minutes, okay? Daniel? You hear me?'

'Yes. I hear you.'

'Martin? You hear me?

'Momma ... momma ...'

'What'd you do to Billy?'

'What did I do to Billy? Mickey, I didn't do nothin' to Billy, why you lookin' at me like that? Talkin' to me like that, man, you talk like I did somethin' wrong to Billy. I didn't do nothin' wrong with him. That snake got old, that's all. That snake died, that's what happened. Probably had a heart attack.'

'Snakes don't have heart attacks. Pneumonia, renal failure, parasites, predators, old age if you can't put a name on it, but they don't have heart attacks.'

'What? You think snakes live for ever or somethin'? Snakes die, man, just like people. They get old, they get sick, they die, don't kid yourself.'

'Yeah? So how come my mother's where she is now? How come she can't even talk now? How come nobody ever comes to see her? They come to see her they gotta sneak. Why's that, Josie? Why they have to sneak?'

'Mickey, Mickey, you gotta understand, it was time for your mother to retire. She wasn't feelin' good, she wasn't lookin' good, Mickey, hey, everybody's got to move on, sooner or later. One thing about life, it keeps changin' – that's the one thing stays the same, my man. Everything's all the time changin'. All the time, the one thing never changes is everything changes.'

'She wrote to me, Josie, she told me. She wrote to me all the time. She told me what was happenin'.'

'What was happenin'? What? What was happenin'? I'm not followin' you.'

'She told me you kept on her, tellin' her it was time to quit.'

'' Cause I wanted her to retire? That's what this is about? Well, that's right, I did. I did want her to retire. I had to get new talent in here, my man, we were starvin', we were goin' down. Nobody wants to look at same-old faces all the time, you know that. There's VCR's, man. People can get anything on those videos. You wanna see people doin' it with horses, donkeys, dogs, whatever, man, you can see it. Don't have to leave your house. You wanna compete with that, you gotta give 'em somethin' they can't see on their VCR. C'mon, man, figure it out, you're smart. You always been smart. Know how I knew you were smart, huh? You were always askin' questions. How's this work, how's that work, always askin'. Only dumb thing you ever did was not work for me. I coulda showed you how everything worked, Mickey.'

'She didn't want me to work for you. You're not answerin' my question. How come her friends have to sneak around to see her?'

'What're you askin' me for? Ask them. Maybe they ain't as good a friends as she thinks, ever think of that?'

'I'm gonna ask them lotsa things. I'm gonna find out what you did to Billy—'

'Oh, man, grow up, I didn't do nothin' to that snake. People get old, snakes get old, people get sick, snakes too, what the fuck you think? This is new to you? You never heard this? Happens to everybody, man, everybody and everything. I own the show, but I ain't God. What, you think I punished that snake cause I caught it feedin' apples to your mother or somethin'? Hey, this is the world here, Mickey, I didn't do nothin' to that fuckin' snake. It died, that's all. Understand? What your momma don't wanna understand is she don't look good no more. She ate too much, she wanted to eat sausage every day. I told her, you could eat when you're young, when you're twenty, thirty maybe, but you can't keep eatin' that when you get old, all that grease. Not if you're takin' your clothes off for guys to look at. She didn't wanna listen to me, she let herself go, nobody wants to look at that.'

'At that? Look at that? You talkin' about my mother? Is that the that you're talkin' about?'

'Hey, Mickey, listen to me, man. This ain't nice what I'm gonna say, okay? But if people laugh at you, man, the only way you make money is if you're a comedian, understand? And your mother, she wasn't Lucille Ball, understand? She was a snake dancer. And snake dancers, they got to look good, understand? Guys don't wanna get up off their money to see nobody old, fat, so weak she can't lift the damn snake over her head – you understandin' anything I'm sayin' here, Mickey? Or those Goddamn marines turned your brain to shit or what?'

'I'm learnin' a lot from them, you can quit worryin' about what's happenin' to my brain.'

'I'm not worried. I just don't understand you, that's all. I thought we was tight, man. Then, boom, away you go, joinin' up. I mean that's somethin' I'll never understand, Mickey, why you joined up with that outfit. I had a trucker worked for me one time, know what he told me? He says, you know what USMC stands for, those initials, man? Uncle Sam's Misguided Children. And listenin' to you now, I'm thinkin', yeah, he was right. 'Cause if you're not a misguided child, talkin' all this nonsense what I did to Billy, man, if you're not a USMC, I never seen one.'

'So, uh, Daniel, what's it gonna be, son? You two decided yet?'

Daniel, looking first at the floor and then at the top of his brother's head as he held him, said nothing for a long moment. Then he said, 'I know what you said you have to do, but he can't do it. He's too scared. You just have to ask me what you wanna know. I can't let him go now. He told me, don't go away, don't go away, that's all he can say. Honest, just ask me what you want, I'll tell you. I won't lie, just let him stay with me, okay?'

So much for all my tough talk about keeping them together, Latusek thought. 'Just know that it's gonna happen and it's gonna happen in the next couple minutes.' Yeah, right.

Beaumeyer tapped Latusek on the shoulder and whispered, 'I'm not tryin' to tell you how to do your job, Chief, but, uh, in my experience, I mean, lookin' at that boy? You're not gonna get anything outta him anyway. Not tonight. Maybe not ever. What can it hurt if he comes along?'

'Can hurt everything,' Latusek whispered back. 'Keepin' 'em together goes against everything I've ever learned.'

Latusek bent over again, hands on knees, his face inches away from Daniel's face. 'Okay, Daniel. You can keep him with you. We're gonna go to Mister Beaumeyer's office now, okay? But, Daniel, listen to me. If I ask you a question and he answers it? Or if I ask you a question and you look at him before you answer me? If that happens just once, Daniel, do you understand? Either one of those two things happens? I bring him back here and I handcuff him to the bed – do you understand what I just said? If you do, I want you to say that you do, okay? Say it now.'

Daniel hesitated, nodding slowly.

'No, uh-uh, Daniel. I have a tape recorder in my pocket – look, see here?' Latusek pulled it out of his shirt pocket and held it in front of Daniel's eyes. 'This here? The sound of our voices turns it on, I don't have to turn it on, it's been runnin' the whole time we've been talkin' here, so what I'm sayin' is, you can't nod your head or shake your head, you have to speak, you have to say the words, you understand me?'

'Yes.'

'Yes what?'

'Yes, I understand you.'

'And what about the other thing I just said about if you look at your brother when I ask you somethin' – did you understand that too? And what'll happen if you do that?'

'Yes. I understand.'

'Okay. Good. Let's go. We're goin' to Mister Beaumeyer's office now.'

Inside the office, Beaumeyer got a couple of folding chairs out of his closet, set them up beside his desk, and motioned for the boys to sit.

'Wait a second,' Latusek said. 'Don't sit just yet. You can, Martin, but not you, Daniel. I want you to take your clothes off, Daniel. Not everything, just your shirt and pants. Keep your underwear on. Don't leave, Mister Beaumeyer, please, I want you to witness this, okay?'

'What're you doin'?' Beaumeyer said.

'Why you want me to do that?'

'Just do it, son, okay? I wanna examine your body, take some pictures. Don't argue with me, just do it.'

Latusek took off his cap, ran his fingers through his hair a couple of times, and then set the tape recorder on the corner of the desk, identified everyone in the room, and stated the time, date, and place of the interview. He then said that Daniel was removing his shirt and pants.

When Daniel was standing awkwardly in his cotton briefs, Latusek told him to extend both arms out in front of himself and then to hold over his head. There were two very bright red marks on Daniel's body: one on his right torso, starting in the middle of his ribs and extending downward for nearly two inches; and another one right below the bottom of his briefs on his right thigh.

Latusek pointed them out to Beaumeyer and asked him if he saw them. Beaumeyer said that he did. Latusek then took six photographs of Daniel, two showing his face and torso down to about the midpoint of his thighs, then two closeups each of the red mark on his ribs and the other two of the top of his thigh. He knew without doubt that Daniel had fired the shotgun. The mark on the ribs had to have resulted from the shot fired into the ceiling, the one on the thigh from the shots at his father's legs.

Latusek put the camera on top of a file cabinet, put his cap over it, ran his fingers through his hair, and told Daniel to put his clothes back on and sit beside his brother in the folding chairs. He pulled Beaumeyer's swivel chair around so that it was close to the corner of the desk and sat so that his knees were only inches away from Daniel's knees. Martin Jr huddled close to Daniel, trying to press himself into his brother's armpit.

'You boys hungry? Thirsty?'

'No, uh-uh. He got us some cheese crackers and a Pepsi before.'

'So you don't want anything now?'

Daniel shook his head.

'You have to speak, Daniel. Remember? This is a sound recorder, all right? And your answers have to be on the tape.'

'Forgot. Sorry. No, I don't want anything – I mean we don't want anything.'

'Okay. But if you want anything, at any time, okay? Just say so, and if I can get it for you, I will. If you have to go the bathroom? Just speak up, all right?'

'Yes. All right.'

'All right.' All right, Latusek, he thought, time to get to it. And don't waste anybody's time here, get right to it. 'Now, Daniel, I want you to understand some things, okay? You're eighteen years old – is that correct?'

'Yes.'

'You understand that makes you an adult?'

'Yes.'

'Okay. Now, what I'm gonna say next is very important and I want you to say that you understand it, okay, and if you don't I want you to say that too, okay? I want you to know that I'm gonna be asking you questions about your father's death and that anything you say can and will be used against you in a court of law. Do you understand that?'

'Yes.'

'And also that you can have an attorney present if you want one – do you understand that?'

'Yes. But I don't know any.'

'That's all right, you don't have to know any. If you want one, the courts have to get one for you, okay? You understand that?'

'Yes.'

'Do you want one?'

'Uh-uh.'

'Is that a no?'

'Yeah. I mean that's a no.'

'You sure, Daniel? You positive that you don't want an attorney here, right beside you?'

Daniel shrugged and looked at the floor. 'You already seen where the shotgun kicked me. My ribs're real sore. I'm not gonna lie even if I could.'

'Okay, Daniel. Just tell me where you were standing when you shot your father the first time, okay? Approximately, it doesn't have to be exactly where you were standing, okay? I know nobody can remember exactly where they were when these things happen, but just try, okay?'

'Uh, well. I was, uh, I guess we were, uh, by the couch. At the end there. Of the couch. Yeah.'

'Toward the kitchen? That end of the couch, you mean?'

'Uh-huh, yeah.'

'And when you said "we" just now, you were talkin' about who? You and Martin, or you and your father? Who did you mean when you said "we"?'

'My dad. Not Junior. Just my dad and me.'

'And why were you by the couch? Did you get up from the table? Where you were havin' cereal? Is that where it started? At the table when you were havin' cereal – who had the Wheaties? You? You had the Wheaties?'

'Uh-uh, no, I had the Cheerios. Junior and me, we had the Cheerios. Dad, he, uh, he always had Wheaties.'

'And that's where it started? At the table? Was it over the cereal or what?'

'Over the cereal? No it wasn't over – uh-uh, didn't have nothin' to do with the cereal.'

'What was it over, then?'

'It was over the gun. Uh, you know, the gun, that's what it was over.'

'The gun? Now, when you say the gun, do you mean the shotgun or the rifle?'

'No, the shotgun. It didn't have nothin' to do with the rifle – well, I mean it did but it didn't. Maybe if it did, maybe it wouldn't've happened, I don't know.'

'Uh-huh. Whose shotgun was it, by the way? Yours? Or your dad's?'

'Oh, it was his, my dad's, it wasn't mine, uh-uh.'

'Uh-huh. So you're sayin' if it had been about the rifle, it might not've happened? Why're you saying that?'

'I'm not sure, I don't know, but maybe, you know. I mean, when I think about it, maybe it would've, uh, been different. But Junior, he's, uh, the shotgun is just, you know, it's too loud. It's way too loud, it makes him cover his ears. Used to crawl under the bed. Not any more, but he used to.'

'The shotgun scares Junior, right?'

'Scared me, too. Scared us all.'

'Well, okay, you said it's too loud for him. Why's it scare you?'

' 'Cause you don't know, I mean, none of us, you know, we didn't know when he was gonna get, uh, you know, like he'd get ... and, uh, go outside and start shootin'. Could be the middle of the night, could be early in the mornin'. Well, it was never in the daytime. Was always at night. Woke everybody up. 'Specially Junior. He'd start cryin', couldn't stop. Mom'd get so mad at him, she'd start cryin'.'

'At your dad?'

'Yeah. Oh, yeah.'

'Would he be drinkin'? When he'd go shoot it?'

'You mean like beer? Or whiskey? No, he didn't drink. I mean, all he ever drank was diet pop, that's all.'

'So what was he shootin' at when he was out there? Animals?'

'Oh, no. Viet Congs. He was always sayin', you know, these Viet Congs were out there, they had tunnels all over the mountain, that's why he couldn't work no more. He didn't have time to work, he had to quit.'

'Had to quit because of the Viet Cong? Which job was that?'

'At the quarry. Drove a truck for the quarry. But he kept sayin' the guy that owned the quarry, he knew what he was up to. He was all nice and polite durin' the day, but at night he'd give the Viet Congs a signal and they'd come outta their tunnels and he had to go on patrol, my dad. And he'd be out there shootin'. Scared Junior so bad ... Mom ... me, too. All of us...'

'Uh-huh. So, uh, Daniel, the second shot. You move? Or were you still standin' more or less by the end of the couch?'

'Yeah ... he got up. I didn't know how he got up ... I didn't think he could get up ... I mean, he was down there so long ... on the floor ... and he just kept talkin' how he had to teach Junior how to guard the perimeter ... he said Junior was old enough, he was at least as old as some of those Viet Congs, thirteen, you know ... he kept sayin' Junior had to start pullin' his own duty, he couldn't loaf out on the rest of us, dope off ... he had to learn how to shoot ... when he came back, you know, with the gun, Junior just started screamin', he was terrified...'

'And your dad wanted to teach him how to shoot it? Is that what this was about?'

'Yeah. He taught me when I was twelve. He kept sayin' if I could learn when I was twelve, Junior could damn sure learn when he was thirteen, and I kept tellin' him, Dad, you didn't teach me with the shotgun, you taught me with the .22. The .22 don't kick, it don't have any, uh, oh, what's the word?'

'Recoil?'

'Yeah, recoil. Couldn't think of it for a second. I mean, I couldn't shoot the shotgun either when I was twelve, I told him, I said you can't expect Junior to shoot it, look how little he is, he shoots that, you make him shoot that, you know, it'll hurt him. I know, he made me shoot it once. God, my shoulder was messed up for about a week. Thought it was broke. I mean it wasn't, but I thought it was.'

'And this is what you were tryin' to tell your dad?'

'Oh, yeah. But he wouldn't listen. Mom said he wouldn't listen to anybody, wouldn't listen to her, wouldn't listen to the people at the VA ... but I couldn't just, you know, just ... do nothin'. Couldn't just sit there. Had to try.'

'So it was your dad brought the shotgun into the dining room, right? Your father went from the dining room to his bedroom, correct? And when he came back he had the shotgun with him right?'

'Yeah, uh-huh. I mean we were just sittin' there, you know, eatin'. And he seemed real ... okay, you know? We were just talkin', and he was askin' Junior how he was doin' in school and we told him school was out for the summer and stuff like that. And the next thing, oh, man, he starts in about the Viet Congs, and the perimeter, and the tunnels, and how old Junior was, and thirteen was time to learn, time to start pullin' his own duty like everybody else, and then he jumped up ... and when he came back, you know, he was, uh, he walked up to the table real fast, and he had some shells in his hand, and he said, Junior, look at me. Stop that bawlin'. Look. This is all you gotta do, this is how you load it, and he started loadin' it, and Junior was bawlin' and he just started shakin', and I said, Dad, he's scared, you're scarin' him, and he said, Cut it out, cut out that cryin', you're not a baby, you're thirteen, them Viet Congs, they were nine years old, some of 'em and they wouldn't come up to your shoulder, the top of their heads, and they killed us, boy. They killed your momma, don't you know that? You gotta be ready, they're out there, they killed her, they'll kill you in a heartbeat, and he just kept on, and he wouldn't stop ...'

'Jesus,' Beaumeyer said.

'And you got the gun away from him? How did you do that?'

Daniel shrugged. 'I just asked him for it. I said, Dad, let me show him, okay? He's scared – I didn't wanna say he was scared of you, you know. So I just said, Here, let me show him.'

'And he handed it over?'

'Oh, yeah. He got real proud. Started tellin' Junior, Look, look at your brother, that's how a man pulls his duty, quit your bawlin' and look. Show him, Danny boy, attaboy, show him. Listen, there's one on the roof now, I can hear him, he's up there, shoot the son of a bitch, shoot him now, Goddammit! Just kept sayin' it, Shoot him now, Danny, shoot him now, he's right over your head, shoot him! Blow his balls off, he ain't a man, he don't need 'em, shoot the son of a bitch right between the legs, do it! He just kept hollerin' and ... God, he was real close to me ... That's an order, private, you disobeyin' me? That's an order, Goddammit, shoot him or I will, and then I'll shoot you. You and your bawl-baby brother, I'll shoot you both you don't shoot him ... So, you know, I shot him. There wasn't anybody up there, but I thought, God a'mighty, what am I supposed to do? So I shot. Right through the ceilin'. It kicked so hard, thought I broke my ribs or somethin'.

'And Junior just, God, he just started screamin' and he stood up and he peed all over himself and Dad just started hollerin' how the Viet Congs didn't pee themselves, they were nine years old and they were men and you hada kill them or they'd kill you, blow their balls off so they damn sure couldn't make any more Viet Congs. He just kept sayin' all that crazy stuff ... then he started grabbin' for the gun and hollerin' how Junior was some kinda Vee Cee and his eyes were just ... I don't know, he was gone, I never saw anybody like that, he was just ... I don't know how to say how he was ... he was ... ugly. Ugly. Junior was screamin', Dad was grabbin' the gun and I don't know how it happened, honest to God I don't, but he jerked on the barrel real hard and I let go, and the handle, the butt, you know? Soon as I let go when he was jerkin' on it so hard? The butt hit him right between the legs, and he just let go of the gun, and he doubled over and he fell down on his knees and he was holdin' himself, and he was ... groanin' and swearin', and he looked at me and he said, Gimme that gun, and he stood up and I don't even know how I was holdin' the gun again, I don't know how I got it back ... but he was comin' for it, or for me, or both, I don't know, and he was ... God, his eyes were ugly ... and I said, Don't, please, Dad, don't ... and he was snarlin' at me, and makin' this noise, God, he sounded like some dog, and I was cryin' ... and he said, I'm gonna kill all you Vee Cees ... and he jumped at me and I don't even remember pullin' the trigger.

'I don't even remember puttin' another shell in, honest. I just felt this, uh, this wham in my leg and he screamed and Junior was screamin' and there was blood all over his leg . . . and he was on the floor . . . and then, oh, man, he started gettin' up, and I didn't wanna hurt him, honest, I didn't wanna hurt him . . . but we were all screamin' or cryin' and he was screamin', Vee Cee, Vee Cee, Vee Cee, and I felt this wham in my leg again and the noise. My ears were ringin' and Junior was hollerin', Momma, Momma . . . and he just was layin' there . . . and I put the gun down and sorta shoved it under the couch with my foot, I remember shovin' it under there, I don't know why I did that but I did, and I remember goin' to the phone and we have this party line and these two women are always talkin', they never let anybody else get on the line without makin' a real big deal, and they wouldn't let me get on, and I said, Please, I have to call somebody, and they said you don't need to call anybody, and they were askin' me who I thought I was interruptin' them and they wouldn't listen to me . . . and I turned around and there was blood everywhere . . . it was just shootin' up out of his legs like a fountain, just shootin' straight up in the air, I couldn't believe it . . . and I tried to call again and those ladies wouldn't let me talk, they wouldn't . . . and I just screamed at 'em, Let me call somebody, please, you gotta let me call somebody, I just shot my dad, he's hurt real bad, he's bleedin', and then they finally hung up and let me call . . .'

'Mickey, he finds out I been talkin' to you, he'll put me out.'

'You mean like he put my mother out?'

'Listen, Mickey, I didn't have nothin' whatsoever to do with that. That was between them.'

'I didn't say you did. You listen, Herman. He might put you out, but he can't strip your tattoos off you, he can't put you out by takin' somethin' away from you. You are your work, you know? It was a little different with my mother.'

'Oh, we're all just hangin' on here, Mickey. Hell, most places now, little girls got tattoos. On their ankles, on their backs, on their backsides. Whole damn country's freaky. I don't stand out no more. Freak shows on TV all the time. MTV, all them rock 'n' rollers? You ever see that guy plays basketball for the Chicago Bulls? Fifty years ago he'd be happy to carry my bags, now he's all over TV.'

'Remember what Josie used to say?'

'I know, I know, "Spare me the sermon, Herman." I ain't tryin' to give you one—'

'You're not answerin' me. And you're not listenin' to me. There's nothin' I can do about Josie, Herman. Listen to me. Even if I could get a humane officer to pay attention to me, there's no way he could get anybody to corroborate what I'm sayin' he did to Billy, understand me? Herman? You understand?'

'I'm listenin', I'm listenin'.'

'You look like you're listenin', Herman, I can see that, but what I'm askin' you is, do you understand? I can't do anything to Josie. Most anybody could get him for is cruelty to animals, I haven't looked up the law yet. Pay a fine maybe, three hundred bucks or somethin', probation maybe, I don't know what it is. That's if it was a dog. Somebody's little poochie. But nobody's gonna get real worked up about him killin' a snake, and, anyway, we both know nobody's gonna do that 'cause nobody in the show's gonna trash him, Herman, am I right? You see what I'm sayin'?'

'Yeah, I see it, I see it. So whatta ya want from me?'

'I wanna know what he did with Billy.'

'Why? What difference does it make? He's gone, that's all. And your mam's gone too now, so what difference does it make?'

'Herman, just think a minute, okay? When you go down, your tattoos are goin' down with you, right? When Tiny goes down, all his fat's goin' down with him—'

'If they can find a box big enough—'

'And when Hairy Mary goes down her beard's goin' too, right?'

'Yeah, so? When we go down, we take our schtick with us, so what?'

'Herman, open your eyes for a second, will ya? My mam's goin' without Billy. That's not right. How would you like it if Josie skinned you?'

'That's not funny, Mickey.'

'I'm not tryin' to be funny. Just think about it. How about if he skinned you and all your movin' pictures disappeared? You went down in one place and your art gallery went down someplace only Josie knew where. You think that'd be right? C'mon, Herman. That'd be right?'

'Man, Mickey, how'd you get so weird? That's disgusting, I don't even wanna think about that.'

'Well, try thinkin' about it, 'cause that's the way it's gonna be with my mom. She did her whole life with Billy. Raised me on money she made with him. Sometimes I hated that fuckin' snake, sometimes I was so jealous of that snake, man, I'd be lyin' if I said there weren't times I wanted to kill that snake myself. But I didn't. But in two days, Herman, two days, she's goin' down without him. And you know what happened to him. If anybody in the show knows, you know.'

'That's all you wanna do? Just put him in the box with your mom? You swear?'

'That's all.'

'He's in his trailer. Just the head. He had it taxidermed.'

'He had him mounted? Billy's head?'

'I don't think it's mounted on nothin'. You mean like a deer head?'

'Yeah.'

'No, I don't think so. I only seen it once, but I don't remember no plaque or nothin'.'

'What'd he do with the rest?'

'Huh? Oh. I was thinkin' about my gallery bein' buried someplace else. What'd he do with the rest? I don't know, threw it in some lake, reservoir, somethin'. Green County, I think. We were workin' some firemen's festival or somethin'. I think that's where we were, but I'm not sure now.'

'So, uh, how'd he kill it?'

'How you think? His precious little .32. Yeah. Has the bullet on his keychain.'

'On his what?'

'His keychain, I said. Either he got it from the taxidermy guy, or maybe it went through, I don't know. But he says it's the one that did it. That I heard. Heard him say that myself. You sure this ain't gonna come back on me, Mickey? 'Cause you're startin' to get a funny look.'

'I'm not gettin' any look. Don't worry about it, it'll never come back on you. Not from me. Unless you're the only one he told.'

'You kiddin'? This here, Josie wanted everybody to know.'

John Beaumeyer was putting the folding chairs back in his closet when he asked Latusek what he thought.

'About what?'

'You believe him?'

'I still have a lotta people to talk to. People at Franklinburg, I haven't talked to anybody there yet. Man was there four years at least. In and out a couple years before that. Maybe somebody there heard him carryin' on about the "Viet Congs", I don't know. His former employer'll have something to say. His neighbors. Either they heard him shootin', carryin' on, or they didn't. For the kid's sake, I hope they back him up because I think you're right about the younger one. I don't think he's gonna be able to talk to anybody for a long time. Just losin' your momma is enough to shake anybody up. Shook the hell outta me. But then you see your father go down the way his went down? And his brother's holdin' the gun? You hear a lotta people throw this word "traumatized" around, but in this case, though I don't pretend to be any expert, I think this time the word that applies here is "traumatized." '

Latusek shrugged and headed for the elevator. 'Doesn't matter what I think, anyway. After I've interviewed all the people I can find who might know somethin', asked all the questions I can think of, then, hey, it's not up to me to think about anything. It's up to the coroner and the DA. I'm just another witness. I just have to be the best witness I can, that's all. Which means I got a lotta writin' to do.' Latusek shook hands with Beaumeyer, told him it was nice to meet him, and said good night.

Once outside, Latusek loosened his tie and unbuttoned his collar in the humid, almost balmy night air. He got in the Galaxy and drove slowly to the Protestant section of the county cemetery, glancing occasionally at the quarter-moon. He had no trouble finding his mother's grave, even without a flashlight. He squatted down beside it, took off his cap, patted the damp grass, and said, 'Hello, Momma. It's me again. Worked my first case today. You know, as chief. God, that still sounds so strange. Anyway, needed a lotta help, didn't work it myself. And I got a ton of work to do yet. But I couldn't wait to tell you; it's very, very satisfyin'. It really is. Not as satisfyin' as when I nailed Josie's ugly ass, but, what the hell, nothin's ever gonna be as satisfyin' as that.

'These poor kids, Momma, God, I feel so sorry for 'em. There's almost nothin' left. Their momma died, seventeen days ago, I think. Kidneys. Then their father, he's on paranoid patrol, sounds like he did some real hard time in Vietnam, not sure about that, have to check ... anyway, he wants to show his younger son how to shoot a shotgun. The wind-up is, his older boy, Jesus, I hope he gets a good lawyer, he shoots the old man, twice, once in each leg, guy bleeds to death. Right in their dining room, living room. Hell, their trailer, it was a lot bigger than ours, Momma, it was like a little house, you know, but it still got me thinkin' right away about us, just bein' in it.

'All day long, I kept thinkin' about how it was when you had to go down. Just kept hearin' all those conversations I had with people. Heard 'em as clear as if they were on a tape inside my head. Maybe they are. You. Herman, the game warden, funeral director, the preacher. Those last three were tough. Really. It was all I could do to convince 'em that you weren't goin' down without Billy. What was left of him. But I did. Don't know how I did it, really. I mean I know. But I don't know where I found it in me to stay cool, to stay calm, to do what had to be done, to do it right, 'cause, God, Momma, everything in me wanted to do Josie the way he did Billy.

'I know you've heard this all before. Don't know why I think I have to tell you again. But I do. I think it's 'cause I never believed you about him and I still feel really crappy about that. Crappy. Hell, that's not the word. Guilty. That's the word. No other word like it. Guilty. All the times you told me, kept tellin' me, yeah, right, Josie's fine with you, he wants to act like you're his son, but you're not his son, and don't let him tell you you are. But I wish you'd told me who my father was, Momma. I'll never understand why you didn't. Only thing I can think of is, somehow, for some reason you were ashamed of him. Too late now. I'll never know.

'But when I was talkin' to that poor kid tonight, Momma, I felt it so hard. Honest to God, I know it's gonna sound like I'm exaggeratin', but my goddamn bones hurt, I mean it. It hurt me in my bones, I felt so bad for that kid. And I knew half of it was I was just feelin' sorry for me. Couldn't help it. It's hard not to know, Momma. Sometimes, like tonight, when I had to ask that boy if he killed his own father, and he said, in the softest, sweetest voice . . . I mean, this boy's eighteen, he doesn't look like he's gone through puberty yet. Tall, skinny, got a face like a baby. And he spoke so soft I had to keep tellin' him to speak up, son, speak up.

'Speak up, son. Exactly what the game warden said to me.'

'Speak up, son. You want me to do what now? You want me to arrest a man for killing your mother's boa constrictor?'

'Yes, sir. I can prove it too, sir. But you have to help me. We have to surprise him. If he knows we're comin', he'll get rid of everything. Get rid of Billy's head, and he'll get rid of the bullet, which he keeps on his keychain. He brags about it. It's how he keeps everybody in line, all the people who work for him. He caused my mother to die, sir.'

'He did what now?'

'She died, sir. People told me that when she heard the shot and she went to see what was goin' on, when she found Billy thrashin' around and she saw all that blood, she didn't know what to do, she couldn't help Billy, couldn't do anything for him, his head was dead, gone, you know, the bullet went through his brain, his body was there, but it was just thrashin' around, it wasn't alive. And she knew she couldn't help him? And she knew what was gonna happen to her? Without Billy?'

'What was gonna happen to her, son?'

'Without him, she didn't know how to make money. I know it sounds stupid, but that's all she thought she knew how to do.'

'What did she do?'

'She had a stroke, sir. Right there. And a month later, she had another one. And she died with that one.'

'No, no, I mean with the snake.'

'She was a performer, sir. A snake dancer. She danced with Billy. In a carnival, you know? A travelin' show?'

'So the snake wasn't just a pet, it was part of her livelihood.'

'He was part of her life. She had Billy almost as long as she had me. She got him about when I was like four, five months old.'

'And this man who shot Billy – he was her employer?'

'Yes, sir.'

'And you're also saying he killed your mother?'

'No, sir, that's not what I'm saying. He didn't actually kill her. But when he killed Billy? When he shot Billy? He might as well've shot my momma, might as well've put that bullet right through her brain.'

'Well, son, don't be upset about what I'm going to say, but that's a little farfetched for me. I'm just a game warden, son. Crimes against persons are not what I do.'

'I know what you are. That's why I came to you. I know nobody can get him for killin' my mom. But I know you can get him for killin' Billy. Killin' a zoo animal, sir, I looked up the law. That's a second-degree misdemeanor in Pennsylvania. You get him convicted of that, he could get two years. Plus a fine, plus costs. And I want him to get as much of *that as any judge will give him, sir. I want to do it right, sir, because I'm a military policeman now, and I want to be a policeman when I get out. I want to do the right thing, sir. Please, help me.'*

'And he did, Momma – which I know you know. Just love tellin' it. He got a search warrant for Josie's person, truck, and trailer. Found the bullet on his key-chain, found the .32 Colt, and found Billy's head in a coffee-can in his bedroom closet. Matched the bullet and the Colt – I know, I know, I've told you this a hundred times. Can't help myself, Momma. I never get tired of tellin' you. I just wish you were here sometimes. So we could talk the way we used to.

'You said somethin' to me, oh, coupla times. Every once in a while I think about it. First time you said it, you were real mad at me, remember? When I first started talkin' about joinin' the Marines? Remember how you said when I was little I used to think about why you danced with Billy, but then I grew up and turned into a smart-ass and stopped thinkin' about it? I never stopped thinkin' about it, Momma. I just think it's somethin' I'm never gonna be smart enough to understand. You knew somethin' about you and dancin' with Billy and why men wanted to watch you that I don't think I'm ever gonna understand. Not the way you did. Wish you were here so we could talk about it. Lotsa other stuff, too.

'Well, time to go, Momma, my butt's really draggin'. See you soon, let you know how things are goin'. Goodnight, Momma. Give my best to Billy.'

STAYING AWAY FROM AMY

Jane Haddam

There was a clutch of flies weaving in and out of the blades of the ceiling fan the day the judge handed down her second restraining order – and all the time the droning was going on, Bobby Shear watched them. It was easier to watch the flies than to look straight ahead. The judge had a truly awful face, the most awful face Bobby had ever seen, and it bothered him no end that she didn't wear make-up. None of the women around Amy these days wore make-up, although Amy still did. If Bobby turned his head a little to the right, he could see the side of Amy's face, with her hair pulled back in a barrette and her eyelashes blackened and stiff, the way they always were. If he did that, he would want to reach across and grab her by the arm, the way he had the night before, which was what had gotten him into this mess. He would also have to see the bruises, which he would rather not do. Amy had two black eyes and a broken right arm this afternoon. Bobby vaguely remembered one of the ambulance men worrying that he might have cracked her skull. He was so hung over, he was sick to his stomach. It didn't help that the air-conditioner was on the blink and this was South Carolina in July. Nothing helped, really. He was nineteen years old and his life was over. The last good time he could remember having was over a year ago, on the night of Amy's senior prom, when they had driven out to the lake at dawn and gotten laid four times on a mattress in the back of his daddy's flatbed truck. Bobby hadn't had a senior prom of his own because he had dropped out of high school at the end of his sophomore year.

The judge was looking pained. She had taken her glasses off and begun to rub the bridge of her nose between her thumb and forefinger. Sometimes, when he was feeling particularly clear-headed, Bobby wondered what it would be like to get this woman by the throat and pop her eyes out of her head. Sometimes he just imagined everybody else in the world already dead.

The judge put her glasses back on. She looked out over the bench and said, 'Mr Shear? Have you been listening to me?'

Bobby felt an elbow in his ribs – his court-appointed attorney, telling him to stand up. His court-appointed attorney was a woman who didn't wear make-up. Bobby stood up.

'Yes,' he said.

'You're listening to me,' the judge said.

'Yes, ma'am,' Bobby said.

'Good. Because I am going to be saying this to you for the second time, and I don't want to have to say it for the third. If there is a third time, Mr Shear, I will put you in jail. Have I made myself clear?'

'Yes, ma'am.'

'If the law made any sense, I would jail you for assault right this minute and you wouldn't get out again unless you managed to get yourself acquitted at trial. But the law doesn't make any sense. I am therefore doing what I can do. Have you been told that you will be arraigned on assault charges this afternoon?'

'I wasn't assaulting anybody. I was just—'

'You can save the argument for the judge in that case, Mr Shear. I don't want to hear it. You broke this woman's right arm. You bruised her extensively. You gave her a concussion from which she is still recovering. And that was this time. When you were already under a restraining order. Which required you to keep at least five hundred feet of space between yourself and Amy Stepman at all times. You were aware of this restraining order, Mr Shear?'

'Yes, ma'am.'

'Fine.' The judge put her glasses down again. Without them, her eyes looked like pinpricks. 'I am giving you another restraining order, Mr Shear, except this time you will be enjoined against approaching any closer than one thousand feet to Miss Stepman. You are not to go to her place of employment, not at any time or under any circumstances. You are not to go to her house. You are not to approach her car. You are not to telephone her. You are not to have any contact with her in any manner whatsoever. Because if you do, and if I hear about it, I will put you in jail. And I will keep you in jail, Mr Shear, if I have to reinvent the laws of the State of South Carolina to do it. Have I gotten through to you at all, Mr Shear?'

'Yes, ma'am.'

'Marvelous.' The judge put her glasses back on and stood up. Everybody stood up with her, except for Amy who was having trouble standing. Amy's lawyer had her hand on Amy's bare arm, just where Bobby wanted his own hand to be. There were days when he could lie in bed and feel her skin against his own as plainly as if she had still been lying beside him, stark naked and twisted in his sheets.

Bobby's court-appointed attorney was named Cassie Halloran. She was short and plump and angry-looking, and she didn't like him at all.

'Pay attention this time,' she hissed, as people began filing out of the courtroom. 'She could do you a lot of damage. Especially if you go to trial for assault.'

'I thought we were going to do a deal with the assault.'

'We're going to try to do a deal, Bobby, we're going to try. That doesn't mean we're going to succeed. You aren't exactly popular around here these days.'

'I wasn't assaulting anybody,' Bobby said. 'I was just—'

'Stuff it up your ass. Nobody's interested.' Cassie Halloran had her briefcase packed. She tucked it up under her arm and stalked into the court's center aisle. 'Pay attention this time, Bobby, I mean it. You're in a lot of trouble already. Don't get into any more.'

Bobby rubbed his hands against his eyes. When he looked up, Cassie was going out of the great double doors, propped open now to let in the air. Her ass moved in circles when she walked. Her high heels looked too thick and heavy for her feet.

Bobby went into the center aisle himself, then down it and out of the double doors. He went through the foyer and out onto the courthouse steps. Meldane looked small and mean and pinched in the hard light of the sun – but mostly it looked low-rent.

'Hey, Bobby,' old Mr Tucker said, walking along the sidewalk in the direction of the benches the town had built near the bus stop for senior citizens to sit on. Old Mr Tucker was as senile as hell, and always had been, as far back as Bobby could remember.

A little way down the block, Amy was getting into the front passenger seat of a navy blue, brand-new Volvo station wagon, with her lawyer behind the wheel. At the very last moment, she looked up and caught his eye – but her expression remained blank, her mind seemed empty. It was as if she had made him invisible, so that no matter what he did she would never again be able to see him at all.

*

In the beginning, of course, she had seen him. Bobby had never felt so alive in anyone else's presence, or so little like an Ultimate Loser. That was the summer they were both sixteen, the summer before the summer he dropped out of high school. He had wanted to drop out then, but he had just completed his freshman year. The idea of having only one year of high school made him a little queasy, as if it would end up being a brand of some kind, rendering him truly worthless for ever. Amy was a year ahead of him in school, because she had never been held back. She had a little stack of psychology books she carried around to read on her breaks at the Ultra Burger. That was where Bobby had met her, face to face, for the first time – although he had run into her off and on for years, the way people run into each other in small towns. This time he noticed her hair, which was bright red and fell like a waterfall down her back. Her hips looked too narrow and too delicate even in her clunky Ultra Burger uniform. In her tight worn jeans, they looked as if they might have been made of thread.

'Listen,' Amy would say, when he drove her out to the lake to neck. 'It's all a matter of planning. You've got to get focused and put your mind to things. That's the only way to get ahead.'

Bobby wasn't interested in getting ahead. He was only interested in getting along. Every time Amy let his hand move another inch down her back, or dropped another piece of clothing on his car's littered floor, Bobby felt as if he had won the lottery. He even rubbed his real lottery tickets against her skin to bring them luck. Her skin was soft and smooth and very white. The rough places around her nipples were so pink they reminded him of the odd color her father had painted her bedroom. He wanted to get out of the car and lie on the grass in full sight of the sun, where the air could keep them both warm. Mostly he just wanted to be inside her and inside her and inside her, over and over again. When he was inside her, the world was a perfect place, and he was a perfect person in it.

'What are you thinking?' she would ask him when they had finished making love, and, 'When are you going to decide what to do with your life?'

Then there was the prom, and after the prom there was the fight. Bobby remembered it as clearly as if he had it on videotape, to play back for himself whenever his memory started to wane. The prom had been wonderful and the morning after had been wonderful, too – but then The Revelation had happened, and it was only later that Bobby realized that Amy didn't think there had been a revelation at all. When he was very happy, he didn't listen very hard. He heard her voice the way he heard instrumental music on the radio. She had probably told him a hundred times before and it had meant nothing to him, just notes, jazz wafting across a parking lot at him from somebody else's car.

They finished making love for the fourth time and Amy sat up. She put his tuxedo shirt on as if it were a robe and reached for her evening bag. Inside her evening bag she had a lipstick and a comb and a change purse and the little round disc for her birth-control pills – which Bobby didn't know she was taking.

'I knew we were going to be out all night,' Amy said, popping one of the pills out of the case and into her mouth. 'You have no idea how hard it is to take precautions.'

'You're taking pills,' Bobby said, feeling his stomach turn over. He was washed in fever, sick. 'You're taking birth-control pills.'

'Of course I am. I have to. You won't wear a safe.'

The fever got higher and higher, higher and higher. It seeped into his blood vessels and made him feel as if he were burning up. It made the air around him feel cold.

'How did you get them?' he asked her. 'I thought you couldn't get them without permission. Did your mother give you permission?'

'Don't be a goop. I got them in Columbia. There's a women's health-care center there right near the university that will give them to anybody.'

'And you've been taking them, all along.'

'Bobby, make sense,' Amy said. 'I can't get pregnant now. I don't want to get pregnant now. I've got tons of money saved. I've got good grades. I want to go to college.'

'College.'

'I'm going to go to graduate school, too,' Amy said, sitting down again. 'I'm going to be a psychologist before I'm finished. Just you wait. I can't get pregnant now. And I really don't want to have an abortion.'

Birth control. Abortion. College. Psychologist. The world had become a jigsaw puzzle with none of the pieces put in order. Bobby knew what would happen to Amy if she ever got up to the university in Columbia. She would start to look at him the way everybody else looked at him, and then his only safe place would be gone. What frightened him was that she might already look at him this way. She might be seeing him only because she was using him, so that she wouldn't look like too much of a grind before she left town.

What happened next was so strange that he never told anyone about it, not even his lawyer, when he finally had a lawyer: the air around him seemed to clear; the fog in his head, made up of marijuana cigarettes and hard-edged fear, seemed to clear, too. For the first time in his life, he thought he was perfectly aware of everything, inside himself and out. He saw his hand rise in the air on the end of his arm. He saw the frown on Amy's face, quick-drawn and annoyed; he felt the flat of his hand hit the smooth plane of her cheek. It sounded like a gun going off in a metal room.

After that, he did lose control – and sense, too. He balled his hands into fists and started to windmill.

'You bastard,' Amy was screaming at him, her legs up in his direction and kicking out. 'You bastard, you bastard, what the hell do you think you're doing?'

They were out in the open, at the lake, where anybody could hear them. There were always a dozen couples at the lake on the dawn after a prom. Amy caught him in the jaw with a single spiked heel. The point went into the side of his neck like a blunt needle. He staggered back and cried out.

'What are you *doing*?' somebody said, over his head – and that was the first he knew that he had an audience.

It was Garrett Fairchild who had hold of him – Garrett Fairchild, whose father was a doctor in Columbia and who was going North to Yale at the end of the summer. Somebody else came up and got hold of him on the other side, but Bobby didn't notice who it was. He was watching Garrett's face get redder and redder. He was watching Amy, too. She was scrambling around the back of the truck, picking up clothes and trying to cover herself. Her nose was bleeding big gobs of red down the front of her face.

She was crying. Bobby could see that. He thought it was good she was crying. It might make her know what he was feeling. It might make her even care. He thought he should have done more to her than break her nose and give her a couple of bruises around the eyes. He should have done something permanent, that she would carry with her always, that she would never be able to forget.

'Jesus Christ,' Garrett said.

'Garrett, honey?' some girl said. When Bobby's brain began to clear again, he knew it was Carla Walters, the girl Garrett had been going with all this year, the girl who was going to be left behind when Garrett went North. Or maybe Carla was going North, too. Bobby's head ached.

'We could take you home,' Garrett was saying – to Amy, Bobby knew. 'You want us to help you call the cops?'

Carla Walters made a strangled little sound.

'I want to take his clothes and leave him here,' Amy said, sounding furious. 'I want him to have to get back to town looking the way he looks and explain himself to people.'

Carla Walters started to giggle. The other guy said, 'Oh, Lordy Lord Lord,' and Bobby suddenly knew who it was: Johnny Ray Moore. Johnny Ray wouldn't be going away to college, but his father owned the Texaco station right in the middle of town, and Johnny would own it after him. Johnny Ray would be sitting on Main Street for the rest of Bobby's life, sniggering.

'Wait a minute,' Garrett said. Bobby felt him go over to the truck. He heard the metallic pings as Garrett got up on the flatbed and looked around.

'Is this all?' Garrett asked.

'He would have had shoes,' Johnny Ray said.

'He can keep the shoes,' Amy said.

Carla Walters giggled again.

Garrett stepped over Bobby's naked body and went to the front of the truck. Bobby heard him opening the cab.

'Might as well take the keys,' Garrett said. 'Just to make sure the boy really has to walk.'

Carla's giggle this time was high and shrill and hysterical – and almost at once it started to fade. They were moving away from him. They were going off to wherever Garrett had parked his car. Bobby felt the hot morning wind streaming over him like melted butter. He knew he should get up and do something about himself. He couldn't make himself move.

Somewhere in the distance, a car had started up: Garrett's or Johnny Ray's, it was impossible to tell. He was alone out here. The water was only a couple of feet from his head. If he walked in the wrong direction, he could drown in it. Instead, he wrapped his arms around his knees and squeezed his eyes shut as tightly as they would go, more tightly than they had ever been before.

And then he started to cry.

She stayed in town all summer, working at the Ultra Burger. She had to, because her father was not a doctor like Garrett Fairchild's. Her father worked construction on the new subdivisions that were going up all around Columbia for the people who were moving South to work at the universities or one of the new companies that did things with computers. Bobby saw him sometimes, in the diner or the post office, dressed in heavy clothes that always seemed to be filthy. Sometimes he was with Amy. At those times, Bobby would press himself back against the nearest wall he could find and watch them. They went to the post office to mail off things the university needed before Amy could start classes at the end of August. They went to the hardware store to buy an alarm clock with a bell loud enough to wake Amy for school no matter how late she'd been out the night before.

'I can guess what it's going to be like,' Mr Stepman said, 'being on your own for the first time. Might as well take precautions.'

Mostly, Bobby went to the mall, where the Ultra Burger was, and sat at a table near the window while Amy was working behind the counter. The first time he sat there, Amy marched over to him to ask him what he was doing. She stood towering over his table with her hands in the pockets of her apron and nearly spat at him.

'I'm getting a burger,' Bobby said, looking away from her, out of the window at the shoppers in the concourse. 'I just got off work. I'm starving to death.'

'You didn't just get off work,' Amy said. 'You got fired two days ago. I heard about it.'

The shoppers in the concourse all looked richer than he was – richer and different, in that odd way he was never able to put his finger on. Amy didn't look different in that way yet. Her hair still fell down her back. Her eyes were still heavy with make-up. Her nails were still very long and very red. He thought if he could just put his hands out and draw her to him, he would be able to change her mind about everything.

'I'm not going to do anything,' he said, instead. 'I'm just sitting here. I don't know why you're picking on me.'

'I'm not picking on you. You're picking on me. You're bothering me.'

'I'm not bothering you.'

'You're here.'

'I can go to the Ultra Burger. No law says I can't.'

'Go down the hall to McDonald's.'

'I don't know what's wrong with you, anyway. We had a fight. People have fights. They don't stop talking to each other just because they have fights.'

'You broke my nose, you asshole,' Amy said.

Then she turned her back to him and walked off. It was true that he had broken her nose. She still had bandages on it, halfway through the summer.

After that, Bobby went to the Ultra Burger every time Amy was on shift and he wasn't working. He wasn't working most of the time, because that summer he kept getting fired from one job after the other. It was as if nothing he could do was right. He sat in the Ultra Burger until five minutes before Amy was supposed to get off. Then he went to the parking lot in the back and stood against the wall of the building until Amy came out to get her car. Sometimes she didn't have a car and her father came to pick her up. That was bad. Sometimes she came out with another girl and there was nothing Bobby could do about it. Mostly she came out alone, carrying a big shoulder bag with a book sticking out of the top of it.

'Listen,' Bobby would say then, moving in her direction. 'Amy, listen to me. We've got to talk.'

The psychology books said no woman should ever have anything to do with a man once he'd hit her. Bobby knew that because it had been part of the battering unit in his health class that last year he'd spent in school. In the book, there had been pictures of women whose husbands and boyfriends had beaten them up. Some of them had bruises all over their bodies. Some of them had cigarette burns on their breasts. The pictures were in black and white. The nipples all looked as if they were surrounded by dead skin. The arms and legs were bent at funny angles, where the bones had broken.

'It's not like that,' Bobby would call at her, as she slammed the door of the car and started the engine. The car had air-conditioning. The windows all stayed rolled up tight.

'You still love me,' Bobby would scream, as loud as he could, as he ran at her. She always managed to get the car moving before he could get to it. He never started running soon enough. He never ran fast enough. She backed the car out of the space it was in without looking at him. She shifted gears and drove off as if she were alone in the lot. Once or twice, she came close to running him down.

In August, Amy went away to Columbia and Bobby started a job with the South Carolina Department of Transportation. It was just digging ditches and clearing roads – what Bobby would have called 'nigger work', except that he knew he wasn't supposed to use that word any more outside the little two-block neighborhood where he lived with his mother – but it paid better than minimum wage, and the hours were decent. With Amy gone, he didn't know what to do with himself in his off hours. He started to have as few off hours as he could. He put in for overtime whenever it was available. He learned to sleep more than he had ever slept before. When he couldn't stand it any more, he went into town and tried to listen to the conversations of people who knew her, in case they had any information he needed to hear. None of them ever did.

Thanksgiving came and went. One of the girls at the Ultra Burger told him that Amy had not come home for the long weekend because she had to study. The Department of Transportation job was seasonal work, and he was itchy. He got another job, this time at a self-service gas station out near the Interstate. He sat hour after hour in a bullet-proof plastic booth while people handed over their cash and credit cards before working the pumps. Sometimes he sold motor oil. Sometimes he tried to explain to older people who didn't seem to be able to understand how to put their credit cards into the machine at the pump so that they didn't have to come to the booth at all.

He was in J. C. Penney's at the mall when he saw her again and, although there was a lot about her that was the same, he almost didn't recognize her. Her hair cascaded down her back. Her eyes were still heavy with make-up. Her nails were still long. All of it seemed to have taken on a new ambience, as if they had changed her *aura* or something up there at the university. She was with her friend DeeDee Holt, picking through a big bin of plastic brush-and-comb sets that Penney's had on sale. She had her back to him, so that he didn't have to hurry off into a safe distance. He could get up close and hear.

'It's not all the way I expected it to be,' she was telling DeeDee, 'but it pretty much is. And I love it. It's a whole different attitude. It's a whole different way of thinking about your life.'

'If you keep talking that way, you'll end up running off to New York,' DeeDee said. 'I don't want a whole different way of thinking about my life. I like it here.'

'I'm getting out of South Carolina as soon as I graduate,' Amy said. 'Just you watch.'

It was the clothes that were different, that was it. The Amy of Meldane High School had liked bright colors and fabrics that looked hard and shiny to the touch. This Amy still wore jeans, but her shirt was soft and heavily embroidered, like something a hippie would wear. The jeans were looser than Bobby remembered them. They seemed to leave a lot of open space around her thighs. He wished he could nail it down. She was becoming a different person, but he didn't know how. He didn't know why. He didn't know what it would mean.

He held out until the week after New Year's. New Year's Eve, there had been a party at Garrett Fairchild's house and Amy had gone. Bobby had been waiting outside her house, parked a block down the street, to see if she would come out to go partying. When she came out and got into DeeDee's car, he followed them. When he got to Garrett's house, he parked a little ways away and watched. There seemed to be some kind of reunion going on. Most of the kids Bobby remembered from Amy's high-school class were in attendance, even people – like Amy and DeeDee and Johnny Ray Moore – who had not been part of Garrett's rich kids' crowd. The Fairchild house was a massive French Provincial with stucco siding painted a pale creamy green. There was a terrace out back where couples were dancing to slow songs, clutching at each other while they moved.

Back home the next morning, Bobby tried to think, but couldn't. He tried to go in to work, but he couldn't do that either. He lay on the same bed he'd had as a child and stared at the cracked ceiling above his head. The phone rang and rang, but he didn't pick it up. There was a six pack and a half of beer in the refrigerator. It belonged to his mother, but he didn't know where she was. He took the beer back to his own room and drank it.

The next morning, he woke up to find that he had lost his job and lost Amy, too. She had gone back to Columbia to start the new semester. He felt stupid about the job. If he had been able to lie effectively, he could have held onto it. He knew from experience that you could always lie your way out of trouble the first time. When he thought about Amy, he just felt bad – and then he felt something else, something that made him nervous. He remembered balling up his fists and going at her, and the way her flesh had felt when it yielded. He remembered the sound of her nose cracking against the side of his hand. It was aphrodisiac music. It made him swell and grow hard. His penis hurt against the tight confines of his jeans. He thought about her backed up on the flatbed near the cab of the truck, naked and kicking at him, scared to death. He thought he could remember her eyes grown twice their normal size and full of fear. He started to move his hips rhythmically against his bed. The air around him was as thick and wet as mayonnaise. The room was so close, he could barely breathe. He stopped remembering and started imagining: Amy laid flat out underneath him with her arms tied and her mouth gagged; Amy with her legs open and staked out with handcuffs; Amy with her red hair. There were all those magazines you could get in Columbia and Charleston. There were all those pictures of women screaming and held down. He had seen them a million times. They had never made any impression on him at all. He had thought they were stupid and unrealistic. When men did things like that they could get prosecuted for rape. Even if they didn't, they had to ask themselves: what was wrong with them that they couldn't get a woman to go to bed with them and want it?

Now, thinking about Amy, it was all different. He had suddenly seen the point. He imagined himself bringing the flat of his hand down hard against the side of her face, over and over again, until her cheeks began to bleed. He imagined himself biting her nipples so hard that the skin of them came off in his mouth. He imagined his fist going into the side of her chest, over and over again. He knew he was pumping up and down on the same sheets he would have to sleep in tonight and every night after for the rest of the week. He couldn't stop imaging the red of her blood on the white of his hands.

And then he exploded.

It was a week after New Year's when he finally went up to Columbia. He drove with a map open next to him on the seat of his car, and paid close attention to the signs that said *University of South Carolina*. It wasn't that far from Meldane, but Bobby had never made the trip before, not even to buy dope or booze. It was as if the placed glowed with one of those auras the girls at the Ultra Burger were always talking about, as if it were haunted in a particularly nasty way. Amy didn't believe in auras, though. When he tried to tell her he felt the presence of the dead in the cemetery behind his house, she gave him a book by somebody named Bertrand Russell, which he couldn't read. He leafed through it a couple of times and then stuffed it under the driver's seat of his truck. It was probably still there, soaking up dirt and oil, causing trouble for whoever was using the truck now.

The university was bigger than he had expected it to be. It was bigger than Meldane, and the buildings were more impressive, too. He followed signs that said they were taking him to a visitors' parking lot, but he didn't like where he was going – off to the side somewhere, out of the center of things. He drove around and around, looking for some place more central to park. Every parking place had a sign on it that said that it was reserved for permit parking only. The last thing he wanted was to get his car towed in Columbia. It would be, he thought, like being buried alive. There would be no marker for his grave. The sorority girls would come and stand on it, tapping their heels into the soft earth over his chest.

He was on his fourth circuit through a thick cluster of buildings with brick sides and tall white columns when he saw her: Amy, standing on the broad front steps of the biggest building of all. He slowed the car down. The cars behind him started to honk. He squinted at the front of the building and caught the word 'library'. Amy had a backpack slung over her shoulder. It looked heavy and full of books. She was talking to a tall boy in jeans and a T-shirt. The T-shirt had a muddied-up picture on it that Bobby couldn't recognize and the words, *Smash The Welfare State*.

Bobby made the curve in the road, because he had to. Amy and the boy passed out of sight. There was nowhere it was really okay to park, but there were a lot of cars parked anyway. All of them, Bobby could see, had bright red windshield stickers on their drivers' sides, which were probably permits. Bobby pulled between two of them anyway. Now that he knew where Amy was, he wouldn't have to be gone long. He would just get hold of her and go.

He got out and ran down the walk in the direction he had come. When he got around the curve again, he saw the library and the boy Amy had been talking to, but Amy was gone. For a moment he panicked. He really had had no idea that the university was this big. He had thought of it as a kind of high school, maybe like one of those regional high schools they had in the northwest corner of the state. Amy could have disappeared in this crowd and gone anywhere.

The walkways were all full of people. The boys were all dressed in jeans and T-shirts and worn brown loafers. The girls were either like Amy, in jeans, too, or dressed to kill, like women in a magazine. Bobby wove in and out between them, feeling worse than out of place. Nobody paid attention to him.

He was halfway up the walk to the library steps when he realized that she was still there, just not talking to the boy she had been talking to when he first saw her. His attention had been so riveted on the boy, he hadn't seen Amy standing just a single step down, talking to one of the magazine girls. She had dropped her backpack at her feet and taken out a notebook. The magazine girl had a notebook, too.

Bobby went to the bottom of the steps and looked up. Amy had not seen him. It was chilly this morning for South Carolina. She had on a thick red cotton sweater over her jeans.

'Moskowitz wants the survey papers in by the twenty-third,' she was saying, 'but it's crazy, because none of us is going to have our surveys done in time, and he knows it. I hate it when they care more about their schedules than they care about—'

'Amy,' Bobby said.

He thought he'd whispered it, but he must have shouted. Half a dozen people turned to look at him. Amy's head shot up and swivelled in his direction. She looked instantly furious.

'Jesus Christ,' Amy said.

The magazine girl shook her head. 'Are you all right, honey? I don't think it's a good idea to take the Lord's—'

'Amy,' Bobby said again.

Amy picked up her book pack and walked down to him. The magazine girl was watching them both. Bobby was sure she would be able to pick him out of any line-up in the world for the rest of her life.

Amy got down to where he was and stopped. 'What are you doing here?' she asked. 'I can't believe you've gotten ambition after all these years. I don't think you're even back in high school.'

'I want to talk to you,' Bobby said.

'We've got nothing to talk about.'

'Yes, we do. We do. We've got us to talk about. We—'

'There is no "us", Bobby. I don't make "us" with someone who broke my nose. I don't even talk to someone like that. I want you to get out of here.'

'I want you to come with me.'

'Go to hell.'

They had been walking all the time they were talking. Bobby was surprised to realize that they had been walking in the direction of his car. He took it as a sign. It was Amy who was doing the moving. If it had been up to him, they would have been standing still. He thought that deep in her brain she must want what he wanted. When she thought with her gut instead of her head she came right at him.

They came around the curve in the sidewalk. Bobby could see his own car, parked where he had left it, right ahead.

'This was over last summer,' Amy was saying, so angry she was having difficulty getting out the words. 'This was over when you ruined my senior prom for me for ever. This was over the first time you put your hands—'

'They're brainwashing you up here,' Bobby told her. 'That's what's happening. When you get out of here, you'll see this really isn't what you want.'

They were right up next to his car. He never locked his car doors. He never remembered to. Now he grabbed the passenger side doorhandle with one hand and Amy's wrist with the other. He swung the door open and Amy at the car in one jerky movement. He felt great, better than he had ever felt before – as if he were Harrison Ford in an adventure movie, or James Bond. Amy went careening towards the car, off balance. The side of her body smashed into the sharp edge of the open door.

'You bastard,' Amy said.

Bobby took a step towards her and pushed her into the car. Her head hit the top of the doorframe and she cried out, resisting. Bobby stepped closer and pushed again. He got her into the car and slammed the passenger door shut. Then he ran around the other side and got in behind the wheel. Amy was clutching at the doorhandle. It was one of the old-fashioned ones, plated with chrome. This was the 1972 Buick Bobby had bought to replace his pick-up truck, which had died some time around Thanksgiving. The passenger side doorhandle stuck. Amy didn't know the trick of it. Bobby leaned across her and pounded the lock down to make it even harder for her to figure out. Then he got the engine going and raced the gas.

'Let me out of here,' Amy said.

They were on the road and moving. Luck was with him. There was almost no traffic. He got going as fast as he could on this curving street. He didn't want her to be able to jump out. He came around another curve and saw the signs for the visitors' parking lot. He headed in that direction because he knew it would bring him back the way he had come.

'Let me out of here,' Amy said again. 'Let me out of here now, you bastard. I'm going to have you arrested for kidnapping. I'm going to have you locked up for good, you two-bit redneck son of a—'

Bobby leaned across the seat and grabbed a big fistful of bright red hair. He yanked, hard. She wasn't afraid. That was the thing. She was angry at him, but she wasn't afraid. He yanked again. Amy cried out. A matted swatch of hair came off in his hands. There was blood at the ends of it.

'You shut up,' he yelled at her. 'Shut up, shut up, shut up. I'll break your jaw if you don't shut up.'

'I'll break your balls,' Amy screamed at him.

The entrance to the Interstate was right up ahead. Bobby swung onto it. Once they really got going, everything would be all right. Amy wouldn't be able to jump out of the car if it was going seventy-five miles an hour. He got to the top of the ramp and swung onto the empty highway and pushed his foot down on the gas. Amy was still screaming at him, but he couldn't hear her voice. The car seemed to be full of wasps, buzzing in his ears.

'Shut up,' Bobby said again.

Then he reached out and grabbed Amy's throat with his right hand. He felt his fingers close around the delicate bones there and his penis got hard. He shoved his arm out as far as it would go and felt Amy's head crack against the glass of the window over there. It felt so good, he did it again and again, again and again – even though Amy wasn't screaming at him any more, even though she wasn't even moving. It was as if the world had been out of focus all his life, and now it had become clear. It had become right. Amy's head was bleeding. Her tongue was hanging out of her mouth. Everything was gorgeous and perfect and wonderful about this day. The sky was as blue as he had ever seen it. The grass was as green as a crayon. He was flying, weightless, off in outer space.

When the police sirens started up behind him, he paid no attention to them at all. He was sure they couldn't be for him. He was sure that he was invisible.

He had no idea that he was doing one hundred and five miles an hour.

He had been all the way to Meldane when they caught him, and that was his good luck. It was old Judge Harmon's last month on the bench, and old Judge Harmon was a man of the old school. *He* understood how a woman could provoke a man into doing something stupid. *He* understood how women sometimes just needed to be hit, even wanted to be hit, because if they didn't get hit they would go right out of control. If Bobby had been up before any other judge, he would surely have gone to jail. Amy was in the hospital with a concussion. She was going to have to drop out of the university for the semester to recover. If it had all happened a month later, he would have gone to jail, too, because by then That Woman would have been on the bench, the one who would later issue the restraining orders. As it turned out, Bobby had nothing to worry about from anybody except Amy's father, who was gunning for him.

'If you go near her again,' Mr Stepman had said, when they all came out of court after the sentencing, and all Bobby had gotten was six months' probation, 'I'll kill you myself.'

Bobby had gone near Amy, though, several times, although he had been careful not to let anyone see him do it. He had gone out to the county hospital and looked at her sleeping. Once or twice, he had picked wild flowers at the side of the road and left them in her room when it was empty, because she was off at physical therapy or taking a shower. He was sure that she would know the flowers were from him when she got back. He was sure that she had come to her senses now that she was free from the university. On the day she was supposed to come home from the hospital, he parked a little ways from the front gate and watched her father pick her up. After she was home, he drove out to her house at least once a day to see if he could catch a glimpse of her in the back yard. Mostly what he did was make plans. His six months' probation wouldn't last for ever. When it was over, he would go to claim her. He had it all worked out. He would get his high-school equivalency and train for a trade, maybe carpentry or plumbing. She would go back to work at the Ultra Burger until they had saved up enough for a wedding and then again until they had saved up enough for a house. He even had the house picked out, in a new development of small neat ranches out on the Crosswell Road.

'Bobby's got religion,' his boss at the time said, and then laughed so hard he spilled his beer.

Bobby used to mind being laughed at, but he didn't any more. He could see his future plain, and there were so many good things in it.

Winter passed into spring and spring into summer. Bobby signed up for a night course in high-school English at the community college, but there was too much going on in his life. He couldn't make himself concentrate. He went over to Amy's every evening after work. Now that the weather was getting hot, she was outside more often than not. She lay stretched out on her mother's wicker chaise with a sun umbrella over her head, reading books. It was the books that made Bobby nervous.

'What's she reading those books for?' he asked Amy's friend DeeDee, when he caught DeeDee in the Ultra Burger.

DeeDee looked him up and down as if he were a kind of insect. 'What were you doing over at Amy's house? Isn't that a violation of your probation?'

'I didn't talk to her, DeeDee. I didn't bother her. I just saw she was reading a book.'

'You're going to get yourself in trouble if you keep this up. You're already in trouble. You're going to get yourself in trouble again.'

'I'm not going to get myself in trouble—'

'She's going to do the summer session up at Columbia, just to make up some time. She's only going to do one course. But it'll help. After what you did to her.'

'She's going up to Columbia?'

'I hope she graduates from the university and gets rich and famous. I hope she writes a book and turns you into a case study. I hope she tells the world what a psychopath you really are, Bobby Shear.'

'She's going up to Columbia,' Bobby said again.

He should have gone back to work then, but he didn't. He didn't want to and he couldn't think. Instead, he drove out to Amy's house and parked his car up close. It wasn't the same car he had been in when he had been arrested – that one had died just like the truck had – so he didn't think it would be recognized, but he didn't really care. He walked down the block and stood in front of Amy's house. He thought about ringing the doorbell and decided against it. He went around to the side and pressed his body into a thick evergreen tree that marked the dividing line between the Stepmans' property and their neighbors' to the left.

Amy was sitting on the chaise, with books piled all around her. Her bright hair was pulled back in a ponytail, tied with a terrycloth bow. Her face was free of bruises. Her arms were white and perfect. The book in her lap was as thick as a dictionary.

Bobby moved closer. 'Amy,' he whispered.

She didn't hear him. She was making notes in a spiral notebook. Bobby edged closer still.

'Amy,' he said again, 'listen to me.'

Amy looked up and turned her head in his direction. She saw him right away. He might as well not have tried to hide at all. Amy dumped her book on the ground and jumped up.

'Get out of here,' she shouted at him. 'Get out of here.'

'Amy, listen,' he said.

Amy started to scream. It was a high-pitched, insistent scream, as piercing as needles, and all of a sudden all Bobby cared about was making it stop. He ran all the way into the yard and tripped on the book Amy had been reading. He picked it up off the ground and started tearing pages out of the middle of it. He threw pages onto the green grass of the lawn, pages everywhere. The back door opened and Amy's mother came out. When she saw him she started screaming, too, so that the air was full of darts. Bobby grabbed Amy by the arm and started to pull. Amy pulled back, trying to get away from him. Amy's mother disappeared into the house and came back with a broom. By then the whole neighborhood had heard what was going on. A woman ran out of the house next door and then back in again. Bobby knew instinctively that she would be calling 911 right this minute, that he didn't have very much time. He started to pull Amy around the side of the house.

'You can't go back there,' he kept shouting at her, over and over again. 'You can't go back there.'

Amy's mother came at him with the broom, hitting him over the head, hitting him and hitting him. He hit back, but he hit at Amy, pounding his free fist into any part of her he could find. The woman next door had come back out of the house again. She was standing right next to him, screaming in his ear.

'You can't go back there,' Bobby kept shouting.

He was still shouting the same thing when the police showed up and took him away from her. He was shouting as if only by shouting could he go on holding up the universe.

It was only later, when he was in jail waiting to be arraigned, that he heard what he needed to hear: he had done some damage. Amy was in the hospital again. She would not be going back to Columbia for the summer session.

That had been in early June – Southern, but not technical, summer. It was now late July, summer by anybody's standards all over the northern hemisphere, and Bobby thought the heat might be affecting his brain. He could barely remember this last incident at all, although he did remember what had set it off. Amy had gone back to work at the Ultra Burger after the June trip to the hospital, and he had hung around there, trying to determine what was what. What was what turned out to be another trip up to Columbia, to get things straightened away for the fall term. Amy was going back again, no matter how hard he tried to make her see reason. It was as if he didn't matter, or didn't even exist. He thought she might have one of those mental illnesses. It was the only reason he could think of why she would go back time and again when by now she ought to know it was going to end up costing her her life.

There was a parking ticket stuck under the windshield of his car. He saw it flapping in the breeze as soon as he turned onto Polk Street. The breeze didn't amount to much. July in South Carolina was worse than hot. He had little rivers of sweat running down the back of his neck and into the unyielding harshness of his stiff white shirt.

Bobby took the pink parking ticket out from under the windshield and stuffed it into his pocket. Then he got into the car and sat down behind the wheel. He'd left the windows open while he was in court. Nobody stole cars in Meldane, and nobody anywhere would steal this car. Still, the heat was nearly unbearable. Every part of him felt slick. He almost thought that he was melting.

He put his forehead down on the steering-wheel and closed his eyes. If he stayed in town this afternoon, they would all be looking at him. Guys he had known in high school would sit on the revolving stools in the diner and talk about what an ass he was, just loud enough so that he could hear as he was going by. All the muscles in his body seemed to be screwed up tight. Every part of him hurt. He could see himself in another ten years' time: spending his Saturday nights drinking beer and getting into fights at some roadhouse off Route 79; spending his Sunday mornings lying on the floor of his room in his mother's house, too sick to sit up straight.

If he had Amy in front of him now, he could change everything. He could pin her shoulders to the floor and go after her face. He could hit her and hit her and hit her until all there was to see of her was blood. The blood would flow freely down her cheeks and into the carpet under her head.

He was pounding the steering-wheel so hard he was setting off the horn. The sound made him take a deep breath that hurt his chest. He sat back again. It was his own hands that were in danger of being bloody. He had hit them into the hard plastic ridges of the steering-wheel over and over again. They were red and raw.

He got his cigarettes out of his pocket and lit one up. Then he got his car key into the ignition and started the car.

July in South Carolina was no joke. It was the middle of the day. The sun was beating down out of a clear sky. It had to be over a hundred degrees.

Bobby pulled the car onto Polk Street and went down Polk to Main. He headed down Main Street in the direction of the Interstate. He stayed well within the speed limit. He looked neither right nor left. If the good old boys who sat on the bench outside Johnny Ray Moore's father's gas station had something to say to him, it wasn't something he wanted to hear.

In no time at all, he saw the big green signs that marked the ramp onto I-95.

At first, Bobby thought he might really be going somewhere – to Atlanta maybe, or to Jacksonville. He thought he would do well in Florida, where there was a lot of new construction going on. He could get a job driving a truck and rent an apartment near the beach. He could make a lot of money and buy a microwave oven like Amy's mother had, so that when Amy came to visit she would know that he wasn't poor. Amy would miss him if he were gone. She wouldn't be able to live without him.

He saw the junction signs for Route 22 and headed towards them without thinking. He was on the off-ramp with no way to turn around before he realized that he was headed for Columbia. He wondered what he had been doing on the highway. It was much later than it should have been if he had simply driven up the Interstate in a straight line. He must have gotten off before and done a loop or two, he had no idea why. He couldn't remember anything about it. He only knew it was suddenly late afternoon. There were shadows everywhere.

At the bottom of the ramp, he turned left in the direction of Columbia proper. There was a truck stop in the dirt across from the ramp, selling Shell gasoline and souvenirs. The building was made of dark brown wood and looked ready to fall over. It would have a room in the back with shelves full of painted plywood tomahawks and praline cow patties.

'She should have learned to appreciate me by now,' Bobby said to the air. It felt good. He liked the sound of his own voice, strong and clear like that. Mostly when he talked to people, he mumbled.

'She's never going to find anybody who will love her as much as I do,' Bobby said. His voice was so deep he made the glass of the windshield rattle.

He was almost at the point where there would be no going back. He would be at the university and forced to go through it if he wanted to go out. He pulled the car over to the side of the road and looked around. There were small houses scattered here and there, square wooden ones, like the one he and his mother lived in back in Meldane. That meant that there would be a bar somewhere, if he could only find out where.

He turned down a side street and drove under a leafy canopy of trees. This was a mistake. The houses were getting better and better. He turned around in somebody's driveway and headed back the way he had come. For some reason, it seemed very important not to ask for directions.

He crossed Route 22 and went down another side street. This one was better.

Here and there there was a trailer – and not a double-wide trailer, either, but one of the small ones, with a metal awning over its cramped main window. Bobby turned on the radio and began to bop along to the music that came on. Some of the front yards here had junk in them: a broken refrigerator without its door; a car that had lost all four tires and rusted out half its hood. There were broken beer bottles along the side of the road.

He slowed down as the road began to narrow. He tried a couple of wider side streets and found himself in a world of nothing but trailers. These were the worst kind of trailers, though. They didn't even have metal awnings. They did have TV antennae. Every once in a while, somebody came out of one and that somebody was always black.

Bobby doubled back and tried another circuit. He doubled back again. He was beginning to think he might be wrong. Every neighborhood like this one that he'd ever been in had had a bar. A bar within walking distance, that was the ticket. A bar for people who had had their cars repossessed.

He tried another side street, just about ready to give up. He thought about what it would be like to go into one of the bars where the college kids drank. The thought of the college kids made him sweat in a way that had nothing to do with the heat of the season.

She really should have learned to appreciate me by now, he told himself again, silently this time—

—and then there it was, right in front of him. It was painted black. It had a neon Budweiser sign blinking next to its narrow front door. It seemed to have no windows at all.

Bobby pulled into the big dirt parking lot and killed his engine. Next to the Budweiser sign there was another one, hand-painted, that said Tattoo Professionals. He got another cigarette and lit up again. There weren't many vehicles in the lot. Most of them were wrecks, just like his own.

He got out and looked around. There was no sign giving this place a name. He got out his wallet and looked inside it. He had two hundred and twelve dollars. Twelve of it was his own. Two hundred belonged to his mother. He had taken it out of the jelly jar she kept it in, after she'd gone to work this morning. He had wanted to have some money on him in court. He could never stand sitting there in the middle of all the lawyers, knowing he was flat broke.

He put the money back in his wallet and the wallet back in his pocket. He walked across the lot to the front door and pulled it open. The smell of cigarettes was overwhelming, but it didn't quite cover the smell of piss.

There were three men sitting at the bar, hunched down at one end. They were all old, and they all looked like bums. Bobby went down to the bar's other end and sat on a stool. There was a mirror on the wall in front of him, but it was so dirty he couldn't see himself in it.

The bartender was a woman with her hair pulled back in a silver clip and not much else on. Her high heels made her look taller than she was. Her camisole top was too small for her large, firm breasts. They were too large and too firm to be real. She came over to Bobby and put her hands on the bar.

'Get you something?'

'Budweiser.'

'Bottle or draft?'

'Bottle.'

She turned away, leaned down over a silver metal cooler chest, and came up with a bottle. 'Buck fifty,' she said, putting it down in front of him. 'You want a glass?'

Bobby didn't want a glass. The bottle was so cold that water was condensing down the side of it. Bobby wiped it with his palms and put two dollars down on the bar.

'Sign says you've got somebody to do tattoos.'

'Right.' The woman took the bills and gave him back fifty cents.

'Who?' Bobby asked her.

The three old guys at the other end of the bar looked as if they could nurse what they had for ever. The woman looked at them blankly, as if they were part of the furniture. Maybe they were. She turned back to Bobby.

'Me,' she said. 'I do tattoos.'

'Who're you?'

'Shelby.'

'Where did you learn to do tattoos?'

Shelby leaned over and rested her elbows on the bar. Bobby could see right down the front of her camisole, but she didn't seem to notice.

'I learned to do tattoos in New York,' she said. 'I went to New York to be an actress. But it didn't work out. So I learned to do tattoos. Do you want a tattoo?'

'Maybe.'

'Well, I can't do anything fancy. If you want art, you've got to go to Herb Breeland out on the other side of town. He does art. I do stuff.'

'What stuff?'

'Names. Little pictures. You know, like hearts. And roses.'

'Does it cost a lot of money?'

'It depends on what you want. I do a little heart for ten. I get five dollars a letter for names. It's like that.'

'It's like that,' Bobby repeated. For twenty-five dollars, he could have a heart and Amy's name put right on his arm. He sucked on his beer. Getting a tattoo was supposed to hurt. Most of the guys he knew who had them got stoked up right before they went in for a session. He wished he had some grass to help him make up his mind.

Down at the other end of the bar, the three old guys were getting ready to leave.

'Just a second,' Shelby told him.

She went down the bar to them and said something in a voice too low for Bobby to hear. They shrugged their shoulders and scratched their heads. Shelby shrugged her shoulders and turned her back to them.

'They never leave tips,' she told Bobby, when she got back to him. 'I've threatened them a million times, I'm going to cut them off and not let them come back, but it doesn't do any good. They don't have any money.'

'They don't look like they have any money.'

'They're just drunks,' Shelby said. 'This town is full of drunks. Drunks and no-accounts. Welcome to the New South. Why do you suppose that is?'

'I'd like to get a tattoo,' Bobby said. 'Get it right up on my left shoulder. A heart with the name "Amy" in it. Do you think you could do that?'

'Is Amy your girlfriend? I could do that.'

Bobby's beer was gone. He pushed the empty bottle across the bar to Shelby. She picked it up and dropped it into a big box of bottles at her feet.

'Give me a second to set up,' she said, 'then you come on down the back there and take off your shirt. I could make you the heart in red and the name in blue. There won't be anybody in this place to bother us for hours.'

Bobby had forgotten that he was still wearing his court clothes. He had stopped feeling the stiffness of his shirt and the tightness in the waist of his one good pair of pants. While Shelby was setting up, he went out to his car and took these things off. He had jeans and a T-shirt on the back seat. The T-shirt was filthy, but even filthy it felt better on than the white shirt had. The good pair of pants had cut into the soft skin around his waist and left a welt. He rubbed it and winced when he felt the sting. He took off his black socks and black shoes and put his Reeboks on over bare feet. The black shoes were supposed to be 'good' shoes, too, but they weren't really. He'd bought them for ten dollars at the Payless store out at the strip mall, and the soles were already beginning to come apart from the uppers.

There was no other car in the parking lot any more except for his own. There was no sound anywhere, not even from the highway. He could have been on the moon.

He walked back into the bar and found Shelby standing next to a new bottle of cold beer. He picked up the beer and drank from it.

'I thought you'd changed your mind,' Shelby said. 'A lot of guys change their minds.'

'Nah.'

'As long as you don't change your mind after it's over. I can't do anything for you after it's over. Once it's on, it's on.'

'Don't worry about it.'

'Come on out in back, then. I got a little room I use to do it in. You're going to have to take off your shirt, but there won't be anybody to see you there. Or maybe you don't care if people see you without your shirt.'

I'd like to see you without your shirt, Bobby thought – but he really didn't mean it. That was knee-jerk. That was horniness talking. He never in his life wanted to see another woman naked, unless it was Amy.

Shelby was going down a narrow corridor that opened to the side of the bar and motioning for him to come along. Bobby picked up his beer and followed her.

'You just sit there,' she told him, pointing at a square low stool in the middle of what was really only a cubicle, created by three thin curtains hanging on rods.

Tacked to one of the curtain-walls was a series of pictures – men wearing tattoos that Shelby had made for them. One or two of the pictures showed only the tattoo, floating on what seemed to be a disembodied body part. A stray upper arm. A loose wrist. Bobby pulled his dirty T-shirt off and put it across his lap.

'I don't do too badly if I stick with what I know,' Shelby said, 'but Herb, he's a kind of genius. Does big snakes that go all the way around your arm. Did a bird once on this guy's back, called a phoenix. Did this picture with it coming up out of a fire. It was awesome.'

Bobby had his head turned away from her. It made him feel wrong to be looking at her skin. She was showing a lot of skin. Her skirt was cut high on her thighs. She wasn't wearing stockings. Her legs were covered with hard blue veins.

Besides, Bobby didn't want to see the needles. If he saw the needles, he was sure he would chicken out.

'You ready?' Shelby asked him.

Bobby grunted. He could still hear his mother last night, coming in from a night out with her best friend and drinking buddy, this old woman named Kiley who lived a couple of doors down. They were both drunk and his mother was angry. She'd spilled something down the front of her dress. It made the cheap polyester look even cheaper, ruched and mottled.

'My son the trash,' she'd said to Kiley, shrieking out the words as if she were being slain in the spirit at some tent revival and wanted the whole universe to hear about it. 'My son the trash, beats up girls who don't even want to do it with him.'

He could have put his fist in *her* face then. He could have broken her bones. He could have taken the house apart.

'Hey,' Shelby said.

The first needle that went in hurt so much that Bobby almost cried. He did cry out, and jump, which made Shelby back up.

'You can't move,' she told him. 'You can't ever move while I'm doing this. It will screw everything up.'

'All right.'

'Most guys get stoned before they do this. I should have given you a shot of whiskey instead of another beer.'

'Why don't you get me the shot of whiskey.'

'Just a minute.'

She was gone. Bobby closed his eyes. Something was happening to his brain. He seemed to be floating in a different kind of world, not outer space but like that. This room was not real. He was not real either. The pain had happened to somebody else in another country. He wondered what was going on in Meldane, now that he was not there to watch it happen.

Shelby came back with two shot glasses full of dark amber liquid. She handed him one and said, 'Shoot it. Do it fast.'

Bobby did. His throat burned. His body got hot.

'Do the other one,' Shelby told him.

Bobby did the other one. This time, it didn't burn as badly. The shot glass was made of very thick glass. He handed it back to Shelby and stretched.

'Give it a second to work and then I'll try again,' Shelby said. 'If it still doesn't work we'll have to think of something else. I've never had a tattoo myself. I've heard too many grown men scream.'

'Do you believe people ought to do what they want to do?' Bobby asked her.

Shelby blinked. 'I don't get it.'

'I had this teacher in school. He was always saying that people ought to follow their dreams. They ought to express themselves. They ought to get out there and do what they wanted to do, instead of just doing what they were expected to do. You ever hear anything like that?'

'No. I don't know. You're not making a lot of sense.'

'You ever been in love?'

'Yeah, I guess. I was married once.'

'And?'

'And he couldn't get his shit together, so I threw him out. What's your point?'

What *was* his point? That really was the problem. He felt the way he sometimes did when he had smoked too much marijuana. He felt so calm, he might as well have been part of the carpet. Everything really was floating now, out there and away from him. He was out of space and out of time, with this woman and her silicone breast implants. He wondered what it had cost her, to get her breasts to look like that. He wondered where she had gotten the money.

'Do you hook?' he asked her.

The tattoo needle was actually a black plastic gun that looked a little like a hair dryer, but smaller. Shelby was holding it in the air when he turned to look at her. He could tell by the lines in her face that he had made her furious. He wanted another shot of whiskey.

'Hey,' he said.

'You didn't have no call to say that. I didn't give you any reason at all to say that.'

'I was just wondering. About the money. You can't make a lot of money, working in a place like this.'

'I ought to throw you out of here on your ass. I ought to dump you in the parking lot and leave you there.'

'So maybe you go to school up at the college and I just didn't know.'

'I'm going to go get myself a beer.'

One of the pictures pinned to the curtain was of a rose high on the back of a woman who didn't seem to have anything on the top half of her. Her face was turned away, so that all Bobby could see was her permed blonde hair.

'Wait,' he said to Shelby.

He stood up and walked over to her. She was getting nervous. He could see the twitching in the muscles of her cheeks. He felt as if he were sleep-walking. There was no tension anywhere on earth. He only wished he'd thought to feed some quarters into the jukebox. It was too quiet in this place. He could hear himself breathing.

'Wait,' he said again.

'Wait what?' Shelby asked him. She backed up a little.

'Her name is Amy. My girlfriend's name. Did I tell you that?'

'I want to go get myself a beer.'

'She's a student up at the university. She isn't supposed to be. But she is. That was the trouble.'

'I don't think I should have given you that whiskey,' Shelby said. 'Jesus Christ.'

'I'm supposed to be staying away from Amy,' Bobby said.

There were no real walls here. She could have moved any time she wanted. She seemed to be rooted to her place.

Bobby went towards her and put his hand up on her shoulders. She flinched, but he had no idea why. He hadn't hurt her. He was going to hurt her, but he hadn't hurt her yet.

'I want to go get myself that beer,' she said again. Her voice was a high, thin whine.

Bobby put his hand up to her neck. She had a small neck. He could get his one hand almost all the way around it. She tried to step back and he held onto her. Her eyes were very large. His fingers were digging into her flesh. The skin under his hands felt too hot to hold for very long. She was not as pretty as Amy. She was not as young, either. He thought she was lying, saying that she had never sold herself. He thought she sold herself every night after the bar closed, to whatever drunk lasted the longest standing up.

He let go of her neck and stepped away from her. She stumbled on her high heels and nearly fell.

'Get out of here,' she said. Tears were coming out of her eyes, but she didn't sound as if she was crying. 'Get out of here. Get in your car and leave or I'm going to call the police.'

'I want you to come out to my car.'

'Like hell I will.'

'If you don't come out to my car, I'll do it again. I'll break your neck in half.'

'You're out of your mind. Do you know that? You're crazy as a loon.'

He probably *was* crazy as a loon. He could accept that. There was a kind of honor in that. He took her shoulders in his hand and turned her around. He pushed her down the corridor and back into the bar. The bar was still empty. The peace that had settled around him suddenly felt even deeper than it had been. Everything was changed. Everything was different now. Even his luck was different.

'I knew it was all going to come apart when she said she was going to college,' he said. 'In a lot of places they don't let women go to college. In the Arab countries, those places. And they're right. They know what women are like. They know it only makes them unhappy.'

'Jesus Christ. What's wrong with you?'

The front door seemed to be the only one. He pushed her toward that. It was hard to move her. The heels of her shoes caught on the carpet.

'If you yell when we get outside to the parking lot, I'll finish you right where you stand.'

This time she said nothing. He pushed open the door and they stepped outside. The parking lot was just as empty as it had been. It was nothing but packed dirt, and the surface of it was turning to dust. The nearest house was too far away to see clearly. The only thing he could make out was the pile of rusted gasoline cans in the front yard.

He pushed Shelby over to his car, got out his keys and opened the trunk. He had a spare tire back there, a retread he had paid less than twenty dollars for. The tread was already beginning to separate from the rest of the tire.

'If I don't do something, I'm going to lose it all. Can you understand that? I have to do something. I have to be somebody else. That has to happen now.'

'I'm not getting into any God-damned trunk.'

'You can see the university from here. I didn't notice that when I came in. You can see that tower thing up over the trees.'

She tried to run. He saw it coming seconds before it happened. He saw it in her face. She ducked under his arm and darted to the side of him. He turned in a full circle and came up behind her. She was still crouching when he grabbed her around the waist.

'Wait.'

'You're not putting me in any trunk.'

He lifted her off her feet. She was much lighter than he'd expected her to be. He was much stronger than he remembered being. She twisted in his hands.

He laid her down across the tire.

'Now,' he said.

'Don't,' she said.

He leaned into the trunk. Her neck was very small. He put both hands on it this time and pressed down with all his weight. She was kicking out, but her legs kept getting caught in the side of the trunk. They were too far away to be a danger to him anyway. The thread on the tire looked like it was graying into ash. He pressed down and pressed down. Finally, he felt it. The bones under his hands were fine and thin. When they broke, they snapped like the bones in a chicken wing. Shelby's eyes got wide. She began to choke.

Bobby stepped back and closed the trunk. It would take her a while to die, of course. You didn't just die because your neck was broken. People broke their necks and had them fixed and lived for years. He would have to listen to her thrashing for half an hour at least. He wouldn't have to listen to her choking, because the sound of the engine would drown that out. He was glad he had waited to kill her in the trunk, even so. It would have been much too much trouble to kill her back there and drag her body out here. It would have brought him much closer to getting caught.

He went around to the front of the car and opened the driver's side door. He looked up over the trees and saw the clock tower or the bell tower or whatever it was rising up over his head. They seemed to have built everything at the university out of red brick. He wondered why.

He got into the car and put his keys into the ignition. He started the engine and waited for it to stop hitching. He thought about all the movies he had seen where men killed women. They had all turned out to be wrong. He wasn't angry. He wasn't even upset. He was just hungry, and feeling a little light-headed.

The car stopped rocking and he put it into gear. He bumped carefully across the parking lot and onto the road. It would be dark in only an hour or two, but it was still hot. The steering-wheel felt almost liquid under his hands. He went down the road past the trailers and into the neighborhood of small wooden houses. He wondered why he hadn't noticed before that these houses were shacks. He turned and turned and turned again and found himself at the entrance to the Interstate.

On any day other than today, he would have been lost.

He stopped at the McDonald's outside Coucherville to eat. He was so hungry, his stomach seemed to be grinding glass inside him. He and Amy had once barricaded themselves into the ladies' room at this McDonald's and made love on the floor. The ladies' room was just one room, not a large space with stalls. That was back in the days when Amy had been as reckless as he was himself. She liked taking chances and making out in strange places. She liked kissing his neck while he drove, to see if she could distract him.

He went around to the trunk and listened. There was no sound in there at all. Either Shelby was already dead, or she was unconscious and on the way. It didn't matter. She would be dead by the time they reached Meldane.

He put a couple of quarters into the newspaper dispenser and got one out – The *Meldane Herald*, not the paper from Columbia. He went in and walked up to the long empty counter. It was one of the new ones, made of stainless steel. The girl who came to wait on him was no one he knew. He asked for a number four extra-value meal, supersized, and got his wallet out of his back pocket. He still had all of his mother's money in there. The way things were going, he was going to be able to give almost all of it back.

Back in the car, he put the food on the seat next to him and looked through the paper. The story about himself and Amy was on the third page, a little paragraph no more than an inch long at the bottom of the page. It said nothing important. *Amy Stepman received an expanded restraining order against Robert William Shear . . .*

Bobby pulled out of the McDonald's and headed back for the Interstate. It was, somehow, seven o'clock at night. Whole patches of the day seemed to have disappeared while he wasn't paying attention. Big chunks of time were missing. He thought he should have taken a couple of beers for the road, or a whole bottle of whiskey, while he had the chance.

Back on the Interstate, he bumped along in traffic so thin he was sometimes the only car on the road. The trees on either side of him were thick and dark. The street lamps were spaced too far apart. Counting exits felt like counting sheep. He almost fell asleep at the wheel.

When he and Amy were first going out, she would wind a length of red yarn around the spiral of her notebook and make him do the same. She said that that way they would be secretly bound by love. Red was the color of valentines. In the afternoons, she got out of class before he did. She sat on the steps near the north corridor entrance and waited for him to be finished with health citizenship class. She wasn't ashamed of him then. She wasn't embarrassed to have him sitting next to her in the Sycamore, even when the people she was with were part of Garrett Fairchild's rich kids' crowd.

He wondered if Shelby was dead in the trunk by now. He wondered if she was in a lot of pain. The answers to those questions did not seem to have anything to do with him.

In Meldane, by the time he got there, it was full dark. Main Street was deserted. Even the stretch of sidewalk in front of the courthouse was empty of parked cars. The diner was closed and dark. Nobody ate in town at night. They went out to the roadhouses or the malls. At the last intersection that was part of town proper, one of the two town cop cars was pulled into a shadow, waiting for tourists coming through too fast. Bobby honked at him when he passed, and the cop honked back.

Funny, Bobby thought, *he's got to know where I'm going.* Anybody who saw him would have to know where he was going. There was nothing out this way but the road to Florida and Amy's house, nestled in a neighborhood of houses just like it. He wondered if any of them cared if he stayed away from Amy or not. He wondered if they were all secretly on his side.

He went down to Candor Street and turned left. He was coming up on it from behind, in case she had posted sentries, or her lawyers had. He had no idea if they would do something like that. He went from Candor to Markham and from Markham to Broad. There were lights in the living rooms of most of the houses. The doors and windows were all tightly shut. The houses all had air-conditioning.

Bobby got to Amy's street and eased down the block. Usually when he came here these days, he parked a few houses away, so that nobody would notice him. He couldn't do that tonight. He came to a stop right in front of Amy's front door. There was a light on in her living room, too, but nobody seemed to be in it. Maybe they were all out in the back yard eating barbecue.

He got out of the car and went around to the back. He opened the trunk and tried to get a good look at Shelby's body lying inside. There was a street lamp right above his head, but for some reason it made everything harder to see. Shelby didn't look like anybody he had ever seen before, although he remembered perfectly the bones of her neck breaking under his hand.

He leaned into the truck and got his arms under the body. He lifted it up – it was true, all the things they said about dead weights – and backed away from the vehicle. He expected someone to come running out of one of the houses, screaming at him. Nothing happened.

He brought Shelby's body around the car and to the walk in front of Amy's house. He put it down on the steps and looked around. Then he picked it up again and headed for the back. Mr Stepman had talked about getting some extra fencing to keep people coming around that way, but he hadn't done it.

Bobby edged past the big evergreen tree and into the back yard. It was empty, too, but there was a green plastic chaise still out on the lawn, and a round table with an umbrella that was stuck through a hole in the center. The back yard seemed better lit than the street. For a while, Bobby couldn't figure out why. Then he saw that Mr Stepman had begun putting in his new security arrangements after all. There was a big security light hanging from the back of the house. It was blazing.

Bobby put Shelby's body down on the chaise. Stretched out like that, she looked almost alive. She looked ready to whine at him.

'Just a minute,' he said to her.

He went to the sliding glass doors that led into Amy's kitchen and tried to open them. They were locked. He got a stone from the ground and pounded it into the glass until he caused a crack. He used the stone to make the crack worse and then put his finger in to pull the glass loose. The glass cut him and made him bleed.

'Damn,' he said to himself.

'I'm going to call the police,' Amy said to him, calling down from a window above his head. 'I'm going to get on the phone right now.'

Bobby stood back and looked at her. Her red hair was falling down, like Rapunzel's in the tower. Her face in the brightness from the security light was white and clean, unlined, undamaged, unreal. He thought of the way she looked when she walked down the corridors of the high school, her hair flowing, her books held close to her chest, the boys turning as she passed to watch the way her jeans fit against her thighs. He should have stayed in high school just to watch her walking there.

And then it hit him.

'You're alone,' he said.

'I'm not going to be alone in a minute and a half.'

'You're *alone*.'

Amy retreated from the window. Bobby raised his foot and smashed it through the glass door. Then he turned back to the chaise and got Shelby again.

He was a different person now, that was the thing. He was an entirely different man, not the boy she didn't want any more. He had died and been resurrected.

He edged himself and Shelby through the smashed glass door and started through the kitchen. It didn't matter if she was calling 911. They wouldn't be here in time. Nobody could be here in time. Nothing mattered except that Amy should take a good look at Shelby and feel the bones in her neck. Once she had her hands on those bones she would finally understand.

When they were first going steady, they skipped lunch every afternoon to go out in back of the bleachers on the athletic field and neck in the hot sun. They stretched out together on the grass and pressed their bodies against each other. They braided their fingers together and kissed the palms of each other's hands. On those afternoons he had sometimes felt released beyond description, past pain, past weakness, past that awful sense that failure was the only thing he would ever have the right to call his own. He had known right then and there that he would never be able to leave her.

Right now she was probably upstairs making phone calls. She was calling her parents and her lawyers and the town police. It didn't matter.

In a minute or two, he would have it all straightened out.

In a minute or two, she would finally realize how *much* he had changed.

THE HONEYED AXE

H. R. F. Keating

One

Inspector Ghote decided to approach the place on foot. He was determined not to be hurried. There were problems ahead. One beehive of problems. This was not just any murder. It was the murder of the Headmaster of one of the altogether posh, for-rich-only schools of India. Already it was splashed across the headlines. The whole reputation of Bombay's famed Crime Branch, almost immediately called in to supervise the investigation, rested now on his shoulders.

Perched up in the hills within a hundred miles of Bombay itself, the Matthew Arnold School, named long ago after some top-notch Angrezi schools inspector-cum-poet believed to have come to give some advices, it was where many, many of the city's Number One big fries had their sons and heirs. Inspector Pendharkar, who had gone up from the police station in the little town below when the death had been reported, had underlined the difficulties twice over.

'Inspector, I am telling you. Offsprings of three-four very-very well-known Bombay smugglers are there only. Bigwig politicians sending also. Not at all matter for local officer.' Quick look out of the corner of his eyes. 'Inspector, you are thinking I am one damn *kaamchor*, no?'

A shirker. Yes, Pendharkar was that. But it was easy to understand why he had been intent on shifting the whole investigation on to a supervising officer from Bombay. His English none too good, and each and every one up at the school bound to be hundred per cent English-speaking.

Okay, so far as I am concerned there need be no nonsenses about that aspect, but nevertheless I am not very much looking forward.

Yet Inspector Pendharkar, however bad his English, had done good work when he had been summoned to see the body of Anglo-Indian Mr Arnold Thomas, son and grandson of Arnold Thomases before him, each in turn the school's Head-master. To begin with, he had observed the curious fact about the single deep wound in the dead man's skull. The tiny altogether unexpected circumstance that surely must eventually led to the murderer.

'Yes, Inspector, one damn funny thing. Death, you are knowing, caused by blow from heavy weapon, cutting also. Not at all blunt instrument. One axe, is looking like.'

'Yes? What funny thing?'

'Honey, Inspector.'

'Honey?'

'*Ji haan*, inside that wound I was after some time spotting some unexplain substance. Yellowish by colour. Medical ointment, *ek dum* I am thinking. Then I was thinking, why would a murderer be applying some kind of ointment to wound they only are inflicting. So I was looking more of close. Smelling also. Believe, not believe, but in that wound six-seven, seven-eight smears honey.'

'First-class observation, Inspector.'

'But – but – is more also.'

Pendharkar's eyes had gleamed with self-satisfaction.

'More, Inspector?'

'Yes, yes. You are knowing this school-bool is just only by itself up there. Nothing else near. No houses, not any shop. So I was wondering where from is coming this honey-punny. And there were one or two fellows there I could be asking. In good round Marathi. Bearer, cook, *malis* working in gardens. And soon I was finding out simple truth.'

'Which was?'

'Yes, okay. Always possible-possible said honey coming from some woods. Some junglee finding one bee-nest. But, most likely, honey, I was thinking, coming from school itself. *Chota sahibs* getting best bread and honey. So I was asking-asking. Offering *beedi* to smoke, offering boot up arse. And I was finding answer. Big five-kilo tins honey kept in storeroom refrigerators, storeroom under key and lock also. In end I must be asking gentleman they are calling Bursar to be opening up. And what I was finding inside one big-big refrigerator? One tin honey, full to top and solid-solid. Inside same, deep-deep mark looking like one blow of axe.'

Something stirred in Ghote's mind. The faintest memory. But it was not to be called back.

'*Shabash*, Inspector, damn good work,' he said encouragingly. 'But this axe, the weapon in question, it is safely stored in your Muddamal Room here? Important to guard all evidences.'

'But, no, Inspector. No. Weapon not yet found.'

'No? Not so good, that. You have instituted thorough search?'

'Inspector, *ji haan*. But that axe may be anywhere. That place is big-big, and all round are woods. Miscreant could have thrown down same at one hundred and one good spots. It has a handle marked with red as Matthew Arnold School property, but how to find one red mark in one *lakh* green places?'

'I see. Well, we shall have to hope.'

But hurry on. Vital to wring every drop of information out of Pendharkar before going up to that élite establishment above the town. Already he had been deprived of a chance to inspect the body, found early the morning before. 'In front of one statue by main entrance, look almost like some sort sacrifice, temple goat,' Pendharkar had said. The heat, even up in the hills, had rendered imperative the Christian burial the Headmaster's religion demanded.

'Now, the locked store you were mentioning – it is always key-fastened?'

'*Ji haan*, locked-locked day and night also.'

'And this Bursar fellow ... what is it he is called?'

'He is by name one Dr Washikar. Is not at all doctor-doctor. Is just only Science Master there. But carrying double profession, master-cum-bursar.'

'I see. And he is the one with a key to this store where you were finding that honey tin, yes?'

'*Ji haan*, Inspector.'

'But is he the only one with access?'

'Access, what is?'

He had tried to suppress a dart of irritation. 'Access, access. Who was able to get to that honey tin. Who else is having keys?'

'Ah, that I can tell. Yes, yes. Three more only itself.'

'Three people only? But – but how can you be certain?'

'Dr Washikar Sahib telling and explaining.'

'Explaining what?'

'It is now not term-time, yes?'

'Of course. No school opens till first of June.'

'But not all the masters at that school are going away when term is over. Most going. But some, when they are not married men itself, staying. Four only. Now, in that storeroom is being kept two-three bottles whisky.'

'Ah, I see. Whisky should be kept under lock and key, but all four of those masters who stay on at the school after term is over like to drink.'

'No and yes, Inspector. You see, Dr Washikar is having key because he is Bursar. But he is not drinking-pinking. Also Hindi Master, one by the name of Mr Shreeram Vidyarthi is also good Hindu and not at all taking wines. But because the two others are having key to that room for getting their whiskies Vidyarthi Sahib also was given.'

'And these two others? Who are they?'

'Yes, yes. Number one, Mr Batheja, Mathem— Matheth—'

'Mathematics Master, yes?'

'*Ji haan*. Mr Batheja, Mathematics Master. And number *do*, Colonel Majumdar, Indian Army retired, the in-charge Sports.'

'Good, good. And no one else has a key to that storeroom? Not any *khansamah*, not any cook?'

'No, no. When any such is wanting provision they must be applying to Washikar Sahib.'

'You are one hundred per cent certain of this? You realise, isn't it, what it is meaning?'

'No, Inspector.'

These backwood fellows. No wonder they sent an officer from Headquarters. But the officer they have sent, will I cope up to situation? Howsoevermuch I am Headquarterswalla?

'Inspector? I am not fully understanding. What meaning it is about keys?'

'Simple, my friend. If the axe that killed Mr Arnold Thomas, Headmaster of Matthew Arnold School, was, as you have said, first somehow used on a tin of honey, and if four only people had access to the locked store where that tin was, then one of these four must be the murderer – Mr Washikar, Bursar and Science Master, Mr Shreeram Vidyarthi, Hindi Master, Mr Batheja, Mathematics Master and Colonel Majumdar, Sports Master. Those four only.'

By the time Ghote had reached the outskirts of the Matthew Arnold School he was beginning to regret his determination not to approach the place, as Inspector Pendharkar had wanted him to, with a screech of a police Jeep's tyres coming to a halt in a swirling cloud of dust. On to his hastily donned best shirt and trousers, already less than morning-clean from the enveloping red dust of the road from Bombay, he had now added a clinging under-layer of sweat from his toiling climb up to the plateau.

In the state he was in how was he going to face his four suspects? Three of them full to top with academic qualifications, the fourth an army colonel?

He came to a halt where the steep path broke through a tangle of thorny trees beside a thin waterfall tumbling into a deep gorge and contemplated the sight in front of him. An enormous stretch of beautifully green turf, wonderfully cool to the eyes after the aridity of Bombay in the full heat of pre-monsoon May, lay cut off from the outer world by the surrounding wide circle of scrubby trees. Well separated on the wide, green, beautifully mown extent, the squares of no fewer than three cricket pitches could be made out, slightly browner than the surrounding grass, neat, precise and promising of endless hours of calm pleasure. At the far side a *mali* guided a bullock slowly drawing along a big mower, the sound of its whirring blades coming to his ears like the buzzing of a wasp.

For a moment he thought of the many cheek-by-jowl squares on the Oval Maidan back in Bombay, reduced from incessant use to dull areas of pale dust. How different everything was here. Here no boy would play unless dressed in proper whites from top to toe and with all his gear correct to the last detail, pads whitened to unsmirched chalkiness, bat oiled and hundred per cent clean, ball gleaming in red leather, each stitch of its seam firmly in place.

Across the wide glowingly green stretch stood the buildings of the school itself. A solidly impressive mass, its rough-hewn dark stone echoing that of his own Headquarters building at Bombay's Crawford Market built at the height of the British Raj, its long range of stone-edged, pointed-arch windows like, again, pictures of the churches in the UK. At the centre of the whole a tall square tower rose up, topped by a large clock, white-faced and with, of course, Roman numerals. Below, a magnificent *gul mohar* tree in full red-orange blossom shaded a pure white statue.

A statue. Yes, he thought with a sudden thrust of grim reality, that must be where only forty-eight hours ago the body of Mr Arnold Thomas had lain, blood from the deep cleft in his skull oozing on to the paving stones beneath.

And it was now his duty to go forward across that cool, green stretch and into the dark stone building on the far side, so alien to the surrounding climate even up in the cooler hills here, filled somehow with the presence of the fair-skinned rulers of the distant British Raj, the presence that still wafted out towards him from the very clock tower at just that moment sending ringing out eleven sonorous strokes of its bell – cold, confident and, yes, admit it, awe-inspiring.

He stood watching the deserted scene, unable to make up his mind to drop down to the well-watered area of green, green grass – not one scrap of dirty paper, not one cow's dropping to sully it – and go through the tall entrance arch to seek his witnesses. His four suspects.

Suddenly, from behind the tangled clump of scrubby trees overhanging the waterfall at his back, there came the sound of a voice. A boy's voice. Speaking in English, though without the pinched vowels of British visitors to Bombay.

But what was it saying? What?

'"It matters not how strait the gate, how charged with punishments the scroll..."'

He turned and began softly to move forward.

'"...I am the master of my fate..."'

Frowning, he took two more steps nearer.

'"I am the captain of my soul."'

The piping voice fell silent. Another step forward.

Sitting perilously at the very edge of the steep drop beside the crystal cascading water of the falls was a boy aged about twelve, something of a roly-poly figure, dressed in a white shirt and grey half-pants held up with a bright-striped elastic belt.

What was he doing? With those clothes he must belong to the Matthew Arnold School. But why was he here when the next term would not begin for two or three weeks? And what – whatever? – did those words mean? *Straight the gate ... charged ... the scroll*?

Surely they could not be some sort of confession before, feeling somehow he had betrayed some trust, that he was not at all captain of his soul, he launched himself to death down the steep sides of the gorge? Could it be?

My God, he thought, once before in my life I rescued a boy from drowning like this. Have I got to do it again?

He measured the distance between himself and the chubby white-shirted figure.

Yes. Near enough. Just.

Two

Set, at the first sign of any movement from the boy at the edge of the gorge, to fling himself outwards with outstretched, grabbing arms, Ghote leant one further inch nearer.

Beneath the shifted weight of his foot a dry twig cracked with a tiny popping sound.

Lazily, the boy turned to see what had made the small, inoffensive noise.

'Helloji.' A sudden beaming smile on his podgily round face. 'Can I help you?'

'No. Yes. What – what it was you were saying?'

For an instant the boy seemed not to understand.

'Oh,' he said after a moment. 'Was I saying the poem aloud?'

'It is a poem?' He shook his head. 'That is perhaps explaining the whole thing.'

'Well, yes. It's a bloody silly poem by an old-time Britisher by the name of W. E. Henley. Every newie is made to learn it in his first days at Matthew Arnold, and has to explain each time he is asked that this gate is not going straight to anywhere but is just narrow. You spell it s-t-r-a-i-t. Whole thing is meant to fill your head with first-class ideals. I was sitting here thinking about the days when I first arrived, and the words must have just come popping out. Hope I didn't disturb you.'

'No, no. Not at all. But – but why is it you are here?'

'Here? You mean out at Chinaman's Falls? Or do you mean here at the school? Simple answer to both questions, actually. I'm here at Chinaman's Falls, so called because there used to be Chinese convicts hereabouts in British days, because it's a nice out-of-harm's-way spot. And I'm here at school in the middle of the bloody vac because my father went to the US on business and took my mother with him. Plus, no one in the family back in Madras was willing to put me up. Or put up with me, more likely.'

'To put up with you?'

'Yes. My appalling behaviour, you know. Reason I was sent to Matthew Arnold in the first place. One and all agreed I was badly in need of discipline, and discipline is the one thing they know how to dish out here. At the end of the cane.'

Something in the cheerful way the boy – who, he saw now, did look distinctly South Indian – had spoken made Ghote suddenly think that meeting him had been a piece of luck. He might well be able to learn from him, without him at all knowing how important it was, a good deal about those four suspect masters.

'Well,' he said, treading a little cautiously and, he hoped, with cunning, 'I have just only come up here to look at your very fine school.'

Could he add he was thinking of sending a son of his to it? No. No, considering his dust-red and sweaty state, that would be stretching likeliness a bit too far. He did not look the sort of *crorepati*, money falling out of each and every pocket, who would be sending a son to this place. Definitely not.

'Just to look?' his potential informant answered, as quick as a mongoose. 'Not to investigate murder of one headmaster? You are a policewalla, isn't it?'

After just an instant Ghote gave a wry grin.

'Hundred per cent correct,' he said. 'I can see I must not try any pulling wool over eyes with you. I am one Inspector Ghote, Bombay Crime Branch. And, please, what is your good name?'

'Bulbul. I am always called Bulbul.'

Again a little disconcerting. He had hardly expected the boy to hand him his card, but this much informality was surprising. Yet not unwelcome.

'Very well, Bulbul. No beating about the bushes. Your headmaster has been murdered. You have somehow learned that, and—'

'Somehow? No way. You don't find out things here by chance only. What you have to have at Matthew Arnold School is sharp eyes, plus sharp ears. Cunning also, if you are wanting to survive. Very soon after I came I learned, as almost the only South Indian in the place, that however much they were saying "Be a good loser", if I didn't want to be victim of all sorts of nasty jokes, from boys and masters also, I must learn how to deceive. So I was finding out it paid to act the fool in class so as to make others laugh instead of twisting arms. Then I learned how to gain popularity by cheeking masters, and at the same time making them believe I was after all a hard worker. To act their "Play up, play up and play the game", but to play my own game for myself. Good preparation for life, you know.'

Well, Ghote thought, Bulbul he is by name – *bulbul* a nightingale – and certainly he is able to sing, altogether sweetly. So I wonder ... How much altogether will he sing for me? Tell me all the things I would never get to know about this school, its murdered Headmaster and, most of all, about those four teachers I have sooner or later got to question?

'But,' he asked still with some caution, 'are you never caught out for your nefarious classroom doings?'

Wide smile lighting up the smooth round face.

'Oh, yes, yes. I am letting myself get caught. Price of fame. Or price at least of popularity itself. Record number of canings per term, record offers of tuck.'

'I see,' Ghote said, guessing that 'tuck' – did the word come from UK? – must mean sweetmeats and other treats. 'So, is each and every one of the masters often caning yourself, or are some being more kind?'

'Oh, all of them. All of them. You know, you don't get to break records without putting in some effort. Direct quote by old Colonel Majumdar, Majjidumdum.'

Yes. First of the four neatly brought up.

'He is the Sports Master, isn't it? Is he then very tough on you?'

Bulbul grinned.

'Not at all,' he said. 'Behind the tiger face, and when you see him you will know what I mean by that, behind it is one cotton heart. So you will not be finding your killer there, Inspector.'

So much for wool-over-the-eyes.

But after all, he told himself, Bulbul's judgment may not be hundred per cent accurate. Twelve years of age only.

'And now are you wanting to hear about caning powers of the others Inspector Pendharkar has told you must be suspects? Don't answer. I will tell anyhow. Number one – who shall I make number one? Okay, let's choose Vidyarthi Sahib. The one Agatha Christie would make into Least Likely Suspect. You are reading Agatha Christie, Inspector? First-class training manual for Crime Branchwallas?'

'No,' Ghote answered, a little stiffly. 'Or, rather, yes. Yes, in my boyhood I was going through one or two of those books.'

'Okay. So, Least Likely Suspect, which is meaning one you must straight away arrest, isn't it? Pandit Shreeram Vidyarthi, Hindi Master. Though why we should be made to learn that awful language hour after hour, I don't know. Even for boys from the Hindi Belt it is only useful for giving orders to servants. You can't talk about sport or films or rock in Hindi, not even any sort of modern business. But—'

'Yes, yes,' Ghote interrupted, anxious to get Bulbul off that well-worn track. 'And were you collecting many, many of your record punishments by not paying attention in Hindi class?'

'Oh, well, some. Yes, if you knew the old pandit, with his long white beard and his altogether gentle manner, you would think he would never take up the cane. But he does. When he thinks it is deserved, and then he is not so gentle. But fair always. Yes, that I must admit. Fair always. So could still be your murderer, Inspector.'

'All right,' Ghote said. 'This method of detection of yours might not be approved at Police Training School. But I do not altogether discount same.'

'But in any case,' Bulbul went on, paying no attention to the contrived compliment, 'there's a better way of getting out of Hindi.'

'Yes?'

Let this witness, this odd sort of witness, talk about whatever comes into his mind. In that way any witness is likely to produce at least some useful evidence.

'Yes. All you've got to do is to say something in class that leads old Panditji into telling one of his stories. Then no more Hindi.'

'Stories? What sort of stories it is?'

'Oh, still absolute Hindi stuff. But the old pandit's always decent enough to tell them in English. Not at all James Bond, but a lot better than Hindi grammar. I expect a chap like you had them all from your mother's lips – the tale of the crow and the sparrow, the story of the monkey and the crocodile.'

As the boy spoke, the very tales themselves, as told him by his mother, sprang to life in Ghote's mind. He had forgotten them, as he usually forgot most of the stories she had told him. Until some spark brought them to sudden light again. Another of them, he had no idea which, seemed to be poised just behind his ears at that moment. But he knew it would be no use trying to drag it into hearing. If he waited, one day suddenly for no good reason . . .

'And do you play such tricks on all your teachers?'

'Or, put it your way, Inspector: which of the teachers you are suspecting do you want to hear about next?'

He smiled at that, if with a little difficulty.

'All right,' he said. 'Tell me about— Well, start with Dr Washikar, Bursar-cum-Science – what should I be knowing about him?'

'First of all, he also is not your murderer. No guts. That I am knowing. The hard way. When he thinks he has to punish me. Only it is not at all hard way. I tell you, when Washikar Sahib gives you the cane you have to pay very much attention to know he is doing it at all, like late lamented Headmaster Thomas in fact. Except for the times when Tommy gets into one of his monster rages. No fun then to be bent over before him. Like when he beat the whole senior class, beat each one of them like a madman only, boys seventeen-eighteen years of age screaming and yelling. Till in the end Tommy fell down on the ground, altogether exhausted. And very much *hangama* after to keep it all damn quiet.'

'He beat those boys that hard?'

'Oh, yes. Weeks before all marks were gone. Personal inspection, in return for many, many jokes told.'

Wait, Ghote thought. Could one of those victims have taken revenge? Such a revenge?

'When did that all happen?' he asked.

'Two years past.'

'So all the boys involved have left the school?'

Bulbul grinned.

'Oh, Inspector, no luck for you there. Not one Old Rugbee was up here when Tommy met his horrible end.'

'Old Rugbee? What is that?'

'It is what they call Matthew Arnold School former pupils. That is because school was founded to be copy of famous English school Rugby College, where – so they are always telling and telling us – the great Headmaster was one Dr Arnold. But, brutality victim or not brutality victim, not a single Old Rugbee was here. I can tell you that for certain. Even in the vac I still keep my eyes wide open.'

'I see. And it was by keeping open those eyes of yours that you knew Mr Arnold Thomas had been murdered?'

'Of course, as soon as they found old Tommy with that hole in his head I knew about it. And I know about everything else that's gone on since.'

Ghote decided this ought to be tested.

'You managed to listen even when Inspector Pendharkar was here making initial inquiries?'

'Of course. And, you know, in spite of the sort of English that fellow is speaking, he is not altogether a damn fool.'

'He will be glad to hear your opinions.'

Bulbul gave him another of his flashing smiles.

'But you will not be telling, isn't it?'

'Yes. I am thinking he would not altogether like praise from a schoolboy itself.'

'And no bloody cheeky comments on standard of English, yes? But you, I am guessing, are one little bit different. I am guessing you would be very interested in knowing who one schoolboy is thinking is the murderer.'

Bulbul smiled, white teeth glinting broadly.

'Very well. Tell only.'

Another face-splitting cheeky smile.

'Inspector, I will admit it. I am as much in dark as you. But you have not heard my assessments at cane end of all your suspects, yes?'

'Right, then, let me hear about number four, Mr Batheja, Mathematics.'

'Now, there is one cunning devil. When you see him punishing some other fellow you would think, Oh, that's not going to be too much of bother. But when it comes to you yourself on receiving end, then you are learning that he has a way of flicking wrist to achieve maximum effect from minimum effort. If there is any master I am as much as possible taking care not to find myself in trouble with it is Oxford-returned Batheja Sahib. Consequently, myself becoming one ace mathematician. Which will please my father to the utmost when he is making me join his business.'

So, Mr Batheja a cunning fellow. And I am going to have to tackle him. Sooner or later. England-travelled, almost like some British itself. No doubt, one brilliant mind. And cunning, cunning. But cruel also. Relishing to inflict pain.

And so, if he had some reason, to kill? Would it be—?

His tentative train of thought was abruptly interrupted. A shout, a bellow, from just behind the clump of scrubby trees which had hidden Bulbul from Ghote struck at them like a roar of unexpected thunder.

'Chintamani!'

For a long moment they both sat seemingly stunned by the sheer noise. Then Bulbul spoke.

'God, that's for me.'

'For you?'

'Well, my name is Chintamani, so I suppose it must be me Colonel Majumdar is wanting. And, come to think of it, I know why.'

'Why?'

'He has ordered me to run three times round the sports field every day before tiffin. And I have been sitting here talking to you itself.'

And then the colonel appeared.

Ghote's first impression was of a moustache. An enormous moustache, seeming to obscure the whole face behind it. Black, deep-dyed black, and bushily curling, waxed at each tip, it reached beyond the ears, totally covering the upper lip and most of the cheeks beyond. After a little, as Colonel Majumdar took Bulbul to task for his 'appalling slackness', Ghote was able to ignore the hairy mass and see the man behind it. Sharp beak of a nose, ferocious grey eyes seemingly fixed in a permanent glare. Body, clad in bright-striped, if faded, blazer, upright as a post and as thin and hard.

Eventually the colonel took him into his notice.

'And who the devil are you, sir?'

He swallowed, just once. Now it had to begin. However much it had been arrived at by chance, the first interrogation of the case.

'Good morning,' he said. 'Please, is it that I am speaking with Colonel Majumdar, Sports Master at this school? I am Inspector Ghote by name. From Bombay itself. Here on orders to investigate sad death of your late Headmaster, Mr Arnold Thomas.'

'Hah. Are you indeed? Then what the devil are you doing up here, keeping this idle boy from his exercise?'

He felt bound to get his bubblingly cheerful informant out of as much trouble as he could.

'I was happening to meet him as he was running round this playing field,' he said. 'And he was kindly giving brief account of aims and objects of Matthew Arnold School.'

Bulbul was quick to accept this gift.

'Oh, yes, sir,' he said to Colonel Majumdar. 'I was trying to explain to you, sir. You see, I had run one and a half circuits already when I found this gentleman and he was asking his way to the school. So I was doing my best to help him.'

'Hah.' Colonel Majumdar did not sound wholly convinced. But with one final glare he gave Bulbul his marching orders.

'Right, go and run the other circuit. And a half. And I shall be timing you, boy. So don't you dare slack off.'

'No, sir. Oh, no, sir.'

Bulbul set off at a fast trot. Only, as soon as the colonel's back was safely turned, to drop into an easy, backward-glancing lope.

Ghote hoped the lie he had told for him would earn eventually some return. There was likely to be more he would need to find out about his four suspects, or what there might be in the murdered Headmaster's life which might have made someone want to take that missing axe – that mysteriously honey-smeared axe – to him.

But then he realised that Colonel Majumdar was standing with his back to half-heartedly trotting Bulbul because he had something he wanted to impress, forcibly, on the investigator from Bombay.

'Glad we happened to meet like this, Inspector. One or two small points I'd like to make clear before you get talking to any of, well, put it in a nutshell, any of my colleagues here.'

'Yes, sir?'

'I'm an old Army man, Inspector, as you will have realised.' Colonel Majumdar trod cautiously onwards. 'And as such accustomed to speaking my mind. Never does when you're going into action not to let every officer under your command know exactly what the objective is. Get that?'

The last two words, suddenly banged out like two quick shots from a rifle, caused Ghote to recoil for a moment as if the rifle was not aimed at him but tucked, rather inefficiently, into his own shoulder.

'Yes. Yes, sir. Yes, I am well understanding,' he managed to say at last, though whether he had fully understood or not was still a question.

'Right, then. Take this on board. You'll hear some fairy stories about me. Right? Right, damn great pinch of salt needed every time.'

Ghote, assailed by so many metaphors, could only try to look sympathetic.

'Hah. Thought you were the sort of chap who'd understand. Bloody embarrassing having to say it, but best to spit it out. No good ever comes of trying to confuse the enemy with a lot of fake manoeuvres, whatever certain senior officers tried to tell me.'

Ghote thought for a moment about those senior officers. Were they right, those major-generals, lieutenant-generals, generals? Or was Colonel Majumdar right to despise those men senior to himself? In which case, was he a man who thought he always knew best? And, if he was, did that mean, despite young Bulbul's deduction from his surprisingly unvigorous punishing powers, that he had taken an axe to the person who was, in a way, his commanding general here? Mr Arnold Thomas, Headmaster?

'Yes, sir,' he said, inventing hastily. 'I myself am finding assistant commissioners, additional commissioners, even commissioners themselves are sometimes talking through hats.'

He saw a flash of reassurance in the grey eyes above the sprouting dyed black curls and whirls of the moustache.

'Right. Then you'll appreciate my position. You see, thing is, I was threatened at the end of last term with, not to put too fine a point on it, the sack. Age-barred, old Thomas said. Claimed I was lacking in blasted efficiency.'

Ghote planted an astonished expression on his face.

'Well, I'm not the sort of fellow who boasts about what he can do. Can't stand chaps like that. But I tell you this, Inspector. I'm a damned sight more efficient than most of the rest of the staff. Some pretty odd fish have come here in recent years. I'm an Old Rugbee myself, you know. This is the blazer, matter of fact. And when I say place is going to rack and ruin, don't you let anybody tell you different.'

'But, sir,' Ghote ventured, determined to get at the truth of the situation, 'many sons of the riches are coming still, isn't it? And fathers paying also?'

'Dare say they are. Know they are, poisonous little devils. My day, Inspector, morning parade, you had half a score sons of princely houses standing there with the best of them, three hundred boys, every one of them dressed alike, all at attention like damned good soldiers. And now what? Little swine jerking and jabbering. No discipline, no discipline at all. Know why? Damned fathers don't pay their bills, and the little blighters know they're getting away with it. Thought of that, have you? Eh? Eh?'

Ferocious glare back again now.

'No, sir, no. I had not at all thought.'

'Right. Well, dare say you'll see for yourself, once you start poking and prying about like a damned policeman.'

There were limits.

'Sir, it is my bounden duty to be poking. And prying also.'

Colonel Majumdar seemed momentarily taken aback. But eventually acknowledged he had gone too far.

'Course it is, course it is. Like to see a man who knows his duty and does it. But – but – what the devil was I saying?'

'That . . .' Ghote paused.

To what point in the machine-gun splutter of revelations should he take his witness back? Where could he fix on without causing some sort of an explosion? An explosion that might put an abrupt end to this useful stream of disclosures?

In the end he chose the daring course.

'Sir, you were saying you yourself had been threatened with a sack.'

'Hah.'

Half a step back. Was the explosion coming?

'Yes. Yes, well, Inspector, I dare say it's best you should hear about that from my own lips, rather than get the garnished version from one of my brother masters. The fact of the matter is, it wasn't a threat. I was actually given formal notice by old Thomas. Got till the end of the year. Then I'll find I'm shifting for myself. Pension getting smaller every week with the damned price hikes. Nobody wanting to employ an ex-officer who's done his damnedest for his country. Bit of a black lookout really.'

'Yes, sir. I can see it is very, very bad thing.'

But behind the hastily put together response his mind was working furiously. Was the colonel painting, without fully realising it, the picture of a desperate man? A man who might murder in order possibly to obliterate the sentence of dismissal passed on him?

'Course, I know where the trouble really was.'

'Yes, sir?'

What was this?

'Trouble springs from that appalling brother, half-brother whatever, of Thomas's. Know about him, do you?'

'No, sir. No. Not at all.'

'Right. Well, he's that fellow Jagadir Thomas, same father, different mother. Very different mother, I dare say. Chap who made all that money on the Bombay Stock Exchange back in the sixties. Came up from nowhere, and now has half a dozen high-ups in politics in his pocket. If you can believe all you read in the damned newspapers.'

'Oh, yes, sir, I am knowing such.'

But only by reading the newspapers Colonel Majumdar had just condemned as damned.

'Well, it's common knowledge – at least it's common knowledge to me – that this place, the Matthew Arnold School, my own alma mater, dash it, would have been closed down years ago if Arnold Thomas hadn't managed to squeeze sums of money out of Jagadir. Probably had some hold on him, I don't know.'

Again Ghote's mind began to go leaping from one point to another.

Jagadir Thomas involved in the affairs of this school? Jagadir Thomas, politicians' crony. This could be a case bringing very much of troubles down on any investigating officer. And Arnold Thomas perhaps knowing something to the detriment of his half-brother. So, if he had, would Jagadir Thomas, well known as ruthless, have decided to dispose of this too knowledgeable ghost from his past? Either with his own hands, or using some hired help?

But how, if all this was true, did that honey come into it? Why would Jagadir Thomas, or one of the *goondas* he might have employed, dip that axe into honey before doing the deed?

And why did *honey* still say something in the very back of his own mind?

Three

Questions raced and tumbled in Ghote's mind. Was Jagadir Thomas using this school for nefarious purposes? What might it be that his half-brother knew? Could he himself learn it, and somehow use it? These were not to be immediately answered. Colonel Majumdar, as he had spoken the words 'alma mater', had turned aside. Was it, Ghote asked himself afterwards, to hide a tear emerging from one of those grey eyes and instantly lost among the growth of that fierce moustache? Looking away, the Sports Master must have spotted, at the other side of the green expanse of the playing field, none other than Bulbul Chintamani. Sitting down at his ease.

'*Chintamani!*'

Once more there came the wrathful blast. But this time Colonel Majumdar, perhaps guessing that even his lion roar would not reach across the huge extent of green between himself and idling Bulbul, set off at once in hot pursuit.

Watching him cut across the grass with long, scissoring strides, shouting all the while, 'Chintamani! Chintamani! Play up, boy! Play up, play up and play the game!' Ghote could not help thinking the dead Headmaster must have been more than a little unjust in dismissing him on grounds of inefficiency. Which, first, increased the strength of his possible motive for the murder, and, second, made it all the more physically possible that he had dealt that single skull-penetrating axe blow.

But, damn it, a productive interrogation, of a sort, had been cut short. Young Bulbul would have to come up with a lot more of his useful gossip to make up for what abandoning his run had brought about.

And – an abrupt, dark thought – three more interrogations, at none of which was he likely to be able to take advantage of lucky informality, lay ahead.

However, duty dictated just one thing.

With leaden steps he set off in his turn across the wide stretch of grass, heading for the arch in the long, dark line of the school buildings immediately behind the blazing *gul mohar* tree and the white statue – Who was it of? – in front of which the body of Arnold Thomas had been found.

At least, he thought when eventually he stood in front of the statue, glancing for a moment at traces of dark blood at its foot, here is one question I have found the easy answer to. Who is remembered here? DR ARNOLD THOMAS – FOUNDER AND FIRST HEADMASTER – THE MATTHEW ARNOLD SCHOOL – SI MONUMENTUM QUAERIS CIRCUMSPICE.

The final part baffled him. Latin, he supposed. Had it been Sanskrit, he might have had a shot at working out the meaning.

But then the very last word burst in on him. With a message. *'Circumspice.'* Whatever it might actually mean, it said to him just one thing. Be circumspect. Watch out.

He had to make yet more of an effort to venture through the dark arch behind into the school itself. Once through, he found everything cold, sunless. And apparently deserted.

Puzzled and depressed, he wandered further and further on, glancing into room after room just in the simple hope of seeing someone, anyone, who could tell him where any of his three suspects might be found. But all he saw in each room he came to were ranks of wooden desks, deeply carved and cut about with layers of initials, and, at the front teachers' podiums, empty but somehow forbidding. Marching along the seemingly endless, high-ceilinged corridors, his footsteps echoing plonkingly, he did at last come across one room with a slight difference. In place of a podium it had a long scarred bench littered with dusty scientific apparatus. Dr Washikar's classroom, he thought. But no Dr Washikar to question. A curse? Or a blessing?

Eventually he found his way out to a big inner building in the same dark stone, with above its pair of tall doors the carved words BUILT AT THE EXPENSE OF HIS HIGHNESS RAVSINHJI, THAKOR SAHEB OF SATARA. Venturing to pull one leaf of the doors an inch or two open, he saw a vast, echoingly empty assembly hall, lit by dim stained-glass windows, with at the near end four tall wooden boards inscribed with the names of past pupils who had achieved honours of various sorts, and, distantly at the far end, a gloomy painting of – it must be – Victoria, Queen–Empress.

A little later he found another huge room, as big as the assembly hall, with above its doors, beside which there hung from a massive rosewood stand an immense brass gong, the word REFECTORY. Taking a quick look inside, he was relieved to see, under some dark portraits on the walls and the huge cross-beams of the roof, that up on a dais four places had been laid for tiffin. Down below, too, on one of six long, long, bare teak tables with shiny wooden benches beside them another single place had been set.

For Bulbul, he thought. So at least when tiffin time comes I may find here my useful little informant. And perhaps all four of my suspects.

Nevertheless, he felt he had to set off on his search again and ventured to climb a wide wooden stairway to the floor above. But there again he found nothing, only dormitories, each named after British heroes, Drake, Marlborough, Nelson, Wellington, and filled with cheerless rows of empty iron-framed beds.

It was only when, making his way down again, he thought to try a classroom door he might have missed before that he saw, sitting tranquilly reading at the tall, upraised teacher's podium, the blackboard behind it covered with phrases in *devanagri* script, a mild, long-bearded figure in pure white kurta-pajama. Surely Shreeram Vidyarthi, Hindi Master.

Taking a deep breath, he stepped in and introduced himself.

'Ah, yes, I suppose an investigator from Bombay was bound to appear before long. What can I tell you that might be helpful, Inspector?'

Something about the direct and simple way he had been addressed made Ghote decide not to go through the early stages of an interrogation, the gradually getting nearer and nearer the key question. Instead he asked it at once.

'Sir, did you have any reason to wish the late Mr Arnold Thomas dead?'

A steady look from the mild brown eyes in the aged face above the flowing white beard.

'Oh, yes, Inspector, you could say that I did. He had just dismissed me, without explanation, from the well-remunerated post I have held at this school for the past many years.'

Another master dismissed. What had got into murdered Mr Thomas's head? Had he been proposing to fill the school with even more new faces? Had he flown into one of the weak man's rages Bulbul had vividly described and was he throwing out anybody and everybody he came across? And if he was, why was he?

But perhaps these sackings had been just only for Colonel Majumdar and Shreeram Vidyarthi. One thing to ask when I find Dr Washikar and Mr Batheja. If I ever do.

However, Shreeram Vidyarthi had not, it seemed, finished his mildly frank piece of self-incrimination.

'Though I suppose, Inspector,' he said in his softly dreamy voice, 'that I ought in justice to you, if not to myself, to add that being dismissed was not something that greatly worried me. I have for some time been contemplating taking *sannyas* in holy Varnasi.'

Sannyas. Total retirement from the world. Stepping down into utter anonymity on the banks of the Ganges. Under a new name, or none at all. All contact with the past relinquished. Bare sustenance sought with a held-out begging bowl.

Well, if Shreeram Vidyarthi was contemplating that, then he had no reason to have killed his Headmaster, however much of a sack he was threatened with.

Must check with Bulbul of the ready ears whether he has heard anything of this. But, if I had to go by my judgement only, I would say without hesitating that what I have been told is altogether likely.

So one more suspect eliminated. If Colonel Majumdar with what Bulbul had called his 'cotton heart' can also really be put out of account. Then only two now remaining.

He took an instant decision. If need be he could get back later both to the colonel and to this gentle, white-bearded figure. But at this moment, as quickly as possible, he ought to pursue the more hopeful lines.

'Sir,' he said, 'could you kindly be telling me where I may find Dr Washikar, Bursar of this school?'

Eliminate him, as Bulbul had indicated he might easily be able to, and then there would be just one left. An arrest before the sun went down? It could be.

He allowed himself the smallest flicker of anticipated triumph.

'You would doubtless find Dr Washikar in the school storeroom at this moment,' Shreeram Vidyarthi said. 'He is much concerned, obsessed I may say, with checking the contents of the shelves and refrigerators there. You would find the storeroom through the kitchens, and the kitchens you can best locate by the simple expedient of sniffing. Tiffin cannot be far off and there would be some cooking taking place.'

The mention of the storeroom refrigerators put Ghote at once in mind of the big tin of honey in which Inspector Pendharker had found the mark of an axe. The link between axe and honey, something which had plagued him from time to time ever since Pendharkar had first mentioned his discovery, now asked its question once more. But the answer was as elusive as ever. For an instant he thought of asking the Hindi Master, the teller of tales, whether the conjunction of honey and axe meant anything to him. But he decided it was by no means likely, and in any case he could hardly wait now till he had confronted his last two suspects, however formidable they might be.

He offered his thanks and hurried out.

True enough, as soon as he lifted his nose and gave a tentative sniff the odour of spicy cooking came to his nostrils. Spices, he thought, one touch of India in this atmosphere of British Raj.

At once his spirits perked up, and he found it was only a matter of a brisk walk down the corridors which ten minutes before had seemed so chill and interminable before he came to the kitchens where a solitary cook, sweaty in singlet and wrap-around *lunghi*, was busy preparing a meal that would meet the needs of just four masters and one boy. A quick request for directions and in ten seconds more he was standing at the open door of the storeroom he had heard so much about. And there in front of him, reaching up to a high shelf, notebook in hand, was a tall, flappily thin man, partially bald, his face dignified with a pale wisp of moustache and a pair of gold-rimmed spectacles.

'Please, I am talking with Dr Washikar?'

The Bursar wheeled round like – the very opposite of what he was – a thief caught in the act.

Hastily Ghote explained why he was there.

Dr Washikar dropped his notebook.

'But – but—' he said.

'Yes? What it is?'

'I thought— I was thinking— There was a police officer here earlier. Surely he noted all the relevant particulars?'

'Yes, sir. Inspector Pendharkar from the town police station was extremely thorough. But after particulars have been noted there comes the time for conclusions to be drawn. I have been sent from Bombay itself to draw such.'

'But – but what conclusions, Inspector?'

'The conclusion as to who was murdering the late Mr Arnold Thomas.'

'Murdering?' Dr Washikar asked, as if the word itself was altogether new to him.

'Sir,' Ghote said sharply, 'you were not thinking that a deep axe wound has occurred in Mr Thomas's head without human agency?'

'Oh.'

It was plain that somehow Dr Washikar had been thinking just that. Or perhaps that he had not been thinking about the death at all. Or was it that he was pretending to be so innocent?

'Sir,' he said to him, sharply as before, 'let me be telling you what are implications of the death of Mr Thomas. Sir, some person struck the fatal blow, and—'

'A dacoit. A dacoit from somewhere, Inspector. It must have been such a passing robber.'

Dr Washikar seemed delighted with the explanation that had occurred to him.

'No, sir. You see, in that wound in Mr Thomas's head there was a quantity of honey. And, sir, in this storeroom itself Inspector Pendharkar was seeing one honey-tin with in it the mark of an axe.'

'Yes, yes. I was here when he took that tin from the refrigerator. I made a note that there was one fewer than previously. Look, look, I can show it to you in my book.'

He scrabbled on the floor to rescue the fallen notebook.

'Sir, that is proving nothing.'

'Nothing? Then let me show you the very tin. I put it aside after Inspector – what did you say his name was?'

'Pendharkar, sir.'

'After Inspector Pendharkar had seen it. Here it is. Here.'

He stooped and from one of the lowest shelves in the big room produced a five-kilo tin prominently marked BEST NILGIRIS HONEY. He levered off its partly opened top with eager fingernails.

Ghote peered. Saw only a melted sloshy swirl of dark liquid.

'It was evidence,' he said, unable to keep a note of forlorn disappointment out of his voice.

'But it is here still.'

'Evidence that some person had plunged into same one axe-head. When we are finding axe, which unfortunately appears to be missing, we would have one good link in chain of evidences leading to conviction of the murderer.'

'But now that link is lost?'

Dr Washikar did not sound as dismayed as a respected citizen ought to have been.

Was he, in fact, secretly triumphing? Had all that almost unbelievable lack of common knowledge been a hasty attempting at bluffing when a Bombay detective had come on him unawares? Was the Bursar after all his man? Had he, too, been dismissed by an enraged Mr Arnold Thomas?

And, if so, how now can I—? The scrabbling thought was cut short by a sudden tremendous, reverberating sound.

All speech became impossible.

Then, when at last the prolonged rising and falling boom had sunk to a level that made it possible to be heard, Dr Washikar, the expression on his smudgily moustached face noticeably happier, spoke. 'Yes,' he said. 'Head Bearer has just struck the gong. Time for tiffin.'

From a hook on the back of the storeroom door he plucked a tattered black academic gown and, muttering 'Must be properly dressed', rapidly shrugged his narrow shoulders into it.

Then he looked at Ghote, much as if he were seeing him for the first time.

'Inspector – Inspector – I am not sure you gave me your name.'

'It is Ghote, sir.'

'Ah, yes. Well, then, Mr Ghote, would you care to join us for tiffin? I am sure the kitchens, however few the vacation cooks, will be able to rise to one extra meal.'

Ghote, the sight of the single sweat-stained cook at work still fresh in his mind, had some doubts. But, salivatingly aware ever since he had stepped out of Shreeram Vidyarthi's classroom of the fragrance of spices, he gratefully accepted the invitation.

At the entrance to the huge room labelled REFECTORY there stood the man who must have sounded that reverberating stroke on the big gong beside the doors – the Head Bearer, a magnificent sight in a red-sashed white tunic and elaborate turban. For a moment Ghote wondered where he had sprung from in the almost deserted school. But, he thought, no doubt he had been in his quarter somewhere, putting on the magnificent turban ready for his ceremonial duty.

'Ah, Bearer, we have an unexpected guest. Would you . . .?' As the Bursar's voice trailed away he was answered.

'No problem, Dr Washikar Sahib. No problem itself.'

Stepping into the high-beamed hall, Ghote saw his other three suspects, each like Dr Washikar wearing a gown and, standing at the table on the dais, looking like so many crows perched round a rubbish bin. Colonel Majumdar's gown hung in neat military folds from his broad shoulders, as black as his curling moustaches. Shreeram Vidyarthi's looked more than a little odd against his flowing white kurta-pajama. But it was the third master, wrapped in his gown as if he were protecting himself from a monsoon downpour, who sent a shiver of anticipation through him. Mr Batheja, England-returned Mathematics Master, and, according to young Bulbul, 'one cunning devil'.

He looked over towards him as intently as he dared. A man of below average height even, from the crouching way he was standing inside that wrapped-round gown, somewhat *kubra*, hunchbacked. And with a narrow, jackal-like face, pock-marked.

I cannot question that villainous-looking fellow in front of those other three, he thought. And if I attempt, sitting up there, not to ask any questions whatsoever I would be reduced to mumbling only. Then, when later I am wishing to exercise authority, how would I do it?

And, he saw, the Head Bearer was now advancing towards the dais with, on a small tray, the silver cutlery without which, plainly, at the Matthew Arnold School no morsel of food could be consumed.

He went quickly over to him.

'No,' he said. 'Kindly put my place on the table over there. I am knowing young Bulbul Chintamani, and I will keep him company.'

He turned and offered the same explanation to Dr Washikar, contriving to imply that he had somehow been acquainted with Bulbul long before. Dr Washikar looked on the whole relieved to be freed of the presence of a man who might ask him things he would prefer his colleagues not to hear.

'Very well, Inspector. It is good of you to spend time with the boy. I trust you do not find him a nuisance. He can be distinctly impertinent on occasion.'

'Oh, I am sure he would not be so with me.'

He sat himself down on the bench at the opposite side of the table from Bulbul's place. Impertinent or not, he said to himself, I have done well to get this opportunity to hear more from him.

Looking at the distance between himself and the table on the dais where the four masters had yet to take their seats, he calculated that nothing Bulbul said would be overheard there. Unless, teasingly, the boy chose to say something just a little too loudly.

But where was he?

Suddenly the big double doors clattered open again with much more noise than could have been necessary. Up on the dais four scandalised faces glared at Bulbul as, strolling carelessly, he went across to his place.

'Chintamani,' Dr Washikar squawked, 'why have you kept us waiting? You know tiffin cannot commence until grace has been said.'

'Oh, sir,' Bulbul answered, the picture of bright-faced innocence, 'I somehow did not hear the gong. Was it sounded?'

All four masters standing there, even mild Shreeram Vidyarthi, looked as though they wished they had a cane to hand.

'Well,' the Bursar said at last, 'now you have chosen to come, kindly proceed.'

Bulbul placed his hands neatly together and sent issuing out a stream of incomprehensible sound.

'Latin,' he said to Ghote as, the moment he had finished, he vaulted over his bench and dropped down on to it. 'Don't ask what it is meaning. We have to learn it, but I can never remember.'

'Listen to me,' Ghote hissed at him. 'There are things I am wishing to ask. But if you are making one damn fool of yourself all of them up there will sit with ears like cockroaches wanting to know what more of cheek you are giving out.'

Bulbul's grin faded right away.

'Oh, okay,' he said. 'From now on I'll be one perfect schoolboy.'

And he did put on a fine act, quietly eating and occasionally pointing to one of the big oil paintings hanging on the walls as if he were explaining them to this guest. Ghote, glancing surreptitiously up towards the dais, saw after a few minutes that they were no longer under close observation.

'Right,' he said to Bulbul, attempting to look as if he were asking him some question or other about life at the Matthew Arnold School, 'tell me, were you knowing that Mr Arnold Thomas had told Colonel Majumdar his time at this school was over?'

Surreptitiously Bulbul grinned.

'You are asking if I was by some chance standing just beneath the window in the Headmaster's house when he was ranting and roaring at poor old Majjydumdum? Why should you think I would behave in that disgraceful way?'

Ghote gave him a look. Half of irritation, half of admiration.

'All right. So, Vidyarthi Sahib?'

'Him also. But not so much of ranting-raving. Hard to rant at that old fellow. Will not rant back.'

He paused, evidently thinking about the scene he had contrived to overhear.

How did the boy know when something to interest him was going on? Sixth sense? Seventh even?

'Well, not quite true, that. About not ranting back. He did not rant. But near the end he was saying what I could not catch, and all of a sudden old Tommy was going silent.'

Ghote's antennae pricked up.

'It was some kind of threat he was making?' he asked, wondering whether after all the Hindi Master should still be one of his likely suspects.

'Could be. Vidyarthi Sahib is capable of uttering threats. Quiet threats, if you like. But threats. He has uttered to myself. With mention of cane. Followed, if I was not sensible, by threat carried out.'

Ghote decided to store this away. Perhaps he had misjudged the gentle, white-bearded old man. Or had been deceived by him?

'And Dr Washikar?' he asked.

'Not so much rant-rant. But same message. Services no longer required after year's end.'

'Mr Batheja?'

Bulbul looked downcast.

'Too cunning to make his way to Headmaster's study in such a manner that I am wanting to know what will be going on there.'

'So you do not know whether he also has had a sack?'

'Touch gold and speak true, I have not at all been able to find out.'

Another pointer to the cunning mathematician?

Ghote laid down the knife and fork he had been using in conformity with the unIndian atmosphere. The food had not been nearly as good or plentiful as he had expected. But such appetite as he had greeted it with had abruptly faded away.

Four

When the meal at last came to an end Dr Washikar, up on the dais, got to his feet.

'Chintamani,' he bleated out. 'Grace, please.'

Once more Bulbul yammered out an almost uninterrupted string of Latin words. The same ones as at the start of the meal? Or different? No telling.

Then Ghote, still idly puzzling about it, saw to his appalled astonishment that Mr Batheja, unlike his three colleagues who were leisurely proceeding out of the room, was coming directly over towards him. Still wrapped in that enveloping black academic gown, his head emerged from its flowing folds sharp, pock-marked, jackal-like.

Coming to me in one beeline, he thought.

And Bulbul, he realised, had promptly deserted him. Not that he blamed the boy. He had said he always did his best not to get on the wrong side of the Mathematics Master, and if he had lingered when a private talk was plainly in the air then he would be very firmly on that wrong side.

'Inspector, I am about to give you some information that should bring your inquiry to a swift conclusion.'

No beating about the bushes now.

'It is Mr Batheja? You are teaching Math—'

'Come, Inspector. You know who I am. I know who you are. So no more nonsense, if you please.'

So much for conducting any interview with authority.

But he did his best.

'Very well,' he said. 'You have information about the murder of Mr Thomas. It is incumbent upon you to give it to me.'

Mr Batheja merely smiled. Pointed jaws ready to bite.

Ghote decided that his only possible course was to wait and let the fellow say what he had to say in his own way and his own time.

'Inspector, are you aware that the Hindi Master at this establishment, Mr Shreeram Vidyarthi, was dismissed in ignominy some twenty-four hours before Mr Thomas met his death?'

He was not going to put up with this sort of bullying.

'If I am aware,' he said, 'it is confidential matter.'

'Yes, I was right. You do know. I thought so. I suppose that wretched little spy Chintamani has been talking to you. Well, let that pass. But now, answer me this – what steps do you intend to take if I inform you that furthermore Vidyarthi has plans to disappear somewhere among the riffraff inhabiting the banks of the Ganges at Benares? Or Varnasi, as no doubt he likes to call the place.'

'Sir, I know very—'

He stopped himself.

No, howsoevermuch I am on wrong foot with this cunning devil I am not going to fall for one old trick like that.

'I am not at all interested in whatever insinuations you are making against one of your co-masters, Mr Batheja,' he said. 'What I am wanting to know is, were you yourself also dismissed by Mr Thomas in the last hours of his life?'

For just an instant Mr Batheja hesitated.

So you were, Ghote said to himself.

'Inspector, whatever makes you think just because Mr Thomas was engaged in clearing out some of the dead wood that has brought this establishment in recent years to the verge of ruin that I should be among that number?'

Bluster only. But let him think he has got away with same.

'Please, then, tell me, sir, how did it happen that this fine school is on the verge of, as you are saying, ruin itself?'

Mr Batheja gave him a sharp look.

'I cannot believe that with all the questions you must have been asking since your arrival, Inspector, you cannot have come to see for yourself what the situation is. What did you learn from that long talk I observed you having at the far side of the playing field with that palsied fire-eater Majumdar? And, if you learned nothing from him, no doubt your ear was bent by whatever malicious gossip young Chintamani dreamt up for your benefit. Not to mention your secret conference with that pious idiot Vidyarthi and you frightening that worm Washikar, hiding away in his precious storeroom. But if you really contrived to see nothing in front of your eyes, then let me tell you plainly that, unless Arnold Thomas had persuaded that half-brother of his to give him further large funds, this school would have ceased to be in existence within two years at most.'

Much what he had learned from Colonel Majumdar. But had he been a biased witness?

'Sir,' he said, giving Mr Batheja as sharp a look as he could summon up, 'I have not seen so many evidences of that. Many very, very well-off fathers are sending here their sons, and paying and paying for privilege. So why should there be any talking of close-down?'

'Nevertheless,' the little man answered, 'I assure you that expenses are considerably exceeding receipts. Has it not occurred to you to wonder why the school is at present almost deserted? Until this year all the servants were as a matter of course kept on from one year's end to another. And what did you find put before you at the table just now? A meal only fit for some roadside *chaikhana*.'

Well, Ghote reflected, if his meal had been a cut above what he might have got with a cup of tea by the road somewhere, it had by no means lived up to the spicy odours he had been greeted with beforehand.

So is this unpleasant fellow correct at least about the state of the school's finances? And what does it mean if he is?

He could think of no way in which it made any of the four possible honey thieves – but why on earth had one of them dug that axe into it? – more likely to have killed the Headmaster than any of the others.

But, if one of them had to be picked out, it was this little, hunched-up, pock-marked individual now smiling wolfishly up at him. What to say to him that would make him somehow betray himself?

'All that is most interesting,' he said, stiffening himself up, 'but what I am wanting to know is, if this school is truly on last legs, what will you yourself do when you are no longer having, like Mr Vidyarthi, one well-remunerated job?'

Mr Batheja gave a sharp bark of a laugh.

'Come now, Inspector, have you, in spite of my assurances, got it into your head that I was dismissed in a moment of rage by Mr Thomas, and that I then killed him to prevent my dismissal taking place? Well, if so, let me tell you that I happen not only to be a mathematician of more than average skill but I have also, for better or worse, the knack of making ignorant little boys understand mathematics. Ask anyone.'

And Ghote realised that, if he had not gone round asking how good a teacher Mr Batheja was, he had learned from as reliable a source as Bulbul Chintamani – when he was off guard – that under Mr Batheja's teaching he was becoming 'one ace mathematician'.

So, even if he was right about the Headmaster having in his last hours alive begun instantly dismissing all of the teachers who had chosen not to go away after term was over, that did not mean that Mr Batheja at least had needed to worry. If he was as good at teaching as Bulbul had reluctantly indicated, he could get another post easily enough.

And what other reason could he have for murdering the Headmaster? None that had in any way emerged.

And, for the matter of that, what reason could Shreeram Vidyarthi have? Or Dr Washikar – that obsessive counter-up of oily tins of *vanaspati*, bright-labelled packets of Det ('Removes All Tea, Coffee, Blood, Haldi and Masala Stains'), sticky tins of honey? He was certainly not falsifying his accounts. True, Colonel Majumdar had admitted to being despondent about his prospects of finding further employment. But if he had killed the Headmaster so as to negate his dismissal, surely he would not have spoken about his fears for the future as openly as he had done? And in any case he had been certified by Bulbul Chintamani as being cotton-hearted.

No, all those high hopes of mine of an arrest before the sun goes down were destined to be cast into the dustbin. Getting at which of those four with access to that honey-tin by finding out who had a motive for the killing has got me nowhere. And, more, it would be no use trying to break any alibis. All four of them were bound to have been asleep in their beds during the long hours of the night when the murder took place. Or, rather, three of them would have been asleep while the fourth, axe in hand, prowled.

But which of the four was that? Which?

And how else to find out? What questions more to ask?

He could think of only one. And that not a question any of the four, bar the murderer who would never volunteer the answer, could help with. *Why was the Headmaster's body there in front of the pure white statue of his own grandfather, founder of the Matthew Arnold School?*

A question as baffling as: *Why had the missing murder weapon been smeared with honey?*

That, too, was never surely going to be resolved. But it was possible, just, that the question of where the murder had taken place might provide the answer to who had committed it. Was it possible that the killing had not happened there in front of the statue but somewhere else? The murderer might for some reason, good or bad, have carried the bleeding corpse to the symbolic place where with the coming of daylight it had been found.

Why did I not ask Pendharkar about the blood there? It was the sort of thing he would have paid attention to. Was it too little to have spread from the wound? Or was there so much of it that the murder must have happened in front of the statue? Were there perhaps telltale drops or smears indicating that the body had been carried from somewhere? If there were, then a careful search of the whole place might reveal where the killing had, in fact, happened. And that might show which of those four was responsible. Which was the honey thief. But a search of that sort was not something he could do on his own.

No, only one thing for it. Go back down to the town and talk to Pendharkar. No solution by sunset now. Definitely.

Five

The sun in mid-afternoon was baking, even in the cooler air of the hills. Toiling across the wide green playing field, Ghote cursed himself even before he had reached the third of the cricket squares for not telephoning down to Inspector Pendharkar and asking for transport. But, setting out from that very statue of the school's founder where Headmaster Arnold Thomas's body had been found, he had somehow felt if he left the place so to speak officially he would not be the one who brought the case to a successful conclusion. If the end came about through a wide-scale search carried out by constables under Pendharkar's command, then the credit would go to the local force. He would have failed entirely in the task he had been given.

Sweatily he climbed the small wooded ridge surrounding the plateau of the playing field. Chinaman's Falls, he thought. That is the noise of falling water I can hear. And how much of hope I had this morning when I first saw that cascade. And yet more when I heard that rascal Bulbul reciting his poem.

It matters not how straight – no, strait – the gate,

How charged with punishments the scroll,
I am the master of my fate:
I am the captain of my soul.

But – but— What is this I am hearing? It is not at all in my own head. It is Bulbul's voice itself.

And a moment later he saw the boy's white shirt through the screen of scrubby trees. He was sitting just as he had been before, perched on the very edge of the gorge, the falls tumbling down only feet away from him.

Shall I speak to him again? No. No, if I do, he will guess, clever monkey that he is, that I am going back down defeated.

Then just as he set off, treading warily to avoid this time any telltale crack of a twig underfoot, he changed his mind. Bulbul had been altogether helpful. Pity, if he was never to see him again, not to be saying goodbye.

'Bulbul,' he called out, very quietly so as not to frighten him on his dangerous perch.

The boy did not even turn round.

'Well, Inspector,' he said, 'I was thinking you were going to creep past without one word.'

'You knew I was here?'

'Inspector, fact is, climbing up you were puffing and panting like a zoo-fat lion. Not a very good advert for our Indian police.'

Ghote smiled, in spite of himself.

'So what are you doing once more up here at Chinaman's Falls?' he asked.

'Well, number one, reciting that bloody poem again. And, number two, I am wondering what is that piece of wood with red paint on it that came to light just now when a branch down there was swept away.'

'Red paint? Were you saying *red paint*? A piece of wood? Let me see.'

Pendharkar had said the missing weapon had a red-paint identifying mark on it. Could this...?

He felt new vigour coursing through him.

A moment later he was lying beside Bulbul, flat on his stomach for safety's sake, peering hard down at the spouting and spilling tumble of water at the foot of the falls. It seemed impossible at first to see what the boy had spotted. But then he glimpsed it. And, yes, it looked very like the haft of an axe. With a splodge of red paint on it. Very like. Very like.

'You know,' he said to Bulbul, before cautious thoughts about not putting words into a witness's mouth had prevailed, 'I am almost certain that down there is the very axe that was killing Headmaster Thomas.'

'The missing weapon,' Bulbul said, eyes shining with excitement. 'You want me to go and get it?'

'Go down there? No, no. That would be madness itself. I will make my way back to the school and telephone Inspector Pendharkar to come up with each and every necessary rope.'

'And lose the kudos of solving the case?'

Ghote looked at the boy.

'How did you know?'

'Oh, just only guessing. But now I know my guess was good. And, let me tell you, it would not be too difficult for me to climb down there. In the gym, under

Havildar Dharamjit Singh, Physical Training Instructor – only one of staff I am truly respecting – I am the fastest boy on the ropes. Up and down, up and down.'

Then Ghote glimpsed a prize he ought perhaps to renounce.

'You are certain, hundred per cent, you could do it?' he asked.

Bulbul, by way of answer, swung himself round and down on to the edge of the gorge.

Fear suddenly now snickering inside him, Ghote did see that there was at least plenty of wiry-looking vegetation growing all the way to the bottom.

Nevertheless, he watched with lip-biting anxiety Bulbul's round dark head going swayingly down foot by foot as he sought different handholds and footholds. Five feet away. Six. Seven. Eight.

And a sudden fear-lurching slip as whatever thin branch he had been clutching went tearing out of its cranny in the rocks. At once he saw Bulbul's face looking up at him, grinning.

'Take care only,' he heard his own strangulated voice say.

'Okay, okay. No problems.'

But there were still, he calculated, fifteen dangerous feet to go before even one of Bulbul's toes touched the bottom.

Then what different dangers might await him? Thin though the torrents of the falls were, there were three or four of them cascading down, mingling, splitting apart at some jutting rock, rejoining each other. And when at the foot they combined and, leaping out of the deep pool their forceful descent had made, went tearing away along the gorge they made up together a fast-flowing, confined and powerful stream. Bulbul had only to put a foot wrong to fall into it and in minutes to be swept away, his body battered on the rocks that littered the gorge's bed.

Even if he succeeded in getting safely to the bottom and what he found there proved to be an axe with its haft marked in red, he then had to get back up again, bringing with him the precious piece of evidence. If it was the missing weapon . . .

God, what an idiot he had been to let the boy do it. And all, really, because of his pride.

What business have I got having pride? he asked himself bitterly. Am I some – what is it they were called? – am I some Old Rugbee? Was I taught at some such élite place as this Matthew Arnold School? Traditions of courage. All that 'Play up, play up and play the game' *tamasha*. Why was it I did not simply say constables under Pendharkar would sooner or later find spot where murder was committed, if it was not committed in front of that statue, and then case most likely will be resolved? And if that brought no kudos for Inspector Ghote, what of it? Murderer would be charge-sheeted under Indian Penal Code section 302 whoever was getting credit. And that is what—

'Inspector! Inspector!'

Bulbul's voice, yelling out in sudden fear from the foot of the gorge.

What has happened? Why did I not watch each and every foot of descent? What for was I day-dreaming only?

No, not lying there injured. Not caught in that stream. But what has made him shout like that? Certainly not triumph at finding the axe. No, instead fear. More fear than the cheerful young fellow is able to take.

'Bulbul, I am coming. Stay still. I am coming.'

When, after more heart-stopping slips and arm-wrenching moments suspended from almost nothing, he reached the foot of the falls at last – there was a ridge of rock barely wide enough to stand on – he saw that Bulbul, frozen into speech-lessness, was pointing at something on the far side from where he was standing himself.

A body.

Then, as he began to look more closely, he saw that the corpse – it was, as the phrase had it, suited and booted – was in an advanced state of decomposition. From the contorted position it lay in, half on its back, it had almost certainly been thrown down into the gorge. And a good many days ago. Even some weeks, to judge by the almost bare bone of the one leg where the trousers of the smart white suit had been ripped away.

And across the thighs lay the axe Bulbul had gone down to find, the red-daubed missing weapon that had surely killed not this corpse but the one in front of the statue outside the school, Headmaster Arnold Thomas. It looked as if it had been thrown down at some time much later than when the body had been sent to lie almost totally hidden under the richer growth of vegetation by the pool at the foot of the falls. It lay across the trousers, visibly denting the putrid flesh of the thighs, its red-daubed shaft protruding just far enough out from under the low overhanging bushes for Bulbul to have glimpsed it from his perch above once that concealing branch had been swept away.

He turned now and looked at the boy more intently.

'You are all right?' he asked him. 'One hundred per cent safe and sound? Keep one tight hold of that branch. Take some deep breaths also.'

'It – it – it – it is just like old Tommy all over again,' Bulbul gabbled out at last.

'Not at all nice to have to see, I am knowing only too well,' Ghote said. 'But, you know, I must be doing my duty. You also. Can you flatten yourself well against the side so I am able to pass?'

After a moment or two Bulbul did as he had been asked, his face still grey with shock. Ghote managed to slide past him without slipping into the stream boiling and bubbling an inch or two away. Beside the body, he managed to find space to kneel, noting the fine cotton of the suit it wore, the heavy silk necktie, its end jutting out from beneath, the good-quality black shoes on the large, well-spread feet, and, inescapably, the smell of flesh dead for days reeking in the air despite the fine spray from the falls that was soon solidly soaking the back of his shirt.

Closing his mouth tightly, he pushed a hand in under the suit jacket where he had detected a bulge that might be a wallet. It was. Still kneeling, he pulled its two sodden sides apart.

Inside, it seemed reasonably dry. And at once, jutting up from one of its many little slit pockets, he saw a thin bunch of visiting cards. He drew one out and read.

Jagadir Thomas. Swirling script printed in a bright pink colour, two addresses underneath in black.

But he did not need to take those in. The pink-printed name was enough. Jagadir Thomas, Mr Arnold Thomas's half-brother. The man who had made a fortune, and more, on the Bombay Stock Exchange, and who had in the past put some of it into rescuing the Matthew Arnold School from its Headmaster's weak management. The man who had all those politicians in his pocket – or scraping as much as they could out of it.

And was dead.

He gritted his teeth and carefully turned the slack corpse on to its front. Imme-diately he saw what it was that had produced the flow of blood still faintly staining the rocky ledge. A deep wound in the skull made with something like an axe. The twin of the single blow which had brought his half-brother's life to its end.

But, he asked himself perplexedly, if the axe that killed Arnold Thomas was the red-marked one lying across the legs of this putrifying corpse, how could it have come about, if it had, that it had killed Jagadir days and days earlier?

Impulsively seeking an answer, he bent down close to the wound. A wriggling cluster of blackness broke up into half a hundred bloated flies. He forced himself to peer yet more closely. But there was no trace of the honey he had against his better judgement half expected to see smeared in the depths of the wound. Only white sucking maggots wriggling and feeding. No trace at all of the honeyed axe that had killed the Headmaster.

And then, extraordinarily, as he knelt with his nose almost inside the foul-smelling, maggoty wound in the dead man's head, a story which his mother had told him when he had been no more than eight years of age came back into his mind. He could almost hear her voice.

Long, long ago before the British came, before the Mussalmans came, up in the hills there were men and women who were the most peaceful people there have ever been in the world. They were so peaceful that they never, never wished to hurt a single thing. Not any man, not any woman, not any child, not any animal, not even any growing thing. But even in those days of peace there were the monsoons, coming every year as they still do now. And when the monsoons come, as you are very well knowing, everybody must have some shelter from these pouring, pouring rains. And to have shelter you must have houses. And to have houses you must have some wood to build them. But only on living trees is there wood strong enough to build houses that will stand up when the winds coming with the monsoons blow and blow. So from time to time those gentle people have to cut down a tree. But when they do so they first of all ask pardon of the tree for what they will have to do. And then they take the axe they are going to chop that tree with, and they dip it in honey so that they will hurt the tree the least amount that they can.

And then Ghote knew who it was who had murdered Mr Arnold Thomas. And why.

All along, he thought, his nose had been thrust, not into this evil-smelling wound – he jerked back from it and all but fell into the tumbling stream behind – but into the story of the honeyed axe and what it told him. When Inspector Pendharkar had first informed him of the discovery that narrowed the suspects down to the four masters with access to the honey-tin in the refrigerator something had tickled the back of his mind. It had been, he knew now, his mother's story. But at the time, grasping at the sudden tightening of the wide circle of possible murderers, he had let it slide from his mind. Again, in the school storeroom that story had come to momentary life as he had looked down into the liquidised honey in its tin. But equally it had faded into nothingness almost at once. And finally there had been the moment when he had almost asked Shreeram Vidyathi, Hindi Master easily distracted from the intricacies of grammar into telling moral tales, whether the combination of honey and axe meant anything to him.

He rose slowly to his feet.

'Bulbul,' he said, 'I don't want you to do this just only out of you wanting to boast. But would you be able to climb back up out of here?'

Bulbul gave him a grin. A pale version of his usual crescent of dazzling teeth. But a grin nevertheless.

'No need for any boastings and climbings, Inspector. I am happy now to stay where I am, keeping off all those bystanders who may, like you, want to thrust their noses into that nastiness while you go up the way you were coming down – but with more of gracefulness, please – and telephone to Inspector Pendharkar for all those ropes he would need.'

Then he gave Ghote a single sharp look.

'Or would you first want to go and arrest your famous murderer?'

Once again Ghote nearly toppled into the stream.

'But you know who it is?' he asked. 'You were knowing all along? You cannot have known. You cannot.'

'No, no, no. I am not knowing even now.'

'But—'

'But I was just only seeing your face when you were getting up from looking at that body. Then I was learning it: you knew. Listen, you should come back here in term-time when we are playing some poker late in the night. Then we would teach you how to keep one poker-face. Or, no. No, not ever, I am thinking.'

'Cheeky brat.'

'So, are you going to tell me his name? Colonel Majumdar, Vidyarthi Sahib, Dr Washikar – no, it can't be that piece of old chapatti – or Mr Batheja, one I am wanting it to be?'

'Who is the murderer? No, I am certainly not going to tell you that.'

'Well, I suppose I shall have to be pleased with just only being right about you knowing who it was when you identified that horrible mess of a person there.'

'Yes, that only.'

And Ghote comforted himself with thinking that, for once, Bulbul had got it wrong. But the boy had not seen, thank goodness, that there was no smear of honey deep in that wound.

If he had perhaps he, too, would have remembered Shreeram Vidyarthi telling at some time or another the story of the honeyed axe. Though it was doubtful if he would have learned the lesson the tale was meant to convey. That there are times when a cruel act must be carried out. But that the good man first smears his axe with honey.

As Shreeram Vidyarthi had done when he had seen the body of Jagadir Thomas lying, perhaps more visibly, where his half-brother had tumbled it into the gorge out of sight. Then he would have realised, as he could hardly have failed to, that Arnold Thomas in one of his weak man's fits of uncontrollable rage had taken that axe to his half-brother, most likely when he had been refused yet one more large loan. So that must have been when, at the foot of the statue of the betrayed founder of the Matthew Arnold School, he in his turn had struck an axe blow. He must have decided that if justice was to be rendered it should not be the harsh justice of the law, the clapping on of handcuffs, the bundling into a cell. No it should be justice, tempered with honey.

Ghote found it all beginning to become clear in his mind as he climbed up out of the gorge. But he soon came to the conclusion that, unless he wanted to find himself lying dead where Jagadir Thomas was, he had better keep his mind on what he was doing.

After that he made better progress. So it was only some twenty minutes from the moment he had heard Bulbul's frenzied shout from the bottom of the gorge that he arrived back at the school buildings.

There he set off, hurrying, for the classroom where he had earlier seen Shreeram

Vidyarthi quietly reading. But in a moment he checked himself.

Yes, he thought, pacing onwards slowly, it is my duty now to arrest that man. But I will do it with care. With kindness even. None of your *filmi* clapping on of handcuffs and marching into a police truck. No, my axe also must be dipped in honey.

But when he quietly opened the classroom door he found, for all his expectations, that Shreeram Vidyarthi was not there.

Instead on the blackboard, where earlier sentences of Hindi grammar had jostled each other, on the wiped clean surface were words. Written, considerately, in English.

When I first saw you, Inspector Ghote, I knew that before long you would be faced with arresting me. But, as I told you, I have for some time been thinking of taking *sannyas*. If you still wish to find me you may succeed if you look day after day, week after week, year after year, among the *sannyasis* on the banks of Holy Ganges. But I am inclined to believe you will think you have done enough.

He who was formerly known as Shreeram Vidyarthi

CEMETERY PLOT

Mary Anne Kelly

It all started at the cemetery, the old one in Queens, complete with gargoyles and saints. No, actually, it had started a few days before. I was on my way to the city, just hitting the listen button on my answering machine while I watered the plants and then I was out the door, baby, no parole. My plan was to walk up to the F train, zip into Fifth, bus up Madison and visit the Met. They were having Cézanne; I'm nuts for him. I've had a picture of his *Houses of the Provence* for years and I was finally going to get a look at the real McCoy. So there was no way I was going to pick up the phone.

It was Iris. Iris and me, we go way back. She's this German-Jewish, really wild old lady who understands me and I kind of understand her. We argue a lot. Or did. We made a lot of money together at one point, too, she and I. And I'd still have it if it wasn't for another one of my husband's schemes. This particular one had to do with a Guyanese catering hall and a manager who must have thought we'd said a catering hall just for him in Guyana.

I let Iris ramble on, her cherished music box playing in the background. She was pissed about something ridiculous, the way old people get – spots on the lawn, or the dog chased her crows into the sky. Her crows. So you get the idea. Or there was always Alleletzte, I thought, seeing him out the window shuffling by. He's this bum who circumnavigates Richmond Hill. He tends to leave his smelly shopping cart in Iris's back yard. Whatever it was, it could wait. Her voice did have a catch, though. That wasn't like her. I threw my purse into my prize possession Coach bag, made a cylinder of the *Daily News* and stuck that in, too. You never knew how long you had to wait for the F. And off I went. I caught sight of myself in the hall mirror going out. It's a spectacular mirror, Venetian glass. Old. Iris had talked me into buying it from the owner when we'd first bought the house. It had cost an awful lot at a time when there'd been little to spare, but Iris had said I'd never regret it. And, of course, I never have. I kept seeing my expression in that mirror as I strode towards the station. That expression didn't look as pleased with itself as it had at first. It was so unlike Iris to be vulnerable. Listen, I told myself, you can always stop off on the way back.

The Q37 went bellowing by. If I had decided to wait for it, it never would have come along. I stopped to catch my breath at the top of Park Lane South. Down the hill in Forest Park, the sunlit mist wove through the trees. You had to see it. Like a painting, I thought. I stood there for a moment and took it all in. Oh, well. Those originals never do look as good as you think they will. I turned around and headed back down the hill for Iris's big house. It was a good thing I did. She didn't answer and I had to let myself in. She was sitting in her chair. It's a throne, really. I think she got it from Sotheby's years ago. It's a wreck but she likes it – room for her and the cat. She looked so, I dunno, so desolate sitting there all scrunched over. No matter how badly she felt, she wasn't one to scrunch.

Don't ask me why, but I offered her a drink. Her eyes lit up for a moment. '*Ja,*' she said, 'I'd like that.'

I went to the cabinet with the Italian hand-painted scene of paradise on the doors and I took out a bottle of Madeira. Iris gave an unconvincing little shrug of pleasure. So I put that down and picked up the bottle of Jack Daniels. She nodded lovingly. Both of us knew full well she wasn't supposed to drink at all. Well, we talked for a long time. She talked about Berlin – always a bad sign – and about her days in India – always a good sign. She was sitting up in her chair when I turned from the doorway to go and she gave me a regal salute. We looked into each other's eyes and smiled. A really good, vibes-bouncing-back-and-forth, for ever smile. So when I came to check on her that night, it wasn't so bad that she was sitting there dead. Straight up, cat on her lap, dead. I disentangled the cat's claws from her taffeta robe and I went and called the doctor. There was a record still going round and round on her old RCA. I walked over with the cat in my arms and stopped it and read the label. 'The Blue Danube Waltz.' Some things you just never forget.

And then there I was at the cemetery. Funny thing about death. It's not so bad for the ones left behind if they've done the right thing. And I had. I knew that. Not too many people were at the cemetery. When you're Jewish they bury you quickly. Not like us, with the seven-day wakes. I'd called a couple of people: Howie, the antiques dealer from Kew Gardens; and Jerry, the liquor-store owner. He was pretty broken up. Her lawyer, Mr Snow, was there with his bright-eyed assistant, who introduced himself as Perry. Perry Beverly. Then there was my mother and father, my daughter, dressed for some sort of Mandarin Imperial ball. My son was there in a tie, looking sad. And back off in the shadows, Alleletzte, stooped and weepy beside his shopping cart. I'd never seen him cry. I'd seen him hit by a car and walk away, but I'd never seen him cry. He thinks we are chums because I used to live in Klosters, near his home town in Switzerland. That was back in the days when I made my living as a photographer.

So there we all were. It was a sunny autumn day. I'd stopped listening to the rabbi, my attention drawn to something shining at a nearby grave. It was a knife, jabbed in the dirt. It was disgusting. Dirty. But dirty in a foul way. I don't know why. Under the Angel Gabriel like that. I tried to listen again, but couldn't. The knife was so, I don't know, violent-looking. And there was something all crumpled beside it. I craned my neck to get a better look. It was a rubber glove. I shivered and walked over. Probably the gardener's knife, after all. My mother came and thunked me on the shoulder. 'Place your flower on the coffin,' she hissed. So I did.

Then we all went over to Niederstein's and had lunch. I figured I would pay, me and Iris being such good friends. We had schnitzel and beer, except for Howie who had the blutwurst, which he declared was delicious, and then when I asked for the bill, the waitress said Howie had already paid, which I thought was pretty cool, so I relaxed and enjoyed my dessert. My mother made a little speech, the way she will tend to do if somebody gives her a drink, and then we all went home. Jerry from the liquor store cried all the way. Of course, she'd spent a lot of money in his shop over the years, but Jerry had plenty of money. He never spent it but he loaned it readily enough. I knew, because Howie was always borrowing from him to pay off people who brought him antiques.

The driver took us back. I hated seeing Iris's grand Queen Anne and knowing she wasn't inside it, I tell you.

I don't know what it was that made me think something wasn't right, but I woke up that night and wandered around in the dark. Nothing wakes Johnny. Don't worry about him. The wind was so strong even the cans rattled in the alley. I sat in the window looking out on the street. And there, in the middle of the pachysandra, was Iris's cat. I'd forgotten all about him. Genevieve, Iris's neighbor, had taken him in. Well, here he was now. I went down the stairs, muttering to myself. There was no way I could even consider keeping another animal. I have Floozie and she's enough. I hate the smell of a cat. So down the steps I go and I open the door. 'Lu,' I said, 'Lu, go away.'

Lu just stands there.

'Aw, Lu,' I said, 'if I take you inside, you'll get used to the idea and I just can't keep you.'

'Yaaaaaaaaaaaa,' said Lu. Did you ever hear a Siamese speak? It's horrible. He stood on bowed legs. You could tell he was confused.

Lu looked in my eyes with his blue ones, then turned. With all the dignity of his breeding, he marched carefully down the sidewalk. His name, Iris had informed me, was Chinese for 'the wanderer'.

He'd go back to Genevieve's house. She'd take care of him. I locked the door. He wasn't going to go back to Genevieve's house. He'd go up to the park, get covered in fleas, fall in a ditch. Shit. I pulled my son's boots on, unlocked the door and clomped down the walk.

Respectfully, I greeted him with my palms pressed together. *You* wouldn't do this with a cat but I haven't the slightest compunction. This is why so many things happen to me. I said, 'Look, Lu, I'd like to invite you to sleep over. It's only for the one night, though. Really. We'll figure something else out tomorrow.'

Our eyes, and with them our souls, met. He allowed me to ensconce his pretty heavy body in my arms and together we made our way back up the stairs to my nice warm bed.

The next morning I staggered downstairs. Johnny was hunched and dipping his *biscotti* into espresso.

'Ma,' Anthony said. 'You know what Dharma did? She took her blouse off at her window so Ralphie Antonelli could see!'

'I did not! Shut up, you little shit!'

Johnny laid down the racing form. 'You do something like that once more, I'll send you out to the nuns in Brentwood for two years.'

Dharma screwed in her earrings. I had a vague memory of them as parts of a Christmas ornament. She's always been creative, Dharma has. I was almost relieved to hear of this exhibitionistic interest in Ralphie. She's been reading a little too much Virginia Woolf, if you know what I mean.

'Please don't tattle.' I kissed Anthony on the top of his soft red hair. 'Did you finish your homework?'

'Do I look like I didn't finish my homework?' suave Anthony answered me pityingly.

'Don't answer your mother back,' Johnny warned.

Dharma, eyes closed, was communing with the universe.

'Ow!' Anthony cried. 'I squirted clementine in my eye!'

'So take it away from your eye, you big meatball!' Johnny said. He rolled his shoulders in that particular way Italian men in their undershirts do before they say what they mean to say. 'Won't be home for dinner.'

'OK,' I said.

'Aw, Dad!' Anthony said.

'Gotta pick up a perp.' Johnny stood. I knew he was lying because whenever he lies his right eye twitches, but I would never let on that I know this is so because knowledge is, as they say, power and, who knows, one day I might need a little power.

My mother called the minute Johnny was gone. She couldn't wait to tell me about her Guyanese neighbor, Shanti, who'd run away with her lover, leaving her diligent husband who'd just bought them a Pathfinder. 'And she had little children! The amah told me,' she confided. 'At least I think she was the amah. One of that lot living in the cellar. You know how they are. No end to them.'

'Ma,' I said, 'I don't want to think about somebody else's misfortune. I'm happy being miserable with mine.'

'Claire. Iris had a good, long life. More than most people have.'

'She had shit.'

'Yes, well. Most people have that as well.'

I did remember Shanti. I'd seen her often with the girls as they'd raced home from Mohammed's store, strings of licorice trailing. Shanti hadn't looked so unhappy in her fabric-softened punjabi, her ankles gliding by in golden sandals.

Out on the street, little Alleletzte shuffled behind his shopping cart, making his way through the leaves for the library. Many a morning he'd be out there arguing politics with Iris. No more of that now. Sometimes Iris would find him in her garage sleeping off a bottle and she'd let him stay until he woke up. 'Vot's the harm?' she'd say. She'd probably given him the bottle to start with. Iris had no patience with an inferior Bordeaux.

I got off the phone and took the bike out of the garage. It's an old bike, very crummy and rusty. It's a Columbia, it's got a basket and it gets you there. I glanced at Iris's house and saw coral roses on her porch. Alleletzte. I smiled sadly.

There's a part in Forest Park, between the monument and Woodhaven, where it's so dense you think you're upstate. I pedaled through and found myself near the cemetery. Houdini's buried in there, by the way. It's all steep up and down over there behind the crematorium. If you lose sight of the street you can lose your bearings. Iris's plot is in the older part. Little mansions of marble, cement and stained glass one after the other. The tent was gone and there was dirt over her body.

There was that little bench. Iris must have figured it would be me sitting on it. There was nobody else. I'd been all right until then. I lost it. There I was, sobbing, standing there with golden leaves and wisps swirling around my feet. It sounds almost beautiful, but it was empty and final. She'd always been so colorful, Iris. Always loving and surrounding herself with only the best. I would never know anyone like her again and I knew it. I wasn't even thinking who else might be there. Watching. And waiting.

I felt someone come up beside me and right away, don't ask me why, I remembered that knife I'd seen the day before. I froze. What calmed me was that this fellow was on a bicycle. There's something so harmless about that. I stood and watched him as he arabesqued one leg over the bar and rolled near.

'Everything all right?' he asked.

I was, in fact, glad to see him, handsome and white-helmeted as he was, like a brigadier with brows furrowed, right out of *Fahrenheit 451*. He was one of those bicycle cops, I realized. Anyone who spends all those hours pumping around has to be in terrific shape. The name on the badge said Fogarty. What he must think of me? Disheveled, bloated old bag. Humbly I blew my nose.

'Pretty hanky,' he said.

One thing I do like about me is that I always carry a hand-embroidered, ironed handkerchief. They sell them at the church mini house. Ridiculously cheap. Fresh from the sacheted top drawer of a passed-away bingo lady. I folded it shut with what little bit of dignity I had left. 'I just lost someone,' I explained.

'I see,' he said. His chin went out and his eyes squinted at me over the top of his nose. Greenish bluish malamute eyes. I'm afraid I have a weakness for that particular intensity of Cornish ocean eyes, lit by a fury of white and a drop of a complicated, unruly dark lash. Now I knew. It reminded me of someone I once loved. Love. Still love. Funny how you can after so much time's passed. No excuses. I was as married then as I am now. Nothing happened. I mean not what you're thinking. 'Well,' I said, finally, 'thank you for stopping.'

'No trouble,' he said. 'Sure you're all right now? Good. So long. Take care.' I watched the nice officer ride off, his crisp blue shirt tight against his ribs. I suppose I sighed the wistful sigh of the left-behind.

Suddenly it would feel good to get away from that densely mausoleumed spot, so isolated, sunk in a glacier hole with tall green hills all around. A cloud crept between the sun and me. Something very close to fright closed in. It wasn't the feeling of being physically alone, which never bothers me, it was more the feeling I no longer was. 'Not of the dead we should fear,' my mother always says, 'but of the living.' I pumped away and saw the road with relief. I'd never been so happy to hear a landscaper's obnoxious leaf-blower. Ah, civilization. The warm sun even broke through. I cut down a lane of really fancy crypts, stained-glass windows and wrought-iron grille work. Very impressive.

I stopped. There stood such an unusual little cathedral grave. Light seemed to come from within. There must have been windows on the other side where the sun shone through. I couldn't find the name. I got off my bike and wheeled around to see if it was on that end, but no. I was just about to give up when I noticed an Indian lady sitting there watching me. Her lavendar sari fluttered prettily in the wind.

'Excuse me.' I smiled. 'Would you happen to know who's buried here? It's such a momentous ... er monument ...'

She didn't answer me and I realized she was deaf. So I cranked up the volume and asked her again as I walked carefully over to her, still smiling. I didn't want to frighten her. She looked old and was, no doubt, here to visit her dead husband. There was the strong sound of nearby bees. My God. They were on her necklace! Lots of them. She just looked at me. I reached my arm out to warn her. Her head rolled forward and into her lap.

I tried to scream but no sound came. I tried to run but my feet stayed still. I fled at last by passing out.

When I came to, I lurched frantically to my feet, hugging myself protectively against what I would see. Impossible. She wasn't there. I flung myself around in a circle, searching. She wasn't there. The sound of cars and trucks whizzed by on the road not half a mile away. I ran, berserk, over the ridge in the direction I'd heard the gardeners earlier. I screamed and screamed.

It was the bicycle cop who'd heard me and had come back to see what was up. He must have radioed a squad car because there was a regular little posse around me. The hot-dog guy who stands out on Woodhaven Boulevard brought in some hot tea with a lot of sugar and a female cop was spooning it into me. I suppose I was in shock. They had a crossing-guard jacket over me. I couldn't get over that I'd passed out. Anyway, the cops were very nice. They seemed intrigued that I'd lost consciousness like that. I told them my husband was on the job and how to reach him. I heard the radio squawk back that he wasn't on duty till the night shift. It didn't hit me right away that I hadn't got it wrong. I always assume it's me and, as no one is ever in a hurry to correct me, I usually remain in the dark even when I'm right. They beeped his partner, so Johnny was on the way home. The funny thing was, the Indian woman's body was still nowhere to be found. I had a very hard time convincing any of them that there'd been a body. And when they listened, they looked skeptical. I'd run around so much that I couldn't find exactly the right spot and there was no blood. Two or three uniforms were joking around by the flower dump. Not impatiently, but without the deferential awe that goes along with a true crime scene either.

A female detective questioned me while she drove me home. I just told her what I knew, which was nothing, really, except what I just told you. Johnny pulled up to the house just as I was getting out of the car. The lady cop talked to Johnny in hushed tones but I overheard him telling her that, yes, I'd recently been under an awful lot of strain. I made out the cop shorthand, E.D.P. Lu the cat slinked in and out my legs. And then I got it. Emotionally disturbed person. They didn't believe me. They thought I was having a nervous breakdown. That I'd hallucinated the whole thing.

The next day they kept me in bed. Dharma stayed home and made me lemon grass soup. She goes to this health-food store up in Kew Gardens that thinks it's a Cherokee Indian reservation.

Then this psychiatrist from Johnny's department came over. Dr Bonnefaccio. She kept trying to convince me how no one thought I was nuts so I knew they really must have thought I was. She gave me some great pills reminiscent of Darvon and sat on the edge of my bed wearing tightly woven tweed across a monstrous bosom. She spoke in an innuendo-dripping way I didn't much care for.

'And you say she wore light purple.' Dr Bonnefaccio took notes in a no-nonsense leatherette agenda. It was not lost on either of us that Dharma's room was that same color.

'Yeah. Purple.'

Finally, she got up to go. I was, by now, entirely withered from her gusts of Morroccan musk.

'Here.' I reached over. 'Now, don't forget your book.'

'Not mine.' She redrew her mouth into a sailboat of beetroot.

'H. G. Wells,' I said, approvingly. '*The Time Machine*. Huh. Must be Dharma's. Another overdue library book. Typical. I suppose I'm supposed to take it back.'

'Not today, you're not,' she said.

'Fine.' I nuzzled into the eiderdown. I lay there and read Dharma's book. By night-time I was up making macaroni and butter for Anthony. He was, anyway, lying all over my quilt in his sneakers and monopolizing the remote.

Next day, out of Assam tea, I went up to Austin Street. Who do I see but my sister Zinnie in the Homestead deli. You can always tell Zinnie from the back of her curly, blonde head. I went in and stood behind her and whispered, 'Stick 'em up.' Without missing a beat, her gun's out and she turns around and she's got it to my forehead. The two of us cracked up laughing, but we moved several doddering Hungarians closer to their graves so we decided to leave and go somewhere we could sit down. We walked, me tall, she short, to Agafanny's for a cup of coffee. It's so great in there, it's just a bakery next door to the fruit store, but she's got two tables, one in the window behind a little Belgian curtain of white fleur-de-lis, the window all steamy and swimming, with people walking by outside. Zinnie took the seat with her back to the wall because that's just the way she is. She wanted to hear again exactly what had happened.

As a child, Zinnie would defend us all, even our much older sister Carmela (who was at the moment writing languid poetry at the Palais de la Madone in the south of France and of no actual use to me now. Or ever, Johnny would be quick to add). Anyway, Zinnie was a ferocious, elbows-out kind of kid. Her beat was the block. She was famous for her Chinese burns and every kid feared her. 'Tuffy', they used to call her. 'Tuffy' Breslinsky. It was a pleasure to be related to her. While we were talking it occurred to me that this woman must have been killed before she was decapitated. Why else wouldn't there have been lots of blood? We ate our buttery croissants with deliberation. Who do I see out the window but the bicycle cop from two days ago, Fogarty. He came rolling in.

'I saw you from a block away,' he said. 'How ya feel, how ya feel?' He kept rubbing the top of my shoulder, looking me up and down with his slinky eyes.

'She's fine,' my sister said. 'You can stop treating her like she's a psycho perp.'

He took a step back. 'Hey, lady, I'm just standing here saying hello. I don't know what your problem is.'

'I don't have a problem.'

'Well, then, maybe you'd just back off.'

'I will if you stop treating my sister like we've got us an Aided.' That vertical line she gets between her eyes came out.

'Hello.' I had to step between them to get their attention.

Agafanny stood beside us. 'Coffee?'

'I'm just leaving,' he said.

'So go,' Zinnie said.

I watched Fogarty unchain his bike with a very red face.

'I can't believe how you acted towards him!' I said.

'I didn't like the way he acted.'

'Obviously.'

'So can we finish our coffee here?'

We could. We did. Only I couldn't help noticing that Zinnie had hers with a red face, too.

You'd be surprised how nicely people treat you when they think you're crazy. Even Johnny. I'd hear him downstairs, talking to my mother on the phone in a whispery voice. Part of me kept hoping for another murder so they'd realize I was sane. I felt particularly bitter that my own children pussyfooted around me. There was laundry in the hamper, newspapers behind the basement door, stacked and tied with quadrupled bakery string, the way I like them. But who, I wondered, could murder that terrible way? I closed the door. There was Lu the cat, full lotus on the living-room sofa, looking like someone had just hit him with a bag of quarters. I thought, I really ought to go get a key from Iris's lawyer and get some of his toys. Lu looked up at me. Poor fellow. 'What do you think?' I said. 'Shall we go for a ride?' I took him to Key Food with me and he waited in the car.

Tomorrow was Halloween. I wanted to get back for Anthony, in case he needed me to help him with his costume. Every year he's Alleletzte. He's got a dilapidated derby he was a great hit with years ago and he sticks with that. He chars a cork for his beard. Up the cellar stairs bumps my old shopping cart. He puts on Johnny's shoes. For this I dust off my camera.

I took Woodhaven Boulevard. Automatically you go by the cemetery and Iris. It was as dark as pitch. Flickery lights shone from the graves who'd had visitors. I shuddered. Lu sprang from the back seat and grabbed the driver's seat window with both front paws. He let out this banshee shriek like I've never heard in my life. I was terrified. The stoplight turned green and I drove, right away, home.

On Halloween morning, Anthony came over to me where I stood washing dishes. He put his slender arms around me and asked if this meant I was well. Because, he said, if it did, did that mean he didn't have to make his bed any more? Thriftily I told him no, he still had to as I'm still not one hundred per cent. Displeased but unsure, he went and made his bed. Then, because he'd said that and I figured everyone else must be thinking it, I put on my least crazy-lady clothes (when I'm at my best I look like Fraulein Rothenmeier. You know, long skirt, hobnail shoes, crisp blouse. I go for that.). I walked down to Jamaica Avenue, buttoning my old pea-jacket against the unexpectedly hefty wind. It was dark and beautiful and I was on my mission. I bustled past the ninety-nine-cent stores and the bodegas.

The lawyer's office seemed to be open. I went in. It's a woodworked office with plenty of dust and green lampshades. I sat down on one of those heavy oak swivel chairs because he was on the phone and his assistant wasn't in yet. A handsome, older gentleman is Mr Snow, with a full head of gray hair and patches on his worn elbows. Looks like a lawyer on a daytime soap opera. He had, on his paneled walls, an ikon of President Eisenhower.

Mr Snow was delighted to see me and effusive in his accomodativeness until he realized I wasn't a divorce case but a plea for his already paid up, dead client's house key. (I guess I looked like a divorce case. The right age. The battered expression.) We went back and forth for a little while, him being professionally, ethically correct and me pointing out how his client would have wanted her cat to feel comfortable in its temporary quarters, which didn't move Mr Snow an inch but which gave me an idea, so I suggested he might want to take over the job of providing lodging for the cat. The cat being part of Iris von Lillienfeld's estate. As it really was his responsibility. And, I added, as he was so adamant about – er – ethical procedure. I let that sink in. I smiled. He smiled. It didn't take long. I was out of there with the key before you could say Spam.

'Oh, and if I'm not in when you bring it back, just leave it with my assistant,' said the suddenly offhand Mr Snow. My dad says he's senile, but he seemed sharp enough to me. 'She'll be here if I'm at lunch.' Business couldn't be that bad, I thought. Two assistants. Lunches out.

I walked swiftly up Richmond Hill to Iris's house to get it over with. The front walk was lost in leaves. I put the key in the door. It swung open. The familiar scent of Iris's Givenchy came over me in a reassuring way. The chairs held their empty arms up on their hips. I found Lu's favorite Afghani next to Iris's throne. Comes from Mazar-i-Sharif, north-west of Kabul. Nice and old. I smacked it on the radiator and a puff of dust and cat dander billowed out. I looked up. Funny. For a moment I thought I wasn't alone. But of course I was. I rolled the rug up, listening. I hoped

Alleletzte hadn't moved in. He was always showing up with musty books and noteworthy junk. Iris sometimes bought the stuff he'd get from Howie. Or gave him things to sell to Howie. Only Howie never had cash. He liked the ponies. He'd run next door to Jerry's liquor store and borrow money. Jerry always had cash. Sure. Iris had just paid him. So the money went around the little circle.

Iris kept the economy going. She still had a lot of old Raja silver from Poona and turquoise from McLeod Gange. Things like that from her India days. Always cleaning out a drawer. It wouldn't surprise me if Alleletzte felt entitled to some of it. I wouldn't put it past him. And he never minds going to jail for a couple of days. Iris had a softness for him because he'd spent time in Dachau. He'd suffered as much as anyone had, she'd told me once.

The table beside Iris's throne looked strangely bare without her withered, amber-ringed hand flitting about the lamp. Kleenex tissues. Nivea cream. And a book. I wondered what she'd been reading and picked it up. Thomas Moore. *Utopia*. How sharp her mind, right until the end. It was, however, a library book so I stuck it in my pocket. I'd take it there later, when I took Dharma's back. It had the same due date so I figured Dharma had brought it. It was nice of her to do someone a favor but it was more often me who seemed to tie the bows up on those ribbons.

I knew there was a rubber mouse and a shattered bisque doll Lu particularly liked in the kitchen. I fished them out and put them in a plastic bag. Iris kept plastic bags in a clothes-pin bag. She was always filling them up with home-made ruggelah for me to take home. I clutched that clothes-pin bag to me, you know, like it held some part of her still inside it. There came a swift rap-rapping on the window pane. I jumped, embarrassed to be caught in an embrace with a clothes-pin bag. It was Mr Snow's young man, the assistant who'd been with him at the funeral. Not liking him for catching me, I scraped myself together, nicked my head frostily in the direction of the back door and met him there.

'Hi,' I said. 'Come for the key?'

He shook my hand formally. 'Beverly,' he said. 'Perry Beverly.'

'I remember you,' I assured him.

'From sadder times,' he finished for me.

'Yes,' I said, liking him better. 'I would have brought it right back,' I said. 'What happened? Mr Snow was afraid I'd ransack the house?'

He made a charming, helpless gesture, a what-shall-we-do-with-these-old-people grimace.

'Hang on,' I said. 'I forget where I put the key. Can you come in for a second, Mr Beverly?'

'Perry. Please.' His little teeth were very white, his ears neat and small.

'Perry.' He looked formal in his navy sports jacket and Ivy League tie. I held the door open with one foot. 'Sit a second, OK?'

I fished through my pocketbook. It occurred to me that he was waiting for me so I sat down. He didn't scare me, and, anyway, Mr Snow knew we were here, but there was a tension in the room. He craned his neck and peered into my messy bag. A bit familiarly, I thought.

'How do you find anything in there?' he asked. One eyebrow was permanently higher than the other.

'Oh, I just keep stirring till it comes to the top.'

His clean hands were on his khaki knees, palms down. I try to get Johnny to wear Dockers but they just stay in the closet and out come the black jeans again and again. Perry looked about him. 'This is a great house.'

'Isn't it?' I opened up the bread box and took out the Pepperidge Farm.

'A shame, really.'

'What?' I put the bread in my pocket.

'I was just thinking. I mean, some foreigner will turn it into an apartment house.'

'Oh, God, I hope not.'

'No one who appreciates these houses can afford them.'

'I know, it's true,' I commiserated. 'Why don't you buy it?' I said suddenly.

'I wish I could.' He smiled. He had a mocking way about him.

'Just passed the Bar, huh?' I said, to put him in his place.

He smiled, I must admit, humbly.

Took him long enough, I thought. He wasn't a kid, from the lines on his face. 'Joined the Liar's Legion, eh?'

Then he said something I thought very odd, for a lawyer. 'Act with the scheme of the lowly,' he said, 'and you become it.'

'Lao-tzu?'

'Perry Beverly.' He winked.

I laughed. 'Aha. Here it is.' I handed him the key. Perry had that old-money ring to him. I liked the thought of old money. It excited me.

He held the key without taking it. For a moment I thought he was going to say something important, the way his eyes lit up. I even had a momentary flash of sex, hot sex, right there on the table. And he wasn't even my type. He was medium in just about every aspect. Now, I like a man with a big head. Orson Welles. Spencer Tracy. And a remarkable voice. Perry here had neither. Maybe that was the point, I concluded, retrieving my hand. I walked out with him and watched him lock up, feeling very warm. Startled sparrows took off as we came out the door. Iris had spent years arranging for their comfort and now they were highly put out. They didn't go far. Straight up into the branches to supervise this latest what next. I took the still-soft bread from my pocket.

'Where are you from, Perry?' I stood beside him, close to the house.

'Lefferts Boulevard.' He turned the key with care and pushed the door with a rattle to make sure it was well shut. A thorough man.

'No, I mean originally.' I threw the bread out, far as I could.

'Born and raised right here.' He looked at me in a puzzled way. Was I supposed to know?

'Lefferts Boulevard, huh? I thought you were going to say the North Shore. The way you dress.'

He gave the key a short little ride into the air and caught it. His eyes were a nondescript gray color but the light behind them dazzled. 'So you like the way I dress,' he said, pleased.

Crows flew down and were getting all the crumbs. I looked up at the kitchen window. Iris used to stand there and shush me off with her little claw reaching out of her shawl.

'Thanks for coming all the way up,' I said. And then I just left. The hell with this was what I thought. I remember very well.

Johnny was waiting for me when I went in the back door. He was sitting there at the table in his black T-shirt. He had that look. I know Johnny. He likes it in the afternoon. So, for that matter, do I.

It beats me how you can be as close as him and me and as far apart two seconds later.

He was rolling on his socks.

'I love you,' I told him.

'I love you, too,' he said. Only his right eye twitched. And then we both had to go do stuff. When I came home, someone was in my driveway. It was, of all people, Fogarty.

'Well, hello,' I said.

'Hello, yourself,' he said.

We stood looking at each other. I remembered what had happened to me last time I'd run into him. He's a skinny, dodgy kind of guy. I juggled the great bags of candy I'd picked up at Woolworths. I had everything – Sky Bar, buttons on paper, Tootsie Rolls and Chunkys. I would have offered him some, but the truth was that I'd molested every bag and I was ashamed.

'I've got your bike,' he said.

'So you have.'

I rode it over.' He shrugged.

'Thank you, Fogarty. So much. Where did you find it?'

'They had it at the station house. Since ...' he ducked his head tactfully '... the other day.'

Something warned me it could be dangerous if I asked Fogarty in for a cup of coffee. Then I wondered if Johnny had sent him over to keep an eye on me. No, I decided, Johnny wasn't that complicated. Nor was he that considerate. We walked together to the garage to put the bicycle away. My car was in there. It's an old Mercedes from the fifties. I found it in Germany years ago. I thought he'd be impressed with the running boards, but he was more like Johnny who thinks old things are just that. There was a heavy silence between us. I stood very still. I noticed his knife in his sheath.

He said, in a hemming, hawing sort of way, 'Your sister. She lives with you?'

Aha. So that was how it was. I looked over the rusty hood at him and smiled, disappointed and relieved at the same time.

'My sister is divorced since years, has a kid in high school and, as you may have gathered, will not be trifled with.' Actually, Zinnie's marriage was annulled by the tribunal, but you can't say things like that right off the bat.

Fogarty got this faraway look in his eyes. He shook his head. 'I'm no good at women anyhow.' He sighed with such distress that he made me his champion.

'Oh, well, never mind,' I comforted him, ushering him out of the garage. 'Come inside. I'll give you some rum stollen and we'll make a plan and—'

'Naw,' he interrupted me. 'She wouldn't like that. She can't stand me anyway.'

'I'm not so sure about that,' I reassured him, the two of us suddenly in cahoots.

'I dunno. I sort of like to do things my own way.' He tilted his head at me miserably. 'My own speed.'

Hmm. This was better than I'd thought. He'd evidently been hit by what the Sicilians call the thunderbolt of love.

'Of course.'

'What kind of kid does she have?'

'Who?'

'Zinnie.'

'Oh. What kind? Oh, I see. A boy. Michaelean. Mick. Big into sports.'

He bit his lip and shook his head, putting this news into his pocket. Well, he had what he'd come for. 'Now, you take care of yourself.' He pressed my hand when he shook it. There was pity in his eyes. 'Oh. And Happy Halloween.'

'Likewise.' I knew what was happening. Visions of baseball games with Zinnie's boy at Yankee stadium danced in his head.

On the sill was an envelope of dried seeds I'd harvested in August.

I went and got my bike and rode to Iris's grave. There are things worse than fear. The pity in that nice cop's eyes was one of them.

I found it right away. I knew just what I was going to do. Three rows of foxgloves lengthwise down the gravebed. Hers would be the most beautiful in the cemetery. There was nothing to clear away, no weeds or grass. I got to work and made my three nice rows, then sowed them with double seeds. In the spring, they would rise up like peach and lemon cockle shells. I leaned back on my haunches and contemplated my work. I patted the dirt smooth. It was almost as if I was daring something to happen.

'What the hell is all this going on?'

It was the gardener, a Mr Harry Dhundee, from the script on his breast pocket. I stood up and brushed my knees, knowing I was in big trouble. Never, Johnny warns, move onto the turf of a uniformed squit, but I'm afraid I lost my temper and yelled right back at him. He stormed away in the direction of his landscaper truck, head down. I stomped clear across the meadow to the only working fountain and lugged my watering-can back, overflowing, to moisten the seeds. By now I felt a little ashamed of my behavior, chastened as I was by all this physical exertion, until I looked down and saw my seeds had been methodically churned out.

I went home in a stew and found another of Dharma's confounded library books tossed onto the porch. I washed up to my elbows. There was a note from Anthony. He'd gone trick or treating and would be home before supper. I felt so guilty. It was the first time I'd missed him gussying up. And all for nothing.

I trotted to the library. Even so late in October its front lawn was blooming with, what, maybe fifty different kinds of roses. It's a good thing they're there because before you reach them you have to walk through a small delegation of derelicts. They hang out there on the benches, waving empty bottles, the flags of their dreams. Alleletzte was out there by this time, whistling 'Ramona'.

'*Gruetzi, Schatzilii*,' he greeted me.

'*Tag, Herr Alleletzte*,' I replied, respectfully. In India the wanderers are revered and given the benefit of every doubt. Not that this applies to Alleletzte, who is a scoundrel, but I mean in general. Respect also infers distance, which is what you want to keep with a guy like this.

It was warm and quiet in the library. Perry Beverly was sitting there reading at the study table.

'Hello,' I whispered.

You'd have thought I'd stuck him with a pencil, the look on his face. He was reading *Looking Backward*.

'Good?' I asked.

He snapped it shut. 'Very.'

I kept on going.

'Mrs Benedetto,' he whispered. No one calls me Mrs Benedetto but the dry-cleaners.

'Claire,' I corrected him, then immediately regretted encouraging any intimacy.

'Let me give you one of these.' He smiled, sticking his collar out to show me what he had on. It looked like a piece of yarn with eyes and a hat on it.

'What is it?'

'A bookworm.'

'Sorry?'

'Here. I've got lots.'

'No, that's OK.'

'Oh, sure. It's for the library. Reading awareness.'

'Oh. Oh, all right.'

I didn't really want the red and yellow one in my hand but the alternative was to let him pin another on me. 'So,' I said. 'Thanks.'

'I'll show you something,' he said, assuming I would follow him. Reluctantly, I did. We went together down the dark rows of books. He wore no aftershave. My mouth felt a little dry. I remembered the lady's head falling into her lap and I looked at Perry. 'It's not here.' He smiled and shuffled across the room to retrieve his attaché case. No, I sighed. Something unfortunate about him, surely; where he went he lumbered, but he was sweet. And kind. No murderer.

'What do you think of the mural?' he asked, returning.

It occurred to me that he might have heard what happened in the cemetery. Was that why he looked at me so piercingly? The fluid, greenish people flounced across the mural. Richmond Hill's milk-fed Utopia. They contrasted to the living, dark-skinned readers underneath them. I didn't know what to say. And yet he wanted something. 'I like a story mural,' I managed.

He regarded me disapprovingly.

'And so huge,' I pursued, still eager to please.

'One hundred sixty square feet,' he answered knowledgeably.

There is nothing more boring to me than the actual size of anything. He seemed to sense this and told me instead about the architects of Richmond Hill.

I didn't dare to steal a look at my watch. Funny, I thought, I'd never seen him around before. I wondered again how much younger he was than I. There is a part of me that wishes I had married a man like Perry. A man who would share newspaper articles from the *Times* across the breakfast table. Who would come up the stairs at night with what he thought would interest us both – a pear on a plate, or the news that a foreign film was on channel thirteen. Then I remembered Anthony out there trick or treating, possibly for the last time. And I wasn't with him. I turned to go. 'Gotta run.' I smiled and I went, knowing that Mr Beverly, er, Perry was very angry that I did.

I went to the antique shop to see Howie. The sleigh bells on the door jingled, announcing my arrival. Howie was sitting behind the counter, his left eye scrunched into a jeweler's loop and his right ear attached to a cellular. Has quite a few clandestine tattoos, Howie does, when he rolls back his sleeves. I feel compelled to look. Which is his hope and dilemma, I suppose. Classic shirt tucked into motorcycle pants. He motioned me to sit down. 'Wait till I tell you about the dream I had last night.' He leered. 'Did you hear who wants to buy the von Lillienfeld house?' He covered the speaker with his hand.

'No,' I said, shocked, intrigued. But at that moment whoever had him on hold came back. I could never sit in an antique shop, though, because I love snooping around. I was inspecting a collection of English teapots when I came to a stop.

There, in the locked glass cabinet, was Iris's music box, the one always on her table beside the throne. Of course, I thought, that's what had been missing!

It was so lovely. Victorian Indian, black enamel, hand-painted with figures of the finest detail. A story in miniature scenes, I remembered her telling me once. The story of Divali. Given to her by some swami. There was certainly no other box like that in New York. It was antique and, if I wasn't mistaken, hellishly valuable. It played, when it did, the 'Waltz of the Flowers'.

I stood, spellbound, for longer than I'd planned. Howie was still on the phone. I moved slowly away from that spot and pretended to study a burled walnut cabinet, then I drew my hands in the air as though I'd just remembered I hadn't put a quarter in my meter and flew out the door.

I had to think. I couldn't imagine that Howie would have stolen anything from Iris's home but, then, I couldn't imagine what had happened at the cemetery either. Of course, it could have been that Iris had given the music box to Howie on spec. She was known to do things like that. But I couldn't imagine she would have with this. It had been too special to her.

The truth was I'd been too frightened to ask Howie what it was doing there. As I walked along it occurred to me that it must have been Alleletzte. He'd somehow got his hands on the music box. Easily done for him. Just climb in a window. Those locks were as old as the house. Iris wasn't one for reform. And if anyone asked, he'd point out the roses he'd left on her porch. Big faker. Of course he'd stolen them from the library. And he would know just where to bring a music box for instant cash.

I went home. I made dinner. Lamb chops. After I did the dishes I took the dog out. I always do just before it gets dark. But it was dark already, much earlier than usual. I had put the issue of the music box on the back shelf for the moment, in order to worry about the system of feng shui, you know, rearranging your furnishings and doorways so good fortune can come to you unobstructed, and I was looking at my house. I was trying to figure out if, as my daughter Dharma had insisted at the table, the tree in front of our house was, in fact, obstructing good luck, and whether the woman who'd lost her head, for example, had cared about such things, when I noticed all these lights being set up on a lot of the doorsteps and in the windows. Raj, one of my neighbors, was coming spryly home from work and he stopped to pet Floozie. I watched him go.

'Raj!' I called out.

Raj, in his business suit, stopped.

'What are all the little lights out for?'

'Divali.' He pronounced the word with gentleness. 'The festival of lights.'

My heart beat quicker. Divali. The scenes on Iris's music box were of Divali. 'But what does it mean?'

'Oh. It is the night of the longest darkness. There's a story behind it all. If you're really interested . . .'

'Yes. Yes, I am.'

'Stop off this evening and I'll give you a small book.'

I didn't waste any time. I took the dog home, brushed my teeth, brushed my hair and went back down the block. Raj had the old McAfferty house. I went around back and knocked at the basement door. I peeked in. The hallway was a marvel of Formica. His wife let me in. Nice lady. Very shy. I took my shoes off and was shown into the inner sanctum, a many-carpeted sort of drive-in theatre for sultans with oriental rugs strewn around the sports-bar-sized TV screen. I sat, patiently crosslegged, while he shared with me his nightly meditation, *Jeopardy*. Finally, he switched the TV off and we were face to face.

'In a nutshell, the story of Divali is this,' he said. 'Long ago, in India, Crown Prince Ram was banished by his stepmother's wish to a forest for fourteen years. She wanted the crown for her own son, Bharat. But Bharat despised his mother for her wish. He took Ram's slippers and put them on the crown, promising to keep them there for the fourteen years. But if Ram was one day late coming home, Bharat would burn himself to death.'

'So did Ram come back in time?'

'On the last day of the fourteen years, Bharat, on his ready funeral pyre, saw Ram coming. Ram was guided by "divali," the string of lights he had prepared. Joyously, Bharat went and put the crown of slippers on Ram's head.'

Raj handed me a well-worn leather booklet. 'I want you to have this,' he said.

I smiled at him. 'Thank you. I'll keep it.'

I left and walked up the block quickly. I don't mind the dark but it felt like there were whispering sounds and I was nervous. You know the way brittle oak leaves sound in the wind, nice but a little like an animal hissing? My parents' house is on the way home so I ran to their doorway.

They were standing in the dining room, deep in the process of wrapping a care package with brown paper to be sent to Carmela.

'What are you sending her?'

'Food.'

'I can't believe you're sending food to France.'

'Like sending coals to Newcastle,' my father muttered.

'I stopped at Raj's house,' I said. 'Look what he gave me.'

'Fancy leather.' My dad swept a knowledgeable eye across it.

'Good soda bread,' I said, stuffing a piece in my mouth.

'Officer Fogarty said he saw you going into Mr Snow's.'

'The lawyer? Gee, you can't get away with anything around here. Suppose I'd wanted to talk to him in private? Does everybody know everybody else's business?'

'Things are all right with you and Johnny, aren't they?' My matter peered at me suspiciously.

'No worse than usual,' I joked. I supposed I was being flippant. I knew she was worried about me. 'I went there to get Iris's key so I could get the damn – I mean, darn – cat's things. What was Fogarty doing here? Am I being watched?'

'I told you everything was fine.' My dad's reassuring eyes twinkled at my mother.

'Officer Fogarty stopped off with your bicycle yesterday,' my mother said primly. 'He was looking for you.'

'Looking for Zinnie, you mean,' I said.

'Oh, so that's it,' Mom said. 'I had a feeling he liked Zinnie. All those questions...'

'You women know everything.' Dad laughed. 'You ought to go into business.'

'And just what business, I'd like to know? I haven't got five minutes to myself. What business would have me?'

'Now, Mary—'

'Don't "Now, Mary" me! I'm tired, Stan. I haven't had a moment all day and look at me, I'm still at it.'

'Ma.'

'Listen, Mary, I haven't exactly been sitting around doing nothing all day either, you know. It's all double drill and no canteen around here lately!'

'Uh, Ma? Dad? I've got to go.'

'Oh, that's brilliant! What have you got to complain about, I'd like to know?'

'Well, so long. I'll talk to you tomorrow, then.'

'Now you see what you've done?'

'Oh. Say, Mom?' I stopped at the front door. 'Did you know the Beverlys?'

'Beverly?' She looked at Dad puzzled. 'Can't imagine why that rings a bell. Seems I just heard something about a Beverly.'

'You're the one remembers everyone.' Dad snorted.

Thus placated, my mother squinted her well-informed eyes. 'Oh, sure, you remember. Grace Beverly. She just died. A month or two ago. The son didn't eat for weeks. I knew I'd heard the name recently.'

'Did I know her?'

She looked at me. 'I think you did. Well, you might have. Don't you remember? She worked at the big houses up in the Gardens. Laundry, was it? No, she was dreadful untidy. Cooked, I think.'

'No, I don't think so. These have money. Son went to law school.'

'Some people stash away plenty, cookin',' my dad said.

'Had a little boy,' my mother went on, ignoring us. 'Keen on animals he was. A nice little boy. Stout. About your age, wasn't he?'

We thought together.

'Maybe Zinnie's age, then.' My mother sighed. 'Let's see.' She rubbed her face absently. 'Protestants, I remember that.'

'Hmm,' we all said.

'There was something...'

'Why don't you stay for a cup of tea?' Dad said.

'Can't, thanks,' I said. 'I'll be up all night. So what about him?' I pressed. 'Do you think you remember him? The boy?'

My mom put her cheek in her hand. 'Worked up at one of those mansions for a while, she did. I remember that. So many of those big houses had foreigners in them.'

'Huh,' I said. I didn't like to say she was a foreigner herself.

'Why do you want to know?'

'He's Mr Snow's assistant. Oh, you saw him at the funeral.'

'Who, the one blubbering all over the place?'

'No, Mom, that was Jerry, the liquor-store owner.'

A look of disapproval passed between my parents. Jerry'd only been in Richmond Hill these fifteen years.

'I've got to go,' I said. 'Anthony will be watching television.'

'Fancy Mr Snow hiring that Beverly boy,' my mother said.

'Should have retired long ago,' my father said.

'I thought Daisy Webster was Snow's assistant.' Mom's face wrinkled. 'Did I put the trash out? What night is this?'

'I put it out.' Dad swatted her rump with the funny sheets.

They waved me out, friends again. The front door closed on the smell of soda bread and meatloaf.

'Mom.' Anthony looked up from the television screen when I came in the door. 'Somebody called you.'

'Who?'

'Uh. I forget.'

'Well, try and remember. Did you brush your teeth?'

'Yeah.'

'Tell the truth.'

'No.'

'So do it. Do it now. Or I'll come in there and we'll have a war.'

'Aw, Mom, it's just at the end...'

'Go brush your teeth,' I said.

'It's my favorite show!'

'They're all your favorite shows. Anthony? Anthony, you do as I say or I'll call your ... Johnny! Johnny, can you tell Anthony to—?'

Anthony stood in the doorway. 'Dad had to go out.'

'Out? Now? Where?'

We looked in each others' eyes. Anthony shrugged.

'Go brush your teeth,' I said, more gently.

He marched away. He turned around. 'Oh, yeah. It was Howie who called.'

'Thank you. Is Dharma in bed?'

'She's studying her shitty Latin verbs.'

'OK. Up in a minute. And don't say shitty.'

'You do.'

'Goodnight.'

' 'Night, Mom.'

I picked up the phone. I held my breath. I dialed the one-oh-two. 'Could you put me through to the bicycle squad, please?'

'Bike Squad,' somebody said.

'Hello,' I said in a small voice. 'I'd like to leave a message for Officer Fogarty, please.'

'Yeah? What's the message?' the voice barked. I surmised from his tone that Officer Fogarty got his share of female callers. I gave him my number and hung up. I noticed my palms were all wet. Floozie was asleep on the couch but I couldn't see Lu. He was probably curled up under a radiator, deaf and as warm as toast.

I climbed the stairs and knocked on Dharma's door.

'What?'

'It's me.'

'I'm studying.'

'May I come in?'

A rude amount of time elapsed, but Dharma is fourteen so just about everything she does is accompanied by some form of standard rudeness and therefore not to be taken personally.

The key turned grudgingly in its lock. The door opened a crack.

'Have you seen the cat?' I asked.

'I guess it's too much to ask if he's run away,' she said.

'I don't know,' I admitted.

'Listen, we've got to talk about this.' She opened the door, sat down and crossed her legs in a grown-up, no-nonsense, I've-seen-enough-Oprah-to-know-this-is-within-my-rights way. 'I can't have this cat coming in here, like spraying my stuff. I can't go to school smelling like this sick old cat. No matter how responsible you may feel, I mean.'

'He's not sick.'

'Well, old then. Same thing.'

'Ouch. I'll let him know how you feel next time I see him.'

'I'm serious.'

'So am I.' I made to go.

'Mom?'

I turned with what I prayed was not shining hope in my eyes. 'What is it?'

'Are you still taking those pills?'

'No. I only ever took the one.'

'Can I try one?'

'No.'

'Why not?'

'Because it was too much fun. And I don't want you to have fun.' I walked to Anthony's room. He was asleep, his comic books all over the bed. I took them away and covered him up.

The phone rang just as I was going to go and get myself a glass of wine. Jerry's recommended inexpensive but terrific '95 Merlot, as a matter of fact.

I picked up the hall phone. 'Hello?'

'Fogarty.'

'Hi, it's Claire Breslinsky. Uh, Benedetto, sorry, Benedetto.'

'Claire.' His voice warmed. 'How's it goin'?'

'I'm sorry to bother you but—'

'You're not bothering me. What's up?'

'Well, maybe it's silly, but I just thought maybe it was important...'

'What?'

'Well, I mean, I'd hate to accuse somebody but—'

'Just come to the point.'

'Oh. OK. I was at Howie's store today, you know, Aunt Howie's Attic?'

'Sure, I know it. Cool place.'

'I happened to see something there that belonged to Iris, my friend who died. I missed it when I went into her house. I should just have asked Howie myself but ... something stopped me. I was afraid.'

'Of what?'

'That he would just lie.'

'So, what was it?'

'A music box. Indian. Victoriana. Very valuable.'

'What's very valuable? Like a thousand? Ten thousand?'

'Yeah.'

'Yeah, what?'

'Ten thousand.'

'That's valuable.'

'Yeah.'

'So. I'll stop in. He's open late, right?'

'What's tonight? Thursday? Yeah, he's open. Till nine.'

'I'll take a look.'

'Okey-dokey.'

He hung up. Then I got an idea. I called Zinnie and told her the same thing. I went to bed and slept like a rock. About four o'clock in the morning the front doorbell started ringing. I jumped up. It was freezing. I realized Johnny wasn't in bed and my first thought was that he was drinking again and his partner was bringing him home. I flung open the door. No one was there. I leaned into the night. 'Johnny?'

'What is it?' Dharma was at the top of the stairs. 'Is it Daddy?'

'No, it's OK. It's not Daddy.'

'Well, if it's not Daddy ...' Dharma narrowed her eyes at me accusingly '...then where is he?'

I went over to her and put my arms around her. To my grateful surprise, her lip loosened up the way it would when she was little, she smiled half-heartedly and went sleepily back to bed.

I woke up in the nudging light of day with a guilty feeling towards Howie. I knew I had to go talk to him. Especially after Zinnie and Fogarty had converged on him at once. I took my bike and came to an abrupt halt when I turned his corner. There were five cop cars, parked this way and that and a lot of people and yellow tape stretched from his shop to the street. I grabbed hold of a woman.

'Ooh,' she said. 'It's the shop-owner there. Mr Edelman!'

'Howie? Howie Edelman? What happened?'

'He's dead!' She lit another cigarette from the butt of her last one. 'They found him dead!'

'What?'

'Yeah, the cops found him. They went in. I just saw him yesterday.'

'How did he die?'

'Murder.' She was a huge woman, stout, but with a beautiful, heavily made-up face. She looked at me suspiciously. 'Say, did you know him?'

'Yes,' I whispered. 'Yes, I knew him.'

'You better go talk to the detective over there,' she said, pointing to the officer in charge. I turned, heartsick. I didn't want to talk to anyone. At that moment, the print man opened the shop door and dusted it. You could see right in. I didn't want to look but I couldn't stop myself either. Howie was slouched on the floor, sitting up. An arrow pierced his chest. On his head was a pair of red slippers.

I went to the barrier cop and asked him to please let me speak to the detective in charge. He took one look at me, hair askew, rusty bicycle, and decided against it. I was told, instead, 'Move along, this ain't no sideshow here.' Then I was given the broad of his back.

I had to speak to someone. Luckily I didn't have to wait that long. Elroy Hamilton was coming out. He's been in Homicide for years. When he saw me, he barged over.

'Mrs Benedetto,' he said, putting his big hand out. 'How the hell are you?' He made the cop who'd barred my way lift the wooden horse. I hoped it was heavy.

'I thought I'd better tell someone,' I said, 'that the slippers on the victim's head might have a special meaning. I mean, it's just like the story of Divali.'

'Who's Divali?'

'Today is Divali. The night that has the longest darkness. It's the Hindu holiday.'

'What are you, some kind of Hindu expert?'

'No. Not at all. But the story of Divali ends with a crown of slippers.'

Fogarty was in the back room. He came over and shook hands with me. I wondered where Zinnie was.

'Let me ask you something,' Elroy said. 'You know any Indians had something against Aunt Howie here?'

'Indians? No.'

My eyes swept around the shop. The music box wasn't there.

'I have to tell you.' I spoke urgently. 'Howie called me last night. It had to have been before nine.'

'And do you have any idea what he wanted?'

'I was here yesterday and I just ran out because I saw a music box that I thought might have been stolen and I—'

'Whoa, whoa, wait a minute. You saw something you thought Mr Edelman might have stolen?'

I looked from his face to Fogarty's. 'I don't think Howie stole it, but I think he might have bought it from someone who did steal it.' I wasn't going to say Alleletzte, but I thought it.

'Let me ask you something.' He lowered his voice. 'Was there anyone you knew of who owed Howie Edelman money?'

'More likely he owed Jerry next door,' I said.

'Jerry.'

'The liquor-store owner.'

He was writing this down.

'Oh, no, Jerry wouldn't have killed Howie. They were like ...' What were they like? Coolly polite.

The photographer arrived and pushed us out of the way. 'Everybody out of here,' the print man cried.

'Excuse me, Fogarty,' I said. 'Have you seen my sister?'

'Yeah,' he said. His face turned red. 'She went next door to talk to the liquor-store owner.' He looked at his pad. 'Jeremiah Husk.'

'Isn't that the nut had the hallucination in the cemetery that time?' I overheard one of the cops say about me. I slipped away. I peeked in the liquor store. My sister, Zinnie, was standing over Jerry. I could tell she'd been up all night. I had a terrible feeling they were going to find the music box with Jerry. That would certainly cover his expenses, I thought miserably. I should have remembered then that the story of Divali not only ended with a crown of red slippers, it started with them as well.

'Hey,' I called to Zinnie.

'What's up?' she said, not wanting an answer. Then her eye was caught by my bookworm pin.

'Where'd you get that?' She pulled me aside.

'At the library,' I told her. 'They're giving them out.'

She took it between her fingers. 'What for?'

'Just like that. Encourage reading. That sort of thing.'

'He had one, too.' She nudged her head.

'Who, Howie?'

'Yeah.'

My eyes filled up with tears. 'Howie loved the library.'

'Too cheap to buy a book, huh?'

'That, too,' I admitted, forgetting my tears. 'Perry Beverly actually gave me mine. Do you remember him? He's about your age.'

'No,' she said. Then added, 'Oh, hell, yes. Fat kid, right?'

I shrugged, unable to imagine Perry fat.

'You knew him,' she said. 'Don't you remember? Got locked in the closet that time with the lady's cat? Up in the Gardens? Then they hushed it up?'

A vague memory stirred. I must have moved on in my interests at that point, ignoring anything having to do with the neighborhood.

'You better get out of here,' Zinnie said.

I stood there.

'What?' Zinnie said. 'You can't believe he would murder his friend?'

'It's just so unbelievable that he'd kill him and stick the slippers on his head like that. I mean, why would Jerry even know it was Divali?'

My sister made an I-could-tell-you-stories shrug. Jerry was sitting on his folding chair in his cornflower-blue shirt and he was crying. I know he's meek and bald and flosses his teeth behind the cash register when he thinks nobody's looking, but until I started patronizing his store, I'd run up against dead stares when I asked which wine I should buy if I was serving, say, fusilli with red sauce. Jerry's eyes would light up and he'd fish around on the bottom shelf for a '94 Chianti Rufina, Il Principe. Or even a nice Côtes-du-Rhône. Something you could afford two or three bottles of, you know? But good.

I know he was mean-spirited with Howie, but that was because Howie only paid him back when he felt like it. All of a sudden, while I'm standing there feeling sorry for him, he jumps up and pushes my sister out of the way; she falls into a display of that boring Mouton Cadet and there's broken glass and red wine everywhere. Before you can say 'boo', Howie's out the back door and the cops are yellin', 'Cop down!'

Elroy and Fogarty were the first ones in there, dancing over the broken glass, and they're trying to get the back door open, but it's not opening. So I run in and help pick my sister up and the two of them are still trying to get out the back door and it's not moving. Meanwhile, there goes Jerry, getting away!

All the cop cars fill up and now they're drifting after him, sirens wailing. My sister was OK, but now she's hot. She wants this guy. Fogarty runs out the front door and she goes right after him. He jumps on his bike so she jumps on mine. I'm standing there, and there's poor Howie dead on the floor of his shop.

I tried to imagine where Jerry would go.

All the cops were heading up towards Austin so, of course, that's where all the people ran. I remembered the train bridge and went that way. We used to go there when we were kids. It was farther off but it was above the action, so you could look back. My sister had had the same idea. There was my bike, tossed in the stickerbushes. I looked over the side and noticed a fluttering or movement of cornflower blue from a back doorway on the station side. I screeched my unforgettable excuse for a whistle. It was too late, though, they'd all turned the corner and were out of sight.

I couldn't do anything. I stood there. At that moment, Zinnie's head appeared back at the station. Darned if she hadn't remembered that screech from when we were kids and it was last call to dinner. I screeched again with all my might, even threw in a little Moroccan women wailing. She looked up, right at me. I flailed my arms in Jerry's direction.

She got him all right. There she was, cuffing Jerry. Fogarty was holding Jerry's arms behind his back. Jerry was just standing there and he's crying again. I thought, Boy, is he stupid. What had he thought, he'd blend in with the crowd?

I saw Zinnie snap at Fogarty. He snapped right back. Well, I figured, he'd have to if he was going to keep up with her. So all's well that ends well. After that, they put him in a squad car. Zinnie looked up and gave me a wave. I cycled off, feeling good, then sad. Iris. Now Howie.

I went to the cemetery from behind, near Franklin K. Lane. I didn't feel like running into that gardener, Mr Dhundee.

The sky was crisp and blue. I tooled over the top of the hill and stopped. You could see all over Queens up here. The wind blew and my hair licked at my eyes. It was a neglected spot, all toppled stones and brush. Perfect for daredevil kids on bikes. Or lovers, I thought wistfully. And then I saw it. The little cathedral mausoleum. The one with no name. There were the lights. They were on again.

I went down the ravine, the bicycle bumping wildly beside me. When I got to level ground I stopped, never losing sight of the tomb. I was afraid if I did, I'd never find it again. I clutched the handlebars with such force that the rubber grips left their imprint on my palms. A tinkering sound came from inside, and a baby crying. I leaned my bicycle on a pale grave and crept forward.

Softly, from behind, a gentle, eerie hand picked up my hair. A thrill ran up my spine.

'You're late,' he said.

That was the moment I could have broken away. I could have fled. My fear would have carried me. But I waited. Something in me held me there. It wasn't curiosity. All my wondering stopped the moment I felt his pickled breath on the curve of my neck. It was something else, something learned, deeply ingrained. Obedience. Locked deep like the memories of childhood.

An anguished cry came from the little tomb.

'It's just the cat,' he said. I turned and looked at him. He still wore his bookworm on his lapel. 'I knew you'd come today.'

'Today?'

'Divali.'

'The festival of lights.'

'You knew you were supposed to be here today?'

'No,' I said. 'I hadn't the slightest idea.'

'Oh, yes, you did. The dates were in the books.'

'The seven-day books.' I still had no idea, but I sensed complicity would serve me best.

He opened the door to the tiny, candle-lit crypt. It was a quarter of a room, with a gray marble shelf for a coffin. His stuff was all around, smudged reading glasses, old deli food, some filthy towels.

'Beautifully made, isn't it?' He patted the limestone-covered walls, like a man kicking tires on a car he just loved. 'Airtight.'

On the sills along the stained-glass windows were pots of ghee lit with wicks. He pulled a rug away from the floor. A stench came at me. I had my handkerchief out and held it to my nose. It was Lu's rug.

My God. He'd been in my house. 'Lights,' was all I could say.

'Enjoy them while you can.' He came closer. 'I'm out of wicks. These won't burn long.'

We stood together inside the door, looking in. There was the music box with the sides taken off. I could still flee. Just that moment I could have run. But Lu the cat was pressed tight in a box on the floor. His front paws and legs had scratched through the bleeding box. That was the crying I'd heard. There were things on top of the box to hold him in. Stones. And something else. Like tenderloin.

I wouldn't go in. I stayed where I was but I leaned forward, towards the hole. It gaped, dark from the earth. The wretched smell came from there. Perry walked out of reach, behind the hole. He wanted me to see. He wanted it with an obscene pursing of the lips. I leaned further in and looked. It was Shanti. Or rather her lavender sari wrapped like flowers all around her. Her slender legs ... And lying beside her, upside down, was Mr Dundhee.

I swooned and fell back against the door. Poor Lu made that awful sound again. Perry watched me and his shoulders went up. Like an excited child's. That was the sound he loved.

Suddenly, I remembered him. I remembered him when he was a boy. I could see him, standing like a potato, in line at the bakery with his potato mother. She with her shopping bags. He being good.

I remembered something else. There was a little park with swings by the Jewish school. There would be no one there after school and my sister Carmela and I would climb the fence and go in. It was wonderful to trespass. One boy wouldn't climb. He wanted our attention, though. He took a kitten and threw it down the sewer. I'd wanted to call someone, but my sister had made us run home. And I'd run. I hadn't told. Never. I was afraid of that boy. Not what he'd done but how he'd laughed as he'd done it.

'I remember you,' I said.

'Of course you do.' He smiled.

And there was something about a house where his mother was working...

'How did you find this place?'

He was putting the murals back on the music box. I'd heard the mechanism working, but without the hammer.

'I was at Mother's grave,' he said, 'and I took a walk and stopped to admire the workmanship with the groundsman. He said this one was lost, it wasn't on the survey map. It was off the border of both caretakers' maps, all these years. A lost mausoleum! Isn't it too romantic? It had to be mine.' Perry flicked a maggot from his clothes. 'I would come to see Mother. We don't have anything as elaborate as this, of course. Dhundee liked to walk along with me. I knew so much about his culture.' Perry smiled. 'Shanti was his niece, you know. He was teaching her to drive. A surprise for her husband for Divali. They would meet here. She would sit out there and sew and wait for him.' His head snapped up. 'But she knew I was going to get her. I could see it in the provocative way she would adjust her sari while I watched. And she would laugh! Her bangles made that sound, they never stopped.'

He's going to kill me, I realized.

'I wanted to get her tongue out,' he confessed. 'I was trying to pull out her tongue so she would look like Kali. You know, the goddess with her tongue sticking out, goddess of destruction. I couldn't get her mouth to stay open, though. I had to cut her head away to get it.'

He reached across the cat, the cat shrieked and I thought he was going to pick up the key to lock me in. But I was closer to the door than he was. And the keyhole, I remembered, was outside. Instead, he picked up the tenderloin. It wasn't that. He held it in front of his mouth and stuck one arm out, his fingers splayed apart. It was Shanti's tongue.

'I thought I'd astonish someone,' he said. 'I was delighted when it was you. That was the lucky part. I had my little house to keep her safe,' he chatted on, touching

137

the walls around him, caressing them. He stopped. 'I had to stop Dhundee with the very knife I'd used for Shanti. I almost lost it once. That's how we met again, did you know?'

I remembered the knife at Iris's grave.

'Such a beautiful day, that was. I just latched on. Nobody questioned me. Do you remember, we went to lunch. I found it thrilling. Do you remember?'

'Yes.'

Perry hugged himself. 'I love it here. It's the way things used to be, you know? So idyllic. So Anglican.'

I looked around. It was a crypt. And there were bars on the insides of the windows.

'I thought I would be buried here one day but, then, I started to visit. It was so peaceful. Mr Dhundee confided in me that he'd used the place for a liaison once. I have to tell you I was shocked. But the more I thought about it the more it excited me. At first I would come here and read. That's when I decided to summon you with the books. With the due dates in the back. I got the key from Dhundee. Then I'd just sleep over.'

I saw his knife. All crudded with old blood.

'Perry. What happened at the big house? It was Indian people your mother worked for, wasn't it?'

'You knew what happened.'

'I didn't.'

'You did, too.'

'I must have been away. I never heard. Honestly. I just remember that big mansion.'

He looked at me suspiciously. Then I could see the raw hurt in his eyes. 'They caught me, those pompous Indians. They discovered me with their stupid cat.' He shrugged. 'I was just doing something with her nails, you know. It was nothing more than that. Mother used to do my nails, cut them down good, so I wouldn't scratch her. If I peed the bed she'd spank me and I might scratch her.'

'How terrible,' I said.

He disregarded me. 'Respectable!' he cried. 'That's a laugh. Trade! That's what they were. Textiles. Dehli. Puh. Mother had to degrade herself to them. Had to. They would have fired her. We shouldn't even let them in the country. Destroying the integrity of the architecture.'

'Yes,' I said.

He looked at me shrewdly. Was I making fun of him? No, he still trusted me. 'You thought I worked for Snow,' he said. 'You just handed me Iris's key.' He took it out of his pocket and put it with the other.

'You think like a lawyer.'

'Yes, that's true. But I never said I worked for him. You gave me that.'

I thought back. He'd never said he was a lawyer. I'd supplied him with the role, hadn't I? I held my head, then took my hands down. I dared not act weak. 'You're right,' I said. I was afraid to take even a step back. I knew he'd jump across that gaping, stinking hole and pull me in. I looked peripherally at that other key. Big, old-fashioned thing with filigree. Beside it was a box of rubber gloves, the top one rumpled, like a box of tissue.

Lu moaned in agony.

Perry sensed my urge to flee.

'What will you do?' I said, willing myself not to look at the cat. Not to look at the key.

'I'll go to prison. Upstate.'

'Yes.' I nodded my head approvingly, hope replacing fear.

'Sing Sing, probably. Right on the Hudson. Used to be extremely famous. They filmed all the old gangster films up there.' He said this like he was talking about going away to school with some difficult courses in front of him. 'Not far,' he added.

I looked at him in surprise. He thought I would come and visit him. That we were in this thing together.

'I'll write.' He screwed the last screws back on the music box.

'I'll write you back,' I lied.

He stopped and looked at me pityingly. He put the screwdriver on the shelf, beside the book with the key. 'I mean I'll write my book. They'll want to make a movie. I'll be sure to put you in it, eh? You and your pretty daughter.' He smiled his charming smile. I felt my color drain.

He knew my daughter. Suddenly I knew why Anthony had thought Ralphie'd been in the bushes. It was Perry who'd been outside, watching her.

Perry stroked the music box. 'She has the softest room,' he whispered in a trembling shiver. 'That's where I found the cat.'

He'd violated her room. That's what Dhorma had smelt. I'd misunderstood. He was going to kill me and then her.

'Of course I'll work on my appeal,' he said, brightening.

I stared at him. I closed my mouth. He was right. That's what would happen. And visitors would come from all around to study his warped mind. The music from the box started up. The 'Waltz of the Flowers'. He'd made sure it would work. Handy, Perry was. Capable. But he didn't love the music. It was all a prop, to make him a more interesting murderer. Now, at least I knew who I was. I'd been allowed to be the witness, the audience. Until I showed fear. Then he would go for me, like a lizard. Quick.

I backed away. But in backing away I was no longer in front of the door. There were bars on the windows both inside and out. I'd never get away. No one would ever hear me. His eyes drove into me.

'What happened to Iris?' I had the wherewithal to sound parental. 'Tell me now. I have to know.'

Perry ran his fingers along the top of the music box. 'I didn't mean for her to die. It just happened.'

'She wasn't hurt?'

Perry screwed up his face, helpful, remembering. 'She was sitting there talking about India. I think she was tight.' He snorted. 'What a great culture they had. She should have only known, I know more about their stinking culture than they do.' He bit his thumb. 'I never wanted her to die, though. She was the only one who came when mother was laid out.' He looked at me with sane, deliberate eyes. 'Mother worked for her. Part time. She was the day lady. You don't remember.'

He was right. I didn't.

He picked up the music box and held it. 'One minute she was saying how you were going to take her to Aunt Howie's Attic the next day so Howie could have a look at her music box.' Perry stopped, surprised. 'And all of a sudden she wasn't talking any more.' He wound it up again. 'So I took it for her. He couldn't fix it, though. And then he wouldn't let me have it back. I got it, though. So.'

I was glad about Iris. I was glad that's how it had been. 'Perry, what happened at the big house?'

'They locked me in the closet. They did it all the time. They tied me to the ironing board. Because I punished their sadistic cat.' He looked at Lu.

'I'm sorry,' I whispered.

His eyes flashed at me. 'It wasn't too bad. Whenever she would punish me, she'd be sorry after. Like all you women.' He let out a laugh. 'She'd let me braid her long black hair while she read to me from Goberdhan's *Joyous Memory Book*. Her hair reached between her legs. You know some of those Indian women never cut their hair. Never.' He looked, caressingly, at mine.

'I was sorry about your mother,' I said, holding his eyes with my own. I hardly breathed.

He put the key down beside the cat and he seemed to change. I was vibrating with fear. The slipper's waltz, I thought. Funny, the things you think. The willing flowers. I wouldn't die still, though. I would fight.

'Let me tell you all about Mother,' he said. 'I'll tell you what that kind lady did. She knew they put me in there. She knew. She knew the first time.' He lowered his head and banged it on the music box. 'She knew it the second time.' He banged his head again. 'She knew it the third time.' Again. 'She knew.' He banged. 'She knew, she knew, she knew!'

I thought he was going to lunge at me but he didn't. In a compassionate voice he said, 'She didn't know. She was so . . .' he put his hand up '. . . alone. And they were so wealthy. So powerful. She thought they knew what was best . . . She used to . . .'

He came closer to me, sidestepping the hole. Megalomaniacs are shrewd, but their own words are golden to them. I poised my knee and rammed. He dropped into the hole, along with my shoe. I snatched the key and took the cat. I went out backwards and shut the door. He was just climbing from the hole, stunned. He'd been so sure I'd wanted to hear what his mother had done. I tried to get the key in the lock. He'd climbed up; he was at the door. He pushed it. That was his mistake. It didn't open unless you turned the knob. I turned the key. He pressed the slender knob. If he had done that first he would be out.

He stood on one side of the door and I on the other.

I waited. I realized I held the cat. I looked into its blue, old eyes.

'Airtight,' he'd said. 'Made to last.'

He was talking now. He'd sensed I'd moved away from the door. It was hard to understand, muffled, but he went on in a reasoning way.

My bicycle was where it had been.

I heard him laugh. Horrible, and hopeful.

Lu slumped into the bicycle basket.

I looked at my hands. They hardly shook. I mounted the bike.

I started going. The trees closed in around me on Myrtle Avenue. Out there on the middle of Victory Field, Iris's crows were grazing in the center of all those weary joggers.

You know, I've always hated those sleek, illustrious birds. I turned around and pointed my handlebars and I drove right through the middle of them. They flew, in fits and starts, into the perfect sky.

*

Not a bad ending, I thought. Only then I remembered Shanti's kids. They'd always think their mother had left them. And another thing. If you act with the scheme of the lowly, you become it, right?

So I went and got the Parky to come back there with me. He walked and I rode, him with his loud walkie-talkie, me with only one shoe on.

We could see it right away when we topped the hill. At first it looked like a dangerous jewel on ropes of sleeping pearls. Flames glittered up from the tomb. He'd set himself on fire, like Bharat's funeral pyre in the story.

'Holy!' The Parky dropped his radio. I put the filigree key in his hand while he called 911, and Lu and I got out of there.

We passed Alleletzte in the tunnel of trees up on Myrtle. He was caught in the sunset, dead west. The wheels of his cart made their own rusty song, wrenching sense from none. And then making it beautiful. Know what I mean?

THE SEDGEMOOR STRANGLER

Peter Lovesey

'Listen.'

'What is it?'

If there was a sound, it was not obvious. All Emma could catch was a scent, the mock orange drifting across the lane from one of the cottage gardens. On this warm June night, hidden among the withies with her dreamboat of a man, she was thinking only of romance.

'Kiss me.'

'No. Listen. Can you hear a rustling sound?'

Emma was not minded to listen. She curved her hand around his neck to draw his face closer to hers.

He resisted, bracing his shoulders. 'It's all around us. What is it – insects?'

With a wriggle of her hips, she let him know she wasn't lying naked on the ground to discuss the wildlife of Somerset.

'Just listen.'

'There's nothing,' she murmured. 'It's only the wind, I expect. Come on, lover.'

He was not her lover yet, and he would not relax. 'Wind? There's no wind.'

She hesitated. Until this minute, he had seemed so confident, so appreciative of her. She really wanted him. Their first passionate coupling would be ruined if she lost her patience.

He insisted, 'There isn't a breath of wind tonight.'

'Then it must be the withies growing.'

'The what?'

'All around us.'

This was true. On a hot day on Sedgemoor, a crop of these fine willow wands may get taller by two or three inches. After dark the process continues, more slowly, yet, in the still of the night, it is audible. The rustle he had heard was the sound of growth itself. Months back, in winter, the withies had been pruned to the stump. Now taller than a man's reach, with graceful foliage, they testified to the richness of the earth that nourished them. This mud that Emma was lying in – call it earth, silt or topsoil – was the life-giver. All you had to do was push a willow cutting into the ground and it would sprout roots and grow.

The crop screened the couple from the row of stone cottages across the lane. A withy bed is not the ideal place to lie down and make love, but you have to take what you can find in the flat landscape of the moor. These two had gone to some trouble to avoid being seen. His car was parked outside the village, up a track leading to a field. They had approached from around the back of the crop, away from prying eyes, regardless that the fading light would shortly bring them privacy anyway. But, then, lovers are not good planners. Persevering, stepping with care to avoid the nettles, eventually they had found this space between the tall willow wands.

The secretiveness was more at his insistence than Emma's. Nobody would recognize her. She was not from withy-growing people. Her parents were middle-aged hippies who ran one of the many 'alternative' shops in Glastonbury, selling trinkets and jewellery with so-called occult properties. Emma had rebelled against all that in her teens, had found work pulling pints in a pub for better money per week than her parents made in a month. She made new friends there. It was such a treat to mix with people who earned enough to take you out for a meal and buy you the occasional present.

By now she was becoming just a little impatient with her partner. 'Is there a problem?' she asked, trying to put some concern into her voice. 'Haven't you done it outdoors before?'

'Keep your voice down.'

'Nobody's about, and if they were it wouldn't matter. They don't know who we are.'

Reassured, or goaded into action, he turned on his side and drew her towards him, slid his hand down her back and over the rise of her hip and announced, 'Your backside is covered in muck.'

She giggled. He was no better at sweet-talk than she was. She squirmed closer, presenting all of her bottom for him to pass his hand over, supposedly to brush off the specks of earth. The undressing had been one-sided up to now. His own rump was still enclosed in denim and whatever he wore underneath. Still, Emma didn't mind – if it led to a result. All blokes were different. This one definitely needed coaxing.

She located his belt and unfastened it. He tensed. She freed the top button of his jeans.

This man was not much of a stud. He came prematurely, when Emma was thinking of other things. Asking herself if that was it, she lay in the mud and looked at the stars.

No, that was not it. Presently she felt his hands around her throat.

The tourist board calls this place the Wetlands or the Levels; to the inhabitants it was, is now and ever shall be Sedgemoor. It needs no glamorizing. It has more of legend, mystery and tragedy than anywhere else in England. If you have heard of Sedgemoor, you probably connect it with the bloody battle that was fought there in 1685, when the Duke of Monmouth's pitchfork rebellion was crushed by the King's army. Sedgemoor, as the locals speak of it, ranges far more widely than the battlefield. It is the entire tract of marshland bounded by Bridgwater Bay in the west and the Mendip and Quantock Hills inland. When the last ice age ended and the waters rose, the region became a stretch of sea, with a few tiny islands. Ultimately the sea receded, drew with it a mass of clay and left a ridge that formed a natural dyke. Sedgemoor was enclosed, a vast floodplain waterlogged each winter by rivers that overflowed. Flooding may devastate, but it also spreads deposits of fertile silt across the earth. In times relatively modern, drainage systems were introduced, and with them cattle, cider orchards and withy beds.

The talk in the public bar at the Jellied Eel in Bridgwater was the usual – who was laid off work and who was about to be. The modern economy had punished the people of Sedgemoor worse than most. Few of those in the pub had full-time work. Farming, the main employer, had shed thousands of workers as a result of automation, quotas and food scares. Beef, dairy products, cider – all were in decline. The demand for withies was negligible. The only viable industry was peat, and that was not a major employer. Peat-cutting machines were job-cutting machines.

The young woman behind the bar, washing glasses, was not thinking about employment. Unemployment was Alison Harker's dream, lifelong unemployment, sunning herself on a yacht in a Mediterranean bay. She had met a man across this bar two weeks ago who was capable of turning the dream into reality. Her pale, Pre-Raphaelite looks, the oval face and the long, red hair had appealed to him at once. She knew. Some fellows practically drooled at the first sight of her.

Tony was one of these, a pushover. He had only dropped in for a quick pint after doing some business in the town, and she wouldn't normally have expected to see him again, but he returned a couple of days later, his eyes shining like chestnuts fresh from their husks. She knew she could have him whenever she wanted, if she wanted – so cool was she about the prospect until someone told her his Mercedes was outside, with the chauffeur sitting in the front listening to the cricket on the radio. Then her knees wobbled.

Their first date was a Saturday lunch at the best hotel in town. She thought about adjourning to one of the rooms upstairs for the afternoon, but she didn't want him to get the impression she was easy, so she kept him – and herself – in suspense.

The next time he offered her an evening meal at a restaurant up near the coast, in the village of Stockland Bristol. She'd heard that it was highly regarded for its cooking, a place that catered mainly for tourists and people from 'up out' who could afford the prices.

Somewhere along the route they were forced to stop because the narrow lane was blocked by cars. There was an emergency in the field on their left. Rather than sitting in the car to wait, they got out to look. It was a situation familiar to anyone from the moors. A cow had stumbled into the ditch and was up to its shoulders in mud and water. A Sedgemoor ditch is more than just a furrow at the edge of a field. It is more than a stream. It is broad, deep and dangerous, kept filled in summer to act as a barrier between fields and provide drinking water for the animals.

A lad scarcely old enough to be in charge of a tractor had tied a rope around the cow's neck and was giving full throttle to this old Massey-Ferguson in the hope of hauling the beast out. The mud was doubly defeating him. The wheels were spinning and the cow was held fast. Alison saw that the poor animal was in danger of strangulation. It was making no sound, yet the distress in its eyes was obvious. The taut rope was around the throat in a knot that could only tighten as force was applied.

Reacting as a farmgirl, she ran across to the kid on the tractor. She had rescued cattle from ditches herself and there was a right way to secure the rope. The boy didn't like being told this by a woman dressed as if she had never been near a farm, but it was obvious from the way she spoke that she was experienced. At her bidding the lad backed the tractor far enough to slacken the tension. She took off her shoes and tights and handed them to Tony. After hitching the skirt of her new midi dress under her knickers, she let herself some way down the side of the ditch. Up to her thighs in the murky water, she strained to loosen the rope. It took all her strength. Twice the cow sheered away, almost dragging her into the ditch. At the cost of some torn fingernails, she finally untied the knot and attached the rope properly behind the cow's horns. She scrambled up the bank and told the boy to try again, pointing out where the tyres would find a better purchase.

The tractor took up the strain and the rope tightened. With a tremendous squelching sound and much splashing the cow was plucked out of the mire and enabled to scramble up the bank, where it stood, shocked, silent, dripping mud.

On the way back to the car Tony said, 'So you're not just a pretty barmaid.'

Alison grinned. 'Pretty muddy. I'm going to make a mess of your car.'

'Blow the car. I'm more worried about your dress. Keep it hitched up until your legs dry.'

'I can't go to a restaurant in this state.'

'Leave it to me.'

'I mean I wouldn't want to. I look disgusting like this.'

'You don't.' And he meant it. He might have been looking at the treasure of Troy. 'But I understand how you feel. Don't worry. The people who own the restaurant live upstairs. They're sure to have a shower.'

Typical of a man to dismiss the problem so lightly, as if it didn't exist. 'I can't march in and ask to use their shower.'

'I can. They know me.'

The chauffeur produced some clean paper tissues from the glove compartment and Alison wiped off the worst of the mud. If she had known Tony better, she might have asked him to help, but this was only their second date and they had made minimal body contact on the first so she coped while he acted the gent and stared fixedly across the fields like a birdwatcher. As it happened, this saved an awkward explanation for when she opened one of the tissues she found a lipstick imprint, obviously made by some previous passenger. Amused, she folded the tissues again and tucked it into her handbag, thinking she might tease him when she knew him better.

You can only do so much with a few paper tissues. She sat self-consciously next to Tony in the rear seat of the elegant car with her smeared legs exposed while they were driven six miles to their destination, an old stone house converted into a restaurant. Tony explained the problem and the woman owner took Alison upstairs as if a shower for the guests was the usual pre-dinner appetizer. The private bathroom was immaculate, with fluffy white towels and everything gleaming. After showering, Alison trimmed her damaged fingernails. Then she looked at her clothes. She was relieved to find that the specks of mud on her dress had already dried, and they rubbed off, leaving no mark anyone else would notice.

Sipping red wine at the candlelit table, she admitted she had been brought up on a farm and was used to dealing with cows. 'My people are dairy farmers. Generations of them.'

'Locally, you mean?'

She nodded. 'We know the moors. Grandfather used to keep a boat tied to the back door because the winter floods were so bad years ago. They regularly got several feet of water. The fields still get flooded to get a nice, rich covering of silt, but it's under control these days.'

'So why did you leave? What brought you to Bridgwater?'

'My pig-headed attitude. Women are supposed to do the same work the men do, or near enough, up to your knees in dung and silage. I wouldn't have minded, but they told me my brother Henry, who is seven years younger than I am, was going to inherit the farm and everything father owned. Blow that. I left.'

Tony's face creased in concern. 'You mean they would have left you penniless?'

She smiled. 'It's not quite so melodramatic. I was expected to work for my brother when the time came. He would have given me a wage.'

'But there was no question of you sharing the farm?'

'No chance.' To shift the attention from her family, she asked Tony about his work. She already knew a certain amount. He was the new money, a marshland millionaire, the owner of a fleet of digging machines that stacked sliced blocks of peat in tidy walls. He lived in an architect-designed villa in the Brue Valley and he had a bigger house in Gloucestershire. He was thirty-four, not bad-looking, curly-haired, dark and as tall as she would have wished.

'Here's a confession. I got my start through inheritance,' he told her with a flicker of amusement, 'but I didn't cut out any sisters. I don't have sisters. My dad saw the potential of peat years ago, before the price jumped, in the days when they called it turf-cutting. He was in there before Fisons, or any of them.'

The peat that was Tony's fortune is the principal asset of the moors. Where there is shallow water there are reeds, and the reeds of five thousand years ago fell into the swamps, rotted down and were compressed. Many generations later, mankind discovered that the soggy brown fibrous stuff had a use. It was cut from the ground, stacked, dried and used mainly for fuel. Some clever entrepreneur even shipped it to Japan to be used in distilling whisky.

But what transformed peat-cutting into an industry was the 1960s boom in natural fertilizers. Millions of people living in tidy suburban homes with patches of garden at front and back wanted the peat to nourish their soil. In the new wood-and-glass garden centres all over the country it was stacked high in bright plastic sacks, and the profits were high as well. An acre of Sedgemoor which you could have bought for five pounds in 1939 was worth at least ten thousand now.

And no one had ever seen Tony with a wife.

After the meal they drove through the lanes to a village at the west end of Bridgwater Bay which smelt of the sea. A bulwark of enormous quarried stones had been heaped along the front to keep back the highest tides. They clambered up and found a place to sit among the stones and watch the sunset. It would lead to some kissing, at the least, Alison assumed. First, there were things she wanted to know. 'Have you brought anyone here before?'

He shook his head. 'Never been here.'

'How did you know it was here, then?'

'I didn't. The lane had to lead somewhere.'

They listened to the mournful, piping cry of a curlew and stared at the sunset reddening the shallow channels that lay on the vast expanse of mud. Down by the water, the tiny figure of a fisherman was manoeuvring a sledge-like structure across the mudflats, bringing in his catch of shellfish from the nets further out. Soon the tide would turn. Along this coast the Bristol Channel has a rise of nearly forty feet and the water rushes in at the rate of a galloping horse, so timing is crucial for the fishermen.

Alison picked up the conversation again. She had not forgotten the lipstick mark on the paper tissue. 'Where do you take your girls, then?'

'What do you mean – take my girls?'

'Women, if you like. Birds, or whatever you call us. Where do you take them after dinner in that restaurant?'

Tony turned to face her. A hurt look clouded his features. 'I'm not the playboy you seem to think I am.'

She asked the big question, trying to sound casual. 'Married?'

'Do you think I would be here with you if I was?'

It was as good an answer as she was likely to get without spoiling the evening.

She guessed there was something he didn't want to discuss at this minute, like a recent divorce or a failed relationship. She didn't mind if he had a past, as long as it *was* over for good. You expected a man to have experience. She had a certain amount herself, come to that.

As if that cleared the way, he kissed her for the first time. He held her bare shoulders and traced the line of her neck. She could feel the links of his gold bracelet heavy and cool against her flesh. She pressed close and rested her head in the curve of his neck and shoulder. But they did not have sex, there in the setting sun, or later. She was not ready to suggest it, and nor, apparently, was Tony. They returned to the car and Hugh the chauffeur drove them back to Bridgwater. After being so direct with her questions Alison half wondered if she would be invited out again, but Tony suggested another meal the following week.

Over the next days she gave sober thought to her needs, sexual and material. No amount of wishful thinking was going to transform this man into a great lover. He seemed content with kisses and cuddles so toe-curling that she was reminded of her pre-teens. So she considered the trade-off. Whoever got hitched to Tony need never work again. She pictured herself in the designer clothes she had seen in expensive magazines at the hairdresser's. With her looks and figure it would be an injustice if she never got to wear such things. She thought of the holidays advertised in the travel agent's window. She weighed the other advantages: being driven about in the car; the choice of two houses; a swimming pool; meals in posh restaurants.

I wouldn't be ashamed of him, she reflected. His looks are all right, quite dishy, in fact. He must be intelligent to be running the business. He treats me with respect. I haven't noticed an aggressive side to him. And his work keeps him busy. Wicked thought: if I felt the urge to go out with blokes who appealed to me more, I could probably get away with it.

At the pub where she worked was a man whom Alison knew from experience would make a more passionate partner than Tony. She had slept with Matt Magellan more times than she cared to admit. Matt understood her needs. He was a tease and an out-and-out chauvinist, but when it came to sex he treated her right. He seemed to know instinctively the fine mix of flattery and passion that inflamed her. His touch was magic. She'd known him since childhood, which was a pity because she could remember him at fourteen when he didn't come up to her shoulder and she'd refused to go out with him for fear of making an exhibition of herself. He had put on some inches since then, but he was still below average height. A lovely mover, though, comfortable with his physique, beautifully co-ordinated on the dance-floor, regardless of what sort of dancing it was.

More than once she had caught herself wondering if she loved him. But how can you love a slaughterman who drinks in the pub each night and has about as much ambition as the cattle he kills?

'Fill them up, Ally,' he called over to her. His round.

She went to his table to collect the glasses.

'Have one thyself?' he offered.

'No, thanks.'

'A half, then?'

'Not even a half.'

'Saving thyself?'

She reddened. 'What do you mean?'

'Isn't that obvious? Who were treated to a tasty supper out Stockland Bristol way the other evening?'

One of Matt's drinking friends, John Colwell, a particular enemy of Alison's, said, 'Tasty supper and tasty afters, I reckon.'

Her contempt came out as a hiss. She could neither confirm nor deny that kind of remark with any dignity. After filling the glasses she carried them to the table and made sure she slopped Colwell's cider when she placed it in front of him.

Matt said, apparently for the amusement of his fellow-drinkers but not without bitterness, 'She'm given up cider for champagne.'

Every barmaid is used to suggestive remarks from the customers and Alison generally laughed them off. This was not like that. It was edged with malice. She said witheringly, 'It isn't the cider I'm sick of.'

Back behind the bar, she turned up the music to drown the crude remarks they were sure to be making about her, thinking how unjust it is that nobody remarks on the company a man keeps. Why shouldn't she go out with a stranger? What a dreary prospect, only ever spending time with clodhopping yobs like that lot.

With no other customers to serve, she picked up the local paper and read once again about the murdered girl they had found at Meare Green a week ago. Only seventeen, poor soul, naked as a cuckoo, and strangled. They reckoned she must have been lying among the withies three weeks before she was found, her clothes beside her. She came from Glastonbury, fifteen miles away, so the police had worked out that she was taken there in a car. It was about the only thing they had worked out. They were still appealing for witnesses. Some hopes, Alison thought. Meare Green always looked empty of inhabitants.

The girl's name was Emma Charles and she had worked as a barmaid. From the picture, one of those brightly lit studio shots with a pale blue background obviously taken when she was still at school, she was dark-haired and pretty, with thick eyebrows, a wide, sensuous mouth and dimples. There was a lot of speculation that she may have met her killer in the pub. Glastonbury, with its legends and ley-lines, has more than its share of freaks and weirdos passing through or camping there in the summer. The girl's parents owned an 'alternative' shop that went in for incense-burning and astrology, mandalas and mysticism. They were pictured in their tie-dye shirts, the father with a blond ponytail, the mother with cropped hair and a large Celtic cross hanging from her neck. But it seemed that Emma had left home and had not spoken to either of them for weeks.

It was easy to identify with her.

The report went on to state euphemistically that Emma was known to have had several close friends. Detectives were questioning a number of men believed to have associated with her.

'So when are you going out with him again?'

Startled, she looked up from the paper. Matt was by the counter. She had not noticed him, assuming that he and the others would be busy with their drinks for some time. His question was best ignored.

He said, 'I want three packets of crisps, vinegar-flavoured.'

Alison reached behind her and put them in front of him without a word. He dropped a couple of coins on the counter and said, 'Keep the change. You never know when you might need to catch a bus home.'

*

The next Saturday she went with Tony to see a film called *Seven*, about a serial killer. She'd have preferred a Woody Allen film which was showing in Glastonbury, but Tony wasn't keen. He seemed to dislike Glastonbury as much as she found Bridgwater a bore. *Seven* shocked her with its violent scenes, well made as it undoubtedly was, but she didn't admit this. 'I couldn't believe in the story,' she said when they had their drinks later. 'Murder isn't so complicated.'

'What do you mean?'

'Real serial killers aren't like that. They simply repeat the same method several times over. They're not inventing wild new ways of killing people.'

'I wouldn't know,' said Tony.

'They're not that intelligent,' she went on. 'They can't be. Take the case of that girl who was found at Meare Green.'

'That's not a serial murder.'

'You can't say,' she pointed out. 'It could turn out to be.'

His eyes slid downwards, staring into his drink. 'All right,' he conceded. 'What were you going to say about the woman at Meare Green?'

'Just this. She was strangled. Manually strangled, the paper said. That means with his bare hands instead of using her tights or something, doesn't it? Now, if that bloke did a second murder, you can bet he'd do exactly the same thing, with his hands around the woman's throat. That's how the police catch these people. They call it their MO. It's Latin, isn't it?'

'You seem to know a lot about it.'

'If you're a woman, you need to know.' She had a sense that he wanted to end the conversation, but something was spurring him on.

'You're saying this man, whoever he may be, isn't capable of thinking of some other way of killing the next one?'

'Yes.'

'But you don't know anything about him.'

'I know he's thick.'

'You can't say that. He might have a degree in astrophysics.'

'Intelligent men don't murder people just at random. Serial killers are thick, so they do the same thing and get caught.'

'The guy in the film wasn't thick. He changed his MO.'

Alison smiled. 'And still got caught. Serve him right.'

It was still warm when they left the pub, so she suggested they walk back to her flat. He told Hugh to drive the Mercedes round to her street and wait there. Having a chauffeur constantly on call was not always such a useful arrangement. It was not unlike having a chaperon.

'Do you ever go anywhere without Hugh?' she asked as they strolled through the silent streets, his arm around her waist.

He laughed. 'Does he cramp my style, do you mean? I give him days off sometimes.'

'Then do you drive the car yourself?'

'I use taxis.'

The Mercedes was waiting in her street when they reached it, on the opposite side from her flat, the lights off.

She looked up at him. 'Coffee?'

'Another time.'

'I have a phone, you know. You could call a taxi.' As she spoke she thought, This is wrong. I shouldn't be rushing him.

He took her hand and squeezed it gently. 'I appreciate the offer. I'm due back in Gloucester tonight. An early appointment tomorrow. Shall I see you next week? When's your night off? Saturday again?'

'Saturday.'

They kissed. Then he walked across to the waiting car.

A man with an old-fashioned haircut with sideburns and a parting at the side came into the pub a couple of evenings later and didn't buy a drink. He went straight to Matt's table and started talking to the group. After a while he took a notebook from his pocket and wrote things down. Then he moved to another table. Matt and his friends stared after him and talked in lowered voices among themselves.

Alison was uneasy about this stranger disturbing the customers. She went across to Matt's table and asked who he was.

'Fuzz,' said Matt. 'Wants to know if anyone here knew that girl who was strangled. We told 'un there's no sense in coming to Bridgwater asking about a girl from Glastonbury.'

'Why is he here, then?' said Alison.

He says they've been to all the pubs in Glastonbury, including the one she worked in, and now they're extending their inquiries.'

'She's never set foot in here.'

'That's what we told 'un.'

'He's wasting his time, then,' said Alison. She returned to the bar counter and continued to watch with disfavour the detective go from table to table.

Finally, he walked across to her. His blue eyes assessed her keenly. The voice had a note of Bristol in it, that soft, unhurried way with words which can be so disarming. 'Detective Sergeant Mayhew, Somerset and Avon CID. You don't mind if I ask you a couple of questions, do you, my dear?'

'What about?'

'I'm sure you know by now,' he said, bringing colour to her cheeks. 'I watched you go to the table under the window and ask the lads what I was up to. Fair enough. You have a job to do. I could be dealing in drugs for all you know. But I'm not, am I? What's your name, love?'

She told him, adding, 'That dead girl has never been in here to my knowledge.'

'Maybe her killer has, though.'

Shocked by the suggestion, Alison retained enough of her composure to say, 'We've no way of knowing.'

'I don't expect you to know, miss. How could you?' He took a leisurely glance around the room. 'But you want to be on your guard.' While Alison tried to look unimpressed, the sergeant went on, 'It was a barmaid who was murdered. We've questioned a number of local men she knew, and they seem to be in the clear. The chances are that he isn't a Glastonbury man. More likely he's the sort of fellow who comes into the pub once or twice and chats up the pretty girl who serves him. You've met a few of them, I dare say?'

'Hundreds.'

'A certain amount of charm, good looks, gift of the gab. Pushing their luck, trying for a date?'

'Some do.'

'Anyone lately?'

She shook her head. Strictly speaking, Tony fitted the profile, but she excluded him. A man too timid to come in for a cup of coffee at the end of an evening was hardly likely to strangle you. 'No one I can recall. What makes you think he'd come to Bridgwater?'

'He wouldn't want to show his face in Glastonbury, would he?'

'I suppose not.'

'Could be Burnham he tries next, or Langport. Burnham and Langport aren't my patch. Bridgwater is, and that's why I'm here, giving you advice.'

Alison said nothing. Let him give his damned advice. She didn't have to thank him for it.

He asked. 'Are there any other girls employed here?'

'Two others help at the weekends. Sally and Karen. It's lads, apart from them.'

'I may look in again, then, Miss Harker, but you'll do me a favour and pass on my advice, won't you?'

After he had gone, business at the bar was brisk and the level of noise rapidly returned to normal. Alison was too busy serving to give any more thought to the murdered woman until near closing time, when she went to Matt's table to collect empties.

Matt grasped her by the wrist. He had a powerful grip. 'I hope you told the copper about your fancy man, him you spent last Saturday night with. Seems to me, he's got to be a suspect, going out with barmaids.'

'Don't be ridiculous, Matt.'

'Ridiculous, is it? I'd have said he's just the sort of bloke they're after, the kind that moves from town to town looking for a woman foolish enough to go out with him.'

'Let go of my arm.'

'We all know he's got wheels. With that great car of his, he could have driven the poor lass from Glastonbury out to Meare Green and strangled her. I'd say you have a duty to mention him to the police – if you haven't already.'

'I bet she hasn't,' said John Colwell.

'Don't you have any brains in your head?' said Alison, wrenching away her arm, which had become quite numb where Matt had gripped it. 'Tony's car is driven by a chauffeur. If he wanted to murder anyone – which I'm sure he doesn't – do you think he'd have the chauffeur drive them to the spot and wait in the car while he did it? What's the chauffeur going to think when he comes out of the withy-bed without the girl? Oh, get with it.'

'Happen he gives the chauffeur an evening off,' said Matt.

'When he does, he uses a taxi.'

'Who told you that?'

'He did.'

'He would, wouldn't he?'

She rubbed her arm. It was turning red. She wouldn't be surprised to find a bruise there. 'You're so puerile, you lot. As a matter of fact, Matt, if I wanted to report anyone to the police, it ought to be you. See this mark coming up? If they're looking for someone violent to women, I can give them a name.'

'They'd laugh at you,' he told her.

'And I could tell them you have a rusty old Cortina you drive around in.'

John Colwell grinned. 'He does, and all.'

Alison had neatly turned the fire on Matt. He could squirm for a change. 'Talk about suspects. What's to stop you from driving over to Glastonbury and picking up some unfortunate girl and killing her?'

Matt tried to laugh it off. 'Little old me, the Meare Green strangler?'

'Killing's your job, isn't it?'

His friend Colwell grinned. 'She's got you there. You've got to admit she's got you there, Matt.'

The seed of anxiety had been sown, not about Matt, whom she'd known all her life almost, and not about Tony either. The worry was over her personal position. She could get into trouble for failing to mention Tony to the police. He fitted the profile Detective Sergeant Mayhew had given her – not a local man, but with charm, good looks and the gift of the gab, the sort who visits the pub only once or twice and gets friendly with the barmaid. She knew Tony was harmless. Well, she felt certain he was harmless, which was almost the same. A guy who passed up the chance to make love after buying her expensive meals was hardly likely to strip the clothes off her and strangle her.

Unfortunately, Matt or his cronies were liable to make mischief and tell the detective about Tony's visits to the pub and his evenings out with her. She knew that crowd and their so-called sense of humour. They would think it hilarious to embarrass her, forcing her to answer questions from the police about her dates with Tony. For Matt, who was jealous, it would be a kind of revenge.

Sergeant Mayhew had said he would probably be back at the weekend to talk to the other barmaids. Alison decided it was in her interest to be on duty on Saturday after all, in case anything was said. If she handled this right, she could get to Sergeant Mayhew before Matt did. She and the other girls could monopolize him.

She spoke to the manager next day and fixed it. She would take Thursday off and come into work on Saturday. Then she called Tony on his mobile and said unfortunately she couldn't go out with him on Saturday as she'd been compelled to change her shift. He was relaxed about it and good enough to suggest they met the following week.

Thursday gave an opportunity of doing some detective work of her own. She had thought of a way of finding out more about Tony's recent past. In brilliant morning sunshine that brought extraordinary clarity to the scene she cycled six miles though the lanes, past fields where sheep and cattle grazed and the wild iris, kingcup and sweet gale abounded. At the edge of the lane baby rabbits crouched and butterflies swooped up. Her destination was Stockland Bristol, the restaurant she and Tony had visited the previous Saturday.

The woman owner remembered her, of course, as the customer who had showered in her bathroom. 'Did you leave something behind, my dear?'

'No. It's just ...' Alison hesitated, uncertain how to phrase this. 'The gentleman I was with – Tony – Mr Pawson – he's a regular customer of yours, I gather.'

'I wouldn't say regular. Occasional describes it better. We're always glad to see him, though. Is anything wrong?'

'Oh, no. Well, to tell you the truth, I've become rather attached to him.'

'I'm pleased for you, my dear. He's a charming gentleman.'

She fingered the ends of her hair. 'I don't know how to ask this. It's a terrible cheek. I thought, being a woman, you might understand.'

'What on earth is the matter, my dear?'

Alison blinked hard, and succeeded in getting a tear to roll down her cheek. 'I keep thinking about the times he came here before. Is there anyone else – I mean is there another woman – he brought here recently, say in the past six weeks?'

Eyebrows raised, the woman said, 'It wouldn't be very discreet of me to say so, would it? We owe our patrons some confidentiality over such matters.'

Alison's hopes plummeted.

'However,' the woman went on, 'since he has only ever brought gentlemen before who were obviously businessmen, I can set your mind at rest without seriously breaking any confidence. Is that what you wanted to know?'

Alison sang as she pedalled home through the lanes.

Detective Sergeant Mayhew's second appearance in the Jellied Eel couldn't have been more convenient for Alison. He came in at about six on Saturday evening, well before Matt usually arrived. John Colwell was already there, but he didn't matter because he wasn't the sort to start a conversation. He wouldn't make trouble.

Just to be certain, Alison came from behind the bar to greet the policeman and escort him across the room to meet the other barmaids. He made his pious little speech about the wisdom of rejecting invitations from customers they didn't know.

Karen, blonde and with more brass than a cathedral, was moved to say, 'Why?'

'Why what?'

'Why should we be careful? Only one girl is dead, and she was in Glastonbury.'

Sergeant Mayhew shook his head slowly at Karen's naivety. 'This isn't your run-of-the-mill murder. Men who kill girls they go out with can easily get a liking for it. And if they do, it's a pound to a penny they move on to another town.'

'What is he – some kind of sex maniac?'

'I can't answer that, miss.'

'The Glastonbury girl was stripped and raped, wasn't she?'

He pondered the matter. 'Difficult to tell. She wasn't wearing anything, it's true. But the body had been lying there some time in hot weather when it was found. Even the best pathologist can't tell much from a decomposing corpse.'

Karen screwed up her face at the thought, and Sally steered the conversation back to the living end of the investigation. 'I expect you've got the names of all the local weirdos and rapists. I hope they all get questioned.'

'That's been done, miss. The trouble with this case is that we don't know which day the girl was murdered so it's no use asking people like that where they were at a particular time.'

'How will you find him, then?'

Karen said cuttingly, 'The way they always find them. Through a tip-off.'

The sergeant didn't seem put out by the comment. 'Young ladies like yourselves can certainly help. Be alert. Get on the phone to us if anyone you don't know tries to ask you out.'

'Will you be calling at all the pubs in Bridgwater?' Sally asked.

'That's a question I'm not at liberty to answer, miss.'

Karen quickly followed up, 'We've been picked out. Why?'

'I just made myself clear, miss. There's nothing I can add. Just be on your guard – here, and especially on your way home.'

Alison decided this was the cue to usher him out. 'Would you like a drink before you go?' She knew he was likely to refuse. To her profound relief, he looked at his watch and agreed he ought to be on his way.

'I can tell you why this pub is being targeted,' said Karen after the sergeant had left, her eyes as wide as beermats. 'One of those perverts on their list has been seen drinking here. They can't arrest him without proof.'

'Keep your voice down, Karen. You'll upset the customers.'

'Sod the customers,' said Karen. 'We're the ones at risk.'

For all her bluster, Karen was only a relief barmaid. When Alison told her firmly to drop the subject, she obeyed. For more than an hour the public bar returned to normal. Then Matt came in and joined John Colwell and the rest of their crowd. When Alison next looked across, Karen was at their table in earnest conversation, undoubtedly passing on her version of what Sergeant Mayhew suspected.

Later, in a quiet moment behind the bar, Alison told Karen, 'If you say one more word about that murder, I'm going to report you for upsetting the customers.'

'Upsetting that lot? You must be joking.'

But the damage was done. Matt came over to order another round and leered at Alison. 'Police were in again, I hear, still looking for the barmaid strangler. They'm watching some pervert, that's for sure. Must be frustrating for 'em, knowing the bastard who did it and not being able to nail him. People have a public duty to report things, I say.'

She busied herself with the order, trying to ignore him. In topping up the first of the five beer glasses, she spilt some.

'Losing your touch?' said Matt.

She said nothing.

'Don't suppose you told 'un about your evening out with the peat millionaire.'

She stood the fifth of the glasses on the counter and told him the price.

He held out a ten-pound note. 'You know the old saying? "Gold dust blinds all eyes."'

She said through her teeth, 'Get lost, Matt.'

'Think about that.'

'One more word, Matt, and I'll spit in your glass, I swear I will.'

He grinned. 'Go ahead. But I'll have my change first, if you don't mind, not being a millionaire myself.'

She turned to the till and took out her anger on the keys. Then she slammed his money on the counter, avoiding his open hand, and went to the next customer.

Matt's words stayed with her. She went to bed with her thoughts too turbulent for sleep. She hated admitting it to herself, but there was some truth in what he had said. Tony's money was an attraction. Her romantic notions had focused on the life he could so easily provide for her. Persuaded that he was generous and inoffensive, tall and good-looking, she could grow to love him, she had told herself. He seemed attracted to her, otherwise why would he have invited her out? She had these looks that turned men's heads, not always men she wanted, so she was fortunate when it happened to be someone she could kiss without flinching. More than that, she had yet to discover. But it was the high life that beckoned.

I feel safe with him, she reasoned. He's a pussy-cat to be with. If I had the slightest doubt of his conduct, I'd talk to the police. Is that a delusion? After all, when I go out with him I'm backing my own judgement with my life.

About four in the morning, aroused from a short, disturbing dream, she needed a cigarette. She reached for her handbag and felt inside for the pack she knew was there. She didn't often smoke these days. Delving deep into the bag, she withdrew the pack and with it came a paper tissue, neatly folded, unlike the others she stuffed into the bag. Remembering where she had got this one, she switched on the light, opened out the tissue and spread it in front of her. The lipstick print looked unusually vivid, and in her heightened state she felt that those slightly parted lips were about to say something to her. She folded it quickly and returned it to the bag.

When she woke it was almost ten. Sunday. She was not on duty until twelve. She shuffled into her small kitchen and switched on the kettle and the radio and started performing those automatic actions which would shortly provide her with the coffee she needed to clear her brain.

The radio was tuned to the local station and the newsreader was going on about some incident in the Iron Age village reconstruction at Westhay, near Glastonbury. Alison continued to potter about without paying much attention. He was saying, '... was found in the largest of the roundhouses by one of the staff when he came on duty this morning. The woman has not yet been identified. A press statement is expected from the police later this morning. Last month the body of Emma Charles, aged seventeen, from Glastonbury, was found at Meare Green, some twelve miles away. No one has been arrested for the crime.'

Roused from her stupor, she reached for the volume switch. Too late. They were talking about the weather. She stood by the radio clutching the front of her nightdress in frustration.

This had to be another victim. They wouldn't have mentioned the first girl unless there were similarities. Sergeant Mayhew's warnings about a possible serial killer were justified.

Alison knew the Iron Age village from being taken there as a schoolgirl. She had squatted with her classmates inside one of the reconstructed dome-shaped huts of wattle and daub, smelling the peat fire that smouldered in the centre, not really listening to their teacher twittering on about the people who had lived on the moors oodles of years ago in huts like that. The history lesson had made less impression than the cosy atmosphere in the building itself. The snug interior had appealed. She had imagined herself sleeping there contentedly under thick furs, her feet warmed by the fire. In no way could she picture it as a murder scene.

The next bulletin would be on the half-hour. She drank her coffee, showered and dressed.

Part of the main statement at the press conference was broadcast live at ten-thirty. 'The Peat Moor Visitor Centre, where the victim was found, has been closed to visitors while the scene is examined by forensic experts. The dead woman, who is believed to be in her early twenties, was white, with dark, shoulder-length hair, slimly built and about five feet six in height. She was unclothed. Her clothes were found beside the body inside the reconstruction of a prehistoric Iron Age hut. She appears to have been strangled.

'We appeal to anyone who saw a woman of this description, wearing a black sleeveless dress with shoulder-straps, black stole and black shoes with silver buckles, in the area yesterday evening, either alone or in company, to get in touch with Glastonbury Police. We also wish to hear from anyone who knows of a woman of this description who did not return home last night.'

No reference this time to a possible connection with Emma Charles's death.

Possibly the police were more cautious than the radio station. But if strangulation was the cause of death and the victim was unclothed, the chances were high that Emma's killer had committed a second murder.

By lunchtime, when Alison came into work, still shaky with the news, the pub was buzzing and there was a rumour that a barmaid at the King's Arms in Langport was missing from home.

Another barmaid in another town. Just as Sergeant Mayhew had warned.

On the one o'clock television news the story was confirmed. An unmarried woman of twenty-two called Angie Singleton had been identified. Saturday was her day off. She was last seen leaving her parents' house at six-thirty that evening. They had assumed she was meeting two of her girlfriends at the pub where she worked and going on to a disco in Glastonbury.

'My God,' said Karen to the pub in general. 'I'm chucking up this job. He's done Glastonbury and Langport. He's got to come to Bridgwater next.'

'Don't panic, love,' one of the older men called across. 'They'll catch the bloke this time. That poor lass who was found over at Meare Green had been dead three weeks. This one is fresh. They pick up all kinds of clues at the scene of a murder. By now they know exactly who they're looking for. They'll have the colour of his hair, the shoes he wears, the make of his car and the size of his John Thomas, I wouldn't be surprised.'

'You watch too much television,' Karen said with scorn. 'Real cases aren't solved that easily. How do you think serial killers manage to do in seven or eight women without getting pulled in?'

Alison kept out of the argument. She, too, was frightened. In truth, she was also relieved that she wasn't the focus of attention she had expected to be.

But later in the day the spotlight turned on her again. A man she had never seen before came into the bar and asked for her by name. He spoke first to Karen, whose silly reaction was to give Alison a boggle-eyed look that meant this could easily be the strangler. The stranger was in his thirties, in a leather jacket, red T-shirt and jeans. His dark eyes assessed Alison with alarming intensity.

He approached, leaned over the bar, beckoned to her to come closer and said in a tone nobody else could possibly overhear, 'I'm DI Briggs, Glastonbury Police. I have some questions. Would you step outside to my car for a few minutes?'

She was about to say, How do I know? Then she realized she was looking at a police ID card masked from the rest of the room by his jacket. She asked Karen to take care of things for a few minutes.

In the car, he came quickly to the point. 'This man you've been going out with. Tony Pawson. You know who I mean?'

Her skin prickled. She was in trouble now, and so was Tony.

'How did you meet him?'

'He's a customer.'

'A regular?'

'I wouldn't call him a regular, no.'

'Chatted you up and made a date, did he?'

'Something like that.'

'When did this start?'

'About three weeks ago. We've only been out three times altogether.'

'Where did he take you?'

'Twice for a meal. And once to a film.' Her voice trailed off revealingly. Until this moment it had not occurred to her that Tony's choice of film was going to interest the police.

'Where?'

'The film? Here in Bridgwater.'

'The meals.'

She was mightily relieved to pass over the film and discuss the meals. 'The first was just up the road, at the Admiral Blake. And he also took me to the Levels Restaurant at Stockland Bristol.'

He asked for dates and times. She told him each outing had been on a Saturday, her day off.

'Have you slept with him?' Responding to the look he got from Alison, he added, 'I wouldn't ask unless—'

'No,' she cut in. 'I haven't.'

'When I say "slept"—'

'You can put down "no". We had a few evenings out together, that's all. Ask his driver if you don't believe me.'

'The driver came too?'

'He waited in the car. If anything happened, he would know. His name is Hugh, and he drives Tony everywhere.'

'You're saying Pawson doesn't drive? Is he banned?'

'I've no idea. I can only tell you what he said to me. Sometimes he uses a taxi.'

He was frowning. 'Let's have this totally clear. On three dates with Pawson, there was no sex.'

'I've said so.'

'It wasn't suggested even?'

'I don't know why you're pursuing this. I felt perfectly safe with him.'

'Maybe the others also did.' He shook his head, chiding himself. 'Disregard that. I'm thinking aloud.'

She felt her skin prickle. 'Those girls were raped. It said in the paper they were raped.'

DI Briggs hesitated. 'If I tell you something confidential, can I trust you?'

She shrugged, guessing that he wasn't doing her a favour. Why tell her anything in confidence unless it was to undermine her? 'I suppose so.'

'In a case like this, we don't release all the details. Some things are known only to the killer and ourselves. Then, you see, we can tell if we've got the right bloke. The signs are that there was sex in both these cases, but it wasn't forced. It was consensual. Do you follow me?'

She stared at him in disbelief. 'You mean they let him make love to them?'

'And then he killed them. Were you with Tony Pawson yesterday?'

She shook her head.

'Why not? It was your day off.'

'I changed my day. I took Thursday instead.'

'Did you go out with him Thursday?'

'No. I expect he was at work.' She didn't volunteer the fact that she had spent Thursday checking on Tony's previous visits to the restaurant at Stockland Bristol.

'Any reason why you changed your day off? Was he due to go out with you last night?'

'Those are two different questions.'

'Answer the first one, then.'

'I changed over because Sergeant Mayhew said he was coming back to the pub at the weekend. Some stupid rumours were being put about and I didn't want people discussing me behind my back.'

'Rumours about you and Tony Pawson?'

'Yes, and there was no foundation for them. I've told you the truth about my evenings with Tony.'

'But you didn't tell Sergeant Mayhew.'

'He didn't know anything about them.'

'So you didn't say anything? A police officer was asking about strangers coming in and chatting you up, inviting you out, and you didn't say anything?'

Her nervousness was being supplanted by annoyance. 'Listen, Tony is nice to me. He treats me decently. Your sergeant was here on a *murder* inquiry. Do you seriously expect me to give you his name as a suspect?'

He started to say, 'If you had ...' Then he stopped and fitted the phrase into another question. 'If you hadn't been working yesterday, would you have gone out with Pawson?'

'Probably.' As she realized what he was suggesting, she felt her fingernails pressing deep into her thighs.

'These rumours. Who exactly was putting them about?'

'Some fellows in the pub.'

He insisted on more than that. She was forced to admit under more questioning that she had been seriously involved with Matt at one time. Matt obviously interested him. He knew about the old Cortina he drove and his work as a slaughterer. This brought the questioning to an end, but the inspector hadn't finished with her. He wanted her to return with him to the pub and point out Matt.

After DI Briggs had finished questioning him and left, Matt behaved like the star witness meeting the press, holding forth to the entire pub about Tony, referring to him as 'our barmaid's fancy man' and insisting that he would be arrested before the day was out for the murders of the two women.

That evening Alison finished work at six and walked in steady rain through the streets of Bridgwater, longing for a few quiet hours at home, free of the tensions in the pub. She was thinking she would not stay in the job much longer.

The sight of Tony's Mercedes outside the house where she lived made her say out loud, 'Oh, God!' She reached for a railing for support. Her first impulse was to turn and walk away. But the car door opened and Tony actually ran towards her, opening one of those huge golf umbrellas. 'You're drenched. Come under this, for pity's sake.'

Controlling herself, she told him she was almost home and didn't care about getting wet, making it as plain as she could that their friendship was at an end. With no chance of being invited in, he asked if she would step into the car for a moment because there was something he wanted to tell her.

Alison couldn't face explanations. She changed tack completely and used the excuse that she was wet through. She asked him to let go of her arm.

He said, 'You believe I killed those women, don't you? I've had two long interviews with the police. Do you think I'd be at liberty now if they knew I was a murderer?'

She said truthfully, 'I can't believe you killed anyone.'

'You're afraid of me. I can see it in your eyes.'

'Tony, all I am is tired. I've had a hard time lately. I just want to get home.'

His voice rose at least an octave. 'That's why I want to talk to you. I know you've been bothered by the police. I don't blame you if it turns you right off me. I want the chance to say sorry.'

'Consider it done. I'm tired and wet through.' She started walking away and he stepped alongside her, turning to face her, appealing to her with those soulful brown eyes.

'Tomorrow, then?'

She said, 'No. It's over, whatever it amounted to. Let's leave it like that.' She was at her front gate.

In an odd, troubled voice which she found chilling he said, 'Can't you understand? I'm not willing to leave it like that.'

Frightened now, she ran up the path to the front door, let herself in and slammed it.

Later, she plucked up courage to look out of the window and was relieved to see that the car had gone.

The murder of Angie Singleton, the Langport barmaid, had happened on Saturday night when Alison would have gone out with Tony if she had not changed her plans. He had been free that evening. The more she thought over what she had learned, the more uneasy she felt. These murdered women had consented to sex so they must have fancied the man who eventually put his hands around their throats.

Suppose it was Tony. Just like her, they could have been attracted by his money, allowed themselves to be driven out into the country, probably treated to a meal somewhere and gone with him afterwards. The difficulty she had with this was in understanding what turned him from the gentle, diffident man she knew into a strangler. Did sex transform him? Was it something deep in his psyche that made him hate the women he went with? Maybe his reluctance for sex came from a recognition that he couldn't control his violence. By not insisting on a physical relationship, had she saved her own life?

That same evening she phoned the Glastonbury police. DI Briggs and Sergeant Mayhew were with her inside the hour. She handed them the paper tissue with the lipstick imprint and explained where it had come from.

'It's been on my conscience. If Tony really is a suspect, it's just possible that this is the mouth-print of the first girl, Emma Charles. I read in the papers that her bag was found beside her. I suppose you can check whether she had a lipstick similar to this.'

DI Briggs agreed with an air of resignation that forensic science was equal to the task. 'We could have done with this the first time you were questioned. This will take at least another week to check. The lab runs all kinds of tests.'

'It's still a long shot,' Alison pointed out.

'Let us be the judges of that,' he said, leaving her with the clear impression that he knew a lot more about Tony's involvement than he was willing to admit. 'Meanwhile, if you value your life, have nothing to do with this man. If he pesters you, call us straight away.'

Ten days went by and there was no arrest. In the Jellied Eel, Matt was increasingly critical of the police. 'They know who did it. We all know who did it. So why don't the buggers pull him in? If they don't act soon, some other woman is going to get stiffed.'

Colwell, quick to fuel Matt's complaints against the police, said, ''Tis evidence they lack. These days they want a watertight case, or the Prosecution Service isn't interested. I was talking to a copper not so long ago and he told me there are murderers and child molesters known to the police, no question, and they can't touch them. They just don't have the evidence.'

'I gave them evidence enough,' said Matt.

'All you gave they is hearsay and rumours,' chipped in one old man who was weary of all the bluster. 'You don't know nothing of what happened down Meare Green or Westhay.'

Matt's credibility was in question and he was loud in his defence of it, hammering the table with his fist. 'I don't know nothing, eh? Why do you think we've had the police call here three times, then, questioning a certain party about the company she keeps?'

'They questioned thee, come to that,' the old man pointed out, and got a laugh for it.

'Took a statement from I,' said Matt, reddening suddenly. 'That's different. There's no suspicion attached to me.'

'So you tell us.'

'I had information, didn't I? Spoke to the driver of that there Mercedes that sat outside on certain occasions when we couldn't get a decent service at the bar. And why couldn't we get served? Because the staff was otherwise occupied, flirting with a fat cat, as she believed. Fat cat be buggered. She were flirting with a bloody tiger.'

Alison heard this in silence and pretended not to listen, knowing it would only encourage Matt if she got involved. If only to put a stop to the innuendo, she longed for an early arrest.

'So what did he tell 'ee, that driver?' Colwell asked Matt.

'Told me his boss used to drink in Glastonbury until a few weeks ago.'

'Glastonbury?' Colwell was impressed.

'Then he switched to here. He likes this pub.'

'The beer?'

'The decor, he reckons.' Matt's eyes swivelled towards Alison and a huge laugh went up from the table.

'Doesn't mean he strangles barmaids,' said the old man, 'else why is young Alison still with us?'

'I warned her in time, didn't I?' said Matt. 'Probably saved her life by telling her what she were getting into.'

'He hasn't been back since the police were here,' said Colwell, as if that confirmed Tony's guilt.

'Made his getaway, I reckon,' said Matt. 'One of them South American countries that don't do the extra—'

'Extradition.' Colwell came to his rescue. 'With his money he can afford to live down in Brazil for the rest of his life.'

'In that case, we can all relax,' the old man said. 'There won't be no more stranglings on Sedgemoor.'

Alison knew how mistaken they were. Tony had not left Sedgemoor. In the past week he had tried to phone her at least a dozen times. Anticipating this, she was not answering calls, but she was certain it was Tony because she checked each time with the computer voice that gives the last caller's number. She didn't tell the police. For one thing, she wasn't truly scared of Tony, and for another she now felt ashamed of handing the lipstick stain to DI Briggs. If it turned out to have no connection with the case, she was going to despise herself. She just wished Tony would give up phoning. Her only genuine fear was that he would turn up at the pub. If he ever did, Matt and the others were liable to lynch him – or whatever passed for a lynching on Sedgemoor.

Whenever Matt came in, the conversation turned to the stranglings. Lately the slurs and reproaches had become more dangerous. No longer were they speculating when an arrest would be made. The talk was now of a police force incapable of acting because the legal system was weighted in favour of the criminal.

'They're bloody impotent,' Matt told his cohorts. 'They dare not make an arrest in case it doesn't stick. They know full well who did it, and they can't touch him. He's laughing at them.'

'Wouldn't do much good if they nicked him,' said Colwell. 'Once upon a time a man like that would have been topped. The worst he'll get is life, and that's no time at all these days. He'll be out in five or six years to start all over again, strangling women. A devil like that wants topping.'

'He won't get no life sentence,' said Matt. 'They'll say he isn't right in the head. He'll see a bloody head-doctor and be out inside a year. Rehabilitation, they call it.'

'Rehabilitation, my arse,' said Colwell. 'He wants putting down like a mad dog.'

'Who's going to do it, though?' one of them asked. 'Not I.'

Silence descended like the last edge of the sun.

Colwell started up again, letting the words come slowly, as if he had already calculated their effect. 'I could tell you a way. They dealt with a sex pest when I were a lad living up Burnham way, on the estuary. He was a right menace to all the women. Can't recall his name now, but I know the police couldn't do nothing about him. He were soft in the head or something. Anywise, the men took care of him. One night he disappeared off the face of the earth.'

'What happened to him?' Matt asked.

'He were never seen again.'

'Come off it, John. You just said you could tell us about it.'

'And so I did.' Colwell seemed to savour the attention he was getting. 'He were given a ride on a mud horse.'

'What's that?'

'Come closer. I'll tell thee.'

The rest was delivered in a voice pitched deliberately low. All Alison heard were some laughs at the end that made her flesh creep.

'When you think on it,' Colwell finished up in his normal voice, 'it's foolproof.'

'If it worked once,' said Matt, 'it could work again. Save the police a heap of work, wouldn't it?'

Alison seriously thought of speaking to Tony if he phoned again, warning him not to set foot in Bridgwater or anywhere near it. She had no idea what a ride on a mud horse meant, except that it was a death sentence.

The next day, Saturday, Tony didn't phone at all. Alison hoped he had seen sense at last and given up.

This was her day off. She spent it quietly, watching a movie on TV for most of the afternoon, the sort she liked, with pirates and gorgeous women in crinolines and nothing more violent than the baddies being poked with swords and falling into the sea. Later, she went out for some shopping. Among other things, she picked up a copy of the *Bridgwater Mercury*. Seeing the headline, she felt pole-axed. MERCEDES CLUE IN BARMAID STRANGLINGS.

The police had now established that a black Mercedes had been seen parked by the entrance to a field at Meare Green one evening in the week Emma Charles was thought to have been murdered. A similar vehicle had been seen in the car park at the Peat Moor Visitor Centre on the Saturday night Angie Singleton was killed there. The police national computer had been used to check on the owners of all Mercedes registered in Somerset.

Until this moment she had not been willing to believe Tony was the strangler. How could she have been so stupid, going out three times with a man like that, and actually inviting him to spend the night with her?

She needed a brandy, or something, just to stop this shaking. The Jellied Eel was only a short walk up the street. She stuffed the newspaper in with the other shopping and made her way there, moaning to herself like a demented person.

The bar was empty except for three old men playing dominoes. Karen was on duty, looking bored. She said, 'You look terrible, darling. What's up?'

Alison produced the newspaper. 'Haven't you seen this?'

'Of course I have. First thing this morning.'

'I only just saw it. God, I need a brandy.'

Karen reached for a glass and pressed it to the brandy dispenser. 'Surely you knew he was odd?'

'He wasn't odd with me.'

'You're bloody lucky, then.'

'I'll drink to that.' Alison shuddered, took a sip, and felt better as her throat warmed.

'Why do you reckon you were spared, then?' Karen asked.

The answer came candidly, with no artifice. 'I don't know. He never threatened me, never tried anything heavy. There wasn't a hint of it. He was a slow starter, if you know what I mean.' She added in the same honest vein, 'The police told me something I suppose I can tell you now. It wasn't rape. They let him do it to them.'

'Go on,' said Karen in disbelief.

'So I wonder if they were killed because they hustled too much. You know?'

'Forced the pace?'

'Yes. And if he wasn't much good at it, lacking confidence or something, maybe he lost control and strangled them.'

Karen grimaced as she visualized the scene. She drew in a sharp breath. 'Nasty.'

'As you say, I had a lucky escape.'

'You don't know how lucky.'

'What do you mean?'

'Only that he was in here asking for you this afternoon.'

Alison wondered if she had heard right. 'What? Haven't they picked him up? I thought he was under arrest.'

Karen shook her head. 'But it's all right. He's no danger to you now, love.' She

165

glanced across at the domino-players and lowered her voice. 'Matt and some of the lads were here. They grabbed the bastard.'

'Oh, no!'

'What's the problem? He's guilty as hell. They took him off in Matt's car. He'll be riding a mud horse by now.'

'Doing *what?*'

'You must have seen them in Bridgwater Bay – those things the fishermen use to cross the mud. Like something between a surfboard and a sledge?'

Alison knew at once. Simply hadn't linked the name with the contraption. The mud horses were used at low tide to slide over the most treacherous stretches of the flats, where a man would swiftly sink into the ooze if he tried to stand upright. The fisherman would lean on the superstructure, letting it bear his weight while he propelled it with his feet. And they had put Tony on one of these?

The grotesque thing reared up in her mind.

'I'm going to call the police.'

Karen shrilled in alarm, 'You can't do that. You'll get them all arrested.'

'It's vile.' She ran across to the public phone.

'Don't be so bloody dense.' Karen pushed up the hinged flap on the bar and dashed after her. The domino party suspended play and watched in awe.

Alison had the phone in her hand and was dialling the emergency number. 'Keep away from me, Karen.'

Karen made a grab for the phone and felt the force of Alison's foot against her belly. The kick would not have disgraced a karate expert. Karen was thrust backwards, tipped off balance and slid across the wood floor.

Alison made her call. It took some explaining, but she conveyed the urgency of the matter.

After a short interval filled with foul language from Karen, who was too winded to fight, a police car arrived outside, with siren wailing. A constable in uniform came in and asked for Alison.

Inspector Briggs was waiting in the back seat of the car. Alison got in beside him and it moved off fast. He had been at a meeting at Bridgwater police station when the emergency call came in, he explained. A response car was already on its way to Stolford, the village at the west end of the bay where the mud horses operated.

'He'll be dead by now,' said Alison. 'They'll have tipped him into the mud and left him to die. I don't care what he's done. That's no way to treat anybody.'

Briggs weighed what she had said. He glanced at his watch. 'We should be in time.'

'No chance. They've been gone for *hours.*'

'You're forgetting something, miss. If they're planning what you say, they have to wait for low tide, and it isn't due for another half-hour.'

'I hope to God you're right.'

'Still like the man, do you?'

She didn't answer.

Briggs said, 'You heard about the sightings of the car?'

'I saw it in the paper.'

'That isn't all. This morning we had the result of the lab tests on the tissue you handed in, the one with the lipstick mark you found in his car. It's a variety called Love All by Miss Selfridge. Emma Charles was carrying a lipstick of that brand in her bag, just as you expected. It's the proof we needed.'

'Why didn't you arrest him this morning, then?'

'We were just about to nick him. The meeting I mentioned was to finalize the arrest. I'm from Glastonbury, remember. We had to liaise with our colleagues here.'

Liaise with colleagues. She didn't trust herself to speak.

Briggs aired his theories as to a motive. 'You know why you weren't killed like the others? Because it didn't come to sex. That's when he's dangerous. It's all love and roses until he climaxes, and then some kink in his brain turns him lethal. Maybe he's just bad at sex, and knows it, and takes out his resentment on the women. Or it could be a power thing. Whatever the reason, you've been dating Jekyll and Hyde.'

There was a sense of urgency now. Siren blaring across the countryside, the car swallowed the fast road towards Hinkley Point, only marginally cutting its speed after turning right along a minor road. The hedges along the lanes were eight or nine feet high at this northern edge of the moor, making it impossible to see more than a few yards ahead. Alison knew from her cycle ride to Stockland Bristol through lanes very similar that farm traffic used these ways. The driver seemed to have blind faith that any approaching tractor would hear the siren and have time to move aside into a passing point.

But cows were less amenable. Suddenly the way was blocked by the back end of one tractor that would not be making way, for it was herding about sixty Friesians back to the field from the milking sheds. Black and white cows filled the lane, ambling along at a leisurely rate. They could not be moved aside, turned back or hustled.

Betraying no emotion, Briggs ordered the siren and light to be turned off in case they panicked the cows. The patrol car was forced to crawl behind the tractor.

A message came over the radio. The first car had reached Stolford. They had spotted some people out on the mud and were going to investigate.

'If they really mean that, they'll regret it,' said Briggs in his deadpan voice. 'It's suicidal, walking on the flats.'

Five or six minutes were lost before the cows were all off the lane and the farmer eased the tractor up to the gate and waved the car by.

Stolford was less than a mile off, and still there was no view of the coast. Finally they reached a cluster of farm buildings and cottages that had to be it. The pulsing blue light of the first police car was visible ahead on the skyline. They crossed a humpback bridge, moved up the ridge that kept the tide from encroaching, pulled up beside the other police car and got out. Matt's rusty Cortina was standing nearby.

Beyond a thin bank of shingle and scattered rocks, the mudflats opened out, a vast no man's land exposed by the low tide. Somewhere below the grey outline of the Welsh headland, the soft oozy mass met the water of the Bristol Channel. A couple of miles to the left at the western extremity of the bay was the citadel-like structure of Hinkley Point, the nuclear power station, the hum of its turbines carrying to them. Five miles in the other direction was the resort of Burnham-on-Sea.

'I can't see anyone,' said Alison.

'They'll be way out. You want field-glasses.'

The low sun reflecting on the streams and channels dividing the mudflats produced a pattern like lacework across the scene, but by no stretch of the imagination could it be described as anything but desolate. Gulls and wading birds patrolled the margins.

No one was in the second police car. An elderly man with a dog stood beside it.

'Where did the policemen go?' Briggs asked him.

The old man gestured vaguely across the great expanse of mud with his stick. 'They tried, but they had to come back. Then they were off up the coast path like blue-arsed flies.'

'Which way?'

He nodded towards Hinkley.

'Has the tide turned yet?'

'Any time now.'

'Did you see the other men go out?'

The old man nodded. 'They took two of my son's mud horses without so much as a by-your-leave. Serve 'em bloody right if they come to grief, I say.'

Briggs opened the boot of the car and took out a pair of binoculars.

He made an agonizingly slow scan of the shoreline along the limit of the mud. Then he put down the glasses and said to his driver, 'We'll have to cut them off ourselves. They're heading towards Steart.'

'With Tony?' Alison asked.

'Pawson? No. He's still out there.'

Appalled, she cried out, 'Where?'

He pointed. 'You could easily take it for a piece of wreckage, but it looks to me like a man up to his waist in mud.'

'What? Let me look.'

He handed the glasses across and Alison looked through, getting only a blur at first and then, as she worked the focus control, a clear sight of a large seabird, a herring gull that took flight just as she spotted it. A slight move to her left and she was presented with the disturbing image of a man held fast by the mud with little more than his torso above the surface, his arms held high, and waving. No one was near.

'Oh, my God!'

This, then, was Matt's idea of justice, leaving a man stranded in mud that would hold him helpless until the huge tide rushed over him and drowned him.

'We've got to get out there and save him.'

'We can't reach him,' Briggs told her in his staid voice. 'We'd go under ourselves. The best we can do is radio for help, and I'll see to it. But we can nick the idiots who did this to him. You wait here. For Christ's sake, don't do anything stupid. The tide comes in so fast you'd have no chance at all.'

He was in the car and had slammed the door before she could react. It reversed and drove away fast. She turned to the old man and asked, 'Do you have a phone?'

He shook his head. 'What would I want with a phone?'

She turned and looked at the nearest farmhouse and saw the telephone wires leading to it. She wasn't convinced that Briggs wanted Tony to survive; his laid-back manner suggested otherwise. It would be easy for him to delay and say later that he'd been distracted in the chase. She resolved to call the emergency services herself. She dashed down the slope and across the little bridge towards the farmhouse.

Before reaching it, she became aware of a movement to her left and a glimpse of a tall man, smartly dressed, with a black tie and grey suit, standing out of sight against the wall of a barn. She stopped and turned towards him. His face was known to her, yet in her agitated state she couldn't place him until he spoke.

'Were you looking for help, miss?' The voice – quiet, considerate, with just a suggestion of deference, prompted her memory. Of all people, he was Tony's chauffeur, Hugh. It wasn't so remarkable she had failed to recognize him. After all, she knew the back of his head far better than the front.

She blurted out the words, 'Tony is—'

'I know,' he said, as calm in his way as Briggs. 'I was waiting outside the pub when they bundled him into their car and drove off. It's all right. I phoned ten minutes ago from the car. There's a rescue helicopter on its way.'

'Thank God,' she said. 'Oh, Hugh, how could they do this?'

He shook his head. If he knew anything at all about the suspicion Tony was under, he was unlikely to speak of it. So the headshake was in disbelief at the savagery of Matt and his friends. 'I followed their car some way and then lost them in the lanes. When I got here they were halfway across the mud.'

'Where's your car?'

'Out of sight behind the farmhouse.'

'Over there?'

'I'll show you. We can move it closer now.'

He led her around the side of the farmhouse to where the Mercedes stood. He opened the front door and Alison got in. This was the first time she had not been seated in style in the rear seat. Hugh got in beside her and started up.

Under the stress she was in, she put her hand over his arm and squeezed. 'Thank God you're here.'

His pale blue eyes crinkled at the edges in amusement. How is it, she thought, that some men have this capacity to give you confidence?

Instead of turning right, to go over the humpback bridge and up on the ridge beside the police cars, he swung the car towards the road.

'Where are we going?'

'Not far.'

Not understanding, she said, 'We don't want to go away from here. We want to see what's happening.'

He said, 'Relax.'

Relaxing was far from her mind. They headed off along the lane, out of the village and away from the waterfront where everything was happening. The air rushed through the open roof, blasting her ears and tugging her hair back.

She cried out in alarm, 'Hugh, what's going on? I want to be here. I want to get out.'

'Shut up.'

The rebuke came like an electric shock. Alison did go silent, but only because she was so stunned. Even in this emergency he shouldn't have spoken to her like that.

The Mercedes belted between the high hedges. Anything coming towards them would have no chance of stopping in time.

She gripped the safety belt with both hands, trying to understand what was happening, wondering if Hugh had some plan of his own for going to Tony's aid from a different stretch of beach. What else could explain this?

Then they left the road. A sudden swing of the wheel and they were bumping through an open gate into a field. About thirty yards on, out of sight of the lane, he braked.

Alison felt for the door handle. To her total amazement, Hugh leaned right over and pressed down the lock. Then he grabbed her right arm and forced it under the safety belt. He snatched the slack part of the belt and jerked it so tight that she was held rigid against the seat-back. His hand slipped under the collar of her blouse and pressed against her neck, and she understood.

Hugh was the strangler.

He had killed those other women after driving them out to some lonely spot and having sex with them. Suspicion had fallen on Tony because of the car, but it was his chauffeur who was the killer, using the car on days when it wasn't required. The tissue marked with lipstick proved it. Poor Emma Charles must have sat here, in this seat beside Hugh, and placed the used tissue in the glove compartment in front of her.

Now she herself was about to die because she had found him at the scene. He must have been unable to stay away, compelled to watch Tony being dragged across the mud on the mud horse just to be certain that someone else took the rap. No doubt he had fed Matt with lies about Tony's guilt.

His hand was halfway around her throat, choking her. She managed to blurt out the words, 'This won't save you. They know all about you.' Of course they did not, and of course he knew it.

He swung towards her, still with his right hand gripping her neck, manoeuvring himself out of the driver's seat across the divider where the handbrake was. He was trying to get fully over her, to get a better grip on her throat. She felt his knee slide across her thighs. His weight was on her, his hot breath in her face, both hands around her neck. He braced, straightening his arms to bear down on her.

With her left hand – the only one that was free – she clutched at his wrist and tried desperately to break the grip that would asphyxiate her in seconds. Hopeless.

She stared up at him, and saw his teeth bared with the effort. His face was outlined by the blue sky. Some instinct for survival sparked an idea in Alison's brain. She realized that his head was poking through the gap in the roof. Instead of clawing at his hands, she groped upwards, behind him, reaching above the windscreen. Her vision was blurred. The blood supply to her brain had almost ceased.

Her middle finger located a button just below the roof. She pressed it. There was a whirring sound as the electrical control activated the sliding roof. She kept her finger on the button.

Hugh gave a yell, more of fury than pain. His grip on Alison's neck loosened. The roof panel had already closed against his chest, and then, as he ducked, it trapped him even more effectively by closing against his neck. There was no way he could bring his head through the gap.

In the car, his stranglehold loosened. Alison gasped for breath, found the catch of the seat belt and released it. She unlocked the door, squirmed from under Hugh's legs and fell out onto the grass. She didn't stop to see if he had any way of escaping. Sobbing, she stumbled to the gate and up the lane.

At about the same time, an RAF rescue helicopter passed over, heading inland towards Woolavington. The crew estimated that Tony Pawson had been within two or three minutes of death when they snatched him from the rising tide.

*

Two weeks later, Tony took Alison for a meal at the restaurant in Stockland Bristol. They went by taxi.

They had many more meals out before he asked her to marry him. No one could accuse Tony of rushing things. In fact, Matt Magellan and John Colwell were out of prison by then and drinking again at the Jellied Eel, but with one difference. Alison had long since given up her job as barmaid and was spared having to serve them.

She and Tony were married in St Mary's, Bridgwater, the following spring. Hugh the chauffeur was not among the guests. He was a long-term guest elsewhere, with a recommendation that he should remain so for the rest of his life.

LOVE AND
OTHER CRIMES

Michael Malone

Maybe saints don't care about their reputations – though any saints you ever heard of managed to get themselves written up in books – but as for the rest of us, we've all got some notion of who we are that we'd like the world to agree with. With me, it's my brains; I admit I think of myself as smarter than most. Whenever the *Hillston Star* mentions that I'm the youngest police chief our small Piedmont city ever appointed, and that Hillston has the lowest per capita crime rate in the Southeast United States, I take a personal pride in the notice, because my brains get the credit. Conversely, if there's a homicide in Hillston, I take that personally, too, because I think any potential murderers ought to worry so much about me coming after them that their ugly impulses just shrivel away.

Other types of reputation are low on my list, including the one that around here they call social prominence. I don't live in the best part of town, and I don't belong to the Hillston Club, like all the people who do live in the best part of town, and nobody's ever asked me to join. So I was only in the Hillston Club on this particular night because I was curious about why Patty Raiford had invited me to her fifth wedding. She and I weren't what you'd call close. But, then, her wedding turned out not to be exactly on an intimate scale anyhow – more like Haver Stadium for Homecoming, so I didn't take it as a bid to get personal. Besides, she'd sent the invitation to 'Chief Cuthbert Mangum, c/o Hillston Municipal Building, Please Forward,' and my name isn't Cuthbert – it's Cudberth, which my mother possibly mistook for Cuthbert, but, still, anybody who knows me knows I live at River Rise, and even at the Municipal Building everybody just calls me Cuddy.

Patty'd had good luck with the weather. It was a late-summer night, hot and clear with a full North Carolina moon the color of a ripe peach. A moon that looked like it was going to come in through the French doors of the Hillston Club like a balloon God was sending Patty to say congratulations. The moon would have fit right in with the rest of the decorations. It was clear from the size of the flower arrangements that the bride was a party-thrower of robber-baron pro-portions, and willing to treat even folks she didn't know to at least a hundred thousand dollars' worth of bands and booze on the flimsy excuse of her getting married again.

Money was nothing to Patty; she'd been born with plenty and, when that ran out, collected more from various husbands, and spent a considerable portion of it throwing these type of fêtes. People said Hillston'd be a lot duller without Patty Raiford's parties, and probably it would be for them. She was such a favorite with the *Hillston Star* that they referred to her in headlines by her first name only, like she was Elvis or Princess Di. For her wedding announcement they had a big picture of her in a floppy lace hat under the headline, 'PATTY TO TIE KNOT # 5 WITH SEAFOOD KING.'

The knot was tied by the elderly minister at First Presbyterian Church. He was brought out of retirement to officiate at Patty's fifth, and seemed to have some doubts about its permanence, judging from the tone of his homily; since he'd officiated at weddings one through four it was hard to blame him. Maybe it wasn't an accident when he flipped his Bible into the choir stall, startled by the blast of trumpets Patty had hired to strike up some loud Handel as she raced out of the church. She'd had a fleet of busses waiting to take her guests from there to the Hillston Club, which is where about two hundred of us were still celebrating at midnight when – as the *Star* put it the next day – 'the joyful festivities turned to tragedy in one horrible moment.'

I'd strolled through the ballroom looking for a fellow police officer, Justin Savile the Fifth – the most likely of my friends to get invited to this event – but I didn't see him. Not having a date to dance with myself and tired of analyzing the crime rate – all the country club set appeared to think they could politely talk about to a chief of police – I took a bottle of champagne on to the verandah, and out there under Patty's big moon listened to the Jimmy Douglas Orchestra play slow songs to keep people on the dance floor. But there was a problem with the air-conditioning and it was too hot for any guests who hadn't fallen in love that very night to want to sway up against each other to the tune of 'Unforgettable'. Most of them crowded instead around large tables that ringed the walls and kept on drinking, smoking and laughing loudly together.

I heard somebody in the shrubs between the verandah and the pool, and turned to see a man about my age headed up the steps. He was a tall, blond fellow with a tan, who looked like he'd taken off weight too fast, and seemed lost inside his green polo shirt. Just as he stumbled past me with a polite apology, there was a sudden drumroll inside the ballroom. We both moved over to the French doors where a spotlight turned our attention up to Patty. She was leaning over a little balcony that jutted out from the end of the room off the second floor. Across its rail there was a banner that promised in gold letters JOE AND PATTY FOR EVER. Together the blond man and I watched the bride shake a blue lace garter over her head then spin it down at the squad of men in tuxedos waiting below. As they grabbed for the garter, it fell to the floor near a huge ice sculpture. They scrimmaged for it in a violent huddle.

The man in the polo shirt muttered in that soft slur of the wealthy South, 'You'd think it was a basketball in the last five seconds.'

I nodded companionably. 'A national play-off game, too. Victory!' One of the younger males had got hold of the garter; he held it aloft like a scalp, then ran off with it. Patty announced from the balcony that she and Joe were leaving for a few minutes to change for their honeymoon drive to the Carolina coast. The man in the green polo shirt ground his teeth. As he hurried away towards the side of the verandah, a business envelope stuffed in the rear pocket of his khakis fell out.

'Hey, you dropped something,' I called after him.

He picked it up and said, 'Thank you so much.' Then he was gone. If I'd known who he was, I would have stopped him.

The balcony scene with the garter reminded me of the first time I'd met Patty Raiford. A few years ago Justin had dragged me along to 'Patty's divorce party' at her big family home on Catawba Drive. For some reason, no matter who she was married to, everybody always referred to Patty by her maiden name – Raiford. I guess it was less confusing, considering how often her last name changed.

And for some other reason, Patty always went back between husbands to the family house she and her brother had inherited. Her brother still lived there by himself, except when Patty got divorced. She had dubbed this particular divorce party 'Nostalgia Night' – husband number three was on his way to becoming a sentimental memory – and everybody was supposed to dress up as their favorite childhood television show.

She was Cher. Justin came in a Nehru jacket as *The Man from U.N.C.L.E.* I didn't want to come as anybody, so I just wore my summer police chief's uniform and said I was Andy Griffith on *Mayberry, RFD.* Could be that's why folks ran up and asked me to do something when Patty's husband number three arrived at the party with a U-Haul and tried to load into it various pieces of furniture he claimed were his. He was dragging a chair through the door with Patty's brother still sitting in it, yelling for help. I made him put everything back, and Patty got the last laugh by dropping a drawer full of women's underwear down on his head from a second-floor window, shouting – I guess facetiously – that he'd bought them for her, but worn them himself. Turning a black-purple that didn't look good for his blood pressure, he'd stomped off, tearing a strapless bra out of his hair.

Patty's laugh was appealing, I admit, though she didn't look a thing like Cher. So I invited her to dinner, but I got nowhere. She said she was devastated and busy, and next thing I knew she'd married number four. And next thing after that, she'd divorced number four, and got herself engaged to Joe Raulett, the Seafood King, and she'd invited me to her wedding c/o the Police Department.

Number five was a change of pace for Patty. All her previous husbands had pedigree. Famous old Southern families had produced both #1, an All-Star quarterback with a drinking problem, and #2, father of her twin sons, a New Orleans portrait painter of considerable private means – just as well because all his portraits looked like his mother and nobody wanted to buy them. Then #3, the one with the U-Haul, was a millionaire heart surgeon addicted to tennis. He was followed not by dinner dates with me but by #4, Wilson Tedworth, Junior, vice president of the bank his daddy owned.

But #5, Joe Raulett, the Seafood King, was a self-made man. By his own admission, Joe 'came from nothing', but by his boast, he came fast and hard. He now owned a chain of big blue restaurants dotted through the Carolinas, all called Neptune's, and all with the same menu of fish and crustaceans fried 'in 100% pure Georgia peanut oil' – as we were told every night in bright blue television ads.

No doubt that's why at the Hillston Club there were so many mounds of lobster tails and crab claws, and why at the end of the high-ceilinged ballroom, right below the little balcony from which Patty had thrown the garter, there was this statue of Neptune. It stood seven feet tall, carved out of blue ice, in a vat the size of a community hot tub packed with dry ice so it steamed. You could tell it was the Greek god of the sea because he had a spiky ice crown on his head, and in his right hand he raised a big ice trident skyward. A circle of irregular icicles around the base appeared to represent the foaming waves out of which the ocean god was rising buck naked. His private parts had been tastefully minimized by the artist. All night long I overheard drunk guests making cracks about whether or not the groom had personally posed for the thing. Not many of them even knew Joe Raulett. The few relatives from his side of the family were huddled together in one corner, drinking iced tea and worrying about the long drive home.

My wedding invitation had invited me to Patty's 'fifth and final marriage', but maybe she'd made the same rash pledge last time, too, and maybe then the big banner had read PATTY AND WILSON TEDWORTH, JUNIOR, FOR EVER. According to Justin, Patty had always had lots of men in her life, most of them coming to some

177

kind of grief. Even her dad had gotten killed in a car crash, speeding to pick her up from an eighth grade dance.

When she was in college, two boys – a cadet down from West Point and a Deke at Haver University – fought a duel over her. An actual old-fashioned duel with real pistols. They shot each other in the cemetery behind the football stadium on Saturday morning, after discovering at an ΣAE party on Saturday night that Patty was engaged to both of them. The cadet died in the hospital, and the frat boy almost did. The incident made her famous all over the state, and after that it was like men just got in the habit of violence where she was concerned.

Now, long after Patty had gone off to change out of her wedding outfit, the man who'd got hold of the blue lace garter was tearing around wearing it on his head like a laurel wreath, while two rivals snatched at it as he dodged by them. So I guess I ought to be glad she'd said no when I'd asked her out to dinner since it was clear that dating Patty was like sneaking a stack of sirloins past a pack of starving Dobermann pinschers – you didn't want to do it unless you were heavily insured. Course, in what Patty and Justin called 'their circle', suitors could afford the premiums. Their circle circled the best parts of town where I didn't live, and cul-de-saced here on Catawba Drive at the Hillston Club. It was the circle where you golfed all day and partied till you puked all night, and the names of its members were the names you saw on Hillston street signs. They still call themselves 'the young circle' but I think it's time they dropped the label. Not even Patty Raiford could ring up five husbands fast enough to belong in something called 'the young circle'.

But younger, prettier women just faded away in comparison with Patty, and they seemed to know it. When she walked back into the ballroom in her travel outfit, I saw a half dozen men shoot over to her like a floor full of tacks sucked into a magnetic field. She wouldn't dance with them, and they sulked back to watch the Atlanta Braves on a portable TV. Two of the baseball fans' abandoned wives came over to where I was standing by the French doors onto the verandah. They called back to Patty, 'Oh, come look at this moon!' as if they'd never seen a moon before in their lives, or at least never expected to see another one. Or maybe it was just a tactic to get Patty out of the room where their husbands were. They got so overcome by the moon that they gave high-pitched shrieks, ran past me across the verandah and jumped into the club pool in their cocktail dresses.

The shrieks of the swimmers did bring out Bubba Percy, star reporter – according to him – of the *Hillston Star*. Bubba was a big, pretty man with Bambi eyelashes, a pudgy face, and the kind of glossy hair they make TV commercials about. His by-line was the most popular in the state, but he was even more conceited about his looks. Before he saw me, he pulled out a little comb and worked on his hair.

I stepped out of the shadows. 'Bubba, vain as you are, I'm amazed you'd come out here, because those girls have so splashed up the water in that pool you won't be able to see your reflection in it.'

Undisturbed, he gave his cuff links an admiring glance. 'Cuddy, if you were as good-looking as I am, you'd make it a law so every stop sign in Hillston had your picture on it. 'Bout to arrest somebody?'

'No, the bride invited me.'

He was surprised. 'Yeah? Me, too.' Bubba unbuttoned his gold-brocaded vest and fanned himself with the lapels. 'Hot in there,' he informed me. 'That ice dick of Joe's is melting right off his statue. The air-conditioning doesn't kick in soon, the old Seafood King's gonna turn into the Seafood Queen.' He looked over at the women paddling around in the pool. 'Women'll do anything,' he added after a while.

'Just about.'

We watched as a third young lady, Blue Sunderland, reputed to be – so I was told – the best-looking married woman in Hillston, cannon-balled into the deep end with an explosion of water that crashed over her two friends' heads. They came bobbing up to her. All three laughed. Bubba clamped a cigarette in his white teeth and grinned. 'Yep, women'll do anything. Men won't. You ever notice that?'

'Men are boring,' I agreed. 'You covering society news for the *Star* now?'

'Captain Pig, I wouldn't miss one of Patty's weddings for another week in the sack with Hillary Clinton. We go way back.'

'You and the First Lady?'

'Me and Patty.' He rolled the cigarette with his tongue from one side of his mouth to the other, but didn't light it. 'Yeah, Patty gave me a blow job in a hot-air balloon once. Over the state fairgrounds. Everybody thought I was just up there by myself having an epileptic seizure.'

I didn't bother to answer. Bubba was famous for his tales of outlandish and physically risky sexual adventures, which might or might not be true – the one about him and my mother certainly had no basis in fact; my mother never went anywhere but the Baptist Church and the A&P, much less got it on with Bubba Percy, as he had claimed, out on the observation deck of the Empire State Building one New Year's Eve.

I offered him some champagne, and he took the whole bottle. 'You notice I don't bother saying I don't believe you.'

'Believe me. It was real. Me and Patty, hot-air balloon.' He pointed the champagne bottle at the sky in a toast. 'Now look at me, not even married once, and look at her, number five and she's only thirty-eight.'

I agreed. 'There's no denying Patty's predisposed to a faith in connubial bliss that defies her statistical experience.'

He laughed. 'Her poor brother Pascal. He's given her away five times and he keeps getting her back.' Bubba pointed at somebody inside.

It was Patty's brother, coming into the ballroom like he was looking for something he couldn't find – maybe somebody to dance with. He was a stocky man in a black velvet dinner jacket. I said, 'Aren't they supposed to be twins? He sure doesn't have her looks.'

'Yeah. Pascal got the brains and Patty got everything else.' Bubba and I stood watching the party while we drank our champagne.

I asked his opinion. 'You think five's the lucky number? You think it's Joe and Patty for ever like that banner says?'

Bubba interpreted the conventional wisdom: Patty's circle was hoping for the best. That meant they figured she'd be divorced again by Christmas. They couldn't get over her break-up with Wilson Tedworth, Junior, who'd always been called Dink, for reasons Bubba felt free to speculate on. That meant they'd had no hopes for that marriage either. The young circle said Patty'd been truly crazy about Dink but the problem had turned out to be that Dink was just truly crazy, and there'd been 'a few episodes'. That meant he'd tried to kill any man who'd talked to her since the honeymoon.

Bubba said 'the final episode' had happened right here where we were standing.

Tedworth had suddenly swerved off the golf course, raced his electric cart around the pool and onto the verandah, careened through the lunch crowd and crashed into the golf pro who was drinking Bloody Marys with Patty. 'The final episode' ended both the golf pro's career – his hip was broken – and Dink's and Patty's marriage. In court, Dink apologized and got off with a warning from the judge, who happened to be a friend of his father, Tedworth Senior, President of Central Carolina Trust. According to Bubba, Patty's divorce judge didn't like the Tedworth-family-friend judge, so he gave Patty her freedom, Dink's house and a lot of the Tedworth assets at Central Carolina Trust. The consensus of the young circle was that Dink had been a good sport about being told to hand over just about everything he owned to Patty. Indifference to money was a big part of their code.

A year had gone by since then, but the young circle said Wilson Tedworth was still not reconciled to the loss of his wife. And for months they had been enthusiastically predicting trouble at her wedding to Joe Raulett, the Seafood King who'd come from nowhere fast.

Bubba flicked his unlit cigarette into the night as he stared transfixed by the breasts of the wet, pregnant Blue Sunderland whose friends were hauling her out of the pool. The three young women then ran off onto the adjoining golf green, where they stripped down to their bras and panties, and stretched out beside the ninth-hole flag. 'Look at that.' Bubba angled for a better view. 'I'd love to make it with Blue Sunderland, wouldn't you?'

'Bubba. Give it a rest.'

'Aw, lighten up, Porcus Rex. It's just the old Eurocentric sexist rhetoric fighting extinction.' He greedily popped another cigarette in his mouth.

I pointed out, 'You don't even light those things.'

He shook his head, careful not to mess up the wave in his auburn hair. 'Nah, I quit. I want to go national, and North Carolina's about the only place you *can* smoke any more.' He pointed back at the crowd inside.

Between the cigarettes and the dry ice steaming up from the Neptune statue, it did look like Patty was close-dancing with her new husband in a rain forest. The Seafood King was a good-looking man – sort of like Ted Turner with the prematurely gray hair and the Clark Gable mustache – but he was an awful dancer.

Suddenly Bubba gave a sharp whistle, grabbing my arm in melodramatic style and spilling my champagne. 'Step back from the fan,' he warned. 'Tedworth's here.'

'Wilson Tedworth Junior? At Patty's wedding? That's tacky.'

'Damn right. Your pal Justin would have a fit. This is black tie and Dink's in a damn polo shirt!'

Bubba shoved me through the French doors and pointed out Patty's fourth husband over near the Neptune statue. It was the tall blond man who'd come out of the bushes onto the verandah earlier and watched Patty throw the garter with me. Not only was he under-dressed, he was drunk and crying, and hauling at Patty. Patty's brother Pascal was ineffectually trying to pull Tedworth away, and Patty was yelling about why didn't Dink just drive his car through the wall and smash into them, like last time! It was obviously this sort of thing the circle was talking about when they mentioned that Patty and Dink Tedworth had 'episodes'.

The fact that Tedworth was crying – which presumably he hadn't been doing when he ran down the golf pro – made the scene more embarrassing than it would have normally been. Southern men are often drunk and often hauling at people, but they don't cry in public unless their mothers have died or their alma mater's lost a Bowl game. At my side, Bubba gave a disgusted snort. 'Look at that – he's bawling his eyes out!'

Tedworth managed to drag the five people pulling at him halfway across the ballroom before they pinned him to the floor. Rather than leave well enough alone, Patty ran over and told the Jimmy Douglas Orchestra to play 'Can You Feel the Love Tonight?' from *The Lion King*, which must have had some special meaning because Tedworth went nuts and threw a vase of flowers at her, instead hitting the Neptune statue so icicles flew off the waves at its base. A half-dozen men piled on top of him like they were sacking the quarterback, and Patty leaned over them and shouted into their midst with what smacked of sarcasm, '*I can feel the love tonight, Dink. How 'bout you?*'

At this point, the groom, Joe Raulett, rushed into the middle of the scene, but Patty's brother stopped him before he could reach the huddle. Tedworth got loose and took a swing at them. The others piled back on top of him. Bubba and I looked at each other, shrugged, ran inside and pulled the top layers off the drunk man. Hauling him to his feet by his green polo shirt, I warned him, 'That's enough.' He seemed to give some thought to the possibility. 'You okay?' I waved my hand in his face. Weaving, he nodded; he had the glazed look of a dying bull, and jerked his head dully from one cluster of gawking guests to another. His nose was bleeding, and his wiping at it wasn't an improvement.

Patty suddenly appeared beside me and took my hand. 'He's fine,' she assured me. She raised my arm as if I'd just won a boxing match. 'Y'all know Cuddy Mangum, our chief of police? And I didn't even call 911.'

Faces nodded hello. Her husband and brother fought to hold onto Tedworth's arms; all three turned red and grim in the face from the struggle.

Bubba grinned. 'Man, Patty, you still bring it out in them, don't you? Well, that was fun. Now if Dink had just come in on the golf cart...'

Just then Tedworth broke loose, and lunged towards Patty and me. He told Patty he was so sorry, he loved her and he was going to have to hurt her. Then he toppled into me, apologizing with a bizarre pattern of polite pats.

Patty pulled me away from him. 'Come on, Cuddy, let's dance. Pascal, do something about Dink.'

Dink told Raiford not to touch him but Joe Raulett grabbed hold of one arm and then Raiford took the other. The Seafood King urged me to indulge his bride. 'Dance with her, Chief Mangum. We've got it under control here.' He called out to the crowd. 'It's under control. Everybody get on back to having fun.' The groom kept his hand in a hard squeeze on Tedworth's arm as he and his wife's brother fast-walked the drunk away like they all three might be going to foxtrot together as soon as they found an open spot. I had to admire the Seafood King. He was a take-charge kind of guy, and wasn't going to let his new wife's ex-husband ruin his expensive party. I lost them in the crowd.

Bubba picked up two champagne bottles and a plate of jumbo shrimp, and with a kiss blown at Patty headed back outside, no doubt to the women lying on the golf course.

Patty wrapped her arm around me as she steered me nearer the band. 'Where'd Bubba go?' she asked.

'Ran off after three young ladies cavorting in the swimming pool.'

'Oh, them.' She puffed them away with a dismissive breath. 'You gonna dance with me or not?'

As she and her husband both seemed to think it was such a good idea, I figured, Why not? She was a good dancer; a palm's pressure on her back was enough to lead her into a complicated pattern without a falter. And she had a warm, generous hand that felt at ease in mine. Maybe that easiness was the source of Patty's appeal; she was at home with men. After all, she'd been with a man since the womb – her brother Pascal was a twin – and she had given birth to twin boys herself.

As other couples joined us on the floor, and the band segued into another syrupy show tune, I said I was sorry Tedworth had to cause such a scene at her wedding.

'Ummm.' She shrugged as if to add, What else can you expect?

'You know I saw your ex outside a while ago; he didn't act all that drunk. How'd he get so wasted so fast?'

She lifted her shoulders again, slipping off responsibility. 'He doesn't drink,' she said. 'I heard you were a great dancer.'

I guess we weren't going to talk about how her fifth husband was now tossing her fourth husband out of her wedding party. 'Who told you?'

She smiled as we deftly sidestepped a couple loudly counting out the box step as if they'd be marched in front of a firing squad if they messed up. 'Justin Savile.'

'Justin?'

'A dancin' champ, he said.' I gave her a spin and a reverse dip. She laughed. 'He was right.'

'Where is Lieutenant Savile tonight?' I looked around. 'Weren't y'all friends?'

She frowned with a little smile. 'Well, I asked him, but Justin and Dink go way back, so he sent his regrets.'

'Ah.' I nodded. 'Opposed to you divorcing Dink Tedworth?'

'To me marrying Joe.'

'Too bad,' I said. 'I know Justin loves any chance to wear those little patent leather ballet slippers with bows on them.'

She laughed the laugh that had made me want to take her to dinner a few years ago. 'He even has buttons on his trousers instead of zippers.' I wondered how she knew that, but maybe it was common knowledge in the circle. She walked her fingers along the back of my neck. 'Justin said it was some big dance competition you won.'

'It was a Shag contest at the Tucson Lounge.'

'Okay, Cuddy, let's show 'em how to do it.' We'd already had two dances together and I offered to let somebody else cut in, but she pulled me over to the band leader and squeezed his hand. 'Jimmy, honey, play me and the police chief a fast old shag, okay? Like "Kansas City", something like that.'

Jimmy Douglas shook his head in mock despair. 'Patty, how many these honky tunes you gonna make me run tonight?'

Patty gave Douglas a little back rub. 'You just play something fast. You know you love me, Jimmy. I'm your best customer.'

He laughed. 'Well, that's true.'

'But I'm settling down. This is my last wedding.' She crossed her heart with two fingers.

'Then I hope it's a good one.' Douglas smiled and turned back to his band. They took off in a hurry with Little Richard's 'Tutti Frutti', and Patty and I stayed with them. We must have been doing okay, because the other dancers fell back and made a circle around us and clapped when it was over.

'How 'bout another one?' Patty panted. I just nodded, not wanting to admit I was out of breath. The band kicked into 'Sea Cruise'. She and I were good together, no doubt about it, and were headed for a big finish when we got pre-empted. Somebody screamed. Loud.

I had Patty on an outswing and let go of her too fast as I spun around in the direction of the scream. She skidded into the couple behind us. Then she looked up, and she screamed, too. The band stopped playing with the sharp squeal of a distressed clarinet. Everybody was staring at the ceiling. At the end of the room, under the balcony, Wilson Tedworth Junior hung head first on top of the giant ice Neptune statue, with the points of the crown stuck in his neck and his head dangling in air. Two forks of the huge trident were poked through his midriff. Blood spurting over his green polo shirt spread in bright lines down the sides of the sea god, turning the blue ice purple.

For two or three seconds, it looked like Neptune had lifted Tedworth up over his head, ready to pitch him somewhere. He stayed there, poised in the air, while the whole room went dead quiet. Then the statue's head and arm snapped off, and Tedworth crashed down, splattering vivid red on the ice as he fell. The statue toppled over sideways and shattered. Tedworth landed with a loud thud on top of the hors d'oeuvres table, then bounced off. The table held dozens of glass platters and punch bowls and candlesticks and vases. Most of them broke.

By now we had a stampede headed for a look. It wasn't easy to push them back. Once I got close I knew Dink Tedworth was dead. He looked right at me, but his eyes were blank. When I yelled for a doctor, three guests stepped forward and agreed with me. I looked up at the little balcony right above us on the second floor. It was empty. The banner JOE AND PATTY FOR EVER was hanging sideways from a rope. Tedworth must have ripped it loose as he plummeted head first onto the ice statue ten feet below. He'd gone over that rail in one of three ways. He fell, he jumped, or somebody pushed him. I was going to have to find out which one.

It was a relief to the guests to have the police chief already on the scene, and after I got them corralled and asked for their cooperation, they called 911, and shut the French doors to the ballroom so no one could get in or out. The guards lunged for their stations, full of importance. Everyone else stood staring at Patty as she stepped out of the crowd, and asked, 'Is Dink dead?'

I nodded. With a long look at my face, she nodded back at me, then sat down carefully in the nearest chair.

I ran out into the lobby, and up the curving stairs to the second floor, now chased by the hysterical club manager, who kept telling me he was Mr Bowe, as if that would explain everything. We ran through an empty dimly lit dining room and reached a door that led into the small balcony area from which Tedworth had fallen. Nobody was there. Mr Bowe – a prissy little man torn between a tremulous horror and an institutional effort to pretend nothing was wrong – prattled on compulsively about how the balcony was a musicians' gallery modeled on an eighteenth-century Royal Governor's mansion in Virginia. It was used only once a year when a brass quintet played fanfares to introduce the new crop of Hillston debutantes, daughters of local doctors and merchants, who – he whispered, raising a pale little eyebrow – would never minuet again in their lives.

In the thick dust on the balcony floor I could see dozens of smeared footprints. According to the manager, the entire club was thoroughly cleaned once a week, but a glance at the cobwebs suggested that 'thorough' didn't include this little area. On the other hand, there was no dust at all on the rail over which Tedworth had taken his tumble, but Mr Bowe felt confident that his staff must have wiped off the rail before attaching Patty's banner.

Mr Bowe was frantically opposed to the notion that Tedworth had accidentally leaned over the rail and lost his balance. It conjured such nightmares of lawsuits slapped on the club by the Tedworth family that he had to press his satin handkerchief against his eyes to squeeze out the image. Balling each of his small hands in the grip of the other, he urged me to consider suicide. 'I'm afraid we have to face it, poor Mr Tedworth jumped to his death, heaven help him. You saw how he was acting. We all saw it. And there have been other ... well, there have been incidents, even here at the club. Incidents.'

'Yeah, I heard about the golf pro.'

'If you want my opinion, I think poor Mr Tedworth, and I always liked him, I think he jumped to spoil his former wife's wedding reception.'

'That'll do it,' I agreed.

He peered at me anxiously from behind his handkerchief. 'Don't you think he jumped?'

I was shining my pen light into the corners. 'Maybe he just fell. Maybe somebody pushed him.'

The little club manager turned the color of key lime pie. Pushed him? That would be even more sordid. He had to go take an aspirin; at least he said he needed an aspirin but he looked like he needed a fistful of Valium to me.

Among other dusty things on the floor I noticed a dead infant mouse, a little strip of leather half the size of a match, a folded sheet of nice white blank paper, and a piece of moldy sandwich. I made the embarrassed Mr Bowe leave them all where they were. As he walked me back through the dining room, I saw a little red chair knocked over near one of the rear windows, and under it there was a bottle of champagne spilled out on the carpet. The manager was nearly in tears when I stopped him from picking up the chair. 'You can't touch things, all right, Mr Bowe?'

Alarm fluttered through him. 'Why? You're not bringing in the police, are you?' I reminded him again that I was the police. He waved his shiny handkerchief in a frenzy as he led me back downstairs, as if he were a nervous escort leading a surrender party.

While, of course, none of Tedworth Junior's family had been asked to come celebrate Patty's wedding to Raulett, many of his friends were there, being friends of Patty's as well. Women collected at tables, crying, men at the bar, talking too fast as they told each other what all of them had just seen. Patty still sat staring straight ahead in the chair where I'd put her. Her husband Joe was holding his ribs like he was going to be sick as he paced around making calls on a mobile phone. Pascal Raiford, sweaty and shaky at the same time, was trying to help out by putting the wedding presents in shopping bags then removing them when they didn't fit. Dr Honeycutt was amazed that he had played golf with Dink only two days before, and from that excursion, 'You sure couldn't have predicted this.' He was contradicted by his wife Caryn who assured me that Dink was so despondent over losing Patty that his close friends had been 'seriously worried' about him.

I sat down beside Patty. Two women had joined her and kept rubbing her hands as if they were trying to keep her circulation going.

I leaned towards her. 'I'm real sorry, Patty, but I've got to ask you a few questions.' She took a drink of the water her friend held out, and nodded at me. 'Did you have any other conversation with Tedworth tonight – other than what we all heard? Do you know what he meant by he was going to have to hurt you?' She shook her head. 'Did you understand him to mean he might—'

'Do this on purpose? He did, didn't he?'

The women around her nodded eagerly, murmuring, 'Yes. Of course he did. Don't blame yourself. He just couldn't move on without you. He came to say goodbye.'

She burst out crying. 'I'm just so damn mad at him.'

Pascal Raiford hurried over and pulled his sister into a hug. I asked to talk to Raiford, and when we'd stepped aside I questioned him about where Dink Tedworth had gone after he and Joe Raulett had dragged him out of the ballroom. Pascal explained that Joe had taken Dink into the men's room to do something about his nosebleed, and that he hadn't seen either of them again until Dink fell off the balcony. Like Dr Honeycutt, Raiford was sure Dink's death was an accident and not suicide, though he admitted that at times lately Dink had seemed to be on the verge of a nervous breakdown, and that he had been behaving erratically at the bank where they were both vice-presidents.

I could finally hear sirens as Joe Raulett strode towards me, pointing at his watch, urging me to let their guests go home. I said I was sorry, but we needed names and addresses for their statements. Patty's new husband was making an effort to keep his voice pleasant, but the strain gave his face a waxy look. 'You count the band, there're still two hundred people here. They're exhausted.'

'And Tedworth's dead.' I sat Raulett down. 'Pascal Raiford says you took Tedworth into the men's room—'

He interrupted to ask if it wasn't obvious that Wilson Tedworth had killed himself, and had come to Patty's wedding reception expressly to do so.

'I don't know.' There was an unbroken bowl of crab claws on the floor. I leaned down and took a couple. 'That true, you got him in the men's room?'

Reluctantly Raulett told me that, yes, he had led Tedworth into the men's lounge, where he'd drunkenly tried to clean himself up, after which he'd agreed to depart from the club without further trouble.

'He did?' I ate a crab claw. 'Sort of a change of mood?'

Raulett tightened his arms around his midriff. 'Maybe he knew he'd made an ass of himself. I told him if he didn't get out, I'd have him arrested.'

'Did he? Leave?'

Raulett loosened his tie. 'I thought he did. He left the men's room.'

'But you didn't watch him leave?'

'I'm not a crossing guard. I kept trying to wash off the damn nosebleed he'd gotten on me, and he wasn't in the lobby when I came out of the john.'

'And you went straight back to the ballroom.'

'Yes.' He shook his head distractedly. 'I think so.'

I looked at him a while. 'He make you mad, Joe?'

'Damn right.' Raulett jumped to his feet, and pointed at the verandah. 'The guy's a nut. You heard what he did a couple of years back right out there?'

I nodded. 'Ran over the golf pro with his cart. Yeah, I heard.'

'Right. A nut. The things Patty and I had to put up with . . .' He started towards where her brother was leading her out of the room.

I sat him down again. 'Just a second. Tedworth say anything that suggested he was getting ready to kill himself?'

After a struggle, Raulett admitted, 'Just how he loved her and she was too good for me. But I wouldn't put it past him,' he added angrily.

'Seems like shoving you over the rail would have done the trick even better, and left him around to enjoy Patty.' I ate another of the Seafood King's crabs, and wiped my hands on the little napkin that said 'Joe and Patty' above today's date. 'You see him fall?'

'No. First thing I heard was everybody screaming.'

'See anybody up there on the balcony tonight?'

'Well, just Patty when she threw the garter. But that was before Tedworth busted in on us. Oh, and Mr Bowe's people put up the banner.'

'You ever up on the balcony yourself?'

'No. Why should I be?'

So Justin Savile, head of our homicide division, had to show up after all at the wedding party he had refused to attend because he'd known Wilson Tedworth Junior since kindergarten. Though I'd gotten Justin out of bed at one in the morning, he'd arrived at the Hillston club ten minutes later dressed in a three-piece seersucker suit with a blue bow-tie and socks to match. He hugged Patty and told her how sorry he was about Dink, then he came over to look at the blood-soaked body.

'I knew this wedding to Joe Raulett was a bad idea,' he told me by way of greeting. Justin's convinced he has psychic insights. 'See what I mean?' He lifted the corpse's hand, and let it fall. 'Accident?'

'Probably not.' Looking at the body, I suddenly remembered something. 'He had an envelope sticking out of this back pocket earlier tonight – it fell out. I told him he'd dropped it, and now . . .' I checked all his pockets. It wasn't there.

Justin looked at the dead man sadly. 'A goodbye letter?'

I said, 'Maybe. Maybe not.'

Justin sharply turned his head up to me. Then he pulled the cloth back over his old schoolmate.

While Justin worked his way through the guests huddled in the lobby, Forensics gathered what evidence they could. In a fret, I hounded them to hurry their photos. The cause of death was disappearing on us fast. Even if Tedworth's blood was cooling it was warm enough to melt the broken-off pieces of the ice statue stuck in the side of his neck and poking out of his ribs.

Our medical examiner, Dr Dick Cohen, kept yawning as he made notes. He couldn't get over why so many Hillston corpses had to pick an ungodly hour like this one to croak in; he took it personally.

'That's right, Dick, they're dying just so you'll have to haul yourself out of bed in the middle of the night when you haven't had eight straight since you left Brooklyn in '75.'

'It's God's truth. I can't sleep down here in the South.'

'Well, since you're awake, what'd Mr Tedworth officially die of? And don't tell me he choked on a piece of ice in his throat.'

Dick Cohen speculated that Tedworth had expired after the sharp point of a triangle of ice four inches long punctured a carotid artery in his neck while simultaneously two eight-inch prongs of an ice trident perforated his lung and heart. Carefully pulling the pieces of ice out of the body, he packed them in iced containers.

'Suicide?' I asked him.

He scratched at his black stubble. 'Nutty way to kill yourself. Course, you can't tell with a drunk. I had one cut off his own head with a circular saw.' He hauled himself wearily to his feet. 'Come see me at the morgue.'

They'd just hoisted the body bag onto the gurney when Bubba Percy ran in from the verandah. I'd forgotten he was still out there. Bubba was now looking like he'd done a few cycles in a washing machine. He was barefoot and bare-chested, his hair and pants were soaking wet; the rest of his clothes were missing. I said, 'Those ladies roll you?'

Bubba quickly took in the scene. And its significance. 'I fuckin' missed it, didn't I? I just heard somebody killed himself. Who?' As he'd asked the room at large, nobody bothered to answer him. Undeterred, he loped with squishy steps after the gurney, leaving behind big puddles of water, and before the attendants could stop him he unzipped the body bag. I yanked him back from it.

'Dink Tedworth. Goddam it!' Bubba was squirming with annoyance. 'I can't believe I missed the whole fuckin' thing. What'd he do, shoot himself in front of Patty? Is that it?'

I told Bubba he'd have to wait to read about it in the *Raleigh Observer*. He growled at me and went racing after Dick Cohen.

We couldn't find the missing envelope that should have been in Tedworth's pocket, and no one had seen it, and he hadn't given a letter to anybody willing to say so. Justin's team asked the same questions of one hundred and eighty-seven people, and got the same answers, and sent everyone home to start nursing their hangovers. None of them had seen Wilson Tedworth Junior from the moment he was escorted out of the ballroom until half an hour later when Caryn Honeycutt – the doctor's wife – screamed as she caught sight of him dropping through the air. The drummer of the Jimmy Douglas Orchestra did think he'd caught a glimpse of a couple on the balcony shortly before Tedworth fell; they'd looked like they were necking. But the drummer wasn't sure. The little balcony was all the way across the ballroom, and it was dark, and it was none of his business. Nobody admitted to being a part of that hypothetical necking couple.

The feeling around the department was that Justin Savile could get anybody to blab anything; he could coax the sexual fantasies out of a mother superior under a vow of silence. So I believed him when he said none of the guests or staff was going to be of much help. There had been a few people in the lobby during that half-hour, but they hadn't noticed Tedworth coming out of the men's room and climbing the staircase to the second floor. They were Braves' fans who had hauled a TV out there; it had been the fourteenth inning with the bases loaded, and they wouldn't have noticed if the cast of *Baywatch* had danced by naked, shaking tambourines.

While of no use as witnesses, the guests were all too eager to explain that where Patty was concerned, 'jealousy was an issue for Dink' – which I'd already guessed. We heard a dozen other 'episodes' to add to the one about the golf pro: on their honeymoon, Dink had cracked a man's head open on a granite bar top in St Kitts for presuming to buy Patty a pina colada. This man had needed fourteen stitches and a check for $25,000 in order to recover from his injuries. A week after their first Christmas, Dink had smashed open the door of a hotel suite in Charlotte, expecting to find Patty there with a stranger, when she was, in fact, visiting her sister in Savannah just as she'd told him. Instead, he'd terrorized an Israeli diamond salesman taking a shower. Tedworth claimed he'd gotten an anonymous phone tip telling him to go to that room of that hotel, and he'd apologized and paid for the door.

According to their friends, things had just gotten worse after Patty left him and took up with Joe Raulett – though ironically enough it had been Dink and her brother Pascal who had sponsored Joe's membership in the Hillston Club, where Patty had met him. I assume Dink had regretted it. Once, finding them kissing at the Pine Hills Inn, he'd challenged Joe to a fight, and when his offer was declined had smashed his rival's face into a plate of tortellini. He'd paid for the damages. I asked Justin why Patty hadn't gotten a restraining order against her former husband. Justin shrugged. 'I guess she just expects it. Back in college, these two guys actually fought a duel and one of them got—'

'Killed. I heard.'

But while on the one hand the guests conceded that Dink Tedworth was 'insanely jealous' of Patty – emphasis on 'insane' – and 'maybe had a problem with his temper' on the other they were quick to defend him against the assumption that he'd also had a problem with his drinking. They wanted it understood that Dink didn't drink, by which they presumably meant he didn't drink all the time, the way most of them did. His intoxication tonight explained why he had lost his balance and fallen off the balcony, or had lost his mind and jumped off the balcony – the majority view.

Most of the guests had – like Justin – preferred Dink Tedworth – one of them – to Joe Raulett – not one of them – although they had nothing specific against the Seafood King except that his Cadillac was the bright blue color of his restaurants, and so was his cummerbund. Some dismissed him as new money – most of theirs was at least thirty years old – but they didn't doubt that he loved Patty. They just worried that this tragic thing with Dink was going to get the marriage off to a bad start. Bless her heart, sighed Caryn Honeycutt. Patty seemed to be living under a curse like the Kennedys or something. Why, if you counted her father, this was the third man who'd gotten himself killed over her. Mrs Honeycutt sounded a little envious to me.

By three a.m. we'd sent almost everybody home. Justin was leaving to break the news to the Tedworth family. He found me poking around under the collapsed table, looking for that letter of Dink's. He couldn't resist pointing out that my tuxedo pants looked like they'd been made in the sixties and worn every night since. I allowed it was possible. Justin sighed, 'Cuddy, is this another one of those Rubin's Rentals on Tuscadora?' He flipped open my jacket and read the label, which indeed did say just that. 'Why don't you at least *buy* a tux?' Justin's were custom-made.

I swatted away his hand. 'The day I see you in a polyester Hawaiian shirt is the day I buy a tux. Get out of here.'

In the lobby, Joe Raulett was bluntly informing Mr Bowe that the club had better not bill him for all the breakage when the table collapsed. Tedworth had caused that breakage, and he hadn't been on their guest list and wasn't their responsibility so the club could forget it, he wasn't paying a cent. Flushed and trembling, Mr

Bowe fluttered away. I heard him unburdening himself to Dr Honeycutt about Raulett's unprecedented attitude. 'My heavens, if Mr Tedworth had been alive he wouldn't have dreamed of not offering to pay for the damages.'

The Seafood King then surprised his wife by revealing that he planned for them to take off on their honeymoon in the morning. When I told him no trip until after the coroner's inquest, he accused me of bullying him because he didn't have the social clout of the Tedworths. Patty stared at him as if she'd mistaken a stranger for somebody she knew. She said, 'Let's go home, Joe. We're tired.' I agreed with her.

Bubba Percy caught up with me as I headed for the car lot by the tennis courts. By now the moon was gone, and a hot, black wind was whipping leaves off the enormous oak trees that shielded the club from outsiders. Bubba had on a waiter's jacket over his bare chest. He was shivering in his soaked pants. 'Dink didn't shoot himself,' he told me.

'Nope. You lose your clothes?'

'Maybe didn't even jump. Fuckin' tripped. You see him?'

'Bubba, if it's any consolation, I missed it, too.'

He pulled a pack of cigarettes from the waiter's pocket, and this time lit one and took a deep drag. 'Dink Tedworth's caused scenes before.'

'Yeah.' I nodded impatiently. 'The golf pro. The guy in St Kitts. Yeah yeah yeah.'

Bubba leaned on somebody's BMW and got conversational. 'One night Raulett was making out with Patty in his car right out there on Catawba Drive, and Dink drives up behind them and rams them. They jump out, and Dink's BMW shoves Raulett's Cadillac straight down the hill into a power-line pole. It took out the lights in North Hillston for six hours.'

'I hadn't heard that one.'

He smoked with great pleasure. 'Yeah, well, you want news, come to a newsman.'

'Why didn't the lovebugs stay home 'stead of going at it in public all over town? Considering dink's well-known "problem with jealousy"?'

'Pig Chief, you can't let people intimidate you. So I got my headline. NEW HUBBY'S ICE MAN KILLS PATTY'S EX. Like it?' He grinned, shaking his wet hair like an Irish setter. 'Ask me what I was doing.'

I looked him up and down. 'Go home. Sky's gonna let loose.'

But he jabbered on despite the fact that I was loading evidence bags into my trunk and not paying attention. 'We ran off to the ninth fairway, Blue Sunderland and me. We got it on. That's why I missed it all. When we got back to the pool, the other two pushed me in, and we messed around. We were sitting on the side, and who knows what could have happened, but somebody chucks some ice out the window at my damn head, hurt like hell, blood everywhere, and that kind of broke the mood, and then before I can get it going again, we hear all this shouting and screaming – we're laughing how some jerk in there's probably mooning Raulett's grandmother and then Blue's husband runs out looking for her, yelling about somebody's dead.'

I slammed shut the trunk.

'I heard the sirens but I figured some geezer'd just had a stroke.'

'Bubba, goodbye.'

'Yeah. I better get a photographer over here.' His teeth were rattling.

'Where's your car?'

He pointed at his new convertible, felt in his pants for his keys, then cursed.

'Damn it. I left my jacket by the pool. I hope nobody took my damn gold vest. I got it at Harrod's in London.'

I opened my car door. 'I thought maybe you stole it the last time you went to the Liberace Museum.'

Bubba grinned, having fun again. 'Yeah. I went with your mother. And she was a wild woman once we crawled under his white baby grand.' I watched him trot off just as a bombardment of thunder let loose. Rain splatted out of the black clouds like God had turned them upside down, like He'd changed his mind about celebrating Patty's fifth wedding with that big pink moon. Bubba broke into a gallop; his brand new convertible was fast filling with rain, which couldn't be all that good for his white leather seats.

The clouds came to a standstill right on top of Hillston, and it rained all night. Fat drops were still rolling morosely down my office windows on Monday morning when Justin came in with the report from Forensics.

He pulled off his raincoat, revealing yet another new outfit, an ivory linen suit that he didn't buy on his salary. I licked chocolate glaze from my donut. 'Don't you think you're looking jest a little too massa of my old Kentucky home for a cop in Hillston, North Carolina, at the end of the twentieth century?'

'Cuddy, you're just jealous. And given your misguided loyalty to your regular haberdasher – K Mart – I can understand why.' He threw his Panama hat on a chair and tossed a pad of notes at me. 'Lab report.'

There were fifty-two different people's fingerprints on the balcony. The only clear shoeprint was one of Mr Bowe's. Tedworth's blood – perhaps from his earlier nosebleed – was on the rail. At some point last night somebody'd been up on that balcony sniffing cocaine: there were traces on the piece of folded white paper left behind, and it hadn't been lying there long enough to get dusty. Also interesting: there were not only no prints on the balcony rail, there were none on the champagne bottle spilled on the carpet by the dining-room window. Justin said Forensics thought they looked wiped. I asked if Dink Tedworth was a coke-head.

Sipping his expresso out of his porcelain cup, Justin gave me a computer handout of a print match. 'I got a partial off that paper. Guess what? Patty's brother Pascal has a bad habit. He didn't want to say anything last night, but when I told him I had a match with his Navy file he admits he was on the balcony last night—'

'Indulging in an illegal substance?'

'I'm afraid so, but he doesn't want Patty to find out. Now, Pascal says when he headed back from the balcony after his snort up the nose, there was somebody standing there in the dark in that dining room—'

'Who?'

'He says Dink. He says this was before Dink caused the scene on the dance floor. Dink was drinking champagne from the bottle, and now Pascal wonders if he was trying to get up the nerve to jump because he tried to talk to him and Dink told him to go away and tell Patty to have a good life, or words to that effect. Pascal now worries it may have been suicide.'

'Join the crowd.' I looked out my window at the rain beating on umbrellas moving down below. 'Dink kills himself in front of her?'

'It happens.'

'I know it does.' I ate another chocolate donut out of sadness at the way people are so determined to break their own hearts.

Justin handed me a folder. 'But Patty was just one of Dink's problems, I'm sorry to say.' Justin had pushed Pascal Raiford hard on what he'd meant last night about Dink's behaving erratically at work, and Pascal had finally broken down and confided that Dink had recently gotten himself into 'real trouble' at Central Carolina Trust.

'And why didn't Pascal mention any of this last night?'

'Wanted to protect Dink's name, he said. Plus, he admits he didn't want to say he was up on the second floor, scared we'd get on to his coke habit.' He tapped the folder. 'But this bank business was going to come out anyhow. Dink messed up.'

He sure had. This morning Pascal Raiford had taken Justin to the bank where he and Tedworth Junior had both been vice-presidents under Tedworth Senior, and filled him in. It turns out that while Dink never spent much time at Carolina Trust, preferring the golf links or tailing Patty around town, he'd spent enough time in it to skim off a million dollars, and had fudged the books successfully for two years to hide the fact. The branch manager had confirmed it. Dink had robbed them blind.

Justin flipped through the file. 'I wouldn't have thought Dink had the brain power for big-time embezzling.'

I pointed out, 'He didn't. He got caught.'

'After two years. It was just last week.'

Only six days ago there'd been a blow-out at the bank when the 'misappropriation of funds' was traced back to the owner's son. Lawyers were called into a long meeting with Tedworth Senior, as a result of which Tedworth Junior was yanked off the golf course and confronted with the evidence against him. Dink had immediately confessed. He acknowledged that he'd gotten in way over his head, and had been too embarrassed to admit it, having always been a disappointment to his father anyhow. When asked to return the funds, he claimed to have lost the entire million dollars in bad investments. His father threw a coffee pot at him – bad temper was apparently a family trait – and instructed him to take a 'leave of absence' till they sorted things out. If Tedworth Senior hadn't been the majority shareholder of Carolina Trust, Junior might have been in jail, and alive.

Justin said Pascal was the one they'd sent to the golf course to bring Dink back to the bank so they could confront him. 'Pascal said it was the hardest thing he ever had to do. And Patty doesn't know about it and he hopes she doesn't have to.'

'Why should she care?' I asked. 'She divorced the guy.'

'Well, maybe so, but Dink never stopped loving her. Dink's dad said Dink made a will *after* the divorce and still left her everything.' Justin swung his raincoat over his shoulders like a cape. 'Course, she'd already taken most of it anyhow.'

'Right.' I lobbed the donut bag in the trash. 'Go find out about those bad investments. You don't just lose a million dollars.'

'Sure you do,' said Justin, whose family was real old money, and had misplaced most of it somewhere between now and the Revolutionary War.

On my way to the morgue I ran into our assistant DA. She'd read Justin's report and leaned towards suicide. She said he had a long history of violent and irrational behavior. We had a man who'd lost his wife, his money, his job and his reputation, and who had mixed – we'd discovered – champagne with enough barbiturates to make a hippopotamus sail over high hurdles. I couldn't argue with any of it. But I was still fretting over those wiped fingerprints and that missing letter. She said I was always fretting and should give it up and take her to dinner.

Dick Cohen sat in the morgue hunched over Dink Tedworth on the autopsy table. He was shivering, even in his bulky sweater. I don't know why the man leaves Brooklyn for the South because he hates the cold, and then spends all his time in a freezing morgue. He turned Tedworth's jaw to the side, and with a plastic pointer showed me the hole in his neck. There was a huge bruise on the jaw and teeth had bitten through the lip. 'Point of the ice crown went right in here.' Dick wanted me to take a closer look at the wounds in the ribcage. He was always wanting me to miss things so he could explain what I was too ignorant to see. But this time I got it right away. There were three wounds in the chest; not two, three.

'Right.' Dick's narrow balding head gave its unvaried nods. He touched two gashes on the corpse. 'The two forks from the trident did these.' Then he moved the pointer to a third hole off at an angle. Something thicker and deeper than the trident prongs had gone 8.38 inches into the chest cavity, penetrating the pericardium and puncturing the tricuspid valve. 'So what was it?' He pulled his glasses down on his nose to add weight to his question.

We checked through the death scene photos. I found the shot that showed the third prong of the trident as we'd remembered it, broken off, lying on the floor beside the collapsed hors d'oeuvres table, nowhere near the body. We examined Tedworth's bloody polo shirt again. There were definitely three separate rips in it, and all had faint traces of the blue dye that had coated the ice statue.

'How 'bout these?' I pointed at a photo showing the base of the Neptune statue with its circle of high jagged spears of ice that were supposed to look like ocean waves. Dozens of the spikes lay broken on the floor.

Dick looked begrudgingly at the print. 'Yeah. 'Cept they came off the statue's base, and Tedworth got stabbed seven feet higher, when he hit the head and arm. And he landed a good yard from the base.' He used his pointer on the photo. 'So there's no way one of those spikes...'

I threw the pictures down. 'You stupid idiot!'

Alarmed, Dick stepped back. 'Hey, there's no need to—'

'No, not you. Me!' I started dialing Bubba Percy at the *Hillston Star* on my mobile phone.

'Hey, where you going, Cuddy?'

'We've definitely got a murder.'

'What else is new?' Dick sneezed.

At the Hillston Club, there was nothing even the rich could do to stop the rain, which had soaked the golf course, flooded the tennis courts, and frustrated the young circle, who, swinging their rackets and clubs, paced impatiently in the lounge, glaring out at the torrent. Mr Bowe, the nerve-racked manager, scurried among them, apologizing for the weather and for the intrusive yellow police tape that kept them out of the bar as well.

We finally found Tedworth's BMW; it looked like he'd been living in it. He had a lot of pictures of Patty in the glove compartment.

Nobody at the *Star* knew where Bubba Percy was, and I left my fourth message for him to call me immediately. Heading upstairs, I ran into a pleasant-looking man who said he was Dink's lawyer; he told me that yesterday Dink had made an appointment to see him this morning, claiming it was an 'urgent matter'. The lawyer asked about our investigation, and I told him most people seemed to be leaning towards suicide. He was adamant. 'No way Dink killed himself at Patty's wedding reception, no way.'

I asked him what made him so sure and he answered, 'Bad taste.'

I patted his shoulder. 'I couldn't agree with you more.'

Mr Bowe took me furtively into his office and whispered that he wanted to help and possibly this wasn't relevant and it was true that Mr Raulett was a club member though a very recent one and perhaps the admissions committee regretted their decision anyhow but last night he had seen Mr Raulett down in the kitchen. He had seen him lift his shirt to press an ice pack on some terrible-looking bruises on his ribs. And so Mr Bowe thought I might want to wonder – as he did – how did Mr Raulett get those bruises when he hadn't really been part of the subduing of Mr Tedworth on the dance floor? I nodded. Mr Bowe nodded. He fluttered away.

Up on the second floor, I found Justin waiting for me with a pallid Pascal Raiford. In the daylight I could see more of his resemblance to his sister Patty, but, naturally or not, she'd definitely come out ahead in the looks department. Justin had bad news. They'd been back at the bank. It seemed unlikely that anyone would ever find out how and where Dink had lost the million dollars; he'd covered his tracks and destroyed any records. But Tedworth Senior was going to replace the money personally, and there would be no public exposure of Dink's crime after his death.

I whistled. 'That's a dad.'

Raiford now confided that Dink had explicitly told him he was going to commit suicide; he'd said so last night up on the second floor.

I got a little nasty-sounding. 'Is there some reason why you're handing out vital information like this on the installment plan?'

Rattled, Raiford answered Justin instead of me. 'Try to imagine how tortured I've felt. Wanting to tell the truth. Wanting to spare Dink's reputation, for Patty's sake.'

I turned to Justin. 'For Christ sake, did she divorce Tedworth or not?'

Justin ignored this and asked Raiford what he'd told Dink when he threatened suicide.

Raiford mumbled, 'To go home and sleep it off.'

I asked him why he hadn't taken Dink home himself if he was so worried about him. 'I should have,' he admitted. 'Oh, God, I should have.' I sent him off with a cop to give his statement.

We checked the window by the overturned chair, where the champagne had been spilled. I picked up an ashtray, leaned out the window, and threw it into the pool below. It was an easy throw. Justin cut a square out of the still damp carpet to take to the lab. Mr Bowe saw us and had a fit.

On our way downstairs, Justin stopped at a club photograph on the wall. It showed a golfing foursome a few years back, holding a small trophy. There stood Joe Raulett and Wilson Tedworth Junior, side by side and smiling, with Pascal Raiford and Dr Honeycutt. Justin pointed at Raulett's tasseled golf shoes in the picture. 'That's it,' he told me, chagrined. 'That tiny strip of leather you saw up on the balcony? It's part of a shoe tassel. And you know what . . .?' He flipped through last night's crime scene photos to one with Joe in it. 'Damn it, I noticed his shoes last night!' He was stabbing his finger at Raulett's shoes. 'Tassel loafers with a tuxedo?' With the magnifier you could see the tip of the groom's shoe; it had black tassels and one was torn. Raulett had been on that balcony last night, and had lied about it.

'So it's another duel over Patty.' Justin said. '*Cherchez la femme, mon capitaine.*'

'Talk American,' I ordered him.

After Justin left, Bubba Percy came bouncing into the lobby. 'Bubba, don't you answer your pager? I've been calling since—'

'Listen to this first!' Bubba had just heard from Patty's 'best friend', Amanda Dixon, one of the young matrons in the pool with Blue Sunderland last night, that Patty had only married Joe Raulett for 'spite' and was still in love with Dink Tedworth. This morning Patty was all to pieces on the phone to Amanda, blaming herself for driving Dink to suicide by torturing him. (Clearly, her best friend saw no reason to preserve Patty's privacy.)

'Torturing him how?' I asked.

Bubba took me aside enthusiastically. 'Whenever Patty saw Dink following her, she'd put the make on some jerk like that golf pro, so he'd go nuts. Patty was the one – listen to this, Cuddy—'

I gave up trying to get a word in.

'Patty got Amanda to call Dink and drop that anonymous phone tip about her banging somebody in the Charlotte hotel Christmas before last when actually she was in Savannah. Patty did it just to see if he'd drive to Charlotte and make a fool of himself.'

Bubba had my attention. 'Patty married Joe Raulett just to upset Dink Tedworth?' He nodded. 'Well, I'd say she succeeded.'

'You heard it here.' He tapped my shoulder with his rolled-up newspaper.

I grabbed his arm. 'Last night you were talking about being at the pool with those women...'

'It was wild.'

'Bubba, shut up! Didn't you say something to me about somebody chucking ice in the pool? It sounded like your same old bullshit, but it came back to me that you said ice. Did you? Was it from that Neptune statue? Was it dyed blue?'

Bubba stared at me; he knew from my eyes he was now holding the end of a major piece of string, and he played it out. Yes, last night while he was sitting at the edge of the club pool with 'the Three Graces of Hillston', somebody had actually thrown a 'stick' of ice from somewhere, and hit him on the head with it. Maybe it was blue; it was too dark to see much. It was like an icicle as thick as his fist and a foot long, and it had broken on his skull. A long piece had actually stuck in his hair, and when he pulled it out it had blood on it. It could have killed him. With a deep sense of injury Bubba bent over and showed me a very tiny scab beneath his thick wavy hair.

I made Bubba come out in the rain to show me where he'd been sitting, and from where he thought the ice had been tossed. From the pool, across the edge of the patio, he pointed up at the second floor of the club. ''Round there.' He shrugged. 'How should I know?' I could see the open window.

'What'd you do with the ice?'

Baffled, he was trying hard to hide it. 'Are you kidding? I took it home and stuck it in the freezer for a souvenir. What do you think? I dropped it in the pool.'

I looked at the rain spattering into the big rectangle of warm empty pool water. 'Bubba, please tell me you haven't washed your hair since last night.'

He was indignant. 'I wash my hair twice a day. Look at it.'

'Did you touch anything after you grabbed that icicle? I don't mean women, I mean your clothes. Did you wipe—'

'Okay, what's up, Mangum? It's a homicide, right? Who killed him?'

'Did you wipe the blood on your clothes?'

He decided he'd find out more if he helped. Dramatically, he struggled to remember. 'I think I leaned over, let's see, and wiped my hand on something, and it was my gold vest, and I had a fit and said to myself, Why the hell did you do that, you paid three hundred—'

I rushed him back inside. 'You're going with Pendergraph here ...' I called over an officer. 'Wes! And give him that gold vest.'

Bubba balked. 'I took it to the dry cleaners this morning.'

'Goddamn it! Go call them quick! Stop them from cleaning it.'

Pendergraph made a move for Bubba, but he dug in. 'Mangum, come on, fair's fair. You owe me. Off the record.' He stared at me solemnly, but I knew he'd be on the phone in a nano-second with whatever I told him.

He yelled after me, 'She killed him, Patty killed him?' The club manager walked into the lobby, heard this, pressed his yellow handkerchief against his mouth and scurried back to his office.

I told the assistant DA we had a homicide and couldn't have dinner. There was blue vegetable dye from the statue and type A blood and type O blood on Bubba's brocade vest. The type O was Bubba's; the type A was Dink Tedworth's. There was also dye and Dink's blood on the section of carpet fabric we'd taken from the second floor. Somebody had taken an ice spike from the base of the Neptune statue and, concealing it, followed or led Dink Tedworth upstairs, stabbed him in the heart, then tossed the ice out the window, figuring it would soon melt, destroying the evidence. Instead, it had landed on Bubba Percy; for the only time in his life the man was in the right place at the right time. The murderer had dragged Tedworth onto the balcony and shoved him over the rail so that he'd crash down onto the statue. (The struggle to do so had looked like the 'necking couple' the Jimmy Douglas drummer had seen.) Afterwards he had spilled champagne over the carpet stain and wiped the bottle clean of prints. Hurrying back into the ballroom, he'd joined the horrified crowd clustered around Dink's body.

The assistant DA said, 'Meet me at Pogo's and we'll work on who's the murderer.'

I told her I had to go pick up some shoes first.

Patty Raiford Raulett was alone at the Raiford's eighteen-room Colonial on Catawba Drive. Her twin sons were in New Orleans with their father. Her brother Pascal was at the bank. And when I asked for her husband Joe, she said he was off closing a deal. I expressed surprise that Joe would be doing business the day after he'd gotten married when he'd planned to be at the beach on his honeymoon. Not to mention that his wife's ex-husband had died the night before.

Patty shrugged. 'Can I help?'

'Matter of fact, I want the tassel loafers Joe was wearing last night.'

She gave me a look, then flung my raincoat over a brocade chair. 'I'll be right back.' She took her Bloody Mary and left.

I wandered around a mammoth living room crammed with handsome furniture that looked very old and very expensive. There were pictures of Patty everywhere. There must have been five photos of her for every one of Pascal, even though it was his house. But, then, there'd been five marriages of Patty's for every one of Pascal's – and I'd heard that the one he'd had only lasted six months.

She returned with the loafers and her Bloody Mary. I held up the piece of leather we'd found on the balcony floor. It fit the torn tassel. I said, 'I'm going to have to talk to your husband.'

Patty motioned for me to follow her. 'Well, you're welcome to wait. What have Joe's shoes got to do with this?'

We went out through a sun room onto a patio. I said, 'Nice garden.'

'Thanks. Pascal tries to keep up the old family style without the old family income.' (And she didn't even know what he was shelling out for cocaine.) The rain had stopped, and we sat down under an umbrella on the patio. There was a green plastic alligator floating in the pool with a *Vogue* magazine lying on his stomach. A maid suddenly appeared beside us. She poured me an iced tea and gave Patty another Bloody Mary. Patty squeezed her hand thankfully, and she left. Did they have a signal, or had the maid been looking out the window, waiting for when to bring the next drink?

I said, 'The shoe means your husband was up on the balcony last night. So when he tells me he wasn't, I wonder why he lied. Also I wonder where he got those bruises I've heard are on his ribs, since he wasn't in the scuffle on the dance floor.'

She didn't beat around the bush. 'You think Joe killed Dink?'

'That's what you think?'

'No. Dink jumped.'

I let that go for now. 'A friend of yours told Bubba Percy you deliberately set out to make Dink jealous even after your divorce.'

'Amanda Dixon?' She didn't seem angry at her gossipy friend.

'Didn't you worry something like this might happen? Or was it more important to keep on being the North Carolina belle of the ball? Isn't that your reputation?'

She blushed. 'Don't say things like that.' We looked at each for a while. I waited. She stared sadly into her Bloody Mary, and whispered, 'I never thought he'd kill himself. That's God's truth.'

'How 'bout old Joe?' I held up his tasseled loafer. 'You just using Joe to make Dink jealous?'

'Miz Raiford?' We were interrupted by the maid returning with a cordless phone. She didn't say who it was. Patty answered it, said 'Hi, Joe' and told him come home right away, that I wanted to see him. She hung up and said he'd be here in about twenty minutes.

She stirred her drink with the celery stalk. 'It's my fault he jumped.'

I said, 'He didn't. Bubba Percy wonders if maybe you killed him.'

'Bubba thinks he has a sense of humor.'

'He says women'll do anything.'

'He's right.' She made an effort at a smile. 'They will. But I didn't kill Dink.'

'Your brother Pascal says Dink told him flat out last night that he was going to kill himself, but Dink's lawyer thinks he wouldn't have done it in front of people at your party because it'd be in bad taste.'

She nodded. 'Everybody always said Dink had the best manners.'

'Except for that little problem with his jealousy. But I don't think he was going to kill himself there or anywhere else.' I put on my sunglasses; it made it easier to watch her face. 'Somebody had already stabbed Dink in the heart before he went over that rail.'

She took this in, shaded her eyes to look at me.

'So, does your husband know you married him just to spite Dink? A thing like that could annoy a groom.'

Patty wasn't liking me as much as she had on the dance floor. 'You're pretty sarcastic.'

'Murder rubs me the wrong way.'

She spent the next half-hour asking me questions. I kept looking at my watch. After forty minutes I called the desk sergeant and told him to send a car out to find Joe Raulett. Patty followed me back through the huge, cool house, promising me Joe was just stuck in traffic. The maid was mopping the floor of the marble foyer, and pointed silently for me to walk around her. I asked her if that had really been Mr Raulett on the phone. She turned to look at Patty. Patty nodded, and the maid said, yes, it was Mr Raulett on the phone, and she went back to her mopping.

At the door, Patty said, 'So Bubba Percy thinks I murdered Dink?'

My raincoat felt sticky and heavy in the hundred-degree August sun. I nodded. 'He also says the two of you had oral sex in a hot-air balloon over the state fairgrounds.'

She smiled and closed the door.

Justin yawned as I took another bite of jelly donut. 'Admit it, Patty pulled a fast one on you.'

It was true. I don't know who she was talking to on that cordless phone, but it wasn't Joe Raulett because he'd already left town on a plane to San Juan. Where he'd gone from there we still hadn't found out. Justin studied me for a while. Then he said, 'You're not happy. It's that stupid envelope, and for all you know it was Dink's damn phone bill.'

It's a strange thing. We had nothing in common, and yet Justin knew me better than anybody else in my life. (Admittedly my relatives are dead and I live alone.) I said, 'So where did the letter go?'

'More to the point.' He looked at me. 'Where'd Joe Raulett go?' He threw a dart at the photo of my predecessor that I kept on the door for just that purpose.

I headed back to the big house on Catawba Drive.

The maid didn't look happy to see me. Patty, Bloody Mary in hand, didn't look any happier. She said Joe really had told her he was coming home, and she had no idea where he'd gone or why.

I got sarcastic on her again. 'Well, where'd he tell you he was going when you helped him pack, and drove him to the airport, and then sat there with me pretending he'd be back any minute?'

She ignored this, and tried to get me to look at things differently. 'You can't call this murder. They got in a fight about me and Dink fell over the rail. It could just as easily have been Joe who got killed.'

'Would you care? Or is it just to the victor go the spoils?'

'You're not very nice,' she said, and closed the door on me.

I called Bubba. The *Star* broke the story with a big photo of Patty.

SEAFOOD KING KILLS PATTY'S EX AT SOCIETY WEDDING
Second Man Murdered for Love of Seventies Campus Queen

She was back in the news. Dink Tedworth had died for love of her. And Joe Raulett had killed him. A waiter finally remembered seeing Raulett and Tedworth headed up the lobby stairs together. A print of Raulett's was found on the overturned chair. A guest recalled Raulett threatening Tedworth's life in a restaurant once. Pascal

Raiford admitted he'd had his suspicions of Joe all along. None of the young circle seemed too surprised – after all, that blue cummerbund. But I wanted the satisfied feeling I get when I bid five no-trump and I make five no-trump. And I didn't have it. Why hadn't a tough man like Raulett toughed it out, admitted the fight and claimed the fall was an accident or self-defense? The whole town knew how often Dink had attacked him in public. Why run away?

The diminutive and pompous Hercule Poirot, another great believer in brains, says it's always the little gray cells that solve murders. But in this case it was what the little gray cells forgot. I got a call from Rubin's Rentals on Tuscadora. They wanted their tuxedo back, which I'd stuffed in my closet after coming home the night of Tedworth's death and forgotten all about. I had it in the car and Justin was with me, so I thought I'd run it into Rubin's while he waited. Justin was checking the garment's pockets. I told him I'd already gotten all the change out, but I could lend him a dollar if he was that desperate.

'How jocular,' he said. Then he stuck his hand in a little diagonal side pocket of the jacket that I hadn't even known was there and pulled out an envelope. 'I guess you don't use a cigarette case,' he said. 'That's what the pocket's for.' He handed the envelope to me. 'Look familiar?'

'Patty' was written on the front in a big sloping script. Here it was, the envelope missing from Dink Tedworth's khaki pants, the envelope I'd torn the Hillston Club apart for. Justin shook his head. 'You'd be lost without me ... Did you find it and forget?'

'No.' I pulled over to the curb. 'Shut up and let me think.' I flashed back to how Tedworth had lunged against me after I'd broken up the fight on the dance floor, and how he'd patted me so many times while apologizing. He must have put the envelope in my jacket then. Justin wondered if maybe he'd been so out of it with pills and alcohol that he'd believed he was returning something *I'd* dropped. But I decided that Dink had put it there deliberately because he knew I was the police chief, and that I'd make sure Patty got it. I read the letter to Justin. Then I sent him over to Central Carolina Trust to arrest Patty's twin brother for murdering Dink Tedworth.

The next day Patty burst into my office without waiting to be announced. I have to admit she looked good angry. Justin was with me but she didn't say hello to either of us. She said 'Pascal's in jail! Is he some kind of witness? Why won't they let me see him?'

'Hi, Patty.' I smiled at her. 'Guess what! You were right. Joe didn't kill Dink.' This took her aback, and she stopped talking. I said, 'Joe *was* up on that balcony and he did have a fight with Dink. But he left Dink up there alive as can be. Somebody else came along and killed Dink. Oh, and it wasn't *Cherchez la femme* – it was that other phrase, Follow the money.'

Now she looked at Justin. 'What is he talking about?'

I answered for myself. 'About Dink and your brother Pascal, about the million dollars they embezzled from Carolina Trust. Honey, it didn't have a thing to do with you. You're back down to only one guy murdered for love.'

Justin hurried over to her, and helped her into a chair. He looked at me. I told him to go ahead and tell her. He tried to do it gently.

I hadn't been 'very nice' to her again, because the truth is the murder did have a lot to do with Patty. Dink had gotten himself into such a state by the night of her wedding that he'd crashed the reception to see her 'for the last time', not because he was going to kill himself but because – as he put it in his letter – he planned to 'face the music in the morning' by pleading guilty to embezzlement. He also wrote that he was sorry to have to hurt her but he planned to tell her brother Pascal that if Pascal didn't turn himself in at the same time Dink would have him arrested. Because Pascal had been his partner in the embezzlement.

In fact, Pascal was the senior partner, the know-how behind the computer wizardry that had made all that money disappear without the bank ever noticing. At the end of Justin's interrogation – I listened behind the glass – Pascal had been almost bragging about his clever scheme. But he'd needed Dink's access to bank codes so he'd lured him into the scheme by claiming it was really just a game on paper and that they could put everything back whenever they wanted to. Dink had always loved Pascal because he was Patty's twin and because Patty loved him. And so he'd given Pascal the information he needed. Once involved, Dink was trapped not by the money but by the specter of his father ever finding out.

Pascal, on the other hand, did want the money; he had expensive tastes. Privately he invested in the fast-growing Neptune restaurant chain owned by a new golf buddy of his, Joe Raulett. Unfortunately, it was around the same time that Dink's marriage broke up and Joe Raulett went after Patty and Dink went after Joe. Pascal couldn't let Dink find out that he and the hated Seafood King were building Neptune restaurants as fast as they could with money that belonged to Central Carolina Trust. So Pascal told Dink that he'd lost all the money investing in bad stocks, that he hoped Dink could forgive him, that they had to forget the whole thing that ever happened and pray the bank never found out.

The bank found out. And traced the embezzlement to Dink alone. When the board called in Pascal and told him to go to the golf course to bring Dink back, he almost panicked and fled. Luckily he didn't. For as it turned out, he didn't even have to beg Dink to keep quiet about his involvement. Dink volunteered! Since they didn't suspect Pascal, Dink would take the full blame on himself and leave Pascal out of it 'for Patty's sake'. And Dink might have stuck to this noble gesture had he not discovered that – far from losing the money – Pascal had used it to get filthy rich in partnership with the creep who'd stolen Dink's wife.

He found out because he spent a lot of time spying on Joe Raulett. He broke into Raulett's Cadillac the night before the wedding to see what he could find there. What he found were contacts in a briefcase that made it clear even to someone of his banking simplicity that Pascal Raiford owned seventeen per cent of Neptune, Inc., for which he had paid $738,000.

At the wedding reception Dink told Pascal he wouldn't protect him any more – that Pascal had lied to him and betrayed him, and that if he didn't return the money and turn himself in, Dink would call the police on him in the morning. Poor Pascal, he hadn't been kidding when he'd told us he was 'tortured' that night at the Club. Buying time, he'd told Dink that he'd do as he asked. Then he followed Dink around, watched him getting drunker with alarm, tried to stop him when he rushed onto the dance floor and grabbed at Patty. What if Dink drunkenly shouted out the truth right then and there? Pascal couldn't risk it.

So, fortified by cocaine, Pascal seized the opportunity, the way you have to if you want to get ahead in business these days. After Raulett strong-armed Dink into the men's room, Pascal snatched up one of the thick icicles which had been knocked off the statue's base when Dink had thrown the vase at Patty. He saw Dink run back into the lobby from the men's room, spot Raulett and chase him upstairs. Pascal followed. While he watched from the shadows, the two men started fighting. Dink broke two of Raulett's ribs with a kick. Raulett slammed Dink in the face with the little red chair, knocking him out. He left him lying there.

Instantly Pascal ran over, stabbed Dink, dragged him to the balcony, toppled him over the rail, and ran downstairs to join the crowd. He was even luckier than he'd hoped. The body not only hit the statue, it was speared on it. Pascal then did what he could to make everybody think, first, that it was an accident, then, when that didn't work, a suicide, and then, as a last resort, a fight between Dink and Joe over Patty. The Hillston Club set was predisposed to believe men would fight to the death for love of Patty. It was something they were used to, even admired. She had that reputation.

DRIVING LESSONS

Ed McBain

The girl looked sixteen and blonde, and the man looked thirty-two and dazed. The responding blues were questioning the girl and trying to question the man who'd been in the vehicle. They weren't expecting much from the man, not in his condition.

They thought at first he was drunk even though he didn't smell of alcohol. The girl was cold sober. Hysterical because she'd just run somebody over, but cold sober nonetheless. She was the one who'd been driving the car.

'What's your name, miss?' one of the blues asked.

'Rebecca Patton. Is she all right?'

'May I see your license, please?'

'I don't have a license. I'm just learning to drive. I have a learner's permit. Is the woman all right?'

'May I see the permit, please?'

The officer should have known, but didn't, that in this state, within many sections of the Vehicle and Traffic Law, a learner's permit was deemed a license to drive. All he knew was that here was a sobbing sixteen-year-old kid who'd just run over a woman who looked like she was maybe twenty-eight, twenty-nine years old.

They were standing outside the vehicle that had knocked her down, a blue Ford Escort with dual brake pedals and oversized yellow and black STUDENT DRIVER plates on the front and rear bumpers. The impact had sent the woman flying some five feet into the air, tossing her onto a pile of burning leaves stacked on the sidewalk near the curb. One of the witnesses had dragged her off the smoldering fire, onto the lawn, and had immediately called the police. Other blues at the scene were still searching for the handbag the witness said she'd been carrying. But the stricken woman was wearing red, and the leaves on the ground were thick this fall.

They kept scuffing through the fallen leaves, searching for the camouflaged bag, hoping to find a driver's license, a business card, a phone bill with a name and address on it – anything that would tell them who she was. Anonymous, she lay in the gutter some twenty feet from where a highway patrol car was just pulling in behind the Ford. Red coat open over a blue skirt and jacket, white blouse with a stock tie. Eyes closed. Hands at her sides, palms upward, fingers twitching.

The blues took the highway patrolmen aside and informed them that they'd tested the guy's skills and he'd failed with flying colors and seemed to be high on something. Nobody smelt alcohol but they gave him a breathalyzer test, anyway, and discovered no trace whatever of methyl alcohol in his system, the guy blew much lower than point-one-oh. One of them asked him his name, which the blues had already done. He still didn't know. Shook his head and almost fell off his feet. They opened the door on the passenger side of the Ford and let him sit.

'He's Mr Newell,' the girl said. 'He's been giving me driving lessons. I don't know how this happened, she just stepped off the curb. Oh my God, is she all right?'

'Can you tell us his first name?'

'Andrew. Will she be all right?'

The ambulance arrived along about then. It was almost three thirty. Paramedics lifted the woman onto a stretcher and hoisted her inside. The ambulance pulled away from the curb. Nobody yet knew who the woman was. The street seemed suddenly very still. A fresh wind sent withering leaves rattling along the curb.

'I think you'll both have to come along with us,' one of the blues said to the young blonde girl and the man who seemed stoned.

The girl nodded. 'Will you call my father, please?' she asked.

The phone was ringing when Katie got back to the apartment that afternoon. She put the two bags of groceries on the table just inside the door and went swiftly to the kitchen counter, sitting on one of the stools there and yanking the phone from its wall hook at the same time.

'Logan,' she said.

'Katie, it's Carl.'

'Yes, Carl.'

'Can you get down here right away? Lieutenant needs you to question a female juve.'

'Sure,' she said. 'Give me ten minutes.'

'See you,' Carl said, and hung up.

Katie sighed and put the phone back on its hook. This was supposed to be her day off. But she was the only woman detective in the department and whenever they got a young girl in, the job went to her. She was wearing, on this bright fall afternoon, a tan plaid skirt with low heels, opaque brown pantyhose and a matching brown sweater. The skirt was on the short side; she'd have to change before driving downtown. She'd also have to call Max again to see if there was any further word from her dear departed husband. Worst thing about a detective squadroom in a small town was the lack of privacy. River Close claimed a mere 50,000 inhabitants – well, some fifty-five during July and August, but all the summer renters were gone now.

She went to the kitchen window and cranked it open. A gust of cool air rushed into the apartment, carrying with it the aroma of woodsmoke. From the junior high school across the street, she could hear the sounds of football practice. Today was the sixteenth of October, a clear brisk day during one of the most glorious falls Katie could recall. Spoiled, of course. Autumn spoiled for ever. Stephen had left her on the twelfth of September. Easy come, easy go, she thought. She'd only known him since she was sixteen.

Until now, she'd always thought of autumn as her time of year. Sometimes felt she even *looked* like autumn, the reddish-brown hair and freckled cheeks echoing the season's colors, her eyes as blue as any September sky. She'd hated the freckles when she was a little girl, but at thirty-three she felt they added character to her face. Made her look a bit more Irish, too, as if she needed any help with a name like Katherine Byrne Logan.

She wondered all at once if she should go back to her maiden name after the divorce. She was so used to being Katie Logan, so used to being Detective Logan, so used to being just plain *Logan* that . . .

Call Max, she thought.

She looked at the wall clock. Ten minutes to four. Better get cracking.

First the frozen stuff, she thought, and began unpacking the groceries.

*

Max Binder had been recommended to Katie by a lawyer she knew in the State Attorney's Office. A portly, avuncular man with white hair and chubby cheeks, he seemed uncommonly well suited to the task of consoling forlorn women seeking divorces. Katie supposed she fell into this category. A forlorn woman. Deserted, desolate and forsaken. If she were any more Irish, she'd be keening. Instead, she was dialing the three Bs and hoping Max wasn't in court.

'Binder, Benson and Byrd,' said a woman's voice.

'Ellie, it's Katie Logan,' she said. 'Is he in?'

'Second.'

Max came on the phone a moment later.

'Hi, Katie, what's new?' he asked.

Same question every time. What's new is my husband left me and is living with a twenty-two-year-old waitress is what's new.

'Have you heard from him?' she asked.

'Not yet.'

'What's taking him so long?'

'He only got our counter-proposal a week ago. You're being eminently fair, Katie. I can't imagine him refusing at this point.'

'Then call Schiffman and light a fire under him.'

'Schiffman's trying a big case this week.'

'Shall I call him myself?'

'Schiffman? No, no. No. No, Katie.'

'How about Stephen, then? My alleged husband.'

'No. Certainly not.'

'I want a divorce, Max.'

'Of course you do. But be patient just a little longer, Katie. Please. I'm handling it. Please.'

'OK, Max.'

'OK, Katie? Please.'

'Sure,' she said. 'Let me know.'

She hung up and looked at the clock.

'On my way,' she said aloud.

Rebecca Patton's dark brown eyes were shining with tears. Behind her, the high windows of the room framed trees bursting with leaves of red, orange, yellow and brown. They were sitting in what the local precinct had labeled the 'interrogation room', after those in big-city police departments, though normally the cops at Raleigh Station didn't put on airs. Katie hadn't yet told her that the woman she'd hit was in a critical condition at Gardner General Hospital. She hadn't yet told her that so far the woman hadn't been able to speak to anyone. Still anonymous, the hospital had admitted her as Jane Doe.

'Rebecca,' Katie said, 'your father just got here. If you'd like him to come in while we talk ...'

'Yes, I would, please,' Rebecca said.

'And if your mother would like to join us ...'

'My mother's in California.'

A sudden sharpness of voice which startled Katie.

'They're divorced.'

'I see.'

'I hope no one called her.'
'I really don't know. I'm assuming the –'
She almost said 'arresting officers'.
She caught herself.
'– responding officers called whoever . . .'
'I didn't give them her name. I don't want her to know about this.'
'If that's your wish.'
'It's my wish.'
'Let me get your father, then.'

Dr Ralph Patton was sitting on a bench in the corridor just outside the squadroom. He got to his feet the moment he saw Katie approaching. A tall spare man wearing blue jeans, a denim shirt, loafers and a suede vest, he looked more like a wrangler than a physician – but Wednesday was his day off. His dark brown eyes were the color of his daughter's. They checked out the ID tag clipped to the pocket of Katie's gray tailored suit, and immediately clouded with suspicion.
    'Where's Rebecca?' he asked.
    'Waiting for us,' Katie said. 'She's fine, would you come with me, please?'
    'What's she doing in a police station?'
    'I thought you'd been informed . . .'
    'Yes, the officer who called told me Rebecca was involved in an automobile accident. I repeat. What's she doing here?'
    'Well, there are questions we have to ask, Dr Patton, I'm sure you realize that. About the incident.'
    'Why? Since when is an accident a crime?'
    'We haven't charged her with any crime,' Katie said.
    Which was true.
    But a young woman lay critically injured in the hospital, knocked down by the automobile Rebecca Patton had been driving. And the only licensed driver in the subject vehicle had been under the influence of something, they still didn't know what. If the woman died, Katie figured Andrew Newell was looking at either vehicular homicide or reckless manslaughter. But whereas the law considered the licensed driver to be primary, if the learner behind the wheel *knew* that he wasn't in complete control of all his faculties, they might *both* be culpable.
    'Are we going to need a lawyer here?' Dr Patton asked, brown eyes narrowing suspiciously again.
    'That's entirely up to you,' Katie said.
    'Yes, I want one,' he said.

Technically, the girl was in police custody.
    And in keeping with the guidelines, as a juvenile she was being questioned separately and apart from any criminals who might be on the premises, of whom there were none, at the moment, unless Andrew Newell in the lieutenant's office down the hall could be considered a criminal for having abused whatever substance was in his body when he'd climbed into that Ford.
    The Patton lawyer was here now, straight out of Charles Dickens, wearing mutton chops and a tweedy jacket and a bow tie and gold-rimmed spectacles and sporting a checkered vest and a little pot belly and calling himself Alexander Wickett.
    'How long have you been driving?' Katie asked.

'Since the beginning of August,' Rebecca said.

'Does she have to answer these questions?' her father asked.

Wickett cleared his throat and looked startled.

'Why, no,' he said. 'Not if she doesn't wish to. You heard Miss Logan repeating Miranda in my presence.'

'Then why don't you advise her to remain silent?'

'Well, do you *wish* to remain silent, Miss Patton?'

'Did I hurt that woman?' Rebecca asked.

'Yes, you hurt her,' Katie said. 'Very badly.'

'Oh God.'

'She's in critical condition at Gardner General.'

'God, dear God.'

'Do you want to answer questions or don't you?' Dr Patton said.

'I want to help.'

'Answering questions won't—'

'However I can help, I want to. I didn't mean to hit her. She stepped right off the curb. There was no way I could avoid her. I saw this flash of red and ... and ...'

'Becky, I think you should—'

'No. I want to help. Please.' She turned to Katie and said, 'Ask whatever you like, Miss Logan.'

Katie nodded.

'Do you consider yourself a good driver, Rebecca?'

'Yes. I was planning to take my test next week, in fact.'

'How fast were you going at the time of the accident?'

'Thirty miles an hour. That's the speed limit in that area.'

'You've been there before?'

'Yes. Many times. We drive all over the city. Main roads, back roads, all over. Mr Newell's a very good teacher. He exposes his students to all sorts of conditions. His theory is that good driving is knowing how to react instantly to any given circumstance.'

'So you've been on that street before?'

'Yes.'

'When did you first see the woman?'

'I told you. She stepped off the curb just as I was approaching the corner.'

'Did you slow down at the corner?'

'No. There are full stop signs on the cross street. Both sides of Grove. But Third is the through street. I wasn't supposed to slow down.'

'Did Mr Newell advise you to use caution at that particular corner?'

'No. Why would he?'

'Did *he* see the woman before you did?'

'I don't think so.'

'Well, did he say anything in warning?'

'No. What his system is, he asks his students to tell him everything they see. He'll say, "What do you see?" And you'll answer, "A milk truck pulling in," or "A girl on a bike," or "A red light," or "A car passing on my left," like that. He doesn't comment unless you *don't* see something. Then he'll say again, "What do you see *now*?" Emphasizing it. This way he knows everything going through our heads.'

'When you approached that corner, did he ask you what you were seeing?'

'No. In fact, he'd been very quiet. I thought I must have been driving exceptionally well. But it was a pretty quiet afternoon, anyway. No video games.'

'No what?'

'Video games. That's what he called unexpected situations. When everything erupts as if you're driving one of those cars in a video arcade? Six nuns on bicycles, a truck spinning out of control, a drunk staggering across the road. Video games.'

'Did you at any time suspect that Mr *Newell* might be drunk? Or under the influence of drugs?'

'Not until he got out of the car. After the accident.'

'What happened then?'

'Well, first off, he almost fell down. He grabbed the car for support and then started to walk towards the police officer, but he was weaving and . . . and stumbling . . . acting just like a drunk, you know, but I knew he couldn't be drunk.'

'How'd you know that?'

'Well, he wasn't drunk when we started the lesson, and he didn't have anything to drink while we were driving, so how could he be drunk?'

'But he couldn't even give the police his name, isn't that right?'

'Well, he could hardly talk at all. Just . . . you know . . . his speech was slurred, you could hardly understand him.'

'Was this the case while you were driving? During the lesson?'

'No.'

'He spoke clearly during the lesson?'

'Well, as I said, he didn't make very many comments. I think there were one or two times he asked me what I saw, and then he was quiet for the most part.'

'Was this unusual?'

'Well, no, actually. He never commented unless I was doing something wrong. Then he'd say, "What do you see?" Or sometimes, to test me, he'd *let* me go through a stop sign, for example, and then tell me about it afterward.'

'But this afternoon, there weren't many comments?'

'No.'

'He just sat there.'

'Well, yes.'

'Before the woman stepped off the curb, did he ask you what you saw?'

'No.'

'Did he hit the brake on his side of the car?'

'No.'

Andrew Newell didn't come out of it until eight forty-five that night.

Detective Second Grade Carl Williams sat on the edge of a desk in the lieutenant's office, and watched the man trying to shake the cobwebs loose from his head. Blinking into the room. Seeing Carl, blinking again. No doubt wondering where he was and who this big black dude was sitting on the edge of the desk.

'Mr Newell?'

'Mmm.'

'Andrew Newell?'

'Mmm.'

'What are you on, Mr Newell?'

'What?'

'What'd you take, sir, knocked you on your ass that way?'

Newell blinked again.

Go ahead, say it, Carl thought.

'Where am I?' Newell asked.

Bingo.

'Raleigh Station, River Close PD,' Carl said. 'What kind of controlled substance did you take, man?'

'Who the hell are you?'

'Carl Williams, Detective Second, pleased to meet you. Tell me what kind of drug you took, knocked you out that way.'

'I don't know what you're talking about.'

Good-looking white man sitting in the lieutenant's black leather chair, blondish going gray, pale eyes bloodshot after whatever it was he'd taken. Coming out of it almost completely now, looking around the room, realizing he was in some kind of police facility, the lieutenant's various trophies on his bookshelves, the framed headlines from the *River Close Herald* when Raleigh Station broke the big drug-smuggling case three years ago. Blinking again. Still wondering what this was all about. Tell him, Carl thought.

He told him.

'According to what we've got, you were giving Rebecca Patton a driving lesson this afternoon when she ran into a woman. We don't yet know her name. She's in critical condition at Gardner General. Car was equipped with dual brakes. You were the licensed driver in the vehicle, but you didn't hit the brake on your side of the car because you were too stoned either to see the woman stepping off the curb or to react in time to avoid the accident. Now I have to tell you seriously here, Mr Newell, that if the girl didn't know you were under the influence, if she had put her trust in you as her instructor and, in effect, you broke this trust, and this accident occurred, then most likely – and I'm not speaking for the State Attorney here – but most likely you would be the person considered culpable under the law. So it might be a good idea for you to tell me just when you took this drug, whatever it was, and why you knowingly got into a vehicle while under—'

'I didn't take any damn drug,' Newell said. 'I want a lawyer right this goddamn minute.'

Working in the dark on Grove Avenue, playing his flashlight over the leaves on the lawn and in the gutter, Joseph Bisogno kept searching for the red handbag he'd seen the woman carrying just before the car hit her. The police had given up finding it about a half-hour ago, but Joseph knew it was important to them, otherwise they wouldn't have been turning over every leaf in the neighborhood looking for it.

Joseph was sixty-eight years old, a retired steel worker from the days when River Close was still operating the mills and polluting the atmosphere. These days the mills were gone and the town's woman mayor had campaigned on a slogan of 'Clean Air, Clean Streets'. She was about Joseph's age. He admired her a great deal because she was doing something with her life. Joseph had the idea that if he found the handbag, he might become a key figure in this big case the police were working. Newspaper headlines. 'Retired Steelworker Key to Accident.' Television interviews. 'Tell us, Mr Bisogno, did you notice the woman *before* the car struck her?' 'Well, I'll tell you the truth, it all happened so fast . . .'

But, no, it hadn't happened that fast at all.

He'd been out front raking leaves when he saw the woman coming out of the church across the street, Our Lady of Sorrows, the church he himself attended every now and then when he was feeling particularly pious and holy, which was rarely. He enjoyed exercising out of doors, made him feel healthier than when he worked out on the bedroom treadmill. Mowing the lawn, picking weeds, raking leaves the way he'd been doing today, this kind of activity made him feel not like sixty-eight but forty-seven, which was anyway the age he thought of himself as being. Think of yourself as forty, then you'll feel like forty, his wife used to say. But that was before she got cancer.

He was willing to bet a thousand dollars that Mayor Rothstein thought of herself as forty-seven. Good-looking woman, too. Jewish woman. He liked Jewish women – had dated a Jewish girl named Hedda Gold when he was seventeen; she certainly knew how to kiss. Mayor Rothstein had hair as black as Tessie's hair had been before she passed away seven years ago. Maybe if he found the handbag, the mayor would ask him to head up a committee, give him something to do with his life other than mourning Tessie all the time – poor, dear Tessie.

The woman had come down the church steps, red coat flapping open in a mild autumn breeze, red handbag to match, blue skirt and white blouse under it, blue jacket, head bent as if she had serious thoughts on her mind. Leaves falling everywhere around her. Coins from heaven, Tessie used to say. He wondered if Mayor Rothstein believed in heaven; he certainly didn't. Next door, his neighbor had already started a small fire of leaves at the curb. Woman coming up the path from the church now, turning left where the path joined the sidewalk, coming toward where Joseph, on the other side of the street, was raking his leaves.

He thought . . .

For a moment, he thought the car was slowing down because the driver had seen the woman approaching the curb. A blue Ford, coming into the street slowly, cautiously. But then he realized this was a beginning driver, big yellow and black plate on the front bumper, STUDENT DRIVER, the woman stepping off the curb unheedingly, head still bent, the car speeding up as if the driver hadn't seen her after all. And then, oh God, he almost yelled to the woman, almost shouted, *Watch it!* The car, the woman, they . . . he *did* shout this time; yelled 'Lady!' at the top of his lungs, but it was too late. The car hit her with a terrible wrenching thud, metal against flesh, and the woman went up into the air, legs flying, arms flying, the collision throwing her onto his neighbor's leaf fire at the curb, the shrieking of brakes, the driver leaning on her horn too late, too late, all of it too late.

The girl driving the car did not get out.

Neither did the man sitting beside her.

The girl put her head on the steering wheel, not looking at Joseph as he dragged the woman off the fire and rolled her onto the lawn. Joseph went inside to call the police. When he came out again, the girl still had her head on the wheel. The woman's red coat was charred where the flames had got to it.

He remembered all of it now.

Visualized it all over again. The woman going up into the air, legs and arms wide, as if she were trying to fly, arms going up into the air . . .

The handbag.

Yes.

Flying out of her hands, going up, up . . .

He suddenly knew where it was.

*

Newell's attorney didn't get to Raleigh Station until almost ten o'clock that night. His name was Martin Leipman; a smart young man Carl had met on several prior occasions, usually while testifying in court. He was wearing a shadow-striped black suit with a white shirt and a maroon tie that looked like a splash of coagulated blood. He had no objection to Carl reading Miranda to his client – as why would he? – and he listened silently while Carl ascertained that Newell had understood everything he'd explained, and was ready to proceed with answering the questions put to him. Since this had got so serious all of a sudden, Carl had also requested a police stenographer to record whatever Newell might have to say about the accident.

'You understand we can call this off any time you say, don't you?' Leipman asked him.

'I do,' Newell said.

'Just so you know. Go ahead, Detective.'

Carl said, 'Do you remember anything that happened on Grove and Third this afternoon?'

'No, I don't,' Newell said.

'You don't remember the automobile striking that woman?'

'I don't.'

'You don't remember the responding police officers asking you your name?'

'No, I don't.'

'Do you remember taking any drug that would have put you in this altered state?'

'No.'

'Tell me what you do remember.'

'Starting when?'

'Starting when you got into that car.'

'That was after school. I teach Art Appreciation at Buckley High, and I give driving lessons after classes, twice a week. Rebecca Patton is one of my students. She had a lesson today, at ten minutes to three. I don't know who's on the schedule until I see the chart posted in the Driver's Ed office. I go there after my last class, look at the chart and then go out to the trainer car. I was waiting in the Ford at a quarter to three, behind the area where the busses pull in. She knew where to go. She began taking lessons with me over the summer vacation, started at the beginning of August actually ...'

... actually, he's known Rebecca since the term before, when she and her father moved from Washington, D.C. to River Close. Art Appreciation is what is known as a crap course at Buckley High, a *snap* course if one wishes to be politically correct, but Rebecca takes it more seriously than many of the other students do, going to the public library on her own to take out books on the old masters, copying pictures from them by hand ...

'I'm certain she would have gone to a museum if River Close had one, but of course we don't ...'

... so the library had to suffice. She brings her drawings in every week – the class meets only once a week – and asks specific questions about composition and perspective, and color and design, but especially about tension, playing back to him his theory that all works of art are premised on the tension the artist generates within the prescribed confines of the canvas, the painting tugging at the frame in all directions to provide the thrill a spectator feels in the presence of genius.

'I got to know her a little better in August,' Newell said, 'when we began the driving lessons. She told me she wanted to do something creative with her life. She didn't know quite what, whether it'd be music, or art, or even writing, but *something*. She'd just turned sixteen, but she already knew that she didn't plan to spend her life as a bank teller or a telephone operator, she had to do something that required imagination. She told me I'd been responsible for that. My class. What I taught in my class.'

'How'd you feel about that, Mr Newell?' Carl asked.

'I was flattered. And I felt ... well, that I'd done my job. I'd inspired a young mind to think creatively. That's important to me. When I'm teaching art, I always ask my students, "What do you see?" I want them to scrutinize any given painting and tell me in detail what they're seeing. That's how I forge a link between my students and the artist, by asking them to actually *see* what the artist saw while he was executing the work. I try to expand their horizons. I teach them to dare. I teach them to ...'

'Let's get back to this afternoon, shall we?' Carl said.

'We've already covered this afternoon,' Leipman said. 'Unless you've got something new to add.'

'Counselor, I still don't know what your client took.'

'I told you ...'

'He told you ...'

'Then how'd he get in the condition he was in?'

A knock sounded discreetly on the door.

'Come in,' Carl said.

Johnny Bicks, the third man on the squad's afternoon shift, poked his head around the door. 'Talk to you a minute?' he asked.

'Sure,' Carl said, and went out into the hall with him.

'Some guy just came in with what he claims is the victim's handbag,' Johnny said.

'Where is he?'

'Downstairs, at the desk. I already told Katie.'

'Thanks,' Carl said. He opened the door to the lieutenant's office, leaned into the room and said, 'Excuse me a moment, I'll be right back,' and then closed the door and headed for the steps leading downstairs.

The man standing with Katie at the muster desk was telling her that he'd found the bag in one of the trees on Frank Pollack's lawn; his neighbor's lawn. Caught in like one of those forks in the branches, you know? Hard to see because it was red and so were the leaves all around it. Besides, the police officers had been searching the *ground*, you know? Nobody had thought to look up in the trees.

Katie asked the desk sergeant if he had any gloves back there, and he reached under the desk and handed her a pair of somewhat filthy white cotton gloves that had been used in accepting evidence two or three times before, she guessed. As she pulled on the gloves, she realized Mr Bisogno here had already handled the bag but no sense adding insult to injury.

'How do you know it's the victim's?' Carl asked.

'I saw her carrying it,' Bisogno said. 'I'm the one told the officers she was carrying a red handbag.'

Katie was reaching into the bag for the woman's wallet.

212

'You witnessed the accident?' Carl asked.

'I did.'

Katie opened the wallet.

The phone on the muster desk was ringing.

'Raleigh Station, Sergeant Peters.'

Katie pulled out the woman's driver's license.

'Just a second,' Peters said. 'Katie, for you. It's somebody at Gardner General.'

She took the phone.

'Detective Logan,' she said.

'This is Dr Hagstrom in the Emergency Room at Gardner,' a man's voice said.

'Yes, Dr Hagstrom?'

'The Jane Doe we received at three fifty this afternoon?'

'Yes?'

'She's dead,' Hagstrom said.

'Thank you,' Katie said, and handed the phone back to Peters. 'We've got a homicide,' she told Carl.

Carl nodded.

Katie looked at the license in her hand.

The name on it was Mary Beth Newell.

The State Attorney who came to Raleigh Station that night at twenty to eleven was dressed in blue tailored slacks and jacket, no blouse under it, a Kelly green silk scarf at her throat picking up the virtually invisible shadow stripe of the suit. Alyce Hart was wearing blue French-heeled shoes as well, no earrings, no make-up except lipstick. Her brown hair was cut in a wedge that gave a swift look to her angular face, as if she were a schooner cutting through the wind. Katie liked everything about her but the way she chose to spell her first name. Carl liked her because he felt she thought like a man, which Alyce might have considered a dubious compliment. The three of them had worked together before; this was a small town.

'Breathalyzer was negative, right?' she asked.

'Yeah,' Carl said.

'So what was he on?'

'Who knows?'

'Whatever it was, he's wide awake now,' Katie said.

'Can we do a blood test?' Carl asked.

'Under Miranda, you mean?' Alyce said.

'Yeah.'

'Not without his consent. Nothing I'd like better than to see what kind of juice is running through his veins, have him pee for us, too. But we'd need a court order for that, and we can't get one till he's arraigned. This was New York, Chicago, any other big bad city, we'd find an open court, have him arraigned tonight. River Close, though, just *try* to wake up some judge this hour of the night. We'll be lucky if he's arraigned by two, three tomorrow afternoon.'

'Which may be too late,' Katie said.

'Depending on what kind of shit he took,' Carl said.

'If we can't show he was on *something*,' Alyce said, 'we've got no case.'

'Well, we've got witnesses at the scene,' Carl said.

'The girl's a witness, too,' Katie said.

'Sure, but Newell's attorney might . . .'

'No question,' Carl said.

'Right, claim he ...'

'You can bet the farm on it,' Alyce said. 'He'll say the *accident* caused it. Shock, whatever. Couldn't walk, couldn't talk, couldn't remember his own name. Anyway, let's charge him and hold him. We may be able to get an early-morning arraignment. If not, we pray it was a drug with a long half-life. You agree with vehicular manslaughter?'

'I wish we could go for reckless,' Carl said. 'Guy pops pills, and then knowingly gets in a car with a *learner*? He's not only risking *her* life, he's courting disaster with everybody on the street.'

'Let me offer the grand jury a choice,' Alyce said. 'Shoot for reckless manslaughter, settle for vehicular. How does that sound?'

'Good to me,' Katie said.

'Me, too,' Carl said.

'Let's get some sleep,' Alyce said.

Don't let the bimbo answer, Katie thought.

She was sitting at the kitchen counter, sipping a Scotch and soda. The clock on the wall read three minutes to midnight. The phone kept ringing. Three, four, not the bimbo, she prayed.

'Hello?'

The bimbo.

'Let me talk to Stephen, please,' she said.

'Who's this?'

'Mrs Logan,' she said.

'His mother?'

Sure, his mother, Katie thought.

Who happens to be dead.

'His *wife*,' she said, hitting the word hard.

'Oh.'

Long pause.

'Just a sec, OK?'

Sounding like a teeny bopper. Twenty-two years old, Katie thought. The minute hand on the wall clock lurched. Eleven fifty-eight. My how the time flies when you're having ...

'Hello?'

'Stephen?'

'Yes?'

'Katie.'

'Yes, Katie. Do you know what time it is?'

'I spoke to my attorney today ...'

'Katie, we're not supposed to be doing this.'

'Doing what?'

'Talking. The attorneys are supposed to do all the talking.'

'Oh dear, am I breaking the law?' she asked.

'You know you're not breaking the law. But ...'

'Then hear me out. We sent you a counter-proposal last week, and we haven't yet heard from you. I'm eager to get on with this, Stephen. I thought you were, too. Instead ...'

'I am.'

'That's what I imagined. You're the one who left, Stephen.'

'Katie, I really think we should let the lawyers handle this, is what I think, really.'

'I really think you should tell me what's taking you so long to study a one-page document, is what *I* think, really.'

'Katie ...' he said.

And hesitated.

She waited.

'Give me a little time, OK?' he said softly. 'Please.'

And all at once she was bewildered.

In bed that night, all night long, she kept remembering. Because, honestly, you know, she'd had no clue. Smart cop, first in her class at the academy, promoted to detective after a year on the force when she'd walked into a silent-alarm hold-up and apprehended two guys twice her size who were wanted for armed robbery in Indiana, a hell of a long way away, but who was measuring? Smart detective. Had no clue at all that Stephen was cheating on her.

Well, married to the same guy for ten years, who would have guessed? Such a lovely couple, everyone said. High-school sweethearts, everyone said. She'd waited for him while he was in the army, waited for him when he was called up again and sent to yet another distant nation. There was always something to defend, she guessed, honor or oil or some damn thing. But, oh, how handsome he'd looked on the day they were married, Captain Stephen Gregory Logan, in his dress uniform, Miss Katharine Kyle Byrne, all in white, though certainly no virgin. Well, high-school sweethearts, you know. Met him when she was sixteen.

Who would have guessed? Not a clue.

There were the hours, of course.

A policeman's lot is not a happy one, the man once wrote, and he'd been right. The graveyard shift was the worst. You wouldn't think there'd be much crime in a small city like River Close but there were drugs everywhere in America these days, and drugs moved day and night, so you had to have round the clock shifts, and you had to have cops who caught those shifts, on rotation, every three months. Whenever she jammed what was officially called 'the morning shift', Katie left for work at eleven fifteen to get to the squadroom at a quarter to midnight, and didn't get home till a quarter past eight, by which time Stephen had already left for work. During those three months, she saw him maybe five, six hours a day. That wasn't too good for the marriage, she realized now, but who would have guessed then? They're so much in love, everyone said.

So last month, she gets home from a long hard afternoon shift, four to midnight, gets home at about a quarter to one in the morning, and he's sitting in his pajamas in the living room, the lights out, a drink in his hand, and he tells her he's leaving.

Leaving? she says.

She doesn't know what he means at first. Well, the thought is inconceivable, really. His job doesn't call for travel, he's never been *sent* anywhere in all the years of their marriage, so what does he mean, he's leaving? He's a vice president at the bank. In fact it was *his* bank the two hoods from Indiana were trying to rob that day she caught the squeal, away back then when she was twenty-five and riding shotgun in a patrol car with Carl Williams. She always kidded Stephen that he got his promotion to vice president only because she thwarted the hold-up. So what does he mean, he's leaving?

You, he says. I'm leaving you.

Come on, she says, I had a hard day.

Irish sense of humor, right?

Wrong.

He was leaving her.

The police had confiscated the training vehicle the school used for its Driver's Ed course. Technicians from the lab had searched it for evidence that Newell – as instructor and supervisor – had, in effect, been 'driving' the car in violation of subdivision four of section 1192 of the Vehicle and Traffic Law, which stated: 'No person shall operate a motor vehicle while the person's ability to operate such a vehicle is impaired by the use of a drug as defined in this chapter.' The drugs referred to were listed in the Public Health Law and constituted a virtual pharmacology of every opiate, opium derivative, hallucinogenic substance and stimulant known to man. And woman, too, Katie thought.

On Thursday morning, the day after the fatal accident, they drove over to Our Lady of Sorrows in one of the Pontiac sedans set aside for the Raleigh Station's detectives. Carl was driving, Katie was riding shotgun beside him.

'Guess what Annie cooked again last night?' Carl asked.

'Asparagus,' Katie said.

'Asparagus,' Carl said. 'We're married six years, she *knows* I hate asparagus, but she keeps making asparagus. I told her why do you keep making asparagus when you know I hate it? First she says, "It's good for you." I tell her I don't *care* if it's good for me, I don't like the taste of it. So she says, "You'll *get* to like the taste of it." So I tell her I'm thirty-seven years old, I've been hating asparagus for thirty-seven years, I am *never* going to like the taste of it. You know what she says next?'

'What?' Katie asked.

'She says, "Anyway, you *do* like it." Can you believe that? I'm telling her I hate it, she tells me I like it. So I tell her one more time I *hate* asparagus, please don't make asparagus again, I *hate* it! So she says, "When you get to be President of the United States, you won't have to eat asparagus. Meanwhile, it's good for you."'

'That was broccoli.'

'Just what I told her.'

'There's the church,' Katie said.

Bright morning sunlight was flooding the churchyard as they entered it through an arched wooden door leading from the church proper. Katie had expected to find Father McDowell on his knees in prayer. Saying matins, she imagined, wasn't that the one they said in the morning? The good father was, in fact, on his knees – but he was merely gathering flowers. Katie guessed he was a man in his early seventies, with a ruddy face which led her to believe he enjoyed a touch of the sacramental wine every now and again. He greeted them warmly and told them at once that he himself had planted the mums he was now cutting for the altar. Planned the garden so that it bloomed all through the spring, summer and autumn months. The mums he was carefully placing in a wicker basket were yellow and white and purple and brown. They reminded Katie of Stephen, damn him! Excuse me, Father, she thought.

'We're here to ask about a woman named Mary Beth Newell,' she said. 'We have reason to believe she was here at Our Lady of Sorrows yesterday. Would you remember her?'

'Yes, of course,' McDowell said.

He snipped another stem, carefully placing stem and bloom alongside the others in the basket.

A football game. Stephen bringing Katie a bright orange mum to pin to her white cheerleader's sweater. The big letter B on the front of the sweater. For Buckley High.

'Is it true her husband has been arrested for killing her?' McDowell asked.

'He's been charged with vehicular homicide, yes, Father.'

'But why? I understand a young girl was driving.'

'That's true. But he was the licensed driver.'

'It still seems ...'

'The girl didn't know he was under the influence. State attorney believes the fault was his. *Did* Mrs Newell come here yesterday?'

'She did.'

'Can you tell us what time she got here?'

'Around two fifteen, two twenty.'

'And left when?'

'An hour or so later.'

They were here to learn whether or not the priest had seen the accident. They were building a list of reliable witnesses, the more the merrier. But McDowell's response stopped Katie cold. Her next question should have been, 'Did you see her leaving the church?' Instead, she said, 'Mrs Newell spent a full *hour* with you?'

'Well, almost, yes.'

Katie suddenly wondered why.

'Father,' she said, 'we know Mrs Newell lived in St Matthew's parish, some ten blocks from here.'

'That's right.'

'Is that where she worships?'

'I have no idea.'

'Well, does she worship here?'

'No, she doesn't.'

'Then what was she doing here, Father?'

'She'd been coming to me for spiritual guidance.'

'Are you saying that today wasn't the *only* time she ...?'

'I can't tell you anything more, I'm sorry.'

Katie knew all about privileged communication, thanks. But she was Irish. And she sniffed something in the wind.

'Father,' she said, 'no one's trying to pry from you whatever ...'

McDowell was Irish, too.

'I'm sorry,' he said, and snipped another stem as though he were decapitating someone possessed by the devil. Katie figured he was signaling an end to the conversation. Gee, Father, tough, she thought.

'Father,' she said, 'we don't want to know *what* you talked about ...' Like hell we don't, she thought. '... but if you can tell us when she first came to see you.'

'Is that why you're here?' McDowell said. 'To invade a dead woman's privacy?' Wagging his head scornfully, he rose from where he was kneeling, almost losing his balance for a moment, but regaining it at once, his prized basket of cut flowers looped over his arm. Standing, he seemed to be at least six feet tall. 'She got here at around two fifteen,' he repeated, 'and left about an hour later. Does that help you?'

'Sure, but when's the *first* time she came here?' Carl asked.

He'd been silent until now, letting Katie carry the ball. But sometimes a little muscle helped. Unless you were dealing with a higher authority. Like God.

'I'm sorry, I can't tell you that,' McDowell said.

So they double-ganged him.

'Did she spend an hour *each* time she visited you?' Katie asked.

'How many times *did* she visit, anyway?' Carl asked.

McDowell shook his head in disbelief. He was striding swiftly toward the entrance to the church now, the basket of flowers on his arm, the black skirts of his cassock swirling about his black trousers and highly polished black shoes. They kept pace with him, one on either side.

'She wasn't here to discuss her *husband*, was she?' Carl asked.

'Some problem her *husband* had?' Katie asked.

'Like a *drug* problem?' Carl asked.

McDowell stopped dead in his tracks. Pulling himself up to his full height, he said with dignity, 'The only problems Mary Beth discussed with me were her own. Good day, detectives.'

And went into his church.

So now they knew that Mary Beth Newell had problems.

Just before noon, Alyce Hart called the squadroom to say that Newell still hadn't been arraigned and if there were any further questions they wanted to ask, they'd best do it now. 'The irony of our judicial system,' she said, 'is that we can ask the accused anything we want *before* he's arraigned, but after that we need his lawyer's permission to talk to him.'

Katie wasn't quite sure what 'irony' meant, exactly. Besides, she couldn't think of anything she wanted to ask except what kind of dope Newell had taken and when he'd taken it.

At a quarter past one, the phone on her desk rang again. She picked up, identified herself, and listened as a member of the search team told her that the steering wheel had yielded no evidence that Rebecca Patton had, in fact, been driving the car when it hit Mary Beth Newell. Any prints on the wheel were hopelessly overlayed and smeared because too damn many students used the same training vehicle. The techs had also found palm and fingerprints on the driver's side dashboard, presumably left there by the several instructors who used the same car and who'd reached out protectively and defensively whenever a student's reaction time was a bit off. But these, too, were smeared or superimposed one upon the other, and did nothing to prove that Andrew Newell was effectively unconscious at the time of the accident.

Katie kept listening.

The next thing he said puzzled her.

At first she thought he'd said they'd found *cocaine* in the car. She *thought* he'd said, 'We also found a cup with a little *coke* in it.' Which was what he *had* said, but at the same time *hadn't* said.

A moment later, she learned that what he'd *actually* said was, 'We also found a cup with a little *Coke* in it.' Coke with a capital C. Coca-*Cola* was what he was telling her. In the Ford's center console cup holder on the passenger side, they had found a medium-sized plastic cup with the red and white Coca-Cola logo on it, which cup they had immediately tested.

Katie held her breath.

'Nothing but Coca-Cola in it,' the tech said. 'But the guy sitting there could have used it to wash down whatever shit he ingested. A possibility, Kate.'

But . . .

He didn't have anything to drink while we were driving, so how could he be drunk?

How indeed? Katie wondered.

Katie got to the school at two twenty that afternoon. She went directly to the general office, showed a twenty-year-old brunette her shield and ID card, and asked for a copy of Rebecca Patton's program. The girl hesitated.

'Something wrong?' Katie asked.

'Nothing,' the girl said, and went to the files.

Katie waited while she photocopied the program. It told her that Rebecca would be in an eighth-period French class till the end of the school day.

'Where's the Driver's Ed office?' she asked.

'What do you need *there*?' the girl asked.

Katie looked at her.

'Down the hall,' the girl said at once, 'second door on the left. You're trying to send Mr Newell to jail, aren't you?'

'Yes,' Katie said, and walked out.

What she needed in the Driver's Ed office was a feel of the place. This was where Andrew Newell came at the end of each school day to consult the chart that told him which student would be driving that day. This was where he'd come yesterday, before getting into the car that would run down his wife. Here was the wall. Here was the chart. Here were the teachers' names and the students' names. Was this the room in which he'd ingested the drug – whichever the hell drug it was – that had, minutes later, rendered him incompetent?

'You're the detective, aren't you?' a man's voice said.

Katie turned from the wall chart.

'Saw you on television last night.' He was sprawled in an easy chair, open newspaper on his lap. 'Right after Andy was charged,' he said. 'Eleven o'clock news. The red hair,' he explained.

Katie nodded.

'Ed Harris,' he said. 'No relation.'

She must have looked puzzled.

'The movie star,' he said. 'Ed Harris. Besides, he's bald.'

This Ed Harris was not bald. He had thick black hair, graying at the temples, brown eyes behind dark-rimmed eyeglasses. He rose and extended his hand. Katie guessed he was half an inch short of six feet. Forty, forty-two, or thereabouts. Lean and lanky, like Abe Lincoln. Same rangy look. She took his hand.

'Are you going to send Andy to jail for the rest of his life?'

'Hardly,' she said, and almost shook her head in wonder. Their case was premised on the presumption that Newell had knowingly entered the training car while under the influence of a drug that had rendered him incapable of performing in his supervisory capacity. This constituted a criminally negligent act which had caused the death of another person. But the penalty for vehicular manslaughter in the second degree was only imprisonment not to exceed seven years. 'If he's found guilty,' she said, 'the maximum ...'

'I sincerely hope he won't be.'

'Well, *if* he's convicted, the maximum sentence would be seven years. He could be out in two and a third.'

'Piece of cake, right?'

Katie said nothing.

'Two and a third *days* would destroy him,' Harris said.

She was thinking, If you can't do the time, don't do the crime. She still said nothing.

'For a lousy accident, right?' Harris said. 'Accidents *do* happen, you know.'

'Especially if a person's under the influence.'

'Andy doesn't drink.'

'Ever see him stoned?'

'Andy? Come on. If you knew him, you'd realize how ridiculous that sounds.'

'I take it you're good friends.'

'*Very* good friends.'

'Do you know Rebecca, too?'

'Sure, she's in my algebra class.'

'Is she a good student?'

'One of the best. Smart as hell, curious, eager to learn. And from what Andy tells me, a good driver, too.'

'Not good enough. That's why there's a brake pedal on the instructor's side of the car.'

'Let me tell you something,' Harris said, and immediately looked up at the wall clock. She had seen his name on the chart for a driving lesson at two fifty with a student named Alberico Jiminez. The clock now read two thirty-five. In five minutes, Rebecca would be coming out of her French class. Katie didn't want to miss her.

'Andy and I both teach Driver's Ed,' Harris said. 'The classes are two hours long, twice a week. I teach them on Mondays and Thursdays, Andy teaches them on Wednesdays and Fridays. This is class time, you understand, not road time. Four hours a week. We try to teach *responsible* driving, Miss Logan, and we spend a great deal of time on how substance abuse affects ability and perception. These are teenagers, you know. Some of them drink, some of them smoke dope. We're all aware of that. Rebecca would have known in a minute if Andy had been under the influence. She knows all the signs, we've been over them a hundred times.'

'We have witnesses who saw him staggering, saw him—'

'Your witnesses are wrong.'

'My witnesses are police officers.'

Harris gave her a look.

'Right,' Katie said, 'we're out to frame the entire nation.'

'Nobody said that. But you know, Miss Logan ...'

'Newell *should* have hit the brake. The responsibility was his.'

'No. If anyone was responsible, it was Mary Beth. She's the one who wasn't looking where she was going. She's the one who stepped off that curb and into the car.'

'How can you possibly know *what* she did?'

'I read the papers, I watch television. There were witnesses besides your police officers.'

'And she was your friend . . .'

'She was.'

'Any idea what might have been troubling her?'

'Who says she was troubled?'

'You didn't detect anything wrong?'

'No. Wrong? No.'

A bell sounded, piercing, insistent, reminding her that this was, in fact, a school, and that she was here to see a student.

As she turned to leave, Harris said, 'You're making a mistake here, Miss Logan. If nobody hit that brake, there simply wasn't *time* to hit it.'

'Good talking to you, Mr Harris,' Katie said.

'Ed,' he said. 'Don't hurt him.'

Rebecca came down the front steps of the school at a quarter to three, her books hugged to the front of her pale-blue sweater. Girls and boys were streaming down the steps everywhere around her, flowing toward where the idling yellow school busses were parked. A bright buzz of conversation, a warm consonance of laughter floated on the crisp October air.

'Hey, hi,' she said, surprised.

'Hi, Rebecca. Give you a ride home?'

'Well . . . sure,' she said.

Katie fell into step beside her. Together, they walked in silence across the curving drive and into the parking lot. Leaves were falling everywhere around them, blowing on the wind, rustling underfoot. Katie reached into her tote bag. Her keys were resting beside the walnut stock of a .38 caliber Detectives Special. She dug them out and unlocked the door of the car on the passenger side.

'I sometimes think I'll never get in another car again,' Rebecca said.

'It wasn't your fault,' Katie said.

'It wasn't his, either.'

'Tell me something. When you said . . .'

'I don't want to say anything that will hurt Mr Newell.'

'His negligence killed someone,' Katie said flatly.

'You don't know he was drugged. Maybe he had a stroke or something. Or a heart attack. Something. It didn't have to be drugs. You just don't know for sure.'

'That's what we're trying to find out.'

'He must be *heart*broken, his own *wife*!'

'It doesn't matter who it was, he—'

'*I* was the one driving! Why should Mr Newell . . .?'

'You were in his custody.'

'I was *driving*!'

'And he was *stoned*!' Katie said sharply. 'His responsibility was to—'

'Please, please, don't.'

'Rebecca, listen to me!'

'What?'

Her voice catching. She's going to start crying again, Katie thought.

'Did you know he was drugged?' she asked.

'No.'

'Then you're not culpable, can you understand that? And protecting him would be a horrible mistake. I want you to answer one question.'

'I can't, please, I—'

'You *can*, damn it!'

Her voice crushed the autumn stillness. Leaves fell like colored shards of broken glass. In the distance there was the rumble of the big yellow busses pulling away from the school.

'You told me Andrew Newell didn't drink anything while you were driving,' Katie said. 'Is that still your recollection?'

Silence.

'Rebecca?'

The girl hugged her schoolbooks to her chest, head bent, blonde hair cascading on either side of her face. The sounds of the busses faded. Leaves fell, twisted, floated. They stood silently, side by side, in a stained-glass cathedral of shattered leaves. Gray woodsmoke drifted on the air from somewhere, everywhere. Katie suddenly remembered all the autumns there ever were.

'We stopped for a Coke,' Rebecca said.

'This was right after the lesson began,' Katie told Carl. They were sitting side by side at wooden desks in the squadroom. Most of the furniture here went back to the early forties when River Close first established a detective division. Until that time, any big case here, the chief had to call in detectives from the county seat up Twin River Junction. 'Say five after three; Rebecca didn't check her watch. Newell said he was thirsty, and directed her to the drive-in on Olive and High. They ordered a Coke for him at the drive-in window, and were on their way in five seconds flat. Newell kept sipping the Coke as they drove.'

'Did Rebecca see him popping any pills?'

'No.'

'So all we've got is the tech's guess.'

'Plus Newell stoned at the scene some fifteen minutes later.'

Both of them fell silent.

At four this afternoon, Newell had finally been arraigned, and they'd got their court order for blood and urine tests. They were waiting for the results now. Meanwhile, they had statements from all the various witnesses, but that was all they had.

It was now a quarter past five and dusk was coming on fast.

At six thirty, just as Katie and Carl were packing it in, the phone on her desk rang. It was Alyce Hart, calling to say that Newell's blood had tested positive for secobarbital sodium.

'Brand name's Seconal,' she said. 'Not often prescribed as a sedative these days. From what the lab tells me, fifty milligrams is the sedative dose. For Newell to have presented the effects he did at the scene, he had to've ingested at least three times that amount.'

'A hundred and fifty mills.'

'Right. That's the hypnotic dose for a man of his weight. Full hypnotic effect of the drug usually occurs fifteen to thirty minutes following oral or rectal administration.'

'Think somebody shoved it up his ass?'

'Unlikely. Effects would've been very similar to alcoholic inebriation. Imperfect articulation of speech, failure of muscular coordination, clouded sensorium.'

'What's that?'

'Sensorium? State of consciousness or mental awareness. I had to ask, too.'

Which was another thing Katie liked about Alyce.

'How long would these effects last?' she asked.

'Three to eight hours.'

'Fits Newell, doesn't it?'

'Oh, doesn't it just?'

'Think he was an habitual user?'

'Who cares? We've got a case now, Katie.'

'We've also got what he washed the pills down with.'

'Oh?'

Katie told her about Newell stopping to buy a Coke just before the accident. She also mentioned that she'd been to Our Lady of Sorrows and had learned that Mary Beth Newell had taken her problems to the priest there, seeking spiritual guidance.

'Problems. What kind of problems?'

'He wouldn't say. But Our Lady of Sorrows isn't her parish.'

'What is her parish?'

'St Matthew's.'

'How far away?'

'Ten blocks.'

'Mm,' Alyce said, and was silent for a moment. 'What are you thinking, Katie?'

'Well ... if Newell *knew* his wife was troubled about something, his lawyers might claim her state of mind was such that she caused the accident herself.'

'Yeah, go ahead.'

'By not paying attention to where she was going. Or even by deliberately stepping into the car's path.'

'It's a defense, yes,' Alyce said thoughtfully.

'So, what I was thinking is maybe we should try to find out exactly *what* was bothering her. Before the defense does. In fact, I thought I might drop in on her sister tomorrow morning.'

'OK, but don't expect too much. This may turn out to be nothing. Everybody has problems, Katie. Don't you have problems?'

'Me?' Katie said. 'Not a worry in the world.'

Thing she used to do when she and Stephen were still a proper man and wife, would be to ask him questions. 'Stephen, what does "irony" mean, exactly?' And, of course, he would tell her. He'd been telling her things ever since she was sixteen. Anything she wanted to know, she'd ask Stephen and he would tell her. So what she wanted to do *now* was pick up the phone and call him. Say, 'Hi, Stephen, I hope I'm not interrupting you and your bimbo at ... what time is it, anyway? My oh my, is it *really* one fifteen in the morning? I certainly hope I'm not intruding. But someone used the word "irony" in my presence, and it occurred to me that although I often use that word myself, or even its sister word "ironic" I've never been really quite sure what *either* of those words mean exactly. So, Stephen, if it's not too much trouble, I wonder ...'

But no.

Because you see, she and Stephen were no longer proper man and wife, she and

Stephen were separated, that was the irony of it, that was what was so very damn ironic about the situation. So she got out of bed in her pajamas and padded barefoot to the little room Stephen had used as a study when he still lived here, and went to the bookshelves behind what used to be his desk and found the dictionary and thumbed through it till first she found 'iron' and then 'ironclad' and 'iron hand' and finally, bingo, there it was, 'ironic'. And guess what the definition was? The definition, according to Mr Webster himself, was: 'meaning the contrary of what is expressed.'

Huh? she thought.

How does that . . .?

She ran her finger down the page and found the word 'irony', and its first definition seemed to echo what she'd just learned about 'ironic'. In which case, she wondered, what's so damn *ironic* about them not being able to question Newell after he was arraigned? But hold it, kiddies, not so fast, here came the *second* definition. Katie took a sip of Scotch. 'Irony,' she read out loud. 'A result that is the opposite of what might be expected or considered appropriate.'

So if you can question a man because you *hope* to charge him with a crime, but then you can no longer question him after he's been *charged* with that crime, she guessed that was sure enough ironic.

Yep, that's irony, she thought.

How about that, Stephen?

How about that, hon?

A fine Friday-morning mist burnt away as Katie drove through the small village of River Bend, and then into the countryside again, where narrow streams wound through glades covered with fallen leaves. She drove onto a covered bridge, the interior of her car going dark, brilliant sunlight splashing her windshield a moment later. She hoped she wouldn't get a migraine, sudden changes of light often brought them on. Stephen would fetch her two aspirin tablets and advise her to lie down at once. No migraine, please, she thought. Not now. No Stephen to offer solace, you see.

The towns, hamlets, villages and occasional city in this part of the state suffered from a watery sameness of nomenclature due to a natural abundance of rivers and lakes. Mary Beth Newell's sister was a kindergarten teacher in Scotts Falls, named after the rapids that cascaded from the southernmost end of Lake Paskonomee, some twenty miles north-east of River Close, and within shouting distance of Twin River Junction, the county seat. If Andrew Newell had been charged with reckless endangerment, his attorney most likely would have asked for a change of venue and Alyce would have had to prosecute in Twin River J, as the town was familiarly known to the locals. Even with the lesser charge, Leipman might ask that the case be moved out of River Close. Either way, Alyce would go for the jugular.

Katie found Helen Pierce in a fenced-in area behind the elementary school. Katie had spoken to her only once before, on the telephone the night they learned Mary Beth Newell was dead. She had seen only police photographs of the dead woman's body, and could not form any true opinion as to whether or not the sisters resembled each other. The woman now leading a chanting band of feathered and painted five-year-olds in what appeared to be a war dance was in her late thirties, Katie guessed, with soft brown hair and deep brown eyes. She wore no make-up, not even lipstick. She had on a plain blue smock and Reeboks with no socks. She was also wearing a huge feathered headdress. Calling a break, she told Katie that this was an authentic Lakota Sioux ritual rain dance, and that she and the children were trying to break the twenty-seven-day drought that had gripped the region.

'Keeps the foliage on the trees,' she said, 'but the reservoirs are down some fifty per cent.' She waved her feathered dancers toward a long wooden table upon which pint cartons of milk and platters of cookies had been set out. Keeping a constant eye on the children, she walked Katie to a nearby bench, where they sat side by side in dappled shade.

'Did your sister ever mention her visits to a priest at Our Lady of Sorrows?' Katie asked.

'No,' Helen said at once, and turned toward her, surprised. 'Why would she go there? Her church is St Matthew's.'

'The priest indicated that something was troubling her. Would she have mentioned that to you?'

'No. But why is it important?'

Katie explained what a possible defense tactic might be. Helen listened intently, shaking her head, occasionally sighing. At last, she said, 'That's absurd, nothing was troubling my sister that deeply. Nothing she confided to me, anyway. Well . . . but no.'

'What?'

'She and Andy were trying to have a baby. Without any luck.'

'Would that have bothered her enough to . . .?'

'Well, Andy's *attitude* might have annoyed her. But I don't think she'd have gone to a priest about it.'

'What attitude?'

'He didn't want a "damn baby", as he put it. Went along with her efforts only because she threatened to leave him if he didn't. But they argued day and night about it, even when other people were with them. He kept saying if they had a damn baby, they'd never be able to go back to Europe the way he wanted to. He studied art in Europe, you know, and his big dream was to go back there. That's what he'd been saving for, and having a baby would ruin all that. I sometimes felt the reason she couldn't conceive was because of Andy's negative stance. I know that's dumb, but it's what I thought.'

'But she never once mentioned seeing Father McDowell?'

'No.'

'Never mentioned whatever was troubling her?'

'Never.' She was silent for a moment, and then suddenly, as if the idea had just occurred to her, she asked, 'Have you looked for a diary?'

'No, did she keep . . .?'

'Why don't you look for a diary or something?' Helen said. 'She always kept a diary when we were kids. Little lock on it, kept it in her top dresser drawer, under her socks. I'll bet anything she *still* keeps one, you really should take a look.' And then, all at once, she realized that she was speaking of her sister in the present tense, as if she were still alive. Her eyes clouded. 'Well, we were kids,' she said, and fell silent. Across the yard, the children were beginning to get restless. 'This whole damn thing,' she said, shaking her head, 'the damn *stupidity* of it . . . the . . . the very *idea* that some smart lawyer might try to get Andy off on a ridiculous claim of . . . of . . . Mary Beth being *troubled*!'

She rose abruptly.

'Send him away,' she said. 'Send the son of a bitch away for life.' Katie was about to explain yet another time that all you could get for vehicular homicide was a maximum of seven years. But Helen had already turned away, and in an overly loud voice she shouted, 'OK, let's make *rain!*'

The request Katie typed into her computer read:

1. I am a detective of the River Close Police Department, assigned to the Raleigh Station, where I am currently investigating the vehicular homicide of Mary Beth Newell.
2. I have information based upon facts supplied to me by Father Brian McDowell, pastor of the Church of Our Lady of Sorrows in River Close, that Mrs Newell had been coming to him 'for spiritual guidance' regarding personal problems.
3. I have information based upon facts supplied to me by Mrs Helen Pierce, the deceased's sister, that she kept a locked personal diary in the top drawer of her . . .

Well, now, she thought, leave us pause a moment, shall we? Am I telling the absolute truth here? On an affidavit that will be sworn to before a magistrate? True, Helen Pierce told me her sister *used* to keep a locked diary when she was a kid, *used* to keep it in the top drawer of her dresser, is what Helen told me, Your Honor, I swear to that on a stack of bibles.

But she also said, and I quote this verbatim, 'I'll bet anything she *still* keeps one, you really should take a look,' is what she told me. Those were her exact words. So, whereas I *do* fervently wish to send Andrew Newell away for a very long time, the son of a bitch, I don't think I'm lying or even stretching the truth here when I say that I have information – based on facts supplied by her sister, Your Honor – that Mary Beth Newell kept a locked personal diary in the top drawer of her dresser, although not under her socks.

So, Your Honor . . .

Based upon the foregoing reliable information and upon my own personal knowledge, there is probable cause to believe that Mrs Newell may have confided to her diary information regarding her state of mind at the time of the incident, which information would help determine whether Mrs Newell was sufficiently troubled or distracted to have recklessly contributed in some measure to her own demise.

Which is exactly what Newell's lawyers would love to prove, and that's why I want to get my hands on that diary, if it exists, before they do, Your Honor.

Wherefore, I respectfully request that the court issue a search warrant in the form annexed hereto, authorizing a search of the premises at 1220 Hanover Road, Apartment 4C, for a diary belonging to the deceased.

They tossed the apartment high and low and could not find a locked diary in Mary Beth's top dresser drawer or anyplace else. They did, however, find an appointment calendar.

In plain view, as they would later tell Alyce Hart.

Which meant they were within their rights to seize the calendar as evidence without violating the court order.

The calendar revealed that starting on the twenty-first day of August, Mary Beth Newell had scheduled appointments at two fifteen every Wednesday and Saturday afternoon, with someone she'd listed only as 'McD'. These meetings continued through to the day of the accident.

'Well, even beyond that,' Katie said. 'Take a look. She had another one scheduled for tomorrow, and another two next week. Now unless she was going to McDonald's for hamburgers, I think we can safely assume the "McD" stands for McDowell. In which case ...'

'Let's revisit the man,' Carl said.

Father McDowell was alone in a small chapel off the side portal, deep in silent prayer when they entered the church through the center doors at three that afternoon. A blazing afternoon sun illuminated the high arched stained-glass windows, washing the aisles with color. They spotted the priest at once, and waited respectfully until he made the sign of the cross and got to his feet. He stood staring at the crucifix over the altar for a moment, as though not quite finished with his Lord and Savior, adding a postscript to his prayers, so to speak, and then made the sign of the cross again, and started backing away into the main church. He turned, saw them at once, scowled with the memory of their earlier visit, and seemed ready to make a dash for the safety of the church proper – but they were upon him too swiftly; he was trapped in the tiny chapel.

'Few questions, Father,' Katie said at once.

'I have business to attend to,' he said.

'So do we,' Carl said.

'We have Mary Beth Newell's appointment calendar,' Katie said. 'It shows she'd been coming to see you twice a week since the third week in August.'

Father McDowell said nothing.

'That sounds pretty serious to us,' Carl said. 'A woman walking all the way over here, twice a week.'

'What was troubling her, Father?'

'We need to know.'

'Why?' he asked.

'Did Andrew Newell know she was coming here?'

From the organ loft, quite abruptly, there came the sound of thick sonorous notes, flooding the church. The glorious music, the sunlight streaming through the stained glass, the scent of incense burning somewhere, the flickering of votive candles in small red containers on the altar behind McDowell, all blended to lend the small church the sudden air of a medieval cathedral, where knights in armor came to say their last confessions before riding off to battle.

'Why was she coming to see you?' Katie asked.

'Why not her own parish?' Carl asked.

'Help us, Father,' Katie said.

'Why?' he asked again.

'Because if her husband knew she was coming here, if he *knew* his wife was troubled about something ...'

'Then his attorney might try to show she was distracted at the time of the accident ...'

'... walked into that car because her mind was on something else.'

'Worse yet, walked into it *deliberately*.'

'She was not suicidal, if that's what you're suggesting,' McDowell said.

'Then tell us *what* she was.'

'Help us,' Katie said again.

The priest sighed heavily.

'Please,' she said.

He nodded, almost to himself, nodded again and then walked into the church proper, up the center aisle to a pew some six rows back from the main altar. The detectives sat one on either side of him. As he spoke, McDowell kept his eyes on the crucifix hanging above the altar, as if begging forgiveness for breaking faith with someone who had come to him in confidence. From the organ loft, the music swelled magnificently. McDowell spoke in a whisper that cut through the laden air like a whetted knife.

'She came to see me because she suspected her husband was having an affair,' he said. 'She was too embarrassed to go to her parish priest.'

But twice a week? Katie thought. For eight weeks? Ever since the twenty-first of August?

As McDowell tells it, at first she is uncertain, blaming herself for being a suspicious wife, wondering if her doubts have more to do with her inability to become pregnant than with what she perceives as her husband's wandering. He doesn't want a baby, she knows that; he has made that abundantly clear to her. As the weeks go by and she becomes more and more convinced that he is cheating on her, she wonders aloud and tearfully if perhaps her incessant campaign, her relentless attempts to conceive, her strict insistence on observing the demands of the calendar and the thermometer chart, haven't transmogrified what should have been a pleasurable act into an onerous experience, something dutiful and distasteful, something rigid and structured that has forced him to seek satisfaction elsewhere.

'By the end of the summer, she was positive there was another woman,' McDowell said.

'Did she say who?'

'No. But she was becoming very frightened.'

'Why?'

'Because someone was following her.'

'She saw someone following her?'

'No, she didn't actually *see* anyone. But she felt a presence behind her. Watching her every move.'

'A presence?' Carl asked, raising his eyebrows skeptically.

'Yes,' McDowell said. 'Someone behind her. Following her.'

'Good!' Alyce said on the telephone that evening. 'This only makes him more despicable!'

'You think he was the one following her?' Katie asked.

'Either him or his bimbo, who cares? Here's a woman trying to get pregnant and her darling husband's fooling around. Just *let* the defense try to show her as a troubled woman – I dare them. The trouble was her *husband*. Gets into a car stoned out of his mind and causes the death of an innocent wife who's faithfully attempting to create a family while he's running around with another woman. Seven years? The jury will want to *hang* him!'

Katie hoped she was right.

228

'Let's nail it down,' Alyce said. 'I want a minute by minute timetable, Katie. I want to know who saw the training car leaving the school parking lot at exactly what time. Who served Andrew Newell that Coke at exactly what time. Who saw Mary Beth Newell step out of that church and start walking toward her rendezvous with death at exactly what time . . .'

Sounding like she was already presenting her closing argument to the jury . . .

'. . . who saw the car approaching the crossing of Third and Grove at exactly what time. Who saw the car striking that poor woman at exactly what time. It takes fifteen to thirty minutes for Seconal to start working. OK, let's prove to a jury that he had to've swallowed the drug on the way to Grove and Third and was incapable of preventing his own wife's death! Let's prove the cheating bastard *killed* her!'

Amen, Katie thought.

The accident had taken place on Wednesday at approximately three twenty in the afternoon. This was now eleven a.m. on Saturday morning, the nineteenth day of October, and the drive-in at this hour was virtually deserted, the breakfast crowd having already departed, the lunch crowd not yet here.

Katie and Carl asked to see the manager and were told by a sixteen-year-old kid wearing a red and yellow uniform that the manager was conducting a training session just now and wouldn't be free for ten, fifteen minutes. Carl told her to inform the manager that the police were here. They ordered coffee and donuts at the counter, and carried them to one of the booths. The manager came out some three minutes later.

She was nineteen or twenty, Katie guessed, a pert little black woman with a black plastic name tag that told them she was JENNIE DEWES, MGR. She slid in the booth alongside Carl, looked across at Katie, and said, 'What's the trouble?'

'No trouble,' Katie said. 'We're trying to pinpoint the exact time a Coca-Cola would have been purchased here on Wednesday afternoon.'

Jennie Dewes, Mgr looked at her.

'You're kidding, right?' she said.

'No, we're serious, miss,' Carl said.

'You know how many Cokes we serve here every day?'

'This would've been a Coke you served some time around three o'clock this past Wednesday,' Katie said.

'You mind if I see your badges, please?' Jennie said.

Katie opened her handbag, fished out her shield in its leather fob. Carl had already flipped open his wallet.

'OK,' Jennie said, and nodded. 'This would've been drive-in or counter?'

'Drive-in,' Katie said.

'Three o'clock would've been Henry on the window. Let me get him.'

She left the booth, and returned some five minutes later with a lanky young blond boy who looked frightened.

'Sit down, son,' Carl said.

The boy sat. Sixteen, seventeen years old, Katie guessed, narrow acne-ridden face, blue eyes wide in fear. Jennie sat, too. Four of them in the booth now. Jennie sitting beside Carl, Henry on Katie's left.

'We're talking about three days ago,' Carl said. 'Blue Ford Escort with a student driver plate on it, would you remember?'

'No, sir, I'm sorry, I sure don't,' Henry said.

'Don't be scared, Henry,' Katie said. 'You're not in any trouble here.'

'I'm not scared, ma'am,' he said.

'Blue Ford Escort. Yellow and black student driver plates on the front and rear bumper.'

'Young blonde girl would've been driving.'

'Pulled in around three, ordered a Coke.'

'Not at the window,' Jennie said suddenly.

They all looked at her.

'If this is the right girl, I saw her inside here. Pretty white girl, blonde, sixteen, seventeen years old.'

'Sixteen, yes. Brown eyes.'

'Didn't notice her eyes.'

'Man with her would've been older.'

'Thirty-two.'

'Wasn't any man with her when I saw her.'

'What time was this?' Katie asked.

'Around three, like you say. She was coming out of the ladies' room. Went to the counter to pick up her order.'

'Picked up a Coke at the counter?'

'*Two* of them was what she picked up. Two medium Cokes.'

They found her at a little past noon in the River Close Public Library, poring over a massive volume of full-color Picasso prints. The table at which she sat was huge and oaken, with green-shaded lamps casting pools of light all along its length. There was a hush to the room. Head bent, blonde hair cascading over the open book, Rebecca did not sense their approach until they were almost upon her. She reacted with a startled gasp, and then recovered immediately.

'Hey, hi,' she said.

'Hello, Rebecca,' Katie said.

Carl merely nodded.

The two detectives sat opposite her at the table. A circle of light bathed the riotous Picasso print, touched Rebecca's pale hands on the open book, and Carl's darker hands flat on the table top.

'Rebecca,' Katie said, 'what happened to the second Coke container?'

'What?' Rebecca said, and blinked.

'You bought two Cokes,' Carl said. 'The techs found only one empty container in the car. What happened to the other one?'

'I guess I threw it out,' Rebecca said.

'Then there *were* two containers, right?'

'I guess so. Yes, there probably were.'

'Why'd you throw it out?' Katie asked.

'Well ... because I'd finished with it.'

'Rebecca ... the container you threw out wasn't yours, was it?'

'Yes, it was. I'm sorry, I don't know what you're ...'

'It was Mr Newell's, wasn't it?'

'No, I distinctly remember ...'

'The one *he* was drinking from, isn't that true?'

'No, that was in the holder. The cup holder. On the center console. I'm sorry, but I'm not following you. If you can tell me what you're looking for, maybe I can help you. But if you ...'

'Where'd you toss the container?' Carl asked.

'Somewhere on the ... the street, I guess. I really don't remember.'

'Where on the street?'

'I don't remember the exact location. I just opened the window and threw it out.'

'Was it somewhere between the drive-in and the spot where you ran down Mrs Newell?'

'I suppose so.'

'We'll look for it,' Carl said.

'We'll find it,' Katie said.

'So find it,' Rebecca said. 'What's so important about a stupid *Coke* container, anyway?'

'The residue,' Katie said.

And suddenly Rebecca was weeping.

The way she tells it ...

This was after she'd been informed of her rights, and after her attorney and her father had both warned her, begged her not to answer any questions.

But she tells it, anyway.

She is sixteen, and so she must tell it.

The video camera whirs silently as the little blonde girl with the wet brown eyes tells the camera and her lawyer and her father and the state attorney and all the assembled police officers exactly how this thing came to pass.

She supposes she fell in love with Mr Newell ...

She keeps referring to him as 'Mr Newell'. She does not call him Andrew or Andy, which is odd when one considers the intimate nature of their relationship. But he remains 'Mr Newell' throughout her recitation. Mr Newell and his passionate love of art, which he transmits to his students in a very personal way, 'What do you see? What do you see *now*?'

And, oh, what she sees is this charming, educated man, much older than she is, true, but seeming so very *young*, burning with enthusiasm and knowledge, this sophisticated world traveler who studied in Italy and in France and who is now trapped in a shoddy little town like River Close with a wife who can only think of making babies!

She doesn't learn this, doesn't hear about his wife's ... well, obsession, you might call it ... until she begins taking driving lessons with him at the beginning of August. They are alone together for almost two hours each time, twice a week, and she feels confident enough to tell him all about her dreams and her desires, feels privileged when he confides to her his plans of returning to Europe one day, to Italy especially, where the light is golden and soft.

'Like you, Rebecca,' he says to her one day, and puts his hand on her knee and dares to kiss her, dares to slide his hand up under her short skirt.

There are places in River Close ...

There are rivers and lakes and hidden glades where streams are drying in the hot summer sun, no rain, the trees thick with leaves. The little blue Ford Escort hidden from prying eyes while Mr Newell gives her lessons of quite another sort. Rebecca open and spread beneath him on the back seat. Mr Newell whispering words of encouragement and endearment while he takes her repeatedly, twice a week. Rebecca delirious with excitement and wildly in love.

When she suggests one day toward the middle of September ...

They are in a parched hidden glade; if only it would rain, the town needs rain so badly. Her panties are off, she is on the back seat; they have already made love, and she feels flushed and confident. He is telling her he adores her, worships her, kissing her again, calling her his blonde princess, his little blonde princess. I love you, I love you, kissing her everywhere, everywhere ...

'Then leave your wife and marry me,' she suggests. 'Take me with you to Italy.'

'No, no,' he says, 'I can't do that.'

'Why not?' she says. 'You love me, don't you?'

'I adore you,' he says.

'Then marry me.'

'I can't,' he says.

'Why not?' she asks again.

'I'm already married,' he says.

There is a smile on his face as he makes his little joke – I'm already married – which is supposed to explain it all to the little sophomore who was stupid enough to fall in love with the worldly art professor. How could she have been so goddamn *dumb*?

What do you see, Rebecca?

What do you see *now*?

She sees killing her.

Mr Andrew Newell's beloved wife Mary Beth.

'At first, I could only follow her on Saturdays. I go to school, you know. But I had to figure out a way to kill her with the *car*, so he'd be blamed. I take Driver's Ed courses so I knew that the licensed driver is the one responsible in any accident. So I wanted him to be in the car with me, so he'd be blamed. That way he'd be charged with murder and get sent to prison for life.

'But I needed to know where she'd be on the days I had my driving lessons, Wednesdays and Fridays. So one week, I stayed home from school and followed her on Wednesday. She went to the church again, same as on Saturday. And the next week I stayed home on Friday and followed her, but she was just doing errands and such, it would've been too difficult to plan a way our paths would intersect. Her path and the car's path, I mean. During a driving lesson. A Wednesday driving lesson. It had to be on a Wednesday, because that's when she went to the church, you see.

'I take Driver's Ed courses, I know all about drunk driving, I figured the only way Mr Newell could be blamed was if I got him drunk. But he didn't drink. I once brought a bottle of wine to the woods with us, this was the second time we made love. I wanted to show him how sophisticated I was, so I bought this bottle of very expensive Chardonnay, it cost me twenty-two dollars. But he wouldn't drink any, he told me he didn't drink. That was when I still thought he loved me. That was before I realized he was making a fool of me.

'There are lots of medical books in my father's library – he's a doctor, you know – books on pharmacology and toxicology, everything I needed. I started browsing the books, trying to find something I could give Mr Newell that would make it *look* as if he was drunk when I ran her over. Make it look like *he* was the responsible party. Any of the barbiturates looked good to me. I searched through my father's bag one night and found some Seconal capsules and decided to go with them. I dropped two big red caps in his Coke before I carried it out to the car. Two hundred milligrams. I figured that would do it. The rest was easy.'

'Did you intend killing her?' Alyce asked.

'Oh, yes.'

'Why?'

'Because he was making a fool of me. He loved her, you see, otherwise he'd have left her to marry me. I did it to pay him back. If this worked the way I wanted it to, he'd have gone to prison for life.'

'Do you know what the penalty for vehicular homicide is?' Katie asked.

'Yes,' she said at once. 'Prison for life. Homicide is murder.'

'Seven years, Rebecca.'

Rebecca looked at her.

'It's seven years.'

The room went utterly still.

'I didn't know that,' Rebecca said.

'Well, now you do,' Alyce said.

It began raining along about then.

Driving home through the rain, Katie thought how goddamn sad it was that a girl as bright and as beautiful as Rebecca could have made the tragic mistake of believing in love and romance in a time when vows no longer meant anything.

Sixteen years old, she thought. Only sixteen.

I'm in love with someone else, Katie.

I'm leaving you.

The irony, she thought, and brushed hot sudden tears from her eyes.

'Enough,' she said aloud.

And drove fiercely into the storm ahead.

NO CONNECTION

Susan Moody

There's nothing pretty about a corpse.

Death drains away all significance, all humanity. What's left is nothing more than a piece of dead flesh. Though even the word 'flesh' is misleading. The word 'flesh' implies a certain meatiness, something sanguine and blood-filled, like a piece of steak or a plate of raw liver, whereas the average corpse is yellowy-white, the colour of tripe.

They talk about the dignity of death. Looking down at Peggy's body, Dorothy could see nothing dignified about the tallowy face, the slightly open mouth, the revolting shine of eyeballs in the slit between the upper and lower lids.

She took hold of the corpse's hand. The fingers lay inert between her palms, the nails sharp-pointed. There were white hairs between the knuckle joints, coarse, like the bristles left on the skin of a ham. She cleared her throat. She said aloud, 'Goodbye, Peggy.' Feeling foolish. Feeling elsewhere. That wasn't Peggy, lying under the sheet. Peggy, too, was elsewhere. The radiator clicked beneath the window. Peggy's glasses lay on the night-table beside the high, hard bed. The faint disgusting smell of bodily functions was heightened by the air freshener which lingered in the corners of the room.

'Goodbye' seemed little enough to offer as a farewell. But what else was there to say? Besides, Peggy had left long ago. During the past nine weeks, the occupant of the bed had been a stranger, a person who wept with pain, stared with half-mad eyes, muttered, drooled. Dorothy had stayed beside her – there'd been no one else – but she was never going to be hypocritical enough to pretend that she'd wanted to be there.

And now, at last, as well as being absent, Peggy was dead.

All Dorothy could think was, Don't let it be like this for me. Not like this, slow, cruel, undignified. Let it come suddenly. Please let me not die a little bit at a time.

Life's supposed to begin at forty. In Dr Dorothy Metcalf's case, the start had been delayed by almost twenty-five years, since she was not quite sixty-five as she came out of the door of Broadcasting House one Monday morning in December. Walking down towards Oxford Circus, she was on a high, a definite high. She caught sight of herself in a shop window and nodded with satisfaction at her carefully crafted image. Slim black trousers over polished black boots with a wedge-cut heel, black silk polo-neck, a brilliant poncho, black fedora. She looked what she was. Feisty feminist. Gutsy woman. Ball-breaker.

She strolled towards Piccadilly. There was an exhibition she wanted to see at the Royal Academy; she could have a cup of coffee there. Relive the radio interview. Congratulate herself on her performance as the birthday guest on *Start The Week*. She'd been good. Damn good. Not allowed the beady-eyed radio host with the nasal delivery to patronise her, which he'd been inclined to do at first. She'd taken control from the start, shown him what was what.

'Mermaids?' he'd said, sneeringly. It sounded like a soft subject. Could have been one. But she'd taken it and run, showed the mythologising reconstructive spin applied over the centuries by men. Women as siren, woman as temptress and seducer, luring men to their doom. A masculine construct, she'd said, a sea-fable adapted, via myths of Neptune and other fish-tailed gods, to bolster male prejudices, to rationalise otherwise inexplicable male failures of seamanship, navigation, captaincy, and from there spreading insidiously into the various myth-ologies, temptress, predator.

'It's fair to say that your previous books have not reached anything like the success of this one,' he'd said. 'Can you account for this?'

She'd been cool. 'Easily.'

'How?' he'd prompted.

'This time I deliberately set out to write a popular book,' she'd said.

'Well, you've certainly succeeded in that.'

'Yes. As a feminist, the mermaid seemed to me to provide a seductive sym-bolisation of the way women have always been perceived in male-dominated societies.'

'Is that why the book's appealed so strongly to the reader in the street?'

'The mermaid legend is a particularly potent one,' Dorothy had said, con-centrating on the selling points of the book – after all, she was there to pitch herself, not to raise the banner of feminism. 'The mermaid myths provide an alternative to the Greek Olympians; all I've done is set out these fairly diffuse and discrete stories so that the pattern is more easily observable.'

'And given them a feminist slant?'

'Not really. The fascination with the mermaid as a symbol is universal, and not confined to any particular culture. Part of the appeal is undoubtedly to something primeval in us, an atavistic recognition of the fact that the mermaid inhabits the ocean, the source of life. For women, she represents safety – she can enthral without any danger of being ravished, since she is, although definitely, and even defiantly, female, nonetheless impenetrable, possessing no sexual parts. For men, she provides them with the best protection of all against the thing they fear most – sexual impotence.'

'It's an interesting theory but—'

'It's an explanation for the popularity of the book, rather than a theory.'

'What about mermen?'

'There are mermen, indeed, even mercats and merdogs. But they are later accre-tions to the original myths. The merman, for instance, is usually grotesque and ugly, an embodiment of the asexual, though always credited with a kind heart, whereas the mermaid is neither. However, some of the most potent stories concern the sacrificial aspect, a female trait. We all grew up on Hans Andersen's little mermaid, the proto-martyr who died for the man she loved.'

'And I believe there is talk of a television tie-in?'

She had smiled invisibly, made her voice humble yet delighted for the sake of those beyond the mike. 'I don't want to tempt the fates but, yes, negotiations are taking place.'

Drinking coffee at the Royal Academy, Dorothy smiled again. It had all been extremely satisfactory. A fitting reward. After all these years of obscurity, and before that of struggle, life was suddenly beginning to bloom as it had not done since her parents had died, fifty years ago.

In a week's time, she'd be sixty-five! Thirty years older than her own mother had been when she died. It hardly bore thinking about. There was no getting round the fact that sixty-five was old. She didn't *feel* old. She didn't totter, or have funny turns, or press a hand to her chest when she went up a flight of stairs, the way other people her age did, the way Peggy used to before they took her to the nursing home. Oh, there was sometimes a certain stiffness when she got out of bed, and a tendency to bruise easily, those funny purple marks which come up under the skin, but other than that she was as fit as a flea. She still played tennis all through the summer. Practised yoga every day. Enjoyed the same things as she had done twenty, forty years ago.

The fact was, she hadn't time to be old. It didn't fit into her agenda. Quite apart from the mermaid book, and the celebrity it had brought her, there was her real work. For instance, she was already halfway through the planning stage of a trip to South America. She'd been invited to present three separate papers at various symposia. There was the Herman Bauer bibliography to complete, and the possibility of a visiting fellowship for next year to consider. In Australia, too – nice money, a bit of prestige, can't be bad, as her research students put it.

Or maybe she'd drop work altogether. *Work* work, that is. She could easily afford to now the book had attained global cult-status. Fame was heady stuff. Fame beat prestige every time. She liked these appearances in the media, stalking on in her heels, confounding expectation, being butch where they wanted womanly, being ultra-female where they looked for tough academism.

The television series gleamed somewhere at the back of her mind. Still in the very earliest stages of discussion, she nonetheless knew it would happen. She'd met the producer for lunch two or three weeks ago and been deeply impressed by her commitment to the project. A TV series: what a birthday present!

She looked at her watch. She ought to be back in Oxford by five-thirty at the latest. David was picking her up at seven, and she'd want a bath before then. A bath and a drink. Champagne, she rather thought. There was a lot to celebrate.

Hearing her voice after so long made him feel a bit funny. He wasn't sure he'd have recognised it, to tell the truth. If the programme presenter hadn't announced who it was, he'd just have thought it was another of those arty-farty women they liked to have first thing on a Monday morning, as though a little bit of culture would start you off right. But the name had kind of leapt at him and, of course, he'd rushed over and turned up the volume so he wouldn't miss a syllable.

The same, but not the same – that's how she sounded. More certain of herself. Not surprising, given what she'd managed to do since they last met. All those books, for a start. And a distinguished career at Oxford University to her credit. An anthropologist, that's what he called her, the presenter chappie. A social anthropologist.

He'd always known she was clever. It seemed incredible that she should also be sixty-five. And there was going to be a television tie-in. He'd get a sight of her, then, as well as hear her voice. See what she looked like after all these years.

Jack glanced out of the window at the street below. Even when it was grey and raining, the little Cotswold town looked beautiful. He'd never regretted leaving Liverpool to move down here. Not once. Across the way, he could see the Christmas tree blinking on and off in the window of the bookshop. Later, when he'd shaved and had a cuppa, he'd go downstairs and switch his own tree on. It would be his first Christmas without Gwen: he wondered how that would be. Sad, of course, but there was no point in looking back. He prayed that his own passing would be easier than hers, and immediately thought of Dorothy again. She'd done fine. He'd bought all her other books, of course. Had to order them special. Felt a certain pride at seeing them lined up in the bookcase. Not that he'd ever read any of them, way above his head, but he liked to have them there. Not just to remind him, but also as a kind of thank-you.

The mermaid book was different, of course. It had pictures, for a start. He kept it by his bed, together with Gwen's brooch. Liked to look through it last thing at night. He and Gwen had celebrated their twenty-fifth anniversary by going to Paris on an overnight excursion, and they'd seen the brooch in a window, a silvery mermaid, her tail studded with pearls. Gwen had fallen in love with it, so he'd bought it for her. The fact that Dorothy had written a book about mermaids seemed significant, though he didn't really know why. He just wished Gwen could have seen the book.

He looked at his watch. He ought to be getting ready for the day. Maybe he'd send Dorothy a card, a birthday card, mention that he'd heard her on the radio, just so she knew he hadn't forgotten. Sometimes he fantasised about her walking into the teashop, whether he'd recognise her, or she him. He'd sent a card when they first opened up, just so she'd know where he was, and what he had done, thanks to her, but she'd never replied. No reason why she should. No reason at all. Just so long as she knew how he felt. That he'd never forget.

There was a stab of pain under his ribs and he winced. He'd have to go to the doctor about it. If there was one thing he feared more than anything, it was a messy death. A death like Gran's. A death like Gwen's. Sometimes he'd find himself muttering things. 'No, please.' Or, 'Don't let it be like that.' Or, 'Let it be quick.' Probably sounded a bit barmy. But with Gwen gone, and Susie miles away in Chester, there wasn't anyone else to talk to but himself. He'd have to watch it, or they'd have him put away.

Susie. He smiled again. Any day now and he'd be a grandad. He couldn't wait. There was something soothing about the way life went on, in spite of the bad bits. If only Gwen could have lasted until the baby was born. A Christmas baby. Susie'd already said they were going to call it Noel. Or Noelle, if it was a girl. Nice name.

He looked at the cover of Dorothy's mermaid book, stroked the glossy jacket, picked up the mermaid brooch, fingered the knobbly tail. It was only a cheap thing, he could see that now. Some of the pearls had dropped out – not that they were real pearls, of course not – and the silver was rubbing away so you could see the plaster stuff underneath. But he'd always remember Paris, and Gwen, and how extraordinary it had seemed to him that they'd been married for twenty-five years.

The phone rang. He picked it up and cleared his throat, knowing it would be Susie. 'Hello?'

'Hi, Dad, it's me.' His daughter's voice, as always, reminded him of her mother's, when they'd been young and courting. The plans they'd made. The dreams they'd shared.

'Hello, sweetheart,' he said. 'How's himself?'

'If you mean the baby,' she said, mock-severe, 'don't forget it might be a girl.'

'As long as she takes after her mum, and not her dad, she'll be gorgeous.'

'I hope you're not saying you think Graham's ugly.'

'Ugly?' Jack said, trying to sound solemn. 'He makes gargoyles look good.'

'Dad!'

'Seriously, everything OK?'

'Seriously, yes. And you?'

'Fine,' he said. 'Jimmy Knapp and his sergeant dropped in yesterday for a cuppa. Asked about you and the baby. I told them they how much we're all looking forward to it. Oh, and they sent a message for Graham, told him to find out which end is up before he starts changing any nappies.'

Susie laughed. 'Cheeky.' Three years ago, she'd married Graham, a popular local copper who was still remembered by his mates, even after his move up north.

'Anyway,' said Jack, 'I'm just about to go down and open up. We're always extra busy this time of year.'

In fact, it was busy all year round. The plan had worked. The dream had come true. Only the other day his accountant had told him the teashop was a little goldmine. And so it was. He had everything he could want, really. Except Gwen, of course. Still, no use crying over spilt milk, and he had friends and the club, and golf. He never had any problem filling the days if he wanted to. And soon there'd be Noel. Or Noelle. He pretended to Susie that he didn't mind which it was as long as the baby was healthy, but secretly he couldn't help hoping it was a boy. Just to start off with. He'd have liked more kids himself, but after Susie the doctor had said it probably wouldn't be a good idea to try for any more, since it wouldn't be good for Gwen's health. So Susie had been an only child.

'Enjoying your birthday?' A week later, David smiled at her across the restaurant table.

'Enormously,' said Dorothy. 'I don't know how they knew the date, but the department put on quite a show.' She raised a glass of the Moët he'd ordered and toasted him. 'They wheeled in a cake, with candles, and made me blow them out. And champagne.'

'Moët?'

'Certainly not, especially with all the cuts. And Professor Malling, the head of department, presented me with a clay figure of a mermaid, a replica of the one in the Volksmuseum in Copenhagen. I must say, I was quite touched.'

She smiled. She was used to personal autonomy – in fact, she preferred it to the kind of interdependence she saw in other couples, especially after the disastrous mistake she'd made with Robert. But there was no denying that David brought her a great deal of comfort. Even pleasure. She still found it extraordinary that at this late stage in her life she had found what she ironically thought of as Lurve. David was so solid. So good. There were not many people who could say that about. Certainly not about herself, as she'd be the first to admit.

He'd brought her a little packet tied in green ribbons with a label that read *To my evergreen Dottie*. She wasn't sentimental, hadn't got time for it, but she would have admitted to a kind of softening as she read the label. Then she wondered what in Christ's name could be inside. The box was so small that it more or less had to be jewellery. She hoped not. She had no wish to disappoint him, but she and jewellery didn't get on. So much so that she'd always suspected that the problem between Robert and herself had stemmed from the time she dropped her engagement ring overboard as they were crossing the Channel. Not deliberately, of course. Though, looking back, it might have been construed as an act of Freudian wish-fulfilment. With this ring I thee wed. By dropping this ring into the Channel, I thee unwed. But it had been a genuine accident, she really hadn't meant to. Especially when it had been his mother's. She'd been fiddling with it as they'd stood at the rail, watching the cliffs of Dover fall away, and then suddenly ... He'd been absolutely livid, but there wasn't much either of them could do about it. And later she'd left her wedding ring in a longhouse in Bhutan, and when he replaced it she'd managed to lose that too.

The truth was that she wasn't a very feminine woman, if feminine meant being sentimental about fripperies and such things. On the other hand, it was impossible to deny the significance of certain gifts, so there would be something pleasingly symbolic about being given jewellery by David. A milestone in their feeling for each other. Opening it, she found that he'd bought her a pendant. Pre-Columbian, in beaten gold, rather massive and very beautiful. Difficult to lose. Once again, she marvelled at the fact that she had found so good a companion at such a late stage of her life.

Over coffee, David said, 'Why does that man keep staring at you?'

'Which man?'

'Behind you. Over in the corner, by the window. He's been watching you ever since we sat down.'

'Perhaps he recognises me from the photo on the back of my book.'

David shrugged. 'Maybe. Writers are the most anonymous people in the world, even the famous ones. But I suppose in Oxford...'

Later, coming back from the washroom, Dorothy glanced over at the table by the window, but the man who'd been there had gone and a waitress was clearing away the covers.

'What did he look like?' she said, sitting down.

'I don't know. Average. Smallish. A bit thin on top, glasses. Good suit.'

'Maybe it wasn't me he was staring at,' she said. 'Maybe it was you. Or maybe he was wondering what we'd ordered because he wanted the same thing.'

'I'm sure it was you he was watching.'

'Maybe I reminded him of his mother.'

'He wasn't that much younger than you are.'

It wasn't until David had left that Dorothy got round to looking at her mail. Bills, some photocopied reviews from her publishers, more birthday cards she'd brought back from her pigeonhole at college. One of them wasn't strictly a birthday card since it had no printed greeting inside, just a blank page on which someone had written, *Glad your book's doing well. And now you're sixty-five! Don't worry – I haven't forgotten what you did. Nor what you wanted me to do. I'll never forget.* There was a single letter signature underneath: a T or a J. Maybe an I.

What was this? Who'd sent it? What did the message mean? *I haven't forgotten what you did.* Like what? Was it from one of her former graduate students? In that case, she'd know the writing, wouldn't she? But this writing was completely unfamiliar. *Don't worry*: the words seemed threatening. It was one of those phrases which ought to be reassuring, but never is. Even if you weren't inclined to worry, telling you not to immediately made you do so. *And now you're sixty-five*: it was an odd way to refer to her age.

On the front was a picture of four plump women of a certain age, playing bridge and smoking cigarettes in a suggestive manner. Hmm. Thank you *very* much. I love you too, you bastard. Not that she could tell whether it was from a man or a woman. Royal-blue ink – though these days it was probably one of those felt-tipped pens – which isn't what men usually go in for. An uneducated hand, scrawled, as though the writer was impatient, anxious to get the card in the post.

Don't worry – but, of course, she did. She studied the envelope again but couldn't read the smudged postmark. So someone had sent her a card from somewhere unreadable, which contained a faintly disturbing message and she wasn't supposed to worry?

She worried about it all through the night until she fell asleep around dawn, and consequently got up much later than she was used to. She didn't feel like going into the department, but knew she had to. She'd written over a hundred letters asking for sponsorship for the South American trip and responses were coming in every day. By the end of the afternoon she was feeling shattered. The prospect of cycling home through the cold of a damp winter evening in Oxford didn't exactly thrill her, but at least the house would be warm when she got there, and a good slug of whisky would go down very nicely.

She had turned off the Iffley Road into Daubney Street, and was about to turn left at the next intersection when a car came bombing up the narrow street towards her, cutting in so close that she couldn't keep her balance and was knocked off her bike into the gutter. She fell awkwardly, hitting the road with a thump which set all her bones rattling. If she hadn't been wearing a helmet she'd have smashed her head against the kerb. As it was, she hit it with a hell of a whack. Jesus. Aching, clutching her head, she stared after the car. Bloody idiot. The driver hadn't even noticed her, and had gone roaring off down the road, doing at least sixty miles an hour in a residential zone. Stupid bastard.

She limped on home, had a whisky, took some painkillers and spent another restless night, so much so that in the morning she called in to the department. When the department secretary answered she said she wouldn't be in today: if there was anything urgent, perhaps someone could drop it off to her at lunchtime. The woman immediately went into one of those irritating female routines.

'Oh dear, are you all right?'

'Of course I am.'

'I thought you were looking a bit tired yesterday.'

'Nonsense.'

'Sure you haven't been overdoing it?'

'Overdoing what, precisely?' Dorothy asked sharply.

'Well, at your age ...' The secretary's voice trailed off.

'How do you mean?'

'Easy to tire yourself.'

'Rubbish, woman.' Dorothy slammed down the phone and went upstairs, feeling like a ninety-year-old.

It was dark when she suddenly awoke, her head full of Peggy, the sound of her sucking breath as she inched laboriously towards death, the pain which had swollen the skin around her eyes, the convulsive clutch of her fingers on the sheet. They were things Dorothy had no wish to remember. Things she'd never been able to forget. Perhaps that was because in all those years, her only acquaintance with death was Peggy's. Her parents died abroad, suddenly, when she was fifteen, and it wasn't deemed suitable for her to fly out to Lagos for the funeral – one of the few times when she'd felt grateful to her dreadful old bat of a headmistress. And as for Robert's death, by then it had been none of her business.

Peggy's had been. Appointed Dorothy's guardian while her parents were overseas, she had surely never expected to fulfil the role. What she'd felt on having to take Dorothy under her wing had never been discussed. The two of them had rubbed along in the holidays companionably enough. Neither of them had made demands on the other. There was probably affection between them, but little demonstration of it. It wasn't their way. Once Dorothy had married and moved away they had kept in touch, telephoned from time to time, sent cards for special occasions. Not much else. Peggy didn't come to visit Dorothy and Robert, but three or four times a year Dorothy travelled up to Liverpool to spend a few days with her.

It had been on one of these visits that Peggy received her death sentence. Opening a letter at the breakfast table, she stared at the piece of paper in her hand while the blood slowly receded from her face. Dorothy asked her what was wrong but she just went on gazing at the letter, gently shaking her head. Finally she cleared her throat.

'They want me to go back,' she said, huskily.

'Who do?'

'The clinic. On Monday.'

She passed over the letter and Dorothy read it quickly, gathering that she'd gone in for a routine check-up ten days ago and this was the result. 'I don't expect it means anything.' It wasn't a very sympathetic response, but Dorothy only had a few seconds in which to weigh up whether Peggy wanted her to go into unchar-acteristically concerned mode or try to behave as matter-of-factly as she herself would have done were the situation reversed.

'Will you come with me?'

Peggy never normally made such requests, being a strong believer in inde-pendence, and Dorothy was suitably taken aback. And shocked. 'Of course I will.'

'It must be serious,' Peggy said.

'You don't know that. Anyway, I'll not only come with you, I'll stay with you till we have a clearer idea of what's going on,' Dorothy said briskly.

It wasn't as if she had anything else to occupy herself with. She was thirty-four, with no children – thank God – and since she had a rich husband, no need to work, nor any desire to – how odd that seemed, looking back.

On the way to the clinic, Peggy was philosophical. 'I know what they're going to tell me,' she said.

'What's that?'

'That I've got cancer.'

'I wish you'd stop bloody talking like that.'

'I can feel it,' said Peggy. 'Like bindweed. Choking me.'

'You spent hours trying to get rid of that bindweed.' Dorothy negotiated a roundabout, checked the indicator, ignored the panic seeping through her brain. If anything were to happen to Peggy, there'd be nobody left in her life but Robert. Nobody at all. She had no other family. No friends. She'd always been solitary, from choice. But nobody chose to be *that* solitary.

'Yes,' Peggy said tiredly. 'And I never did manage to root it all out.'

'Tenacious stuff, bindweed.'

'So's cancer.'

'You can't be sure that you—'

'Most of the time I don't know it's there. That's probably how it's got its claws into me. But sometimes I get a rush of such agonising pain that if it lasted for more than a second or two, it would kill me right there on the spot.'

'Why didn't you go to the doctor about it before this?'

'I don't know. We're all brought up not to make a fuss, not to make demands . . .' Her voice trailed off. Dorothy made a soothing noise, still not sure whether it was better to sympathise or to play it down. She didn't want to be confronted with the fact of Peggy's possible death. It demanded responses from her which she wasn't able to give. Yet it wasn't like Peggy to exaggerate. Again came the feeling of dread.

'I shan't accept treatment,' said Peggy, her voice growing firmer. 'If I'm going to die, let's get on with it. I'm not going in for all that chemotherapy, and losing my hair and being sick all the time. Not at my age. I'm nearly seventy – it's not a bad age to go.'

'Let's not assume the worst until we have to, OK?' Chillingly, Dorothy was aware that events had already been set in train, that there was no getting off, no stopping the irrevocability of what was going to happen. 'Until then, I'd rather you didn't talk like that.'

'I'm only facing the facts.'

'You don't know that. They may just want to repeat the tests. I met a woman the other day who had to go back for a second test because they got her boobs squashed up the wrong way. You don't know *what* they're going to tell you.'

Peggy didn't respond. Only as Dorothy pulled into the parking lot behind the clinic did she speak. 'As long as it's not too painful,' she said quietly. 'I can't bear the thought that it'll be so long and painful. I'll let myself down.'

'How could you do that?'

'Scream. Behave badly. Wet myself. Or worse.'

'Peggy . . .' Dorothy put a hand on her arm. 'Please, don't.'

'I know what it's like,' Peggy said. 'I've seen it. I nursed my own mother during her last illness. It took her nearly a year to die. I don't want that for myself.'

Nor me, Dorothy thought.

Watching Peggy die wasn't exactly what she'd have opted for, given the choice, but she did it. Duty played a part in her decision to stay on in Liverpool and see Peggy through her dying days. Duty and gratitude. Besides, who else was there?

He hoped she'd liked his card. He'd chosen it from the bookshop especially, because they'd mentioned on the radio that she played bridge. He wasn't good with words, but he'd tried to tell her that he hadn't forgotten her kindness. Nor what she'd wanted him to do: make a success of things. He'd done that all right. He'd thought about telling her where he lived, but in the end he didn't, thinking she might feel obliged to come and see him. He didn't want that, not really. Embarrassing for them both after all this time. He'd just wanted her to know that he'd never forget. No idea where she lived, so he'd sent it to the college they mentioned in the radio programme. She'd be bound to get it there. At least, he hoped so. At sixty-five, you'd think she was retired. Maybe they did things different in these Oxford places.

'Look,' David said.

'What at?'

'See that Jag, three houses down on the other side? I'm sure it's that man again. The one who was watching you in the restaurant the other day.'

'Aren't you being a little paranoid?'

'Maybe. Or maybe not.'

'Why should the same man be parked outside my house? How could he possibly have discovered where I lived?'

'He could have followed us back here that night.'

'He left before we did.'

'Maybe he waited outside. Maybe he was watching you for ages before that.'

Dorothy remembered the birthday card. *I'll never forget what you did.* Could it have been this same man who had sent it? If so, what did it mean? And what exactly was she supposed to have done to him, anyway? She was not a fanciful woman, but unease glided down her spine as she thought about it. Who was he? A former colleague with a grudge? A graduate student indulging in some silly game? Someone who had fixated on her for some reason? It was part of the price of fame, she knew that, but didn't these madmen choose people in the public eye, rather than academics, even if they were the author of a worldwide best-seller?

'I'm going to go out and ask what the hell he thinks he's playing at,' David said.

'That's ridiculous. There's absolutely nothing to connect him with me.' Dorothy spoke more sharply than she meant to.

David turned away from the window. 'I'll pop out to my car – it's parked further down. I'll look in his window as I go by and see if it's the same man.'

'And if it is?'

'I'll ask him what he's doing.'

'He might take exception to some complete stranger interrogating him for no reason, especially if he's just visiting someone in the street.'

'I'll say I'm sure I've seen him before somewhere.'

As the front door opened and David emerged on to the path, the grey-blue Jaguar murmured into life and pulled away. He looked back at Dorothy and shrugged. So much for that. Dorothy went into her study, a little room at the back of the house, and took the mysterious birthday card out of the bottom drawer where she'd placed it under a couple of bulky files. However hard she stared at them, neither card nor envelope provided any more information than they had when she'd first seen them, over a week ago. Even supposing the watcher in the Jag and the sender of the card were one and the same man, how had he known it was her birthday? *I haven't forgotten.* The words cast shadows of pain and ugliness and a distilled kind of grief. Something struggled for recognition at the back of her mind but she couldn't pin it down.

Was there any significance in the picture of the four plump women? Perhaps the card had been sent by one of her bridge-playing friends. But, if so, why the cryptic message? In any case, most, if not all, of the people she knew at the bridge club wouldn't have a clue when her birthday was, and if they did wouldn't have sent a card.

Damn. There was bound to be a simple explanation. It was the phrase *Don't worry* which really bothered her. What exactly was it that she wasn't supposed to worry about?

A couple of days later, she started from a sound sleep into the darkness of her bedroom. Sweat had dampened her nightdress; her head was pounding. The hammering of her heart made the bedsprings vibrate. She had no idea what had woken her, she just knew she was terrified. All the more so for not knowing exactly why.

For years she had struggled to make up for lost time. Leaving Robert had taken courage, going back to nothing, making a new life for herself. She'd achieved what she set out to do: as Peggy was always saying, she was a clever woman. Here she was, sixty-five years old, and by her own efforts she had won through not only to success but to a considerable measure of personal happiness with David. And with just a few words, all that had been destroyed. Just when she'd had something to enjoy and so much to live for. There was a time, ten, twenty years ago when if someone had offered her the alternative of peaceful and immediate death to carrying on living she might well have accepted. Now, however . . .

Oh, God! Oh, no!

Explanations hit her with the force of a rockfall. She fumbled for the lamp beside the bed and switched it on.

No! It couldn't be.

She knew who must have sent the mysterious card. The words suddenly made horrifying sense.

It was Jack. It had to be.

She tried to tell herself that she'd got the wrong end of the stick. He couldn't possibly have taken what she'd said seriously. Especially given the circumstances in which she had said it. And yet, looking back, remembering his earnestness, perhaps he had believed she meant it. It was even possible that at the time she *did*. How could he have not realised that she had spoken in the heat of the moment? Under stress. Thirty years ago.

Jack. The more she thought about it, the more certain she became. The single initial fitted, too. J for Jack. Remembering last night's near-miss on her bike, once again terror sluiced through her body. Was *that* Jack? Had he been trying to run her down? And the man in the restaurant? The man outside the house? Was that him, too? She told herself not to be foolish. There was no reason to believe such a thing. Except that . . .

. . . years ago, he'd sworn that he would kill her.

What on earth was she to do?

What on earth *could* she do?

The obvious answer was that she could go to the police.

Sure she could.

They'd assume she was in the first stages of Alzheimer's. A paranoid old dear who was losing her marbles. They wouldn't take a blind bit of notice. And who could blame them? She had no proof. Nothing to substantiate her claim. Only the memory of the absolute commitment in Jack's eyes, all those years ago. Of that damned simple-minded pledge he'd made. Dorothy had seen that look of total obsession before, in graduate students who'd been determined to succeed – and had, indeed, done so. At the time she'd recognised their ambition and applauded it, knowing how hard it was to succeed, what guts it took not to be waylaid. Now she remembered the same determination in Jack.

'I swear to you,' he'd said, his mouth set. 'Wherever you are, I'll find you. And then I'll kill you. When you least expect it. Count on it.'

She rested her head on her knees and groaned aloud. Ruthless she might be, successful too. Independent. But at that moment there was a knot of tears in her throat. The words she'd spoken to him returned in their full horror. Oh, *Christ*. She'd known from the first time she'd met him that he was thick, but could he really have been so bloody stupid as to believe them? Carried them around with him all this time?

For the more she thought about it, the more she knew she'd hit on the truth. This was Jack, all right, returned to fulfil a promise made more than thirty years ago. He must have been biding his time, waiting, brooding, while she hadn't given him a thought. After Peggy's death, she and Robert had lived in Australia for several years before the inevitable split. And when she came back to England, it was to pick up the pieces, establish herself, get some qualifications, do what she'd always wanted to do. Would have done long before if she hadn't fancied herself in love.

Peggy had always disliked Robert. When Dorothy got engaged to him, Peggy was appalled.

'You're a clever girl,' she'd said. 'You should be doing something with your brain.'

'I can be married and still do that.'

'Of course you can't. Marriage and study are an almost impossible combination. Besides, Robert's going to make you unhappy.'

'How can you possibly know that?'

'Because I've met his type before. Handsome, selfish, a high-class layabout. He'll want your undivided attention, and the hell with wasting the benefits of a fine education, which is what you've had. Besides...'

'Besides what?'

'You're not the marrying sort.'

'What do you mean?'

Peggy hesitated. Said, 'You're too selfish, Dorothy. Too self-obsessed.'

Later, Dorothy had been forced to accept that she was right. It was the reason she had avoided falling for a man ever since.

Until now. Until David. And just when she'd found the kind of contented happiness she'd never known before, Jack had decided to kill her.

At lunchtime, Jack slipped upstairs to his flat. A twenty-minute sit-down, that's what he wanted. He'd been doing that more often since Gwen died. He picked up the mermaid book, stroking the glossy cover. If Gwen had still been around, he'd have bought the book for her. As it was, he'd bought it for himself, knowing that he'd done so in a pathetic attempt to convince himself there was still some kind of link between Dorothy and himself.

It was silly, really. They'd come together so briefly, and even then he'd known how little they had in common. Worlds apart. Socially, financially, intellectually. The only thing they had in common was death. Nonetheless, having heard her voice again, after all this time, he found he couldn't stop thinking about her. She'd played an important part in his life. Very important. He didn't think it was fanciful to imagine that those few weeks they had shared had bonded them permanently, even if they hadn't set eyes on each other from that day to this.

What did she look like now? There was a photograph of her on the back cover of the book, but you didn't need to be a professor to recognise that it had been taken some time ago. She'd look different now.

When he went down again, the teashop was chock-a-block. Emmie and Karen, the two girls he'd taken on for the Christmas rush, seemed flustered, and even Janet, his senior waitress, looked grim. He set to himself, weaving in and out among the tables, greeting known customers, sorting out mismatched orders, providing calm where it was needed.

What would Dorothy say if she could see him? Would she be pleased that he made good use of what he'd been given? King of his own domain, that's what he was. And it was all thanks to her. He'd never forget what she'd done for him. Never.

It was years ago now that they'd met. When Gran was dying. Putting a brown pot of tea and cups and saucers on the table in front of the customers in the window, he grimaced briefly. What a way to go. He'd hoped never to see anything like that again, and only six months ago it had happened all over again with Gwen. The same slow and agonising passing. When his turn came, he just hoped it would be quick.

Dorothy'd been the same. He brought scones, little blue dishes of jam and clotted cream, curls of butter, smiling at his customers without really seeing them. Bags of Christmas shopping under the table. The day already closing in. A kid at the next table, banging on the table with a spoon, the parents taking not a blind bit of notice. He stopped. Took the spoon away, smiled at the kid, said something inane. Something bland. Stop the kid's noise without getting up the parents' noses. It was all about public relations, his job.

Dorothy. They'd met at the nursing home. Used to find themselves sitting in the lounge in the small grey hours, staring into a cup of coffee. Exhausted from watching over their respective responsibilities. His gran. Her Auntie Peggy, who wasn't really her aunt. Eventually they'd got talking. 'Gran brought me up,' he'd told her.

'Did she?'

He could tell she wasn't really interested. But it helped him to talk about Gran. Remember what she'd been like when he was just a kid. Seaside outings. The school Nativity play. The way her skirt stretched across her knees when she sat in her chair in front of the fire. He never dared look up it, in case she caught him. Just the dark shadows at the top of her legs. Bulging flesh. 'Never knew me dad,' he'd said. 'And me mum went off when I was seven. So Gran took care of me. Now it's my turn to look after her.'

'Circles,' she said.

'You what?'

'The wheel spins. Her turn, then your turn.'

'See what you mean.' Staring at the wall, his chin quivering. 'I wish she'd go quick, that's all. I can't bear to see her in pain.'

'That's the worst part. Not the losing them, but that it takes them so long to go.'

'Right.'

Peggy's deterioration had been slow and relentless and painful. They gave her medication, painkillers to start with, then morphine injections, but nothing helped very much. She had hoped to die well, but for most of the slow weeks that had not happened. Watching the agony on her face, listening to her hoarse cries, Dorothy wished she had the guts to put a pillow over her face and end it right there. Sometimes, holding the wasted hand, she whispered, 'Don't fight it, Peggy. Just let go.'

But Peggy battled on, refusing to give up, her lungs drawing in yet one more painful breath, her heart sending the blood round and round her system. Dignity was lost. Her ravaged body erupted, long bubbling farts, foul-smelling belches. Thick snot clogged her nose, her eyes were encrusted with yellow mucus. Wiping her face with dampened cotton wool, Dorothy felt her affection turn to nauseated repulsion as Peggy became little more than a vehicle of smells, noises, slime and excretions. She did not want to be there, watching while a human being decomposed, became no more than rotting flesh trapped between sheet, between feeds, between injections.

The only respite came when she went home to Peggy's house to sleep and wash, or in the occasional breaks she allowed herself during the bitter metallic hours between midnight and dawn. Sometimes it seemed as if there'd never been anywhere else but the four pale green walls of the lounge, the table with magazines on it, the comfortable armchairs where a weary watcher could catch a few minutes of sleep. Pot plants flourished on the window-sill; the walls were decorated with reproductions of Blake prints. The nursing-home staff had done their best to minimise the vast gulf which yawned between life and death, but it was an impossible task when the living could not help but be aware that the dying were doomed to lose.

Over the weeks, she began to be aware of the young man who so often shared those grey-washed hours when reality teetered. One evening, he looked up from his coffee and put out his hand. 'I'm Jack,' he said. 'Jack Barclay.' As though it was important that they held on to their identity in that place geared to letting go.

She hadn't wanted to talk. To exchange information. Nonetheless, she had nodded, eyelids gritty with fatigue. 'Dorothy Metcalf.'

That was when he told her about his grandmother. She didn't attempt to define for him her relationship with Peggy. It was easier to call her an aunt, and let it go at that. But from that first self-introduction, they had gradually begun to talk. Dorothy had learned that he was rigid in his views, that he saw everything in black or white. Right was right, wrong was wrong. He understood no middle ways, none of the soft blurs and blendings which help to ease the complex days. He seemed incapable of compromise.

In return, she told him something, minimally, of herself, about her failing marriage. Sometimes they had shed tears together.

'It's so cruel!' he burst out one evening, as they took time off from their separate vigils. The coffee was grey in their cups.

Feeling the same way, she couldn't offer palliatives.

'It gives you a new perspective on things, doesn't it?' he said. 'Makes you realise you shouldn't waste your time.'

'*Carpe diem.*'

'What?'

'Seize the day,' Dorothy said.

'That's what I mean. You never know the hour or the day, do you?'

'When all this is ... over, what will you do with your life?' she asked, for something to say. By now she knew about his pathetic job in the kitchens of a local hotel, his dreary-sounding girlfriend. Gwen.

'I'm not sticking to this shit job a minute longer than I have to,' he said vehemently. 'Going to work for myself, I am. Stuff lining the pockets of some fat-cat boss.'

'Work at what?'

'Wouldn't mind a little restaurant of my own,' he said shyly, looking at her to see if she found this odd. 'Nothing fancy, mind. Not even a restaurant. Just a teashop.'

'Sounds good to me.' A teashop, she thought. It wasn't exactly reaching for the stars, was it?

'That's why I'm working at the hotel,' he said. 'Experience. Learning the trade.

Gwen's all for it, too. She's just finished a City and Guilds in catering.'

They'd smiled wearily at each other and went back to watch over their dying.

On other occasions they discussed films they'd seen, the kind of music they enjoyed, even books. He liked westerns, he told her. Read a lot of westerns. Louis L'Amour, that sort of thing. And *Shane*. He loved *Shane*, must have read it a hundred times.

Once, pushing away her coffee-cup, Dorothy said, 'This teashop of yours – have you got any plans? Concrete plans? Or is it going to stay a dream?'

'Gwen and I have been talking about it a lot,' he said. 'Since Gran got took sick. When we get a moment, we even go round looking at suitable places.'

'Found anything yet?'

'Plenty. Saw one the other day, round the back of the park, which would've been perfect.'

'Would have been? Or is?'

'Is, I suppose.'

'So what did you do?'

'What could we do? Property costs a bomb. We both got savings, but not enough for a mortgage. Even though we aim to start out small, it's still expensive. There's lawyers' fees and furnishing and kitchen equipment to buy, all that sort of stuff. We'll have to wait a bit longer, that's all.'

'What does the bank say?'

'Banks?' He made a scoffing noise. 'I didn't bother going in.'

'I thought they were quite keen on investing in small businesses these days.'

'Might have been once, but not in the current economic climate. Too many people going to the wall.' He drained his coffee. 'Got to be philosophical about it, haven't you? We'll get there in the end. Long as prices don't rise faster than we can save. Anyway . . .'

'Anyway what?'

He stared at her for a moment as if wondering whether to let her in on his secret, then said, 'I don't really want to live up here any more. Not after . . . after Gran goes. Wouldn't be the same without her.'

'Got anywhere else in mind?'

'As a matter of fact, yes.'

'Where's that?'

'The Cotswolds.'

'Why there?'

Again the hesitation. 'Went there once with the Scouts. It was . . . lovely.' He grinned. 'Better get back to Gran, in case she wakes. She won't like it if I'm not there.'

He'd told her he wanted to leave Liverpool, with its salty winds and its dreary back streets. Mentioned the Cotswolds. What he couldn't explain, because he didn't know how to, was the way his heart had lifted at the sight of broad streets lined with corn-coloured houses, green lawns, streams. Blue hills in the background. So different from the wind-swept bleakness of the north. He'd been there with the Scouts, gone to Blenheim by bus, and on the way back to camp they'd driven through a series of small towns and villages. He'd known then that this was where he wanted to live.

'The Cotswolds are expensive,' Dorothy had said.

'I know. And going to get more expensive if we don't get a move on. Cars and that. I've been reading up about it. People commuting. London's within easy reach, see.'

'How much are you short?'

'Too much,' he'd answered brusquely.

'What sort of money are you talking?' He looked at her pityingly. She flushed. 'I'm not very good with money.'

'That's 'cos you've never been without it.'

It was true. Her parents had left her well off, and Robert, the bastard, had more money than he knew what to do with. 'How much, Jack? I don't know anything about these things. Hundreds? Thousands? Tens of thousands?'

'Gwen reckons ten thousand would get us started,' he said. 'Twenty'd be nearer the mark but, then, I'm more cautious, like.'

'I see.' It wasn't an enormous amount, but Dorothy could see how long it would take him to save it.

'We're nearly halfway there,' he said. 'Gwen's uncle left her a bit. And the both of us, we don't go out much, rather stay home with the telly than go spending money on rubbish.'

Returning to Peggy's house to change her clothes and take a bath, Dorothy slept uneasily. She was racked with misery and loneliness, not just about Peggy but about Robert, too. And guilt. She lacked some essential human component: compassion, perhaps. Empathy. The ability to put herself in another's place. The young man with whom she had shared the nights had become, in a way, more real to her than the inhabitants of the world beyond the nursing home. She was jealous too. He might not ever make his dream come true, but at least he had one. She had nothing.

'Tell me about your teashop,' she said the next night. The walls of the lounge shimmered through a haze of exhaustion. She saw a Cotswold street, stone walls, honey-coloured light reflected in broad wet streets.

'... yellow-checked tablecloths,' Jack said. 'And nice china. Not this thick stuff you get in some places, something dainty. Pine walls.'

'Sounds good,' Dorothy said.

'Fresh flowers on the tables. Start out small, scones and that, and maybe move on to high teas, if there's the demand.' Enthusiasm had brought colour to his usually dough-white face. 'Even lunches one of these days.'

For a moment, Dorothy was gripped by the desire to join him. Preparing lunches for the wives of wealthy commuters suddenly seemed infinitely preferable to the options which lay before her. Yellow-checked tablecloths. Scones. She longed to be part of some endeavour, rather than floating as she did.

Weariness overcame them sometimes. Sentences drifted, words slurred. Her mind focussed on the two dying women. She wished that it wasn't so slow. She wished she couldn't smell Peggy's flesh decaying, or watch the life-force fading behind her eyes. Sometimes she was manic, despite her weakness, and they would hold her down, bind her to the bed. She ranted, talked nonsense, remembered wrongs done. Cursed. Dorothy didn't want to be there. Knew that Peggy herself – the real Peggy – would have been mortified to know that she was witnessing this. Jack became Dorothy's only link with normality. More than anyone else, Jack, pathetic creature though he was, knew what she was going through.

His gran went before Peggy did. He stopped coming. She missed him. The day that Peggy finally died he turned up at the nursing home. Dorothy was packing away the pitiful bits and pieces which were all that was left of the strong woman who'd given her a home. 'I just wanted to say that I wouldn't have got through these past months without you,' he said. 'That's God's honest truth.'

'I feel the same way,' she said.

He shook her hand. 'All the best, Dorothy.'

'And the same to you, Jack. I hope you get your teashop soon.'

'Sooner than we thought, maybe. Gran's left me a bit of cash.'

Dorothy surprised herself. Opened her handbag. 'What's your surname?'

He told her, looking surprised. She took out her cheque-book, wrote him a cheque and passed it to him.

He glanced down, did a double take, looked at her, slowly turning red. 'What's this?'

'What's it look like?'

'I can't accept this,' he said. 'No way. Besides . . .'

'What?'

'Gwen and I don't want to start out in debt. It's one of the things we've promised ourselves.'

'It's a gift, Jack,' Dorothy said.

He handed it back. 'Sorry. Can't accept it.'

'Call me a sleeping partner in your teashop.'

'But you don't know me.'

'I know you enough. And I can afford it. Please, take it. For your gran's sake, as much as your own.'

He was reluctant.

'*Carpe diem*,' Dorothy said.

'Seize the day, right?' He looked at the cheque again, and for a minute both he and Dorothy saw the checkered tablecloths, the fresh flowers.

Finally he folded it up and put it into his breast pocket. 'One of these days, I'll pay it back,' he said.

'No. I don't want you to. It's a gift.'

'Is there something I can do for you in return?'

'Yes. Make it happen. Make a success of it. And also . . .' In a vague, unformulated way, she had thought about this, never dreaming that the moment would come – *had* come – when she could express it. For a moment she pressed her lips together, then said, 'Yes, there is.' And told him what else she wanted him to do in return.

'Kill me. When I'm sixty-five, find me and kill me.' Her face had been white. All the strain. And losing her auntie.

That's what she'd said. Her mouth had kind of quivered. Remembering it now, Jack shook his head. Pressed the channel changer, flicked from a programme on crocodiles to some stupid quiz show. Flicked back again. The crocs were more fun.

Kill me . . . They were both a bit strung up that night. He'd been feeling guilty about the excitement of having Gran's money, and at the same time grieving for the loss of the only family he had. And she was suffering from her own loss, the auntie who'd brought her up, though she wasn't an auntie at all.

He put his arms round her. The only time he'd ever touched her. 'I swear to you that I will find you and kill you,' he'd said. Not meaning it, of course. Just calming her down. It hadn't even sounded ridiculous. Not then. Only after, when he got home and had a chance to think about what he'd said. But she'd never have expected him to mean it. A clever woman like that. He hadn't even told Gwen. *Kill* her? It was barmy. 'Even if I plead with you not to,' she'd said. Sobbing, shaking in his arms. 'Just do it, Jack. I don't want to know where or when. I want it sudden. And if I change my mind, if I find you and start saying I didn't mean it, don't listen. All right?'

'OK,' he'd agreed. 'All right.' Soothing. Thinking that if it was him, he'd want to know, if only to be able to say goodbye to the people he loved. Trying not to make a joke out of it because he could see how serious she was. As if he could ever kill someone. Especially in cold blood, the way she was suggesting. 'Yeah, I'll do it.'

'You *promise*?'

'I swear.'

'Say it.'

'I swear I will find you when you're sixty-five and I will kill you.'

She'd crumpled against him. Her face was all shiny with tears. 'Thank you, Jack. Thank you.'

She couldn't see how to stop him. But there had to be a way, if she could only work out what.

Obviously the first thing was to find him. Then she could plead with him. Circumstances have changed, she would say. *We* have changed. Nobody could be insane enough to believe that something said in the heat of the moment over thirty years ago had any relevance now. Not that it had much relevance then, either. Words spoken out of distress. Peggy's body, shrunken under the covering sheet, her skin the colour of a candle, tiny hands lying on the thin white blanket, like the skeletons of crabs. Nobody could have believed she'd meant what she'd said.

Yet he was a simple-minded man. Dense. The sort who'd undertake a commission and carry it through to the bitter end. There'd been that look in his eyes. Commitment. The remembrance was chilling. She felt even more despairing.

Find him first. That was the most pressing need. Secondly, she must watch her back at all times. She got out of bed and went round the house, checking that the doors and windows were safely locked. She had been burgled a couple of years ago and had installed a burglar alarm. Normally it was not switched on at night – now she set it. When daylight came, she went through the house, keeping close to the walls, away from the windows. Walking cautiously.

Because he could do it at any time.

If she had some idea what his plans were, maybe she could forestall him. Was he going to shoot her? Or knife her? Run her down in his Jaguar – if that had been his car parked outside in the street – and claim that she'd stepped off the pavement in front of him? Dozy old pensioner, not taking any notice of where she was – no jury would convict him, especially when no one had any idea that there was a connection between the two of them.

He'd want to avoid awkward questions. He'd want to get away with it. Which ruled out firearms – she was hardly the sort to be gunned down in a drive-by shooting after all. Which also ruled out a faked suicide. Especially given the circumstances of her life, the success of the mermaid book, the possibility of the television programme, David. It was obvious that he'd spent time tracking her down. Perhaps he'd kept tabs on her ever since she'd given him that cheque. The only good thing about this nightmare situation was that he'd have to make it look like an accident. Which meant he couldn't just walk up and do it – he'd have to choose his moment.

She found herself standing at the bedroom window, peering out into the street. There were no strange cars, as far as she could tell. Nobody loitering under a lamppost or bending down to tie a shoelace, the way they did in the movies. Which didn't mean that he wasn't somewhere nearby, watching. She clenched her fists. The situation was absurd.

The Cotswolds. That was the only clue she had. She'd have to drive out to the middle of the area, and do a methodical sweep. Use the *Yellow Pages*. See if anything rang any bells. He'd sent her a postcard years before, but she'd binned it immediately. She'd not been very interested, frankly, was almost ashamed that she'd been so uncharacteristically benevolent. She'd never remember where it had come from. And even if she did, there was no kind of guarantee that he'd still be there. He and his wife had just established themselves, he'd written. They could well have moved on to something bigger or better. Finding him could be a tedious task but not necessarily a daunting one. She was a clever woman, used to research. Tracking down mermaid references had toughened her. Taught her to be remorseless. Once you had established that the facts were there, it was only a matter of time before you dug them up. Somewhere there would be a reference which would lead to a further reference and eventually to what you were searching for. And it had to be easier to find a person than an elusive piece of esoterica about something which had probably never existed in the first place.

Right?

There were private detectives, of course. She could certainly afford to hire one. But how long would it take to find one she could trust? And how much time would he need to delve back into the past and come up with the information she wanted? Too long. Besides – the possibility crouched at the back of her brain, waiting for her to acknowledge it – besides, there was the worst-case scenario to be considered. That Jack wouldn't be budged. 'You told me not to listen if you pleaded,' he might say. 'So I shan't.'

In that case, there would be only one thing left for her to do. And in that case, the last thing she wanted was a trail connecting her with Jack.

So, no detective.

She was on her own.

She settled on a small hotel in Chipping Norton. The Roebuck. Knowing she had to make contingency plans, she had used an Irish accent when booking a room. She'd even thought up a cover story, in case they should ask what she was doing in their part of the world: she was a freelance journalist, researching for an article. These were just emergency plans, she told herself. Not to be used except in a crisis. But they had to be in place from the word go – it would be too late to lay her false trail after the event. If event there had to be.

In her bedroom, she planned her campaign. She couldn't remember his surname. Had no means of knowing what name he'd given his café. She'd have to blitz the Cotswold teashops. Unless brain finally produced the surname she wanted, in which case she'd have much less of a problem.

Each place she visited, her strategy was the same. Open the door, walk into a fug of coffee-scented air, order a pot of tea and a scone. Then ask if Jack was around.

Already, on two occasions, he had been. Just not the Jack she was looking for.

On her sixteenth pot of tea, Dorothy got lucky. She had a feeling about the place as soon as she walked in. There were yellow-checked tablecloths and a fresh flower on each table, set into a cheerful yellow ceramic vase. The crockery on the occupied table was yellow, too. He'd said that was what he wanted, all those years ago. She could hear his voice as if it were yesterday, the thin uneducated whine of it buzzing in her ear like an irritating mosquito. Looking back, she wondered how she could have been so foolish as to give the man money, though at the time it had seemed right, even a good thing to do.

When the waitress came over with the scone she'd ordered, Dorothy asked for Jack.

'He's out, I'm afraid.' The waitress was young, probably a schoolgirl doing a Christmas job. Her name was Karen, according to the lettered wooden beads strung round her neck on a leather lace.

'Any idea when he'll be back?'

'Not really.' The girl positioned the butter dish close to Dorothy's plate. 'Have you got everything?'

'Yes, thanks. Er ... any idea where I might find him?'

'He's gone down to the shooting range.'

The words struck a chill. 'Shooting?' Dorothy said.

'Yeah. Took it up after his wife died.'

'Gwen's dead?'

'Yes.'

Further confirmation. How many Jacks owned teashops in the Cotswolds and were married – or had been – to a woman called Gwen. 'That's terrible news. When did it happen?'

'Six months ago.'

'I used to know them in Liverpool,' Dorothy said smoothly. 'I've been out of touch.' She emphasised her Irish vowels. 'I'm sorry to hear about Gwen. So Jack went out and joined a gun club, did he?'

'To take his mind off, he said.'

'How did she die?'

'Mrs Barclay, you mean? It was cancer. Pancreatic.'

Barclay. *That* was his name. Jack Barclay. Final proof that this was the right place. Dorothy tried to look concerned. 'That's too bad. At least it must have been quick. Pancreatic cancer usually is, once they find it.'

'Took her the best part of eighteen months,' said the girl. 'It was awful, really, watching her go downhill. Jack had a terrible time, trying to look after her himself. Nurse her at home, and run this place. His daughter did what she could, of course. Susie. But she lives up north somewhere, a long way from here, and it was difficult. You can just imagine.'

'I can indeed,' said Dorothy.

'Fifty-eight,' Karen said. 'A terrible shame, really. They'd got such plans, too. They were going to go round the world when she was sixty, see all the things they'd heard about. Egypt, Sydney Harbour, India, that sort of thing.'

'Poor Gwen. And poor Jack.'

'Yeah.' The girl nodded. 'That's why he joined the gun club. He wanted something which wouldn't give him the chance to brood. Not like his fishing.'

'He's a fisherman, is he?'

'Angler, more like. He's got places along the river where he likes to go. And there's Burnham Pond – he really likes that because there's hardly ever anyone else there.'

'Gun clubs and fishing – you can't get much more polarised than that, can you?'

'If you mean different, no. Not really.'

An elderly couple came in, shivering inside their coats, exclaiming over the warm brightness of the yellow paint and fresh flowers. Karen looked over at them. 'Better go,' she said. 'Can't bend your ear all day.'

'It's me who's been asking the questions.'

'Anything you want, give me a shout. Hot water. Another scone.' Karen drifted towards the other table, pulling up the pad which hung from her waist.

Dorothy poured another cup. So Jack Barclay's wife had recently died in tragic circumstances. He must have been painfully reminded of his grandmother's death. That, in turn, would have recalled the woman he'd met in the nursing home back in Liverpool, her hysterical plea, the promise he'd made. He probably thought he owed it to her, that it was the least he could do. It wasn't in the least fanciful to imagine him working out how best to fulfil it. Especially in the stress of recent widowerhood. Deciding on a gun, joining a club where he'd learn how to handle a weapon which would kill cleanly and swiftly.

Using a gun to kill her would make it clear that this was no random attack. But since there was no connection between the Oxford academic and the teashop-owner, why should anyone suspect him?

Back in her hotel, she took off her shoes and lay down on the bed. The room seemed to have been decorated by a florist gone berserk. There were flowered curtains, a flowered coverlet, roses on the carpet, roses on the walls. The effect was nightmarish. Lying on the big double bed, she wondered if there was any point in pleading with Barclay. Would he relent? Would he accept that what she'd said had been in a moment of intense stress? More and more she doubted it.

Which left the other option.

If she was going to resort to that then it was best not to contact him at all. There was always the risk that they would be seen together, and someone, afterwards, would remember.

Getting up, she crossed the room and took a bottle of whisky from her bag. She poured a healthy amount into a glass from the bathroom and sat down with pen and paper.

First of all, method. She didn't have time to join a gun club herself, even supposing she wanted to. Poison, arson, stabbing, strangulation: the traditional blueprints of violent death passed through her mind and were dismissed. If she was really going to go through with it, a top priority was a method which didn't involve blood. Nor noise, screams, seeping brains, bulging eyes. She couldn't handle any of that. Nor was she up to faking a suicide. The police weren't stupid. They were able to tell whether a person had killed himself or not.

Thoughtfully sipping whisky, she tried to envisage herself in a scenario where she and Jack Barclay were in the same room, in circumstances where she was able to make him take poison. Nothing sprang immediately to mind. There'd be the business of getting him to write a note first, to alert someone to the fact that it was self-administered. And then the engineering of a situation in which they could meet. There wasn't any way she could see which wouldn't compromise her in some way. Especially if he told someone he was meeting her. Like the waitress.

Which left what? An accident. Or something which had the appearance of an accident.

What kind of accident should it be? She was a clever woman. Surely she ought to be able to figure something out. She swallowed more whisky. She knew so little about this stranger who had been so briefly in her life and now re-entered it all these years later. Only that his wife was dead, that his modest business was flourishing, that he fished, that he'd recently joined a gun club.

She frowned. Murdering Jack Barclay before he could murder her was, she reminded herself, the last resort. In spite of the heating, she shivered. Could she kill? Deliberately take another person's life? Surely not. Yet she'd already set things up, adopted a fake accent, given a false address, left her car several streets from the hotel, so that when – *if* – Jack Barclay's body was found, there could be nothing to connect her with it.

Restless, she walked back and forth across the flowered carpet. Was it possible that she was mistaken, that the message on his card could be interpreted in some other way? She fished it out of her leather shoulder-bag. Rereading the words, they seemed almost more menacing now that when she had first read them.

Glad your book's doing well. And now you're sixty-five! Don't worry – I haven't forgotten what you did. Nor what you wanted me to do. I'll never forget.

It seemed unequivocal. *I haven't forgotten what you wanted me to do.* She was right: he was going to murder her. There could be no other interpretation.

So the law of the jungle would have to prevail.

Kill or be killed.

She set her mind to the problem again. Contriving an accident with his gun was out of the question. There was her car, but that was awkward. It meant waiting for him to appear. In a town this size, she was sure to be noticed. What was left?

He fished. Could she make something out of that? Anglers usually sat in clumps, didn't they? She remembered them by the river outside Oxford. Regularly spaced along the bank. Surrounded by tackle. Stools and rod-holders and keeping-nets and disgusting trays of maggots, like swollen grains of rice. With so many witnesses, it would be impossible to fake a drowning.

Her brain grabbed and held on to something out of her conversation with the waitress. Burnham Pond. Hardly anyone ever goes there, the girl had said. Where was it? Presumably somewhere reasonably local. She opened the Ordnance Survey map she'd bought in Blackwell's bookshop before she left Oxford, and scanned the area in widening circles.

There it was: Burnham Pond. No more than eight miles from here. Surrounded by woods, nearly a mile away from the main road. Footpaths approached it across farmland.

The more she looked at it, the more it seemed a possible place for what she'd got in mind. The two dimensions of a map might prove misleading, of course. She'd check it out tomorrow. After that, it was a question of finding him there unawares.

It was going to work, she knew that. Even if the police were suspicious about the death, there was absolutely nothing to connect her and Jack. No reason on earth why an elderly Oxford academic should wish to dispose of a country-town teashop owner. No reason at all.

'Some woman came in,' Karen said. It was her turn to stay late. 'Had a scone and a pot of tea.'

'Good,' said Jack. 'That's what we're in business for, after all.'

'Funny! No, but she knew you. Had an Irish accent.'

'Irish?' Jack shook his head. 'Doesn't ring any bells.'

'Seemed a bit put out to hear about Mrs Barclay and everything.'

'Could've been anybody, really.' Shrugging, Jack poured himself a cup of tea and began buttering a scone. 'Someone who's been here before, I should imagine.'

'Dunno. She didn't say. Seemed interested in you, though. I told her about you joining that club.'

'Good.' Jack slipped half a scone into his mouth and, round it, asked, 'Busy afternoon?'

'Nothing I couldn't cope with,' Karen said.

'Good girl.' Jack smiled at her. He wiggled his toes inside his shoes, already thinking of the evening ahead, closing up, putting his feet up, a whisky, browsing again through Dorothy's mermaid book. He was thinking about Dorothy a lot these days. Even dreaming about her. Sexy dreams. Had she got a bloke? He seemed to remember that there'd been a husband in the background. The marriage already on the rocks, if he remembered right. Clever woman like that, you'd think she'd have been able to hold things together. Till death us do part. She'd be bound to have someone else by now.

Gran, Gwen and Dorothy: the three women in his life. Mind you, a bit fanciful to say Dorothy was *in* his life. On the other hand – he looked round the teashop, windows steamed up against the cold outside, fairy-lights twinkling round the windows – in a manner of speaking, she was. No question that it was her generosity had set him and Gwen on the road to prosperity. Being comfortable, at any rate. Which was all you could really ask, wasn't it?

Kill me. He laughed, spluttering his tea. She'd really thank him, wouldn't she, if he suddenly appeared at the door with a knife in his hand, saying, 'I've come to kill you, like you asked me to, all those years ago.' Especially with her book so successful. All over the place, it was. Advertised in the papers. Displays in the bookshops. Not that he spent much time in bookshops, never been a big reader. Louis L'Amour, Micky Spillane, that was the sort of thing he liked. Didn't tax the brain at the end of a hard day. But it'd been a point of honour with him to buy all her books even though he couldn't make head or tail of them. Didn't really try, to be honest, nothing but long words and complicated sentences which went on for pages. Except for the mermaid one. He was pleased for her. Really pleased.

'Bye,' Karen was saying, and he looked up from his thoughts. 'See you tomorrow.'

'Right.' He nodded at her. 'Should be another busy day.'

'Yeah.'

'Hope you're getting lots of tips.'

She put her head on one side. 'Enough.'

'Still planning that trip to India after your exams?'

'Course I am.'

'Tell you what.' He was suddenly struck with an idea.

She stood by the door, her woollen scarf wrapped round her neck against the cold outside. 'What?'

'You've been a good girl, Karen. Worked hard.' He opened the till, pulled out a handful of notes. 'Take this.'

'What for?' Slowly she walked back across the room towards him. 'What's this?'

'Call it a Christmas bonus.'

'But there's masses here. Look ...' She splayed the notes in front of him. 'Are you sure?'

'Absolutely. A Christmas bonus. Put it towards the India thing.' He smiled at her, wishing Gwen was waiting upstairs with his supper, toad-in-the-hole or chops or something. Chips. A nice jug of gravy. 'Someone once helped me on my way, and I'd like to do the same.'

'Wow.' Karen looked down at the money. 'Thanks, Mr Barclay. Thanks ever so much. I'll put it in the bank tomorrow.'

'One condition, though.'

'What's that?'

'You send me a postcard, right?'

She laughed. 'You bet. Lots of them.'

'Good.'

When she'd gone, he sighed. Nice girl. Reminded him a bit of his Susie when she was that age. Eager. Ambitious. He wished he and Gwen could've had more kids. Really did. Maybe there'd be lots of grandchildren instead.

Before he went to bed he listened to the weather forecast. Cold but dry. Maybe he'd go fishing tomorrow. Seemed wrong somehow, to mess about with guns on a Sunday. Fishing would be good. And even on a Sunday the pond was usually deserted, he never understood why. Perhaps they preferred the camaraderie of the river. Different sort of fishing, mind you. But he liked sitting there under the trees, watching the water, listening to the birds. Not so much as he used to, of course. Didn't want to brood, wasn't good to brood over something you couldn't have.

He thought about Gwen as he got into the big double bed. They'd both worked hard, but she hadn't had a bad life with him. Though he said it himself, he'd been a good husband. Nothing to reproach himself for. Never even so much as glanced at another woman. She'd never gone short of anything. And even though she was gone, and he missed her something cruel, there was still plenty to look forward to. The baby. Maybe another one in a couple of years. Grandchildren. Who'd ever have thought he'd be a grandad?

And there'd be young Karen's postcards from India next summer. The way kids travelled about the world these days. When he was young it was about as much as they could manage to get to London, never mind India. It sounded right exciting. Fakirs and that. Turbans and little bells tinkling. Sean Connery and Michael Caine in that film.

He fell asleep, his mind full of elephants.

At first sight, the place seemed ideal. Dorothy had parked in a layby, climbed a stile and tramped across the fields, cursing the mud and the damp, cow-patted grass. Once inside the wood, there was almost no sound except for the wood-pigeons clattering among the leaves and the distant cawing of rooks. She walked round the pond, a fair-sized stretch of water, surrounded by muddy banks and damp brambles. It was quiet. Isolated, even. She'd be bound to find him here eventually. Maybe the weather was a factor. She'd heard on the radio in her hotel bedroom that it was going to be cold but clear over the rest of the weekend. Maybe he'd seize the opportunity to come here tomorrow while he worked on his strategy for disposing of her. On the other hand, this close to Christmas ...

She smiled a little grimly. He'd reckoned without her counter-attack. It was stupid of him to warn her. *I'll never forget what you wanted me to do ...* or words to that effect. Even more stupid to sit outside her house in his flashy car. Had he really thought that she'd wait for him, a sitting duck, until he'd carried out his plan? No way. She was safe here because, for one thing, he didn't know where she was and, for another, he wouldn't be expecting her. She felt impatience stirring. Would he come tomorrow? The sooner the better, frankly.

She found a call-box and telephoned David. 'I'll be back soon,' she said. She wanted to tell him she loved him, but the words were too unaccustomed. 'I'll ring you,' she said.

There were a lot of ifs in her plans. *If* Jack showed up. *If* no other anglers appeared on the scene. *If* she actually succeeded in eliminating him. If all those ifs, she'd be a murderess. The word was heavy. A murderess. But it was that or be murdered herself. And she knew which one she preferred. Putting down the receiver, she rang into her answering-machine. A number of messages were waiting, in particular one from the woman producer who wanted to set up another meeting about the TV show.

Excellent. Wonderful. The future beckoned brightly.

The following day was, as forecast, cold but dry. Clouds moved across the sky, showing intermittent patches of blue. By noon the sun had burned through the cloud cover, dimly radiant. Jack drove down to the garage on the edge of the town and ran his Anglia through the car wash. He'd often hankered after something a bit more flash but, as Gwen had always pointed out, where was the point wasting money on expensive cars? She was right, but he could easily afford it. Maybe he should start indulging himself a bit more. Holidays. Upgrading the car. Eating out in fancy restaurants. Trouble was, none of that was any fun on your own. Frankly, *nothing* was any fun any more.

He knew he was feeling out of sorts. A sense of waste overtook him, opportunities not taken and life not lived. There'd been a lot of that since Gwen died. He drove out towards Burnham Pond. A spot of fishing would soon sort him out.

Dorothy paid her hotel bill and put her suitcase in the back of the car. Away from the hotel, she stopped to buy a newspaper, a sandwich and a couple of bottles of water which she stowed in her backpack. If anyone saw her heading towards Burnham Pond, they'd take her for a hiker.

There were two or three cars parked in the layby, but none was a Jaguar. She experienced a moment of doubt. But a man like Jack Barclay would probably have several cars. Or, if he wasn't already at the pond, he might come later. She had supplies, reading matter. She could wait.

When she reached it, the pond was ruffled by a breeze. She approached cautiously, not wanting to be heard. Through the bramble thickets she glimpsed someone sitting on a folding stool of chrome and canvas, staring into the water. Was that Jack? Silently, she circled, hoping to get a better view. It would be pretty stupid to dispose of the wrong person.

The man on the other side of the pond was grey-haired, slight, wearing glasses. Wasn't that how David had described the man watching her in the restaurant? Even as the adrenalin pumped and sparkled through her body, she couldn't be sure it was Jack Barclay. She thought back to Liverpool. Distinguishing characteristics? She couldn't remember any. His hair had been mousy-brown then, his eyes a muddy hazel. No protruding teeth, birthmarks, scars. Only an overwhelming ordinariness. Nothing about this man was familiar. She waited, racking her brains. And then, suddenly, carrying across the water, she heard the beeping sound of a mobile telephone. The man opposite her set his fishing-rod carefully into its bracket and reached into his pocket.

'Hello?' he said, having flipped down the mouthpiece. 'Jack Barclay here.'

He spoke to the caller for a few more sentences, but Dorothy didn't hear what he said. Her heart was thudding. This was the man she'd come to find. Her target. She moved round the pond until she was directly behind him. There was no one else around. Just the two of them. And the noisy birds. As soon as he ended his call, she would do it.

When he folded the phone up and began to replace it inside his anorak, she sprang forward. She was bigger than he was. She remembered that now, re-membered relaxing against his shoulder and thinking how slight he was, how insubstantial.

He had no warning. His stool tipped forward into the pond, and she was on him, both feet on his shoulders, pressing him down into the mud. He writhed for a bit, his arms in their thick sleeves threshing at the bubbling water, but it was no contest. She waited at least five minutes, then stepped back. He didn't move. His body rose and fell with the slight movement of the water caused by his actions, then gradually stilled.

Dorothy stood on the bank. It would have been better if there'd been a suicide note. But it might be seen simply as an unfortunate accident, a fatal heart attack, with no one to help. And the beauty of it, the absolute marvel of it, was that nobody could possibly connect her with him.

She set off across the fields back to her car. She took the country roads towards Oxford, stopped somewhere for tea, bought a Crown Derby plate in an antique shop. She'd expected to feel excited, strung up, but she didn't. Just relieved at a problem solved.

'It can't have been suicide.' Jimmy Knapp stood in Jack Barclay's flat above the shop. 'He'd never have killed himself with Susie about to have a baby.'

'He was a bit down over losing Gwen,' his sergeant said.

'Yeah, but he'd come to terms with it, sorted it out. And Susie was his whole life. It definitely wasn't suicide.'

'So an accident. Heart attack, something like that, he falls forward into the water and drowns?'

'Not a heart attack, according to the path. boys.'

'So he slipped in, got that heavy anorak on, weighs him down so he can't get out. It wouldn't be the first time someone's drowned like that.'

Knapp shook his head. 'I took a damn good look round. Whatever happened, it wasn't like that. Someone else was there around the same time. Standing right behind him at one point. Small footprints. Could be a woman.'

'Why'd she want to kill Jack Barclay?'

Knapp shrugged. 'God knows. There's a lot of nutters around these days.'

'You think it was that? A nutter?'

'I don't know.' Knapp picked up the book which lay on the table beside Jack's bed. There were mermaids on the glossy cover, sinuous and busty. He'd read about it. A number one best-seller. His own daughter had put it on her Christmas list. 'Important overview of woman's role in society, Dad,' she'd said impatiently, when he'd asked why she wanted it. He'd bitten back something about women's role being under rather than over – not the sort of remark you'd make to your daughter, whatever might pass as a joke down at the station. 'Dorothy Metcalf,' he said.

'You what?' His sergeant was looking at the bookcase with its load of westerns and adventure stories.

'She wrote this.' Knapp held up the book.

'Dorothy Metcalf?' The sergeant pulled a book from a set of five similar ones. 'She wrote this one, too.'

'What is it?'

'*Myth and the Woman*,' the sergeant said. 'Bloody unreadable crap if you ask me. Can't see why they bother to print it.' He opened the book, read the short author biography. 'Professor Dorothy Metcalf, Head of Anthropological Studies at St Hildegarde's College, Oxford. Blah-blah-blah.'

'Wonder why old Jack would have a copy of it. Didn't seem to read anything but cowboy books, far as I can tell.'

'Dunno, really.' The sergeant put the book back. 'And not just one of them, but several. Look at this. *From Leda to Europa: The Demythologising of Rape.*'

'Funny,' Knapp said. 'Doesn't fit in.' He looked thoughtful. 'It's a long shot, I know, but maybe we'll drive over to Oxford, the two of us, and have a word with this lady professor. See where she was yesterday afternoon, if there's any connection between her and Jack.'

A DISH TAKEN COLD

Anne Perry

Celie stared at her in total disbelief. It could not be true. Jean-Pierre dead? How could it be? He had been perfectly all right when she had left him with Amandine only a few hours ago. And there had been no violence in this area last night. Revolutionaries were swarming all over Paris as they had been ever since the storming of the Bastille just over three years ago. The city was in a ferment of ideas, tearing down the old, reforming everything, creating sweeping changes that needed the force of arms to carry them through. The power of the Church was destroyed. The monarchy itself teetered on the edge of an abyss. There was economic chaos, and the hunger and fear that went with it. France was at war, and the Prussian armies were massed on the borders. But for all the imprisonments and executions, no one had yet slaughtered women, let alone babes in arms.

'He can't be!' she said desperately. 'He was ... he ...'

Amandine was white-faced with shock herself, and guilt, her eyes hollow. Celie had left the baby in her care because the usual nurse had been called away on some family emergency of her own. Such care was necessary because, since her husband's death over a year ago, Celie had worked for that extraordinary woman of intellect, letters and dazzling conversation, Madame de Staël. She was daughter of Necker, the great minister of finance, and now wife of the Swedish Ambassador, although she was in her late twenties, no older than Celie herself.

Amandine stood in the middle of the kitchen, the smell of cooking around her.

'It is true,' she said quietly. 'He was asleep in his crib when I left him, and when I went back two hours later he ... he was no longer breathing. He never cried out or made the slightest noise. He was not sick or feverish. I cannot tell you how much I wish I had sat up with him in my arms all night! If I had guessed ...' She stopped. Words were no use, only an intrusion into an intolerable pain. Celie was filled with it, every part of her mind consumed, drowned by it.

'I want to see him,' she said at last. 'I want ...'

Amandine nodded and turned to lead the way back to the small room with its window overlooking the courtyard. The crib was in the corner. Celie hesitated, putting off the moment when it could no longer be denied. She went over slowly and stared down at the tiny form, still wrapped in blankets as if he could feel the cold, although it was the hottest August in years. His face was white. He looked asleep, but she knew in her heart he was not. The frail spirit was no longer there.

Still, she picked him up and held him in her arms, rocking him gently back and forth, the tears running down her cheeks.

She had no idea how much later it was when Amandine took him from her and made her drink some hot soup and eat a little bread. There were no formalities to be observed except the civil ones. There were no priests to turn to in Paris. Religion was outlawed; it belonged to the greed, the oppression and superstition of the past. This was the age of reason. But she would have liked the comfort of ritual now, even if it was foolish and meant nothing. There must be a better way to say goodbye to someone you loved, who was a part of your body and your heart, than simply a cold acknowledgement by some citizen official.

*

She returned the next morning to her work at Madame de Staël's house. Thérèse the seamstress met her at the door.

'Where have you been?' she demanded. 'Madame has been looking for you. My God, you look terrible! Whatever's happened?'

In a shaky voice Celie told her.

'Jean-Pierre?' Thérèse said incredulously. 'He can't be! Oh, my dear Celie, how appalling!' Her fair face was slack with horror, amazement filled her eyes. 'I've never heard anything so awful! Amandine let him die! Why? How? What was she thinking of?'

'Nothing ...' Celie shook her head. She was finding it difficult to speak. Her voice choked. 'It wasn't her fault. He had no fever, no sickness. He just ... died. Now, please ... I ... I must go and tell Madame why I am late.'

Thérèse stood helplessly.

Celie left and went to the salon to find Madame. It was a gracious room. Only a short time ago the finest minds in France, both men and women, had exchanged wit and philosophy here, talking long into the night, while the Revolution was still a thing of great ideas, of hope and of reason.

Germaine de Staël was not beautiful, but she captivated men and women alike with her charm and her brilliant intelligence. When she saw Celie she drew breath to chastise her, then she saw her face and the words died on her lips.

'What is it? What have you seen, or heard? Sit down. You look about to faint.' She moved a little awkwardly. She was visibly pregnant, although her husband was not presently in Paris.

Celie wanted to get it over quickly. Saying the words again made it more real.

'Jean-Pierre is dead. Last evening. He was with Amandine Latour. I don't know the cause. He just ... died.'

'Oh, my dear.' Madame put her arm around her and held her tightly. 'How very dreadful. Such things happen sometimes. No one knows why. There can be no grief like it.' She did not offer any more words. She knew there was nothing to say or to do.

Days and nights passed in a grey succession and Celie did not count them. Her tasks were not onerous. For all her proclamations of brotherhood and equality, Madame was heiress to one of the largest fortunes in France, and she still kept an excellent household. It would be a foolish person in these days of hunger and uncertainty who gave up a comfortable position in it.

However, on the evening of 9 August events began which would change that for ever. Celie had gone to bed exhausted, but she could not sleep beyond the first hour or two. She drifted in and out of dreams, memory returning cold and agonizing with each wakefulness. Then at midnight she heard the alarm bells start to ring somewhere over to the north. It was a wretched sound, rapid, hollow and monotonous. Almost immediately it was echoed from another direction, and then another, until it seemed to be everywhere. The darkness was alive with the clangour of fear.

She rose and lit a candle. There was no need for a robe in the heat, but she felt a prickly sense of vulnerability without it, as if she might be caught in her shift without the protection of clothes. There were other sounds in the house now, other people up.

Her throat tightened as she opened the door and went through the outer room where Thérèse slept. She was not there. She went to the stair. What was happening? The alarm bells were ringing all over the city.

There was another candle at the bottom of the stairs, and in its yellow light she saw the frightened face of one of the menservants.

'What's happening?' she called out. 'What's all the noise?'

'I don't know, he answered breathlessly. 'It's everywhere.'

Celie went down the stairs and across to the salon. Madame was inside, a dozen or more candles lit and filling the room with yellow light and dense shadow. The curtains were drawn back so she could see out of the windows. Thérèse was at the other door.

'Are we being invaded?' she asked, her voice rising sharply to a shriek.

'No, no!' Madame answered with a shake of her head. She, too, must have felt the need to dress, because she had a plain morning skirt and blouse on. She looked extraordinarily calm, although the hand that held the candelabra was not completely steady. 'Jacques said there is a rumour that the suburbs have risen and are marching on the Palace of the Tuileries.'

'The king!' Celie gasped. 'They are going to murder the king!'

'They may try,' Madame replied grimly. 'They say it is Santerre at the head, and I would put nothing past him. But don't worry, my dear.' She lifted her chin a little higher. 'There are nine hundred Swiss Guard to protect him, two hundred gendarmes and three hundred royalist gentlemen, not to mention about two thousand National Guard. The rioters will quickly be driven back.' She turned to the manservant just as there was a loud noise from the street. 'Still, it would be a good idea to bar the doors and make sure all the bolts are shot. It will all be perfectly all right, a lot of shouting, I dare say, but no more. We should go back to our beds and get what sleep we can.'

But the bells went on all night with their hollow, soulless sound, and then at seven in the morning there was the violent shock of cannon-fire. Celie sat up in bed, the sweat trickling down her body. The air was hot already. Outside there were still people shouting and the tramp of feet. Then the cannon-fire came again, louder and more rapid.

She had kept most of her clothes on and she scrambled out of bed, put on her shoes and ran to the window. There were a dozen men in the street below, bare-armed, many of them wearing the red bandannas and kerchiefs of the rabble who had marched from Marseilles, dregs of the seaport slums and prisons. They were all armed with pikes or sabres. A woman on the far side grabbed at a child and scuttled away into a courtyard, avoiding looking at them. An old man shouted something incomprehensible, a precious half-loaf of bread clutched in his hand.

Celie drew her head in and went downstairs to the salon where Madame and Thérèse were standing in the middle of the floor. Madame was pale but composed. Thérèse's fair gold hair was dishevelled, her blouse was fastened crookedly and she was quite obviously terrified.

'Philippe says the suburbs have risen and are marching on the Tuileries!' she said the moment she saw Celie. 'There are thousands of them and they have cannons! We shall all be killed—'

'Nonsense!' Madame snapped sharply. 'Why on earth should they hurt us? We are daughters of the Revolution, as much for freedom and reform of injustice as they are!' She went over to the window and looked down, but standing back a little so as not to be seen from below. Then she turned. 'I think we should have something to eat, and perhaps some hot coffee.'

It was an order. Celie went to obey and Thérèse followed her. In the kitchen

Celie riddled out the old ashes and built a new fire in the stove. It was airless in the room but neither of them wanted to open the door, even into the courtyard.

'How are you feeling?' Thérèse said, her voice dropping with pity. 'I suppose you can hardly care about the king, or anyone else, right now. I wouldn't if I were you.'

Celie watched the flames catch hold, and closed the stove door. There did not seem to be any sensible answer to make. She did not want to talk about Jean-Pierre, although she knew Thérèse meant to be kind. She had no children of her own. She could not be expected to understand. She had had a lover a while back, but apparently it had come to nothing. She had not talked about it.

Thérèse was putting cups onto a tray. They could hear the noise from the street even in here. 'I don't blame you for hating Amandine,' she went on.

'I don't hate her.' Celie denied it, filling the pot with water from the ewer. She was glad she did not have to go out to the well to draw it. 'It wasn't her fault.'

'You're very charitable,' Thérèse said drily.

Celie looked at her, wondering what she meant.

Thérèse shrugged, a little smile curling the corners of her lips. 'Come on, my dear, she did leave him alone! She should have known better. He was so little...'

'Stop it!' Celie blurted out. In her mind she saw him lying there, alone, dying. She should not have left him with Amandine. She should have stayed with him herself. Pain filled her till it seemed she could barely hold it.

Thérèse put her arm around her. The gesture did not even touch the coldness inside; it only suffocated, although it was intended as sympathy.

'You are blaming yourself,' Thérèse said softly. 'You mustn't. It is not your fault. No mother stays with her child every minute. You left him with someone you thought you could trust. You must never chastise yourself!'

The water was boiling.

'I can't help it,' Celie admitted. 'I should have been there.' She moved away and fetched the ground coffee. She poured the water and brewed it automatically, smelling the bitter, pungent aroma. There were no clear thoughts in her mind. The noise outside was getting worse.

They returned upstairs and waited in the salon. Some of Madame's friends arrived and watched with her from the windows. News came every now and again, sometimes shouted from the street, sometimes in the mouth of a breathless servant or visitor.

'The streets are sealed off!'

'All the shops have been closed.'

'The people are evacuated!'

'The Marseillaise are storming the Palace!'

They had known that. They sat huddled together and stared towards the window and the street. Someone else arrived, hot and dirty from running, fighting her way through angry crowds.

'There's a terrible battle going on around the Tuileries!' She dropped her shawl where she stood, a plain brown thing over a drab skirt and blouse. It was the only dress that was safe these days. 'They're killing people everywhere! I saw half a dozen Marseillaise hack a man to death just a hundred yards from here. They've gone mad.'

Thérèse stifled a scream.

Celie felt only a distant horror, but it was something of the mind. Her heart was already numb.

'There are two thousand National Guard at the Palace,' Madame said with confidence. 'Not that they will be needed. The Swiss Guard will turn the rabble.'

Celie and Thérèse went to fetch more coffee. It was not really needed, but it was something to do.

'I wish I were as brave as Madame,' Thérèse said confidentially as they were boiling the water again. She looked at Celie with wide, frightened eyes. 'And I admire you so much. Your courage is superb. And your forgiveness.'

'The Marseillaise have done nothing to me,' Celie replied.

'Not the Marseillaise,' Thérèse said impatiently, waving her hand. 'Amandine ... and, of course, Georges.'

Celie was confused. 'Who is Georges?'

Something tightened in Thérèse's pretty face and her voice changed tone. 'Her lover, of course. You didn't know that?'

'Why should I be angry with him?' She did not care; it was simply automatic to ask, easier than trying to convince Thérèse that none of it mattered. Jean-Pierre was dead. Nothing else was completely real.

The water was boiling but Thérèse ignored it, staring back.

'Because if Georges hadn't been there, Amandine would have been holding your baby, talking to him, instead of in bed with Georges! Are you really so stunned you had not yet thought of that?'

It had never occurred to her. Jean-Pierre's death had been accidental, one of those terrible tragedies one never understands, something for which there is no reason.

'I'm sorry,' Thérèse said with quick gentleness. 'Perhaps I shouldn't have said anything. It's just that in your place I wouldn't have the forbearance you have, and I wanted you to know that I admire you. I would want revenge! A life for a life. I wouldn't be able to think about anything else.'

Before Celie could reply there was a noise in the courtyard, footsteps, shouting, then Jacques, one of the menservants, hurled himself in through the door, his face streaked with blood.

'The National Guard have turned!' he gasped. 'They've gone over to the Revolutionaries! Half the Swiss Guard is massacred. The king's gentlemen are being slaughtered and their bodies thrown out of the windows. In the streets everyone who even looks like an aristocrat is being put to the sword.'

The pot boiled over and no one noticed.

An hour later they were upstairs, terrified to hear the news that came up from the street about quarter-hourly. Six hundred of the Swiss Guard were dead. All the king's gentlemen. No one knew what had happened to the gendarmes. Probably they were dead too. The Tuileries was on fire. The flames were not visible from here, but the pall of smoke hung in the sky, darkening the sun, closing in the heat.

Noon came and went.

It was true. Santerre was at the head of the mob. He had demanded the king's surrender.

'Never!' Madame said fiercely. She was mortified at the slaughter of her compatriots in the Swiss Guard. 'He has more courage!'

But in that, too, she was mistaken. The queen made as if to resist, but the king, perhaps to save even greater bloodshed, walked out and calmly submitted, offering up himself and his family to be taken into imprisonment at the Temple.

Madame was distraught. She had many personal friends among the Swiss Guard and, in spite of all that anyone could do to dissuade her, she insisted on taking out her carriage, and going to see if she could save or help anyone. She seemed oblivious of the danger to herself.

Celie went to bed exhausted and frightened, but the heat was intense, the air seemed to clog in the throat and there was still shouting and the march of feet outside in the street. She ached with loneliness, and when snatches of sleep came, Jean-Pierre was there in her arms again, alive, smiling up at her. On each awakening the cold hand of grief tightened inside her with the same shock as the first time. It was hard not to hate Amandine and the unknown Georges. Perhaps she had been to blame. Maybe she had lied, and Jean-Pierre had cried out, but she had been too busy making love to hear him, or maybe she had simply ignored him, thinking it would not matter.

That day, 11 August, there was more news which outraged Madame de Staël.

'Take away the liberty of the press!' she said furiously, her face flushed, her eyes blazing. 'That's impossible! It is against everything the Revolution stands for! What liberty have we if we cannot write what we believe?'

It was typical of her that she should think of writing first. She was a passionate and eloquent writer of articles, novels, pamphlets, memoirs, anything and everything. To communicate was the breath of life to her, the purpose of existence. Now the new order had in one stroke betrayed all who believed in it. She stormed back and forth, wringing her hands, then at midday, disregarding her condition, she went out without an explanation or any word as to when she would return.

Thérèse went to see if she could buy bread, cheese, perhaps a few onions, and some more coffee. Celie tidied the salon and had Jacques draw water so she could do a little laundry.

Thérèse came home with bread and onions, but no cheese. Her face was smutted and even her hair had tiny flakes of ash from the still-smouldering ruins of the Tuileries. 'I don't know why you're bothering to wash!' she said angrily. 'It'll be worse than when you started. I can hardly breathe for the smell of smoke, and there are flies everywhere. It's as hot as damnation, and the corpses are beginning to smell already. I wish I were anywhere but Paris. I don't know why we stay here!'

'There's civil war in the Vendée and Brittany,' Celie replied flatly. 'We're at war with Prussia. Where do you want to go?'

'Well, I can understand you staying here,' Thérèse said with a shrug. 'But you'd better do whatever you're going to before Madame decides to leave. You can't remain alone! What will happen to you? You have no one.'

Celie thought of Amandine. She had believed her a friend, but perhaps she was wrong.

'What is this Georges like?' she asked curiously.

Thérèse's lips tightened. 'He's handsome enough, in a brash sort of way.'

'I don't care what he looks like!' Celie said sharply. 'I mean what does he believe? Is he clever or brave? Is he honest?'

'Georges?' Thérèse laughed, a curiously brittle sound in the hot, close air of the kitchen filled with the smell of steam and wet linen. 'I don't know what he believes. Whatever is popular at the moment. The king, Necker, Mirabeau, Lafayette, everybody in their turn. Now I suppose it is the Girondins, and if the mob rules then Marat, or whoever.'

'That's contemptible!' Celie said with disgust. 'Why does Amandine have anything to do with him?'

'Because he's charming and funny, he tells her what she wants to hear, and I suppose he's good in bed!' Thérèse said bitterly. 'Haven't you ever been in love ... with someone who made you feel happy, and it wasn't difficult to let yourself believe they meant all they said?'

Celie thought of her husband Charles. It had been a pleasant relationship, friendly, reliable. She could not recall him making her laugh, or telling her the things her heart wanted to hear. But he had been honest and, in his own way, brave.

'Georges knows how to make people like him,' Thérèse went on. 'It's a very useful talent, and he knows that.'

Celie turned away. It sounded shallow and manipulative. How could Amandine have given her body, let alone her heart, to someone so worthless? And while she was with Georges, Jean-Pierre had died ... alone ... no one holding him, no one helping, no one even knowing. It was a cheap and shabby betrayal of trust, of what she had thought was friendship. Thérèse was right – if Madame left, there would be nothing here in Paris for Celie. She would be alone.

A week went by. The weather was suffocating, but slowly the ash cleared, the bodies of the dead were taken away. A new rhythm settled in. The press was censored, but in all the streets one could buy Marat's *L'Ami du Peuple*, filled with cries for vengeance, rivers of blood to wash away the corruption of the old ways. Hebert's *Père Duchesne* made the vulgar laugh with its coarse lampoons of the royal family. Madame de Staël visited her friends, grieved with them in their losses, planned for the future and, as always, talked of ideas.

On the 19th came news that shocked her deeply. The Marquis de Lafayette, hero of the American struggle for independence, early champion for new freedom in France, had defected to the Austrians – the enemy whose armies were even now poised to invade France!

Celie had expected Madame to shout, to explode in words of anger or hurt, disbelief, even the all too understandable desire for revenge. Instead, Madame sat beside her bed in the candlelight looking startlingly tired. She was so young, not yet thirty, but now she had deep circles under her eyes and no colour in her skin. She was visibly heavier around the waist and hips with the child she was carrying. This time last year, in the heat of the summer, Celie had been like that. She could feel it as if it were only a day ago.

'How could he do that, Celie?' Madame asked, staring up, her eyes shadowed. 'How can he betray everything he's stood for – and to the Austrians, of all people?'

'I suppose he was afraid,' Celie replied wearily.

'That's no reason! We're all afraid! God knows, there's enough to be afraid of. I don't know which is worse, the armies on the borders or the mob here.'

'The mob here at least are French,' Celie said, setting down the water jug, forgetting for a moment that Madame was Swiss and her absent husband Swedish.

'A coward?' Madame said bitterly. 'Not Lafayette! Never!'

'Then perhaps he just stopped believing in anything,' Celie suggested.

'That is the ultimate cowardice,' Madame retorted with ringing conviction. 'If you haven't even the courage to hope, to care, to want, to what purpose are you alive at all?' She shook herself impatiently. 'Of course we all despair at times, but only for a moment! You rest, or you mourn, you heal: then you take heart and begin again.' She stood up and came to Celie, putting her arms around her. 'You will heal, my dear. Not quickly, of course – and you will never forget. But you will go on. It has always been women's lot to give life, to love, to have joy and fear, and sometimes to lose. But we do not stop living. That would be a dishonour to life itself, and Jean-Pierre was part of life.'

Celie took a step back, willing herself to be angry rather than weep. She swallowed on her aching throat.

'Doesn't Lafayette's betrayal make you angry?' she demanded. 'Can you bear that Lafayette, of all people, deserted us for the enemy, and not hate him for it?'

'No, I can't,' Madame admitted, going back to the bed and flopping onto it, her fists clenched. 'I want to shout at him, to hit him as hard as I can with my bare hands and feel the sting of flesh. I want him to know how I feel. But, since he's in Austria and I'm here, that's impossible!'

Celie went back through Thérèse's room to her own. She knew Thérèse was still awake, but she said nothing. Amandine was not in Austria – she and Georges were both still here, in noisy, suffocating, blood-drenched Paris. There was one betrayal at least which could be avenged. She did not yet know how, but there would be a way. It was only a matter of finding it.

On 23 August the Prussian armies advanced and Longwy fell before them. The news reached Paris with a high, sharp pitch of fear, as if invasion were only days away. Madame was still struggling to assist those of her compatriots she could find, and for whom there was any encouragement or assistance to give.

Celie had not seen Amandine since Jean-Pierre's death. It was a friendship whose loss cut her. She had expected Amandine to visit her more often, not less, after the tragedy. She said nothing about it, but nevertheless she caught a knowing look in Thérèse's eye, and was pleased she had the tact not to put words to it.

The following afternoon they were out walking slowly in the sun, talking of nothing in particular. Incredibly, there were still acrobats performing on the pavements, and a marionette show, as if life were just as always.

'The theatres are still playing,' Thérèse remarked with wonder. 'I don't know how they can.'

'I suppose they have to eat, like anyone,' Celie answered, turning to watch as a group of National Guardsmen came around the corner, red, white and blue cockades in their hats, muskets over their shoulders.

'But everything they put on is so boring,' Thérèse went on. 'It's all the same propaganda now. Half of it doesn't even make sense!'

'Because all the meaning has been censored out of it,' Celie agreed, moving closer to Thérèse as a youth raced past them and ran into the opening of a courtyard. His feet clattered over the cobbles and they heard him banging with his fists on the wooden door beyond.

The guardsmen drew level with them and stopped.

'Is that Citizen Carnot's house?' one of them asked Celie, pointing to where the youth had disappeared.

'I don't know,' Celie replied.

'Don't lie, Citizeness,' he said grimly, fingering his musket. 'His father-in-law is an enemy of the Revolution. We have a warrant to search his house. Who was it who just went in?'

'Not his father-in-law!' Celie said tartly.

'So you knew him!' The man was triumphant, his suspicion proved. One of the men behind him brought his gun to the ready.

Thérèse grasped hold of Celie's arm tightly, her fingers biting into the flesh.

'No, I don't know him.' Celie kept her voice level, her eyes steady. 'But he was about eighteen. He couldn't be anybody's father-in-law.'

The man looked at her narrowly, then apparently decided he could not exactly name the fault he saw in her and turned away. He waved his arm peremptorily and ordered his men into the courtyard.

'Poor devil,' Celie said quietly.

'You don't know who he is,' Thérèse pointed out. 'He could be anybody. He could be a real enemy of the people. He might be hoarding food, planning to help the royalists, or harbouring a priest or something.'

'The priest could be his brother!'

'Everybody's somebody's brother,' Thérèse said sharply. 'That doesn't make it all right to hide them. Come on! If we stay here they might think we are involved!' She tugged at Celie's sleeve.

'Amandine lives only a few doors away from here,' Celie retorted without moving. She had not been here since that night. 'I wonder if she knows these people...'

'What does it matter?'

There was shouting from inside the house. Someone was banging a gun butt furiously against the door. A woman screamed. There was a volley of shots, and then silence.

Somewhere opposite a child started to cry.

Two old women were quarrelling at the end of the street, regardless of the whole thing.

The guardsmen appeared again, marching out of the courtyard, a man, his arms pinned by his sides, between the first two. He was bruised and bloody. He looked about thirty, dressed in ordinary, brown working clothes. Behind him, also held close by guardsmen, was a second man, older, his hair thin, his face very white but held high as if he would not give in to the fear which shook his body. After them a single guardsman half dragged a woman who was cursing at him, swearing and pleading alternately, her feet tripping as she fought to keep her balance.

'They must have been hiding him after all,' Thérèse observed with a grimace. 'The boy was too late to warn them. It doesn't do to hide a wanted person. It brings ruin down on your whole family, and it doesn't save them in the end.'

The guardsman let the woman go and gave her a little push. She stumbled and fell, remaining where she was, tears running down her face.

Perhaps it was not a wise thing to do, but Celie went over to her. She considered for a moment trying to help her up, then changed her mind and squatted down beside her.

'Is it your father they've taken?' she asked.

The woman nodded.

'What has he done?'

'Nothing! A few pamphlets, but that was before the press was stopped!'

'Then he'll probably be all right. Have you someone you can go to?'

The woman shook her head.

There was a noise further up the street, doors opening and closing. Celie was aware of someone standing over her.

'Where did they take him, Minette?' It was a man's voice, very deep, almost husky.

'I don't know,' the woman on the pavement replied. 'They didn't say.'

Celie looked up. The man who had spoken was very dark; his hair sprang back from his brow in heavy waves. His eyes were almost black as she looked at him with the sun at his back. There was gentleness in his face, and it seemed as if in other times he would laugh quickly, and perhaps lose his temper just as quickly.

He held out his hand to Minette and, against her will, hauled her to her feet.

'Well, we had better find out,' he said, his jaw tightening. 'You're no use to anyone sitting here. I suppose it was the pamphlets again? It will probably be the Commune. What did he write this time?'

'Nothing!' Minette lied futilely.

The man looked at Celie, a slight smile on his lips. 'Are you all right, Citizeness?'

Celie scrambled up, dusty and rather awkward. 'Yes ... thank you ...'

His smile broadened, then he took Minette by the elbow and walked away. He did not seem to have seen Thérèse who stood half in the shadows against the far wall, her face set hard, her mouth thin, eyes narrow and bright.

Celie walked more slowly, without talking again. Thérèse kept darting sidelong glances at her, but she held her tongue. Celie could not get the 'domiciliary visit', as they were known, out of her mind. She had seen them before, of course, and heard of them from friends. Everyone in Paris knew that the Revolutionary powers could search your house any time they suspected you of harbouring a wanted person, an enemy of the Commune or of the government. All priests were automatically in that category. Religion was a superstition from the past, an oppressor of the poor. To sustain it, even to the least degree, was to stand in the way of progress, and justice, and the true freedom, that of reason, enlightenment and the brotherhood of equality.

She could not forget Amandine, sneaking off and leaving Jean-Pierre alone so she could be with her lover, the flattering, manipulative Georges. It was the betrayal which hurt. She had liked Amandine as much as anyone. She had trusted her completely – she would never have left Jean-Pierre with her otherwise. Just one hour's selfishness, indifference to a tiny child – and look what it had cost! Celie would pay the price of it for ever.

Another domiciliary visit in that street, that would be the answer. A march down to the Commune between guardsmen, a trial, the fear and the humiliation. Then the sick misery as you thought of the short journey in the tumbrels, the scarlet blade of the guillotine, the plank slippery with blood, the waiting crowd ... and then oblivion.

Of course they could not execute Amandine. She would be innocent of any wrong as far as they were concerned. What she had really done would not interest them. They would let her go again. And Georges? Well, if he were not really guilty of anything, they would have to let him go too. That was less important. From what Thérèse had said, Amandine would only be hurt by him, sooner or later. Perhaps it would be easier to grieve for him as a martyr than have him live on, and be disillusioned. Then even the past was soiled and stripped away.

She did not yet know how to do it, but that would come.

It took her another two days to call up the nerve to visit Amandine. She found she was shaking as she combed and pinned her hair in front of the piece of glass. The reflection she saw was pale, wide eyes dark with pain and anxiety, mouth turned down a little by sadness, looking vulnerable and lonely. She turned away and walked swiftly downstairs. Madame was out again. She was always out these days. Where she found the strength no one knew.

This was a private matter. She went out into the street and turned left. It was still most unpleasantly hot. The air was sticky. There were little flies everywhere and the smell of the drains was worse than usual. There had been no rain to carry the effluent away. The heat shimmered up from the stones, making them seem to waver.

She walked quickly. Never do anything to attract the guardsmen, or the mob, least of all the Marseillaise with their open shirts and red kerchiefs. Avert your eyes as you pass, in case you seem to be challenging them or, worse, inviting them.

She passed a few people she knew.

She reached Amandine's house and hesitated, gulping and swallowing air. She thought of Jean-Pierre and knocked, then wished she had left it a little longer. But it was too late. The door swung open. Amandine stood there, her eyes blue and smiling, the sunlight on her hair.

'Celie! I'm so glad you've come. I called to see you twice, but you were out or not well.'

'Did you?' Celie said doubtfully.

'Thérèse told me. But it doesn't matter.' She stood aside. 'Come in. Let me get you a little wine and water. It's too hot for coffee. Have you noticed the leaves are beginning to die? And it isn't even September yet.' She led the way into her cool kitchen looking towards the north.

She poured the wine and water and offered Celie a glass. The kitchen was homely, lived in. There was a faint aroma of bread and coffee. Amandine sat down opposite her, her hands cupped around her own glass, as if the coolness of it were welcome.

Then Celie noticed with a jolt a man's coat on a hook on the back of the door to the courtyard, hung casually, as if he knew he would be back. Georges? Was he so comfortable here he took it all for granted?

'How are the people down the street who were arrested?' she blurted out.

'The father-in-law is still in prison,' Amandine replied, looking down at the table. 'They let René go. I think for Marie's sake he pleaded innocence.'

'What do you mean?'

'Said he didn't know his father-in-law was wanted,' Amandine explained. 'It's not true, of course, but what good does it do anyone for him to be executed as well? He feels wretched … guilty for being alive, desperately relieved, ashamed. How did you know about it?' Her eyes searched Celie's.

'I was passing at the time,' Celie said truthfully. 'How is Minette?'

'Terrified,' Amandine answered with a twisted smile, looking up at Celie sadly. 'Angry, confused, waiting for them to come back again, trying not to hope her father will be freed because she wants it so much, and trying not to face the fear that they'll guillotine him because she can't bear it. She wanted René to say what he did, but she's furious with him, too, for being alive.' She was watching Celie as she spoke, to see if she understood.

Celie had not lost anyone to the Revolution. Charles had died in an accident. Jean-Pierre's death had been due to carelessness, neglect.

Amandine looked down at her hands again. 'Anyway, how are you? Madame de Staël must be very upset about the censorship. I know she is a great writer.'

Before Celie could reply, the door from the courtyard opened silently and a man came in. He was handsome in an easy, obvious way. Celie recognized him immediately. It was he who had tried to help the woman Minette in the street two days ago. He looked first at Amandine with a quick light of pleasure, almost a softness; then he turned to Celie, and just as she knew him he, too, remembered her. He smiled and it lit his dark face.

Celie felt herself stiffen.

'Hello, Georges,' Amandine said gently. 'You don't know Celie Duleure. She works for Madame de Staël.' She turned to Celie. 'Georges Coigny.'

'Citizen Coigny,' Celie answered with a cool smile. She was disconcerted that he should be the man who had seemed to behave with such gentleness at that incident. She did not wish to share anything with him. She wanted to leave, but she would be spoiling her own purpose if she did. She ought to stay and learn something about him. It was ridiculous to rely on the snatches that Thérèse had told her. She thought of Jean-Pierre alone and dying in this very house, only a few yards from where she was sitting now, and steeled herself.

Georges sat down as if he did not need to be invited, and Amandine accepted it. There was not even a flicker of surprise in her face. She looked equally comfortable, except that there was concern in her soft features as she regarded Celie.

'Will you stay and eat with us?' she asked. 'It is only vegetable stew, but we should enjoy your company.'

'Thank you.' The words sounded hollow, as if she were speaking a foreign language she barely understood. 'It is just what I should like. And this room is lovely and cool.'

Amandine smiled and stood up, ready to busy herself with the meal, like a good hostess. Celie watched her with envy for her quiet, domestic happiness. She glanced across at Georges, and saw his eyes on her as well. She loathed him for his complacency. He was as much responsible for Jean-Pierre's death as Amandine. But for his selfishness, his intruding appetites, Amandine would never have left him.

Georges turned to Celie. 'How are managing with the food shortages, Citizeness?' he asked. 'I heard the baker on the Rue Mazarine has bread most days. It's a little walk, but it's worth it.'

Celie did not want his helpful advice. She stared at him. There was nothing in his eyes even to suggest Jean-Pierre crossed his thoughts. Was he tactful, not wanting to hurt her, not bring it to her mind unnecessarily? Or was he simply callous? He could not be unaware of it. He must have been there, seen Amandine's horror ... the guilt.

'Thank you.' She hoped she did not sound as stiff as she felt. He must not suspect. Her slowly unfolding plan depended on them both being unaware. She made herself smile. 'I shall remember that. Rue Mazarine?'

'Yes. I think times may get harder.'

'Do you?' That was something she had not thought of. All her emotions were in the past; the future hardly mattered, except to find some sort of justice.

His face was grave. 'I can't help but think so. They are talking of trying the king, and I think it is bound to happen.'

'Trying the king?' It had not occurred to her. 'Who? The Convention?' It seemed a preposterous idea, but even as she questioned it she recalled hearing one of Madame de Staël's friends speak of it.

'Naturally,' he said, biting his lip. 'It will give an appearance of legality to whatever they do to him afterwards.'

Amandine was busy with pans on the stove, chopping more herbs to add. She shot a warning glance at Georges, but he was not looking at her. His attention was focused on Celie. There was a warmth in him as if he liked her. It was a facile charm, deliberate and false, and she despised it. Manipulation of people's emotions was contemptible.

'You mean to imprison him?' she asked, frowning.

'Or the guillotine,' he said quietly.

'The guillotine! Execute the king?' Suddenly the room seemed not pleasantly cool in the August heat but chilly, a shiver passing over the skin. 'Do you think so?'

'They'll have to.' He leaned forward a little, his dark eyes troubled. He smelled very faintly of clean cotton and the warmth of skin. A wave of loneliness engulfed her for Charles, not for his nature or his words but for the closeness of being cared for. She stared at Georges, blinking back her misery.

He must have seen the wretchedness in her, and mistaken it for awe or fear.

'They have to!' He searched for the right words with which to explain to her. 'As long as the king is alive, there will be plots centred about restoring him. He isn't an evil man, but you know yourself he tends to take whatever counsel was given him last. Each faction thought they had persuaded him to reason, and then someone else spoke to him, and he changed his mind. No one will trust him ... they can't.'

She knew it was true. She had lived through all the changes of fortune from the first pleas for reform, through the ascendancy of Madame de Staël's father, then of Mirabeau, then the Girondins. Now the real power seemed to be with the Commune of Paris, and the fearful Jean-Paul Marat.

As if picking her thoughts out of the air, he continued. 'Can you really believe Marat and his hordes would let him live?' he asked softly. 'Have you seen Marat, or heard him?'

She had done both. Marat was half Swiss, half Corsican, swarthy, pock-marked and now riddled with some scabrous disease which broke out in suppurating lesions and caused him to hop, almost crabwise, in his pain. His hair had been matted with filth, he wore rags and a red bandanna around his head. Sometimes he even went barefoot, as if in total identification with the sunken-eyed, copper-faced crowds of the dispossessed whom he led. Celie had been no closer to him than three or four yards, and yet she had been aware of the stench of his body. His voice had been hoarse when he spoke, as if his throat were permanently sore. But it was his rage which she remembered above all else, his demand for rivers of blood to avenge past injustice, the tearing out of tongues, the splitting of limbs, the cutting of endless throats.

'No ...' she said huskily. 'No ... I suppose not.'

'And then everything will change,' Georges went on.

Amandine turned from what she was doing, her brow puckered. 'Won't that be good? Then we can have the real reforms! We can have some proper equality, pensions for the old and the sick, for widows, especially of soldiers. They were talking about that in the Convention only the other day. Alphonse told me, at the Café Procope.'

Georges's eyes were tender as he looked back at her.

'Alphonse is naive, and wants to please. God help him, he wants to be happy! But think about it – we will be leaving behind all the known boundaries of our society. We have outlawed the Church and done away with God, or the hope of divine justice. When we have got rid of the king, and the aristocracy as well, what is there left to fear, or to respect, or even to be certain of—'

'Stop it!' Amandine said sharply, her face tight and pale. 'If you speak like that, people will think you are against the Revolution! Celie's all right, but you don't know who else is! Be careful, Georges!' There was urgency in her voice, and a rising note of fear, not for herself but for him.

Celie waited, her heart pounding. She could not help staring at Georges. His words whirled in her head. What he said was true. They would be entering a new and totally unknown age, everything familiar hurled away. It was frightening.

'All the old restraints would be gone,' Amandine went on firmly, looking at Georges, then at Celie and back again. 'The rules that crippled us and held us back, the bonds that kept us to our place.'

'The chains of slavery,' Georges mimicked Marat, sounding hoarse and gravelly as he did it. 'And the rules that protected the weak, the old, the foolish and the uncertain will be gone too. Now tell me that we can't have change without blood, and some lives being lost!'

Amandine touched him gently, with no more than a brush of the fingers over his hair. He may barely have felt it, but there was familiarity in it and the certainty of acceptance.

'You know very well I wouldn't tell you anything of the kind,' she answered. 'You can't justify anything with someone else's life. Now, are you going to stop frightening us so we can enjoy our supper? Celie has enough of politics at Madame de Staël's house. You never talked this way with Thérèse.'

His face tightened and he looked away, then turned to Celie.

'I'm sorry, Citizeness,' he said quickly. 'Perhaps I let my tongue run away with me. I thought ...' He stopped. She knew what he had been trying to say, that she felt the same. She had, and it angered her because for almost an hour she had been snared by his mind, his charm. She had forgotten who he was, and why she hated him.

'There is no need to apologize,' she said very quietly. 'The press is not free, but you can speak your mind in the company of friends. Perhaps you are right, and the changes will not be freedom but chaos instead.'

'He didn't mean that!' Amandine interrupted, her face flushed. She moved a little closer to Georges, and as if unaware she did so, put out her hand. 'Only that we must be cautious not to abuse it. We shall have to take great care ...'

'I understand,' Celie lied. 'They will be dangerous times – for all of us.' She made herself smile again.

Amandine relaxed. 'Of course. I shouldn't be so ... nervous. I'm sure you must be hungry. Please, be comfortable. Georges, pass this over, and make room at the table.'

Over the next days Celie's mind was in a fever. Georges's face haunted her dreams. Sometimes even awake she could bring him to memory so sharply it was as if he had been in the room with her. And Amandine, whom she had truly believed her friend, had put a few moments' cheap pleasure ahead of Jean-Pierre's life. Her soft eyes, her frank smile, seemed to rest on Celie's closed eyelids so she could never escape.

But now she needed only a little more knowledge and she would know how to execute justice. Georges's words came back. He had seemed to doubt the very fabric of the Revolution. The more she thought about it, the more she realized he had even questioned the fundamental goodness of change itself! He had said that executing the king could destroy what was precious, as well as what was evil, oppressive and unjust. He had predicted things which to some people could be viewed as disastrous.

Maybe she did not yet know of anything active that he was doing against the Revolution, but it could surely be only a matter of time before he did something.

He had spoken disrespectfully of Marat, even disparagingly. He would not only deserve arrest for his corruption of Amandine and his part in Jean-Pierre's death, but for quite genuine political reasons. No stretching of the truth would be necessary for Celie, as a good citizen, to warn the officials of the Commune that he was an enemy of the people and, if left free, might do serious harm to the cause of the reforms which, heaven knew, were generations overdue.

But to be effective, to catch Amandine as well, Georges must be arrested in her house. Celie needed to know more of his actions, his habits, his comings and goings.

It was not difficult to find an excuse to call again: a few buttons borrowed for Madame's blouse when she could not purchase them; a pair of boots Madame no longer wanted, which fitted Amandine; she was passing on the way home with a few extra onions; a word of thanks about the baker Georges had recommended.

Amandine seemed to suspect nothing. Had she no conscience at all? She still did not mention Jean-Pierre, as if he had not existed. His brief life meant nothing at all. Celie's hope, her joy and her grief did not cross the horizon of Amandine's own happiness with Georges. He was there twice when Celie called, and he behaved with the same manipulative charm, the dark eyes looking at her so directly, the deep velvet voice, the white smile. Her loathing of him increased, for the gulf between what he was and what he pretended to be.

But she learned his comings and goings. He was arrogant enough, sure enough of his charm, and her feminine weakness to it, to be quite unguarded with her. He did not hide his views; he did not even moderate them, except when Amandine warned him. But even she was too sure of herself, and of Celie, to conceal his movements, and the nights he spent in her house ... assuredly also in her bed. They must have so little regard for Celie, underneath their pretended warmth, that for them she was not even a part of their real lives, the threads of it that mattered. She was not important enough to be any danger.

But she was! She was very real, and capable of passion and hunger and pain, intolerable pain. There was an aching loneliness in her, a grief for a lost baby which filled the world!

She had all the information she needed. She went to the Commune, up the stone steps, the heat reflecting back in a blistering wave carrying the smells of sweat and dirt. She passed a group of men lounging against the railings. Many had open shirts and wore red scarves, or bandannas. Most were unshaven. One was asleep in the shade, a fly crawling up his arm.

Inside there were self-important citizens going about their business, footsteps light and quick, eyes sharp, the intoxicating taste of power on their lips.

She found the right person quickly, almost as if he had been waiting for her, and fortune guided her footsteps. She told him what he needed to know: Georges's doubts of the Revolution; his reluctance to try the king before the people; his dark fears for the rightness of the cause. Then she told him where she knew he could be found, on 2 September, for certain. He was a greasy little man, earnest and fussy. He praised her loyalty and her honour, and wrote down everything she said.

She left, telling herself she had served justice and the greater good. She had avenged the loneliness and the pain of Jean-Pierre, who had been too small and too frail to do it for himself. But there was no lightness inside her as she returned home. Her sense of achievement was a hard, tight knot inside her.

Of course, the authorities might not even bother with Georges Coigny. There were dozens of people wanted, maybe hundreds – even one of Madame's own lovers, Louis de Narbonne. In days past she had exerted her influence, and intrigued endlessly to have him made Minister of War. Celie had heard from someone else that Marie Antoinette had laughed aloud, and made a sarcastic remark that now Germaine de Staël would be happy to have all the armies of France at her command! The days when the Queen could joke about anything were long gone. It seemed like another world. And Louis de Narbonne was hunted, as Georges Coigny would be, and probably for as little reason.

She had not meant to think that! The words had slipped out without intent. They were both counter-Revolutionaries, men who would retain the old order with its privilege and oppression and, above all, its injustice.

Then that very evening she learned accidentally that Madame was hiding de Narbonne here in the house. She should not have been surprised. He had been her lover, which meant he was intelligent, charming, articulate, well read and unquestionably had a vivid sense of humour. Nevertheless, when she came into Madame's bedroom a little after eight, to return some mended clothes, and found Louis de Narbonne, dressed in plain brown breeches and a stained shirt, she felt a chill of fear stab through her and settle like ice in her stomach.

He swivelled around as he heard her footsteps, his hand poised as if to reach for a weapon. He was a handsome man, in a calm, measured way; all intellect and wit, nothing like the obviousness of Georges Coigny.

She smiled at him, as if to see him there was nothing remarkable. Then, when it was too late, she thought she should have said something. He had never worn a countryman's clothes before. He had been elegant, immaculate. This was an attempt at invisibility. A disguise would have been an admission he was hiding.

She laid the clothes down on the chest at the end of the bed, then turned and left. Neither of them had spoken.

Downstairs Thérèse was about her business in the kitchen. Jacques was moving bottles of wine, Eduard was busy outside in the courtyard. There was no one else around. The housemaid had gone home, and the grooms and coachmen were above the stables.

'There are more of these awful men from Marseilles in the streets,' Thérèse said angrily. 'Between them and the National Guard, you can hardly walk a dozen yards without being accosted.' If she knew Narbonne was in the house, there was not the slightest sign of it in her manner. She clattered pots about, expressing her irritation with frequent words of exasperation.

Jacques returned and set down bread for the next day, but his face was pale.

'What is it?' Celie demanded.

'I saw a poster on the corner of the street,' he replied, his voice sharp and unhappy. 'Louis de Narbonne is wanted by the Revolution!' He knew Narbonne had been one of Madame de Staël's lovers. All Paris knew it.

Outside in the street someone shouted and there was a roar of laughter. It was all exactly as if there were no one new in the house, certainly no one hunted by the Revolutionary police.

A little before midnight, when Celie was almost asleep, there was a violent banging at the door, as if with a gun butt. She sat up in bed, the sweat breaking out on her body in the hot, suffocating night. Fear knotted inside her. There was a moment's prickly silence, then the banging again.

Celie scrambled out of bed, fishing for a shawl, and went to the door. Thérèse was sitting up, her candle lit.

'What is it?' she demanded. 'What's happening?'

Celie walked past her. 'I don't know.' The banging was still going on. 'I'm going to see if Madame is all right.'

'Why shouldn't she be?' Thérèse said irritably. 'We've got nothing to hide.'

Celie made no reply, but went to the farther door and opened it, peering out. She saw the flicker of a candle as Madame de Staël went downstairs.

Celie hurried after her and Jacques came through from the back of the house, fastening his breeches with clumsy fingers. At any other time he would have been the one to answer the door.

Madame opened the latch just as the National Guardsman raised his musket to bang again.

'Good evening, Officer,' she said courteously, looking at the leader. 'How can we help you?' Her hair was loose down her back, and untidy, and she was dressed for bed, but she spoke as if she had been receiving guests and he was one of them, simply a trifle unexpected.

He was tired and angry, and had felt certain of his errand. Now his expression changed to one of surprise and suspicion. He was perhaps thirty, tall, brown-haired. He might have been pleasant enough to look at had he not been unshaven and exhausted.

'Citizeness de Staël?' he said aggressively.

'Of course.' She smiled at him.

'I've a warrant to search your house.' He made no effort to show it to her. No one argued with the National Guard. That was an offence in itself, and they both knew that.

Her voice did not shake in the slightest nor did her smile waver, but, standing behind her, Celie could see her hands clench and the nails dig deep into the flesh.

'Then you must come in,' Madame said, stepping aside to allow him past. She swallowed and took a deep breath, her shoulders rising and staying high, knotted with tension. 'Who are you looking for?'

'Louis de Narbonne,' he answered immediately. 'He's wanted for treason against France.'

'Oh dear!' She made an effort to keep her voice steady. 'How people change. He used to be an excellent servant of the people, patriotic and loyal. I haven't seen him lately.'

'No?' the man's eyebrows rose sarcastically. 'We know your relationship with him, Citizeness!'

She smiled and looked down. 'I'm sure you do,' she conceded, 'but we are sophisticated people. We understand these things. I'm sure you have been ... admired ...'

We! Celie thought in disbelief. She was speaking to this ruffian as if she thought of him as an equal. Everything in him shrieked that he was a peasant, not even a petit bourgeois.

The man stared at Madame de Staël.

'Can I offer you a little wine and water?' she said graciously, still looking only at him, not the half-dozen men behind him. 'It is arduous work you are doing for us. No doubt you have been on your feet all day.'

'Yes, I have,' he conceded.

'Jacques, wine and water for the gentleman,' Madame ordered, barely turning her head as he signalled his men to wait outside. 'Where are you from, Citizen?' she continued. 'I detect a touch of the south in your voice.'

'Provence,' he replied, following her in and closing the door. He seemed pleased she had noticed.

Her face softened and she moved to sit down in one of the large, comfortable chairs. He sat opposite her, glad to rest himself.

'What a beautiful region,' she continued. 'You must find Paris hard, especially this summer with the terrible heat. I've never known it so stifling. And dirty, too, of course, in comparison. Still, Paris is the heart of things, is it not? Surely here we are creating a new order of justice and equality, greater than that in England or Spain or Austria – greater even than the Americas because we have so much more wisdom and greater experience of the past.' Her eyes did not leave his for a moment. 'And then, too, we have a culture and a civilization second to none. Look at our writers! Our scientists, our artists, our poets and painters, and, of course, above all our philosophers. I think philosophy is a French art, don't you?'

'Yes . . .' he answered, struggling to keep up but refusing to admit ignorance of anything. Here was Germaine de Staël, daughter of Necker himself, writer, novelist and supreme conversationalist, addressing him as if he were her equal, as if in another time he might have been invited to her famous salon. 'Certainly,' he answered with gathering conviction. 'We are the most civilized of people. It is in our nature.'

'Don't worry.' She leaned forward confidentially. 'The rest of the world will understand that one day. History will vindicate us totally, Citizen. History will one day say what you and I know now.'

'Of course it will!' he agreed with more feeling. His body relaxed a little. 'We shall be known as heroes then!'

'Your grandchildren will envy you for the time in which you lived,' she said warmly. 'The sights you saw which they will only read about.' She allowed herself to smile at him. 'We are a part of history, Citizen.'

He straightened his shoulders a little.

Jacques returned with the wine and water and hesitated. Celie took it from him quickly and offered it first to the guardsman, who accepted it with relish, then to Madame herself.

The conversation continued. The guardsman ignored Celie and Jacques. Neither dared leave the room. Celie did not even know if Jacques was aware of Louis de Narbonne upstairs in Madame's bedroom. She could think of nothing else. She was cold inside with terror. She was sweating and her hands were sticky and numb. Surely the guardsman must smell the fear in the room? Or perhaps he was so used to it he no longer recognized it. What did the men outside think he was doing? Searching?

Madame continued to talk. She was interesting, sophisticated, amusing. Now and then the guardsman was reduced to laughter. She spoke of the theatre, of recent inventions, of political and moral philosophy, of art. Celie had never heard her more dazzling. Only the pitch of her voice betrayed to one who knew her so well the fear that tightened her throat and held painfully rigid the muscles of her neck and shoulders.

The guardsman was entranced. Never before had anyone spoken to him as if he, too, were clever, articulate and entertaining. It was the ultimate compliment, the one courtesy no aristocrat had ever afforded him. In his mind he despised her, but it was a hatred born of envy. Tonight she had treated him as if there were no need for it, no cause. For a brief hour he also was of the élite.

He left without searching the house more than perfunctorily.

As the door finally closed behind him Celie found she was shaking uncontrollably. She was gulping as if she could not find enough air to fill her lungs, and her knees had no strength at all. Only now she realized her bodice was soaked with sweat, the ice-cold, clinging sweat of terror.

She looked at Madame de Staël, and saw the recognition in her eyes of exactly the same drenching emotions. For an instant they, too, were equals, their common humanity binding them as one and outweighing everything else.

After a measureless moment Celie turned to Thérèse and saw in her blue eyes only contempt because Madame de Staël had treated Revolutionary ruffians as if they were gentlemen. She did not know about Louis de Narbonne upstairs.

Celie felt colder still, her clothes sticking to her.

'Lock up and blow out the candles,' Madame requested in a voice that trembled. 'We had best all return to our beds.'

Thérèse started to say something, then changed her mind and obeyed.

Celie went up with Madame, a step behind her on the stairs. At the top she turned and smiled. Celie smiled back, hesitantly, her eyes in the candlelight frightened and questioning.

Celie admired her more than anyone else she could think of, her courage, her willingness to face the enemy and fight with her heart and her wits to save a man she had once loved, even at the risk of her own life. Celie had watched her. She knew the consuming fear, the knowledge of what the cost would be, and yet there had been no hesitation, no weakness or thought of her own safety. It was what she herself wanted to be. She hungered to have that same courage and honour. It was a blazing light in the darkness of corruption, violence and betrayal, disillusion and futility which was engulfing Paris.

But she was not. Sick shame twisted inside her. She had saved no one ... far from it! The only decisive act she had taken was to betray a man and a woman because they loved each other, and with an hour's indulgence of that love had left a baby alone. Perhaps that made Celie's betrayal justified. It could never make it beautiful.

And she ached for beauty, honour, pity in the tide of hate which rose around her, drowning everything in its ugliness.

She went to her bed with turmoil raging inside her. She had made of herself something she looked at now with loathing. Tomorrow she must find Georges Coigny and warn him, whatever the danger. To fail would destroy her own inner core, the heart and soul of what she was.

But the following morning she had no opportunity to do more than think of

Georges Coigny with a dull ache of anguish. Madame had been granted a passport to leave for Switzerland, but she was deeply worried about some of the deputies of the Convention whom she knew were imprisoned in the Abbaye and in grave danger of facing the guillotine.

Citizen Louis Pierre Manuel, the Procurator of Paris, was a well-read man and an admirer of literature. Indeed, he had written the preface to an edition of Mirabeau's letters which he had recently had published. Execrable, in Madame's opinion, but nevertheless at least an attempt at the art of writing. He was approachable. She had written to him requesting an appointment and it had been granted for the democratic hour of seven o'clock this morning.

'You can come with me, Celie,' she said as she walked from her dressing room towards the salon. 'It would be more appropriate if I did not go alone.'

'But . . .' Celie began, but Madame had already passed her and was through the salon door, her back straight, walking very upright. She would not even hear an argument, let alone heed one.

They set out together through the early morning streets. The gutters were worse every day. The smell of coffee-vendors on the corner was pleasant, but they had no time to stop. Every now and then they passed groups of men carrying either muskets or pikes. Some were lounging against walls or the parapets of bridges, others moved idly from one place to another, apparently without purpose, looking for something to occupy their time and feed their anger.

Celie and Madame de Staël walked briskly, eyes forward. There were a few yells and cat-calls, but they were not seriously troubled. At the town hall Madame marched straight up the steps. A National Guardsman at the door moved forward to bar her way, his face sharp, unshaven, suspicious.

'I have an appointment to see Citizen Manuel,' Madame said with great dignity. 'There is a small service I may be able to render him—'

'Indeed?' the man replied with open disbelief. 'And just what service could you render to the Procurator of Paris?'

'That is a private matter of his own, Citizen,' she answered unflinchingly. 'Please tell him Madame de Staël is here, and that I have considerable admiration for his literary works.' That was a brazen lie, and she told it without a flicker.

Celie was longing for the task to be completed so she could begin the search for Georges. She had named 2 September. She had only twenty-four hours, and now to save him was the thing she wanted most in the world. But Madame had only one thing uppermost in her mind as well, and she was unaware of Celie, except as she needed her for her own support.

They were shown to Manuel's offices and found him more than willing to spare time for a famous lady of letters. Like many other, greater revolutionaries, he had burning aspirations to leave behind him some immortal writings.

Unconsciously he used the manners of the past, his face eager as he recognized her. Celie was invisible.

'Citizeness! In what way can I be of service to you?'

She equivocated only briefly. 'Sir, I appeal to you as a civilized man, which I know you are from your excellent foreword to Mirabeau's letters. And I cannot but believe you are a wise man also . . .'

He flushed with pleasure, although he tried to conceal it.

She did not wait for a reply. She affected not to notice, as if he must be used to such candid praise and it were no more than his due.

'Monsieur, I came to plead for you to exercise the power you have to save the lives of some, at least, of the deputies who now lie imprisoned in the Abbaye, particularly for de Lally and de Jaucourt. They are held for trial and certain death. They are not evil men bent on the betrayal of the ideals both you and I hold so dear. They are simply caught in a misfortune of timing when fear among the masses has caused indiscriminate assets. You and I both know that.' She smiled briefly, not in any lightness of mood but as a mark of her friendship towards him.

Manuel nodded, watching her carefully, his face a trifle pale, his shoulders tight under his brown coat.

'These are times of violent change, often without warning,' she continued. 'Today's heroes are tomorrow's villains. You and I cannot say that next week we shall not find ourselves before a hasty judgment, and taking our last ride in the tumbrels to the Place de la Révolution. In six months you may perhaps no longer have any power. Exercise clemency, Monsieur, so that at least in history you may be found a place among those judged to be above the petty shifts of envy and fear, a man worthy of honour for his ideals and his humanity, as well as his art with words. Reserve for yourself a sweet and consoling memory for the time when it will perhaps be your turn to be outlawed.'

He looked at her, his eyes wide, barely blinking.

Celie wanted to scream, Hurry! Make your decision! There are not only deputies to save, there is Georges Coigny. Innocence and guilt don't matter any more – stop making tiny pointless judgments of an act here or there, preserve a life ... let me undo what I have done.

Words burst out of her. 'Citizen Manuel ... in the future we may all be remembered as a violent and bloody people, but what rested in your own heart is what matters. You can do little to help what France does, but what you yourself do lies wholly within your hands.'

Madame looked at her with surprise, but she did not interrupt.

'I long above all things to have a small part in the beauty of compassion,' Celie went on urgently, her voice shaking.

'Of courage, of ... of ...' she fought for simple words for the hunger aching within her '... of the love for humanity, not the hatred. I want something good of myself to cling to when my own black hour comes!'

Manuel lowered his eyes. 'Of course,' he said very quietly. 'Of course, Citizenesses. I shall do what I can, and I believe it may be enough...'

Madame de Staël inclined her head in a gesture of gratitude reminiscent of the days of the old regime, and Manuel's face lit with pleasure and at last his body relaxed.

They took their leave, and as soon as they were out of the door, even before they had reached the steps outside or passed the guards, Celie spoke.

'Madame, I, too, have someone I must warn before he is arrested.' It was not necessary to add that arrest in itself almost certainly meant execution. 'Please let me go and search for him!'

Madame's face lit with surprise and pleasure. 'You have found someone to love! I'm so glad, my dear. One should not remain forever a widow, especially someone as young as you are. And Charles was not a great love for you, I know that. You have mourned enough. Do go and warn this man.'

Celie did not bother to explain that Georges was anything but her lover – he was as much as anyone responsible for Jean-Pierre's death, the greatest pain she had ever known. But seeing him executed by the Revolution, and seeing Amandine imprisoned or executed also, would not restore her baby; it would only make of her something ugly she did not want to be. It would rob her of the only beauty left. She simply thanked her and went, breaking into a run as soon as she was in the street.

But where should she go? She knew where Georges would be tomorrow, but not today. The only place to begin was with Amandine, and she dreaded that. She might have to explain!

She would lose Amandine's friendship for ever. There was still a strong yearning of memory and sweetness of hours shared, small kindnesses from her, and it would hurt. Amandine had been careless, selfish, but not with malice. Celie was only too aware of times when she had done the same, grasped at love without thinking of the price. Georges was shallow, manipulative, but he was full of charm and intelligence, and perhaps courage of a sort.

First she tried the places she knew he frequented from her earlier search for enough knowledge to betray him, but he had not been to any of them. Precious time was passing. The sun was high. She was tired. Despair rose inside her. It was mid-afternoon already, and she had accomplished nothing!

With pounding heart and clenched fists she made her way through gathering crowds towards the Rue Mazarine. There seemed to be people everywhere, all talking, shouting, their voices sharp with urgency. She did not bother to listen to what they were saying. She must get to Amandine, and ask her where she could find Georges. She could say she had heard he was wanted. He did not need to have been betrayed ... terror and accusation were in the air. Marat and his hordes from the tanneries and slaughterhouses of the Faubourg St Antoine were baying for blood.

She was breathless when she reached Amandine's door. Please, heaven, she was in! She beat on it, bruising her fists.

It flew open and Amandine stood there, white-faced.

Celie choked on her own breath. It seemed as if her heart stopped. She was too late!

'Georges?' she gasped, and choked in a fit of coughing.

'I don't know!' Amandine answered, grasping Celie as if to rescue her physically from her distress. 'Do you need him?' Her face held nothing but innocence and fear.

Celie felt an agony of guilt. 'The Commune is after him,' she said hoarsely. 'I must warn him. Where can I find him?'

'I don't know.' The colour fled from Amandine's face, as if she might faint any moment. 'He might be at Citizen Beauricourt's, in the Rue Dauphine.'

Celie broke loose. 'I'll try there. Where else?'

'The Commune itself.' Amandine's voice was no more than a whisper. She held Celie's arm with hard, strong fingers. 'But you can't go there! You could be killed yourself.'

'No, I won't...'

'Haven't you heard?' Amandine demanded. 'Verdun has fallen! The Marseillaise are on the march! They are everywhere, attacking, looting, even killing! If Madame can take you, you must get out of Paris!'

'I can't get out of Paris!' Celie shouted back at her. 'I must find Georges and warn him, don't you understand? They're after him! If he comes here tonight, and I heard you say he would, then you'll both be arrested ... and arrest means death.'

Amandine gulped. 'I know, but there is no use in you dying as well. When he comes I'll warn him—'

'For God's sake!' Celie cried desperately. 'When he comes they could be waiting for him! There'll be no time! I'm going to the Rue Dauphine, and if he's not there to the Commune.'

'I'll come with you.' Amandine stepped forward as if she would leave without even closing the door behind her.

'No! If you do, there'll be no one here to warn him if I don't find him.'

Amandine hesitated.

Celie threw her arms around her, then let go and turned and ran. She bumped into people, heedless of their annoyance, and plunged on. There were crowds in the streets, milling, jostling, shouting at each other, demanding to know the latest news. She encountered a mob of women on the corner of the Boulevard St Germain, screaming at everyone they saw, faces contorted with rage, hair bedraggled and eyes blazing. Some of them even carried weapons such as kitchen knives and broom handles.

Celie had no time to find another route to the Rue Dauphine. Swallowing her revulsion and a prickle of shame, she hailed them as sisters, and ran on, unmolested, while they surged around a carriage, brought it to a halt and tore open the doors. Celie had no idea what happened to the occupants. She ran on, legs aching, lungs bursting, drenched in sweat.

She came to the house in the Rue Dauphine.

'Georges Coigny!' she gasped to the man who opened the door. 'Is he here? I must speak with him, it is desperately urgent! Please!'

'No, Citizeness,' he replied. 'I don't know where he is.'

She stared at him, refusing to believe his words. His face was bland, suspicious.

'I want to warn him!' she tried again. 'It is for his good! Please, Citizen?'

'He is not here,' he said. 'Try the Commune. He is sometimes there although, with the Prussians attacking, who knows?'

'Thank you.' Every part of her body ached. She had blisters on her feet and her legs were shaking. But she must find Georges. She could not give up now. If she were ever to regard herself with less than loathing, he must be saved. She started off again along the burning pavements, pushing, elbowing her way towards the huge building where the Paris Commune met.

It was six in the evening and she was close to weeping with fear and exhaustion when at last she saw the dark head of Georges Coigny and found the tears of relief running down her face.

'Georges!' She had meant to shout, but her voice could only croak. 'Georges!'

He heard her over the din and turned. 'Celie!' His brows drew down and his face creased with anxiety. He forced his way over to her, pushing past a man with a huge belly and another stained with the grime of the tanneries. 'What are you doing here? Go home!' He was beside her now. 'Better still, get out of Paris. Haven't you heard the news? The men who marched up from Marseilles are looting and killing in the streets.'

'I know!' she gasped, 'but I need to tell you. You are wanted ... there is a warrant out for you. You must get out of the city ... please! They'll guillotine you if they catch you. Go!'

'You must go too,' he urged, putting his arm out as if physically to guide her away. He glanced around, then pushed her along, gently, as if they were old friends. She found herself on the stairs, jostled by people coming and going. The noise was becoming louder, harsher. Someone roared with laughter.

They were out on the street now, Georges's arm still around her, holding her closely. She could feel his body as she was one moment knocked against him, the next almost torn away. A huge man with a barrel chest lurched into her. He stank of stale sweat, onions and rough wine. Involuntarily she cried out, stumbling and only regaining her balance because Georges had not let go of her.

They made their way slowly along the street towards the river. Behind them the shouting grew worse. Someone began to sing, a loud, jubilant sound, like a call to war. Others took it up.

'You must leave Paris!' she shouted at Georges. 'Take Amandine! Get away, be safe . . .' It was the last thing she said to him. A group of men came massing along the street, filling it from side to side, and she was torn from Georges's grip and carried along by them, her cries drowned in their bawdy laughter, and then that song she would come to hate above all others, which would chill the blood in her veins, the 'Marseillaise'.

She could not find Georges again. She looked desperately, knowing it was hopeless. That crowd could have carried him along in any direction. Exhausted and filthy, bruised, her skirts torn, she returned home. She had done all she could. At least Georges knew, and he would protect Amandine.

The following day, 2 September, Madame de Staël determined to leave Paris. Everything she meant to take with her, which was little enough, was piled into a fine coach with six horses, footmen and coachmen in livery, and she and Celie set out.

It was a disastrous plan. They were hardly beyond the entrance to the mews when, at the sound of the postilion's whips, a band of women, gaunt-faced, eyes filled with hatred, hurled themselves at the horses, screaming abuse. The animals were terrified. One reared up, knocking against the others.

'Thieves!' an old woman shrieked, glaring through the windows at Madame and Celie. 'Robbers! Oppressors of the poor!'

'Blood-sucking parasites!' another swore vociferously.

'Plunderer! Looter!' The cries and howls went on. ' "Thief of the nation's gold".'

More people joined in, men as well, until there was a large crowd.

'Take her to the section!' a man yelled, his face twisted with fury. 'Make her answer to the Assembly!' He seized the lead horse's head, while another pulled the postilion from his position, punching him while he did so.

The carriage lurched forward again. Madame was white-faced, but after a glance at Celie she sat back, knowing it would be futile to argue.

At the section offices, they were questioned and abused, charged with trying to smuggle outlaws into exile. Celie thought of Georges with a hope too fragile to dare to dwell on and a fear which filled her with pain. She could not even say Amandine's name to herself. Somehow it had become as important to her to save them as if she were doing it for Jean-Pierre. This was her last gift to him, a gift of saving not destroying, of love above hate. There was hate everywhere, rivers of it, seas of it. It was drowning them all.

The section officer ordered that they should be taken under escort across Paris to the town hall. A gendarme even rode inside on the passenger seat opposite them. At first he was gruff to the point of rudeness, then, as Madame's condition became apparent to him, he treated her with more courtesy. At last, when they were screamed at, abused, buffeted so violently it was a marvel the horses were not injured, he promised to defend them, even should it be at the cost of his own life.

Others were very different, perhaps even touched with guilt at their behaviour towards a woman so obviously with child. Then, the angrier for it, they hurled abuse, even stones, at the proud carriage with its magnificent horses.

At the town hall they alighted amid an armed multitude, all brandishing clubs, staves, pikes and swords. They were forced to walk under a vault of spears. One man with an unshaven face lowered his weapon and pointed it at Madame. Had it not been for the gendarme defending her with drawn sword, she would have fallen, and Celie had no doubt the mob would have been on them both like a pack of dogs.

Inside it was safer, but they were harried and pushed from one official to another, questioned, accused, insulted, until finally, as if God-sent, Procurator Manuel appeared and conducted them to his office. He looked grey-faced, his eyes filled with horror and despair.

He closed the door once they were inside, leaning against the handle as if it supported his weight.

'Thank God I was able to rescue your friends yesterday,' he said huskily to Madame. 'Today I think it would be too late! The Marseillaise are everywhere. Marat's hordes from the slums and tanneries are on the march, howling for blood, and no one seems able to stop them. I don't know if anyone is even trying! Marat calls for seas of blood to cleanse us from the past. Robespierre seems to be going along with him. You must get out of Paris, Madame. I will keep you here safely if I can, then tonight, under cover of darkness, I will get you to the Swedish Embassy. From there you will be able to escape.'

'Thank you, Monsieur,' she said gravely, her voice quivering a little. She sat down on the chair he provided. He offered one to Celie also, and she was glad to sink onto it. Every part of her hurt, the muscles of her neck, her back tight with fear, her stomach knotted, the pulse pounding in her ears, her skin prickling with fear. The room was insufferably hot, and yet she was cold inside.

Manuel left. Hour after hour they sat there, hearing the screams and howls of the mob muted beyond the closed door. Now and again there were footsteps outside. They hardly dared to breathe, looking at each other in a desperate new companionship forged in the face of death.

Then the footsteps passed and they relaxed for a few moments, until the next time.

For six terrible hours they were there, then at last Manuel returned and they made their way in his own carriage under cover of loud and sultry darkness to the Swedish Embassy.

It was one of the worst nights in the history of France. The Marseillaise stormed the prisons and murdered over thirteen hundred of the inmates, sometimes hacking them limb from limb. Many were old men, women and children, incarcerated for no greater reason than poverty. The Princesse de Lamballe, some-time friend of Marie Antoinette, was torn apart and her entrails cooked and eaten. The gutters of Paris ran with human blood.

In the morning Celie and Madame de Staël left a reeking city, a pall of smoke lying over it from the bonfires, the stench of death in the air.

'What will become of them?' Celie said in a whisper as they passed through the city gates. 'What is happening to us?'

'I don't know,' Madame replied, her face ashen. 'It seems that an abyss opens up behind each man who acquires authority, and as soon as he steps backwards he falls into it. It can only get worse! I shudder for all those good and decent people we leave behind.' She leaned across a little, her eyes shadowed by concern. 'My dear, did you manage to warn your friend?'

'Yes!' Celie answered with a sweet rush of gratitude. It was the only precious thing left in this descent into hell. 'Yes . . . I warned him. And he will get Amandine out of the city too. I know he cares for her very much.' Why should it hurt her to say that? It was foolish, a childish pain of loneliness, a yearning for what she could not have.

'Amandine?' Madame said with surprise. 'Oh, I am glad. I always liked her. It was good of you to care, my dear, after what happened. Who does she know that was wanted by the Revolution?'

'Georges Coigny . . . her lover.' Again the words hurt.

'Oh!' Madame tried to laugh, but her throat was dry and it was only a curve of the lips and a little cough. 'He is not her lover – he is her cousin, although they were raised together and are more like brother and sister. He is very handsome, don't you think? Thérèse was in love with him, only she is a very selfish woman, I'm afraid, and he threw her over, not very gently, and she has never forgiven him for it. She holds a grudge, does Thérèse. Not a nice quality. Life is too tragically, desperately short, my dear. One should forgive, for one's own sake as much as anything . . . don't you think?'

Celie leaned back in the seat, tears of relief spilling down her cheeks. She was smiling, filled with an uprushing warmth inside that spread through her whole body.

'Yes . . . yes, I do,' she said passionately.

DEATH IS NOT THE END

An Inspector Rebus Novella

Ian Rankin

For Andrew O'Hagan,
and with thanks to Nick Cave for the title

I wrote this novella at the behest of my friend Otto Penzler. The theme of 'vanishing' has stayed with me ever since, to the extent that I have, in Raymond Chandler's phrase, 'cannibalized' part of it for a sub-plot in the Rebus novel, *Dead Souls*, while altering the histories of the characters involved so that both can be read independently.

One

Is loss redeemed by memory? Or does memory merely swell the sense of loss, becoming the enemy? The language of loss is the language of memory: remembrance, memorial, memento. People leave our lives all the time: some we met only briefly, others we'd known since birth. They leave us memories – which become skewed through time – and little more.

The silent dance continued. Couples writhed and shuffled, threw back their heads or ran hands through their hair, eyes darting around the dance floor, seeking out future partners maybe, or past loves to make jealous. The TV monitor gave a greasy look to everything.

No sound, just pictures, the tape cutting from dance floor to main bar to second bar to toilet hallway, then entrance foyer, exterior front and exterior back. Exterior back was a puddled alley, full of rubbish bins and a Merc belonging to the club's owner. Rebus had heard about the alley: a punter had been knifed there the previous summer. Mr Merc had complained about the bloody smear on his passenger-side window. The victim had lived.

The club was called Gaitanos, nobody knew why. The owner just said it sounded American and a bit jazzy. The larger part of the clientele had decided on the nickname 'Guisers', and that was what you heard in the pubs on a Friday and Saturday night – 'Going down Guisers later?' The young men would be dressed smart-casual, the women scented from heaven and all stations south. They left the pubs around ten or half past – that's when it would be starting to get lively at Guisers.

Rebus was seated in a small uncomfortable chair which itself sat in a stuffy dimly lit room. The other chair was filled by an audio-visual technician, armed with two remotes. His occasional belches – of which he seemed blissfully ignorant – bespoke a recent snack of spring onion crisps and Irn-Bru.

'I'm really only interested in the main bar, foyer and out front,' Rebus said.

'I could edit them down to another tape, but we'd lose definition. The recording's duff enough as it is.' The technician scratched inside the sagging armpit of his black T-shirt.

Rebus leant forward a little, pointing at the screen. 'Coming up now.' They waited. The view jumped from back alley to dance floor. 'Any second.' Another cut: main bar, punters queuing three deep. The technician didn't need to be told, and froze the picture. It wasn't so much black and white as sepia, the colour of dead photographs. Interior light, the audio-visual wizard had explained. He was adjusting the tracking now, and moving the action along one frame at a time. Rebus moved in on the screen, bending so one knee rested on the floor. His finger was touching a face. He took out the assortment of photos from his pocket and held them against the screen.

'It's him,' he said. 'I was pretty sure before. You can't go in a bit closer?'

'For now, this is as good as it gets. I can work on it later, stick it on the computer.

The problem is the source material, to wit: one shitty security video.'

Rebus sat back on his chair. 'All right,' he said. 'Let's run forward at half-speed.'

The camera stayed with the main bar for another fifteen seconds, then switched to the second bar and all points on the compass. When it returned to the main bar, the crush of drinkers seemed not to have moved. Unbidden, the technician froze the tape again.

'He's not there,' Rebus said. Again he approached the screen, touched it with his finger. 'He should be there.'

'Next to the sex goddess.' The technician belched again.

Yes. Spun silver hair, almost like a cloud of candyfloss, dark eyes and lips. While those around her were intent either on catching the eyes of the bar staff or on the dance floor, she was looking off to one side. There were no shoulders to her dress.

'Let's check the foyer,' Rebus said.

Twenty seconds there showed a steady stream entering the club, but no one leaving. Exterior front showed a queue awaiting admittance by the brace of bouncers, and a few passers-by.

'In the toilet maybe,' the technician suggested. But Rebus had studied the tape a dozen times already, and though he watched just once more he knew he wouldn't see the young man again, not at the bar, not on the dance floor, and not back around the table where his mates were waiting – with increasing disbelief and impatience – for him to get his round in.

The young man's name was Damon Mee and, according to the timer running at the bottom right-hand corner of the screen, he had vanished from the world some time between 11.44 and 11.45 p.m. on Friday 22 April.

'Where is this place anyway? I don't recognize it.'

'Kirkcaldy,' Rebus said.

The technician looked at him. 'How come it ended up here?'

Good question, Rebus thought, but not one he was about to answer. 'Go back to that bar shot,' he said. 'Take it nice and slow again.'

The technician aimed his right-hand remote. 'Yes, sir, Mr DeMille,' he said.

April meant still not quite spring in Edinburgh. A few sunny days to be sure, buds getting twitchy, wondering if winter had been paid the ransom. But there was snow still hanging in a sky the colour of chicken bones. Office talk: how Rangers were going to retain the championship; why Hearts and Hibs would never win it – was it finally time for the two local sides to become friends, form one team which might – *might* – stand half a chance? As someone said, their rivalry was part and parcel of the city's make-up. Hard to imagine Rangers and Celtic thinking of marriage in the same way, or even of a quick poke on the back stairs.

After years of following football only on pub televisions and in the back of the daily tabloid, Rebus was starting to go to matches again. DC Siobhan Clarke was to blame, coaxing him to a Hibs game one dreary afternoon. The men on the green sward weren't half as interesting as the spectators, who proved by turns sharp-witted, vulgar, perceptive and incorrigible. Siobhan had taken him to her usual spot. Those in the vicinity seemed to know her pretty well. It was a good-humoured afternoon, even if Rebus couldn't have said who scored the eventual three goals. But Hibs had won: the final-whistle hug from Siobhan was proof of that.

It was interesting to Rebus that, for all the barriers around the ground, this was a place where shields were dropped. After a while, it felt like one of the safest places he'd ever been. He recalled fixtures his father had taken him to in the fifties and early sixties – Cowdenbeath home games, and a crowd numbered in the hundreds; getting there necessitated a change of buses, Rebus and his younger brother fighting over who could hold the roll of tickets. Their mother was dead by then and their father was trying to carry on much as before, like they might not notice she was missing. Those Saturday trips to the football were supposed to fill a gap. You saw a lot of fathers and sons on the terraces but not many mothers, and that in itself was reminder enough. There was a boy of Rebus's age who stood near them. Rebus had walked over to him one day and blurted out the truth.

'I don't have a mum at home.'

The boy had stared at him, saying nothing.

Ever since, football had reminded him of those days and of his mother. He stood on the terraces alone these days and followed the game mostly – movements which could be graceful as ballet or as jagged as free association – but sometimes found that he'd drifted elsewhere, to a place not at all unpleasant, and all the time surrounded by a community of bodies and wills.

'I'll tell you how to beat Rangers,' he said now, addressing the whole office.

'How?' Siobhan Clarke offered.

'Clone Stevie Scoular half a dozen times.'

There were murmurs of agreement, and then the Farmer put his head around the door.

'John, my office.'

The Farmer – Chief Superintendent Watson to his face – was pouring a mug of coffee from his machine when Rebus knocked at the open door.

'Sit down, John.' Rebus sat. The Farmer motioned with an empty mug, but he turned down the offer and waited for his boss to get to his chair and the point both.

'My birthday's coming up,' the Farmer said. This was a new one on Rebus, who kept quiet. 'I'd like a present.'

'Not just a card this year then?'

'What I want, John, is Topper Hamilton.'

Rebus let that sink in. 'I thought Topper was Mr Clean these days?'

'Not in my books.' The Farmer cupped his hands around his coffee mug. 'He got a fright last time and, granted, he's been keeping a low profile, but we both know the best villains have got little or no profile at all.'

'So what's he been up to?'

'I heard a story he's the sleeping partner in a couple of clubs and casinos. I also hear he bought a taxi firm from Big Ger Cafferty when Big Ger went into Barlinnie.'

Rebus was thinking back three years to their big push against Topper Hamilton: they'd set up surveillance, used a bit of pressure here and there, got a few people to talk. In the end, it hadn't so much amounted to a hill of beans as to a fart in an empty can. The procurator fiscal had decided not to proceed to trial. But then God or Fate, call it what you like, had provided a spin to the story. Not a plague of boils or anything for Topper Hamilton, but a nasty little cancer which had given him more grief than the whole of the Lothian and Borders Police. He'd been in and out of hospital, endured chemo and the whole works, and had emerged a more slender figure in every sense.

The Farmer – who'd once settled an office argument by reeling off the books in both Old and New Testaments – wasn't yet content that God and life had done their worst to Topper, or that retribution had been meted out in some mysterious divine way. He wanted Topper in court, even if they had to wheel him there on a trolley.

It was a personal thing.

'Last time I looked,' Rebus said now, 'it wasn't illegal to invest in a casino.'

'It is if your name hasn't come up during the vetting procedure. Think Topper could get a gaming licence?'

'Fair point. But I still don't see—'

'Something else I heard. You've got a snitch works as a croupier.'

'So?'

'Same casino Topper has a finger in.'

Rebus saw it all and started shaking his head. 'I made him a promise. He'll tell me about punters, but nothing on the management.'

'And you'd rather keep that promise than give me a birthday present?'

'A relationship like that . . . it's eggshells.'

The Farmer's eyes narrowed. 'You think ours isn't? Talk to him, John. Get him to do some ferreting.'

'I could lose a good snitch.'

'Plenty more bigmouths out there.' The Farmer watched Rebus get to his feet. 'I was looking for you earlier. You were in the video room.'

'A missing person.'

'Suspicious?'

Rebus shrugged. 'Could be. He went up to the bar for a round of drinks, never came back.'

'We've all done that in our time.'

'His parents are worried.'

'How old is he?'

'Twenty-three.'

The Farmer thought about it. 'Then what's the problem?'

Two

The problem was the past. A week before, he'd received a phone call from a ghost.

'Inspector John Rebus, please.'

'Speaking.'

'Oh, hello there. You probably won't remember me.' A short laugh. 'That used to be a bit of a joke at school.'

Rebus, immune to every kind of phone call, had this pegged a crank. 'Why's that?' he asked, wondering which punchline he was walking into.

'Because it's my name: Mee.' The caller spelt it for him. 'Brian Mee.'

Inside Rebus's head, a fuzzy photograph took sudden shape – a mouth full of prominent teeth, freckled nose and cheeks, a kitchen-stool haircut. 'Barney Mee?' he said.

More laughter on the line. 'Aye, they used to call me Barney. I'm not sure I ever knew why.'

Rebus could have told him: after Barney Rubble in *The Flintstones*. He could have added, because you were a dense wee bastard. But instead he asked how this ghost from his past was doing.

'No' bad, no' bad.' The laugh again; Rebus recognized it now as a sign of nerves.

'So what can I do for you, Brian?'

'Well, me and Janis, we thought ... Well, it was my mum's idea actually. She knew your dad. Both my mum and dad knew him, only my dad passed away, like. They all used to drink at the Goth.'

'Are you still in Bowhill?'

'Never quite escaped. Ach, it's all right really. I work in Glenrothes though. Lucky to have a job these days, eh? Mind, you've done well for yourself, Johnny. Do you still get called that?'

'I prefer John.'

'I remember you hated it when anyone called you Jock.' Another wheezing laugh. The photo was even sharper now, bordered with a white edge the way photos always were in the past. A decent footballer, a bit of a terrier, the hair reddish-brown. Dragging his satchel along the ground until the stitching rubbed away. Always with some huge hard sweet in his mouth, crunching down on it, his nose running. And one incident: he'd lifted some nude mags from under his dad's side of the bed and brought them to the toilets next to the Miners' Institute, there to be pored over like textbooks. Afterwards, half a dozen twelve-year-old boys had looked at each other, minds fizzing with questions.

'So what can I do for you, Brian?'

'Like I say, it was my mum's idea. Only, she remembered you were in the police in Edinburgh – saw your name in the paper a while back – and she thought you could maybe help.'

'With what?'

'Our son. I mean, mine and Janis's. He's called Damon.'

'What's he done?' Rebus thought: something minor, and way outside his territory anyway.

'He's vanished.'

'Run away?'

'More like in a puff of smoke. He was in this club with his pals, see, and he went—'

'Have you tried calling the police?' Rebus caught himself. 'I mean Fife Constabulary.'

'Oh aye.' Mee sounded dismissive. 'They asked a few questions, like, sniffed around a bit, then said there was nothing they could do. Damon's twenty-three. They say he's got a right to bugger off if he wants.'

'They've got a point. People run away all the time, Brian. Girl trouble maybe.'

'He was engaged.'

'Maybe he got scared?'

'Helen's a lovely girl. Never a raised voice between them.'

'Did he leave a note?'

'Nothing. I went through this with the police. He didn't take any clothes or anything. He didn't have any reason to go.'

'So you think something's happened to him?'

'I know what those buggers are thinking. They say we should give him another week or so to come back, or at least get in touch, but I know they'll only start doing something about it when the body turns up.'

Again, Rebus could have confirmed that this was only sensible. Again, he knew Mee wouldn't want to hear it.

'The thing is, Brian,' he said, 'I work in Edinburgh. Fife's not my patch. I mean, I can make a couple of phone calls, but it's hard to know what else to do.'

The voice was close to despair. 'Well, if you could just do *something*. Like, anything. We'd be very grateful. It would put our minds at rest.' A pause. 'My mum always speaks well of your dad. He's remembered in this town.'

And buried there, too, Rebus thought. He picked up a pen. 'Give me your phone number, Brian.' And, almost an afterthought, 'Better give me the address, too.'

That evening, he drove north out of Edinburgh, paid his toll at the Forth Bridge, and crossed into Fife. It wasn't as if he never went there – he had a brother in Kirkcaldy. But though they spoke on the phone every month or so, there were seldom visits. He couldn't think of any other family he still had in Fife. The place liked to call itself 'the Kingdom' and there were those who would agree that it was another country, a place with its own linguistic and cultural currency. For such a small place it seemed almost endlessly complex – had seemed that way to Rebus even when he was growing up. To outsiders the place meant coastal scenery and St Andrew's, or a stretch of motorway between Edinburgh and Dundee, but the west-central Fife of Rebus's childhood had been very different, ruled by coal mines and linoleum, dockyards and chemical plants, an industrial landscape shaped by basic needs, and producing people who were wary and inward-looking with the blackest humour you'd ever find.

They'd built new roads since Rebus's last visit, and knocked down a few more landmarks, but the place didn't feel so very different from thirty-odd years before. It wasn't such a great span of time after all, except in human terms; maybe not even then. Entering Cardenden – Bowhill had disappeared from road signs in the 1960s, even if locals still knew it as a village distinct from its neighbour – Rebus slowed to see if the memories would turn out sweet or sour. Then he caught sight of a Chinese takeaway and thought: both, of course.

Brian and Janis Mee's house was easy enough to find: they were standing by the gate waiting for him. Rebus had been born in a prefab but brought up in a house just like the one he now parked in front of. Brian Mee practically opened the car door for him, and was trying to shake his hand while Rebus was still emerging from his seat.

'Let the man catch his breath!' Janis Mee snapped. She was still standing by the gate, arms folded. 'How have you been, Johnny?'

And Rebus realized that Brian Mee had married Janis Playfair, the only girl in his long and trouble-strewn life who'd ever managed to knock him unconscious.

The narrow, low-ceilinged living room was full to bursting – not just Rebus and Janis and Brian, but Brian's mother and Mr and Mrs Playfair. Introductions had to be made, and Rebus guided to 'the seat by the fire'. The room was overheated. A pot of tea was produced, and on the table by Rebus's armchair sat enough slices of cake to feed a football crowd.

'He's a brainy one,' Janis's mother said, handing Rebus a framed photo of Damon Mee. 'Plenty of certificates from school. Works hard. Saving up to get married. The date's set for next August.'

The photo showed a smiling imp, not long out of school. 'Have you got anything more recent?'

Janis handed him a packet of snapshots. 'From last summer.'

Rebus went through them slowly. It saved having to look at the faces around him. He felt like a doctor, expected to produce an immediate diagnosis and remedy. The photos showed a man in his early twenties, still retaining the impish smile but recognizably older. Not careworn exactly, but with something behind the eyes, some disenchantment with adulthood. A few of the photos showed Damon's parents.

'We all went together,' Brian explained. 'Janis's mum and dad, my mum, Helen and her parents.'

Beaches, a big white hotel, poolside games. 'Where is it?'

'Lanzarote,' Janis said, handing him his tea. In a few of the pictures she was wearing a bikini – good body for her age, or any age come to that. He tried not to linger.

'Can I keep a couple of the close-ups?' he asked. Janis looked at him. 'Of Damon.' She nodded and he put the other photos back in their packet.

'We're really grateful,' someone said. Janis's mum? Brian's? Rebus couldn't tell.

'Does Helen live locally?'

'Practically round the corner.'

'I'd like to talk to her.'

'I'll give her a bell,' Brian Mee said, leaping to his feet.

'Damon had been drinking in some club?'

'Guisers,' Janis said, handing round cigarettes. 'It's in Kirkcaldy.'

'On the Prom?'

She shook her head, looking just the same as she had that night of the school dance ... shaking her head, telling him so far and no further. 'In the town. It used to be a department store.'

'It's really called Gaitanos,' Mr Playfair said. Rebus remembered him, too. He was an old man now.

'Where does Damon work?' Careful to stick to the present tense.

Brian Mee came back into the room. 'Same place I do. I managed to get him a job in packaging. He's been learning the ropes; it'll be management soon.'

Working-class nepotism; jobs handed down from father to son. Rebus was surprised it still existed.

'Helen'll be here in a minute,' Brian added.

'Are you not eating any cake, Inspector?' said Mrs Playfair.

Helen Cousins hadn't been able to add much to Rebus's picture of Damon, and hadn't been there the night he'd vanished. But she'd introduced him to someone who had, Andy Peters. Andy had been part of the group at Gaitanos. There'd been four of them. They'd been in the same year at school and still met up once or twice a week, sometimes to watch Raith Rovers if the weather was decent and the mood took them, other times for an evening session in a pub or club. It was only their third or fourth visit to Guisers.

Rebus thought of paying the club a visit, but knew he should talk to the local cops first, and decided that it could all wait until morning. He knew he was jumping through hoops. He didn't expect to find anything the locals had missed. At best, he could reassure the family that everything possible had been done.

Next morning he made a few phone calls from his office, trying to find someone who could be bothered to answer some casual questions from an Edinburgh colleague. He had one ally – Detective Sergeant Hendry at Dunfermline CID – but only reached him at the third attempt. He asked Hendry for a favour, then put the phone down and got back to his own work. But it was hard to concentrate. He kept thinking about Bowhill and about Janis Mee, née Playfair. Which led him – eventually – guiltily – to thoughts of Damon. Younger runaways tended to take the same route: by bus or train or hitching, and to London, Newcastle, Edinburgh or Glasgow. There were organizations who would keep an eye open for runaways, and even if they wouldn't always reveal their whereabouts to the anxious families, at least they could confirm that someone was alive and unharmed.

But a twenty-three-year-old, someone a bit cannier and with money to hand ... could be anywhere. No destination was too distant – he owned a passport, and it hadn't turned up. Rebus knew, too, that Damon had a current account at the local bank, complete with cashcard, and an interest-bearing account with a building society in Kirkcaldy. The bank might be worth trying. Rebus picked up the telephone again.

The manager at first insisted that he'd need something in writing, but relented when Rebus promised to fax him later. Rebus held while the manager went off to check, and had doodled half a village, complete with stream, parkland and school, by the time the man came back.

'The most recent withdrawal was from a cash machine in Kirkcaldy. One hundred pounds on the twenty-second.'

'What time?'

'I've no way of knowing.'

'No other withdrawals since then?'

'No.'

'How up-to-date is that information?'

'Very. Of course a cheque – especially if post-dated – would take longer to show up.'

'Could you keep tabs on that account, let me know if anyone starts using it again?'

'I could, but I'd need it in writing, and I might also need Head Office approval.'

'Well, see what you can do, Mr Brayne.'

'It's Bain,' the bank manager said coldly, putting down the phone.

DS Hendry didn't get back to him until late afternoon.

'Gaitanos,' Hendry said. 'I don't know the place personally. Locals call it Guisers. It's a pretty choice establishment. Two stabbings last year, one inside the club itself, the other in the back alley where the owner parks his Merc. Local residents are always girning about the noise when the place lets out.'

'What's the owner's name?'

'Charles Mackenzie, nicknamed "Charmer". He seems to be clean. A couple of uniforms talked to him about Damon Mee, but there was nothing to tell. Know how many missing persons there are every year? They're not exactly a white-hot priority. God knows there are times I've felt like doing a runner myself.'

'Haven't we all? Did the woolly suits talk to anyone else at the club?'

'Such as?'

'Bar staff, punters.'

'No. Someone did take a look at the security video for the night Damon was there, but they didn't see anything.'

'Where's the video now?'

'Back with its rightful owner.'

'Am I going to be stepping on toes if I ask to see it?'

'I think I can cover you. I know you said this was personal, John, but why the interest?'

'I'm not sure I can explain.' There were words – community, history, memory – but Rebus didn't think they'd be enough.

'They mustn't be working you hard enough over there.'

'Just the twenty-four hours every day.'

Three

Matty Paine could tell a few stories. He'd worked his way round the world as a croupier. Cruise liners he'd worked on, and in Nevada. He'd spent a couple of years in London, dealing out cards and spinning the wheel for some of the wealthiest in the land, faces you'd recognize from the TV and the papers. Moguls, royalty, stars – Matty had seen them all. But his best story – the one people sometimes disbelieved – was about the time he'd been recruited to work in a casino in Beirut. This was at the height of the civil war, bomb sites and rubble, smoke and charred buildings, refugees and regular bursts of small-arms fire. And amazingly, in the midst of it all (or, to be fair, on the edge of it all), a casino. Not exactly legal. Run from a hotel basement with torchlight when the generator failed and not much in the way of refreshments, but with no shortage of punters – cash bets, dollars only – and a management team of three who prowled the place like Dobermanns, since there was no surveillance and no other way to check that the games were being played honestly. One of them had stood next to Matty for a full forty minutes one session, making him sweat despite the air-conditioning. He'd reminded Matty of the gaffers casinos employed to check on apprentices. He knew the gaffers were there to protect *him* as much as the punters – there were professional gamblers out there who'd psych out a trainee, watch them for hours, whole nights and weeks, looking for the flaw that would give them an edge over the house. Like, when you were starting out, you didn't always vary the force with which you spun the wheel, or sent the ball rolling, and if they could suss it, they'd get a pretty good idea which quadrant the ball was going to stop in. Good croupiers were immune to this. A really good croupier – one of a very select, very highly thought-of group – could master the wheel and get the ball to land pretty well where *they* wanted.

Of course, this might be against the interests of the house, too. And in the end, that's why the checkers were out there, patrolling the tables. They were looking out for the house. In the end it all came down to the house.

And when things had got a wee bit too hot in London, Matty had come home, meaning Edinburgh, though really he was from Gullane – perhaps the only boy ever to be raised there and not show the slightest interest in golf. His father had played – his mother too, come to that. Maybe she still did; he didn't keep in touch. There had been an awkward moment at the casino when a neighbour from Gullane days, an old business friend of his father's, had turned up, a bit the worse for wear and in tow with three other middle-aged punters. The neighbour had glanced towards Matty from time to time, but had eventually shaken his head, unable to place the face.

'Does he know you?' one of the all-seeing gaffers had asked quietly, seeking out some scam against the house.

Matty had shaken his head. 'A neighbour from when I was growing up.' That was all; just a ghost from the past. He supposed his mother *was* still alive. He could probably find out by opening the phone book. But he wasn't that interested.

'Place your bets, please, ladies and gentlemen.'

Different houses had different styles. You either did your spiel in English or French. House rules changed, too. Matty's strengths were roulette and blackjack, but really he was happy in charge of any sort of game – most houses liked that he was flexible, it meant there was less chance of him trying some scam. It was the one-note wonders who tried small, stupid diddles. His latest employers seemed fairly laid back. They ran a clean casino which boasted only the very occasional high roller. Most of the punters were business people, well enough heeled but canny with it. You got husbands and wives coming in, proof of a relaxed atmosphere. There were younger punters too – a lot of those were Asians, mainly Chinese. The money they changed, according to the cashier, had a funny feel and smell to it.

'That's because they keep it in their underwear,' the day boss had told her.

The Asians ... whatever they were ... sometimes worked in local restaurants; you could smell the kitchen on their crumpled jackets and shirts. Fierce gamblers, no game was ever played quickly enough for their liking. They'd slap their chips down like they were in a playground betting game. And they talked a lot, almost never in English. The gaffers didn't like that, never could tell what they might be scheming. But their money was good, they seldom caused trouble, and they lost a percentage same as everyone else.

'Daft bastards,' the night manager said. 'Know what they do with a big win? Go bung it on the gee-gees. Where's the sense in that?'

Where indeed? No point giving your money to a bookmaker when the casino would happily take it instead.

It wasn't really on for croupiers to be friends with the clients, but sometimes it happened. And it couldn't very well not happen with Matty and Stevie Scoular, since they'd been in the same year at school. Not that they'd known one another well. Stevie had been the football genius, also more than fair at the hundred and two hundred metres, swimming and basketball. Matty, on the other hand, had skived off games whenever possible, forgetting to bring his kit or getting his mum to write him notes. He was good at a couple of subjects – maths and woodwork – but never sat beside Stevie in class. They even lived at opposite ends of the town.

At playtime and lunchtime, Matty ran a card game – three-card brag mostly, sometimes pontoon – playing for dinner money, pocket money, sweets and comics. A few of the cards were nicked at the corners, but the other players didn't seem to notice and Matty got a reputation as 'lucky'. He'd take bets on horse races too, sometimes passing the bets onto an older boy who wouldn't be turned away by the local bookmaker. Often though, Matty would simply pocket the money and if someone's horse happened to win, he'd say he couldn't get the bets on in time and hand back the stake.

He couldn't tell you exactly when it was that Stevie had started spending less breaktime dribbling past half a dozen despairing pairs of legs and more hanging around the edges of the card school. Thing about three-card brag, it doesn't take long to pick it up and even a moron can have a stab at playing. Soon enough, Stevie was losing his dinner money with the rest of them, and Matty's pockets were about bursting with loose change. Eventually, Stevie had seemed to see sense, drifted away from the game and back to keepie-up and dribbling. But he'd been hooked, no doubt about it. Maybe only for a few weeks, but a lot of those lunchtimes had been spent cadging sweets and apple cores, the better to stave off hunger.

Even then, Matty had thought he'd be seeing Stevie again. It had just taken the best part of a decade, that was all.

When Stevie Scoular walked into the casino, people looked his way. It was the done thing. He was a sharp dresser, young, usually accompanied by women who looked like models. When Stevie had first walked into the Morvena, Matty's heart had sunk. They hadn't seen one another since school and here Stevie was, local boy made good, a hero, picture in the papers and plenty of money in the bank. Here was a schoolboy dream made flesh. And what was Matty? He had stories he could tell but that was about it. So he'd been hoping Stevie wouldn't grace his table, or if he did that he wouldn't recognize him. But Stevie had seen him, seemed to know him straight off and come bouncing up.

'Matty!'

'Hello there, Stevie.'

It was flattering really. Stevie hadn't become big-headed or anything. He took the whole thing – the way his life had gone – as a bit of a joke really. He'd made Matty promise to meet him for a drink when his shift was over. All through their conversation, Matty had been aware of gaffers hovering and when Stevie wandered off to another table one of them muttered in Matty's ear and another croupier took over from him.

He hadn't been in the plush back office that often, just for the initial interview and to discuss a couple of big losses on his table. The casino's owner, Mr Mandelson, was watching a football match on Sky Sports. He was well built, mid-forties, his face pockmarked from childhood acne. His hair was black, slicked back from the forehead, long at the collar. He always seemed to know what he was about.

'How's the table tonight?' he asked.

'Look, Mr Mandelson, I know we're not supposed to be too friendly with the punters, but Stevie and me were at school together. Haven't clapped eyes on one another since – not till tonight.'

'Easy, Matty, easy.' Mandelson motioned for him to sit down. 'Something to drink?' A smile. 'No alcohol on shift, mind.'

'Ehh . . . a Coke maybe.'

'Help yourself.'

There was a fridge in the far corner, stocked with white wine, champagne and soft drinks. A couple of the female croupiers said Mandelson had tried it on with them, plying them with booze. But he didn't seem upset by a refusal: they still had their jobs. There were seven female croupiers all told, and only two had spoken to Matty about it. It made him wonder about the other five.

He took a Coke and sat down again.

'So, you and Stevie Scoular, eh?'

'I haven't seen him in here before.'

'I think he only recently found out about the place. He's been in a few times, dropped some hefty bets.' Mandelson was staring at him. 'You and Stevie, eh?'

'Look, if you're worried, just take me off whatever table he's playing.'

'Nothing like that, Matty.' Mandelson's face broke into a grin. 'It's nice to have a friend, eh? Nice to meet up again after all these years. Don't you worry about anything. Stevie's the King of Edinburgh. As long as he keeps scoring goals, we're all his subjects.' He paused. 'Nice to know someone who knows the King, almost makes me feel like royalty myself. On you go now, Matty.'

Matty got up, leaving the Coke unopened.

'And don't you go upsetting that young man. We don't want to put him off his game, do we?'

Four

It had taken a couple of days to get the tape from Gaitanos. At first, they thought they'd wiped it, and then they'd sent the wrong day's recording. But at last Rebus had the right tape and had watched it at home half a dozen times before deciding he could use someone who knew what he was doing ... and a video machine that would freeze-frame without the screen looking like a technical problem.

Now he'd seen all there was to see. He'd watched a young man cease to exist. Of course, Hendry was right, a lot of people disappeared every year. Sometimes they turned up again – dead or alive – and sometimes they didn't. What did it have to do with Rebus, beyond the promise to a family that he'd make sure the Fife police hadn't missed something? Maybe the pull wasn't Damon Mee, but Bowhill itself; and maybe even then, the Bowhill of his past rather than the town as it stood today.

He was working the Damon Mee case in his free time, which, since he was on day shift at St Leonard's, meant the evenings. He'd checked again with the bank – no money had been withdrawn from any machines since the twenty-second – and with Damon's building society. No money had been withdrawn from that account either. Even this wasn't unknown in the case of a runaway; sometimes they wanted to shed their whole history, which meant ditching their identity and everything that went with it. Rebus had passed a description of Matty to hostels and drop-in centres in Edinburgh, and faxed the same description to similar centres in Glasgow, Newcastle, Aberdeen and London. He'd also faxed details to the National Missing Persons Bureau in London. He checked with a colleague who knew about 'MisPers' that he'd done about all he could.

'Not far off it,' she confirmed. 'It's like looking for a needle in a haystack without knowing which field to start with.'

'How big a problem is it?'

She puffed out her cheeks. 'Last figures I saw were for the whole of Britain. I think there are around 25,000 a year. Those are the *reported* MisPers. You can add a few thousand for the ones nobody notices. There's a nice distinction actually: if nobody knows you're missing, are you really missing?'

Afterwards, Rebus telephoned Janis Mee and told her she might think about running up some flyers and putting them up in positions of prominence in nearby towns, maybe even handing them out to Saturday shoppers or evening drinkers in Kirkcaldy. A photo of Damon, a brief physical description, and what he was wearing the night he left. She said she'd already thought of doing so, but that it made his disappearance seem so final. Then she broke down and cried and John Rebus, thirty-odd miles away, asked if she wanted him to 'drop by'.

'I'll be all right,' she said.

'Sure?'

'Well...'

Rebus reasoned that he was going to go to Fife anyway. He had to drop the tape back to Gaitanos, and wanted to see the club when it was lively. He'd take the photos of Damon with him and show them around. He'd ask about the candyfloss blonde. The technician who had worked with the videotape had transferred a still to his computer and managed to boost the quality. Rebus had some hard copies in his pocket. Maybe other people who'd been queuing at the bar would remember something.

Maybe.

His first stop, however, was the cemetery. He didn't have any flowers to put on his parents' grave, but he crouched beside it, fingers touching the grass. The inscription was simple, just names and dates really, and underneath, 'Not Dead, But at Rest in the Arms of the Lord'. He wasn't sure whose idea that had been, not his certainly. The headstone's carved lettering was inlaid with gold, but it had already faded from his mother's name. He touched the surface of the marble, expecting it to be cold, but finding a residual warmth there. A blackbird nearby was trying to worry food from the ground. Rebus wished it luck.

By the time he reached Janis's, Brian was home from work. Rebus told them what he'd done so far, after which Brian nodded, apologized, and said he had a Burns Club meeting. The two men shook hands. When the door closed, Janis and Rebus exchanged a look and then a smile.

'I see that bruise finally faded,' she said.

Rebus rubbed his right cheek. 'It was a hell of a punch.'

'Funny how strong you can get when you're angry.'

'Sorry.'

She laughed. 'Bit late to apologize.'

'It was just...'

'It was everything,' she said. 'Summer holidays coming up, all of us leaving school, you going off to join the army. The last school dance before all of that. That's what it was.' She paused. 'Do you know what happened to Mitch?' She watched Rebus shake his head. 'Last I heard,' she said, 'he was living somewhere down south. The two of you used to be so close.'

'Yes.'

She laughed again. 'Johnny, it was a long time ago, don't look so solemn.' She paused. 'I've sometimes wondered ... ach, not for years, but just now and then I used to wonder what would have happened...'

'If you hadn't punched me?'

She nodded. 'If we'd stayed together. Well, you can't turn the clock back, eh?'

'Would the world be any better if we could?'

She stared at the window, not really seeing it. 'Damon would still be here,' she said quietly. A tear escaped her eye, and she fussed for a handkerchief in her pocket. Rebus got up and made towards her. Then the front door opened, and he retreated.

'My mum.' Janis smiled. 'She usually pops in around this time. It's like a railway station around here, hard to find any privacy.'

Then Mrs Playfair walked into the living room.

'Hello, Inspector, thought that was your car. Is there any news?'

'I'm afraid not,' Rebus said. Janis got to her feet and hugged her mother, the crying starting afresh.

'There there, pet,' Mrs Playfair said quietly. 'There there.'

Rebus walked past the two of them without saying a word.

It was still early when he reached Gaitanos. He had a word with one of the bouncers, who was keeping warm in the lobby until things started getting busy, and the man lumbered off to fetch Charles Mackenzie, *aka* Charmer. It seemed strange to Rebus: here he was, standing in the very foyer he'd stared at for so long on the video monitor. The camera was high up in one corner with nothing to show whether it was working. Rebus gave it a wave anyway. If he disappeared tonight, it could be his farewell to the world.

'Inspector Rebus.' They'd spoken on the phone. The man who came forward to shake Rebus's hand stood about five feet four and was as thin as a cocktail glass. Rebus placed him in his mid-fifties. He wore a powder-blue suit and an open-necked white shirt with suntan and gold jewellery beneath. His hair was silver and thinning, but as well cut as the suit. 'Come through to the office.'

Rebus followed Mackenzie down a carpeted corridor to a gloss-black door with a sign on it saying 'Private'. There was no door handle. Mackenzie unlocked the door and motioned for Rebus to go in.

'After you, sir,' Rebus said. You never knew what could be waiting behind a locked door.

What greeted Rebus this time was an office which seemed to double as a broom-cupboard. Mops and a vacuum cleaner rested against one wall. A bank of screens spread across three filing cabinets showed what was happening inside and outside the club. Unlike the video Rebus had watched, these screens each showed a certain location.

'Are these recording?' Rebus asked. Mackenzie shook his head.

'We've got a roaming monitor, and that's the only recording we get. But this way, if we spot trouble anywhere, we can watch it unfold.'

'Like that knifing in the alley?'

'Messed up my Mercedes.'

'So I heard. Is that when you called the police? When your car stopped being a bystander?'

Mackenzie laughed and wagged a finger, but didn't answer. Rebus couldn't see where he'd earned his nickname. The guy had all the charm of sandpaper.

'I brought back your video.' Rebus placed it on the desk.

'All right to record over it now?'

'I suppose so.' Rebus handed over the computer-enhanced photograph. 'The missing person is slightly right of centre, second row.'

'Is that his doll?'

'Do you know her?'

'Wish I did.'

'You haven't seen her before.'

'She doesn't look the sort I'd forget.'

Rebus took back the picture. 'Mind if I show this around?'

'The place is practically empty.'

'I thought I might stick around.'

Mackenzie frowned and studied the backs of his hands. 'Well, you know, it's not that I don't want to help or anything...'

'But?'

'Well, it's hardly conducive to a party atmosphere, is it? That's our slogan – "The best party of your life, every night!" – and I don't think a police officer mooching around asking questions is going to add to the ambience.'

'I quite understand, Mr Mackenzie. I was being thoughtless.' Mackenzie lifted his hands, palms towards Rebus: no problem, the hands were saying.

'And you're quite right,' Rebus continued. 'In fact, I'd be a lot quicker if I had some assistance – say, a dozen uniforms. That way, I wouldn't be "mooching around" for nearly so long. In fact, let's make it a couple of dozen. We'll be in and out, quick as a virgin's first poke. Mind if I use your phone?'

'Whoah, wait a minute. Look, all I was saying was ... Look, how much do you want?'

'Sorry, sir?'

Mackenzie reached into a desk drawer, lifted out a brick of twenties, pulled about five notes free. 'Will this do it?'

Rebus sat back. 'Am I to understand you're trying to offer me a cash incentive to leave the premises?'

'Whatever. Just slope off, eh?'

Rebus stood up. 'To me, Mr Mackenzie, that's an open invitation to stay.'

So he stayed.

The looks he got from staff made him feel like a football fan trapped on the opposition's turf. The way they all shook their heads as soon as he held up the photo, he knew word had gone around. He had a little more luck with the punters. A couple of lads had seen the woman before.

'Last week, was it?' one asked the other. 'Maybe the week before.'

'Not long ago anyway,' the other agreed. 'Cracker, isn't she?'

'Has she been in since?'

'Haven't seen her. Just that one night. Didn't quite get the nerve up to ask for a dance.'

'Was she with anyone?'

'No idea.'

They didn't recognize Damon Mee though. They said they never paid much attention to blokes.

'We're not that way inclined, sweetie.'

The place was still only half full, but the bass was loud enough to make Rebus feel queasy. He managed to order an orange juice at the bar and just sat there, looking at the photo. The woman interested him. The way her head was angled, the way her mouth was open, she could have been saying something to Damon. A minute later, he was gone. Had she said she'd meet him somewhere? Had something happened at that meeting? He'd shown the photo to Damon's mates from that night. They remembered seeing her, but swore Damon hadn't introduced himself.

'She seemed sort of cold,' one of them had said. 'You know, like she wanted to be left alone.'

Rebus had studied the video again, watched her progress towards the bar, showing no apparent interest in Damon's leaving. But then she'd turned and started pushing her way back through the throng, no drink to show for her long wait.

At midnight exactly, she'd left the nightclub. The final shot was of her turning left along the pavement, watched by a few people who were waiting to get in. And now Charles Mackenzie wanted to give Rebus money.

At three quid for an orange juice, maybe he should have taken it.

If the place had been heaving, maybe he wouldn't have noticed them.

He was finishing his second drink and trying not to feel like a leper in a children's ward when he recognized one of the doormen. There was another man with him, tall and fat and pale. His idea of clubbing was probably the connection of baseball bat to skull. The bouncer was pointing Rebus out to him. Here we go, Rebus thought. They've brought in the professionals. The fat man said something to the bouncer, and they both retreated to the foyer, leaving Rebus with an empty glass and only one good reason to order another drink.

Get it over with, he thought, sliding from his bar stool and walking around the dance floor. There was always the fire exit, but it led on to the alley and, if they were waiting for him there, the only witness would be Mackenzie's Mercedes. He wanted things kept as public as possible. The street outside would be busy, no shortage of onlookers and possible good Samaritans. Or at the very least, someone to call for an ambulance.

He paused in the foyer and saw that the bouncer was back at his post on the front door. No sign of the fat man. Then he glanced along the corridor towards Mackenzie's office, and saw the fat man planted outside the door. He had his arms folded in front of him and wasn't going anywhere.

Rebus walked outside. The air had seldom tasted so good. He tried to calm himself with a few deep breaths. There was a car parked at the kerbside, a gold-coloured Rolls-Royce, with nobody in the driver's seat. Rebus wasn't the only one admiring the car, but he was probably alone in memorizing its number plate.

He moved his own car to where he could see the Roller, then sat tight. Half an hour later, the fat man emerged, looking to left and right. He walked to the car, unlocked it and held open the back door. Only now did another figure emerge from the club. Rebus caught a swishing full-length black coat, sleek hair and chiselled face. The man slipped into the car, and the fat man closed the door and squeezed in behind the steering wheel.

Like them or not, you had to admire Rollers. They carried tonnage.

Five

Back in Edinburgh he parked his car and sat in it, smoking his eleventh cigarette of the day. He sometimes played this game with himself – I'll have one more tonight, and deduct one from tomorrow's allowance. Or he would argue that any cigarette after midnight came from the next day's stash. He'd lost count along the way, but reckoned by now he should be going whole days without a ciggie to balance the books. Well, when it came down to it, ten cigarettes a day or twelve, thirteen, fourteen – what difference did it make?

The street he was parked on was quiet. Residential for the most part with big houses. There was a basement bar on the corner, but it did mostly lunchtime business from the offices on neighbouring streets. By ten, the place was usually locked up. Taxis rippled past him and the occasional drunk, hands in pockets, would weave slowly homewards. A few of the taxis stopped just in front of him and disgorged their fares, who would then climb half a dozen steps and push open the door to the Morvena Casino. Rebus had never been inside the place. He placed the occasional bet on the horses, but that was about it. Gave up doing the football pools. He bought a National Lottery ticket when opportunity arose, but often didn't get round to checking the numbers. He had half a dozen tickets lying around, any one of which could be his fortune. He quite liked the notion that he might have won a million and not know it; preferred it, in fact, to the idea of actually having the million in his bank account. What would he do with a million pounds? Same as he'd do with fifty thou – self-destruct.

Only faster.

Janis had asked him about Mitch – Roy Mitchell, Rebus's best friend at school. The more time Rebus had spent with her, the less he'd seen of Mitch. They'd been going to join the army together, hoping they might get the same regiment. Until Mitch lost his eye. That had been the end of that. The army hadn't wanted him any more. Rebus had headed off, sent Mitch a couple of letters, but by the time his first leave came, Mitch had already left Bowhill. Rebus had stopped writing after that . . .

When the Morvena's door opened next, it was so eight or nine young people could leave. The shift changeover. Three of them turned one way, the rest another. Rebus watched the group of three. At the first set of lights, two kept going and one crossed the road and took a left. Rebus started his engine and followed. When the lights turned green, he signalled left and sounded his horn, then pulled the car over and wound down his window.

'Mr Rebus,' the young man said.

'Hello, Matty. Let's go for a drive.'

Officers from other cities, people Rebus met from time to time, would remark on how cushy he had it in Edinburgh. Such a beautiful place, and prosperous. So little crime. They thought to be dangerous a city had to look dangerous. London, Manchester, Liverpool – these places were dangerous in their eyes. Not Edinburgh, not this sleepy walking-tour with its monuments and museums. Tourism aside, the lifeblood of the city was its commerce, and Edinburgh's commerce – banking, insurance and the like – was discreet. The city hid its secrets well, and its vices too. Potentially troublesome elements had been moved to the sprawling council estates which ringed the capital, and any crimes committed behind the thick stone walls of the city centre's tenements and houses were often muffled by those same walls. Which was why every good detective needed his contacts.

Rebus took them on a circuit – Canonmills to Ferry Road, back up to Comely Bank and through Stockbridge into the New Town again. And they talked.

'I know we had a sort of gentleman's agreement, Matty,' Rebus said.

'But I'm about to find out you're no gentleman?'

Rebus smiled. 'You're ahead of me.'

'I wondered how long it would take.' Matty paused, stared through the windscreen. 'You know I'll say no.'

'Will you?'

'I said at the start, no ratting on anyone I work with or work for. Just the punters.'

'Not even many of them. It's not like I've been milking you, Matty. I'll bet you've dozens of stories you haven't told me.'

'I work tables, Mr Rebus. People don't place a bet and then start yacking about some job they've pulled or some scam they're running.'

'No, but they meet friends. They have a drink, get mellow. It's a relaxing place, so I've heard. And maybe then they talk.'

'I've not held anything back.'

'Matty, Matty.' Rebus shook his head. 'It's funny, I was just thinking tonight about that night we met. Do you remember?'

How could he forget? A couple of drinks after work, a car borrowed from a friend who was away on holiday. Matty hadn't been back long. Driving through the town was great, especially with a buzz on. Streets glistening after the rain. Late night, mostly taxis for company. He just drove and drove and, as the streets grew quieter, he pushed the accelerator a bit further, caught a string of green lights, then saw one turning red. He didn't know how good the tyres were, imagined braking hard and skidding in the wet. Fuck it, he put his foot down.

Just missed the cyclist. The guy was coming through on green and had to twist his front wheel hard to avoid contact, then teetered and fell onto the road. Matty's foot eased off the accelerator, thought about the brake, then went back on the accelerator again.

That's when he saw the cop car. And thought: I can't afford this.

They'd breathalyzed him and taken him to St Leonard's, where he'd sat around and let the machinery chew him up. Would it come to a trial? Would there be a report in the papers? How could he keep his name from getting around? He'd worked himself up into a right state by the time Detective Inspector John Rebus had sat down across from him.

'I can't afford this,' Matty had blurted out.

'Sorry?'

He'd swallowed and tried to find a story. 'I work in a casino. Any black mark against me, they'll boot me out. Look, if it's a question of compensation or anything ... like, I'll buy him a new bike.'

Rebus had picked up a sheet of paper. 'Drunk driving ... in a borrowed car you weren't insured to drive ... running a red light ... leaving the scene of an accident ...' Rebus had shaken his head, read the sheet through one more time and then put it down, and looked up at Matty. 'What casino did you say you work for?'

Later, he'd given Matty two business cards, both with his phone number. 'The first one's for you to tear up in disgust,' he'd said. 'The other one's to keep. Have we got a deal?'

'Look, Mr Rebus,' Matty said now, as the car stopped for lights on Raeburn Place, 'I'm doing the best I can.'

'I want to know what's happening behind the scenes at the Morvena.'

'I wouldn't know.'

'Anything at all, it doesn't matter how small it seems. Any stories, gossip, anything overheard. Ever seen the owner entertain people in his office? Maybe open the place for a private party? Names, faces, anything at all. Put your mind to it, Matty. Just put your mind to it.'

'They'd skin me alive.'

'Who's they?'

Matty swallowed. 'Mr Mandelson.'

'He's the owner, right?'

'Right.'

'On paper at least. What I need to know is who might be pulling his strings.'

'I can't see anyone pulling his strings.'

'You'd be surprised. Hard bastard, is he?'

'I'd say so.'

'Given you grief?' Matty shook his head. 'Do you see much of him?'

'Not much,' Matty said. Not, he might have added, until recently at any rate.

Rebus dropped him at the foot of Broughton Street, headed back up to Leith Walk and along York Place onto Queen Street. He passed the casino again and slowed, a frown on his face. At the next set of lights, he did a U-turn so he could be sure. Yes, it was the Roller from Gaitanos, no doubt about it.

Parked outside the Morvena.

Six

'Mind if I join you?'

Rebus was eating breakfast in the canteen and wishing there was more caffeine in the coffee, or more coffee in the coffee come to that. He nodded to the empty chair and Siobhan sat down.

'Heavy night?' she said.

'Believe it or not, I was on orange juice.'

She bit into her muffin, washing it down with milk. 'Harry tells me you had him working a tape.'

'Harry?'

'Our video wizard. He said it was a missing person. News to me.'

'It's not official. The son of an old schoolfriend of mine.'

'Standing at a bar one minute and gone the next?' Rebus looked at her and she smiled. 'Harry's a great one for gossip.'

'I'm working on it in my own time.'

'Need any help?'

'Handy with a crystal ball, are you?' But Rebus dug into his pocket and brought out the still from the video. 'That's Damon there,' he said, pointing.

'Who's that with him?'

'I wish I knew. She's not with him. I don't know who she is.'

'You've asked around?'

'I was at the club last night. A few punters remembered her.'

'Male punters?' She waited till Rebus nodded. 'You were asking the wrong sex. Any man would have given her the once-over, but only superficially. A woman, on the other hand, would have seen her as competition. Have you never noticed women in nightclubs? They've got eyes like lasers. Plus, what if she visited the loo?'

Rebus was interested now. 'What if she did?'

'*That's* where women talk. Maybe someone spoke to her, maybe she said something back. Ears would have been listening.' Siobhan stared at the photo. 'Funny, it's almost like she's got an aura.'

'How do you mean?'

'Like she's shining.'

'Interior light.'

'Exactly.'

'No, that's what your friend Harry said. It's the interior lighting that gives that effect.'

'Maybe he didn't know what he was saying.'

'I'm not sure I know what *you're* saying.'

'Some religions believe in spirit guides. They're supposed to lead you to the next world.'

'You mean this one's not the end?'

She smiled. 'Depends on your religion.'

'Well, it's plenty enough for me.' He looked at the photo again.

'I was sort of joking, you know, about her being a spirit guide.'

'I know.'

He met with Helen Cousins that night. They spoke over a drink in the Auld Hoose. Rebus hadn't been in the place in a quarter of a century, and there'd been changes. They'd installed a pool table.

'You weren't invited along that night?' Rebus asked her.

She shook her head. She was twenty, three years younger than Damon. The fingers of her right hand played with her engagement ring, rolling it, sliding it off over the knuckle and then back down again. She had short, lifeless brown hair, dark, tired eyes, and acne around her mouth.

'I was out with the girls. See, that was how we played it. One night a week the boys would go off on their own, and we'd go somewhere else. Then another night we'd all get together.'

'Do you know anyone who was at Gaitanos that night? Apart from Damon and his pals?'

She chewed her bottom lip while considering. The ring came off her finger and bounced once before hitting the floor. She stooped to pick it up.

'It's always doing that.'

'You better watch it, you're going to lose it.'

She pushed the ring back on. 'Yes,' she said, 'Corinne and Jacky were there.'

'Corinne and Jacky?' She nodded. 'Where can I find them?'

A phone call brought them to the Auld Hoose. Rebus got in the round: Bacardi and Coke for Corinne, Bacardi and blackcurrant for Jacky, a second vodka and orange for Helen and another bottle of no-alcohol lager for himself. He eyed the optics behind the bar. His mean little drink was costing more than a whisky. Something was telling him to indulge in a Teacher's. Maybe it's my spirit guide, he thought, dismissing the idea.

Corinne had long black hair crimped with curling tongs. Her pal Jacky was tiny, with dyed platinum hair. When he got back to the table, they were in a huddle, exchanging gossip. Rebus took out the photograph again.

'Look,' Corinne said, 'there's Damon.' So they all had a good look. Then Rebus touched his finger to the strapless aura.

'Remember her?'

Helen prickled visibly. 'Who is she?'

'Yeah, she was there,' Jacky said.

'Was she with anyone?'

'Didn't see her up dancing.'

'Isn't that why people go to clubs?'

'Well, it's one reason.' All three broke into a giggle.

'You didn't speak to her?'

'No.'

'Not even in the toilets?'

'I saw her in there,' Corinne said. 'She was doing her eyes.'

'Did she say anything?'

'She seemed sort of ... stuck-up.'

'Snobby,' Jacky agreed.

Rebus tried to think of another question and couldn't. They ignored him for a while as they exchanged news. It was like they hadn't seen each other in a year. At one point, Helen got up to use the toilet. Rebus expected the other two to accompany her, but only Corinne did so. He sat with Jacky for a moment, then, for want of anything else to say, asked her what she thought of Damon. He meant about Damon disappearing, but she didn't take it that way.

'Ach, he's all right.'

'Just all right?'

'Well, you know, Damon's heart's in the right place, but he's a bit thick. A bit slow, I mean.'

'Really?' The impression Rebus had received from Damon's family had been of a genius in waiting. He suddenly realized just how superficial his own portrait of Damon was. Siobhan's words should have been a warning – so far he'd heard only one side of Damon. 'Helen likes him though?'

'I suppose so.'

'They're engaged.'

'It happens, doesn't it? I've got friends who got engaged just so they could throw a party.' She looked around the bar, then leant towards him. 'They used to have some mega arguments.'

'What about?'

'Jealousy, I suppose. She'd see him notice someone, or he'd say she'd been letting some guy chat her up. Just the usual.' She turned the photo around so it faced her. 'She looks like a dream, doesn't she? I remember she was dressed to kill. Made the rest of us spit.'

'But you'd never seen her before?'

Jacky shook her head. No, no one seemed to have seen her before, nobody knew who she was. Unlikely then that she was local.

'Were there any buses in that night?'

'That doesn't happen at Gaitanos,' she told him. 'It's not "in" enough any more. There's a new place in Dunfermline. That gets the busloads.' Jacky tapped the photo. 'You think she's gone off with Damon?'

Rebus looked at her and saw behind the eyeliner to a sharp intelligence. 'It's possible,' he said quietly.

'I don't think so,' she said. 'She wouldn't be interested, and he wouldn't have had the guts.'

On his way home, Rebus dropped into St Leonard's. The amount he was paying in bridge tolls, he was thinking about a season ticket. There was a fax on his desk. He'd been promised it in the afternoon, but there'd been a delay. It identified the owner of the Rolls-Royce as a Mr Richard Mandelson, with an address in Juniper Green. Mr Mandelson had no criminal record outstanding, whether for motoring offences or anything else. Rebus tried to imagine some poor parking warden trying to give the Roller a ticket with the fat man behind the wheel. There were a few more facts about Mr Mandelson, including last known occupation.

Casino manager.

Seven

Matty and Stevie Scoular saw one another socially now. Stevie would sometimes phone and invite Matty to some party or dinner, or just for a drink. At the same time as Matty was flattered, he did wonder what Stevie's angle was, had even come out and asked him.

'I mean,' he'd said, 'I'm just a toe-rag from the school playground, and you ... well, you're SuperStevie, you're the king.'

'Aye, if you believe the papers.' Stevie had finished his drink – Perrier, he had a game the next day. 'I don't know, Matty, maybe it's that I miss all that.'

'All what?'

'Schooldays. It was a laugh back then, wasn't it?'

Matty had frowned, not really remembering. 'But the life you've got now, Stevie, man. People would kill for it.'

And Stevie had nodded, looking suddenly sad.

Another time, a couple of kids had asked Stevie for his autograph, then had turned and asked Matty for his, thinking that whoever he was, he had to be somebody. Stevie had laughed at that, said something about it being a lesson in humility. Again, Matty didn't get it. There were times when Stevie seemed to be on a different planet. Maybe it was understandable, the pressure he was under. Stevie seemed to remember a lot more about school than Matty did: teachers' names, the lot. They talked about Gullane, too, what a boring place to grow up. Sometimes they didn't talk much at all. Just took out a couple of dolls: Stevie would always bring one along for Matty. She wouldn't be quite as gorgeous as Stevie's, but that was all right. Matty could understand that. He was soaking it all up, enjoying it while it lasted. He had half an idea that Stevie and him would be best friends for life, and another that Stevie would dump him soon and find some other distraction. He thought Stevie needed him right now much more than *he* needed Stevie. So he soaked up what he could, started filing the stories away for future use, tweaking them here and there...

Tonight they took in a couple of bars, a bit of a drive in Stevie's Beamer: he preferred BMWs to Porsches, more space for passengers. They ended up at a club, but didn't stay long. Stevie had a game the next day. He was always very conscientious that way: Perrier and early nights. Stevie dropped Matty off outside his flat, sounding the horn as he roared away. Matty hadn't spotted the other car, but he heard a door opening, looked across the road and recognized Malibu straight off. Malibu was Mr Mandelson's driver. He'd eased himself out of the Roller and was holding open the back door while looking over to Matty.

So Matty crossed the street. As he did so, he walked into Malibu's shadow, cast by the sodium street lamp. At that moment, though he didn't know what was about to happen, he realized he was lost.

'Get in, Matty.'

The voice, of course, was Mandelson's. Matty got into the car and Malibu closed the door after him, then kept guard outside. They weren't going anywhere.

'Ever been in a Roller before, Matty?'

'I don't think so.'

'You'd remember if you had. I could have had one years back, but only by buying secondhand. I wanted to wait until I had the cash for a nice new one. That leather smell – you don't get it with any other car.' Mandelson lit a cigar. The windows were closed and the car started filling with sour smoke. 'Know how I came to afford a brand new Roller, Matty?'

'Hard work?' Matty's mouth was dry. Cars, he thought: Rebus's, Stevie's, and now this one. Plus, of course, the one he'd borrowed that night, the one that had brought him to this.

'Don't be stupid. My dad worked thirty years in a shop, six days a week and he still couldn't have made the down-payment. Faith, Matty, that's the key. You have to believe in yourself, and sometimes you have to trust other people – strangers some of them, or people you don't like, people it's hard to trust. That's the gamble life's making with you, and if you place your bet, sometimes you get lucky. Except it's not luck – not entirely. See, there are odds, like in every game, and that's where judgment comes in. I like to think I'm a good judge of character.'

Only now did Mandelson turn to look at him. There seemed to Matty to be nothing behind the eyes, nothing at all.

'Yes, sir,' he said, for want of anything better.

'That was Stevie dropped you off, eh?' Matty nodded. 'Now, your man Stevie, he's got something else, something we haven't discussed yet. He's got a gift. He's had to work, of course, but the thing was there to begin with. Don't ask me where it came from or why it should have been given to him in particular – that's one for the philosophers, and I don't claim to be a philosopher. What I am is a businessman ... and a gambler. Only I don't bet on nags or dogs or a turn of the cards, I bet on people. I'm betting on you, Matty.'

'Me?'

Mandelson nodded, barely visible inside the cloud of smoke. 'I want you to talk to Stevie on my behalf. I want you to get him to do me a favour.'

Matty rubbed his forehead with his fingers. He knew what was coming but didn't want to hear it.

'I saw a recent interview,' Mandelson went on, 'where he told the reporter he always gave a hundred and ten per cent. All I want is to knock maybe twenty per cent off for next Saturday's game. You know what I'm saying?'

Next Saturday ... An away tie at Kirkcaldy. Stevie expected to run rings around the Raith Rovers defence.

'He won't do it,' Matty said. 'Come to that, neither will I.'

'No?' Mandelson laughed. A hand landed on Matty's thigh. 'You fucked up in

London, son. They knew you'd end up taking a croupier's job somewhere else, it's the only thing you know how to do. So they phoned around, and eventually they phoned *me*. I told them I'd never heard of you. That can change, Matty. Want me to talk to them again?'

'I'd tell them you lied to them the first time.'

Mandelson shrugged. 'I can live with that. But what do you think they'll do to *you*, Matty? They were pretty angry about whatever scheme it was you pulled. I'd say they were furious.'

Matty felt like he was going to heave. He was sweating, his lungs toxic. 'He won't do it,' he said again.

'Be persuasive, Matty. You're his friend. Remind him that his tab's up to three and a half. All he has to do is ease off for one game, and the tab's history. And Matty, I'll know if you've talked to him or not, so no games, eh? Or you might find yourself with no place left to hide.'

Eight

Rebus searched his flat, but came up with only half a dozen snapshots: two of his ex-wife Rhona, posing with Samantha, their daughter, back when Sammy was seven or eight; two further shots of Sammy in her teens; one showing his father as a young man, kissing the woman who would become Rebus's mother; and a final photograph, a family grouping, showing uncles, aunts and cousins whose names Rebus didn't know. There were other photographs, of course – at least, there had been – but not here, not in the flat. He guessed Rhona still kept some, maybe his brother Michael had the others. But they could be anywhere. Rebus hadn't thought of himself as the kind to spend long nights with the family album, using it as a crutch to memory, always with the fear that remembrance would yield to sentiment.

If I died tonight, he thought, what would I bequeath to the world? Looking around, the answer was: nothing. The thought scared him, and worst of all it made him want a drink, and not just one drink but a dozen.

Instead of which, he drove north back into Fife. It had been overcast all day, and the evening was warm. He didn't know what he was doing, knew he had precious little to say to either of Damon's parents, and yet that's where he ended up. He'd had the destination in mind all along.

Brian Mee answered the door, wearing a smart suit and just finishing knotting his tie.

'Sorry, Brian,' Rebus said. 'Are you off out?'

'In ten minutes. Come in anyway. Is it Damon?'

Rebus shook his head and saw the tension in Brian's face turn to relief. Yes, a visit in person wouldn't be good news, would it? Good news had to be given immediately by telephone, not by a knock at the door. Rebus should have realized; he'd been the bearer of bad news often enough in his time.

'Sorry, Brian,' he repeated. They were in the hallway. Janis's voice came from above, asking who it was.

'It's Johnny,' her husband called back. Then to Rebus, 'It's all right to call you that?'

'Of course. It's my name, isn't it?' He could have added: again, after all this time. He looked at Brian, remembering the way they'd sometimes mistreated him at school: not that 'Barney' had seemed to mind, but who could tell for sure? And then that night of the last school dance ... Brian had been there for Mitch. Brian had been there; Rebus had not. He'd been too busy losing Janis, and losing consciousness.

She was coming downstairs now. 'I'll be back in a sec,' Brian said, heading up past her.

'You look terrific,' Rebus told her. The blue dress was well chosen, her make-up highlighting all the right features of her busy face. She managed a smile.

'No news?'

'Sorry,' he said again. 'Just thought I'd see how you are.'

'Oh, we're pining away.' Another smile, tinged by shame this time. 'It's a dinner-dance, we bought the tickets months back. It's for the Jolly Beggars.'

'Nobody expects you to sit at home every night, Janis.'

'But all the same ...' Her cheeks grew flushed and her eyes sought his. 'We're not going to find him, are we?'

'Not easily. Our best bet's that he'll get in touch.'

'If he can,' she said quietly.

'Come on, Janis.' He put his hands on her shoulders, like they were strangers and about to dance. 'You might hear from him tomorrow, or it might take months.'

'And meantime life goes on, eh?'

'Something like that.'

She smiled again, blinking back tears. 'Why don't you come with us, John?'

Rebus dropped his hands from her shoulders. 'I haven't danced in years.'

'So you'd be rusty.'

'Thanks, Janis, but not tonight.'

'Know something? I bet they play the same records we used to dance to at school.'

It was his turn to smile. Brian was coming back downstairs, patting his hair into place.

'You'd be welcome to join us, Johnny,' he said.

'I've another appointment, Brian. Maybe next time, eh?'

'Let's make that a promise.'

They went out to their cars together. Janis pecked him on the cheek, Brian shook his hand. He watched them drive off then headed to the cemetery.

It was dark, and the gates were locked, so Rebus sat in his car and smoked a cigarette. He thought about his parents and the rest of his family and remembered stories about Bowhill, stories which seemed inextricable from family history: mining tragedies; a girl found drowned in the River Ore; a holiday car crash which had erased an entire family. Then there was Johnny Thomson, Celtic goalkeeper, injured during an 'Old Firm' match. He was in his early twenties when he died, and was buried behind those gates, not far from Rebus's parents. *Not Dead, But at Rest in the Arms of the Lord.*

The Lord had to be a bodybuilder.

From family he turned to friends and tried recalling a dozen names to put to faces he remembered from schooldays. Other friends: people he'd known in the army, the SAS. All the people he'd dealt with during his career in the police. Villains he'd put away, some who'd slipped through his fingers. People he'd interviewed, suspected, questioned, broken the worst kind of news to. Acquaintances from the Oxford Bar and all the other pubs where he'd ever been a regular. Local shopkeepers. Jesus, the list was endless. All these people who'd played a part in his life, in shaping who he was and how he acted, how he felt about things. All of them, out there somewhere and nowhere, gathered together only inside his head. And chief among them tonight, Brian and Janis.

That night of the school dance ... It was true he'd been drunk – elated. He'd felt he could *do* anything, *be* anything. Because he'd come to a decision that day – he wouldn't join the army, he'd stay in Bowhill with Janis, apply for a job at the dockyard. His dad had told him not to be so stupid – 'short-sighted' was the word he'd used. But what did parents know about their children's desires? So he'd drunk some beer and headed off to the dance, his thoughts only of Janis. Tonight he'd tell her. And Mitch, of course. He'd have to tell Mitch, tell him he'd be heading into the army alone. But Mitch wouldn't mind, he'd understand, as best friends had to.

But while Rebus had been outside with Janis, his friend Mitch was being cornered by four teenagers who considered themselves his enemies. This was their last chance for revenge, and they'd gone in hard, kicking and punching. Four against one ... until Barney had waded in, shrugging off blows, and dragged Mitch to safety. But one kick had done the damage, dislodging a retina. Mitch's vision stayed fuzzy in that eye for a few days, then disappeared. And where had Rebus been? Out cold on the concrete by the bike sheds.

And why had he never thanked Barney Mee?

He blinked now and sniffed, wondering if he was coming down with a cold. He'd had this idea when he came back to Bowhill that the place would seem beyond redemption, that he'd be able to tell himself it had lost its sense of community, become just another town for him to pass through. Maybe he'd wanted to put it behind him. Well, it hadn't worked. He got out of the car and looked around. The street was dead. He reached up and hauled himself over the iron railings and walked a circuit of the cemetery for an hour or so, and felt strangely at peace.

Nine

'So what's the panic, Matty?'

After a home draw with Rangers, Stevie was ready for a night on the town. One–one, and of course he'd scored his team's only goal. The reporters would be busy filing their copy, saying for the umpteenth time that he was his side's hero, that without him they were a very ordinary team indeed. Rangers had known that: Stevie's marker had been out for blood, sliding studs-first into tackles which Stevie had done his damnedest to avoid. He'd come out of the game with a couple of fresh bruises and grazes, a nick on one knee but, to his manager's all too palpable relief, fit to play again midweek.

'I said what's the panic?'

Matty had worried himself sleepless. He knew he had several options. Speak to Stevie, that was one of them. Another was not to speak to him, but tell Mandelson he had. Then it would be down to whether or not Mandelson believed him. Option three: do a runner; only Mandelson was right about that – he was running out of places to hide. With *two* casino bosses out for his blood, how could he ever pick up another croupier's job?

If he spoke with Stevie, he'd lose a new-found friend. But to stay silent ... well, there was very little percentage in it. So here he was in Stevie's flat. In the corner, a TV was replaying a tape of the afternoon's match. There was no commentary, just the sounds of the terraces and the dug-outs.

'No panic,' he said now, playing for time.

Stevie stared at him. 'You all right? Want a drink or something?'

'Maybe a vodka.'

'Anything in it?'

'I'll take it as it comes.'

Stevie poured him a drink. Matty had been here half an hour now, and they still hadn't talked. The telephone had hardly stopped: reporters' questions, family and friends offering congratulations. Stevie had shrugged off the superlatives.

Matty took the drink, swallowed it, wondering if he could still walk away. Then he remembered Malibu, and saw shadows falling.

'Thing is, Stevie,' he said. 'You know my boss at the Morvena, Mr Mandelson?'

'I owe him money, of course I know him.'

'He says we could do something about that.'

'What? My tab?' Stevie was checking himself in the mirror, having changed into his on-the-town clothes. 'I don't get it,' he said.

Well, Stevie, Matty thought, it was nice knowing you, pal. 'All you have to do is ease off next Saturday.'

Stevie frowned and turned from the mirror. 'Away to Raith?' He came and sat down opposite Matty. 'He told you to tell me?' He waited till Matty nodded. 'That bastard. What's in it for him?'

Matty wriggled on the leather sofa. 'I've been thinking about it. Raith are going through a bad patch, but you know yourself that if you're taken out of the equation...'

'Then they'd be up against not very much. My boss has told everybody to get the ball to me. If they spend the whole game doing that and I don't do anything with it...'

Matty nodded. 'What I think is, the odds will be on you scoring. Nobody'll be expecting Raith to put one in the net.'

'So Mandelson's cash will be on a goalless draw?'

'And he'll get odds, spread a lot of small bets around...'

'Bastard,' Stevie said again. 'How did he get you into this, Matty?'

Matty shifted again. 'Something I did in London.'

'Secrets, eh? Hard things to keep.' Stevie got up, went to the mirror again, and just stood there, hands by his sides, staring into it. There was no emotion in his voice when he spoke.

'Tell him he can fuck himself.'

Matty had to choke out the words. 'You sure that's the message?'

'Cheerio, Matty.'

Matty rose shakily to his feet. 'What am I going to do?'

'Cheerio, Matty.'

Stevie was as still as a statue as Matty walked to the door and let himself out.

*

Mandelson sat at his desk, playing with a Cartier pen he'd taken from a punter that day. The man was overdue on a payment. The pen was by way of a gift.

'So?' he asked Matty.

Matty sat on the chair and licked his lips. There was no offer of a drink today; this was just business. Malibu stood by the door. Matty took a deep breath – the last act of a drowning man.

'It's on,' he said.

Mandelson looked up at him. 'Stevie went for it?'

'Eventually,' Matty said.

'You're sure?'

'As sure as I can be.'

'Well, that better be watertight, or you might find yourself going for a swim with heavy legs. Know what I mean?'

Matty held the dark gaze and nodded.

Mandelson glanced towards Malibu, both of them were smiling. Then he picked up the telephone. 'You know, Matty,' he said, pushing numbers, 'I'm doing you a favour. You're doing *yourself* a favour.' He listened to the receiver. 'Mr Hamilton, please.' Then, to Matty, 'See, what you're doing here is saving your job. I over-stretched myself, Matty. I wouldn't like that to get around, but I'm trusting you. If this comes off – and it better – then you've earned that trust.' He tapped the receiver. 'It wasn't all my own money either. But this will keep the Morvena alive and kicking.' He motioned for Matty to leave. Malibu tapped his shoulder as an incentive.

'Topper?' Mandelson was saying as Matty left the room. 'It's locked up. How much are you in for?'

Matty bided his time and waited till his shift was over. He walked out of the smart New Town building like a latterday Lazarus, and found the nearest payphone, then had to fumble through all the rubbish in his pockets, stuff that must have meant something once upon a time, until he found the card.

The card with a phone number on it.

The following Saturday, Stevie Scoular scored his team's only goal in their 1–0 win over Raith Rovers, and Mandelson sat alone in his office, his eyes on the Teletext results.

His hand rested on the telephone receiver. He was expecting a call from Topper Hamilton. He couldn't seem to stop blinking, like there was a grain of sand in either eye. He buzzed the reception desk, told them to tell Malibu he was wanted. Mandelson didn't know how much time he had, but he knew he would make it count. A word with Stevie Scoular, see if Matty really *had* put the proposition to him. Then Matty himself ... Matty was a definite, no matter what. Matty was about to be put out of the game.

The knock at the door had to be Malibu. Mandelson barked for him to come in. But when the door opened, two strangers sauntered in like they owned the place. Mandelson sat back in his chair, hands on the desk. He was almost relieved when they introduced themselves as police officers.

'I'm Detective Inspector Rebus,' the younger one said, 'this is Chief Super-intendent Watson.'

'And you've come about the Benevolent Fund, right?'

Rebus sat down unasked, his eyes drifting to the TV screen and the results posted there. 'Looks like you just lost a packet. I'm sorry to hear it. Did Topper take a beating, too?'

Mandelson made fists of his hands. 'That wee bastard!'

Rebus was shaking his head. 'Matty did his best, only there was something he didn't know. Seems you didn't know either. Topper will be doubly disappointed.'

'What?'

Farmer Watson, still standing, provided the answer. 'Ever heard of Big Ger Cafferty?'

Mandelson nodded. 'He's been in Barlinnie a while.'

'Used to be the biggest gangster on the east coast. Probably still is. And he's a fan of Stevie's, gets videotapes of all his games. He almost sends him love letters.'

Mandelson frowned. 'So?'

'So Stevie's covered,' Rebus said. 'Try fucking with him, you're asking Big Ger to bend over. Your little proposal has probably already made it back to Cafferty.'

Mandelson swallowed and felt suddenly dry-mouthed.

'There was no way Stevie was going to throw that game,' Rebus said quietly.

'Matty ...' Mandelson choked the sentence off.

'Told you it was fixed? He was scared turdless, what else was he going to say? But Matty's *mine*. You don't touch him.'

'Not that you'd get the chance,' the Farmer added. 'Not with Topper *and* Cafferty after your blood. Malibu will be a big help, the way he took off five minutes ago in the Roller.' Watson walked up to the desk, looming over Mandelson like a mountain. 'You've got two choices, son. You can talk, or you can run.'

'You've got nothing.'

'I saw you that night at Gaitanos,' Rebus said. 'If you're going to lay out big bets, where better than Fife? Optimistic Raith fans might have bet on a goalless draw. You got Charmer Mackenzie to place the bets locally, spreading them around. That way it looked less suspicious.'

Which was why Mackenzie had wanted Rebus out of there, whatever the price: he'd been about to do some business...

'Besides,' Rebus continued, 'when it comes down to it, what choice do you have?'

'You either talk to us ...' the Farmer said.

'Or you disappear. People do it all the time.'

And it never stops, Rebus could have added. Because it's part of the dance – shifting partners, people you shared the floor with, it all changed. And it only ended when you disappeared from the hall.

And sometimes ... sometimes, it didn't even end there.

'All right,' Mandelson said at last, the way they'd known he would, all colour gone from his face, his voice hollow, 'what do you want to know?'

'Let's start with Topper Hamilton,' the Farmer said, sounding like a kid unwrapping his birthday present.

It was Wednesday morning when Rebus got the phone call from a Mr Bain. It took him a moment to place the name: Damon's bank manager.

'Yes, Mr Bain, what can I do for you?'

'Damon Mee, Inspector. You wanted us to keep an eye on any transactions.'

Rebus leant forward in his chair. 'That's right.'

'There've been two withdrawals from cash machines, both in central London.'

Rebus grabbed a pen. 'Where exactly?'

'Tottenham Court Road was three days ago: fifty pounds. Next day, it was Finsbury Park, same amount.'

Fifty pounds a day: enough to live on, enough to pay for a cheap bed and breakfast and two extra meals.

'How much is left in the account, Mr Bain?'

'A little under six hundred pounds.'

Enough for twelve days. There were several ways it could go. Damon could get himself a job. Or when the money ran out he could try begging. Or he could return home. Rebus thanked Bain and telephoned Janis.

'John,' she said, 'we got a postcard this morning.'

A postcard saying Damon was in London and doing fine. A postcard of apology for any fright he'd given them. A postcard saying he needed some time to 'get my head straight'. A postcard which ended 'See you soon.' The picture on the front was of a pair of breasts painted with Union Jacks.

'Brian thinks we should go down there,' Janis said. 'Try to find him.'

Rebus thought of how many B&Bs there'd be in Finsbury Park. 'You might just chase him away,' he warned. 'He's doing OK, Janis.'

'But why did he do it, John? I mean, is it something *we* did?'

New questions and fears had replaced the old ones. Rebus didn't know what to tell her. He wasn't family and couldn't begin to answer her question. Didn't *want* to begin to answer it.

'He's doing OK,' he repeated. 'Just give him some time.'

She was crying now, softly. He imagined her with head bowed, hair falling over the telephone receiver.

'We did everything, John. You can't know how much we've given him. We always put ourselves second, never a minute's thought for anything but him...'

'Janis...' he began.

She took a deep breath. 'Will you come and see me, John?'

Rebus looked around the office, eyes resting eventually on his own desk and the paperwork stacked there.

'I can't, Janis. I'd like to, but I just can't. See, it's not as if I...'

He didn't know how he was going to finish the sentence, but it didn't matter. She'd put her phone down. He sat back in his chair and remembered dancing with her, how brittle her body had seemed. But that had been half a lifetime ago. They'd made so many choices since. It was time to let the past go. Siobhan Clarke was at her desk. She was looking at him. Then she mimed the drinking of a cup of coffee, and he nodded and got to his feet.

Did a little dance as he shuffled towards her.

A TALE ABOUT A TIGER

S. J. Rozan

'A tale about a tiger is true if told by three persons.'
Anecdotes of the Warring States, Liu Xiang, 1st century BCE

It happened in the Warring States period. In compliance with a peace treaty signed with the king of Zhao, the king of the defeated Wei prepared to send the crown prince to Zhao as a hostage. Minister Pang Cong, who was to accompany the crown prince on his journey to Zhao, spoke to the king before departure.

'If someone comes to report that there is a tiger in the street,' he asked the king, 'would Your Majesty believe it?'

'How can a tiger come into a busy street?' the king replied. 'How can he dare? I wouldn't believe it.'

'Would Your Majesty believe it if two persons say there is a tiger in the street?'

'When two persons report to that effect, I may half believe it,' answered the king. 'Though how can a tiger come into a busy street?'

'If three persons tell Your Majesty the same?'

'I have to believe it,' the king replied, 'if three persons give the same version.'

'But no tiger will dare come into a busy street,' reasoned Pang. 'Your Majesty will accept as true what cannot be true only because three persons allege it. Now, I am going to Zhao with the prince. I believe that there will be more than three persons who will speak ill of me while I am away. I beg Your Majesty to consider carefully before you believe what they may say.'

'I have your meaning,' the king told him. 'You may set out on your journey with an easy mind.'

But sure enough, during Pang Cong's absence from Wei, there were very many people who made malicious remarks against him before the king. By and by, the king came to believe them.

Coin grass, rabbit's seed, ought-to-return. Fisherman's herb; sand snails, dried and wrinkled, packaged in plastic. Sister-in-law's orchid; southern tree lizard, flattened and hanging from a nail behind the counter, looking like a rawhide toy for the large orange cat who lay curled beside the cash register, oblivious to me and all the real customers.

Some of these plants and animals I recognized; some were new to me. I wandered the aisles of the Jiong Mao Pharmacy between rows of glass jars half my size, filled with flowers of some plants, leaves of others; between display cases holding things I knew were fish, and things I didn't know, and things I knew I was glad I didn't know.

Jiong Mao was a herbalist's shop, but not the kind I was used to. Growing up in Chinatown, my brothers and I had been treated for every indisposition by decoctions, concoctions, and infusions brewed by my mother from dried plants and other things wrapped in white paper squares and carefully carried home. The white paper squares always came from Grandfather Gao's apothecary, a dim, quiet, rich-smelling place which had dispensed traditional remedies from the same storefront in Chinatown since Grandfather Gao's great-uncle's uncle had imported its carved wooden screens and shelves from China a century ago.

Sometimes, when I was young, I was despatched there to retrieve some mixture Grandfather Gao had precisely weighed out on the ancient brass scales, and I always liked to go, to sniff the incense Grandfather Gao burned at the altar at the back of the room, to see the carved, low, lion-footed table and the wooden cabinets with their rows of drawers, the brass canisters where the herbs were kept, and Grandfather Gao's kindly, solemn smile.

After my father died it seemed to me I was sent there more often, on errands I was not sure were necessary; and that Grandfather Gao, who was not related to my family in any blood way, always had time to offer me tea and some little sweet, and question me about my schoolwork, giving advice he seemed unconcerned about whether I took. It was usually good advice, the kind my father would have given, and when I understood it – Grandfather Gao talks in riddles and metaphors a lot of the time – I tried to follow it.

This place, Jiong Mao, was different, though it was not unique in Chinatown these days. Bright Fluorescent lights gleamed smartly off new glass and shiny chrome and spotless white tile; the floor was vinyl and the windows wide and filled with neat displays. Most of the tonic herbs and animal parts not sold from glass canisters were plastic-packaged, giving everything a slick and sparkling look. There were no scents at all, but there were sounds: the confident recommendations of the half-dozen white coated pharmacists; the click of customers' heels down the aisles; the whirr of electronic cash registers and the soft jingly thunks as their drawers opened and closed, opened and closed.

All these sounds masked the soft-soled approach of the man I had come to see. Until he spoke from behind me, I didn't realize he was there.

'Miss Chin?' I turned from a jar of delicate ask-for-trouble to see the smile in his voice reflected on his wide, round face. 'I'm so sorry to have kept you waiting. I am Shun Shang Xian.'

Balding, chubby, dressed in a well-cut gray suit, he spoke in English, as a courtesy to me: who can know if an ABC – American-born Chinese – has been taught the ancestral tongue? I responded in English, as a courtesy to him: it would have been rude to imply that I thought he might be more comfortable in Chinese, especially since his English, the little I'd heard of it, was quite good; rude of me to one-up him by accommodating to him when he had opened the conversation by accommodating to me.

'Mr Shun.' I smiled also. 'I'm very pleased to meet you.' Although I left it out because in English it sounds phony, in Chinese I might also have said 'honored', since he was the older of us and a respected and prosperous merchant, while I was young, in a shady profession if you ask my mother, and, if I was lucky, about to become an employee.

'Please.' Mr Shun smiled again as he took my elbow. 'This way.' He steered me through the sparkling aisles toward the back of the store, where he opened a door in the white-tiled wall. Above it was an altar, just a polished granite roof and floor and four pillars, much simpler than the ancient carved wooden construction at Grandfather Gao's. But the statue of General Gung, the god of commerce, and the little pyramid of oranges, and the burned-out sticks of incense were the same. I sniffed the scentless air, wondering when Shun Shang Xian let his incense burn.

I passed through the open door. With the click of the door closing again all the shop's noises stopped. No sound but our own footsteps on vinyl tile followed us down the short hallway, and those were muted: the soles of my shoes were as soft as his. We reached his office and even those sounds ended when we crossed the threshold onto the thick gray carpet.

'Please, Miss Chin, sit down.' Mr Shun gestured me to a lacquered wooden chair with an upholstered seat. 'Do you care for tea?' A kettle, two cups, and a Yixing teapot shaped like a gourd rested on a table beside Mr Shun's broad desk.

I told him that would be lovely and he busied himself with spooning and pouring as I looked around. Each pale-painted wall bore a single Chinese landscape, one of pines, one of mountains, one of horses in the mist. Behind Mr Shun's desk hung three framed certificates, one in English and two in Chinese. Each one, from a different examining body, attested to his training and proficiency as a herbalist.

Mr Shun placed a handleless clay cup glazed only on the inside on a small lacquered table beside my chair. He poured tea for me and for himself, then gave me time to taste and savor it before getting down to business. It was a rich, dark tea, scented with jasmine – the first aroma I'd noticed since walking through his door – and it was really quite delicious.

The first sips behind us, Mr Shun smiled and asked, 'Do you follow traditional Chinese medical practices, Miss Chin? Or are you completely persuaded to the Western way?'

His use of 'Miss' set my teeth a little on edge, but I never correct anyone more venerable than myself on that, which is just about everyone. And I was considering myself lucky that he was even thinking about hiring a female PI.

'One of my brothers is a Western medical doctor,' I told him, 'but my mother always treated us with Chinese medicine when we were young.'

Lydia Chin, neatly sidestepping again, I thought, and smiled and drank my tea.

Mr Shun nodded as though he approved of that. 'Chinese medicine is gaining currency in the West,' he informed me, 'as Europeans come to realize that the world is wider then they thought, and that the answers to some questions had been found before they even thought to look for them.' I smiled politely, waiting to see where this was going.

'However,' he went on, 'I'm sure you know it is often still difficult to have this approach to healing taken seriously in some places. Traditional Chinese medicine is still seen by many as ritual and magic, not science.'

True, I thought, but there's not much I can do about that. It seemed to me this speech sounded a little canned, but maybe it was something he found himself having to say often. I waited some more.

Mr Shun raised his eyebrows in the direction of his shiny scalp. 'I think the English say, quoting Shakespeare, that Caesar's wife must be above suspicion?'

If they did, I didn't know about it, and I didn't know what they meant by it either. 'Yes?' I murmured noncommittally.

'Not because she is more likely to engage in shabby behavior than anyone else, but because she will be more closely watched, and any transgression, or the appearance of one, will be obvious. Do you agree?'

I nodded my agreement, wondering if speaking in roundabout and semi-incomprehensible metaphors was an inevitable result of Chinese pharmaceutical training.

'Many of the ingredients we use in this shop and in shops like this are unfamiliar to Westerners,' Mr Shun went on. 'Some are so alien as to seem frightening, or even possibly disgusting. To Westerners,' he added, smiling.

Yes, and some are disgusting even to Chinese, I told myself, but I didn't tell him. After all, Robitussin is kind of disgusting, too.

'Some,' Mr Shun continued in a conversational tone, as though I were actually a part of this discussion, not just a silent listener, 'make Westerners perhaps somewhat queasy. I shall get to the point, Miss Chin, as we are both professionals, though the matter is delicate: I am talking about the sexual organ of the male tiger.'

Ah, I thought. Well, that clears that up. Mr Shun's eyes stayed fixed on me. The look in them was dubious, as though he were not altogether certain that Lydia Chin, that delicate flower of Chinese femininity, could quite be trusted to have understood what he'd just said. Under his gaze I felt my cheeks flush and ignored them; I went back to the last thing I'd said, and said it gain. 'Yes?'

'The tiger is a noble creature,' Mr Shun, appearing satisfied that I was still with him, announced in a portentous voice. Trepidation gripped me that he was about to begin a long, declamatory oration on the nobility of the tiger. On the other hand, it might give me a chance to bring my cheeks back under control. 'He has a right to prowl his jungle home, to stalk his prey in silence and stealth, to vigorously devour the creatures he requires for his sustenance.'

He hadn't said anything yet that I could argue with, so I kept my mouth politely shut.

Mr Shun went on, 'The tiger's nobility, his swiftness and strength, have made him, in the hearts of our people, lord of the west and of the wind. There is no Chinese person who does not pause in awe of the power of the tiger.'

I was beginning to wonder if Mr Shun himself paused for anything when his tone shifted.

'However,' he said, and his voice lowered, as though we might, if we did not take care, be overheard, 'for some, admiring the potency of the tiger is not enough. Some men, losing what they once had, desire what the tiger has yet. They come to shops such as this, Miss Chin, to purchase that which they believe will restore them to their former state. They believe that a decoction made from the organ of the male tiger to be that marvelous cure.'

Before I could stop myself, I asked the question any sane person would have to ask, under the circumstances, 'Does it work?'

Mr Shun, seeming taken aback, stared. Oh, Lydia, I thought, you and your big mouth. Then he smiled. 'No,' he said. 'Of course not.'

'That's a relief,' I managed. 'For the tiger, I mean.'

'I fear not. Desperate patients and unethical practitioners combine to perpetuate this myth, and its continued currency, Miss Chin, now threatens the very existence of the tiger in his jungle habitats.'

'I think that's terrible,' I said, and I did. 'But I don't see how I—'

'There is a supplier of dried herbs and animal parts to traditional shops such as this one.' Mr Shun held up his hand, a sign for me to be patient. 'Word has reached me that he is offering for sale a quantity of these . . . items. They are illegally taken, no matter where they come from: tiger-hunting is no longer permitted anywhere on earth. I do not deal with him. In fact, I do not know his name, and I know no one who does. But I want you to stop him.'

*

'*What?*' Bill Smith, my sometimes partner, stopped moving with his match halfway to the cigarette dangling from his lips. His jaw might have dropped if he hadn't had to hold onto that cigarette.

'Don't be mean and make me say it again.' I narrowed my eyes at him.

'I'm amazed you said it the first time. Ouch!' His hand sprang back, dropping the match as its flame reached the tips of his fingers. 'Look what you made me do,' he complained, moving the dead match from the café tabletop into the ashtray and lighting another one. I didn't speak again until he'd gotten the cigarette going; it didn't seem fair to distract him from such a complicated task.

Successful, he dropped the new match beside the other one and leaned back in his insecure-looking wire-backed chair. At least, it looked insecure to me, but that's how I'd feel if I were that delicate and someone Bill's size was sitting on me, so maybe I was just projecting.

Although it was still the chilly beginning of spring, we were occupying an outdoor table at Reggio's, a Greenwich Village café – a café so I could have some tea, outdoors so Bill could smoke, Greenwich Village because it's within walking distance of both Bill's Tribeca apartment and Chinatown, where I'm from.

'Can I say it?' Bill asked. 'Once?'

'Once. After that, it's all euphemisms.'

'Tiger penises.' Bill said the words slowly, smiling happily in the pale sunlight. 'You have a client who wants us to smoke out an illegal load of tiger penises—'

'Once, I said!'

'Oh. Quite right. Wants us to smoke out an illegal load of tiger euphemisms, which have been smuggled into the US and are being sold to apothecary shops because your people use them to restore get-up-and-go once it's got up and gone.'

I sighed. 'You know, I almost didn't call you for this case because I knew you wouldn't be able to resist being completely crude and disgusting.'

'And you were absolutely correct. But you called me anyway. I can only surmise that my skills as an investigator, my mental adroitness and ability to improvise, and my fearlessness in the face of danger must have overcome your natural revulsion—'

'They didn't. You're still revolting.'

'Then why?'

I took a deliberate sip of my Lapsang Soochong, a thick, hot tea for a cool, pale afternoon. I replaced the cup carefully in its saucer. 'Chinese medicine,' I told him, 'is based on the concept of balance. Hot balances cold; wet balances dry. Yin balances yang, you see.'

He raised an eyebrow. 'And?'

'You,' I said, 'are vulgar and offensive. That balances me.'

'Hmm.' He pulled on the cigarette, streamed out smoke as if in thought. 'Indisputable,' he said finally. 'Okay, boss. Do you have a plan?'

'I do,' I said smugly, then added, 'Sort of. You want to hear it?'

'I can't wait.'

I shot him a look designed to ferret out the hidden meaning of that line, but he was all innocence. So I sipped a little more tea and outlined the idea I'd had during my meeting this morning with Mr Shun, and had been refining in my head ever since.

When I was finished, Bill drank his coffee in thoughtful silence. He waved the waiter over for another cup. When he'd had about half of that one, he spoke seriously. 'The only part I don't like is not bringing the law in earlier.'

'The Fish and Wildlife Service? I know, but that's what the videotape will be for. We can give it to them any time after we actually meet the guy and see the ... goods. After Mr Shun gets his chance to find out who he is. It's not like he'll get away. Probably,' I added reluctantly, to be fair.

'Probably. But if he turns out to be someone Shun knows, or is somehow connected to, I gather we're supposed to turn around and walk away.'

'Yes,' I said, 'that's true.'

That had been the one stipulation Mr Shun had placed on my investigation, as we drank our tea in his stark, bright office – that I had to let him know who the supplier was before I took the next step.

'And if it is someone Shun knows, he walks away, too? And the guy gets to go on making a fortune, supplying a market for poachers around the world?'

'No, I don't think so. Mr Shun says in that case he'll deal with it. It's a Chinese thing.'

'And he'll deal with it in a Chinese way?' Bill tapped the ash off his cigarette. 'Straight up,' he said to me. 'Will he kill him?'

I stared at him. 'God, no, I don't think so. This isn't something to risk your karma for by getting someone's blood on your hands.'

'Mr Shun thinks like that?'

'Don't you? No, really, the whole point is to maintain the credibility or high character or something like that of Chinese medicine. I don't think killing someone helps you do that.'

'Then what will he do?'

'I gather Mr Shun is fairly well connected in the Chinese communities both here and on the West Coast. If it turns out he does know the guy or his family, he'll just apply pressure of the family kind.'

'What you Chinese do so well.'

'We do. He told me that was why he came to me in the first place, even though I'm a woman – because I'm Chinese and I'd understand.'

'Does he think I'll understand?'

'He doesn't know about you.'

'Ah. You're pretending once again that short, determined Chinese women don't need the help of large, lunky white men? Well, I'll never tell.'

'*Au contraire, mon frère*, I'm trying to protect you. If he knew you existed he'd grind up your parts and sell you as a cure for low self-esteem.'

'At least my parts would have some use.'

'Well, all but one.'

Bill grinned. I almost thought I saw his face redden, but it was probably just a trick of the sunlight. 'God almighty, what's this case doing to you?' he asked. 'I don't believe you said that.'

'I don't either.' I felt my own cheeks flush. 'See what you drive me to? Now, pay attention and let's get back to work. Do you want in?'

'Absolutely. A chance to be on the side of the angels and make filthy remarks at the same time? Who could resist?'

'Certainly not you. Well, then, what about the plan?'

We talked for the next half-hour, sometimes serious, sometimes kidding around. I made suggestions, Bill found the holes in them; he had ideas, I returned the favor. We organized a plan we thought could work, and made contingency plans for each piece of it in case one of them didn't.

'That could be dangerous for you,' Bill said at one point, about my favorite part of it.

I arched an eyebrow, something he can do that I've been practicing in a mirror. 'And?' I said breezily.

He held up his hands. 'And absolutely nothing. Just my job to point these things out, ma'am.'

'Thank you,' I said. 'It will be noted in the minutes that you're doing your job. Shall we continue?'

Doing it that way, over more tea and more coffee and, for Bill, more cigarettes, in the sidewalk café in the thin and breezy air, we cobbled together a first-class plan. Finally, cups empty and ashtray full, we were satisfied we could begin.

I pulled some bills from my wallet, dropped them on the table, and got up to leave. The drinks were on me, because this was my case and Bill was working for me. When it's the other way, when a case comes to him and he needs someone else on it, he calls me. Then he's the boss. That's the way it is with us, the way it's been for some time now. Back and forth, a seesaw, a game of catch, a tug of war: it works for us.

'I'm on my way to set up our next move,' I told him. 'I'll call you when I'm ready.'

Bill lit one final cigarette and watched me go. 'I'll be pining until then,' he called after me while I walked away.

'Good.' I smiled, turned back, and turned away again. 'I like that.'

The next step took me back to Chinatown, back to streets crowded with hard-eyed immigrant women buying glistening fish out of ice-packed cardboard boxes instead of woven wicker baskets smelling of the sea; with young men whose skin had been browned and muscles rounded in the fields of their native villages, now rushing to their jobs in windowless, steamy restaurant kitchens, and old men sitting on chairs in the sun, retired or let go from those same places; with teenagers, dressed in cutting-edge street fashion, calling boisterously to each other in a language their parents didn't understand.

I edged around tourists with guidebooks and cameras, around a group of giggling, uniformed young kids from Transfiguration School. I had to excuse myself twice to get past a trio of sharply dressed young men standing on a corner, all smoking and sporting gold rings and all gesturing and arguing, in Cantonese, about the condition and value of the building across the street: Hong Kong real-estate developers, moving money around.

I stopped at my favorite vegetable stand for four perfect-looking oranges, then at the card shop next door for a shiny red paper bag to put them in. I turned the corner into a street only slightly less crowded than the one I'd come from. In the middle of the block I pushed open an etched-glass door into a shop that wasn't crowded at all.

The dimness and the air's soft scents and the reassuring presence of the heavy, carved woodwork were the same as they had been all during my childhood, and on every visit since then. Grandfather Gao, sitting at his mahogany counter, sipping a cup of tea and turning the pages of his Chinese newspaper, was as I had seen him a thousand times, no more ancient, it seemed to me, then when I was young. He looked up when the door's quiet chimes tinkled, and his long thin face warmed with a smile that was bracketed by the deep wrinkles on either side.

'Chin Ling Wan-ju, and more beautiful than ever!' he welcomed me in Chinese. 'What a pleasure it is to see you.'

'And you, Grandfather,' I answered, also in Chinese, smiling back. 'Though I fear your eyes are failing.'

'What a shame that would be, to be one day unable to see your beauty as clearly as I do now. Will you share a cup of tea with me, or is your errand too urgent to allow such pleasant frivolity?'

'I'd love some tea, thank you. And my errand is ... unusual.' I held out the oranges in their bright red bag. 'I thought General Gung might like these,' I said.

Grandfather Gao took the bag and knew what it meant: that I was here to ask a favor. Without a word he climbed onto a small stool and removed the oranges already stacked on the fine porcelain plate in front of the statue of General Gung. He piled mine in their places. The ones he'd taken down he carried through the door in the back of the shop. Through the open doorway I could see him put them in the shop's small refrigerator. Just because General Gung had already enjoyed the spirits of these oranges didn't mean Grandfather Gao was not entitled to their flesh.

I seated myself on the low, carved bench to wait, gazing at a large glazed porcelain jar bearing delicate images of flowering plum branches, soaring phoenixes, fierce tigers. Grandfather Gao emerged from the door at the rear of the shop carrying a tray which held a plain, elegantly rounded teapot and two small clay cups. He set the tray on the lion-footed table and took a seat on the chair across from my bench, leaving me the honor of pouring out the tea.

'How is your mother, and how are your brothers?' he enquired while we waited for the tea to steep. I gave him a rundown on my family, starting with my mother and working my way down through my four older brothers, eldest first, the Chinese way. I covered my nephews and niece also, and mentioned a letter from my mother's cousin in Hong Kong for good measure. I poured the tea and guiltily realized from the first pungent sip that it was a very costly brew called Silver Needles. This was a tea I'd tasted only a very few times in my life. It seemed to me that Grandfather Gao really should be saving Silver Needles for important occasions and important guests, but it would have been hopelessly impolite of me to say anything beyond what I did say: 'The tea is delicious.'

'Yes.' He smiled. 'This is a favorite of mine. And now tell me, Ling Wan-ju, why you have come on a new spring day to see an old man.'

I put down my tea cup and began. 'I'm working on a case, Grandfather.'

He let his eyes rest on me for a few moments, then nodded silently. Unlike my actual family, who do it all the time, Grandfather Gao has never once objected to my choice of profession. Since he and my father's father were friends in China when they were young, I like to stretch the point and let myself think that my father wouldn't have minded either.

'An apothecary has hired me,' I said. 'Shun Shang Xian, the owner of one of the new shops to the north.' 'North' meant north of Canal Street, for a century Chinatown's border, only breached in the last few years by the sudden flood of poor new immigrants from the mainland and rich ones from Hong Kong. 'He tells me he wants me to stop a black marketeer.'

Telling Grandfather Gao what the goods were that the black market was in required some fancy footwork on my part, since I didn't know either the actual word or any particularly delicate euphemisms in Chinese. Accompanied by what I considered a minimum amount of stammering and blushing, however, I managed to convey my meaning. Grandfather Gao neither smiled nor frowned, just nodded silently as I described the job I'd taken on.

I was about to explain the reason I'd come to see him about it when a sudden thought struck me cold. I felt my face go pale. 'Grandfather,' I asked, 'you don't ... you don't sell...'

He fixed his glittering black eyes on me for a moment before speaking. Then he said, 'No. No, I do not.'

I breathed out the softly scented shop air I'd been holding in. 'Oh,' I said. 'Oh, that's good. I didn't think you would, because it's so ... so ...' I trailed off, unwilling say what I meant: so disgusting. Wasn't that what Mr Shun had said Westerners think, when they think about Chinese medicine?

Grandfather Gao saved me. 'The object in question,' he said quietly, 'has no medical use.'

'That's what Mr Shun said,' I answered gratefully, 'but he said people will pay huge amounts of money for it anyway.'

'The six atmospheric energies,' Grandfather Gao said with his eyes on a spot over my shoulder, 'the seven emotions, the wrong foods, excess fatigue – the causes of disease are never anything but an unbalancing of the body's natural forces. When balance and harmony are restored, so, too, is health.' He brought his eyes back to me. 'The loss of virility in a young man ...' He paused, probably to see whether he could speak so plainly to me. I met his eyes and tried hard not to blush. He went on, seeming satisfied, '... can be treated with herbs and tonics. It is unnatural, and therefore can be cured. But it is not young men who are willing to pay so dearly for the cure you are describing.'

'I thought it was supposed to work on anyone.'

'Old men,' Grandfather Gao said, shaking his head. 'What we are discussing is an old man's cure. And an old man's loss of virility is not a disease which requires a cure. It is natural and to be expected. It will happen when it does, at a different time for each man, but at the right time for each. No, Ling Wan-ju, men who can be cured of this condition can be cured by other means. Men who cannot be cured are men with whom nothing is wrong, except their own fear of age and what lies beyond it.'

I looked at Grandfather Gao as he, unsmiling, rested his eyes again on me. If age, I thought, could account for the subtle richness of layered scents, the calm quiet, the many soft shades of dark in the shadows of this shop, and the stillness of Grandfather Gao's long, thin hands upon the arms of his carved chair, then I was all for it.

'Now,' said Grandfather Gao, almost startling me as he spoke again, so completely had I been caught in the gentle web of this place, 'I do not flatter myself that you have come here solely to hear an old practitioner expound upon his philosophy of healing. Or have you?'

I smiled and shook my head. 'No, Grandfather. Though your words are always welcome.'

He returned my smile. 'And always, Ling Wan-ju, available to you, whether you have requested them or not. Now that you have done me the favor of listening to an old man's thoughts, tell me what it is that I can do for you.'

'This supplier,' I said. 'I need to know his name, and where to find him.'

Grandfather Gao's high forehead furrowed. 'Your client did not tell you?'

'He says he doesn't know. That he's heard this man is operating but he doesn't know who he is. That's part of what he wants.'

'What is that?'

'To know who he is. That's why he hasn't gone to the authorities.'

I explained about Mr Shun's request that he be allowed to learn the supplier's identity before I brought in the law.

'Because it's a small world, your business,' I said. 'And Mr Shun says he's afraid he might turn out to know this man, or be somehow connected to him, even maybe by blood, or home village or something. In that case he couldn't just turn him in. He'd have to handle it another way.'

Grandfather Gao didn't ask me what that other way might be. He's a member of the Three Brothers tong and, although the Three Brothers is largely a merchants' self-help association, 'help' is one of the things they define for themselves.

'Do you know anything about this supplier, Grandfather? The black marketeer?'

In the shadows of his shop Grandfather Gao's look was long, and unreadable to me. Finally he said, 'And why is it that you think I might?'

I tried to tread carefully. I didn't want to offend Grandfather Gao by implying that he might have dealings with a smuggler, a crook. On the other hand, that's why I was here.

'You're a well-known practitioner, Grandfather, with many friends in your profession,' I said. 'If this man is operating in New York, perhaps one of your ... associates has come across him.'

He nodded slowly, his eyes still fixed on me. I had the uncomfortable feeling that he was seeing more than me, or more, anyway, than I'd see if I looked in a mirror.

Finally, he said, 'He has been here.'

'He has?' I blurted. This was more than I'd expected. 'Here?'

'A man of perhaps forty,' Grandfather Gao said, 'originally from Hong Kong, or so he claims. His appearances in this city are rare, but not unknown. The items he is selling now are not his only goods, although this is the first time he has offered them. Bear paws and gall, certain lizards and snakes – he deals in many items whose sale is illegal in this country, and therefore whose price is high. He has come here to my shop before this, but I do not buy from him.'

'Why – if you don't buy from him, why does he come to you?'

Grandfather Gao's brow furrowed, and the shop's ancient shadows seemed to darken a little, and began to close in on me. 'Ling Wan-ju, do you doubt my word?'

I stared at him and grew hot with shame. 'Oh, Grandfather, never! I just – I—' I took a breath and started again. 'I was just trying to get it to make sense. Things have to make sense to me. I just – I need to understand everything. That's why I'm in this business – so I get to understand.'

'And what is it,' he asked quietly, 'that you wish to understand?'

I swallowed. 'Why this supplier came to you, if you never buy from him. And also,' I added, as a thought seemed to rise from the shadows for me, 'if he's going to apothecaries peddling his goods, why he hasn't been to Mr Shun. Why Mr Shun doesn't know who he is.'

'You must tell me, Ling Wan-ju.'

'I . . .' I faltered.

'Why has your client hired you, instead of going to the authorities with his suspicions?'

'Because I'm Chinese,' I answered promptly, feeling like a kid in after-school Cantonese class again. 'So, if it turns out he knows this man and it wouldn't be right for him to get him in trouble, I'll understand and let him handle it his way. Oh. Maybe I see.'

'What is it you see?'

'This supplier came to you because he knows you,' I said tentatively. 'You haven't bought from him before, but with the value of these new goods you might. In any case, you won't turn him in.'

'And why has he not been to see your client?'

'For the same reason, in reverse. He doesn't know him.'

Grandfather Gao sat silent. The shadows receded into their places in the corners of the shop. I got the sense I was supposed to go on, so I did.

'Can you tell me where to find this man?' I asked, almost holding my breath.

'Yes,' Grandfather Gao answered after what seemed to me a very long pause. 'But,' he said, 'he may not agree to see you.'

'Because he doesn't know me?'

Grandfather Gao paused again, and then answered, 'That will be one obstacle, yes. You may, however, tell him you got his name from me – that might ease your way.'

My heart sang with relief, and not just at the prospect of my way being eased.

'But still,' he continued, 'he may not believe you have a serious interest in buying what he sells, or access to the kind of money required to make this purchase.'

'Oh,' I said. 'Because I'm not a man.'

'He is arrogant and thinks much of himself,' he said. 'He does not do himself honor, I think, by the way he acts but, then, neither does he by his choice of occupation.'

Which, of course, is just what my mother says about me.

'I'll think of something, Grandfather,' I said. 'That's what I do. Will you just tell me his name, and where to find him?'

Grandfather Gao nodded, and looked at me, and I got that funny mirror feeling again. He said, 'He calls himself Desmond Ho, though that is almost assuredly not his name. To reach him, call this number.' Slipping his hand into the pocket of his suit jacket – Grandfather Gao had never dressed in anything less formal than a suit and tie in all the years I'd known him – he took out a leather-bound notebook, wrote a phone number in Chinese on a page from it, and tore it out for me. 'Leave a message there, and he will get it. Whether he will respond or not, I do not know. Ling Wan-ju, are you working on this case alone?'

'No,' I said. I smiled. 'I'm working with Bill Smith. My sometimes partner.'

'The large white man your mother so much dislikes?'

'Well, that could be just about any of my friends who aren't Chinese, but, yes, you know who I mean. The one she calls the white baboon.'

'Does your client approve of your choice of associate?'

'He doesn't know. I thought if he's so concerned about handling this in a Chinese way if it turns out he knows the supplier, then he might not be happy if he knew a non-Chinese was in on it from the beginning. But I couldn't come up with any way to deal with this that wouldn't be better with two people.'

He nodded again. 'I must warn you that Desmond Ho is unlikely to be willing to discuss his business at all with a non-Chinese. He deals solely within the Chinese community, for safety.'

'I assumed that, and I think I can come up with a way to get around it.'

'As usual,' he said, 'you are professional and thorough.'

'As usual, Grandfather, you are flattering me.' I smiled. 'However, I'll take my compliments where I can get them.'

'I cannot believe, Ling Wan-ju, that you suffer from any lack of compliments.' He smiled. 'I suspect the white baboon, for example, can be quite generous with them.'

'He's not allowed. He's always got an ulterior motive.'

'A man's motives, Ling Wan-ju—' He broke off and looked up as the chimes on the door tinkled. A woman of my mother's age entered and smiled hopefully as she saw Grandfather Gao. He stood and smiled reassuringly back at her. I stood also; the interview was over.

I thanked Grandfather Gao and left his shop as he, bidding me farewell, turned his attention to his customer. As I stepped out onto the bustling street, I realized that, although I hadn't gotten to hear Grandfather Gao's views on Bill's motives, I had also gotten away without a single incomprehensible nature metaphor.

I called the phone number. There was voice mail on the other end. I left it my number, then called my own machine and, through the miracles of technology, changed the message on it so that if the pseudonymous Desmond Ho called the machine would not give my profession away.

Then I went home.

My mother was there when I got there. I unloaded the vegetables I'd picked up on the way and began stuffing them into the fridge.

'Did you have a good day?' my mother enquired. 'Or did you spend it among criminals and evil men as usual?' She reached into the fridge and moved everything I'd put there to different shelves and drawers.

'Both, Ma,' I answered. As she clucked her tongue I added, 'I had tea with Grandfather Gao.'

'Did you?' she said. 'Well, I hope you showed him the proper respect. And I hope you were not too willful to hear the wise words he no doubt spoke to you, words you are deaf to when your mother speaks them.'

'You're right about that, Ma,' I said. 'What he said to me today I'd never hear from you.'

I called Bill and left a message with his service – 'The hook's been baited but nothing's on the line yet' – just to show that I could produce an animal metaphor if I had to. Then I did a few household chores and waited for the phone to ring.

And it did.

It was the one in my bedroom, the one that rings through from my office when I'm here instead of there. I slid into the desk chair. 'Lydia Chin,' I announced into the phone in English, in a clipped voice I hoped portrayed a woman very busy but always searching for new opportunities.

'This is Desmond Ho. I got a message from someone there.' It was a man's voice, slightly accented and as clipped as mine. It carried with it a sense of being intruded upon, as though the need to call me was cutting into Desmond Ho's very important day.

'Yes, that was from me, Mr Ho. I left my direct number so that we could speak privately.'

Because, of course, otherwise we might be overheard by the huge staff scurrying about the place.

'I see,' he said. 'And what is it, Miss – Chin? – that we have to speak privately about?'

'A gentleman I know suggested we might be of mutual benefit to each other. A man named Gao Mian-Liang.'

There was a pause at the mention of Grandfather Gao's name. 'Yes, I know him. What does he think we can do for each other?'

'I don't want to discuss this over the phone, Mr Ho. Where can we meet?'

'Oh, I'd have to know more about our business before I decide whether we meet, Miss Chin.'

Before *you* decide? Ha. 'You sell. I buy,' I said. 'What more is there to know?' I stuck my feet up on my desk, trying to act as full of myself as he sounded, to see if that would go through the phone.

'Are you telling me, Miss Chin, that you buy the sort of items I sell?' It seemed to me he emphasized the 'Miss' just a little too much, but I admit I'm sensitive on the subject.

'I buy anything, Mr Ho, that I can make a profit on. Goods in short supply are often very profitable.'

'Who exactly are you?'

'I'm Lydia Chin, and there's nothing more than that. I think you'll regret it, Mr Ho, if you don't meet me and hear me out.' And regret it even more if you do, I thought, but that's not my problem.

'Gao Mian-Liang,' Desmond Ho said in a ruminating tone, 'was not particularly interested in my goods when we recently met. Why is he interested in helping me now?'

'He's not. He's interested in helping *me*. He and I have a . . . relationship, Mr Ho. The nature of it is frankly not your business, but it often makes him eager to . . . do things for me.'

I closed my eyes and waited for lightning to strike me, but it didn't, so I went on.

'Look, Mr Ho, I'm a busy woman. The opportunity presented by your goods, as they were described to me, is the kind of thing I'm always interested in, but I'm not about to beg you to consider a deal that would do you at least as much good as it would me. If you want to play games, play them with somebody else.'

'Miss Chin—'

'I want to meet with you today, Mr Ho. In fact, I want to meet with you *now*. Can we do this?'

'You understand the . . . value . . . of what I have to offer?'

'No, Mr Ho, as a matter of fact I don't, but I understand the price. Isn't that what's important?'

So I won. Desmond Ho agreed to meet me that evening, in his hotel suite, at the Holiday Inn, Chinatown.

Bill and I were there right on time.

The first-floor entrance lobby of this Holiday Inn is about the size of a postage stamp, and the second-floor bar, restaurant, and registration area is the size of the postcard you put it on. The hotel was converted about ten years ago from an old office building north of Canal Street, for Hong Kongers coming to New York to look for safe places for their money to ride out the years right after the Chinese takeover, the way people used to send their children overseas in troubled times. From what I've heard, all the spaces in Hong Kong are about the size of postage stamps, so I guess they're used to it.

The clinking of glasses and the tinkling of laughter spilled from the bar and the aroma of grilling steaks drifted out from the restaurant. When in Rome, eat what the Romans eat. The lobby decor was Holiday-Inn-gaudy in shades of red, with a lattice-patterned carpet and gilded molding on the wallpapered walls. I didn't regret the efficiency with which the young Chinese clerk – her name tag read only 'Mona' – greeted us, called up to Mr Ho's room, and then invited us to go on up; I just didn't think it would be any better upstairs.

It wasn't. The hallway was more crimson wallpaper and gilded molding. An occasional piece of furniture with something Chinese about it – a carved-bamboo motif, or little flat brass handles – stood guard along the corridor as we walked to the end. Mr Ho's suite was a little better in terms of interior decoration, but it had Mr Ho in it.

I had been trying not to dislike Desmond Ho based solely on his one conversation with me and his choice of occupation, but half a minute after meeting him I could tell it was a losing battle.

Opening the door to my knock, he stopped at the sight of Bill. Ho was a pudgy-faced man whose thinning hair was combed in a half-circle across his scalp, from ear to shining ear. He wore a pale blue silk shirt and the pants to an expensive gray suit. He scowled; before he could say anything, I announced in English, 'I'm Lydia Chin. This is my partner, Bill Smith. You're Desmond Ho? I believe you're expecting us.'

'I was expecting *you*,' Desmond Ho replied, in the voice I'd heard over the phone, the one that implied he'd been busy with something actually important just before we came. 'You said nothing about bringing someone else.' He remained in the doorway, looked Bill up and down.

'This is my partner,' I repeated. 'We—'

'I'm the money,' Bill rudely interrupted. 'She can have all the bright ideas she wants, but she doesn't buy anything without me.'

'May we come in?' I asked Desmond Ho icily, ignoring my partner. He wasn't all that easy to ignore, as opposed to giggle at, what with the black jeans, open black shirt, jacket with the sleeves rolled up to the elbows, and three gold chains around his neck, not to mention the mirrored sunglasses he hadn't taken off yet, but I did it. I took a step closer to Desmond Ho. I was hoping to be a little difficult to ignore myself, and to that end was wearing a short navy dress my mother had made me, heels, and my own gold chain, very delicate and with a pointed piece of white jade on the end which hung down to exactly the right place.

'I was not prepared for a stranger,' Desmond Ho said, his eyes on my jade.

'You mean a white guy,' said Bill. 'I know all about you Chinese, keeping it in the family and all that crap. Jesus, all this time with her, how could I not know? Well, you just think of Lydia as family, why don't you? And me as the bank. Let us in, we'll talk about it. Otherwise, goodbye.'

Desmond Ho hesitated. Bill said, 'Oh, the hell with it. I thought this was a jackass idea from the start. Come on, Lydia.' He turned to walk away.

'No,' I said. I let my eyes catch Ho's, and rest there. 'Mr Ho is interested in at least discussing doing business with us. Aren't you, Mr Ho?'

Desmond Ho pursed his lips, and once more looked Bill up and down. Bill, who had stopped and turned, blew out an impatient breath.

'Gao Mian Liang will vouch for us,' I reminded Mr Ho. 'I believe he's in his shop, if you'd care to call him.'

So Bill and I waited in the hallway while that happened, watching through the half-open door as Mr Ho, his back to us, spoke rapid Cantonese into the phone on the gilt-trimmed desk. When he was through he hung up, recrossed the room, and peered at me through narrowed eyes. Then he moved out of his doorway, and Bill and I moved into the room.

The room was small, though not as small as the size of the lobby might have led me to expect. It was expensively though loudly furnished in golds and yellows, and the whole place smelt of room freshener and Mr Ho's powerful aftershave. The good news was that it was the outer room of the suite so, after we'd sorted ourselves out and all claimed one piece of furniture or another, no one was left sitting on the bed and pretending that was a normal place for a conversation with a complete stranger.

Bill plopped himself immediately onto the most comfortable-looking chair in the room, a big recliner by the window with Mr Ho's jacket and tie draped on it. He tossed the clothes casually onto the desk. I could see Ho's teeth grinding, so I sat on the sofa and crossed my stockinged legs. Mr Ho hesitated a split second, then came and sat on the sofa with me. Bill did that arched-eyebrow thing, then lit an unconcerned cigarette.

'So,' he said, looking at Mr Ho while he shook out his match and tossed it in the general direction of the ashtray on the desk near him. 'Is it true what she's been telling me?' He nodded at me, took a pull on the cigarette. 'Tiger dicks?'

Mr Ho and I both reddened, him for real, me at least mostly for show. Mr Ho began a reply. 'Traditional Chinese medicine makes use of many healing ingredients—'

'Yeah,' Bill said, 'I'm sure. People really eat that?'

'I told you!' I snapped at Bill. 'You don't just eat it. The ingredients need to be combined, brewed, decocted—'

Bill snorted. 'Sounds like to me it was the tiger that got decocted. Listen, Ho, how much can I sell these things for?'

'I doubt that you can sell them for anything.'

Bill's face darkened. He turned the mirrored glasses to me. 'You said people would pay a lot—'

'Oh, they're very valuable,' Mr Ho said smoothly, 'but no one would buy them from you.'

'Oh,' Bill said, as though the light had dawned. He settled back in his comfortable chair once more. 'From a white guy. I get it. No, see, that's what I keep Lydia around for. A lot of the merchandise we deal in people would rather buy from her. A little Oriental girl, no one ever figures she's trouble, even if the stuff's not particularly Chinese, even if it's hot. You know what I mean? So tell me, Ho, how much can *Lydia* sell them for?'

Mr Ho's lips compressed into a tight line. He glanced at me. I gave him a very small, secret smile, then turned it off as I looked back to Bill. Ho's eyes flickered with confusion. He looked back to Bill, too, and said, 'The going rate at an

341

apothecary shop, if you can find these items, is forty thousand dollars.'

'Say *what*?' Bill grinned incredulously; he sat forward. 'For *one*? You've got to be shitting me.' It was a nice performance, almost exactly the same as his genuine reaction the first time he'd heard that figure, from me.

'Mr Smith,' Ho said calmly, with a condescending smile, 'do you understand what condition it is that this item will cure?'

'Yeah. She told me.' He pointed his thumb at me and smirked.

'And do you suffer from this affliction, Mr Smith?'

'Me?' This time it was Bill's face that flushed. 'What the hell are you, nuts?'

'Precisely,' Ho smiled. 'You are quite obviously a strong and virile man. And were you to lose those qualities, what would you not pay to regain them?'

'Hmmm.' Bill pulled on his cigarette again. 'I see your point. Okay,' he said. 'How many have you got?'

With what seemed to me like pride, Desmond Ho said, 'Nine.'

'Nine,' Bill echoed, with a grin. 'Nine tiger dicks, eight ladies dancing. You bet they're dancing. What's your price?'

'Thirty-five thousand apiece, if you buy all nine.'

'Bullshit, Ho.' Bill squashed the cigarette into the ashtray by his side. I found myself thinking that, unhealthy habit or not, a cigarette was certainly a useful prop. 'Five thousand profit on each isn't worth my time to sit here with you.'

'A forty-five-thousand-dollar profit, easily realized . . .'

'Not that easily, if I'm going to keep the price up. If this is such a great deal, Ho, why are these things still on the market? Why haven't they been snapped up already?'

'I have only just returned to New York,' Ho answered smoothly. 'My goods will be – snapped up? – as soon as it is known they are available. But you can understand that not many entrepreneurs have the ability to buy my entire supply, as you are offering to do. It would be a tempting offer, if the price were right.'

'It's as right as it's going to get. I wouldn't want to flood the market, so I'm going to have to sit on most of them for a while – hey, you suppose that would do anything for me, or you actually have to eat it?' He turned to me with a smarmy grin. I scowled. He went on. 'Anyway, Ho, that means my money's tied up, so that brings the price down. Fifteen thousand.'

'Don't insult me.'

'Bill,' I started, but he didn't let me finish.

'Fifteen, Ho. That's a cool $135,000, in good American cash. Take it and run.'

'That will barely cover my expenses,' Ho objected, 'much less compensate me for the risks I've taken in obtaining these items, and bringing them into this country.'

Meaning, I thought, bribing and poaching and smuggling.

'Not my problem,' said Bill.

'Thirty.'

Bill stood. 'Christ, Ho, you're crazy. No, *I* must be crazy, sitting here dickering over a bunch of dicks. Come on, Lydia, let's go.'

I stayed where I was and turned to Mr Ho. 'I apologize,' I said. 'My partner doesn't understand the opportunity here. Mr Ho, what is your best price?'

'Thirty thousand dollars.'

Without a change in my posture or my expression, I switched to Chinese, and said, 'And if you were to sell them to me and cut him out entirely?'

Bill's eyes flicked suspiciously from me to Ho. I gave Bill a quick wink as Ho responded in Chinese, 'I don't understand.'

'This could be *my* opportunity,' I said. 'I've been trying to end this partnership for a long time. You see how he treats me. I'll give you twenty-five thousand dollars apiece.'

'What are you doing?' Bill demanded, frowning.

'I'm negotiating,' I replied patiently in English. 'I had the sense that Mr Ho would feel more comfortable conducting business in Chinese.'

I smiled at Ho, who said, 'Yes, that's true. My English is weak, you see.' He smiled at Bill, a smile about as genuine as mine at him.

To me, again in Chinese, he said, 'Do you have that kind of capital?'

'I can get it. And I can turn your goods over more rapidly than he thinks, because I have connections he hasn't bothered to pay attention to in Chinese communities beyond New York. He thinks he's so smart.' I smiled prettily in Bill's direction. Then I leaned a little closer to Ho, so that my jade on its filigree chain pointed straight down to the sofa. 'This may,' I told Mr Ho, 'be an excellent chance for both of us.'

Mr Ho once again stared in the general vicinity of my jade. Don't get too carried away, Lydia, he probably just deals in hot jade too, I told myself as I waited for him to speak.

He lifted his bulgy eyes to mine and smiled. 'Twenty-eight,' he said.

Giving him my most deep and meaningful look, I responded, 'Twenty-five, and if I can sell them for more than forty each, half the additional profit.'

'Very well,' he said. 'I accept your offer.'

'Good.' I smiled back, sat up straighter. 'Now, just agree with whatever I tell Bill. I'll be in touch with you later.' I switched the smile to Bill, who was standing there, glowering. 'I've offered Mr Ho eighteen thousand dollars each, in cash,' I told him in English. 'He's agreed to think about it. We'll speak tomorrow.'

'Yeah?' Bill asked suspiciously.

I stood. 'Yes. Thank you, Mr Ho. We'll be in touch.' I extended my hand for him to shake. He took it in both his soft, clammy ones and squeezed. I smiled through the crawling of my skin.

Bill took my arm in a proprietary, caveman sort of way, and said, 'So long, Ho. Pleasure doing business with you.'

'Yes,' Mr Ho said, smiling at him. 'A pleasure indeed.'

He stood in the doorway of his hotel room and watched us go.

'Golly,' I said to Bill, as we rode the vermilion elevator down to the lobby, 'that was positively painful.'

'Uh-huh,' Bill agreed. 'He was a pretty sleazy bastard.'

'No, *you*. I didn't know you had that much crudeness in you.'

'Ah. Well, that's because my normal daily behavior is so entirely refined and elegant—'

'It's because I thought I'd seen you at your crudest any number of times. I didn't know there was any more.'

'You underestimate the red-blooded American male.'

'I didn't think that was possible, but I guess I do.'

'What did you really offer him in your native tongue?'

I scowled up at him as he leered down at me. 'You see, that's what I mean.

Anyway, all I offered him was money. Twenty-five, half the profit above forty, and we cut you out.'

'And he bought that?'

'He thinks I'm trying to ditch you. Why would anyone find that hard to believe?'

The next morning I took myself back to Jiong Mao, to meet with my client, Shun Shang-Xian.

Bill and I, after leaving the Holiday Inn the night before, had sat down together over steamed shu mai at the Excellent Dumpling House to talk over a few things. Mr Shun had been foremost among them. Through the briny taste of shrimp and the gamy aroma of minced pork, we had mused over aspects of this case that had only clarified themselves as things had gone on, and we'd discussed reconciling the client's desires with the requirements of the law.

'I'm not sure it can be done,' Bill had said.

'No, maybe not,' I'd agreed regretfully, 'but it seems to me it's clear what our choice has to be. After all, Mr Shun did come to us.'

'If you're sure.'

'Well, one thing, anyway – if we're wrong it won't work, and no harm done.'

'No harm, except the possibility—'

'Oh, please, don't tell me again that it could be dangerous. You're so boring.' I stifled a theatrical yawn.

'I thought I was crude.'

'*And* boring. It's kind of amazing, really. Not many people can manage that.'

'And not many people can yawn and eat at the same time.'

'I can eat through anything. You know that.'

'Uh-huh. Though why it's not crude to yawn with a half-chewed shrimp dumpling in your elegant little mouth I'll never know.'

'It would be,' I said, 'if you did it.'

At Jiong Mao, the morning sun flowed through the shop's front window, joining the fluorescent lights in sparkling off tile and glass and shrink-wrap. Mr Shun's smile beamed as brightly as either as he ushered me into his office in the back.

'You work so quickly, Miss Chin,' he said admiringly, as he poured me tea. It was the same tea as we'd had yesterday, the sweet-scented jasmine.

'A job's profitability is increased as the time it takes to finish it can be kept to a minimum,' I said, quoting something I'd read in a start-your-own-small-investigations-firm book once, to impress him with my business acumen.

'Yes, that's quite true,' he agreed. 'Please, proceed. I'm eager for your report.'

'I met the subject in question,' I told him, settling my tea cup on its little saucer. 'His name is Desmond Ho.'

Mr Shun's brow furrowed. 'That is not a name I know.'

'Well, most probably it's not his real one. He's a balding, round sort of man.' I described Mr Ho to Mr Shun.

When I was finished, he shook his head. 'I was hoping to be able to know, from your report, whether this is a man with whom I have a connection,' he said. 'But I find I cannot tell.'

'Well, we did think of that,' I reminded him. 'That's why we made the second part of the plan.'

'Yes, indeed. And you are prepared to carry it through?'

'Absolutely. I think it can be tonight.'

'So soon?'

'The profitability ...' I began with a smile.

'Ah, yes.' He answered my smile with his own. 'Very well. Can you tell me how it is to be arranged?'

'I'll have Mr Ho come to me, with his goods, ready to make my purchase, as you suggested. This will happen at a place I've picked out. I'll come up with a plausible excuse not to go back to his hotel, based on the conversation I had with him last night. The video equipment will be set up in the place he comes to, and the whole transaction taped. Of course, I'll have to come up with another plausible excuse not to actually make the purchase, since I won't have all that money.'

He smiled at me, and I at him.

I went on, 'If, after you view the tape, you find you know him, my job is over; you'll deal with it. If you don't, I'll turn the tape over the authorities and they'll pursue Desmond Ho.'

'Very good.' Mr Shun nodded. 'Now, Miss Chin, I must ask you what may be a fairly delicate question. First, let me compliment you on your excellent work so far. You are quite a lesson to those – not including myself in their number – who might be skeptical of the ability of a petite woman such as yourself to accomplish such tasks.'

'Thank you,' I said, trying to accept the remark at face value, and not get involved with those in whose number Mr Shun did not include himself.

'But this place you have chosen, Miss Chin – I do not wish to offend you, and you are, of course, the professional in these matters – but you are certain you will be safe? For Desmond Ho, or whoever this man really is, to feel secure in this exchange, the place must be, I think, more isolated and therefore dangerous for you than I am comfortable with. Because you are there at my behest, you understand.'

'I do understand Mr Shun,' I said, attempting not to bristle. 'But, please, don't worry. I'll be fine.'

'It is a place you know well?'

'Yes. The basement of a tea shop my mother's cousin owns on Mott Street. It's often used as a meeting room for his village association. I'll tell Mr Ho to come in through the entrance on the alley – there's another exit into a rear courtyard. My cousins and I used to play there as children. I know it very well.'

'And it is secure?'

'Well secure – I mean, it's a basement in Chinatown. I don't even remember whether the door locks from the inside. But truly, Mr Shun, I don't believe I'll be in any danger from Desmond Ho.'

'Quite probably not. But to be over-cautious takes little time, and is usually an excellent investment. Tonight, you say?'

'Yes. I'm going to try to get him to meet me just after dark. If it all works out I'll call you as soon as he's gone.'

Shun Shang Xian and I finished our tea and bade each other good day. He saw me to the door and back out into his bright, spotless shop. In our entire conversation, I never once mentioned Bill. There were many good reasons for that.

The basement of cousin Paul Tsang's shop was indeed the place; tonight was indeed the time. I dropped by the shop after I left Jiong Mao Pharmacy, to pick up the keys; I called Desmond Ho, to set the hour; I stopped by my office to pick up the video equipment. Then I went to Bill's.

'Everything's all organized?' he asked from the top of the second flight of stairs after buzzing me in the street door. He came down and met me on the landing, where he took the aluminum case with the two cameras from me. No one but Bill lives in this building, a three-story brick anachronism in a concrete-and-steel warehouse district. The building is owned by a friend of his who runs the bar-and-grill on the ground floor and has his office and storerooms on the second. Bill does a lot of repairs on the building in exchange for cheap rent in the third-floor apartment, where he built the walls and put in the plumbing and windows and things himself.

All of which is to say he's a useful guy to have around when you need to install hidden video equipment in your cousin's basement.

'Yes,' I told him. 'Everyone's set up. I can carry that.'

'No doubt, but think how useless I'd feel. How'd you explain it to Ho, that you didn't want to come to his hotel?'

'I said you didn't trust me after that little Chinese-language episode, and you might be having both me and his hotel watched. I promised I could slip your tail but that we wouldn't be safe at the hotel.'

'He believed that?' he asked, looking wounded, as he held open the door at the top of the stairs for me. 'That I would do that to my own partner?'

'Think of it as a tribute to your acting ability.'

'Hmm,' he said. 'Okay. And your willingness to double-cross me? What's that a tribute to?'

'My acting ability. Are you ready to go down to the tea shop?'

'Now *that's* a euphemism if I ever heard one. What are you really asking?'

'If you're ready to go down to the tea shop.'

'Oh. Well, if that's your best offer . . .'

'It is. I guarantee it.'

So, gathering up a few things, down to the tea shop we went.

Cousin Paul's basement was vinyl-tiled and fluorescent-lighted, with half a dozen card tables and their associated folding chairs scattered across the floor, a big-screen TV at one end, and a primitive but adequately functional bar at the other, where the water came through the wall from the equally primitive bathroom. The men of Cousin Paul's village association were deeply interested in fan-tan, mah-jongg, horse-racing, and drink. But they weren't meeting tonight, and Cousin Paul had been not at all averse to the small pile of Mr Shun's dollars I'd offered him for the use of his space.

The convenient thing about this location for what Bill and I had in mind, besides its isolation and easy access, was the fact that, large-screen TV aside, it was still a basement. That meant that back in the corners and above the hanging fluorescents were gloomy shadows where hot-water heaters and electric fuse-boxes and pipes and ceiling beams were waiting for you to attach video cameras and tape recorders that no one would ever notice.

So we did.

Bill told me what to do with the screwdrivers and clamps and things for the camera mounts, and I figured out for myself about the duct tape for the wires.

'Why do they call this duct tape?' I asked, ripping a length of the shiny, silver, sticky stuff with my teeth and pressing it on the back of a pipe in the corner to hold a microphone. I'd be wearing a mike myself, but when dealing with technology it's always important to have back-up.

'Are you asking that because you really need me to tell you, or because you're nervous and want to hear yourself talk?' Bill spoke from the top of a card table, where he was fixing the angle of a camera he'd clamped to part of the sprinkler system.

'Does the answer have to do with taping ducts?'

'Yes.'

'Then forget it. And I'm not nervous.'

'Yet.'

'All right, wise guy, yet. So what?'

So nothing, apparently, because he didn't say a word, although in the shadows of the ceiling I caught him grinning.

We finished our work, and ran a test of the equipment, sitting at different tables and reciting nonsense poetry to each other in quiet voices to see if our sounds and images were registering. He made me laugh more than I made him smile, but that was probably because he wasn't sophisticated enough to pick up on the subtle nature of the Chinese poetry I was reciting. Or else maybe I was starting to get nervous, and my giggles were the result of that, and my partner wasn't funny at all.

'Probably true,' he said when I proposed that as a theory. 'You, on the other hand, are a riot. Especially with your garage-mechanic jumpsuit and that adorable little grimy smudge on your nose. Mr Ho's going to find that very cute.'

'Mr Ho will never see it. I've thought of everything.'

Standing with a flourish, I unzipped my jumpsuit and shrugged it from my shoulders. I was revealed in all my glory in a pair of black slacks, a deep green, loose-fitting, corduroy blouse, and my white jade dangling from its delicate golden chain.

I stepped out of the jumpsuit. Leaving it on the floor, I picked up some things and walked calmly to the little bathroom, grinning at Bill's expostulation, 'Hey! You can't just *do* that to a guy!' I washed my face, combed my hair, applied some strategic make-up – something I don't normally use, but extraordinary times call for extraordinary measures – and reappeared.

'Now,' I said, slipping into the soft wool jacket that went with the slacks and pointing to the jumpsuit, 'I'm all clean and shiny, and Mr Ho may be here any minute, so you'd better pack that up and disappear with it. If he sees you the jig will be totally up.'

'Well,' Bill sighed, gathering my jumpsuit into his arms, 'at least I'll have this for a memento. I'll hold it close to my heart, breathe deeply its sweet scent, so reminiscent of you ...' Face buried in the cloth, he inhaled, then raised his head. 'Yum. Heavy perspiration becomes you.'

'You know what?' I asked, as he walked away. 'You may not have heard this before, but you're disgusting.'

I sat and waited for Desmond Ho. I had a little time before he was scheduled to show – I like to be early whenever possible – so I clicked on the wide-screen TV and used the ergonomically molded remote to flip through the channels, looking for anything that was worth watching at that size. I had just settled on one of the cable-channel Cantonese soap operas my mother's so fond of when I heard a knock at the door at the top of the stairs.

Instantly adrenaline surged through my veins and set my heart hammering. Calm down, Lydia, I demanded of myself as I rose to answer the door. You're Lydia Ice-water Chin, famous for never once in your life losing your cool. Just please try to remember that. Telling myself all that took me up the stairs leading to the alleyway, where, heart still pounding exactly as before, I opened the door to see the supercilious smile on the face of Desmond Ho.

'Good evening, Miss Chin,' he said smoothly, as though it were perfectly normal for a businessman from Hong Kong to be standing at a basement door in an alley in Chinatown late at night with an attaché case full of merchandise at his side.

Of course, given the business he was in, it might be. I was a little surprised – though I tried not to show it as I welcomed him and led him down Cousin Paul's stairs – at the small size of the attaché case. Could it possibly hold all nine of the items we'd talked about? Of course, he might have the same reaction to Bill's emptied-out briefcase, now full of money, although a great deal of value can be compressed into a very small area when you're talking about paper bills. It hadn't been, in this case – some real ones, some Xeroxed ones, and a lot of carefully trimmed newspaper – but it could have.

Of course, I had no intention of letting Desmond Ho get close enough to the briefcase containing the money, such as it was, to have any real idea what he was looking at. If Bill and I were right and our plan worked I wouldn't have to worry about it; if we were wrong we had Plan B, to be put into effect as needed.

'I'm pleased you're so prompt,' I told Desmond Ho in English, smiling my sweetest smile. There was no need to speak Chinese, since we were alone in the room, and it would just be one step simpler if everything on the tapes were in English. He didn't seem to have a problem with the idea; educated people in Hong Kong grow up speaking both languages anyway, just like we do in Chinatown, and there was in reality nothing weak about Desmond Ho's English.

'I could never keep a woman like you waiting, Miss Chin,' he replied, his smile growing smarmier.

I shrugged. 'Bill does it all the time. I can't tell you, Mr Ho, how thrilled I am at the prospect of this transaction of ours going well, so that I can end the partnership I have with that man. It's far outlived its useful life, believe me.'

'Oh, I do believe you, Miss Chin. Tell me, how did a woman of your obvious ... qualities ... get involved with such a crude man to begin with?'

Aha, I thought, we have it on tape for all posterity. But since Bill's personal defects weren't the point of this conversation, I just smiled perhaps a touch sadly and said, 'How do people get involved, Mr Ho? Now, may I see the merchandise?'

It was a reasonable request, and Mr Ho took it reasonably. He nodded and smiled and spun the tumblers on the case's combination lock. Then he lifted the lid and turned the case to face me.

There were nine, in three rows of three, nestled on foam the way my video cameras were when they were packed in their aluminum box. They were all pretty much the same – grayish-brown, shrivelled, smaller than I'd thought they would be, wrapped in Saran Wrap and fixed with tape. If I hadn't known what they were I might not have guessed. As it was, I barely managed to avoid giving in to the sudden rush of revulsion that turned my stomach over.

'Well,' I said weakly, pulling myself together and smiling a bright smile at Mr

Ho. I straightened up and moved just a little to the side to make sure the camera got as full a view of the goods as I did. 'Do you know, I've never actually seen one of these before.'

'Few people have,' he answered with a touch of pride. 'I had to work quite hard, and was quite lucky, to acquire so many at one time.'

'Your luck is . . . very special,' I told him, and wondered exactly where to go from here. I was just about to ask some foolish, eyelash-batting question, which I hoped would start him on a long digression into his cleverness, skill, and daring in building his unusual business, when it suddenly became unnecessary to continue this conversation at all.

With a crash the door at the top of the stairs flew open. Mr Ho and I both jumped. My chair fell over with a clang. Mr Ho grabbed for, shut, and swung his case to the floor behind him in one very fast move.

At the top of the stairs, holding what looked to me like a very large gun, stood my client, Shun Shang Xian.

'Don't move,' he said calmly, in English, closing the door behind him. Oh, good, I thought automatically over the thumping of my heart, more English for the tape.

Mr Shun started down the stairs. 'Move back, both of you. Yes, you too, Miss Chin. Away from the case,' he added, as Desmond Ho leaned to pick up his merchandise. Ho gave me a baleful stare and stepped slowly back, as I did beside him.

'You're Desmond Ho,' Mr Shun said, as he stepped forward and we stepped back. 'Your reputation precedes you.' He smiled.

'Yours does not, I'm afraid,' Mr Ho answered darkly. 'I don't believe we're acquainted.'

'No,' agreed Mr Shun. 'If we had been, perhaps this might not have been necessary. All I wanted was the chance to do business with you, but I was given to understand that previous acquaintance is your strict criterion for choosing your business partners.'

'Previous acquaintance.' Mr Ho glared at me. 'Or recommendation. Who are you, sir?'

'A simple apothecary,' my client replied, 'desiring nothing more than the opportunity to provide to his customers the best possible ingredients for their treatments and cures.'

'And you?' Ho demanded of me. 'Do you know this man?'

I shrugged. 'I'm Lydia Chin, as I told you.'

He began in an accusatory tone, 'You came to me with the personal recommendation—'

'I work for him,' I said, pointing at Mr Shun. There were some names I would just as soon keep off this tape, assuming the tape were ever to do anyone any good. 'But I didn't know, when he hired me, that he was planning this.'

'You told him about my merchandise?' Ho asked angrily.

'Me?' I said. 'No. He hired me to find you. He told me it was because he wanted to stop you from selling it.'

'Stop me?'

'I'm afraid, Miss Chin, that that wasn't quite the truth,' Mr Shun put in smoothly. 'I grew terribly excited when I heard about your goods, Mr Ho, and I was hoping for the opportunity to make them available to my clientele.'

'How did you hear?' Mr Ho was frowning deeply, as though the answer to that question were of more import than the gun pointed unwaveringly at him. I had a different opinion on the subject, but I was too far from the gun to make any impact on it. This seemed like a good time to ignore the pounding of my own heart and the adrenaline urge to take action, and listen quietly to the conversation of my elders.

However, it didn't seem that there was to be too much more of that. 'I was told,' Mr Shun said simply, and he waved the gun again as he walked forward. This was a clear signal to us to walk backward, and backward we walked, until Mr Ho and I were up against the big-screen TV and Mr Shun had his hand on the combination-locked case.

'I'm sorry about this,' Mr Shun said, 'and especially about you, Miss Chin. I had quite grown to like you, though I must tell you I find you rather indiscreet in the amount of information you are willing to share with your clients, about unlocked doors and meeting times and such. Were you to continue in this profession, I might suggest that you give some thought to that aspect of your work. Ah, well. Perhaps in your next life.' He sighed, almost believably. 'The taking of human life is always regrettable. However, the benefits that will come from the sharing of the power and potency of what you, Mr Ho, have brought here . . .' he hefted the case '. . . will balance the unfortunate—'

'Bullshit, Shun,' came a loud, smiling, steady voice from over Mr Shun's shoulder. From, in fact, the direction of Cousin Paul's primitive bathroom, whose door had just flown open with a bang. Bill stood in the doorway, revolver in two-handed combat stance, bullet-proof vest strapped over his shirt.

My own vest, of course, was smaller, lighter, more expensive, and fastened under my loose green corduroy blouse.

Shun spun around and let a shot fly in the direction of the voice. Bill dove when he saw Shun move. The bullet whined overhead and into a bottle of Cousin Paul's Scotch. Glass and liquor exploded, rained down on Bill. From a crazy angle on the floor he fired at Shun but the shot flew far wide.

By then, though, I'd yanked the .22 from the back of my slacks, leapt across the floor, and stuck the nose of my gun behind Mr Shun's ear. 'Stop it, both of you!' I yelled. 'And you,' I snarled at Desmond Ho, who cowered behind an upturned card table, 'don't move!'

Mr Shun, cold steel pressed against his skin, had the most to gain by obeying me, and he did, immediately. He stopped everything, maybe even breathing, and stood completely motionless, frozen in the position he'd been in when I'd reached him.

I slowly removed the gun from Mr Shun's hand as Bill removed himself from the floor. 'Couldn't you have waited a little longer?' I snapped sarcastically at him. 'I thought you'd fallen asleep in there.'

'Even I couldn't fall asleep in a place that foul,' he said. 'I just thought we should get as much on tape as we could. And you were doing so beautifully. Shun . . .' He grinned as he approached us and took the case from Mr Shun's hand. 'Drop those dicks.'

The next morning, as soon as the shops in Chinatown opened, I went to see Grandfather Gao.

Coming off the street from the bright, already-crowded day, I found the shop steeped in the same textured shadows, soft scents and silence I had always known there. Grandfather Gao stood behind his counter, sliding a pale powder from his brass scale into a cone of white paper. He didn't look up at the tinkling of the door's little chimes. Folding the paper shut and tying it with string, he explained its use to the thin man before him. The man nodded as Grandfather Gao spoke. He took the package, bowed and went out past me, bowing at me also.

Only then did Grandfather Gao's eyes rest on me, but I got the strong feeling he'd known I was there all along.

'Ling Wan-ju,' he said quietly. He smiled, a smile that seemed to have something in it I didn't understand. 'If what I have heard this morning is accurate,' he said, 'your case has reached a satisfactory conclusion. Will you have tea?'

I met his eyes, and nodded, and he disappeared into the rear of his shop. I sat on the carved bench and waited, looking around at the wooden drawers, the brass canisters and the porcelain jars, listening to the quiet.

Grandfather Gao re-emerged, carrying the lacquer tray with the teapot and cups. He settled himself on the chair and waited for me to pour the tea. I did. He reached for his cup, I took up mine, and in Chinese I said, 'Grandfather, you set me up.'

Grandfather Gao cupped his tea in both thin, age-spotted hands. He fixed his shining dark eyes on me, as he had so many times since I was young. I swallowed, but I met his gaze.

'No, Ling Wan-ju, I did not,' he said.

I sipped some tea – it was Silver Needles again, so costly and rare – and found it did little to ease the dryness in my throat. But I went on. 'You must have. Desmond Ho went to a great deal of trouble not to meet people he didn't want to do business with. You knew he was in town, and you knew what he was selling. Shun Shang Xian didn't. Until someone told him.'

Grandfather Gao nodded gravely. 'I set up, as you put it, Shun Shang Xian.'

'And he came to me!'

'I did not anticipate that. Although ...' and he smiled the odd smile again '... perhaps I should have. To discover the identity of a man one very much wants to meet, what more sensible approach could there be than to hire an investigator?'

I filled my head with the steam from my tea, faint with scents I thought I must know but couldn't quite place. 'But why did you do that?' I asked. 'Set him up? I mean, do things in such a complicated, roundabout way?'

'Shun Shang Xian,' said Grandfather Gao, 'is not an honest man. He cheats his customers with short weights and counterfeit ingredients. He fails to pay his suppliers, even his landlord. He has dealt, since his shop opened, in contraband goods. People needing medical assistance remain ill after consulting Shun Shang Xian, and pay for the privilege. And those whose health does improve are nevertheless ... compromised.'

'Compromised how?'

'They benefit, however innocently, from Shun Shang Xian's activities.'

Compromised karmically, that would be. I could see that this was about to become the kind of philosophy discussion I get lost in. I moved on.

'So you decided the world of Chinese medicine would be a better place without him? The way he told me he thought it would be better without Desmond Ho?'

'Do you not agree it will?'

I refused to get drawn into that one, too, although I suspected Grandfather Gao was right. 'And you set him up, told him about Desmond Ho so he'd go after the smuggled goods?'

'I told him there was such a person. A man who was not both greedy and dishonest would not have made any effort to learn more than I told him.'

I thought. 'You're saying it serves him right. That's why you didn't just tell Shun Shang Xian where to find Desmond Ho – why you set him up instead. Because you wanted him to be responsible for his own destruction.'

'Does it not, as you say, serve him right?'

'Yes. Yes, I suppose it does. But what about me and Bill? We could have been killed! What if we hadn't figured it out, that he was planning to double-cross us and steal the ... the goods?'

Grandfather Gao's look was calm. 'How did you do that?'

I blinked. 'Because it was so easy, and at the same time so complicated. I found out who Desmond Ho was with one visit to you. You're very well known in Chinatown – I thought it must have occurred to Shun Shang Xian also to come to you. That was before I knew you'd gone to *him*.'

Grandfather Gao nodded.

'And then I thought, well, all right, maybe you wouldn't tell him. But once I'd found Desmond Ho, there was a very involved plan to have him bring the goods to a secluded place where we could videotape him with them so that if Shun Shang Xian didn't turn out to know him we could turn the tape over to the authorities, but if he did he would deal with the whole situation himself, within the Chinese community – it was ridiculous!'

I took a breath, mentally congratulating myself on having found the Chinese word for 'ridiculous'. 'If Shun Shang Xian wanted a look at the man once I'd found him, why not just come with me to the Holiday Inn and stand across the street until he came out? If he really wanted a videotape, why not let me carry a hidden camera into Desmond Ho's hotel room?

'So Bill and I decided to let Shun Shang Xian's plan unfold, to see what he really intended. I chose a place I knew well, and made sure Shun Shang Xian knew exactly what we were planning and when it was supposed to happen. I'd conveniently never mentioned Bill—' A thought stopped me. 'You liked that, didn't you, Grandfather? The fact that Shun Shang Xian didn't know about Bill?'

'Yes.' Grandfather Gao placed his teacup on the lacquer tray. Automatically I poured him more tea. 'A hidden ally is a valuable thing. And I knew your white baboon would go to some lengths to keep you safe.'

I turned my mind from thoughts of the lengths Bill would go to for me, and asked, 'And you thought I'd need to be kept safe?'

'When you came to me, Ling Wan-ju, I saw what Shun Shang Xian had done, and suspected something of what he was planning.'

'You suspected? You could have warned me!'

'Yes. Yes, I could have. I also could have alerted the authorities to Desmond Ho's activities, but I did not.'

'If you had, you wouldn't have gotten Shun Shang Xian,' I pointed out.

'That is correct. Shun Shang Xian's downfall, just as Desmond Ho's, is a product of his own nature. For each, this is the next step on the path he himself chose.'

I felt my eyebrows knit together. 'Grandfather, are you trying to tell me something?'

He smiled again, and I suddenly realized what the strange element was that I'd seen in his smile: it was pride.

'You have chosen your path, Chin Ling Wan-ju,' he said to me, using my full name, something I'd rarely heard him do. 'It is a path many who love you disapprove of, because they fear for you. But it is yours. Yes, I suppose this outcome might have been different, much worse for you. But worse yet, if I steer you from your path.'

In the soft quiet of Grandfather Gao's ancient shop, I opened my mouth to speak. You could have warned me anyway, I was going to say. I mean, getting killed would knock me right off this path, don't you think? But I could almost hear voices a long way off, behind the hush; almost see shapes, moving like the smoke that rises from incense, in the shadows. When I listened harder, when I looked deeper, of course, there was nothing there; but I was here, and Grandfather Gao was here. And Bill was waiting for me in his apartment at the top of the stairs, waiting to hear what I had to say. And Grandfather Gao was serving me Silver Needles tea. I poured the last of the pot, just enough for another cup for each of us, and we finished our tea in silence.

THE POSTER BOY

Stephen Solomita

One

'Owen?'

Detective Owen Pitt, from his seat behind a small rectangular table, nodded to the fat cop, Sergeant Gregory Baiul, who stood in the doorway.

'Your shyster's here.'

Pitt drew a long breath through his nose. He reminded himself, as he'd been doing all afternoon and well into the evening, that they wanted him angry enough to make a mistake, say something he'd regret. 'I didn't ask for a lawyer.'

'He's from the DBA.' Baiul raised broad, heavy shoulders. His mouth curled into an apologetic smile. 'He comes with the package.'

The DBA was the Detective's Benevolent Association and Baiul was right, the attorney came free of charge. The only problem, as Pitt well knew, was that you could never be sure who a union lawyer represented, you or the people who paid the bill. 'How long?' Pitt finally asked Baiul. 'Until I give my statement? I've been here for six goddamned hours.' His voice, despite the profanity, was rock-solid, a quality he noted with satisfaction.

'Owen, you can take off whenever you want. I already told you this. You can take off, come back tomorrow morning.' Baiul was a short, middle-aged man. At least forty pounds overweight, his cheeks, jowls and chins had long ago merged to form a soft shifting circle. When he smiled, he showed parallel rows of small teeth and a tongue coated with yellow film. 'Like I already said, we gotta interview the witnesses, collect evidence before we talk to you. Otherwise, how do we know what questions to ask?'

Pitt shifted on the plastic chair. He ran his fingers across his forehead, glanced at the one-way mirror on the far side of the room, finally said, 'Tell the lawyer I don't want him.' They were in a basement interrogation room, in Pitt's home precinct, the 77. Pitt had been in this particular room many, many times. Only then he'd been sitting with his back to the one-way mirror, not in the hump seat, staring at his own reflection, knowing somebody was out there, looking in.

'It'd be good,' Baiul said, 'if you told him yourself. So it doesn't look as if you're getting the third degree.' His laugh was unexpectedly thin, a sharp, birdlike chirp that filled the small room.

Pitt watched Baiul step back through the door, hold it open until the lawyer walked inside. The lawyer had his hand extended, palm open. 'Detective Pitt? May I call you Owen? My name is Sam O'Neill.' He waited only long enough to grab Pitt's hand, give it a quick shake, before continuing, 'You talk to anybody yet?'

'I don't want you.' Pitt looked down at the table top. It was covered with graffiti, gang tags, screams of pitiful defiance: BURN ALL PIGS. 'I can't talk to you.'

O'Neill dropped his briefcase on the table. 'Don't worry, Owen. We're not being recorded. They know better than to violate attorney–client privilege.'

'It's not about that.'

'Then what's it about?' The lawyer scratched his ear, looked at his fingertip as if for an answer. 'Because I'm telling you this for the record, Owen. They won't hesitate to use whatever you say against you.'

Pitt took a cigarette from a pack of Marlboros lying on the table, lit it up. He'd begun rationing his cigarettes a few hours earlier when it became apparent that the team was going to sweat him. Now it was equally apparent that he'd be in an advanced state of withdrawal before the night was done. 'If I talk to you I'm dead in the job,' he said. 'I'll be lucky if they don't bust me back to patrol.' He hesitated, finally added, 'And that's just for talking to you.'

'Better to walk a beat than find yourself dismissed. Or worse.' When Pitt didn't respond, O'Neill said, 'Every suspect hopes he can talk his way out of trouble. Reality doesn't sink in until it's too late to fix things.'

'The shooting was righteous.' Pitt dragged on the cigarette, fought to control his rising temper, fought to control an urge to lay everything out for somebody. 'Why should I have to pay for doing my job? The way I learned it, when I was a kid, you did everything right you didn't get spanked.'

O'Neill stood, picked up his briefcase. 'First I had to fight my way past the demonstrators. Then I had to fight my way past the reporters. Then, after I got inside, I had to fight my way past the brass. You *comprende*? There's a whole bunch of winds blowing out there and one of them's gonna pick you up, carry you along. Maybe it'll be the wind called hero cop. Maybe it'll be the one called fuck-up. And maybe it'll be a little breeze that answers to the name of indictable offense.' He walked to the door, glanced at his watch. 'What you oughta do here is keep your mouth shut until you find out exactly what's coming down.'

'I can't.' Pitt refused to look at the lawyer. Instead, he smiled down at his hands. 'But,' he said, his voice almost wistful, 'there's something you can do for me.'

'And what's that, Owen?'

'You smoke?'

'Cigarettes?'

'Yeah, cigarettes.'

O'Neill took a pack of Merits from his shirt pocket. 'They won't give you cigarettes? I don't believe it.'

'It's not that.' Pitt reached for the lawyer's pack. He flicked the top open, saw that it was almost full. 'See, what they want is for me to ask for something. They want me to feel dependent.'

'Is that the way you played it?' O'Neill asked. 'When you questioned a suspect?'

Pitt cleared his throat, wiped the sweat from his forehead. It was very hot in the small room, the air wet enough to grow mushrooms. 'Yeah,' he answered, without looking up. 'I was the good cop.'

Two

'Doesn't look much like the Poster Boy now, does he?'

Baiul ignored the comment. He continued to watch Owen Pitt through the hall window. Pitt was out of his chair, pacing the length of the room. His jacket was lying on the table, his tie on top of the jacket; his shirtsleeves were rolled to his elbows.

'You don't find that amusing?'

Inspector Moses Trager was the ranking officer on the shooting team, but he had no hold on Gregory Baiul. Baiul was Internal Affairs, had been recruited out of the academy. The way he'd come to understand it over the years, Internal Affairs was its own world and nobody wanted to fuck with it. That especially included Trager, who worked out of Borough Command and was looking to advance. Internal Affairs had a file on Trager, a thin file, true, but a file Gregory Baiul had read and copied two days after Trager was assigned to the team.

'Not especially.'

Baiul felt sorry for Pitt. The power of the gun and badge had deserted him, as he'd always known it could; the nightmare had become reality. One of the advantages of working IAD was the near certainty that it could never happen to you.

Pitt kept glancing into the mirror on his side of the wall between them. He was extremely handsome, his broad features matching perfectly, as if they'd been arranged by an editor at GQ. Baiul could see, dimly, his own reflection in the glass before him, but he didn't flinch at the contrast. He liked himself and he liked his job, the challenge of it, the fact that thirty-eight thousand cops despised and feared him.

'You think he's ready?' Trager asked.

Baiul looked down at the witness statements in his hand. He'd been through each of them, had committed every salient fact to memory, had conferred with the ME and the lieutenant who ran the Crime Scene Unit. 'Yeah, he's ready,' Baiul finally said. 'I'll go up for the coffee and donuts.'

Three

When Moses Trager walked into the room without knocking, Owen Pitt experienced a moment of near panic. Though he'd been steeling himself against this moment for nearly six hours, his heart began to pound against his ribs and his rushing blood made a sound in his ears like wind-driven sand against a pane of glass.

'Hey, Owen, I brought you some coffee and something to eat.' Baiul held up the Dunkin Donuts box for Pitt's inspection. He could see that the kid was terrified and he again felt momentary compassion. 'They told me in the squad room that you take your coffee straight up. That right?'

Baiul set the box, a large container of coffee and his briefcase on the table. He opened the box and poked around for a moment before selecting a glazed donut. 'Haven't eaten all day,' he announced, before biting down. 'Busy, busy, busy.'

The ensuing quiet hung over Pitt like the bowl of jello his ex-wife had once tossed in his face. He told himself, as he'd done so many times when he was the interrogator, not to speak first. Baiul wanted him to fear the silence, to show weakness, eventually say something stupid.

'All right.' Baiul swallowed the last bit of his donut. He wiped his fingers on a paper napkin, dropped the napkin on the floor. There was no waste basket in the room, just the table and the three chairs. The floor was brown, the walls a soupy green and covered with graffiti. A single fluorescent light suspended from a pair of chains buzzed relentlessly. 'This is Inspector Trager. He's the ranking officer on the shooting team.' He waited for Trager and Pitt to trade nods, then said, 'We want to know what happened, Owen. That's all there is to it. For the record.'

'You already know what happened.' Pitt was sorry for the words before they were out of his mouth. Nevertheless, aware of a growing recklessness as the fear receded, he continued. 'Being as you've just finished questioning five eye witnesses.'

Baiul opened Pitt's coffee and pushed it closer. He started to speak, but Trager beat him to the punch. 'Hey, hump,' Trager said, 'whatta you think, you get to keep it a secret?'

When Pitt didn't respond, Baiul took a cassette recorder from his briefcase and laid it on the table. 'We'll be video taping from out in the hallway.' He jerked a thumb at the mirror behind him. 'Once I turn on the tape, everything said in this room is on the record. Though you're not a suspect in the commission of a crime, it's my obligation to inform you that anything you say could be used in court against you.'

Pitt reached for his coffee, then realized that his fingers were trembling and he was almost certain to spill it. He stopped with his fingers just grazing the styrofoam cup, wondered if he had only two options: defiance or fear. Like a light bulb has only on or off. 'Would it be all right,' he asked, 'if I made my own tape? If I take it with me when I go?'

'Sure,' Baiul said before Trager could open his mouth. Trager had spent his entire career in Patrol and the art of the interview was as foreign to him as the language of Tibet. 'You have it here?'

'No, it's in my locker.' Pitt looked directly at Trager for a moment, looked into a pair of blank, dark eyes. Pitt had seen eyes like Trager's before, eyes that lacked even the faintest spark of life. The worst of the mutts had that look, the most dangerous, the most cruel.

Baiul cleared his throat, then said, 'Why don't I find somebody to go get it?' He didn't want to leave Pitt alone with Trager, didn't want Trager to drive Pitt away. With a little luck, he'd break the kid by midnight, maybe get home before Louise fell asleep. In fact, he was counting on it.

'I'm gonna get it myself,' Pitt said. 'I gotta take a leak anyway.'

Four

After the quiet of the interrogation room, the mid-evening chaos of the squad room two floors above was nearly overwhelming to Pitt, yet at the same time so beautiful that he wanted to stop where he was and literally take root. The furtive stares of the other cops in the room didn't affect him one way or the other. In a way, he felt that he'd moved beyond them.

Pitt maintained a steady, unhurried pace as he walked between two rows of battered desks toward his own desk at the far end of the room. Though his squad had clocked out long ago, he knew the other detectives well enough. He was sure they supported him, just as sure they wouldn't show it, that if he turned to catch their eyes he'd find an almost primal fear.

Still, after reaching his desk, retrieving the tape recorder and several spare cassettes, Pitt found that he wanted to linger, to sit down, maybe comb the files, make a few phone calls. The urge, even as he turned away, brought a smile to his face. Not the halogen smile he remembered flashing at Sandra Fink, but a genuine smile nonetheless.

The smile carried Pitt into a blessedly empty washroom. As he urinated, carefully washed his hands and face, he began to settle into something approaching his old, confident self. He'd established, he believed, a small measure of independence by demanding to fetch the tape recorder. Baiul's quick assent when he might have taken a stand had acknowledged the heart of that message: if pushed too hard, Detective Pitt would take his story and go home.

Pitt dried his face with a handful of paper towels, then wadded the towels and tossed them in the general direction of an overflowing waste barrel fifteen feet away. He took a comb from his pocket and began to work it through his hair, wondering how Trager would take it if he waltzed back inside the room minus the black stubble that covered his cheeks and throat. Trager was a kind of cop who'd order an execution if he thought it was good for the job. Order an execution or cover one up – it would be all the same to him.

The door opened at that moment and two uniformed cops Pitt barely recognized stepped into the washroom. They hesitated when they saw him, then walked directly to the urinals. As they came by, they nodded. Pitt returned the nods, wondered briefly if the greeting was meant to show support. On impulse, he asked them, 'What's it like out there?'

The shorter of the two uniforms, a blocky Latino, said, 'Reporters up the ass.'

The other uniform said, 'Enough chiefs to open a fucking casino,' then laughed at his own joke before adding, 'The reverends are gathering.'

Pitt scooped up the recorder and the spare cassettes, thinking how stupid the question was. He told himself that he had to narrow his focus, that it was mandatory, that worrying about events beyond his control would get him exactly nowhere. Still, as he left the washroom, he glanced back at the water-stained sinks, the open stalls and gray damp ceiling, and again felt a wistful desire to return to his familiar place. This time the urge brought with it, instead of a smile, a feeling which, after a moment's consideration, he labelled regret.

But regret for what? For himself, for what was happening to him? Or for what he'd done, for Odel Faulkner? Self-pity or remorse?

God, how I wish, Pitt told himself as he descended into the basement as the heat climbed the stairs to embrace him, that I'd shot a white kid.

Five

Pitt stopped outside the interrogation room to light a cigarette. Next to him, a technician, perhaps a cop, stood with his left hand resting on a video camera. The camera was mounted on a heavy tripod, its lens focused directly on the chair Pitt would soon occupy. Inside the room, Baiul sat with his hands spread over his enormous gut. He was listening to Trager go on about a Hong Kong tailor, an immigrant who worked out of Chinatown.

'I try on the uniform,' Trager explained, 'and it's so tight I feel like the toothpaste in a tube. The moron slant-eyes – I swear to Christ, Baiul, he didn't come up to my waist – he tells me, "You get fat, you get fat. It no my fault." Meanwhile, I haven't gained two pounds since I came out of the academy.' Trager slapped his belly for emphasis, once, twice. Finally, he said, 'The fuckin' hump.'

Pitt pulled on his cigarette, blew the smoke out in a slow stream that piled up against the window. He waited a moment, expecting a punch-line from Trager, but Trager settled back in his chair and lapsed into silence.

'No time like the present,' Pitt told the technician as he started toward the door.

The technician said, 'I can't talk to you.' As if Pitt's comment had called for a response.

When Pitt came through the door, Baiul didn't move until the detective was seated. Then he leaned forward, drew a deep breath, said, 'You ready, Owen?'

Pitt looked over at Trager, decided that he'd better be ready, that maybe his small measure of independence was smaller than he'd thought. Still, he took another moment to pop the lid of the styrofoam cup, take a sip of lukewarm coffee. His fingers no longer trembled and he no longer felt either belligerent or fearful. 'Yeah, I'm ready.'

Baiul and Pitt, as if the sequence came as the direct result of a complex and difficult negotiation, started their tape recorders at almost exactly the same moment. Baiul, apparently oblivious, began to label the tape, reciting the day, date, time, case number, and the names of the individuals present. Pitt, the sweat starting on his scalp, glanced at the mirror and wondered if the video was rolling, if the technician was peering into the viewfinder, adjusting the focus. He was hoping the movie was an adventure film, the kind where the hero escapes at the last minute. Instead of a snuff film, the kind where the star never clears the studio parking lot.

'Owen?' Baiul waited for Pitt's full attention. When he was sure he had it, sure the kid wouldn't float off the chair, he said, 'All right, for the record, you are not, at present, a suspect in a crime, but you have a contractual right to have an attorney present for this interview. Do you understand that?'

'Yes.'

'In fact, you've already consulted an attorney. Isn't that right?'

Baiul flicked the question out, a probing jab that found its mark. Pitt fought off the urge to flinch, to lower his eyes. 'I spoke to a DBA attorney, whose name I can't even remember, long enough to tell him that I didn't need him.' His voice, in his own ears, seemed steady enough.

'Whatever you told him is okay with me, Owen.'

Baiul's white shirt, stretched over his soft chest and belly, was gray with sweat. Tufts of dark hair poked from between the top buttons like weeds in a walkway. Pitt, sitting to Baiul's left, wondered if the effect was deliberate, if maybe Baiul had watched too many Columbo movies.

'And you're waiving your contractual right to have an attorney present for this interview. Correct?'

'I'm waiving my right to an attorney. Right.'

Baiul took a lemon-filled donut from the box on the table. 'Why don't you just tell us what happened? In your own words.' He bit into the donut, found the filling especially tart and closed his eyes for a moment in appreciation.

Pitt shifted in the chair. The buzz of the overhead light seemed louder to him, more insistent.

'It was almost noon and I was in the lobby of the 77, talking to Sergeant Gomez who was manning the desk, when a woman came into the precinct and identified herself as a social worker from the Child Welfare Agency named Sandra Fink. She told Sergeant Gomez that she had a court order to remove several children from an apartment about ten blocks from the house and she was requesting a police escort. It just happened that the house was busy and there were no uniformed officers available, so I volunteered.

'I didn't think too much about it at the time because the request was routine and I'd escorted social workers in similar circumstances a number of times when I worked in Patrol.'

Pitt stopped abruptly. He was beginning to sound apprehensive, he realized, a definite mistake. Baiul would sense weakness, would pounce on it like a house cat on a songbird. The important thing here was to get his version out, defend as much of it as he could – not fight off attacks that hadn't taken place. That might never take place.

Six

'We proceeded to the Faulkner residence,' Pitt continued, 'where I knocked on the door and identified myself as a police officer. A black female opened the door and identified herself as Mary Faulkner. Ms Fink, who was known to Ms Faulkner, handed the court order to Ms Faulkner and said, 'We've come for the children, Mary.'

Pitt stopped long enough for another drink of coffee. It seemed to him that Baiul was entirely occupied with the donut in his hand. Dots of powdered sugar hung on Baiul's flushed jowls like dust on a hot iron. As Pitt watched, Baiul's tongue flicked out, caught a tiny drop of lemon filling, then withdrew.

It was an act, of course. Baiul's indifference. Pitt had played a similar game many times in the past. Let the mutts babble until they ran out of steam, then expose the cracks, drive in the wedge until the log split. The problem, for Pitt, was that Baiul knew that Pitt would recognize the game. He knew and he didn't care.

Pitt, as he began to speak, resolved to give Baiul as little to work with as possible. 'Ms Faulkner,' he told Baiul, 'led us into the living room. A white male and two children, one a toddler, were sitting on the couch. There were two plastic bags and a pile of children's clothes on the floor and Ms Faulkner proceeded to go through the clothing. Ms Fink was speaking to the children, telling them not to worry, that everything was going to be okay. At that point, a black male...'

Pitt took a deep breath, steeled himself. 'At that point,' he repeated, careful to enunciate each word clearly, 'a black male child later identified as Odel Faulkner, approximately ten years old, entered the living room from the bedroom. He had a weapon in his hand, a Glock 9mm identical to the one I carry. The child was pointing the weapon at Ms Fink. He walked to within approximately fifteen feet of my position and stopped.

'I told the child to drop the gun and immediately drew my own weapon. The child hesitated briefly, then fired at Ms Fink, and fired again. I then discharged my own weapon.

'The child dropped his weapon and fell backward onto the floor. I instructed Ms Fink to dial 911, then went to the child and began to administer CPR.

'I was still working on the child when two EMS paramedics entered the residence. They pronounced the child DOA. A few minutes after that, Lieutenant Flanagan, the precinct whip, arrived on the scene. He ordered me to return to the house, which I did. I've been here ever since.'

Seven

'That's it?' Trager demanded. 'You think that bullshit's gonna save your miserable ass?'

'Inspector,' Pitt replied without hesitation, 'what I told you is what happened.'

Trager laughed, a full-throated roar that smacked into Pitt like a shock wave, then wiped the sweat off his face with the palm of his right hand before thrusting his wet fingers in Pitt's direction. Trager had removed his jacket but not his tie, and the edge of his shirt collar, drawn tight against his bull neck, was soaked through.

Pitt said, 'I didn't pick the room.' The words were out before he could stop them.

'You're a hump,' Trager said. He wiped his hand, then his throat, with a napkin. 'And the job knows what to do with humps.'

Baiul dropped the last bit of donut into his mouth. He chewed carefully before swallowing, then licked his fingers clean before drying them on a paper napkin. He was taking his time, wondering if Pitt would come apart, maybe punch Trager's light out. He, Baiul, would give a week's pay to see it.

And it wasn't, he believed, out of the question. Pitt's statement had been full of cop-speak – *proceeded to, identified, residence, Ms Fink, Ms Faulkner.* Whereas Trager saw only evasion, Baiul saw fear in Pitt's use of these words. Pitt had pulled away. Maybe, as his career was on the line, he could be forgiven, but it was Baiul's task to give the job as many options as possible. Pitt would have to go back.

'Before Sandra Fink arrived,' Baiul said, 'you were in the lobby of the 77, that right?'

'Yeah.'

'And you were talking to Sergeant Eduardo Gomez who was working the reception desk?'

Pitt nodded, then said, 'Yes.'

'Was there anybody else in the lobby, Owen? Any other cops?'

'There were probably cops going in and out. I don't really remember.'

Baiul slapped his cupped palms lightly against his gut. 'Take a second to think about it. Was there anybody else in the lobby of the 77?'

Pitt fought an urge to close his eyes. What he remembered was that he'd been very tired and thinking about a quick meal at the Bayview Diner and a few hours' sleep before he had to get up again. 'I don't see what this has to do with the shooting,' he said, his anger rising.

After a quick glance at his watch, Baiul asked, 'So you don't remember if there were any other cops in the lobby when Sandra Fink made her appearance?'

'I don't remember. That's right.'

'What were you talking to Sergeant Gomez about?'

'I don't know. The Yankees, the weather. It was just small talk. Shooting the breeze.'

'So you don't remember if there were any other cops in the lobby or what you were talking to Sergeant Gomez about?'

Pitt started to respond, then suddenly remembered exactly what he and Eddie Gomez had been talking about when Sandy Fink walked into the precinct. On the previous day they'd attended the line-of-duty funeral of Clyde Harriman, a patrol sergeant who'd worked out of the neighboring precinct, the 71. Harriman had been killed trying to collar a robbery suspect. The doer had died as well, died at the scene, a fact that had bothered Eddie Gomez. 'The problem,' he'd explained, 'is that there's nobody to hate. Now that everybody's dead.'

'We were talking about Clyde Harriman's funeral,' Pitt said. 'We were both at his funeral.'

Baiul smiled, nodded his head. 'That's good, Owen,' he said, 'because the sooner you remember, the sooner we all go home.'

Eight

The film on Baiul's tongue was now bright yellow, stained perhaps by the lemon filling in the donut. It looked, to Pitt, like a slug he'd found crawling on a reef the last time he and Jeanie had been on vacation. They'd been great together, he and Jeanie, or so he'd thought at the time, but six months later she'd packed up the kids and moved along. 'Before I develop herpes,' she'd explained as he'd carried her suitcase to the car, dropped it into the well of the trunk. 'Or worse.'

When he'd gone after her, begged forgiveness, she'd told him, 'You'll never learn to keep it in your pants, Owen. Not for me, not for anybody.'

As Pitt raised his eyes to the ceiling over Baiul's head, he remembered that Jeanie's voice had been perfectly composed, her expression as well, and that the sudden realization that she was neither sad nor angry had reduced him to tears.

'You with us, Owen?'

Pitt wanted to answer, No, I'm against you, but he shrugged instead. He'd eventually gotten over Jeanie, but he still missed his sons every time he walked into the house.

'You worked a midnight tour yesterday? Is that what happened?' Baiul, as he pulled a well-stuffed file folder and spiral notebook from his briefcase, wondered where Pitt had gone.

'Yeah.'

'And you went off the clock at what time?' He fumbled the notebook open. 'Help me out here?'

'Around a quarter past eleven.'

'Got some overtime, did ya?'

'I got jammed at Central Booking,' he explained. 'It happens to working cops.'

Trager leaned forward. He dug his hands into his knees and said, 'What's that supposed to mean?' Then, before Pitt could respond, he added, 'You're diggin' your own grave, hump. Your own grave.'

Baiul closed his eyes for a moment. If Trager forced Pitt into a corner, if Pitt decided to run, there was nothing Gregory Baiul could do about it. He thought of Louise at home, the health aide in the brown leather chair next to her bed. The dope they gave Louise for the pain would knock her out. If he didn't get home by midnight, she wouldn't feel his kiss.

'I got it right here,' Baiul announced. He tapped the notebook with a blunt forefinger. 'Right here. You went off the clock at 11:19.'

'I said a quarter after eleven,' Pitt insisted.

'So you did. Now, after you clocked out, you went where? Right out to the lobby? You were talking to Sergeant Gomez from 11:19 until Sandra Fink came in at noon?'

'I took a shower first. And shaved.'

'Do you always shower and shave before you go home?'

'Who said I was going home?'

Baiul smiled and looked at the two donuts lying on a sheet of greasy paper in the bottom of the donut box. Instead of taking one, he pushed the box toward Pitt. 'Why don't you have something to eat? You gotta be hungry.'

'What I do on my own time is my own business.' Pitt ignored the donuts. He folded his arms across his chest and settled in the chair.

Baiul flipped through his notebook, pointed to an entry Pitt couldn't possibly read from where he sat. 'Sergeant Gomez owns a bar in Sunnyside, isn't that right? The Blue Line Bar and Grill?'

'That's right.'

'And you've moonlighted at that bar, haven't you?'

'Once in a while. As a favor.'

'You're telling me you weren't paid?'

'No, I'm not saying that.' Pitt again found himself growing defensive. Again, he fought to keep his voice firm. 'What does this have to do with Odel Faulkner?'

'Did you get approval for this job, Owen? Your contract obliges you to get permission.'

'We're talkin' about once a week. As a favor.'

Baiul shook his head. 'I make it ten shifts in the last month. And as many the month before.' He finally picked up a glazed donut and took a bite. 'I gotta say, Owen, it sound like a regular job to me. I mean, I hope you've been declaring the income on your tax returns.'

Trager pulled his chair a little closer to the table. His eyes were glittering now. To Pitt he looked actually happy when he said, 'Your own grave, hump. With your big fuckin' mouth for a shovel.'

Nine

For the following thirty minutes, Baiul questioned Owen Pitt about the nearly three-quarters of an hour between the time Pitt clocked out and the time Sandra Fink arrived with her court order. The questions Baiul asked seemed irrelevant to Pitt who nevertheless continued to respond. Pitt felt slightly ashamed, the little boy caught stealing cookies. Though he knew that moonlighting without permission was a nothing beef, he couldn't stop asking himself exactly how Baiul had found out. The most likely answer, that Baiul's surprise had come from Eddie Gomez, only raised further questions. Did Internal Affairs have an ongoing file on Gomez? Or was Gomez a plant, an IAD snitch recruited at the academy? Or, the most likely of all the possibilities, did the sharks have a file on Owen Pitt, a longstanding catalogue of venial sins ready for presentation to a review board?

Of one thing Pitt was certain. Baiul would never have exposed his leverage so early in the game if he didn't have something more potent in reserve. Any more than Pitt would have flashed his hand if their situations were reversed.

Baiul finally asked, 'Did you put on cologne or a deodorant when you came out of the shower?'

Pitt decided again to assert his independence. 'Why do you need to know that?' he asked Baiul. 'Because if I smell bad, you can just say it out loud. I won't be offended.'

Trager, to Pitt's surprise, burst out laughing, and Baiul, obviously stung, looked down at his hands. Instinctively, Pitt, though he didn't know that Baiul was Internal Affairs and that Trager both feared and hated IAD, tried to drive a wedge between them. 'I thought,' he said to Baiul, 'you told me you were part of a shooting team. Not on hygiene patrol.'

On impulse, and against his instincts, Baiul decided to leave Pitt alone with Trager. He stood and stretched. 'I'm gonna make a donut run,' he announced, as if nothing had happened. 'And while I'm gone, Owen, I want you to make up your mind. You can answer questions or go home. It's all the same to me.'

The warning, Baiul reflected as he stepped into the hall, was as much for Trager's benefit as for Pitt's. Not that Trager was smart enough to read the message. No, the message would go right over Trager's head, but Owen Pitt would understand. His fate was not in Trager's hands.

'Everything all right, John?' Baiul asked the technician as he came alongside. He could see Pitt and Trager through the window. They seemed distinctly uncomfortable together, like two virgins on a blind date.

'Fine, sarge.'

'Good. See if you rustle up a few containers of coffee and a bag of donuts. I've gotta check on something.' When the technician hesitated Baiul added, 'I'd take it as a personal favour.'

'All right.'

'Thanks. And let the video run while you're gone.' As he came up the stairs, Baiul felt the same sense of relief that Pitt had experienced a short time before. The cool air seemed to lift the matted hair on his chest. He pulled his shirt free of his clammy skin, gave his underpants a sharp tug and headed for a payphone on the far side of the room.

As he slammed a quarter into the slot, waited for a dial tone, finally punched in his home number, the lobby door opened and he could hear, faintly, the chanting of demonstrators outside the building. They seemed angry to him, though no angrier than usual, a mass of people who'd decided the facts before the facts were available.

'Hello?'

'Clara?'

'Hello, Mr Baiul. Mrs Baiul's asleep.'

Baiul looked at his watch. It was only nine o'clock. Dr Roman had taken to increasing the strength of Louise's painkillers and sleeping pills whenever she complained. As if it was somehow important that at the time of her death she be already dead.

'Well, don't wake her,' Baiul said. 'I just wanted to let you know that I expect to be home by midnight.' He was about to hang up, but decided that further explanation was necessary. 'In case she wakes up.'

Ten

Baiul went from the telephone directly to the precinct wash room. He stripped off his shirt, drew a handful of paper towels from a dispenser and walked over to a sink. For a moment he did nothing beyond stare into the mirror at his soft, sagging breasts.

Though he loved his wife dearly, had loved her all through their marriage, Baiul had come to recognize a personal fear, a weakness really, which had become more and more threatening as Louise had grown weaker and more remote. When Louise was finally gone – as she would be soon enough – he, Gregory Baiul, would spend the rest of his life alone. It wasn't just his appearance and his age, though both would undoubtedly work against him, but what he'd come to see as an underlying character flaw from which he'd been running for a very long time. Viewed in this light, his marriage was little more than a reprieve, a withdrawn promise that would surely make his fate all the harder to accept.

As Baiul soaped and rinsed his face and his throat, he turned his thoughts to Owen Pitt. The reverends would demand a sacrifice, that was certain. They always demanded a sacrifice. Even so, the job might decide to protect Owen Pitt, might even resist pressure from the Mayor's office. Forces much higher than either Sergeant Baiul or Inspector Trager would make that decision and he, Baiul, had long ago stopped trying to predict which way it would go. He'd seen truly innocent cops thrown to the mob, seen others, the guilty, folded back into the job like chicks beneath the breast of a pigeon. Personally, he hoped the dice would come up seven, that Pitt would be let off the hook.

But nobody would ask him. His job was to find out what had actually taken place and do it quickly, to give the job as much time as possible before it was forced to raise or lower its collective thumb.

When Baiul came downstairs to find the technician, John, manning his video camera in the hallway, he felt immediately buoyed. He had a job to do, a job he loved. Inside the interrogation room, Trager was repeating the story of his custom-tailored uniform for Pitt's benefit, this time adding a fillip. 'Awright, so what am I gonna do? I mean the slope's makin me a *uniform* so I know I'm not gonna scare him with the badge, right?' He thrust his fingers beneath his belt, straightened in his chair and grinned.

'Well, what I did, Owen, was call a friend at Immigration who put a squad together and paid Chung King a little visit. Turned out the gook had three illegals sewing in the back room, a violation of federal law so egregious that the INS felt compelled to pull his green card. So solly.'

Baiul looked at John who rolled his eyes and shook his head. John was Chinese; his last name was Chang. Trager knew that, of course, but was apparently too consumed with righteous indignation to care.

'You decide, Owen?' Baiul asked as he came into the room. Pitt, he noted, actually looked relieved to see him.

'Decide what?'

'If you want to answer my questions?'

'I'm still here.'

'Good.' Baiul sat down, opened the box of donuts. 'Now, why don't you tell us exactly where you were standing when Ms Fink entered the precinct?'

'I was standing at the desk, talking to Sergeant Gomez.'

'About the funeral?'

Pitt drew a breath through his nose, let it out through his mouth. 'I don't remember,' he told Baiul, 'exactly what we were talking about at the exact moment Ms Fink walked through the door.'

'Try, Owen. Take a minute to remember.' Baiul held up a cruller. He inspected it briefly before taking a bite, finally mumbled, 'If you get it right on the first go round, it'll save a lot of time.'

Pitt closed his eyes, more from fatigue than any effort to recall Sandra Fink's entrance. She'd come through the door like she owned the building, a fair, slender woman in a sleeveless blouse and a skirt made of some fabric so sheer that for just a moment, as the door swung shut, daylight from behind had rendered it virtually transparent. As she'd come closer, his eyes had traveled up to her bare arms, her shoulders and throat, her light brown hair. She had a spray of freckles that ran across her upper chest, another running along her cheekbones across the bridge of her nose. Her eyes were green, her smile, or so he'd thought at the time, mischievous and challenging.

Just as Pitt was about to speak, Baiul's tape recorder shut down with a loud pop. Pitt's followed a few seconds later and both men busied themselves with turning the cassettes and restarting the machines. Then Baiul said, 'Owen Pitt interview, tape one, side B.'

'Look,' Pitt said when he again had Baiul's full attention, 'I don't remember exactly what me and Gomez were talking about when Ms Fink arrived. For all I know, we might not have been talking about anything. We might have been having a pregnant pause.'

Baiul ignored the sarcasm. 'Tell you what, Owen,' he said very quietly, 'why don't you just take us through what happened in the precinct. This time in detail.'

Eleven

Pitt stood up, stretched and walked across the room to face the wall. He paused for a moment, wondering if Baiul or Trager would demand that he resume his seat. When they didn't, he said, 'Ms Fink approached the desk and showed Sergeant Gomez an ID card from the Child Welfare Agency.'

'You looked at this identification?' Baiul asked. 'You examined it?'

What Pitt had examined was the curve of Sandra Fink's shoulder, the flow of the muscles in her upper arm when she dropped her ID on the rail fronting Gomez's desk. Then he'd exchanged an appreciative glance with Eddie Gomez. Gomez, a notoriously sour man, had been smiling from ear to ear.

'No,' Pitt said. 'I didn't examine Ms Fink's identification, but Sergeant Gomez did. He checked it and said, "So, you're a social worker." Ms Fink then explained that she had a court order to remove some children from an apartment close by. She—'

'*Some* children,' Baiul interrupted. 'She didn't say how many?'

'Three children. She must have said three.' A movement to Baiul's left caught his attention. He turned his head slightly, saw a tiny coackroach emerge from beneath a strip of molding in the corner of the room.

'Why couldn't she have had an order to remove one of the children? Or two?' Baiul popped the last of the donut into his mouth, then took another from the box. 'Just because there were three kids in the apartment when you walked in doesn't mean they all lived there. Maybe one or two were cousins or playmates.'

Pitt resisted an urge to grind the cockroach beneath the ball of his thumb. It was so tiny that it might not even stain his skin. 'All right, I don't really remember if she said she was gonna pull three kids or two kids or one kid.'

'Well, if you're not sure,' Baiul said, neatly reversing himself, 'you should just say you're not sure.' He made a little circle in the air with his left forefinger, cocked his head. 'Instead of making things up.'

'She wanted a police escort,' Pitt said, 'in case the parent resisted. That was the point. She wanted an escort, but all the sector cars were out on jobs. Sergeant Gomez told her that she'd have to wait.'

'Did that upset her?'

'Not that I could see.' Pitt's head had begun to ache, a continuous, dull pain that seemed to echo the steady, sharp buzz of the light fixture in the ceiling. 'Anyway, though I knew it wasn't my job, I offered to go. It was an impulse. You know, just one of those things you say before you give it a lot of thought.'

He turned to look over Trager's shoulder at Baiul. Trager had his hands folded in his lap and Pitt could see the crown of his scalp through his short gray hair.

'Like I already told you, I'd done this before, escorted social workers who had to pull a kid from an abusive home. It goes real fast because the idea is to get the kids out before the parents can react. What I used to do was tell the parents that I wasn't there to arrest them, and since most of the parents had done pretty awful things to their children, they were so relieved they let the kids go without a fuss.'

Pitt stopped abruptly. He was rambling, almost babbling. If he kept on this way, it was only a matter of time until he began to beg.

'Hey,' Trager said, 'is it true they call you the Poster Boy?'

When Pitt didn't respond, Baiul, who'd been saving the nickname for later, said, 'You wanna tell us anything else about what happened in the house?'

Pitt walked back to his chair, but didn't sit down. Though he hated his nickname, he didn't visibly react to Trager's taunt. In truth, he'd been half expecting it. 'After I volunteered, Sergeant Gomez introduced me to Ms Fink. He said, "This is Detective Pitt." '

'And then?'

And then Owen Pitt had flashed Sandra Fink his best smile, his halogen-floodlight special, the smile he'd been perfecting since high school, since he'd first become aware of the fact that girls had something he wanted. Sandy Fink's green eyes and broad mouth had widened slightly, finally settling into an expression that he, Pitt, had read as an invitation. Not to jump into bed, of course, not that she was about to rip off his clothes. Her smile was an invitation to explore, an admission that the game had begun and she wanted to play.

'Sergeant Gomez wrote out the names of the parents—'

'Wait a minute,' Baiul interrupted. 'One minute you say "parent" and the next "parents". Were you aware of how many adults lived in the household? Or what their names were?'

'I don't know,' Pitt quickly responded. Then he corrected himself, 'I mean, I don't remember Ms Fink specifying the number of adults in the apartment.'

'And you don't remember her specifying the number of children either,' Baiul said. 'Isn't that right?'

'I don't remember specifically,' Pitt said. 'Ms Fink probably did state the number of children and adults in the household.'

'*Probably*,' Trager nearly shouted. 'Now that's what I call fine police work.'

Trager's booming laugh smacked into Pitt's headache like a shock wave. He looked down at his watch, saw that it was almost 9:30. Though he'd been awake for nearly thirty-six hours, he abandoned any hope of sleep. They'd been at it for more than an hour and they were still in the house.

'And what happened,' Baiul asked, 'after Sergeant Gomez took the information?'

'We left the precinct.'

'You didn't go back on the clock?'

'No.'

'You decided to donate your time to the New York Police Department? Is that the way it was? A pure act of charity?'

Pitt had been preparing himself to answer this question for the last six hours. He gripped the back of the chair, let his weight fall toward Baiul. 'Every detective I know works jobs off the clock. Maybe this was a little different, but it wasn't like I was stepping into the fourth dimension.'

Twelve

For the first time, Baiul let his voice rise. He got up and stepped toward Pitt. 'You remember telling us a few minutes ago that your personal time was none of our business?' When Pitt didn't respond, he said, 'Come on, answer the question.'

'Yeah, I remember.'

'Well, that was pure bullshit. That was a lie, wasn't it?'

'It wasn't a lie.'

'No?' Baiul took another step toward Pitt. He frowned, a small movement that nevertheless set his jowls in motion. 'You take new jobs off the clock. You work old jobs off the clock. How's that not our business?' Though he knew he cut a ridiculous figure, especially in contrast to the tall, muscular Pitt, Baiul pressed forward until Pitt took a backward step. Then he said, his voice tight, 'I'd really appreciate an answer here.'

Pitt said, 'All right, in this case it's your business.' Then he lit a cigarette with a red disposable lighter. 'I was speaking in general terms before.' He dropped the lighter into his pocket, folded his arms across his chest.

'In general terms?' Baiul, instead of resuming his seat, crossed the room to stare at his reflection in the mirror. He stayed there, unmoving, until Pitt sat down. Finally, he turned and said, 'No more evasion, Owen. Please?'

'I'm not being evasive. You're asking me for details that I just don't remember. Do you want me to make it up as I go along?'

Baiul took out his handkerchief, intending to wipe the sweat from his face, but the handkerchief was already soaked. He jammed it back into his pocket and glanced at his watch. 'Why don't you just tell us what happened next? Tell us how you got to the Faulkner apartment.'

Pitt sucked on his cigarette. He drew in the smoke as if it contained the answers he needed. 'I used a department vehicle,' he finally admitted, knowing how bad it sounded. 'The same Caprice I used the night before. It was parked in front of the house.'

'You had the keys in your pocket?'

'I took them off the board.'

'Did anybody know?' Baiul, too, resumed his seat. He willed his voice to drop to its gentlest pitch. 'Did Sergeant Gomez know?'

Pitt answered quickly. He'd already decided not to involve Eddie Gomez in anything Gomez hadn't actually seen or heard. 'I don't know,' he told Baiul. 'I didn't tell him, but he might have seen where I went. You'd have to ask Sergeant Gomez.'

'I have.' Baiul could feel the seam of his boxers work its way between his buttocks. He shifted in his seat, resisted the urge to stand. 'Did you go directly to the Faulkner residence?'

'Or did you go to a motel first?' Trager got it off before Baiul could stop him. Then he leaned back in his chair and grinned defiantly.

'We went directly to the Faulkner residence,' Pitt said. He'd been expecting the accusation, though not so soon.

'And what did you talk about on the way?'

Pitt shrugged. 'This and that,' he said. 'Small talk. I don't remember much of what we actually said.' What Pitt did remember was how the sunlight had caught Sandy Fink's light brown hair. The sun had extracted the color, drawn the color up into a soft halo. He'd said something about the air-conditioning actually working as he'd unlocked the door of the Caprice and she'd laughed, revealing strong teeth and the tip of her pink tongue. At that moment he'd been struck by the fact that her beauty, so obvious to him, sprang from inside, that her features, her nose and mouth especially, were too large, too generous. In middle age she would be considered plain.

Baiul sighed. 'Owen,' he said, his voice still gentle, 'you remember I told you that you didn't have to talk to us? You remember that?' He waited for Pitt to nod. 'So what's the point of holding back?' When Pitt didn't respond, he said, 'It's worse than not talking to us at all. Bullshitting. It's actually worse than not talking at all.'

'I—'

'Wait.' Baiul picked up a jelly donut, opened his coffee. 'Now, what I'm gonna do, Owen, is have a donut and some coffee. I really like donuts, but I guess you already figured that out. As for you, I want you to consider what you're trying to accomplish here, the way you're going about it and—'

'We talked about dogs,' Pitt said before Baiul could finish. He rubbed his temples, lowered his head, remembering that after they'd gotten into the car he'd flipped on the air-conditioning, given the car a minute to warm up before pulling into traffic.

As he'd dropped the gear shift into DRIVE, he'd looked at her, drawn by her smile, and his eyes had dropped to the tops of her breasts, then to the tops of her thighs. Her skirt had ridden up a few inches, and he'd felt a strong urge to lightly run the tips of his fingers from her knees to the hem of her skirt, to push her skirt aside, to drop his mouth to hers. When he'd looked up again, Sandy Fink's eyes had told him that it was okay for him to want her, and he'd wondered if, when the time came, she'd carry that open quality, the exuberance, into the bedroom.

'She told me that she had a dog named Pow-Wow, a Husky, and that she paid somebody to walk the dog while she was at work. She said having a dog in the house made her feel safer at night.' Pitt wiped the sweat off his forehead with the back of his hand. For a moment he watched the moisture drop from his fingertips to the tile floor. 'The conversation went back and forth. I told Ms Fink about my own dog, Rusty, the dog I had when I was married. About how I couldn't keep the dog after my divorce.'

Pitt felt the urge to unburden himself grow stronger. For the first time, the word 'confess' passed through his mind. Baiul's puffy face was absolutely still; his dark eyes seemed to absorb the light, as if he was preparing himself to receive a confession, to register every element.

'I told Ms Fink about how I tried to find a home for the dog, how I wouldn't take him to the pound, where he'd be gassed. A lot of time went by while I looked, months and months, and Rusty kept messing up in the house because I was leaving him alone too long. Finally, somebody told me about the North Shore Animal League where they never put an animal down.' Pitt realized that he was again starting to babble, only this time he couldn't stop himself. The impulse to just get through it, get it over, was too much for him.

'Anyway, the Animal League was full up and the best they could do was put me on a waiting list. Six months, that's what they said. Meanwhile, my landlord was bitching night and day about the dog barking whenever I left the apartment.' He took a deep breath, feeling steadier now that he was almost done. 'I couldn't make the six months. No way. So what I did one night was take Rusty over to the Animal League after it closed and tie him to the fence. I figured the dog wouldn't know what was happening, but the look Rusty tossed me as I walked away nearly broke my heart. It was the worst thing that ever happened to me. Until today.'

Thirteen

'Poor Poster Boy,' Trager said. 'He really loved his doggie.'

'Fuck you,' Pitt said before he could stop himself.

'A real nineties kinda guy.' Trager jammed his thumbs beneath his belt. 'I hear the girls get all hot for sensitive types. That right, Poster Boy?'

Baiul waited until he was sure that Pitt wasn't going to respond, then said, 'So that's it, Owen? That's what you talked about on the way to the Faulkner residence? Dogs?'

'One other thing. Ms Fink told me that the parents knew she was coming.'

'She told you the parents were willing to give up the children? She said "parents", more than one?' Baiul, who'd personally interviewed Sandra Fink, let an element of surprise seep into his voice. 'This a new story?'

'Ms Fink told me ... I don't remember the exact words, only that she was definitely expected. She was very calm in the house and on the way over. Not like somebody anticipating a hard time. Like somebody who expected things to go smoothly.'

Baiul found a clean napkin under the donut box. He pressed it to his face, let it soak up the sweat. 'But when you got to the apartment, as you parked the car, you still didn't know how many adults were likely to be in the household. That right?' He pulled the napkin away, threw it on the floor.

'Yes, that's right.' Pitt couldn't take his eyes off a small strip of the napkin clinging to the tip of Baiul's nose.

'And you didn't know how many children you were supposed to remove either?'

'No. Ms Fink might have told me, but if she did I don't remember.'

'And you asked no questions about the parent or parents, whether they had criminal records or a history of violence or if they suffered from an emotional disorder. That's right, isn't it?'

'Yes, right.'

'Okay.' Baiul nodded. 'Anything you need to add, Owen, for the record?'

Pitt started to speak, then stopped himself. He wanted to snatch Sandy Fink's statement off the table, to know what she'd said and what, if anything, she hadn't. Baiul's soft voice seemed, to Pitt, an invitation, as if Baiul was daring him to tell the truth.

'Well, Owen?' Baiul prompted. 'Anything else? Make up your mind.'

'That's what I remember,' Pitt said.

'I see.' Baiul fumbled through the paperwork on the table, finally selected several sheets and studied them closely for a moment. 'According to Ms Fink, you asked for her phone number. You asked her and she gave it to you and you wrote it down.'

'The Poster Boy strikes again,' Trager said. He burst out laughing and this time Baiul joined him.

There was nothing for Pitt to do but take it. Baiul's rapid-fire chirp trilled up and around Trager's relentless boom, holding steady until their laughter seemed to merge, to become purely mechanical. At that moment, as Pitt drifted toward despair, the catch-all charge of conduct unbecoming an officer drifted through his consciousness. He recalled his brief meeting with the DBA lawyer, Sam O'Neill, and the lawyer's succinct warning. What a fool he'd been not to listen, what a purely arrogant fool to believe he could talk his way out of trouble. Now there was nothing he could do but carry the bluff forward.

The relentless buzz of the overhead light seemed to pierce his eyes, to twist and writhe in the nerve endings beneath his scalp. He felt as if he might fall asleep at any moment and he felt as if he might never sleep again. 'Yes,' he said to Baiul when the laughter finally died out. 'Now that you mention it, Ms Fink did give me her phone number.'

'Is that what you called her?' Baiul asked. '*Ms* Fink? As in, "Ms Fink, can I have your phone number?" Like you were asking your fourth-grade teacher for permission to use the toilet?'

Pitt ignored the jibe. 'Like I already told you,' he insisted, 'Ms Fink was very relaxed on the way over. Getting her phone number was just something that happened. It wasn't important to me.' He pulled his chair a little closer to the table. 'In fact, I never asked for Ms Fink's number. She offered it to me.'

It was true as far as it went. As he'd parked the car in front of that devastated tenement, Sandy Fink had turned to him, her green eyes amused, her voice low and teasing. 'Do you want to call me?' she'd asked. He'd smiled then, thrilled by the fact that she'd beaten him to the punch. Desire had rushed through his groin, a purely physical sensation that flashed from his prostate to the tip of his penis. When he'd looked at Sandy, her cheeks and throat had been flushed. With desire?

With embarrassment? He didn't know, but was certain he'd find out.

Baiul wiped a drop of sweat from the inner rim of his left ear and flicked it away. He was almost certain that Pitt, on one level, had already convicted himself, that he'd abandoned all hope of emerging unscathed. That knowledge, even as he noted the terrible fatigue in Pitt's face, lifted Baiul. He looked down at his watch. If he wanted to be home by midnight, he'd have to finish everything, including a written summary of the interrogation, by eleven-thirty. At the latest.

'Ms Fink says that you asked for her number,' he said, his voice deliberately flat. 'Was she lying?'

'*If* she actually said it.'

'I see. Ms Fink is lying. Sergeant Baiul is lying. The whole wide world's out to get poor Owen Pitt. That the way of it?'

Pitt had routinely lied to suspects in the course of various interrogations, usually about witness identifications or the statements of co-conspirators. Baiul, he believed absolutely, would also lie. He'd lie without thinking twice about it and sleep the sleep of the just when he got home.

'I'm telling you that Ms Fink offered to give me her phone number.' To Pitt's disgust, his tone was soft enough to smack of desperation. Again, he felt the urge to unburden himself, to tell his story in such detail that no further questions would be possible.

'Why would Ms Fink lie to us, Owen?' Baiul stretched his legs out beneath the table and laid his folded hands on his belly. 'What's her motive?'

'Maybe she was embarrassed.'

'If she was embarrassed, then why did she tell us at all?'

Baiul knew that Pitt wanted to shout something like, Because you sweated it out of her, which was exactly what had happened, but he was betting that Pitt was too tired to muster the fight.

Pitt started to speak, stopped abruptly, his mouth still open. Though he knew that Baiul would read even this small gesture as a sign of weakness, he closed his eyes and tried to summon a glimmer of that righteous anger he'd felt when Baiul and Trager had first come into the room. Only when it became clear to Pitt that he was stuck with his exhaustion, his fear, his despair, did he finally say, 'I don't know.' Then he repeated himself, 'I just don't know.'

Fourteen

Again, as if a plateau having been reached, the way now had to be made safe for those who came behind, Baiul dragged Pitt back and forth, from the precinct to the Faulkner apartment. The questioning took longer than the original trip; it took Pitt through depths of exhaustion beyond any he'd previously experienced, revealed levels of endurance he hadn't known he possessed. Early on, he accepted the fact that he could do nothing more than stagger forward, repeat the same small set of facts over and over again. To every other question he would have to answer, 'I don't remember,' as if any further admission would lead to immediate and complete ruin.

The worst of it was that Baiul, who seemed moment by moment to grow visibly stronger, was offering the same basic choice that Pitt had offered many times to many suspects. He, Pitt, could run, could demand his union mouthpiece and live to fight another day, or he could plod stubbornly, stupidly, forward and be crushed. He could not, or so he believed, save himself.

Baiul took Pitt from the precinct to the curb in front of the Faulkner apartment six times before he was interrupted. Each time, instead of allowing Pitt to open the door, step out and walk into the building, he posed a demand in the form of a question: 'That story you told Ms Fink, Owen. About your dog. That was a . . . a whadda ya call it . . . a signal. You were just telling Ms Fink that you were divorced. You were flirting, right?'

If Pitt took the bait, said, Yeah, I was putting the make on Sandy Fink, Baiul would let him out of the car. If not, he would keep Owen Pitt behind the wheel of that Caprice until forced to do otherwise. Both men knew it and each, at different times, considered the consequences. Baiul, despite a nearly pleading tone, believed the interview to be at a turning point. If Pitt gave up this little piece, admitted that on the way to the Faulkner residence he had been far more interested in Sandra Fink than in what he might run into when he got there, the dam would break and he'd spill his guts. On the other hand, if Pitt was going to cut and run, he'd do it now, before he talked himself into a indictment.

Pitt as he fought the urge to give Baiul the answer Baiul wanted, kept telling himself that it didn't matter any more, that he was already buried, that Sandy Fink's statement had been only the last shovelful of dirt on an already heaped grave. Unauthorized use of a police vehicle? Failure to notify superior officers? Failure to follow established police procedure? Conduct unbecoming a member of the force? The job could dump him any time it wanted to.

So what was the point in covering the truth? He *had* been flirting with Sandy Fink, *had* imagined his tongue between her breasts, *had* received her phone number with the reverence of a pilgrim entering the Holy land. Baiul wasn't asking for the moon. He was asking for the simple truth.

'My aim was to get the kids out of that apartment,' Pitt answered, as he'd been answering, 'without any problems. Ms Fink had requested a police escort and I was escorting her. If someone else had been available, I wouldn't have been there at all.'

'I just don't see the point of this.' Baiul held a donut aloft, his eighth by Pitt's count. 'If we want your ass, we already have it. I know that you know this, Owen. So what's the point of bullshitting? Fink says you were flirting all the way. She doesn't blame you. She says that she was flirting right back.'

'What about Faulkner and her boyfriend? Does she say she was afraid of them?' Pitt's headache seemed to surround his skull, to be slowly tightening down as if his hair had decided to eat its way into his brain. 'Did she say that she expected violence?'

'What she said, Owen, and the reason we're having this conversation, is that you never asked.' Baiul was about to continue when somebody knocked on the door. For a moment he sat there, motionless, fighting a surge of blind rage. He was so close to the truth he could almost taste it and now he'd have to start again. The timing could not have been worse.

With no choice – Trager hadn't moved a muscle – Baiul stood, opened the door and stepped outside. Pitt, almost as disconcerted as Baiul, looked over at Trager who grinned and said, 'I think that's your executioner.'

Pitt stood and made a slow, almost ponderous circuit of the room. As he passed in front of the mirror, got a good look at himself, he thought for the first time of what he would do if the job cut him loose. Pitt's godfather, his Uncle Stuart, operated a small security firm in Rutherford, New Jersey. Uncle Stu had been the first to warn him about the silks who ruled the job, had told him, 'Cover your ass, Owen. Cover your ass at all times.' Well, not only hadn't he covered his ass, he'd left it hanging so far into the wind that it was now sunburned.

The door opened at that moment and Pitt saw Baiul, in the mirror, enter the room. Baiul looked at Pitt's chair, then at Trager, then, finally, at Pitt himself. Baiul was smiling, his mouth a black line that lifted his jowls high enough to reveal a sharp, pugnacious chin. 'Owen,' he said, 'we gotta take a little break here, have a little meeting. It won't take long. I promise you.'

Fifteen

When Baiul walked into the wash room of the 77th Precinct, ten minutes later, Pitt, stripped to the waist, was sponging his chest with a moistened paper towel. Baiul stopped in the doorway and stared for a moment at the humped muscle on Pitt's back, at Pitt's narrow waist, at the broad, nearly unbroken plane of his chest. Then he stepped up behind Pitt and said, 'It must be hard when you're . . . attractive. It must be hard to keep a marriage going if women throw themselves at you.'

As Baiul waited patiently for Pitt to respond, an image of Louise suddenly came into focus. He saw his wife as she'd been thirty years before, the smile on her face as he'd fumbled with a corsage of pink roses on the night of the senior prom. He'd been so afraid of piercing her breast with the pin that his fingers had trembled uncontrollably. Finally, she'd taken the corsage from his hand and brought it to her nostrils, before pinning it to her gown.

'Hard to be what?' Pitt asked. He'd taken four aspirins and was praying they'd kick in before he had to go back. 'Hard to be a Poster Boy?'

'I didn't mean that,' Baiul said, though he had. 'Not as an insult.'

Pitt nodded glumly. His eyes were rimmed with black circles, shot through with swollen veins. In his own mind, he looked halfway to being Frankenstein. He stared at Baiul's face, suspended next to his own in the mirror, and wondered what it would be like to be trapped in Baiul's body. 'I'm tired,' he told Baiul, 'and I want to get this over with.'

'I know, Owen. That's why I'm here.' Baiul turned his back. He walked over to a urinal and unzipped his fly. 'I was thinking that maybe we could talk privately. Off the record.'

Pitt, taken aback, said nothing. But the urge to get it out in the open, every subjective detail, again beckoned to him.

'I understand why you don't trust me.' Baiul looked over his shoulder at the back of Pitt's head, 'But the thing about it, Owen, like I keep saying, is if we wanna get you . . .' He let his voice trail off while he zipped himself up. Then he walked over to the sink next to Pitt and turned on the water. The basin, slick with dried soap, was stained an intense green around the drain. 'Me, I just wanna get it over with.' He soaped his hands with liquid soap from a dispenser on the wall and began to work up a lather. 'See, I got a sick wife at home and I wanna try to see her before she's out for the night.'

Pitt wadded the paper towels in his hand. 'If you really wanna get out of here,' he said as he flipped the paper towels away, 'why don't you just go with my first statement?'

'Because I'm not the boss, Owen, which should be obvious by now. And also because I just gotta know the truth. It's a thing with me. I just gotta know.'

'You want the truth?' Pitt turned slightly in Baiul's direction. 'What makes you think I know it?'

Baiul rinsed his hands, then splashed water onto his face and neck. 'Gimme a towel, will ya?' His right hand groped blindly in Pitt's direction. 'I got soap in my eyes.'

The paper towel dispenser was empty and Pitt had to go to a pile stacked next to the overflowing waste bin at the far end of the room. When he finally pressed a half-dozen paper towels into Baiul's hand, Baiul's finger closed down, trapping him. 'Just tell me what happened. Tell me what happened and I'll protect you. I swear it.'

Without thinking, Pitt jerked away, the motion quick, instinctive, as if he'd accidentally touched a hot stove. 'You wired?' he asked.

'Frisk me.'

Pitt shook his head. 'Why do you wanna do this?'

'Because, like I said, I wanna get home to see my wife.' As Baiul took a deep breath, he attempted to charge his gaze with sincerity. It was do-or-die time, his last chance. 'And because the way my life is going now ... Look, suppose I told you that what you've been saying so far, it's in your best interest. You were just doing your job; you had no reason to be apprehensive; you only remember about half of your conversation with the Fink woman. Would that convince you?'

'To do what?'

'To tell me what happened. Off the record.' Baiul turned to look Pitt full in the face. 'I swear I'll protect you.'

'That's bullshit. You're IAD. You wouldn't protect your own mother.' Pitt wished that his voice had been a little stronger, that he could have mustered up the contempt he'd felt for the IAD sharks just a few hours before. 'And you know it.'

Baiul took a step forward. 'Suppose I make a deal with you? Suppose I trust you? Would you trust me then?' He wanted to reach out, touch Pitt's chest, but held himself in check. That he should have such power over a boy like this was one of the great pleasures his job afforded. 'I'll tell you a real secret. Something you won't find out about for a couple of days. Something you really need to know. I'll tell you a secret, if you promise to tell me what happened in that apartment.'

'What's the secret?' The words were out before Pitt could take them back. He felt as if he'd taken a step down a ladder, that he could see the ground below.

'You gotta promise me, Owen. You gotta promise that you'll tell me the truth. This is one cop to another, favor for favor. You gotta redeem your marker.'

Sixteen

'You're off the hook,' Baiul told Pitt. 'We're gonna charge the boyfriend.' Baiul watched Pitt's jaw drop, his blue eyes widen, remembering an almost identical expression come over the face of a friend who'd gotten a high lottery number in the draft during the Vietnam War.

'How?' Pitt was smiling now, a soft reflective smile that nevertheless smacked of inner joy. 'Who decided?' He looked up at the recessed fluorescent lights in the ceiling. They were blessedly silent.

'You really need to know this?' He waited until Pitt shook his head. 'That's good, because I don't know myself.'

'Then I guess there's no reason for me to ask why, right? Why you came to this decision.' Pitt turned back to the mirror, decided that if he cleaned up, if he shaved, took another shower and washed the sweat out of his hair, he'd look all right when he left the house. Just in case the reporters were lying in wait by the back door.

'No, the why is simple enough. The gods down at the big house are worried about a lawsuit. They figure if they bury the boyfriend and cut Owen Pitt loose, they'll limit their exposure.' Baiul looked around for a place to sit, found only the toilets in their stalls. His right ankle was throbbing, as it always did when he was forced to stand for any length of time. 'You see, what happened is the mother put it all on the boyfriend. That's Mary Faulkner. She said it was Nikolas Kristova's gun and that he had it lying out on a table in the bedroom. According to the mother, Kristova told the kid that the social worker was gonna put him in a closet where the rats could get him. The kid's got a thing about rats.'

Pitt nodded. 'Is the boyfriend in custody?'

'Yeah.'

'What'd you hit him with?'

'Criminally negligent homicide, possession of an illegal weapon, eight counts of child abuse.'

Pitt leaned back, let his weight drop on the rim of the sink. Baiul, too short to follow suit, felt a momentary twinge of jealousy.

'If the mother gave a statement that incriminated the boyfriend, what makes you think she's gonna sue?'

'Because after we finished with Mary Faulkner, the reverends came calling. Now she won't talk to us.' Pitt shrugged. 'Anyway, it's not me, Owen. It's not me that decides. The silks figure if they dump on you, it'll be used against the job in a wrongful death suit.'

Pitt snorted. 'Wrongful death? the kid fired at least two shots.'

'You're not sure exactly how many?'

'No.' Pitt shook his head, glanced at his watch. 'I've been trying to remember for the last eight hours and I'm still not sure.'

Baiul thought about hopping onto one of the sinks, letting his feet dangle, but he was afraid the sink would come right off the wall. He shifted his weight, tried to ignore the pain. 'Yeah, well, that's another reason we're having this conversation in private. After we finish, you're gonna go downstairs, make a written statement. It'd be good if you got the facts right.'

'What about the tapes we already made?'

'There's no law says we gotta keep 'em.'

'No,' Pitt admitted, 'there isn't.'

Unable to stand it any longer, Baiul walked along the row of sinks to the end of the wash room and removed the waste bin's rounded metal cover. Then he turned the bin on its end, spilling a white mound of crumpled paper towels in the process, and sat down. Finally, he motioned Pitt to join him, explaining, 'I got bad wheels. You know, when I stand up for too long. It's the weight.'

Seventeen

As he crossed the wash room, Pitt jammed his arms into his shirt. The damp, clammy fabric clung to his skin, a reminder that he'd be taking one more trip to the sweltering interrogation room. By the time he reached Baiul, he was already composing a statement.

'Take me into the building,' Baiul said. 'From the car into the building.'

'The place was a real shithole,' Pitt said. 'Everything busted out. The front door, the lobby door, the mailboxes, everything.' He closed his eyes, remembering Sandy Fink climbing out of the Caprice, bouncing up the stairs as if on the way to a party. Her skirt had seemed to move with her, to flow around her hips and thighs like a butterfly around an open blossom.

'Somebody had dropped a quart of milk near the stairs and it had turned sour in the heat. The stink filled the whole lobby. It smelled like baby vomit. Somebody else – or maybe the same mope – took a dump in the corner and there was a cloud of flies, those green flies, hanging over the mess. I remember they flew up in my face and I tried to swat them away, but they were too fast.'

Baiul nodded, said, 'Did you say anything to Sandra Fink? Did she say anything to you?'

'I said, "How can people live like this? I'd rather be dead than live like this." ' Pitt began to button his shirt. 'And she said, "The apartment's even worse." '

'Did that alarm you? Did you think the building was drug-infested?'

Pitt laughed. '*Think*? I was stepping on crack vials as we crossed the lobby. Crunching them like cockroaches.' Then he added, 'This is the 77.'

'But were you alarmed? That's the question.'

'The lobby was empty and there was nobody on the stairs.' It was Pitt's bottom line, the one he'd been trying to draw for the last eight hours.

'So tell me, Owen, who went up the stairs first?'

'She did.' Pitt turned his face away from Baiul. Even at the time he'd known better, known that anyone might be waiting on the next landing, that crack junkies were completely unpredictable. He'd unbuttoned his jacket, made his Glock available, but he'd let Sandy Fink go first. 'She had an ass from heaven,' he finally said.

Relief flooded through Pitt at that moment. He really believed now that he was going to tell his story the way he remembered it. Was sure, too, that he'd never tell it this way again.

'And you wanted to stare at Sandra Fink's ass while she trotted up the stairs.' Baiul's smile widened. 'You wanted to ogle her ass. Isn't that what they say? Ogle?'

'We were playing,' Pitt declared. He wondered if it was even possible to explain what he felt for Sandra Fink to Gregory Baiul, what he'd felt for all the others. The beauty was in that first tension, before you went to bed, knowing you were desired, that someone else wanted you. The light in Sandra Fink's green eyes was more important to him – far more important – than any glimpse he might have had of her thighs or buttocks.

'What'd you say? You were *playing*.'

'Yeah,' Pitt insisted, 'like animals play.'

'Before they have sex?' When Pitt didn't respond, Baiul quickly added, 'You didn't pick a very safe playground. That's your problem, Owen. Nobody plays in a snake pit.'

The door was pushed open at that moment and a uniformed officer, a young black man, stepped into the wash room. Baiul and Pitt fell silent, but didn't look directly at the intruder. Instead, they waited impatiently while he urinated, then washed his hands. When he was finally gone Pitt said, his tone flat to the point of certainty. 'I wasn't asleep on the job. I had my jacket and my eyes wide open. At least while we were on the stairs.'

In Pitt's mind, it was simply true. Maybe he hadn't gone first, checked the landings, the stairwells, but he hadn't buttoned his jacket either. Sandy had climbed the stairs quickly, on her toes, her calves drawing into a tight ball with each step. He'd followed two steps behind, one hand trailing the wall, the other held waist high. His eyes, even if they'd lingered from time to time on Sandy Fink, had been moving. At that point, he'd still been a cop.

'We got up to the apartment without seeing anybody. Sandy knocked on the door and the mother answered. I flashed my shield, but I don't know if she even looked. The woman was stoned. When she turned around it was like she swam into the living room. Slow motion.' Pitt took out a cigarette and lit it, taking his time, seeing it again. 'Sandy was right. The apartment was even worse than the building. Garbage everywhere, half the ceiling gone, water dripping. They had a couch with the legs cut off against the wall and the boyfriend was sitting there. He was in a nod; his eyes were barely open. Two little girls sat next to him, one a toddler, the other maybe six years old. They had on ratty T-shirts and shorts. No socks, no shoes.'

'And you figured those were the kids the Fink woman came to pick up?'

'Yeah.'

'You figured those were the *only* kids.' Baiul let his voice begin to rise. 'That's right, isn't it?'

'I thought it was under control,' Pitt admitted. 'I did.'

'So you didn't check the bedroom.'

'No.'

'Even though you knew you were in the apartment of two heroin addicts? You didn't ask if there was anybody else in the residence? Tell me, Owen, what were you looking at *this* time. Her breasts?'

Baiul, who'd only a short time before wondered if Trager would bear the brunt of Pitt's anger, now wondered if Pitt's anger would fall on him. He watched Pitt's hands ball up, his eyes narrow, and decided that it would serve him right to take a beating for what had been a momentary whim. After all, nothing they said here would matter.

Eighteen

Pitt sucked hard on his cigarette. He was tempted to blow the smoke right into Baiul's face, maybe follow up with a left hook, but he held himself in check. Baiul had as much as told him that he could walk away from this beef and that was what he wanted to do. Nevertheless, Pitt's voice, when he spoke, was edged with contempt.

'There were two garbage bags on the floor next to a pile of clothes. The mother knelt down and began to stuff the clothes into them. She was still moving in slow motion, like the clothes – the *rags* – were made of glass.' He snorted, drew his lips into a sneer, added, 'I wanted to kick her, see if she maybe had a higher gear, but I didn't. I just stood there. Meanwhile, the boyfriend started snoring.'

'You keep saying "the boyfriend". Were you aware of Kristova's relationship with Mary Faulkner at the time?'

'Hey, what I saw in that apartment was a prime cut of white trash. And I didn't need anybody to define his relationship with Ms Faulkner.' He leaned in close to Baiul. 'Because the kids sitting next to him looked just like him.'

Baiul waved his hand in front of his nose, forcing Pitt to retreat. 'But you didn't know who he was, right? You didn't ask and nobody told you.'

'That's right.'

'And you didn't make this individual aware of the fact that you were a police officer? You weren't displaying your shield either?'

'You asking me if I woke him up?'

'I'm asking what I'm asking, Owen.'

Pitt turned away from Baiul. He let his weight drop against the edge of the sink and crossed his legs at the ankles. 'Sandy went to talk to the kids. The scene was very contained.' He flipped the ash from his cigarette into the sink next to him, then added, 'It had to be over a hundred degrees in that apartment. Had to be. Maybe I should have done it by the book, but all I wanted to do was get the kids together and get the hell out. In my judgement, the boyfriend was no threat.'

'No,' Baiul quickly admitted, 'he wasn't.'

Pitt straightened. He dropped his cigarette to the floor and ground it out with the sole of his shoe. 'Look,' he said, 'I've already admitted that I didn't know how many people were in the apartment and I didn't ask. What's the point of going through it again?'

Baiul shifted his weight. The edge of the waste bin was cutting into his thighs. Still, it was blessedly cool in the wash room. 'I just want to get it right,' he explained. Then he smiled and asked, 'Why don't you go ahead?'

'Yeah, why not?' Pitt felt his momentary bravado peel away like an iceberg from the face of a glacier. Though he could remember the scene he'd described to Baiul exactly, could remember what came afterward in great detail, his memory of the few seconds following Sandy Fink's 'Oh, no' had simply been overwhelmed by the emotion of fear. Now, whenever he tried to get back to that moment, his memory of that fear threatened to evoke the equally humiliating emotion of shame. Somehow the world, as he turned toward the bedroom, had narrowed to a small black hole at the end of barrel. Somehow, he'd ceased to be a cop.

'Sandy cried out,' he told Baiul, 'and I spun around. I . . .' Pitt's voice trailed off. He folded his arms across his chest and leaned forward. Baiul watched him closely, but said nothing.

'I saw the gun and I . . .' Again, Pitt stopped. He couldn't recall any of the specifics. He didn't know whether he'd identified himself as a cop or how many shots the kid had fired or even if the kid had fired first. Somehow, when he'd come back to himself, his weapon was in his hand and the kid was lying in a pool of blood on the floor. Then, of course, he'd seen it all, seen that the kid was a kid, seen the burn scars on the kid's chest, the neat hole beneath the kid's left breast.

When Baiul finally spoke, his voice so gentle it surprised him. 'Did you say anything, Owen? When you saw the gun?'

Pitt wavered only for a moment before he decided to go with the official version, the version sure to be included in his written statement. He drew a deep breath, let it out through his nose, knowing, now, that he'd been wrong, that there was a part of the story he would never tell anybody. 'I drew my own weapon and shouted for the kid to drop the gun. The kid fired twice and I shot him. He was less than ten feet away. I couldn't miss.'

'Twice?' Baiul asked in the same tone. 'Are you sure he fired twice?'

'No,' Pitt admitted. 'I'm not sure.'

'What about telling the boy to drop the gun? Are you sure about that?'

Pitt turned slightly to meet Baiul's even gaze. With no clear memory of warning the kid, his story would rise or fall on the statements given by the five witnesses. 'Yeah,' he said, 'I'm sure.'

Baiul got off the waste bin and walked a few feet away, rubbing his buttocks as he went. 'All right,' he said, 'let's finish it up.'

'I secured the weapon and told Sandy to call for an ambulance. Then I went over to the kid. He was bleeding out through his back.' Pitt could see the end coming. In high school he'd run the mile and he felt now as he had at the very end of a close race when he'd somehow forced himself to sprint the last hundred yards toward the tape. 'I checked for a pulse, then I tried to compress the wound. It was hopeless.' He smiled at the back of Baiul's skull. 'But I kept at it, and when he stopped breathing I administered mouth-to-mouth. I figured I was in enough trouble and I didn't want to be accused of not giving a damn.'

Instead of responding to Pitt's statement, Baiul said, 'You know, it's funny, Owen. Nikolas Kristova and Mary Faulkner both swear you didn't give the boy any warning at all, that you drew your weapon and fired it without saying a word.' He, too, was very tired but, unlike Pitt, felt only disappointment. He'd been hoping that Pitt would be completely honest, but that clearly wasn't going to happen. 'By the way,' he told Pitt, 'Odel Faulkner pulled the trigger three times. Three.'

'What about Sandy?' Pitt moved away from the sink. He took several steps forward, stopping when he could again see Baiul's face.

'Ms Fink? What about her?'

'C'mon, Baiul, what did she say? Did she say I warned the kid?'

'Yeah, she backed you a hundred per cent.'

Suddenly, Pitt knew with absolute certainty that he hadn't issued a warning of any kind. He'd drawn his weapon and fired without making a sound because the gun wasn't pointed at him and he didn't want to attract the kid's attention. Worse still, he was now sure that he might have disarmed the kid *because* the gun was pointed away. What would it have amounted to? A couple of quick steps? The boy's arms were as thin as broomsticks. 'And what about the girls?' he finally asked.

'The girls don't know. When they saw their brother with the gun they covered their faces. Then the shots started and ... well, they just don't know.' Baiul shoved his hand into his shirt pocket, found a stick of spearmint gum. He unwrapped it, popped it into his mouth, then said, 'According to Ms Fink, you drew your weapon and ordered Odel Faulkner to, in her exact words, "Drop the gun". Odel responded by firing three shots and then you killed him. It'd be good if your statement agrees with hers.'

Though Pitt registered Baiul's sarcasm, it had no effect on him one way or the other. Sandy Fink had protected him and that was all that counted. He didn't ask himself why, because he already knew. They'd begun sending each other signals almost from the minute she'd walked through the door of the 77 and now she'd opened her heart to him.

Pitt felt a surge of emotion which he quickly identified as love. Though he knew this love was tainted by gratitude, and he was certain it would pass as all his other loves had passed, he allowed the emotion to sweep through his body, to invigorate him. Then he looked down at Baiul, at Baiul's pendulous jowls, his enormous sagging belly, and said, 'Are we done here?'

Baiul looked at his watch. It was 10:30 and he was pretty sure he'd be home before midnight. 'Yeah,' he said. 'Why don't you go back to the room, get started on your statement? I'll be along in a couple of minutes. I gotta make a phone call.'

Nineteen

It took Owen Pitt less than thirty minutes to compose and sign his statement, Gregory Baiul less than five minutes to read and approve it. Then Baiul said, 'You did good, Owen. You held up.'

Baiul stood, but motioned Pitt to remain seated. 'The Inspector,' he told Pitt as he left the room, 'has something he wants to say to you.'

Before Pitt could frame a response Baiul was out the door and Moses Trager inside. Trager, his face expressionless, walked up to Baiul's chair and laid his hands on the top rail. 'What happens next, Poster Boy,' he told Pitt, 'is that you go out on extended medical leave until you testify at trial. You don't carry the badge and you don't work in the bar and you don't talk to anybody about the case. No, what you do, once a week, is see a department psychologist named Howard Pelter. After the trial, when you apply for a disability pension, Dr Pelter will offer the pension board an acceptable diagnosis, something like Advanced Poster Boy Syndrome, and the board will approve your application. Then you're on your own.'

A mix of emotions competed for Pitt's attention. He was angry, yes, mostly because of Baiul's promise. Baiul, without actually lying, had tricked him, led him to believe that he could resume his ordinary life. Pitt was saddened, too, and fearful. Like every detective, he not only loved the gold shield and had worked hard to get it, but to some extent the shield had come to define him. Still, not only would a disability pension leave him on three-quarters pay for the rest of his life, it would also carry lifetime medical benefits. Even, if, at some point, he should recover from his phantom illness and begin a new career.

Suddenly, Pitt began to laugh. He put his hand over his mouth and after a long moment brought himself under control. 'This is the final deal?' he asked. 'No more surprises?'

Instead of answering Pitt's question, Trager straightened and said, 'You try to come back, the department will file against you and you'll be out with nothing to show for it.'

'It's too late for threats,' Pitt said. Then he added, 'You've already arrested the boyfriend. You've already given a statement to the press.'

Trager turned and walked away. As he opened the door, he stole a final glance at Pitt and muttered, 'What a fuck-up you are.'

Left to himself, Pitt debated whether to empty his locker and desk or to get out as fast as he could. Though it meant he'd have to return at some point, again to endure the stares of his friends and co-workers, he decided to leave. It was after eleven and he knew his own squad would be upstairs preparing for the midnight tour. Pitt was certain they would shun him.

Pitt left the 77 through an exit ordinarily used by remand prisoners being transported from the precinct to the Men's House of Detention on Atlantic Avenue. Despite the hour, the air temperature was in the eighties, the humidity oppressive.

At the far end of the block, a blue Toyota pulled away from the curb and Pitt, drawn by the roar of the car's damaged muffler, looked up to see Baiul at the wheel. Instinctively, he raised a hand in greeting, but the Toyota sailed by without any visible reaction from Baiul.

'So long, fat boy,' Pitt called to the Toyota's retreating tail lights. Then he quickly walked the length of the block to a payphone and pushed a quarter into the slot. To his surprise, despite all he'd been through, he didn't have to search for Sandy Fink's number. When she answered on the second ring, he decided that she'd been waiting for his call, that she'd been waiting all night.

Suddenly, though he knew she couldn't see him, Pitt flashed an enormous smile as he came to understand that he would never be able to make it up to her. Not if he lived to be a thousand years old.

'Hey, Sandy,' he said, 'it was terrible about Odel. Just terrible. I can't stop thinking about him and I really need to talk to someone. Do you think I could stop by?'

PORK PIE HAT

Peter Straub

Part One

1

If you know jazz, you know about him, and the title of this memoir tells you who he is. If you don't know the music, his name doesn't matter. I'll call him Hat. What does matter is what he meant. I don't mean what he meant to people who were touched by what he said through his horn. (His horn was an old Selmer Balanced Action tenor saxophone, most of its lacquer worn off.) I'm talking about the whole long curve of his life, and the way that what appeared to be a long slide from joyous mastery to outright exhaustion can be seen in another way altogether.

Hat did slide into alcoholism and depression. The last ten years of his life amounted to suicide by malnutrition, and he was almost transparent by the time he died in the hotel room where I met him. Yet he was able to play until nearly the end. When he was working, he would wake up around seven in the evening, listen to Frank Sinatra or Billie Holiday records while he dressed, get to the club by nine, play three sets, come back to his room some time after three, drink and listen to more records (he was on a lot of those records), and finally go back to bed around the time of day people begin thinking about lunch. When he wasn't working, he got into bed about an hour earlier, woke up about five or six, and listened to records and drank through his long upside-down day.

It sounds like a miserable life, but it was just an unhappy one. The unhappiness came from a deep, irreversible sadness. Sadness is different from misery, at least Hat's was. His sadness seemed impersonal – it did not disfigure him, as misery can do. Hat's sadness seemed to be for the universe, or to be a larger than usual personal share of a sadness already existing in the universe. Inside it, Hat was unfailingly gentle, kind, even funny. His sadness seemed merely the opposite face of the equally impersonal happiness that shone through his earlier work.

In Hat's later years, his music thickened, and sorrow spoke through the phrases. In his last years, what he played often sounded like heartbreak itself. He was like someone who had passed through a great mystery, who *was passing* through a great mystery, and had to speak of what he had seen, what he was seeing.

2

I brought two boxes of records with me when I first came to New York from Evanston, Illinois, where I'd earned a B.A. in English at Northwestern, and the first thing I set up in my shoebox at the top of John Jay Hall in Columbia University was my portable record player. I did everything to music in those days, and I supplied the rest of my unpacking with a soundtrack provided by Hat's disciples. The kind of music I most liked when I was twenty-one was called 'cool' jazz, but my respect for Hat, the progenitor of this movement, was almost entirely abstract. I didn't know his earliest records, and all I'd heard of his later style was one track on a Verve sampler album. I thought he must almost certainly be dead, and I imagined that if by some miracle he was still alive, he would have been in his early seventies, like Louis Armstrong. In fact, the man who seemed a virtual ancient to me was a few months short of his fiftieth birthday.

In my first weeks at Columbia I almost never left the campus. I was taking five courses, also a seminar that was intended to lead me to a Master's thesis, and when I was not in lecture halls or my room, I was in the library. But by the end of September, feeling less overwhelmed, I began to go downtown to Greenwich Village. The IRT, the only subway line I actually understood, described a straight north–south axis that allowed you to get on at 116th Street and get off at Sheridan Square. From Sheridan Square radiated out an unimaginable wealth (unimaginable if you'd spent the previous four years in Evanston, Illinois) of cafés, bars, restaurants, record shops, bookstores, and jazz clubs. I'd come to New York to get an M.A. in English, but I'd also come for this.

I learned that Hat was still alive about seven o'clock in the evening on the first Saturday in October, when I saw a poster bearing his name on the window of a storefront jazz club near St Mark's Place. My conviction that Hat was dead was so strong that I first saw the poster as an advertisement of past glory. I stopped to gaze longer at this relic of a historical period. Hat had been playing with a quartet including a bassist and drummer of his own era, musicians long associated with him. But the piano player had been John Hawes, one of *my* musicians – John Hawes was on half a dozen of the records back in John Jay Hall. He must have been about twenty at the time, I thought, convinced that the poster had been preserved as memorabilia. Maybe Hawes's first job had been with Hat – anyhow, Hat's quartet must have been one of Hawes's first stops on the way to fame. John Hawes was a great figure to me, and the thought of him playing with a back number like Hat was a disturbance in the texture of reality. I looked down at the date on the poster, and my snobbish and rule-bound version of reality shuddered under another assault of the unthinkable. Hat's engagement had begun on the Tuesday of this week – the first Tuesday in October; and its last night took place on the Sunday after next – the Sunday before Halloween. Hat was still alive, and John Hawes was playing with him. I couldn't have told you which half of this proposition was the more surprising.

To make sure, I went inside and asked the short, impassive man behind the bar if John Hawes was really playing there tonight. 'He'd better be, if he wants to get paid,' the man said.

'So Hat is still alive,' I said.

'Put it this way,' he said. 'If it was you, you probably wouldn't be.'

3

Two hours and twenty minutes later, Hat came through the front door, and I saw what he meant. Maybe a third of the tables between the door and the bandstand were filled with people listening to the piano trio. This was what I'd come for, and I thought that the evening was perfect. I hoped that Hat would stay away. All he could accomplish by showing up would be to steal soloing time from Hawes, who, apart from seeming a bit disengaged, was playing wonderfully. Maybe Hawes always seemed a bit disengaged. That was fine with me. Hawes was *supposed* to be cool. Then the bass player looked toward the door and smiled, and the drummer grinned and knocked one stick against the side of his snare drum in a rhythmic figure that managed both to suit what the trio was playing and serve as a half-comic, half-respectful greeting. I turned away from the trio and looked back toward the door. The bent figure of a light-skinned black man in a long, drooping, dark coat was carrying a tenor saxophone case into the club. Layers of airline stickers covered the case, and a black pork pie hat concealed most of the man's face. As soon as he got past the door, he fell into a chair next to an empty table – really fell, as if he would need a wheelchair to get any farther.

Most of the people who had watched him enter turned back to John Hawes and the trio, who were beginning the last few choruses of 'Love Walked In'. The old man laboriously unbuttoned his coat and let it fall off his shoulders onto the back of the chair. Then, with the same painful slowness, he lifted the hat off his head and lowered it to the table beside him. A brimming shot glass had appeared between himself and the hat, though I hadn't noticed any of the waiters or waitresses put it there. Hat picked up the glass and poured its entire contents into his mouth. Before he swallowed, he let himself take in the room, moving his eyes without changing the position of his head. He was wearing a dark gray suit, a blue shirt with a tight tab collar, and a black knit tie. His face looked soft and worn with drink, and his eyes were of no real color at all, as if not merely washed out but washed clean. He bent over, unlocked the case, and began assembling his horn. As soon as 'Love Walked In' ended, he was on his feet, clipping the horn to his strap and walking toward the bandstand. There was some quiet applause.

Hat stepped neatly up onto the bandstand, acknowledged us with a nod, and whispered something to John Hawes, who raised his hands to the keyboard. The drummer was still grinning, and the bassist had closed his eyes. Hat tilted his horn to one side, examined the mouthpiece, and slid it a tiny distance down the cork. He licked the reed, tapped his foot twice, and put his lips around the mouthpiece.

What happened next changed my life – changed me, anyhow. It was like discovering that some vital, even necessary substance had all along been missing from my life. Anyone who hears a great musician for the first time knows the feeling that the universe has just expanded. In fact, all that happened was that Hat had started playing 'Too Marvelous For Words', one of the twenty-odd songs that were his entire repertoire at the time. Actually, he was playing some oblique, one-time-only melody of his own that floated above 'Too Marvelous For Words', and this spontaneous melody seemed to me to comment affectionately on the song while utterly transcending it – to turn a nice little song into something profound. I forgot to breathe for a little while, and goosebumps came up on my arms. Halfway through Hat's solo, I saw John Hawes watching him and realized that Hawes, whom I all but revered, revered *him*. But by that time, I did, too.

I stayed for all three sets, and after my seminar the next day, I went down to Sam Goody's and bought five of Hat's records, all I could afford. That night, I went back to the club and took a table right in front of the bandstand. For the next two weeks, I occupied the same table every night I could persuade myself that I did not have to study – eight or nine, out of the twelve nights Hat worked. Every night was like the first: the same things, in the same order, happened. Halfway through the first set, Hat turned up and collapsed into the nearest chair. Unobtrusively, a waiter put a drink beside him. Off went the pork pie and the long coat, and out from its case came the horn. The waiter carried the case, pork pie, and coat into a back room while Hat drifted toward the bandstand, often still fitting the pieces of his saxophone together. He stood straighter, seemed almost to grow taller, as he got on the stand. A nod to his audience, an inaudible word to John Hawes. And then that sense of passing over the border between very good, even excellent music and majestic, mysterious art. Between songs, Hat sipped from a glass placed beside his left foot. Three forty-five-minute sets. Two half-hour breaks, during which Hat disappeared through a door behind the bandstand. The same twenty or so songs, recycled again and again. Ecstasy, as if I were hearing Mozart play Mozart.

One afternoon toward the end of the second week, I stood up from a library book I was trying to stuff whole into my brain – *Modern Approaches to Milton* – and walked out of my carrel to find whatever I could that had been written about Hat. I'd been hearing the sound of Hat's tenor in my head ever since I'd gotten out of bed. And in those days, I was a sort of apprentice scholar: I thought that real answers in the form of interpretations could be found in the pages of scholarly journals. If there were at least a thousand, maybe two thousand, articles concerning John Milton in Low Library, shouldn't there be at least a hundred about Hat? And out of the hundred shouldn't a dozen or so at least begin to explain what happened to me when I heard him play? I was looking for *close readings* of his solos, for analyses that would explain Hat's effects in terms of subdivided rhythms, alternate chords, and note choices, in the way that poetry critics parsed diction levels, inversions of meter, and permutations of imagery.

Of course I did not find a dozen articles that applied a musicological version of the New Criticism to Hat's recorded solos. I found six old concert write-ups in the *New York Times,* maybe as many record reviews in jazz magazines, and a couple of chapters in jazz histories. Hat had been born in Mississippi, played in his family band, left after a mysterious disagreement at the time they were becoming a successful 'territory' band, then joined a famous jazz band in its infancy and quit, again mysteriously, just after its breakthrough into nationwide success. After that, he went out on his own. It seemed that if you wanted to know about him, you had to go straight to the music: there was virtually nowhere else to go.

I wandered back from the catalogues to my carrel, closed the door on the outer world, and went back to stuffing *Modern Approaches to Milton* into my brain. Around six o'clock, I opened the carrell door and realized that *I* could write about Hat. Given the paucity of criticism of his work – given the virtual absence of information about the man himself – I virtually had to write something. The only drawback to this inspiration was that I knew nothing about music. I could not write the sort of article I had wished to read. What I could do, however, would be to interview the man. Potentially, an interview would be more valuable than analysis. I could fill in the dark places, answer the unanswered questions – why had he left both bands just as they began to do well? I wondered if he'd had problems with his father, and then transferred these problems to his next bandleader. There had to be some kind of story. Any band within smelling distance of its first success would be more than reluctant to lose its star soloist – wouldn't they beg him, bribe him, to stay? I could think of other questions no one had ever asked: who had influenced him? What did he think of all those tenor players whom he had influenced? Was he friendly with any of his artistic children? Did they come to his house and talk about music?

Above all, I was curious about the texture of his life – I wondered what his life, the life of a genius, tasted like. If I could have put my half-formed fantasies into words, I would have described my naive, uninformed conceptions of Leonard Bernstein's surroundings. Mentally, I equipped Hat with a big apartment, hand-

some furniture, advanced stereo equipment, a good but not flashy car, paintings
... the surroundings of a famous American artist, at least by the standards of John
Jay Hall and Evanston, Illinois. The difference between Bernstein and Hat was that
the conductor probably lived on Fifth Avenue, and the tenor player in the Village.

I walked out of the library humming 'Love Walked In'.

4

The dictionary-sized Manhattan telephone directory chained to the shelf beneath
the pay telephone on the ground floor of John Jay Hall failed to provide Hat's
number. Moments later, I met similar failure back in the library after having
consulted the equally impressive directories for Brooklyn, Queens, and the Bronx,
as well as the much smaller volume for Staten Island. But of course Hat lived in New
York: where else would he live? Like other celebrities, he avoided the unwelcome
intrusions of strangers by going unlisted. I could not explain his absence from the
city's five telephone books in any other way. Of course Hat lived in the Village –
that was what the Village was *for*.

Yet even then, remembering the unhealthy-looking man who each night entered
the club to drop into the nearest chair, I experienced a wobble of doubt. Maybe
the great man's life was nothing like my imaginings. Hat wore decent clothes, but
did not seem rich – he seemed to exist at the same oblique angle to wordly success
that his nightly variations on 'Too Marvelous For Words' bore to the original
melody. For a moment, I pictured my genius in a slum apartment where roaches
scuttled across a bare floor and water dripped from a rip in the ceiling. I had no
idea of how jazz musicians actually lived. Hollywood, unafraid of cliché, surrounded them with squalor. On the rare moments when literature stooped to
consider jazz people, it, too, served up an ambiance of broken bedsprings and
peeling walls. And literature's bohemians – Rimbaud, Jack London, Kerouac, Harte
Crane, William Burroughs – had often inhabited mean, unhappy rooms. It was
possible that the great man was not listed in the city's directories because he could
not afford a telephone.

This notion was unacceptable. There was another explanation – Hat could not
live in a tenement room without a telephone. The man still possessed the elegance
of his generation of jazz musicians, the generation that wore good suits and highly
polished shoes, played in big bands, and lived on busses and in hotel rooms.

And there, I thought, was my answer. It was a comedown from the apartment
in the Village with which I had supplied him, but a room in some 'artistic' hotel
like the Chelsea would suit him just as well, and probably cost a lot less in rent.
Feeling inspired, I looked up the Chelsea's number on the spot, dialed, and asked
for Hat's room. The clerk told me that he wasn't registered in the hotel. 'But you
know who he is,' I said. 'Sure,' said the clerk. 'Guitar, right? I know he was in one
of those San Francisco bands, but I can't remember which one.'

I hung up without replying, realizing that the only way I was going to discover
Hat's telephone number, short of calling every hotel in New York, was by asking
him for it.

5

This was on a Monday, and jazz clubs were closed. On Tuesday, Professor Marcus told us to read all of *Vanity Fair* by Friday; on Wednesday, after I'd spent a nearly sleepless night with Thackeray, my seminar leader asked me to prepare a paper on James Joyce's 'Two Gallants' for the Friday class. Wednesday and Thursday nights I spent in the library. On Friday I listened to Professor Marcus being brilliant about *Vanity Fair* and read my laborious and dimwitted Joyce paper, on each of the five pages of which the word 'epiphany' appeared at least twice, to my fellow-scholars. The seminar leader smiled and nodded throughout my performance and when I sat down metaphorically picked up my little paper between thumb and forefinger and slit its throat. 'Some of you students are so *certain* about things,' he said. The rest of his remarks disappeared into a vast, horrifying sense of shame. I returned to my room, intending to lie down for an hour or two, and woke up ravenous ten hours later, when even the West End Bar, even the local Chock Full O' Nuts, were shut for the night.

On Saturday night, I took my usual table in front of the bandstand and sat expectantly through the piano trio's usual three numbers. In the middle of 'Love Walked In' I looked around with an insider's foreknowledge to enjoy Hat's dramatic entrance, but he did not appear, and the number ended without him. John Hawes and the other two musicians seemed untroubled by this break in the routine, and went on to play 'Too Marvelous For Words' without their leader. During the next three songs, I kept turning around to look for Hat, but the set ended without him. Hawes announced a short break, and the musicians stood up and moved toward the bar. I fidgeted at my table, nursing my second beer of the night and anxiously checking the door. The minutes trudged by. I feared he would never show up. He had passed out in his room. He'd been hit by a cab, he'd had a stroke, he was already lying dead in a hospital room – and just when I was going to write the article that would finally do him justice!

Half an hour later, still without their leader, John Hawes and the other sidemen went back on the stand. No one but me seemed to have noticed that Hat was not present. The other customers talked and smoked – this was in the days when people still smoked – and gave the music the intermittent and sometimes ostentatious attention they allowed it even when Hat was on the stand. By now, Hat was an hour and a half late, and I could see the gangsterish man behind the bar, the owner of the club, scowling as he checked his wristwatch. Hawes played two originals I particularly liked, favorites of mine from his Contemporary records, but in my mingled anxiety and irritation I scarcely heard them.

Toward the end of the second of these songs, Hat entered the club and fell into his customary seat a little more heavily than usual. The owner motioned away the waiter, who had begun moving toward him with the customary shot glass. Hat dropped the pork pie on the table and struggled with his coat buttons. When he heard what Hawes was playing, he sat listening with his hands still on a coat button, and I listened, too – the music had a tighter, harder, more modern feel, like Hawes's records. Hat nodded to himself, got his coat off, and struggled with the snaps on his saxophone case. The audience gave Hawes unusually appreciative applause. It took Hat longer than usual to fit the horn together, and by the time he was up on his feet, Hawes and the other two musicians had turned around to watch his progress as if they feared he would not make it all the way to the bandstand. Hat wound through the tables with his head tilted back, smiling to himself. When he got close to the stand, I saw that he was walking on his toes like a small child. The owner crossed his arms over his chest and glared. Hat seemed almost to float onto the stand. He licked his reed. Then he lowered his horn and, with his mouth open, stared out at us for a moment. 'Ladies, ladies,' he said in a soft, high voice. These were the first words I had ever heard him speak. 'Thank you for your appreciation of our pianist, Mr Hawes. And now I must explain my absence during the first set. My son passed away this afternoon, and I have been ... busy ... with details. Thank you.'

With that, he spoke a single word to Hawes, put his horn back in his mouth, and began to play a blues called 'Hat Jumped Up', one of his twenty songs. The audience sat motionless with shock. Hawes, the bassist, and the drummer played on as if nothing unusual had happened – they must have known about his son, I thought. Or maybe they knew that he had no son, and had invented a grotesque excuse for turning up ninety minutes late. The club owner bit his lower lip and looked unusually introspective. Hat played one familiar, uncomplicated figure after another, his tone rough, almost coarse. At the end of his solo, he repeated one note for an entire chorus, fingering the key while staring out toward the back of the club. Maybe he was watching the customers leave – three couples and a couple of single people walked out while he was playing. But I don't think he saw anything at all. When the song was over, Hat leaned over to whisper to Hawes, and the piano player announced a short break. The second set was over.

Hat put his tenor on top of the piano and stepped down off the bandstand, pursing his mouth with concentration. The owner had come out from behind the bar and moved up in front of him as Hat tiptoed around the stand. The owner spoke a few quiet words. Hat answered. From behind, he looked slumped and tired, and his hair curled far over the back of his collar. Whatever he had said only partially satisfied the owner, who spoke again before leaving him. Hat stood in place for a moment, perhaps not noticing that the owner had gone, and resumed his tiptoe glide toward the door. Looking at his back, I think I took in for the first time how genuinely *strange* he was. Floating through the door in his gray flannel suit, hair dangling in ringletlike strands past his collar, leaving in the air behind him the announcement about a dead son, he seemed absolutely separate from the rest of humankind, a species of one.

I turned as if for guidance to the musicians at the bar. Talking, smiling, greeting a few fans and friends, they behaved just as they did on every other night. Could Hat really have lost a son earlier today? Maybe this was the jazz way of facing grief – to come back to work, to carry on. Still it seemed the worst of all times to approach Hat with my offer. His playing was a drunken parody of itself. He would forget anything he said to me; I was wasting my time.

On that thought, I stood up and walked past the bandstand and opened the door – if I was wasting my time, it didn't matter what I did.

He was leaning against a brick wall about ten feet up the alleyway from the club's back door. The door clicked shut behind me, but Hat did not open his eyes. His face tilted up, and a sweetness that might have been sleep lay over his features. He looked exhausted and insubstantial, too frail to move. I would have gone back inside the club if he had not produced a cigarette from a pack in his shirt pocket, lit it with a match, and then flicked the match away, all without opening his eyes.

At least he was awake. I stepped toward him, and his eyes opened. He glanced at me and blew out white smoke. 'Taste?' he said.

I had no idea what he meant. 'Can I talk to you for a minute, sir?' I asked.

He put his hand into one of his jacket pockets and pulled out a half-pint bottle. 'Have a taste.' Hat broke the seal on the cap, tilted it into his mouth, and drank. Then he held the bottle out toward me.

I took it. 'I've been coming here as often as I can.'

'Me, too,' he said. 'Go on, do it.'

I took a sip from the gin bottle. 'I'm sorry about your son.'

'Son?' He looked upward, as if trying to work out my meaning. 'I got a son – out on Long Island. With his momma.' He drank again and checked the level of the bottle.

'He's not dead, then.'

He spoke the next words slowly, almost wonderingly. 'Nobody – told – me – if – he – is.' He shook his head and drank another mouthful of gin. 'Damn. Wouldn't that be something, boy dies and nobody tells me? I'd have to think about that, you know, have to really *think* about that one.'

'I'm just talking about what you said onstage.'

He cocked his head and seemed to examine an empty place in the dark air about three feet from his face. 'Uh huh. That's right. I did say that. Son of mine passed.'

It was like dealing with a sphinx. All I could do was plunge in. 'Well, sir, actually there's a reason I came out here,' I said. 'I'd like to interview you. Do you think that might be possible? You're a great artist, and there's very little about you in print. Do you think we could set up a time when I could talk to you?'

He looked at me with his bleary, colorless eyes, and I wondered if he could see me at all. And then I felt that, despite his drunkenness, he saw everything – that he saw things about me that I couldn't see.

'You a jazz writer?' he asked.

'No, I'm a graduate student. I'd just like to do it. I think it would be important.'

'Important.' He took another swallow from the half pint and slid the bottle back into his pocket. 'Be nice, doing an *important* interview.'

He stood leaning against the wall, moving further into outer space with every word. Only because I had started, I pressed on: I was already losing faith in this project. The reason Hat had never been interviewed was that ordinary American English was a foreign language to him. 'Could we do the interview after you finish up at this club? I could meet you anywhere you like.' Even as I said these words, I despaired. Hat was in no shape to know what he had to do after this engagement finished. I was surprised he could make it back to Long Island every night.

Hat rubbed his face, sighed, and restored my faith in him. 'It'll have to wait a little while. Night after I finish here, I go to Toronto for two nights. Then I got something in Hartford on the thirtieth. You come see me after that.'

'On the thirty-first?' I asked.

'Around nine, ten, something like that. Be nice if you brought some refreshments.'

'Fine, great,' I said, wondering if I would be able to take a late train back from wherever he lived. 'But where on Long Island should I go?'

His eyes widened in mock-horror. 'Don't go nowhere on Long Island. You come see me. In the Albert Hotel, Forty-ninth and Eighth. Room 821.'

I smiled at him – I had guessed right about one thing, anyhow. Hat did not live in the Village, but he did live in a Manhattan hotel. I asked him for his phone number, and wrote it down, along with the other information, on a napkin from the club. After I folded the napkin into my jacket pocket, I thanked him and turned toward the door.

'Important as a motherfucker,' he said in his high, soft, slurry voice.

I turned around in alarm, but he had tilted his head toward the sky again, and his eyes were closed.

'Indiana,' he said. His voice made the word seem sung. 'Moonlight in Vermont. I Thought About You. Flamingo.'

He was deciding what to play during his next set. I went back inside, where twenty or thirty new arrivals, more people than I had ever seen in the club, waited for the music to start. Hat soon reappeared through the door, the other musicians left the bar, and the third set began. Hat played all four of the songs he had named, interspersing them through his standard repertoire during the course of an unusually long set. He was playing as well as I'd ever heard him, maybe better than I'd heard on all the other nights I had come to the club. The Saturday night crowd applauded explosively after every solo. I didn't know if what I was seeing was genius or desperation.

An obituary in the Sunday *New York Times*, which I read over breakfast the next morning in the John Jay cafeteria, explained some of what had happened. Early Saturday morning, a thirty-eight-year-old tenor saxophone player named Grant Kilbert had been killed in an automobile accident. One of the most successful jazz musicians in the world, one of the few jazz musicians known outside of the immediate circle of fans, Kilbert had probably been Hat's most prominent disciple. He had certainly been one of my favorite musicians. More importantly, from his first record, *Cool Breeze*, Kilbert had excited respect and admiration. I looked at the photograph of the handsome young man beaming out over the neck of his saxophone and realized that the first four songs on *Cool Breeze* were 'Indiana', 'Moonlight in Vermont', 'I Thought About You', and 'Flamingo'. Some time late Saturday afternoon, someone had called up Hat to tell him about Kilbert. What I had seen had not merely been alcoholic eccentricity, it had been grief for a lost son. And when I thought about it, I was sure that the lost son, not himself, had been the important motherfucker he'd apothesized. What I had taken for spaciness and disconnection had all along been irony.

Part Two

1

On the thirty-first of October, after calling first to make sure he remembered our appointment, I did go to the Albert Hotel, room 821, and interview Hat. That is, I asked him questions and listened to the long, rambling, often obscene responses he gave them. During the long night I spent in his room, he drank the fifth of Gordon's gin, the 'refreshments' I brought with me – all of it, an entire bottle of gin, without tonic, ice, or other dilutants. He just poured it into a tumbler and drank, as if it were water. (I refused his single offer of a 'taste'.) I made frequent checks to make sure that the tape recorder I'd borrowed from a business student down the hall from me was still working, I changed tapes until they ran out, I made detailed backup notes with a ballpoint pen in a stenographic notebook. A couple of times, he played me sections of records that he wanted me to hear, and now and then he sang a couple of bars to make sure that I understood what he was telling me. He sat me in his only chair, and during the entire night stationed himself, dressed in his pork pie hat, a dark blue chalk-stripe suit, and white button-down shirt with a black knit tie, on the edge of his bed. This was a formal occasion. When I arrived at nine o'clock, he addressed me as 'Mr Leonard Feather' (the name of a well-known jazz critic), and when he opened his door at six thirty the next morning, he called me 'Miss Rosemary'. By then, I knew that this was an allusion to Rosemary Clooney, whose singing I had learned that he liked, and that the nickname meant he liked me, too. It was not at all certain, however, that he remembered my actual name.

I had three sixty-minute tapes and a notebook filled with handwriting that gradually degenerated from my usual scrawl into loops and wiggles that resembled Arabic more than English. Over the next month, I spent whatever spare time I had transcribing the tapes and trying to decipher my own handwriting. I wasn't sure that what I had was an interview. My carefully prepared questions had been met either with evasions or blank, silent refusals to answer – he had simply started talking about something else. After about an hour, I realized that this was his interview, not mine, and let him roll.

After my notes had been typed up and the tapes transcribed, I put everything in a drawer and went back to work on my M.A. What I had was even more puzzling than I'd thought, and straightening it out would have taken more time than I could afford. So the rest of that academic year was a long grind of studying for the comprehensive exam and getting a thesis ready. Until I picked up an old *Time* magazine in the John Jay lounge and saw his name in the 'Milestones' column, I didn't even know that Hat had died.

Two months after I'd interviewed him, he had begun to hemorrhage on a flight back from France; an ambulance had taken him directly from the airport to a hospital. Five days after his release from the hospital, he had died in his bed at the Albert.

After I earned my degree, I was determined to wrestle something usable from my long night with Hat – I owed it to him. During the first seven weeks of that summer, I wrote out a version of what Hat had said to me, and sent it to the only publication I thought would be interested in it. *Downbeat* accepted the interview, and it appeared there about six months later. Eventually, it acquired some fame as the last of his rare public statements. I still see lines from the interview quoted in the sort of pieces about Hat never printed during his life. Sometimes they are lines he really did say to me; sometimes they are stitched together from remarks he made at different times; sometimes they are quotations I invented in order to be able to use other things he did say.

But one section of that interview has never been quoted, because it was never printed. I never figured out what to make of it. Certainly I could not believe all he had said. He had been putting me on, silently laughing at my credulity, for he could not possibly believe that what he was telling me was literal truth. I was a white boy with a tape recorder, it was Halloween, and Hat was having fun with me. He was *jiving* me.

Now I feel different about his story, and about him, too. He was a great man, and I was an unworldly kid. He was drunk, and I was priggishly sober, but in every important way, he was functioning far above my level. Hat had lived forty-nine years as a black man in America, and I'd spent all of my twenty-one years in white suburbs. He was an immensely talented musician, a man who virtually thought in music, and I can't even hum in tune. That I expected to understand anything at all about him staggers me now. Back then, I didn't know anything about grief, and Hat wore grief about him daily, like a cloak. Now that I am the age he was then, I see that most of what is called information is interpretation, and interpretation is always partial.

Probably Hat was putting me on, jiving me, though not maliciously. He certainly was not telling me the literal truth, though I have never been able to learn what was the literal truth of this case. It's possible that even Hat never knew what was the literal truth behind the story he told me – possible, I mean, that he was still trying to work out what the truth was, forty years after the fact.

2

He started telling me the story after we heard what I thought were gunshots from the street. I jumped from the chair and rushed to the windows, which looked out onto Eighth Avenue. 'Kids,' Hat said. In the hard yellow light of the streetlamps, four or five teenage boys trotted up the Avenue. Three of them carried paper bags. 'Kids shooting?' I asked. My amazement tells you how long ago this was.

'Fireworks,' Hat said. 'Every Halloween in New York, fool kids run around with bags full of fireworks, trying to blow their hands off.'

Here and in what follows, I am not going to try to represent the way Hat actually spoke. I cannot represent the way his voice glided over certain words and turned others into mushy growls, though he expressed more than half of his meaning by sound; and I don't want to reproduce his constant, reflexive obscenity. Hat couldn't utter four words in a row without throwing in a 'motherfucker'. Mostly, I have replaced his obscenities with other words, and the reader can imagine what was really said. Also, if I tried to imitate his grammar, I'd sound racist and he would sound stupid. Hat left school in the fourth grade, and his language, though precise, was casual. To add to these difficulties, Hat employed a private language of his own, a code to ensure that he would be understood only by the people he wished to understand him. I have replaced most of his code words with their equivalents.

It must have been around one in the morning, which means that I had been in his room about four hours. Until Hat explained the 'gunshots', I had forgotten that it was Halloween night, and I told him this as I turned away from the window.

'I never forget about Halloween,' Hat said. 'If I can, I stay home on Halloween. Don't want to be out on the street, that night.'

He had already given me proof that he was superstitious, and as he spoke he glanced almost nervously around the room, as if looking for sinister presences.

'You'd feel in danger?' I asked.

He rolled gin around in his mouth and looked at me as he had in the alley behind the club, taking note of qualities I myself did not yet perceive. This did not feel at all judgmental. The nervousness I thought I had seen had disappeared, and his manner seemed marginally more concentrated than earlier in the evening. He swallowed the gin and looked at me without speaking for a couple of seconds.

'No,' he finally said. 'Not exactly. But I wouldn't feel safe, either.'

I sat with my pen half an inch from the page of my notebook, uncertain whether or not to write this down.

'I'm from Mississippi, you know.'

I nodded.

'Funny things happen down there. Whole different world. Back when I was a little kid, it was really a different world. Know what I mean?'

'I can guess,' I said.

He nodded. 'Sometimes people just disappeared. They'd be *gone*. All kinds of stuff used to happen, stuff you wouldn't even believe in now. I met a witch-lady once, a real one, who could put curses on you, make you go blind and crazy. I saw a dead man walk. Another time, I saw a mean, murdering son of a bitch named Eddie Grimes die and come back to life – he got shot to death at a dance we were playing, he was *dead*, and a woman went down and whispered to him, and Eddie Grimes stood right back up on his feet. The man who shot him took off double-quick and he must have kept on going, because we never saw him after that.'

'Did you start playing again?' I asked, taking notes as fast as I could.

'We never stopped,' Hat said. 'You let the people deal with what's going on, but you gotta keep on playing.'

'Did you live in the country?' I asked, thinking that all of this sounded like Dogpatch – witches and walking dead men.

He shook his head. 'I was brought up in town, Woodland, Mississippi. On the river. Where we lived was called Darktown, you know, but most of Woodland was white, with nice houses and all. Lots of our people did the cooking and washing in the big houses on Miller's Hill, that kind of work. In fact, we lived in a pretty nice house, for Darktown – the band always did well, and my father had a couple of other jobs on top of that. He was a good piano player, mainly, but he could play any kind of instrument. And he was a big, strong guy, nice-looking, real light-complected, so he was called Red, which was what that meant in those days. People respected him.'

Another long, rattling burst of explosions came from Eighth Avenue. I wanted to ask him again about leaving his father's band, but Hat once more gave his little room a quick inspection, swallowed another mouthful of gin, and went on talking.

'We even went out trick-or-treating on Halloween, you know, just like the white kids. I guess our people didn't do that everywhere, but we did. Naturally, we stuck to our neighborhood, and probably we got a lot less than the kids from Miller's Hill, but they didn't have anything up there that tasted as good as the apples and candy we brought home in our bags. Around us, folks made instead of bought, and that's the difference.' He smiled at either the memory or the unexpected sentimentality he had just revealed – for a moment, he looked both lost in time and uneasy with himself for having said too much. 'Or maybe I just remember it that way, you know? Anyhow, we used to raise some hell, too. You were *supposed* to raise hell, on Halloween.'

'You went out with your brothers?' I asked.

'No, no, they were—' He flipped his hand in the air, dismissing whatever it was that his brothers had been. 'I was always apart, you dig? Me, I was always into my own little things. I was that way right from the beginning. I play like that – never play like anyone else, don't even play like myself. You gotta find new places for yourself, or else nothing's happening, isn't that right? Don't want to be a repeater pencil.' He saluted this declaration with another swallow of gin. 'Back in those days, I used to go out with a boy named Rodney Sparks – we called him Dee, short for Demon, 'cause Dee Sparks would do anything that came into his head. That boy was the bravest little bastard I ever knew. He'd wrassle a mad dog. He was just that way. And the reason was, Dee was the preacher's boy. If you happen to be the preacher's boy, seems like you gotta prove every way you can that you're no Buster Brown, you know? So I hung with Dee, because I wasn't any Buster Brown, either. This is all when we were eleven, around then – the time when you talk about girls, you know, but you still aren't too sure what that's about. You don't know what *anything*'s about, to tell the truth. You along for the ride, you trying to pack in as much fun as possible. So Dee was my right hand, and when I went out on Halloween in Woodland, I went out with *him*.'

He rolled his eyes toward the window and said, 'Yeah.' An expression I could not read at all took over his face. By the standards of ordinary people, Hat almost always looked detached, even impassive, tuned to some private wavelength, and this sense of detachment had intensified. I thought he was changing mental gears, dismissing his childhood, and opened my mouth to ask him about Grant Kilbert. But he raised his glass to his mouth again and rolled his eyes back to me, and the quality of his gaze told me to keep quiet.

'I didn't know it,' he said, 'but I was getting ready to stop being a little boy. To stop believing in little boy things and start seeing like a grown-up. I guess that's part of what I liked about Dee Sparks – he seemed like he was a lot more grown-up than I was, shows you what my head was like. The age we were, this would have been the last time we actually went out on Halloween to get apples and candy. From then on, we would have gone out mainly to raise hell. Smash in a few windows. Bust up somebody's wagon. Scare the shit out of little kids. But the way it turned out, it was the last time we ever went out on Halloween.'

He finished off the gin in his glass and reached down to pick the bottle off the floor and pour another few inches into the tumbler. 'Here I am, sitting in this room. There's my horn over there. Here's this bottle. You know what I'm saying?'

I didn't. I had no idea what he was saying. The hint of fatality clung to his earlier statement, and for a second I thought he was going to say that he was here but Dee Sparks was nowhere because Dee Sparks had died in Woodland, Mississippi, at the age of eleven on Halloween night. Hat was looking at me with a steady curiosity which compelled a response. 'What happened?' I asked.

Now I know that he was saying *It has come down to just this, my room, my horn, my bottle*. My question was as good as any other response.

'If I was to tell you everything that happened, we'd have to stay in this room for a month.' He smiled and straightened up on the bed. His ankles were crossed, and for the first time I noticed that his feet, shod in dark suede shoes with crepe soles, did not quite touch the floor. 'And, you know, I never tell anybody everything, I always have to keep something back for myself. Things turned out all right. Only thing I mind is, I should have earned more money. Grant Kilbert, he earned a lot of money, and some of that was mine, you know.'

'Were you friends?' I asked.

'I knew the man.' He tilted his head and stared at the ceiling for so long that eventually I looked up at it, too. It was not a remarkable ceiling. A circular section near the center had been replastered not long before.

'No matter where you live, there are places you're not supposed to go,' he said, still gazing up. 'And sooner or later, you're gonna wind up there.' He smiled at me again. 'Where we lived, the place you weren't supposed to go was called The Backs. Out of town, stuck in the woods on one little path. In Darktown, we had all kinds from preachers on down. We had washerwomen and blacksmiths and carpenters, and we had some no-good thieving trash, too, like Eddie Grimes, that man who came back from being dead. In The Backs, they started with trash like Eddie Grimes, and went down from there. Sometimes some of our people went out there to buy a jug, and sometimes they went there to get a woman, but they never talked about it. The Backs was *rough*. What they had was *rough*.' He rolled his eyes at me and said, 'That witch-lady I told you about, she lived in The Backs.' He snickered. 'Man, they were a mean bunch of people. They'd cut you, you looked at 'em bad. But one thing funny about the place, white and colored lived there just the same – it was *integrated*. Backs people were so evil, color didn't make no difference to them. They hated everybody anyhow, on principle.' Hat pointed his glass at me, tilted his head, and narrowed his eyes. 'At least, that was what everybody *said*. So this particular Halloween, Dee Sparks says to me after we finish with Darktown, we ought to head out to The Backs and see what the place is really like. Maybe we can have some fun.

'Well, that sounded fine to me. The idea of going out to The Backs kind of scared me, but being scared was part of the fun – Halloween, right? And if anyplace in Woodland was perfect for all that Halloween shit, you know, someplace where you might really see a ghost or a goblin, The Backs was better than the graveyard.' Hat shook his head, holding the glass out at a right angle to his body. A silvery amusement momentarily transformed him, and it struck me that his native elegance, the product of his character and bearing much more than of the handsome suit and the suede shoes, had in effect been paid for by the surviving of a thousand unimaginable difficulties, each painful to a varying degree. Then I realized that what I meant by elegance was really dignity, that for the first time I had recognized actual dignity in another human being, and that dignity was nothing like the self-congratulatory superiority people usually mistook for it.

'We were just little babies, and we wanted some of those good old Halloween scares. Like those dumbbells out on the street, tossing firecrackers at each other.' Hat wiped his free hand down over his face and made sure that I was prepared to write down everything he said. (The tapes had already been used up.) 'When I'm done, tell me if we found it, okay?'

'Okay,' I said.

3

'Dee showed up at my house just after dinner, dressed in an old sheet with two eyeholes cut in it and carrying a paper bag. His big old shoes stuck out underneath the sheet. I had the same costume, but it was the one my brother used the year before, and it dragged along the ground and my feet got caught in it. The eyeholes kept sliding away from my eyes. My mother gave me a bag and told me to behave myself and get home before eight. It didn't take but half an hour to cover all the likely houses in Darktown, but she knew I'd want to fool around with Dee for an hour or so afterwards.

'Then up and down the streets we go, knocking on the doors where they'd give us stuff and making a little mischief where we knew they wouldn't. Nothing real bad, just banging on the door and running like hell, throwing rocks on the roof, little stuff. A few places, we plain and simple stayed away from – the places where people like Eddie Grimes lived. I always thought that was funny. We knew enough to steer clear of those houses, but we were still crazy to get out to The Backs.

'Only way I can figure it is, The Backs was *forbidden*. Nobody had to tell us to stay away from Eddie Grimes's house that night. You wouldn't even go there in the daylight, 'cause Eddie Grimes would get you and that would be that.

'Anyhow, Dee kept us moving along real quick, and when folks asked us questions or said they wouldn't give us stuff unless we sang a song, he moaned like a ghost and shook his bag in their faces, so we could get away faster. He was so excited, I think he was almost shaking.

'Me, I was excited, too. Not like Dee – sort of sick – excited, the way people must feel the first time they use a parachute. Scared-excited.

'As soon as we got away from the last house, Dee crossed the street and started running down the side of the little general store we all used. I knew where he was going. Out behind the store was a field, and on the other side of the field was Meridian Road, which took you out into the woods and to the path up to The Backs. When he realized that I wasn't next to him, he turned around and yelled at me to hurry up. *No*, I said inside myself, *I ain't gonna jump outta of this here airplane, I'm not dumb enough to do that*. And then I pulled up my sheet and scrunched up my eye to look through the one hole close enough to see through, and I took off after him.

'It was beginning to get dark when Dee and I left my house, and now it was dark. The Backs was about a mile and a half away, or at least the path was. We didn't know how far along that path you had to go before you got there. Hell, we didn't even know what it was – I was still thinking the place was a collection of little houses, like a sort of shadow-Woodland. And then, while we were crossing the field, I stepped on my costume and fell down flat on my face. Enough of this stuff, I said, and yanked the damned thing off. Dee started cussing me out, I wasn't doing this stuff the right way, we had to keep our costumes on in case anybody saw us, did I forget that this is Halloween, on Halloween a costume *protected* you. So I told him I'd put it back on when we got there. If I kept on falling down, it'd take us twice as long. That shut him up.

'As soon as I got that blasted sheet over my head, I discovered that I could see at least a little ways ahead of me. The moon was up, and a lot of stars were out. Under his sheet, Dee Sparks looked a little bit like a real ghost. It kind of glimmered. You couldn't really make out its edges, so the darn thing like *floated*. But I could see his legs and those big old shoes sticking out.

'We got out of the field and started up Meridian Road, and pretty soon the trees came up right to the ditches alongside the road, and I couldn't see too well any more. The road looked like it went smack into the woods and disappeared. The trees looked taller and thicker than in the daytime, and now and then something right at the edge of the woods shone round and white, like an eye – reflecting the moonlight, I guess. Spooked me. I didn't think we'd ever be able to find the path up to The Backs, and that was fine with me. I thought we might go along the road another ten, fifteen minutes, and then turn around and go home. Dee was swooping around up in front of me, flapping his sheet and acting bughouse. *He* sure wasn't trying too hard to find that path.

'After we walked about a mile down Meridian Road, I saw headlights like yellow dots coming toward us fast – Dee didn't see anything at all, running around in circles the way he was. I shouted at him to get off the road, and he took off like a rabbit – disappeared into the woods before I did. I jumped the ditch and hunkered down behind a pine about ten feet off the road to see who was coming. There weren't many cars in Woodland in those days, and I knew every one of them. When the car came by, it was Dr Garland's old red Cord – Dr Garland was a white man, but he had two waiting rooms and took colored patients, so colored patients was mostly what he had. And the man was a heavy drinker, *heavy* drinker. He zipped by, goin' at least fifty, which was mighty fast for those days, probably as fast as that old Cord would go. For about a second, I saw Dr Garland's face under his white hair, and his mouth was wide open, stretched like he was screaming. After he passed, I waited a long time before I came out of the woods. Turning around and going home would have been fine with me. Dr Garland changed everything. Normally, he was kind of slow and quiet, you know, and I could still see that black screaming hole opened up in his face – he looked like he was being tortured, like he was in Hell. I sure as hell didn't want to see whatever *he* had seen.

'I could hear the Cord's engine after the tail lights disappeared. I turned around and saw that I was all alone on the road. Dee Sparks was nowhere in sight. A couple of times, real soft, I called out his name. Then I called his name a little louder. Away off in the woods, I heard Dee giggle. I said he could run around all night if he liked but I was going home, and then I saw that pale silver sheet moving through the trees, and I started back down Meridian Road. After about twenty paces, I looked back, and there he was, standing in the middle of the road in that silly sheet, watching me go. Come on, I said, let's get back. He paid me no mind. Wasn't that Dr Garland? Where was he going, as fast as that? What was happening? When I said the doctor was probably out on some emergency, Dee said the man was going *home* – he lived in Woodland, didn't he?

'Then I thought maybe Dr Garland had been up in The Backs. And Dee thought the same thing, which made him want to go there all the more. Now he was determined. Maybe we'd see some dead guy. We stood there until I understood that he was going to go by himself if I didn't go with him. That meant that I *had* to go. Wild as he was, Dee'd get himself into some kind of mess for sure if I wasn't there to hold him down. So I said okay, I was coming along, and Dee started swooping along like before, saying crazy stuff. There was no way we were going to be able to find some little old path that went up into the woods. It was so dark, you couldn't see the separate trees, only giant black walls on both sides of the road.

'We went so far along Meridian Road I was sure we must have passed it. Dee was running around in circles about ten feet ahead of me. I told him that we missed the path, and now it was time to get back home. He laughed at me and ran across to the right side of the road and disappeared into the darkness.

'I told him to get back, damn it, and he laughed some more and said I should come to *him*. Why? I said, and he said, Because this here is the path, dummy. I didn't believe him – came right up to where he disappeared. All I could see was a black wall that could have been trees or just plain night. Moron, Dee said, look down. And I did. Sure enough, one of those white things like an eye shone up from where the ditch should have been. I bent down and touched cold little stones, and the shining dot of white went off like a light – a pebble that caught the moonlight just right. Bending down like that, I could see the hump of grass growing up between the tire tracks that led out onto Meridian Road. He'd found the path, all right.

'At night, Dee Sparks could see one hell of a lot better than me. He spotted the break in the ditch from across the road. He was already walking up the path in those big old shoes, turning around every other step to look back at me, make sure I was coming along behind him. When I started following him, Dee told me to get my sheet back on, and I pulled the thing over my head even though I'd rather have sucked the water out of a hollow stump. But I knew he was right – on Halloween, especially in a place like where we were, you were safer in a costume.

'From then on in, we were in no man's land. Neither one of us had any idea how far we had to go to get to The Backs, or what it would look like once we got there. Once I set foot on that wagon-track I knew for sure The Backs wasn't anything like the way I thought. It was a lot more primitive than a bunch of houses in the woods. Maybe they didn't even have houses! Maybe they lived in caves!

'Naturally, after I got that blamed costume over my head, I couldn't see for a while. Dee kept hissing at me to hurry up, and I kept cussing him out. Finally I bunched up a couple handfuls of the sheet right under my chin and held it against my neck, and that way I could see pretty well and walk without tripping all over myself. All I had to do was follow Dee, and that was easy. He was only a couple of inches in front of me, and even through one eyehole, I could see that silvery sheet moving along.

'Things moved in the woods, and once in a while an owl hooted. To tell you the truth, I never did like being out in the woods at night. Even back then, give me a nice warm barroom instead, and I'd be happy. Only animal I ever liked was a cat, because a cat is soft to the touch, and it'll fall asleep on your lap. But this was even worse than usual, because of Halloween, and even before we got to The Backs, I wasn't sure if what I heard moving around in the woods was just a possum or a fox or something a lot worse, something with funny eyes and long teeth that liked the taste of little boys. Maybe Eddie Grimes was out there, looking for whatever kind of treat Eddie Grimes liked on Halloween night. Once I thought of that, I got so close to Dee Sparks I could smell him right through his sheet.

'You know what Dee Sparks smelled like? Like sweat, and a little bit like the soap the preacher made him use on his hands and face before dinner, but really like a fire in a junction box – a sharp, kind of bitter smell. That's how excited he was.

'After a while we were going uphill, and then we got to the top of the rise, and a breeze pressed my sheet against my legs. We started going downhill, and over Dee's electrical fire, I could smell woodsmoke. And something else I couldn't name. Dee stopped moving so sudden, I bumped into him. I asked him what he could see. Nothing but the woods, he said, but we're getting there. People are up ahead somewhere. And they got a still. We got to be real quiet from here on out, he told me, as if he had to, and to let him know I understood I pulled him off the path into the woods.

'Well, I thought, at least I know what Dr Garland was after.

'Dee and I went snaking through the trees – me holding that blamed sheet under my chin so I could see out of one eye, at least, and walk without falling down. I was glad for that big fat pad of pine needles on the ground. An elephant could have walked over that stuff as quiet as a beetle. We went along a little further, and it got so I could smell all kinds of stuff – burned sugar, crushed juniper berries, tobacco juice, grease. And after Dee and I moved a little bit along, I heard voices, and that was enough for me. Those voices sounded angry.

'I yanked at Dee's sheet and squatted down – I wasn't going any farther without taking a good look. He slipped down beside me. I pushed the wad of material under my chin up over my face, grabbed another handful, and yanked that up, too, to look out under the bottom of the sheet. Once I could actually *see* where we were, I almost passed out. Twenty feet away through the trees, a kerosene lantern lit up the greasepaper window cut into the back of a little wooden shack, and a big raggedy guy carrying another kerosene lantern came stepping out of a door we couldn't see and stumbled toward a shed. On the other side of the building I could see the yellow square of a window in another shack, and past that, another one, a sliver of yellow shining out through the trees. Dee was crouched next to me, and when I turned to look at him, I could see another chink of yellow light from some way off in the woods over that way. Whether he knew it or not, he'd just about walked us straight into the middle of The Backs.

'He whispered for me to cover my face. I shook my head. Both of us watched the big guy stagger toward the shed. Somewhere in front of us, a woman screeched, and I almost dumped a load in my pants. Dee stuck his hand out from under his sheet and held it out, as if I needed *him* to tell me to be quiet. The woman screeched again, and the big guy sort of swayed back and forth. The light from the lantern swung around in big circles. I saw that the woods were full of little paths that ran between the shacks. The light hit the shack, and it wasn't even wood, but tarpaper. The woman laughed or maybe sobbed. Whoever was inside the shack shouted, and the raggedy guy wobbled toward the shed again. He was so drunk he couldn't even walk straight. When he got to the shed, he set down the lantern and bent to get in.

'Dee put his mouth up to my ear and whispered, *Cover up – you don't want these people to see who you are. Rip the eyeholes, if you can't see good enough.*

'I didn't want anyone in The Backs to see my face. I let the costume drop down over me again, and stuck my fingers in the nearest eyehole and pulled. Every living thing for about a mile around must have heard that cloth ripping. The big guy came out of the shed like someone pulled him out on a string, yanked the lantern up off the ground, and held it in our direction. Then we could see his face, and it was Eddie Grimes. You wouldn't want to run into Eddie Grimes anywhere, but The Backs was the last place you'd want to come across him. I was afraid he was going to start looking for us, but that woman started making stuck pig noises, and the man in the shack yelled something, and Grimes ducked back into the shed and came out with a jug. He lumbered back toward the shack and disappeared around the front of it. Dee and I could hear him arguing with the man inside.

'I jerked my thumb toward Meridian Road, but Dee shook his head. I whispered, *Didn't you already see Eddie Grimes, and isn't that enough for you?* He shook his head again. His eyes were gleaming behind that sheet. *So what do you want?* I asked, and he said, *I want to see that girl. We don't even know where she is,* I whispered, and Dee said, *All we got to do is follow her sound.*

'Dee and I sat and listened for a while. Every now and then, she let out a sort of whoop, and then she'd sort of cry, and after that she might say a word or two that sounded almost ordinary before she got going again on crying or laughing, the two all mixed up together. Sometimes we could hear other noises coming from the shacks, and none of them sounded happy. People were grumbling and arguing or just plain talking to themselves, but at least they sounded normal. That lady, she sounded like *Halloween* – like something that came up out of a grave.

'Probably you're thinking what I was hearing was sex – that I was too young to know how much noise ladies make when they're having fun. Well, maybe I was only eleven, but I grew up in Darktown, not Miller's Hill, and our walls were none too thick. What was going on with this lady didn't have anything to do with fun. The strange thing is, Dee didn't know that – he thought just what you were thinking. He wanted to see this lady getting humped. Maybe he even thought he could sneak in and get some for himself, I don't know. The main thing is, he thought he was listening to some wild sex, and he wanted to get close enough to see it. Well, I thought, his daddy was a preacher, and maybe preachers didn't do it once they got kids. And Dee didn't have an older brother like mine, who sneaked girls into the house whenever he thought he wouldn't get caught.

'He started sliding sideways through the woods, and I had to follow him. I'd seen enough of The Backs to last me the rest of my life, but I couldn't run off and leave Dee behind. And at least he was going at it the right way, circling around the shacks sideways, instead of trying to sneak straight through them. I started off after him. At least I could see a little better ever since I ripped at my eyehole, but I still had to hold my blasted costume bunched up under my chin, and if I moved my head or my hand the wrong way, the hole moved away from my eye and I couldn't see anything at all.

'So naturally, the first thing that happened was that I lost sight of Dee Sparks. My foot came down in a hole and I stumbled ahead for a few steps, completely blind, and then I hit a tree. I just came to a halt, sure that Eddie Grimes and a few other murderers were about to jump on me. For a couple of seconds I stood as still as a wooden Indian, too scared to move. When I didn't hear anything, I hauled at my costume until I could see out of it. No murderers were coming toward me from the shack beside the still. Eddie Grimes was saying *You don't understand* over and over, like he was so drunk that one phrase got stuck in his head, and he couldn't say or hear anything else. That woman yipped, like an animal noise, not a human one – like a fox barking. I sidled up next to the tree I'd run into and looked around for Dee. All I could see was dark trees and that one yellow window I'd seen before. To hell with Dee Sparks, I said to myself, and pulled the costume off over my head. I could see better, but there wasn't any glimmer of white over that way. He'd gone so far ahead of me I couldn't even see him.

'So I had to catch up with him, didn't I? I knew where he was going – the woman's noises were coming from the shack way up there in the woods – and I knew he was going to sneak around the outside of the shacks. In a couple of seconds, after he noticed I wasn't there, he was going to stop and wait for me. Makes sense, doesn't it? All I had to do was keep going toward that shack off to the side until I ran into him. I shoved my costume inside my shirt, and then I did something else – set my bag of candy down next to the tree. I'd clean forgotten about it ever since I saw Eddie Grimes's face, and if I had to run, I'd go faster without holding onto a lot of apples and chunks of taffy.

'About a minute later, I came out into the open between two big old chinaberry trees. There was a patch of grass between me and the next stand of trees. The woman made a gargling sound that ended in one of those fox yips, and I looked up in that direction and saw that the clearing extended in a straight line up and down, like a path. Stars shone out of the patch of darkness between the two parts of the woods. And when I started to walk across it, I felt a grassy hump between two beaten tracks. The path into The Backs off Meridian Road curved around somewhere up ahead and wound back down through the shacks before it came to a dead end. It had to come to a dead end, because it sure didn't join back up with Meridian Road.

'And this was how I'd managed to lose sight of Dee Sparks. Instead of avoiding the path and working his way north through the woods, he'd just taken the easiest way toward the woman's shack. Hell, I'd had to pull him off the path in the first place! By the time I got out of my sheet, he was probably way up there, out in the open for anyone to see and too excited to notice that he was all by himself. What I had to do was what I'd been trying to do all along, save his ass from anybody who might see him.

'As soon as I started going as soft as I could up the path, I saw that saving Dee Sparks's ass might be a tougher job than I thought – maybe I couldn't even save my own. When I first took off my costume, I'd seen lights from three or four shacks. I thought that's what The Backs was – three or four shacks. But after I started up the path, I saw a low square shape standing between two trees at the edge of the woods and realized that it was another shack. Whoever was inside had extinguished his kerosene lamp, or maybe wasn't home. About twenty to thirty feet on, there was another shack, all dark, and the only reason I noticed that one was, I heard voices coming from it, a man and a woman, both of them sounding drunk and slowed-down. Deeper in the woods past that one, another greasepaper window gleamed through the woods like a firefly. There were shacks all over the woods. As soon as I realized that Dee and I might not be the only people walking through The Backs on Halloween night, I bent down low to the ground and damn near slowed to a standstill. The only thing Dee had going for him, I thought, was good night vision – at least he might spot someone before they spotted him.

'A noise came from one of those shacks, and I stopped cold, with my heart pounding away like a bass drum. Then a big voice called out, *Who's that?*, and I just lay down in the track and tried to disappear. *Who's there?* Here I was calling Dee a fool, and I was making more noise than he did. I heard that man walk outside his door, and my heart pretty near exploded. Then the woman moaned up ahead, and the man who'd heard me swore to himself and went back inside. I just lay there in the dirt for a while. The woman moaned again, and this time it sounded scarier than ever, because it had a kind of a chuckle in it. She was crazy. Or she was a witch, and if she was having sex, it was with the devil. That was enough to make me start crawling along, and I kept on crawling until I was long past the shack where the man had heard me. Finally I got up on my feet again, thinking that if I didn't see Dee Sparks real soon, I was going to sneak back to Meridian Road by myself. If Dee Sparks wanted to see a witch in bed with the devil, he could do it without me.

'And then I thought I was a fool not to ditch Dee, because hadn't he ditched me? After all this time, he must have noticed that I wasn't with him any more. Did he come back and look for me? The hell he did.

'And right then I would have gone back home, but for two things. The first was that I heard that woman make another sound – a sound that was hardly human, but wasn't made by any animal. It wasn't even loud. And it sure as hell wasn't any witch in bed with the devil. It made me want to throw up. That woman was being *hurt*. She wasn't just getting beat up – I knew what that sounded like – she was being hurt bad enough to drive her crazy, bad enough to kill her. Because you couldn't live through being hurt bad enough to make that sound. I was in The Backs, sure enough, and the place was even worse than it was supposed to be. Someone was killing a woman, everybody could hear it, and all that happened was that Eddie Grimes fetched another jug back from the still. I froze. When I could move, I pulled my ghost costume out from inside my shirt, because Dee was right, and for certain I didn't want anybody seeing my face out there on *this* night. And then the second thing happened. While I was pulling the sheet over my head, I saw something pale lying in the grass a couple of feet back toward the woods I'd come out of, and when I looked at it, it turned into Dee Sparks's Halloween bag.

'I went up to the bag and touched it to make sure about what it was. I'd found Dee's bag, all right. And it was empty. Flat. He had stuffed the contents into his pockets and left the bag behind. What that meant was, I couldn't turn around and leave him – because he hadn't left me after all. He waited for me until he couldn't stand it any more, and then he emptied his bag and left it behind as a sign. He was counting on me to see in the dark as well as he could. But I wouldn't have seen it at all if that woman hadn't stopped me cold.

'The top of the bag was pointing north, so Dee was still heading toward the woman's shack. I looked up that way, and all I could see was a solid wall of darkness underneath a lighter darkness filled with stars. For about a second, I realized, I had felt pure relief. Dee had ditched me, so I could ditch him and go home. Now I was stuck with Dee all over again.

'About twenty feet ahead, another surprise jumped up at me out of the darkness. Something that looked like a little tiny shack began to take shape, and I got down on my hands and knees to crawl toward the path when I saw a long silver gleam along the top of the thing. That meant it had to be metal – tarpaper might have a lot of uses, but it never yet reflected starlight. Once I realized that the thing in front of me was metal, I remembered its shape and realized it was a car. You wouldn't think you'd come across a car in a down-and-out rathole like The Backs, would you? People like that, they don't even own two shirts, so how do they come by cars? Then I remembered Dr Garland speeding driving away down Meridian Road, and I thought *You don't have to live in The Backs to drive there*. Someone could turn up onto the path, drive around the loop, pull his car off onto the grass, and no one would ever see it or know that he was there.

'And this made me feel funny. The car probably belonged to someone I knew. Our band played dances and parties all over the county and everywhere in Woodland, and I'd probably seen every single person in town, and they'd seen me, too, and knew me by name. I walked closer to the car to see if I recognized it, but it was just an old black Model T. There must have been twenty cars just like it in Woodland. Whites and coloreds, the few coloreds that owned cars, both had them. And when I got right up beside the Model T, I saw what Dee had left for me on the hood – an apple.

'About twenty feet further along, there was an apple on top of a big old stone. He was putting those apples where I couldn't help but see them. The third one was on top of a post at the edge of the woods, and it was so pale it looked almost white. Next to the post one of those paths running all through The Backs led back into the woods. If it hadn't been for that apple, I would have gone right past it.

'At least I didn't have to worry so much about making a noise once I got back into the woods. Must have been six inches of pine needles and fallen leaves underfoot, and I walked so quiet I could have been floating – tell you the truth, I've worn crepe soles ever since then, and for the same reason. You walk *soft*. But I was still plenty scared – back in the woods there was a lot less light, and I'd have to step on an apple to see it. All I wanted was to find Dee and persuade him to leave with me.

'For a while, all I did was keep moving between the trees and try to make sure I wasn't coming up on a shack. Every now and then, a faint, slurry voice came from somewhere off in the woods, but I didn't let it spook me. Then, way up ahead, I saw Dee Sparks. The path didn't go in a straight line, it kind of angled back and forth, so I didn't have a good clear look at him, but I got a flash of that silvery-looking sheet way off through the trees. If I sped up I could get to him before he did anything stupid. I pulled my costume up a little further toward my neck and started to jog.

'The path started dipping *downhill*. I couldn't figure it out. Dee was in a straight line ahead of me, and as soon as I followed the path downhill a little bit, I lost sight of him. After a couple more steps, I stopped. The path got a lot steeper. If I kept running, I'd go ass over teakettle. The woman made another terrible sound, and it seemed to come from everywhere at once. Like everything around me had been *hurt*. I damn near came unglued. Seemed like everything was *dying*. That Halloween stuff about horrible creatures wasn't any story, man, it was the way things really were – you couldn't know anything, you couldn't trust anything, and you were surrounded by *death*. I almost fell down and cried like a baby boy. I was lost. I didn't think I'd ever get back home.

'Then the worst thing of all happened.

'I heard her die. It was just a little noise, more like a sigh than anything, but that sigh came from everywhere and went straight into my ear. A soft sound can be loud, too, you know, be the loudest thing you ever heard. That sigh about lifted me up off the ground, about blew my head apart.

'I stumbled down the path, trying to wipe my eyes with my costume, and all of a sudden I heard men's voices from off to my left. Someone was saying a word I couldn't understand over and over, and someone else was telling him to shut up. Then, behind me, I heard running – heavy running, a man. I took off, and right away my feet got tangled up in the sheet and I was rolling downhill, hitting my head on rocks and bouncing off trees and smashing into stuff I didn't have any idea what it was. Biff bop bang slam smash clang crash ding dong. I hit something big and solid and wound up half-covered in water. Took me a long time to get upright, twisted up in the sheet the way I was. My ears buzzed, and I saw stars – yellow and blue and red stars, not real ones. When I tried to sit up, the blasted sheet pulled me back down, so I got a faceful of cold water. I scrambled around like a fox in a trap, and when I finally got so I was at least sitting up, I saw a slash of real sky out the corner of one eye, and I got my hands free and ripped that hole in the sheet wide enough for my whole head to fit through it.

'I was sitting in a little stream next to a fallen tree. The tree was what had stopped me. My whole body hurt like the dickens. No idea where I was. Wasn't even sure I could stand up. Got my hands on the top of the fallen tree and pushed myself up with my legs – blasted sheet ripped in half, and my knees almost bent back the wrong way, but I got up on my feet. And there was Dee Sparks, coming toward me through the woods on the other side of the stream.

'He looked like he didn't feel any better than I did, like he couldn't move in a straight line. His silvery sheet was smearing through the trees. *Dee got hurt, too*, I thought – he looked like he was in some total panic. The next time I saw the white smear between the trees it was twisting about ten feet off the ground. *No*, I said to myself, and closed my eyes. Whatever that thing was, it wasn't Dee. An unbearable feeling, an absolute despair, flowed out from it. I fought against this wave of despair with every weapon I had. I didn't want to know that feeling. I couldn't know that feeling – I was eleven years old. If that feeling reached me when I was eleven years old, my entire life would be changed, I'd be in a different universe altogether.

'But it did reach me, didn't it? I could say *no* all I liked, but I couldn't change what had happened. I opened my eyes, and the white smear was gone.

'That was almost worse – I wanted it to be Dee after all, doing something crazy and reckless, climbing trees, running around like a wildman, trying to give me a big whopping scare. But it wasn't Dee Sparks, and it meant that the worst things I'd ever imagined were true. Everything was dying. You couldn't know anything, you couldn't trust anything, we were all lost in the midst of the death that surrounded us.

'Most people will tell you growing up means you stop believing in Halloween things – I'm telling you the reverse. You start to grow up when you understand that the stuff that scares you is part of the air you breathe.

'I stared at the spot where I'd seen that twist of whiteness, I guess trying to go back in time to before I saw Dr Garland fleeing down Meridian Road. My face looked like his, I thought – because now I knew that you really *could* see a ghost. The heavy footsteps I'd heard before suddenly cut through the buzzing in my head, and after I turned around and saw who was coming at me down the hill, I thought it was probably my own ghost I'd seen.

'Eddie Grimes looked as big as an oak tree, and he had a long knife in one hand. His feet slipped out from under him, and he skidded the last few yards down to the creek, but I didn't even try to run way. Drunk as he was, I'd never get away from him. All I did was back up alongside the fallen tree and watch him slide downhill toward the water. I was so scared I couldn't even talk. Eddie Grimes's shirt was flapping open, and big long scars ran all across his chest and belly. He'd been raised from the dead at least a couple of times since I'd seen him get killed at the dance. He jumped back up on his feet and started coming for me. I opened my mouth, but nothing came out.

'Eddie Grimes took another step toward me, and then he stopped and looked straight at my face. He lowered the knife. A sour stink of sweat and alcohol came off him. All he could do was stare at me. Eddie Grimes knew my face all right, he knew my name, he knew my whole family – even at night, he couldn't mistake me for anyone else. I finally saw that Eddie was actually afraid, like he was the one who'd seen a ghost. The two of us just stood there in the shallow water for a couple more seconds, and then Eddie Grimes pointed his knife at the other side of the creek.

'That was all I needed, baby. My legs unfroze, and I forgot all my aches and pains. Eddie watched me roll over the fallen tree and lowered his knife. I splashed through the water and started moving up the hill, grabbing at weeds and branches to pull me along. My feet were frozen, and my clothes were soaked and muddy, and I was trembling all over. About halfway up the hill, I looked back over my shoulder, but Eddie Grimes was gone. It was like he'd never been there at all, like he was nothing but the product of a couple of good raps to the noggin.

'Finally, I pulled myself shaking up over the top of the rise, and what did I see about ten feet away through a lot of skinny birch trees but a kid in a sheet facing away from me into the woods, and hopping from foot to foot in a pair of big clumsy shoes? And what was in front of him but a path I could make out from even ten feet away? Obviously, this was where I was supposed to turn up, only in the dark and all I must have missed an apple stuck onto a branch or some blasted thing, and I took that little side trip downhill on my head and wound up throwing a spook into Eddie Grimes.

'As soon as I saw him, I realized I hated Dee Sparks. I wouldn't have tossed him a rope if he was drowning. Without even thinking about it, I bent down and picked up a stone and flung it at him. The stone bounced off a tree, so I bent down and got another one. Dee turned around to find out what made the noise, and the second stone hit him right in the chest, even though it was really his head I was aiming at.

'He pulled his sheet up over his face like an Arab and stared at me with his mouth wide open. Then he looked back over his shoulder at the path, as if the real me might come along at any second. I felt like pegging another rock at his stupid face, but instead I marched up to him. He was shaking his head from side to side. *Jim Dawg*, he whispered, *what happened to you?* By way of answer, I hit him a good hard knock on the breastbone. *What's the matter?* he wanted to know. *After you left me*, I say, *I fell down a hill and ran into Eddie Grimes.*

'That gave him something to think about, all right. Was Grimes coming after me? he wanted to know. Did he see which way I went? Did Grimes see who I was? He was pulling me into the woods while he asked me these dumb-ass questions, and I shoved him away. His sheet flopped back down over his front, and he looked like a little boy. He couldn't figure out why I was mad at him. From his point of view, he'd been pretty clever, and if I got lost, it was my fault. But I wasn't mad at him because I got lost. I wasn't even mad at him because I'd run into Eddie Grimes. It was everything else. Maybe it wasn't even him I was mad at.

'*I want to get home without getting killed*, I whispered. *Eddie ain't gonna let me go twice.* Then I pretended he wasn't there any more and tried to figure out how to get back to Meridian Road. It seemed to me that I was still going north when I took that tumble downhill, so when I climbed up the hill on the other side of the creek I was still going north. The wagon-track that Dee and I took into The Backs had to be off to my right. I turned away from Dee and started moving through the woods. I didn't care if he followed me or not. He had nothing to do with me any more, he was on his own. When I heard him coming along after me, I was sorry. I wanted to get away from Dee Sparks. I wanted to get away from everybody.

'I didn't want to be around anybody who was supposed to be my friend. I'd rather have had Eddie Grimes following me than Dee Sparks.

'Then I stopped moving, because through the trees I could see one of those greasepaper windows glowing up ahead of me. That yellow light looked evil as the devil's eye – everything in The Backs was evil, poisoned, even the trees, even the air. The terrible expression on Dr Garland's face and the white smudge in the air seemed like the same thing – they were what I didn't want to know.

'Dee shoved me from behind, and if I hadn't felt so sick inside I would have turned around and punched him. Instead, I looked over my shoulder and saw him nodding toward where the side of the shack would be. He wanted to get closer! For a second, he seemed as crazy as everything else out there, and then I got it: I was all turned around, and instead of heading back to the main path, I'd been taking us toward the woman's shack. That was why Dee was following me.

'I shook my head. No, I wasn't going to sneak up to that place. Whatever was inside there was something I didn't have to know about. It had too much power – it turned Eddie Grimes around, and that was enough for me. Dee knew I wasn't fooling. He went around me and started creeping toward the shack.

'And damnedest thing, I watched him slipping through the trees for a second and started following him. If he could go up there, so could I. If I didn't exactly look at whatever was in there myself, I could watch Dee look at it. That would tell me most of what I had to know. And anyways, probably Dee wouldn't see anything anyhow, unless the front door was hanging open, and that didn't seem too likely to me. He wouldn't see anything, and I wouldn't either, and we could both go home.

'The door of the shack opened up, and a man walked outside. Dee and I freeze, and I mean *freeze*. We're about twenty feet away, on the side of this shack, and if the man looked sideways, he'd see our sheets. There were a lot of trees between us and him, and I couldn't get a very good look at him, but one thing about him made the whole situation a lot more serious. This man was white, and he was wearing good clothes – I couldn't see his face, but I could see his rolled-up sleeves, and his suit jacket slung over one arm, and some kind of wrapped-up bundle he was holding in his hands. All this took about a second. The white man started carrying his bundle straight through the woods, and in another two seconds he was out of sight.

'Dee was a little closer than I was, and I think his sight line was a little clearer than mine. On top of that, he saw better at night than I did. Dee didn't get around like me, but he might have recognized the man we'd seen, and that would be pure trouble. Some rich white man, killing a girl out in The Backs? And us two boys close enough to see him? Do you know what would have happened to us? There wouldn't be enough left of either one of us to make a decent shadow.

'Dee turned around to face me, and I could see his eyes behind his costume, but I couldn't tell what he was thinking. He just stood there, looking at me. In a little bit, just when I was about to explode, we heard a car starting up off to our left. I whispered at Dee if he saw who that was. *Nobody*, Dee said. Now, what the hell did that mean? Nobody? You could say Santa Claus, you could say J. Edgar *Hoover*, it'd be a better answer than Nobody. The Model T's headlights shone through the trees when the car swung around the top of the path and started going toward Meridian Road. *Nobody I ever saw before*, Dee said. When the headlights cut through the trees, both of us ducked out of sight. Actually, we were so far from the path, we had nothing to worry about. I could barely see the car when it went past, and I couldn't see the driver at all.

'We stood up. Over Dee's shoulder I could see the side of the shack where the white man had been. Lamplight flickered on the ground in front of the open door. The last thing in the world I wanted to do was to go inside that place – I didn't even want to walk around to the front and look in the door. Dee stepped back from me and jerked his head toward the shack. I knew it was going to be just like before. I'd say no, he'd say yes, and then I'd follow him wherever he thought he had to go. I felt the same way I did when I saw that white smear in the woods – hopeless, lost in the midst of death. *You go, if you have to*, I whispered to him, *it's

413

what you wanted to do all along. He didn't move, and I saw that he wasn't too sure about what he wanted any more.

'Everything was different now, because the white man made it different. Once a white man walked out that door, it was like raising the stakes in a poker game. But Dee had been working toward that one shack ever since we got into The Backs, and he was still curious as a cat about it. He turned away from me and started moving sideways in a straight line, so he'd be able to peek inside the door from a safe distance.

'After he got about halfway to the front, he looked back and waved me on, like this was still some great adventure he wanted me to share. He was afraid to be on his own, that was all. When he realized I was going to stay put, he bent down and moved real slow past the side. He still couldn't see more than a sliver of the inside of the shack, and he moved ahead another little ways. By then, I figured, he should have been able to see about half of the inside of the shack. He hunkered down inside his sheet, staring in the direction of the open door. And there he stayed.

'I took it for about half a minute, and then I couldn't any more. I was sick enough to die and angry enough to explode, both at the same time. How long could Dee Sparks look at a dead whore? Wouldn't a couple of seconds be enough? Dee was acting like he was watching a goddamn Hopalong Cassidy movie. An owl screeched, and some man in another shack said *Now that's over*, and someone else shushed him. If Dee heard, he paid it no mind. I started along toward him, and I don't think he noticed me, either. He didn't look up until I was past the front of the shack, and had already seen the door hanging open, and the lamplight spilling over the plank floor and onto the grass outside.

'I took another step, and Dee's head snapped around. He tried to stop me by holding out his hand. All that did was make me mad. Who was Dee Sparks to tell me what I couldn't see? All he did was leave me alone in the woods with a trail of apples, and he didn't even do that right. When I kept on coming, Dee started waving both hands at me, looking back and forth between me and the inside of the shack. Like something was happening in there that I couldn't be allowed to see. I didn't stop, and Dee got up on his feet and skittered toward me.

'*We gotta get out of here*, he whispered. He was close enough so I could smell that electrical fire stink. I stepped to his side, and he grabbed my arm. I yanked my arm out of his grip and went forward a little ways and looked through the door of the shack.

'A bed was shoved up against the far wall, and a woman lay naked on the bed. There was blood all over her legs, and blood all over the sheets, and big puddles of blood on the floor. A woman in a raggedy robe, hair stuck out all over her head, squatted beside the bed, holding the other woman's hand. She was a colored woman – a Backs woman – but the other one, the one on the bed, was white. Probably she was pretty, when she was alive. All I could see was white skin and blood, and I near fainted.

'This wasn't some white-trash woman who lived out in The Backs, she was brought there, and the man who brought her had killed her. More trouble was coming down than I could imagine, trouble enough to kill lots of our people. And if Dee and I said a word about the white man we'd seen, the trouble would come right straight down on us.

'I must have made some kind of noise, because the woman next to the bed turned halfway around and looked at me. There wasn't any doubt about it – she saw me. All she saw of Dee was a dirty white sheet, but she saw my face, and she knew who I was. I knew her, too, and she wasn't any Backs woman. She lived down the street from us. Her name was Mary Randolph, and she was the one who came up to Eddie Grimes after he got shot to death and brought him back to life. Mary Randolph followed my dad's band, and when we played roadhouses or colored dance halls, she'd be likely to turn up. A couple of times she told me I played good drums – I was a drummer back then, you know, switched to saxophone when I turned twelve. Mary Randolph just looked at me, her hair stuck out straight all over her head like she was already inside a whirlwind of trouble. No expression on her face except that look you get when your mind is going a mile a minute and your body can't move at all. She didn't even look surprised. She almost looked like she *wasn't* surprised, like she was expecting to see me. As bad as I'd felt that night, this was the worst of all. I liked to have died. I'd have disappeared down an anthill, if I could. I didn't know what I had done – just be there, I guess – but I'd never be able to undo it.

'I pulled at Dee's sheet, and he tore off down the side of the shack like he'd been waiting for a signal. Mary Randolph stared into my eyes, and it felt like I had to pull myself away – I couldn't just turn my head, I had to *disconnect*. And when I did, I could still feel her staring at me. Somehow I made myself go down past the side of the shack, but I could still see Mary Randolph inside there, looking out at the place I'd been.

'If Dee said anything at all when I caught up with him, I'd have knocked his teeth down his throat, but he just moved fast and quiet through the trees, seeing the best way to go, and I followed after. I felt like I'd been kicked by a horse. When we got on the path, we didn't bother trying to sneak down through the woods on the other side, we lit out and ran as hard as we could – like wild dogs were after us. And after we got onto Meridian Road, we ran toward town until we couldn't run any more.

'Dee clamped his hand over his side and staggered forward a little bit. Then he stopped and ripped off his costume and lay down by the side of the road, breathing hard. I was leaning forward with hands on my knees, as winded as he was. When I could breathe again, I started walking down the road. Dee picked himself up and got next to me and walked along, looking at my face and then looking away, and then looking back at my face again.

'*So?* I said.

'*I know that lady*, Dee said.

'Hell, that was no news. Of course he knew Mary Randolph – she was his neighbor, too. I didn't bother to answer, I just grunted at him. Then I reminded him that Mary hadn't seen his face, only mine.

'*Not Mary*, he said. *The other one.*

'He knew the dead white woman's name? That made everything worse. A lady like that shouldn't be in Dee Sparks's world, especially if she's going to wind up dead in The Backs. I wondered who was going to get lynched, and how many.

'Then Dee said that I knew her, too. I stopped walking and looked him straight in the face.

'*Miss Abbey Montgomery*, he said. *She brings clothes and food down to our church, Thanksgiving and Christmas.*

'He was right – I wasn't sure if I'd ever heard her name, but I'd seen her once or twice, bringing baskets of ham and chicken and boxes of clothes to Dee's father's church. She was about twenty years old, I guess, so pretty she made you smile just to look at. From a rich family in a big house right at the top of Miller's Hill. Some man didn't think a girl like that should have any associations with colored people, I guess, and decided to express his opinion about as strong as possible. Which meant that we were going to take the blame for what happened to her, and the next time we saw white sheets, they wouldn't be Halloween costumes.

'He sure took a long time to kill her, I said.

'And Dee said, She ain't dead.

'So I asked him, what the hell did he mean by that? I saw the girl. I saw the blood. Did he think she was going to get up and walk around? Or maybe Mary Randolph was going to tell her that magic word and bring her back to life?

'You can think that if you want to, Dee said. But Abbey Montgomery ain't dead.

'I almost told him I'd seen her ghost, but he didn't deserve to hear about it. The fool couldn't even see what was right in front of his eyes. I couldn't expect him to understand what happened to me when I saw that miserable . . . that thing. He was rushing on ahead of me anyhow, like I'd suddenly embarrassed him or something. That was fine with me. I felt the exact same way. I said, I guess you know neither one of us can ever talk about this, and he said, I guess you know it, too, and that was the last thing we said to each other that night. All the way down Meridian Road Dee Sparks kept his eyes straight ahead and his mouth shut. When we got to the field, he turned toward me like he had something to say, and I waited for it, but he faced forward again and ran away. Just ran. I watched him disappear past the general store, and then I walked home by myself.

'My mom gave me hell for getting my clothes all wet and dirty, and my brothers laughed at me and wanted to know who beat me up and stole my candy. As soon as I could, I went to bed, pulled the covers up over my head, and closed my eyes. A little while later, my mom came in and asked if I was all right. Did I get into a fight with Dee Sparks? Dee Sparks was born to hang, that was what she thought, and I ought to have a better class of friends. I'm tired of playing those drums, Momma, I said, I want to play the saxophone instead. She looked at me surprised, but said she'd talk about it with Daddy, and that it might work out.

'For the next couple days, I waited for the bomb to go off. On the Friday, I went to school, but couldn't concentrate for beans. Dee Sparks and I didn't even nod at each other in the hallways – just walked by like the other guy was invisible. On the weekend I said I felt sick and stayed in bed, wondering when that whirlwind of trouble would come down. I wondered if Eddie Grimes would talk about seeing me – once they found the body, they'd get around to Eddie Grimes real quick.

'But nothing happened that weekend, and nothing happened all the next week. I thought Mary Randolph must have hid the white girl in a grave out in The Backs. But how long could a girl from one of those rich families go missing without investigations and search parties? And, on top of that, what was Mary Randolph doing there in the first place? She liked to have a good time, but she wasn't one of those wild girls with a razor under her skirt – she went to church every Sunday, was good to people, nice to kids. Maybe she went out to comfort that poor girl, but how did she know she'd be there in the first place? Misses Abbey Montgomerys from the hill didn't share their plans with Mary Randolphs from Darktown. I couldn't forget the way she looked at me, but I couldn't understand it, either. The more I thought about that look, the more it was like Mary Randolph was saying something to me, but what? *Are you ready for this? Do you understand this? Do you know how careful you must be?*

'My father said I could start learning the C-melody sax, and when I was ready to play it in public, my little brother wanted to take over the drums. Seems he always wanted to play drums, and in fact, he's been a drummer ever since, a good one. So I worked out how to play my little sax, I went to school and came straight home after, and everything went on like normal, except Dee Sparks and I weren't friends any more. If the police were searching for a missing rich girl, I didn't hear anything about it.

'Then one Saturday I was walking down our street to go to the general store, and Mary Randolph came through her front door just as I got to her house. When she saw me, she stopped moving real sudden, with one hand still on the side of the door. I was so surprised to see her that I was in a kind of slow-motion, and I must have stared at her. She gave me a look like an X-ray, a look that searched around down inside me. I don't know what she saw, but her face relaxed, and she took her hand off the door and let it close behind her, and she wasn't looking inside me any more. *Miss Randolph*, I said, and she told me she was looking forward to hearing our band play at a Beergarden dance in a couple of weeks. I told her I was going to be playing the saxophone at that dance, and she said something about that, and all the time it was like we were having two conversations, the top one about me and the band, and the one underneath about her and the murdered white girl in The Backs. It made me so nervous, my words got all mixed up. Finally she said *You make sure you say hello to your daddy from me, now*, and I got away.

'After I passed her house, Mary Randolph started walking down the street behind me. I could feel her watching me, and I started to sweat. Mary Randolph was a total mystery to me. She was a nice lady, but probably she buried that girl's body. I didn't know but that she was going to come and kill *me*, one day. And then I remembered her kneeling down beside Eddie Grimes at the roadhouse. She had been *dancing* with Eddie Grimes, who was in jail more often than he was out. I wondered if you could be a respectable lady and still know Eddie Grimes well enough to dance with him. And how did she bring him back to life? Or was that what happened at all? Hearing that lady walk along behind me made me so uptight, I crossed to the other side of the street.

'A couple days after that, when I was beginning to think that the trouble was never going to happen after all, it came down. We heard police cars coming down the street right when we were finishing dinner. I thought they were coming for me, and I almost lost my chicken and rice. The sirens went right past our house, and then more sirens came toward us from other directions – the old klaxons they had in those days. It sounded like every cop in the state was rushing into Darktown. This was bad, bad news. Someone was going to wind up dead, that was certain. No way all those police were going to come into our part of town, make all that commotion, and leave without killing at least one man. That's the truth. You just had to pray that the man they killed wasn't you or anyone in your family. My daddy turned off the lamps, and we went to the window to watch the cars go by. Two of them were state police. When it was safe, Daddy went outside to see where all the trouble was headed. After he came back in, he said it looked like the police were going toward Eddie Grimes's place. We wanted to go out and look, but they wouldn't let us, so we went to the back windows that faced toward Grimes's house.

Couldn't see anything but a lot of cars and police standing all over the road back there. Sounded like they were knocking down Grimes's house with sledge hammers. Then a whole bunch of cops took off running, and all I could see was the cars spread out across the road. About ten minutes later, we heard lots of gunfire coming from a couple of streets further back. It like to have lasted for ever. Like hearing the Battle of the Bulge. My momma started to cry, and so did my little brother. The shooting stopped. The police shouted to each other, and then they came back and got in their cars and went away.

'On the radio the next morning, they said that a known criminal, a Negro man named Edward Grimes, had been killed while trying to escape arrest for the murder of a white woman. The body of Eleanore Monday, missing for three days, had been found in a shallow grave by Woodland police searching near an illegal distillery in the region called The Backs. Miss Monday, the daughter of grocer Albert Monday, had been in poor mental and physical health, and Grimes had apparently taken advantage of her weakness either to abduct or lure her to The Backs, where she had been savagely murdered. That's what it said on the radio – I still remember the words. *In poor mental and physical health. Savagely murdered.*

'When the paper finally came, there on the front page was a picture of Eleanore Monday, girl with dark hair and a big nose. She didn't look anything like the dead woman in the shack. She hadn't even disappeared on the right day. Eddie Grimes was never going to be able to explain things, because the police had finally cornered him in the old jute warehouse just off Meridian Road next to the general store. I don't suppose they even bothered trying to arrest him – they weren't interested in *arresting* him. He killed a white girl. They wanted revenge, and they got it.

'After I looked at the paper, I got out of the house and ran between the houses to get a look at the jute warehouse. Turned out a lot of folks had the same idea. A big crowd strung out in a long line in front of the warehouse, and cars were parked all along Meridian Road. Right up in front of the warehouse door was a police car, and a big cop stood in the middle of the big doorway, watching people file by. They were walking past the doorway one by one, acting like they were at some kind of exhibit. Nobody was talking. It was a sight I never saw before in that town, whites and colored all lined up together. On the other side of the warehouse, two groups of men stood alongside the road, one colored and one white, talking so quietly you couldn't hear a word.

'Now I was never one who liked standing in lines, so I figured I'd just dart up there, peek in, and save myself some time. I came around the end of the line and ambled toward the two bunches of men, like I'd already had my look and was just hanging around to enjoy the scene. After I got a little past the warehouse door, I sort of drifted up alongside it. I looked down the row of people, and there was Dee Sparks, just a few yards away from being able to see in. Dee was leaning forward, and when he saw me he almost jumped out of his skin. He looked away as fast as he could. His eyes turned as dead as stones. The cop at the door yelled at me to go to the end of the line. He never would have noticed me at all if Dee hadn't jumped like someone just shot off a firecracker behind him.

'About halfway down the line, Mary Randolph was standing behind some of the ladies from the neighborhood. She looked terrible. Her hair stuck out in raggedy clumps, and her skin was all ashy, like she hadn't slept in a long time. I sped up a little, hoping she wouldn't notice me, but after I took one more step, Mary Randolph looked down and her eyes hooked into mine. I swear, what was in her eyes almost knocked me down. I couldn't even tell what it was, unless it was just pure hate. Hate and pain. With her eyes hooked into mine like that, I couldn't look away. It was like I was seeing that miserable, terrible white smear twisting up between the trees on that night in The Backs. Mary let me go, and I almost fell down all over again.

'I got to the end of the line and started moving along regular and slow with everybody else. Mary Randolph stayed in my mind and blanked out everything else. When I got up to the door, I barely took in what was inside the warehouse – a wall full of bulletholes and bloodstains all over the place, big slick ones and little drizzly ones. All I could think of was the shack and Mary Randolph sitting next to the dead girl, and I was back there all over again.

'Mary Randolph didn't show up at the Beergarden dance, so she didn't hear me play saxophone in public for the first time. I didn't expect her, either, not after the way she looked out at the warehouse. There'd been a lot of news about Eddie Grimes, who they made out to be less civilized than a gorilla, a crazy man who'd murder anyone as long as he could kill all the white women first. The paper had a picture of what they called Grimes's "lair", with busted furniture all over the place and holes in the walls, but they never explained that it was the police tore it up and made it look that way.

'The other thing people got suddenly all hot about was The Backs. Seems the place was even worse than everybody thought. Seems white girls besides Eleanore Monday had been taken out there – according to some, there were even white girls living out there, along with a lot of bad coloreds. The place was a nest of vice, Sodom and Gomorrah. Two days before the town council was supposed to discuss the problem, a gang of white men went out there with guns and clubs and torches and burned every shack in The Backs clear down to the ground. While they were there, they didn't see a single soul, white, colored, male, female, damned or saved. Everybody who had lived in The Backs had skedaddled. And the funny thing was, long as The Backs had existed right outside of Woodland, no one in Woodland could recollect the name of anyone who had ever lived there. They couldn't even recall the name of anyone who had ever gone there, except for Eddie Grimes. In fact, after the place got burned down, it appeared that it must have been a sin just to say its name, because no one ever mentioned it. You'd think men so fine and moral as to burn down The Backs would be willing to take the credit, but none ever did.

'You could think they must have wanted to get rid of some things out there. Or wanted real bad to forget about things out there. One thing I thought, Doctor Garland and the man I saw leaving that shack had been out there with torches.

'But maybe I didn't know anything at all. Two weeks later, a couple things happened that shook me good.

'The first one happened three nights before Thanksgiving. I was hurrying home, a little bit late. Nobody else on the street, everybody inside either sitting down to dinner or getting ready for it. When I got to Mary Randolph's house, some kind of noise coming from inside stopped me. What I thought was, it sounded exactly like somebody trying to scream while someone else was holding a hand over their mouth. Well, that was plain foolish, wasn't it? How did I know what that would sound like? I moved along a step or two, and then I heard it again. Could be anything, I told myself. Mary Randolph didn't like me too much, anyway. She wouldn't be partial to my knocking on her door. Best thing I could do was get out. Which was what I did. Just went home to supper and forgot about it.

'Until the next day, anyhow, when a friend of Mary's walked in her front door and found her lying dead with her throat cut and a knife in her hand. A cut of fatback, we heard, had boiled away to cinders on her stove. I didn't tell anybody about what I heard the night before. Too scared. I couldn't do anything but wait to see what the police did.

'To the police, it was all real clear. Mary killed herself, plain and simple.

'When our minister went across town to ask why a lady who intended to commit suicide had bothered to start cooking her supper, the chief told him that a female bent on killing herself probably didn't care *what* happened to the food on her stove. Then I suppose Mary Randolph nearly managed to cut her own head off, said the minister. A female in despair possesses a godawful strength, said the chief. And asked, wouldn't she have screamed if she'd been attacked? And added, couldn't it be that maybe this female here had secrets in her life connected to the late savage murderer named Eddie Grimes? We might all be better off if these secrets get buried with your Mary Randolph, said the chief. I'm sure you understand me, Reverend. And yes, the Reverend did understand, he surely did. So Mary Randolph got laid away in the cemetery, and nobody ever said her name again. She was put away out of mind, like The Backs.

'The second thing that shook me up and proved to me that I didn't know anything, that I was no better than a blind dog, happened on Thanksgiving day. My daddy played piano in church, and on special days, we played our instruments along with the gospel songs. I got to church early with the rest of my family, and we practiced with the choir. Afterwards, I went to fooling around outside until the people came, and saw a big car come up into the church parking lot. Must have been the biggest, fanciest car I'd ever seen. Miller's Hill was written all over that vehicle. I couldn't have told you why, but the sight of it made my heart stop. The front door opened, and out stepped a colored man in a fancy gray uniform with a smart cap. He didn't so much as dirty his eyes by looking at me, or at the church, or at anything around him. He stepped around the front of the car and opened the rear door on my side. A young woman was in the passenger seat, and when she got out of the car, the sun fell on her blonde hair and the little fur jacket she was wearing. I couldn't see more than the top of her head, her shoulders under the jacket, and her legs. Then she straightened up, and her eyes lighted right on me. She smiled, but I couldn't smile back. I couldn't even begin to move.

'It was Abbey Montgomery, delivering baskets of food to our church, the way she did every Thanksgiving and Christmas. She looked older and thinner than the last time I'd seen her alive – older and thinner, but more than that, like there was no fun at all in her life any more. She walked to the trunk of the car, and the driver opened it up, leaned in, and brought out a great big basket of food. He took it into the church by the back way and came back for another one. Abbey Montgomery just stood still and watched him carry the baskets. She looked – she looked like she was just going through the motions, like going through the motions was all she was ever going to do from now on, and she knew it. Once she smiled at the driver, but the smile was so sad that the driver didn't even try to smile back. When he was done, he closed the trunk and let her into the passenger seat, got behind the wheel, and drove away.

'I was thinking, *Dee Sparks was right, she was alive all the time.* Then I thought,

No, Mary Randolph brought her back, too, like she did Eddie Grimes. But it didn't work right, and only part of her came back.

'And that's the whole thing, except that Abbey Montgomery didn't deliver food to our church, that Christmas – she was traveling out of the country, with her aunt. And she didn't bring food the next Thanksgiving, either, just sent her driver with the baskets. By that time, we didn't expect her, because we'd already heard that, soon as she got back to town, Abbey Montgomery stopped leaving her house. That girl shut herself up and never came out. I heard from somebody who probably didn't know any more than I did that she eventually got so she wouldn't even leave her room. Five years later, she passed away. Twenty-six years old, and they said she looked to be at least fifty.'

4

Hat fell silent, and I sat with my pen ready over the notebook, waiting for more. When I realized that he had finished, I asked, 'What did she die of?'

'Nobody ever told me.'

'And nobody ever found who had killed Mary Randolph.'

The limpid, colorless eyes momentarily rested on me. 'Was she killed?'

'Did you ever become friends with Dee Sparks again? Did you at least talk about it with him?'

'Surely did not. Nothing to talk about.'

This was a remarkable statement, considering that for an hour he had done nothing but talk about what had happened to the two of them, but I let it go. Hat was still looking at me with his unreadable eyes. His face had become particularly bland, almost immobile. It was not possible to imagine this man as an active eleven-year-old boy. 'Now you heard me out, answer my question,' he said.

I couldn't remember the question.

'Did we find what we were looking for?'

Scares – that was what they had been looking for. 'I think you found a lot more than that,' I said.

He nodded slowly. 'That's right. It was more.'

Then I asked him some question about his family's band, he lubricated himself with another swallow of gin, and the interview returned to more typical matters. But the experience of listening to him had changed. After I had heard the long, unresolved tale of his Halloween night, everything Hat said seemed to have two separate meanings, the daylight meaning created by sequences of ordinary English words, and another, night-time meaning, far less determined and knowable. He was like a man discoursing with eerie rationality in the midst of a particularly surreal dream: like a man carrying on an ordinary conversation with one foot placed on solid ground and the other suspended above a bottomless abyss. I focused on the rationality, on the foot placed in the context I understood; the rest was unsettling to the point of being frightening. By six thirty, when he kindly called me 'Miss Rosemary' and opened his door, I felt as if I'd spent several weeks, if not whole months, in his room.

Part Three

1

Although I did get my M.A. at Columbia, I didn't have enough money to stay on for a Ph.D., so I never became a college professor. I never became a jazz critic, either, or anything else very interesting. For a couple of years after Columbia, I taught English in a high school until I quit to take the job I have now, which involves a lot of traveling and pays a little bit better than teaching. Maybe even quite a bit better, but that's not saying much, especially when you consider my expenses. I own a nice little house in the Chicago suburbs, my marriage held up against everything life did to it, and my twenty-two-year-old son, a young man who never once in his life for the purpose of pleasure read a novel, looked at a painting, visited a museum, or listened to anything but the most readily available music, recently announced to his mother and myself that he has decided to become an artist, actual type of art to be determined later, but probably to include aspects of photography, videotape, and the creation of 'installations'. I take this as proof that he was raised in a manner that left his self-esteem intact.

I no longer provide my life with a perpetual sound track (though my son, who has moved back in with us, does), in part because my income does not permit the purchase of a great many compact discs. (A friend presented me with a CD player on my forty-fifth birthday.) And these days, I'm as interested in classical music as in jazz. Of course, I never go to jazz clubs when I am home. Are there still people, apart from New Yorkers, who patronize jazz nightclubs in their own hometowns? The concept seems faintly retrograde, even somehow illicit. But when I am out on the road, living in airplanes and hotel rooms, I often check the jazz listings in the local papers to see if I can find some way to fill my evenings. Many of the legends of my youth are still out there, in most cases playing as well as before. Some months ago, while I was in San Francisco, I came across John Hawes's name in this fashion. He was working in a club so close to my hotel that I could walk to it.

His appearance in any club at all was surprising. Hawes had ceased performing jazz in public years before. He had earned a great deal of fame (and undoubtedly, a great deal of money) writing film scores, and in the past decade, he had begun to appear in swallowtail coat and white tie as a conductor of the standard classical repertoire. I believe he had a permanent post in some city like Seattle, or perhaps Salt Lake City. If he was spending a week playing jazz with a trio in San Francisco, it must have been for the sheer pleasure of it.

I turned up just before the beginning of the first set, and got a table toward the back of the club. Most of the tables were filled – Hawes's celebrity had guaranteed him a good house. Only a few minutes after the announced time of the first set, Hawes emerged through a door at the front of the club and moved toward the piano, followed by his bassist and drummer. He looked like a more successful version of the younger man I had seen in New York, and the only indication of the extra years were his silver-gray hair, still abundant, and a little paunch. His playing, too, seemed essentially unchanged, but I could not hear it in the way I once had. He was still a good pianist – no doubt about that – but he seemed to be skating over the surface of the songs he played, using his wonderful technique and good time merely to decorate their melodies. It was the sort of playing that becomes less impressive the more attention you give it – if you were listening with half an ear, it probably sounded like Art Tatum. I wondered if John Hawes had always had this superficial streak in him, or if he had lost a certain necessary passion during his years away from jazz. Certainly he had not sounded superficial when I had heard him with Hat.

Hawes, too, might have been thinking about his old employer, because in the first set he played 'Love Walked In', 'Too Marvelous For Words', and 'Up Jumped Hat'. In the last of these, inner gears seemed to mesh, the rhythm simultaneously relaxed and intensified, and the music turned into real, not imitation, jazz. Hawes looked pleased with himself when he stood up from the piano bench, and half a dozen fans moved to greet him as he stepped off the bandstand. Most of them were carrying old records they wished him to sign.

A few minutes later, I saw Hawes standing by himself at the end of the bar, drinking what appeared to be club soda, in proximity to his musicians but not actually speaking with them. Wondering if his allusions to Hat had been deliberate, I left my table and walked toward the bar. Hawes watched me approach out of the side of his eye, neither encouraging nor discouraging me to approach him. When I introduced myself, he smiled nicely and shook my hand and waited for whatever I wanted to say to him.

At first, I made some inane comment about the difference between playing in clubs and conducting in concert halls, and he replied with the noncommittal and equally banal agreement that yes, the two experiences were very different.

Then I told him that I had seen him play with Hat all those years ago in New York, and he turned to me with genuine pleasure in his face. 'Did you? At that little club on St Mark's Place? That was the only time I ever worked with him, but it sure was fun. What an experience. I guess I must have been thinking about it, because I played some of those songs we used to do.'

'That was why I came over,' I said. 'I guess that was one of the best musical experiences I ever had.'

'You and me both.' Hawes smiled to himself. 'Sometimes, I just couldn't believe what he was doing.'

'It showed,' I said.

'Well.' His eyes slid away from mine. 'Great character. Completely otherworldly.'

'I saw some of that,' I said. 'I did that interview with him that turns up now and then, the one in *Downbeat*.'

'Oh!' Hawes gave me his first genuinely interested look so far. 'Well, that was him, all right.'

'Most of it was, anyhow.'

'You cheated?' Now he was looking even more interested.

'I had to make it understandable.'

'Oh, sure. You couldn't put in all those ding-dings and bells and Bob Crosbys.' These had been elements of Hat's private code. Hawes laughed at the memory. 'When he wanted to play a blues in G, he'd lean over and say, "Gs, please."'

'Did you get to know him at all well, personally?' I asked, thinking that the answer must be that he had not – I didn't think that anyone had ever really known Hat very well.

'Pretty well,' Hawes said. 'A couple of times, around '54 and '55, he invited me home with him, to his parents' house, I mean. We got to be friends on a Jazz at the Phil tour, and twice when we were in the South, he asked me if I wanted to eat some good home cooking.'

'You went to his hometown?'

He nodded. 'His parents put me up. They were interesting people. Hat's father, Red, was about the lightest black man I ever saw, and he could have passed for white anywhere, but I don't suppose the thought ever occurred to him.'

'Was the family band still going?'

'No, to tell you the truth, I don't think they were getting much work up toward the end of the forties. At the end, they were using a tenor player and a drummer from the high school band. And the church work got more and more demanding for Hat's father.'

'His father was a deacon, or something like that?'

He raised his eyebrows. 'No, Red was the Baptist minister. The Reverend. He ran that church. I think he even started it.'

'Hat told me his father played piano in church, but . . .'

'The Reverend would have made a hell of a blues piano player, if he'd ever left his day job.'

'There must have been another Baptist church in the neighborhood,' I said, thinking this the only explanation for the presence of two Baptist ministers. But why had Hat not mentioned that his own father, like Dee Sparks's, had been a clergyman?

'Are you kidding? There was barely enough money in that place to keep one of them going.' He looked at his watch, nodded at me, and began to move closer to his sidemen.

'Could I ask you one more question?'

'I suppose so,' he said, almost impatiently.

'Did Hat strike you as superstitious?'

Hawes grinned. 'Oh, he was superstitious, all right. He told me he never worked on Halloween – he didn't even want to go out of his room, on Halloween. That's why he left the big band, you know. They were starting a tour on Halloween, and Hat refused to do it. He just quit.' He leaned toward me. 'I'll tell you another funny thing. I always had the feeling that Hat was terrified of his father – I thought he invited me to Hatchville with him so I could be some kind of buffer between him and his father. Never made any sense to me. Red was a big strong old guy, and I'm pretty sure a long time ago he used to mess around with the ladies, Reverend or not, but I couldn't ever figure out why Hat should be afraid of him. But whenever Red came into the room, Hat shut up. Funny, isn't it?'

I must have looked very perplexed. 'Hatchville?'

'Where they lived. Hatchville, Mississippi – not too far from Biloxi.'

'But he told me—'

'Hat never gave too many straight answers,' Hawes said. 'And he didn't let the facts get in the way of a good story. When you come to think of it, why should he? He was *Hat*.'

After the next set, I walked back uphill to my hotel, wondering again about the long story Hat had told me. Had there been any truth in it at all?

2

Three weeks later I found myself released from a meeting at our Midwestern headquarters in downtown Chicago earlier than I had expected, and instead of going to a bar with the other wandering corporate ghosts like myself, made up a story about a relative I had promised to visit. I didn't want to admit to my fellow employees, committed like all male business people to aggressive endeavors such as racquetball, drinking, and the pursuit of women, that I intended to visit the library. Short of a trip to Mississippi, a good periodical room offered the most likely means of finding out once and for all how much truth there had been in what Hat had told me.

I hadn't forgotten everything I had learned at Columbia – I still knew how to look things up.

In the main library, a boy set me up with a monitor and spools of microfilm representing the complete contents of the daily newspapers from Biloxi and Hatchville, Mississippi, for Hat's tenth and eleventh years. That made three papers, two for Biloxi and one for Hatchville, but all I had to examine were the issues dating from the end of October through the middle of November – I was looking for references to Eddie Grimes, Eleanore Monday, Mary Randolph, Abbey Montgomery, Hat's family, The Backs, and anyone named Sparks.

The Hatchville *Blade*, a gossipy daily printed on peach-colored paper, offered plenty of references to each of these names and places, and the papers from Biloxi contained nearly as many – Biloxi could not conceal the delight, disguised as horror, aroused in its collective soul by the unimaginable events taking place in the smaller, supposedly respectable town ten miles west. Biloxi was riveted, Biloxi was superior, Biloxi was virtually intoxicated with dread and outrage. In Hatchville, the press maintained a persistent optimistic dignity: when wickedness had appeared, justice official and unofficial had dealt with it. Hatchville was shocked but proud (or at least pretended to be proud), and Biloxi all but preened. The *Blade* printed detailed news stories, but the Biloxi papers suggested implications not allowed by Hatchville's version of events. I needed Hatchville to confirm or question Hat's story, but Biloxi gave me at least the beginning of a way to understand it.

A black ex-convict named Edward Grimes had in some fashion persuaded or coerced Eleanore Monday, a retarded young white woman, to accompany him to an area variously described as 'a longstanding local disgrace' (the *Blade*) and 'a haunt of deepest vice' (Biloxi) and after 'the perpetration of the most offensive and brutal deeds upon her person' (the *Blade*) or 'acts which the judicious commentator must decline to imagine, much less describe' (Biloxi) murdered her, presumably to ensure her silence, and then buried the body near the 'squalid dwelling' where he made and sold illegal liquor. State and local police departments acting in concert had located the body, identified Grimes as the fiend, and, after a search of his house, had tracked him to a warehouse where the murderer was killed in a gun battle. The *Blade* covered half its front page with a photograph of a gaping double door and a bloodstained wall. All Mississippi, both Hatchville and Biloxi declared, now could breathe more easily.

The *Blade* gave the death of Mary Randolph a single paragraph on its back page, the Biloxi papers nothing.

In Hatchville, the raid on The Backs was described as an heroic assault on a dangerous criminal encampment that had somehow come to flourish in a little–noticed section of the countryside. At great risk to themselves, anonymous citizens of Hatchville had descended like the army of the righteous and driven forth the hidden sinners from their dens. Troublemakers, beware! The Biloxi papers, while seeming to endorse the action in Hatchville, actually took another tone altogether. Can it be, they asked, that the Hatchville police had never before noticed the existence of a Sodom and Gomorrah so close to the town line? Did it take the savage murder of a helpless woman to bring it to their attention? Of course Biloxi celebrated the destruction of The Backs, such vileness must be eradicated, but it wondered what else had been destroyed along with the stills and the mean buildings where loose women had plied their trade. Men ever are men, and those who have succumbed to temptation may wish to remove from the face of the earth any evidence of their lapses. Had not the police of Hatchville ever heard the rumor, vague and doubtless baseless, that operations of an illegal nature had been performed in the selfsame Backs? That in an atmosphere of drugs, intoxication, and gambling, the races had mingled there, and that 'fast' young women had risked life and honor in search of illicit thrills? Hatchville may have rid itself of a few buildings, but Biloxi was willing to suggest that the problems of its smaller neighbor might not have disappeared with them.

As this campaign of innuendo went on in Biloxi, the *Blade* blandly reported the ongoing events of any smaller American city. Miss Abigail Montgomery sailed with her aunt, Miss Lucinda Bright, from New Orleans to France for an eight-week tour of the continent. The Reverend Jasper Sparks of the Miller's Hill Presbyterian Church delivered a sermon on the subject of 'Christian Forgiveness'. (Just after Thanksgiving, the Reverend Sparks's son, Rodney, was sent off with the blessings and congratulations of all Hatchville to a private academy in Charleston, South Carolina.) There were bake sales, church socials, and costume parties. A saxophone virtuoso named Albert Woodland demonstrated his astonishing wizardry at a well-attended recital presented in Temperance Hall.

Well, I knew the name of at least one person who had attended the recital. If Hat had chosen to disguise the name of his hometown, he had done so by substituting for it a name that represented another sort of home.

But, although I had more ideas about this than before, I still did not know exactly what Hat had seen or done on Halloween night in The Backs. It seemed possible that he had gone there with a white boy of his age, a preacher's son like himself, and had the wits scared out of him by whatever had happened to Abbey Montgomery – and after that night, Abbey herself had been sent out of town, as had Dee Sparks. I couldn't think that a man had murdered the young woman, leaving Mary Randolph to bring her back to life. Surely whatever had happened to Abbey Montgomery had brought Dr Garland out to The Backs, and what he had witnessed or done there had sent him away screaming. And this event – what had befallen a rich young white woman in the shadiest, most criminal section of a Mississippi county – had led to the slaying of Eddie Grimes and the murder of Mary Randolph. Because they knew what had happened, they had to die.

I understood all this, and Hat had understood it, too. Yet he had introduced needless puzzles, as if embedded in the midst of this unresolved story were something he either wished to conceal or not to know. And concealed it would remain; if Hat did not know it, I never would. Whatever had really happened in The Backs on Halloween night was lost for good.

On the *Blade*'s entertainment page for a Saturday in the middle of November I had come across a photograph of Hat's family's band, and when I had reached this hopeless point in my thinking, I spooled back across the pages to look at it again. Hat, his two brothers, his sister, and his parents stood in a straight line, tallest to smallest, in front of what must have been the family car. Hat held a C-melody saxophone, his brothers a trumpet and drumsticks, his sister a clarinet. As the piano player, the Reverend carried nothing at all – nothing except for what came through even a grainy, sixty-year-old photograph as a powerful sense of self. Hat's father had been a tall, impressive man, and in the photograph he looked as white as I did. But what was impressive was not the lightness of his skin, or even his striking handsomeness: what impressed was the sense of authority implicit in his posture, his straightforward gaze, even the dictatorial set of his chin. In retrospect, I was not surprised by what John Hawes had told me, for this man could easily be frightening. You would not wish to oppose him; you would not elect to get in his way. Beside him, Hat's mother seemed vague and distracted, as if her husband had robbed her of all certainty. Then I noticed the car, and for the first time realized why it had been included in the photograph. It was a sign of their prosperity, the respectable status they had achieved – the car was as much an advertisement as the photograph. It was, I thought, an old Model T Ford, but I didn't waste any time speculating that it might have been the Model T Hat had seen in The Backs.

And that would have been that – the hint of an absurd supposition – except for something I read a few days ago in a book called *Cool Breeze: The Life of Grant Kilbert*.

There are few biographies of any jazz musicians apart from Louis Armstrong and Duke Ellington (though one does now exist of Hat, the title of which was drawn from my interview with him), and I was surprised to see *Cool Breeze* at the B. Dalton in our local mall. Biographies have not yet been written of Art Blakey, Clifford Brown, Ben Webster, Art Tatum, and many others of more musical and historical importance than Kilbert. Yet I should not have been surprised. Kilbert was one of those musicians who attract and maintain a large personal following, and twenty years after his death, almost all of his records have been released on CD, many of them in multidisc boxed sets. He had been a great, great player, the closest to Hat of all his disciples. Because Kilbert had been one of my early heroes, I bought the book (for $35!) and brought it home.

Like the lives of many jazz musicians, I suppose of artists in general, Kilbert's had been an odd mixture of public fame and private misery. He had committed burglaries, even armed robberies, to feed his persistent heroin addiction; he had spent years in jail; his two marriages had ended in outright hatred; he had managed to betray most of his friends. That this weak, narcissistic louse had found it in himself to create music of real tenderness and beauty was one of art's enigmas, but not actually a surprise. I'd heard and read enough stories about Grant Kilbert to know what kind of man he'd been.

But what I had not known was that Kilbert, to all appearances an American of conventional northern European, perhaps Scandinavian or Anglo-Saxon, stock, had occasionally claimed to be black. (This claim had always been dismissed, apparently, as another indication of Kilbert's mental aberrancy.) At other times, being Kilbert, he had denied ever making this claim.

Neither had I known that the received versions of his birth and upbringing were in question. Unlike Hat, Kilbert had been interviewed dozens of times both in

Downbeat and in mass-market weekly news magazines, invariably to offer the same story of having been born in Hattiesburg, Mississippi, to an unmusical, working-class family (a plumber's family), of knowing virtually from infancy that he was born to make music, of begging for and finally being given a saxophone, of early mastery and the dazzled admiration of his teachers, then of dropping out of school at sixteen and joining the Woody Herman band. After that, almost immediate fame.

Most of this, the Grant Kilbert myth, was undisputed. He had been raised in Hattiesburg by a plumber named Kilbert, he had been a prodigy and high-school dropout, he'd become famous with Woody Herman before he was twenty. Yet he told a few friends, not necessarily those to whom he said he was black, that he'd been adopted by the Kilberts, and that once or twice, in great anger, either the plumber or his wife had told him that he had been born into poverty and disgrace and that he'd better by God be grateful for the opportunities he'd been given. The source of this story was John Hawes, who'd met Kilbert on another long Jazz at the Phil tour, the last he made before leaving the road.

'Grant didn't have a lot of friends on that tour,' Hawes told the biographer. 'Even though he was such a great player, you never knew what he was going to say, and if he was in a bad mood, he was liable to put down some of the older players. He was always respectful around Hat, his whole style was based on Hat's, but Hat could go days without saying anything, and by those days he certainly wasn't making any new friends. Still, he'd let Grant sit next to him on the bus, and nod his head while Grant talked to him, so he must have felt some affection for him. Anyhow, eventually I was about the only guy on the tour that was willing to have a conversation with Grant, and we'd sit up in the bar late at night after the concerts. The way he played, I could forgive him a lot of failings. One of those nights, he said that he'd been adopted, and that not knowing who his real parents were was driving him crazy. He didn't even have a birth certificate. From a hint his mother once gave him, he thought one of his birth parents was black, but when he asked them directly, they always denied it. These were white Mississippians, after all, and if they had wanted a baby so bad that they had taken in a child who looked completely white but maybe had a drop or two of black blood in his veins, they weren't going to admit it, even to themselves.'

In the midst of so much supposition, here is a fact. Grant Kilbert was exactly eleven years younger than Hat. The jazz encyclopedias give his birth date as November first, which instead of his actual birthday may have been the day he was delivered to the couple in Hattiesburg.

I wonder if Hat saw more than he admitted to me of the man leaving the shack where Abbey Montgomery lay on bloody sheets; I wonder if he had reason to fear his father. I don't know if what I am thinking is correct – I'll never know that – but now, finally, I think I know why Hat never wanted to go out of his room on Halloween nights. The story he told me never left him, but it must have been most fully present on those nights. I think he heard the screams, saw the bleeding girl, and saw Mary Randolph staring at him with displaced pain and rage. I think that in some small closed corner deep within himself, he knew who had been the real object of these feelings, and therefore had to lock himself inside his hotel room and gulp gin until he obliterated the horror of his own thoughts.

THE CASE OF THE SCOTTISH TRAGEDY

June Thomson

One

As my old friend Sherlock Holmes once remarked, his brother Mycroft's life was so routinely divided between his office in Whitehall, his bachelor apartment and the Diogenes Club in Pall Mall that to find him outside these customary haunts was like meeting a tram coming down a country lane.

We were therefore considerably surprised when, on returning to our lodgings late one warm afternoon in August 1887 after one of our rambles about London, we found Mycroft Holmes's portly figure comfortably installed in an armchair in the sitting room, awaiting our arrival.

Seeing the two brothers together, I was again struck by their physical dissimilarities. Mycroft Holmes's huge, overweight body and air of massive indolence were in direct contrast to my old friend's lean frame and quick, decisive manner. However, it was possible to discern in the elder brother's large head and keen grey eyes those unique intellectual powers which had made him indispensable as a government adviser, although ostensibly he was nothing more than a departmental auditor.

'You will forgive me not rising,' Mycroft Holmes remarked, waving a languid hand as we entered. 'I have had a most fatiguing afternoon, closeted with the prime minister, discussing the perennial matter of the Irish Problem, without, it hardly needs saying, coming to any satisfactory conclusion. And then, hardly had I escaped to the peace and solitude of my own chambers, when this telegram was delivered.' Taking a sheet of paper from his inside pocket, he handed it to Holmes, adding, 'As the affair is urgent, I thought it best to bring it straight to you, dear boy.'

My old friend rapidly scanned it before, raising an eyebrow at his brother, he enquired, 'You will not object if I read it aloud for Watson's benefit?'

'Of course not. I assume, if you take the case, you will want the good doctor to accompany you. So pray continue.'

' "Urgently request help," ' Holmes began. ' "My life has been threatened. Stop. Possible connection with Los Halcónes. Stop. Suggest your brother takes up the investigation immediately. Stop. Also suggest he takes a room incognito at Glencastle Hotel on island of Uffa where my wife and I are staying but does not acknowledge our presence. Stop. Vacancies available at hotel. Stop. Grice Paterson." '

'A lengthy message and on the whole comprehensible,' Holmes remarked as he handed the telegram back to his brother. 'But who is Grice Paterson? And who or what are *Los Halcónes*?'

'Henry Grice Paterson, an old acquaintance of mine, is a former diplomat who has now retired,' Mycroft Holmes began. 'It was while he was serving as personal assistant to our consul general in Bogotá five years ago that he became unwittingly associated with an extreme revolutionary party, similar to the anarchist movement in Europe, which calls itself *Los Halcónes*. A *halcóne* is, I believe, a bird of prey, much like a falcon.

'As you may be aware, there has for several years now been considerable unrest in Colombia between different political factions, amounting at times to civil war. The *Halcónes'* intention was to take advantage of the situation and seize power under the leadership of the Herrera brothers, Julio and Gustafo, two young hot-heads from a wealthy family who, in the name of patriotism, seem intent on plunging their country into outright revolution.

'In 1882, an armed raid was carried out on a bank in Bogotá in which a cashier was shot dead and a large amount of money stolen. Grice Paterson happened to be passing as the two robbers fled from the scene of the crime. Both wore bandannas tied over the lower parts of their faces but one of them came loose and slipped down, revealing the man's features. Later, the younger of the Herrera brothers, Julio, was arrested and Grice Paterson identified him as one of the bank robbers by a distinctive scar on his left cheek. Julio Herrera was duly tried, found guilty and executed by firing squad, largely because of Grice Paterson's evidence.

'A few months later, Gustafo Herrera was also captured and, as revolutionary pamphlets were found at his lodgings, he was charged with criminal association and sentenced to life imprisonment. Other members of *Los Halcónes* were either rounded up or fled the country, including Julio Herrera's English wife, who escaped to Mexico.'

'An English wife?' Holmes interjected. 'How did they meet?'

'Presumably in Bogotá. She is the daughter of the managing director of a coffee-exporting firm in the city. Her family disowned her after her marriage to Julio Herrera whose political extremism was already well known.

'But to return to the matter in hand. Before Grice Paterson left Bogotá, he received several threatening letters from members of *Los Halcónes* who were still at large. A gun was also fired at him when he and his wife were in their carriage on the way to some official function. Fortunately, the bullet missed. However, because of the attempt on his life, Grice Paterson was recalled to London and soon afterwards retired from the diplomatic service.

'Since then I have met him fairly frequently at the Diogenes Club of which he is also a member. From our conversations I learned that, since his retirement, Grice Paterson and his wife have spent every August on Uffa, a small island off the west coast of Scotland. Both of them are fond of walking and Grice Paterson is a keen amateur ornithologist. If he is correct, and these renewed threats against his life are indeed the work of *Los Halcónes*, then the elder brother, Gustafo, may be behind them.'

'But I thought he is serving a life sentence in prison,' Holmes objected.

'He was,' Mycroft Holmes corrected him. 'Two years ago, the Foreign Office received a communiqué from our consul general in Bogotá, informing them that some of the surviving members of *Los Halcónes* had regrouped and, in a daring daylight attack on the prison, in which several warders were killed, succeeded in releasing Gustafo Herrera together with other members of the gang. According to the latest information, Herrera is still at large; his exact whereabouts are unknown.'

'But surely you are not suggesting that Gustafo Herrera is at the moment on the island of Uffa, threatening Grice Paterson's life? Why, my dear Mycroft, he would be as conspicuous as our friend Watson would be at a Red Indian powwow!'

'I know your sense of humour is, at times, peculiar, Sherlock, but this is not a matter for amusement,' Mycroft Holmes retorted sharply. 'As I have already told you, the Herrera family is exceedingly wealthy and the brothers were brought up by English nannies and tutors. Consequently, they speak the language as well as you or Dr Watson. Gustafo Herrera could easily pass himself off as an Englishman. The only curious aspects I find about the case are these: why Herrera, if he is indeed behind the threats, has chosen a Scottish island of all places in which to carry them out, rather than London where Grice Paterson is living quite openly; and, secondly, how he managed to find out that the Grice Patersons are spending August on Uffa. No doubt, if you look into the affair, you may find the answer to both those questions.

'However, my dear brother, before you reply,' Mycroft Holmes continued, holding up a broad palm to prevent Holmes from answering too quickly, 'let me warn you of the potential hazards. Gustafo Herrera is a very dangerous man. When *Los Halcónes* were fully active, the group was responsible for at least twenty murders and two bomb attacks which cost forty more lives, among them innocent women and children. If, as I said before, he is behind these threats, then he will be doubly dangerous for he will now have a personal motive – to revenge his brother. And, believe me, Sherlock, he will think no more of murdering Grice Paterson, or indeed you and Dr Watson if you get in his way, than another man would think of crushing a cockroach underfoot.'

Mycroft paused for a moment and directed a keen gaze first at me and then at his brother before continuing, 'Well, dear boy, having heard about the difficulties and dangers of the affair, what is your decision? Will you take the case?'

Holmes looked at me with a quizzical smile.

'What do you say, Watson? Are you game?'

'If you are, Holmes,' I replied without any hesitation.

'Then,' said my old friend, turning to address his brother, 'the verdict is unanimous. We accept.'

Although Mycroft Holmes's plump features remained perfectly bland, I thought I detected a strange expression flicker for a moment in his light grey eyes. It was a look of relief tempered by an uncharacteristic gleam of anxiety, although, when he spoke, his voice betrayed neither, only the brisk, matter-of-fact tones of a man used to dealing with practicalities.

'Very well, then, let us get down to business. I assume you will prefer to travel on the night train from Euston to Glasgow. From Glasgow you will have to take another train to Oban, a fishing port on the west coast from where ferries set out for Mull, their next place of call being Uffa. Incidentally, as you may have noticed, Grice Paterson sent his telegram from Oban where, presumably, the nearest telegraph office is to be found. Now, my dear Sherlock, is there anything else you want to know?'

'Only a description of Grice Paterson and his wife. If, as he suggests, I do not approach them directly, I shall need to be able to identify them from among the other hotel guests.'

'Quite so. Grice Paterson is a tall, grey-haired man with a small moustache who is in his early sixties, although he is still very vigorous for his age. His wife, who is several years younger than he, is fair-haired. You should have no difficulty in distinguishing them. And now,' Mycroft Holmes continued, struggling to raise his portly frame from the armchair, 'I wish you and Dr Watson every success in this enterprise. But, Sherlock, do, please, remember you will be dealing with a man who has killed many times before and will not hesitate to kill again.'

'Well, are you still game, Watson?' Holmes enquired, returning to the sitting room after seeing his brother down the stairs and into a cab. 'Mycroft's warnings have not persuaded you to change your mind?'

'Not at all, Holmes,' I replied.

'Stout fellow! You realise, of course, that Dr Johnson and his amanuensis, Boswell, visited the Western Isles in 1773? We shall be treading in their footsteps when we make our own little jaunt.'

'I hardly think it will be a jaunt, Holmes,' I objected, wondering if Mycroft Holmes had been right in thinking that his brother was not taking the matter seriously enough.

But such is his mercurial nature that later, when he looked into my room as I was packing for the journey, he was in a much more serious mood.

'Remember to take your army revolver,' said he with a sombre expression. 'Judging by Mycroft's account, we may well need it.'

Two

It was almost midday before we reached our destination. After travelling overnight to Glasgow and from there to Oban where we caught the ferry to Uffa, we finally disembarked at the small fishing port of Stranhyde. It was a picturesque place with a straggle of stone houses and cottages strung out along the harbour-front, behind which rose low, green hills. However, despite its modest size, the village boasted a church with a squat tower, two or three shops and a tavern. It was here we hired a trap to take ourselves and our luggage to the Glencastle Hotel which, we understood from the landlord, was situated on top of the cliff about half an hour's drive away. At least, I think that is what he told us; his strong Scottish accent was almost incomprehensible.

We set off along the road which gradually grew steeper, the green hills falling away to be replaced by a higher, bleaker terrain, strewn with great rocky outcrops and stretches of rough grass and heather. The horse began to labour and, to ease its burden, both Holmes and I climbed down to follow it on foot.

Pausing to glance behind me, I saw the landscape had stretched itself out below us, the houses of Stranhyde reduced to a mere handful of small cubes, no bigger than a child's building blocks. Their slate roofs shone pewter in the sun while the sea had spread into a vast, glittering expanse broken only by the dark mass of a distant island rising like a whale's back above the restless surface of the waves.

Ten minutes of hard, uphill slog brought us at last to the hotel which was situated on a high, rocky promontory and which, with its battlemented walls and its two round turrets, put me in mind of a medieval fortress guarding the coast against invaders. This first impression was, however, deceptive for as we remounted the trap and drove through the massive gates we saw that at closer view the hotel presented a more pleasing aspect. The gardens and lawns which surrounded it were well tended and the terrace was bright with urns of gaily coloured flowers.

Its interior was as welcoming, the baronial grandeur of its great hall, which served as a reception area, softened by tapestries and velvet hangings. We were heartened, too, by the genial manner of its proprietor whose accent, unlike the tavern keeper's, we could understand with ease.

As Grice Paterson had stated in his telegram, we had no difficulty in obtaining rooms. While Holmes registered, I glanced about to familiarise myself with my surroundings.

To the left of the desk was a door marked 'Bar' while directly opposite two more doors, both double-leaved, also led off the hall, one labelled 'Dining Room', the other 'Drawing Room'. One half of the latter was ajar, giving me a glimpse of the room beyond, furnished with chintz-covered armchairs and sofas. Over the back of one of these sofas I could just discern the top of a woman's head. Her abundant fair hair, the colour of wheat, was plaited and piled up into a coronet. I wondered if she were Mrs Grice Paterson, whom Mycroft Holmes had described as fair-haired, or some other female guest, but there was no way of telling.

In the meantime, a porter had been summoned to carry our luggage. We followed him up the broad oak staircase to the upper landing and along a passageway, where we were ushered into two adjoining rooms overlooking the front of the hotel with splendid views across the gardens towards the cliff tops and the sea.

Our arrival was well timed for hardly had I finished unpacking than there came the sonorous clangour of a gong downstairs, announcing that luncheon was served. Joining Holmes in the passage outside our rooms, we descended the stairs and entered the dining room together.

It was a large room, facing inland towards the surrounding hills with their vistas of rocks and heather. This bleaker aspect and the rows of mounted antlers and ancient weapons which decorated the walls made it a little gloomy and oppressive.

My interest, however, was taken not so much by our surroundings as by the other guests, many of whom were already seated or who entered soon after our own arrival. There were about fifteen of them, including two family parties consisting of husbands and wives, assorted children and their nursemaids; four young men, evidently together; a middle-aged couple, but not answering to Mycroft Holmes's description of the Grice Patersons; and finally a solitary man wearing pince-nez.

In fact, thanks to Mycroft Holmes, I had no difficulty in picking out the Grice Patersons who were seated at the far side of the room. Henry Grice Paterson was a tall, lean man in his sixties whose keen-cut features, clipped moustache and upright bearing gave him a military air; not the type, I thought, who would overdramatise any situation, however dangerous. His wife, younger than he by about ten years, was an attractive woman who, in her youth, must have been exceedingly pretty although her features now looked haggard with anxiety. She indeed had fair hair which was worn in a simple chignon so she was not the woman I had glimpsed in the drawing room. In fact, that woman appeared not to be present although, out of curiosity, I scanned all the tables one by one. It was while I was thus engaged that the door opened and the lady in question entered.

It would be wrong to describe her as beautiful for her features were too strong and unusual to conform to the conventional idea of feminine beauty. Handsome would be a better word and, although that also hardly does her credit, it conveys something of the powerful effect her straight brows, high cheek-bones and the uncompromising lines of her mouth and chin had on the observer.

There was a queenly air about her as well, which was conveyed not only by the coronet of fair hair but also in her general bearing and the proud, almost disdainful lift to her head. Indeed, so overwhelming was this majestic air that it was only when she passed our table on her way to her solitary place by the window that I realised she walked with a slight limp and had to support herself with the aid of a stick.

During luncheon, my attention strayed from time to time towards her as Holmes and I chatted about general subjects. Holmes had also noticed her presence but he was more concerned with the timing of our meal so that we would not leave the dining room before the Grice Patersons. At last the waiter cleared their plates and they rose from their chairs, passing our table on their way to the door. As they did so, Henry Grice Paterson raised his eyes momentarily towards the ceiling, indicating that we were to meet him upstairs.

We left the dining room about five minutes later and, having mounted the staircase, found Grice Paterson standing alone on the landing, ostensibly absorbed in examining a seascape hanging on the wall. As we approached, he set off down a passageway which led away from our rooms towards the side of the building. With a quick glance behind him to make sure no one was watching, Holmes started after him, with me at his heels, to a door at the far end through which Grice Paterson had gone, leaving it ajar.

Three

We entered – Holmes taking care to close the door behind us – to find the room already prepared for our arrival with three chairs drawn up companionably in a circle around a small, low table. Grice Paterson was standing beside them to welcome us. Having shaken hands and invited us to sit down, he began by apologising for his wife's absence.

'As she finds the whole affair very distressing, she prefers to spend the time reading in the garden. However, she is much relieved, as I am myself, by your presence here, gentlemen, and most grateful that you have agreed to look into the matter.' Turning to Holmes, he continued, 'I assume your brother Mycroft has informed you about *Los Halcónes* and how I became unwittingly involved with them. He has also told you, I imagine, of Gustafo Herrera's escape from prison. Very well, then, allow me apprise you of what has happened since our arrival here ten days ago.'

Reaching into an inner pocket, he drew out two envelopes which he laid side by side on the table. Neither of them bore a stamp and both were addressed in awkwardly formed capital letters in black ink to 'Mr H. Grice Paterson'. The messages contained in the envelopes, which our client removed and unfolded for our benefit, were not, however, handwritten but were composed of words and occasionally single letters apparently cut from a newspaper and pasted onto the sheets. The first stated quite simply: 'A life for a life and a death for a death'. The second: 'Revenge, like wine, improves with keeping.'

'When did you receive these?' Holmes enquired.

'The first, referring to a death for a death, came a few days after we arrived; the second, only two days ago,' Grice Paterson replied. 'Both were found by the hall porter when he came on duty at six in the morning. They were lying on the mat just inside the front door.'

'So they were presumably put through the letterbox before six a.m. by someone not staying in the hotel?'

'That was also my assumption, Mr Holmes. I should add that I received similar letters, although in Spanish, when I was at the consulate in Bogotá which was why I immediately suspected *Los Halcónes* were involved.'

'And no one saw or heard anything?'

'Apparently not. But I have my suspicions as to who on the island has sent them.'

I saw Holmes immediately sit up to attention at this last remark of Grice Paterson's and he asked eagerly, 'And who is that?'

'Before I answer your question, Mr Holmes, allow me to explain a little of the background. It was my habit to take a morning swim from the beach below the hotel at about ten o'clock in the morning. After the tide goes out a large rock pool is left behind as the water recedes. It is a safer place for bathing than the open sea, while the surrounding rocks give one privacy to dress and undress without being seen. I should also add that at that time of the morning the beach is usually empty.

'The Wednesday before last, two days after my arrival here, I was walking back up the beach having had my swim when I noticed a figure standing on the cliff top above me. At that distance it was not possible to pick out any details of his features and at first I did not trouble to observe him very closely, except to note that he was tall and was wearing a long, dark cloak and a wide-brimmed black hat.'

'He?' Holmes broke in. 'You are quite sure it was a man?'

'That was certainly my impression.'

'And did you recognise him as someone you knew?'

'If you mean Gustafo Herrera, Mr Holmes, then my answer must be no. I never saw the elder Herrera brother, only Julio, the younger. By the time Gustafo was arrested and brought to trial, I had already left Colombia. It was only later I began to suspect the man could be Gustafo Herrera.'

'I apologise for interrupting you,' Holmes interjected, 'but these facts are important to the investigation. Pray continue, Mr Grice Paterson.'

'For the next two days he was there every morning, simply watching, and I must confess that his presence began to make me feel uneasy. Although he made no threatening move or gesture, his cloak, and in particular his hat, put me in mind of a Colombian *llanero*, a man from the plains who dresses in a similar fashion. The following morning I received the first of the letters.

'After that I was disinclined to visit the pool and, for several mornings, I kept away altogether. But I missed my daily swim and decided to change my routine and instead go swimming in the early evening when the tide is again low. On two occasions nothing happened. The man did not reappear and I was beginning to think the danger was over when, on the third evening, as I was walking up the beach from the pool, a large boulder came tumbling down from the cliff above and crashed a mere few yards from me. It could, of course, have fallen accidentally for I saw no one on the headland who might have deliberately pushed it over the edge. Nevertheless, I was alarmed by the incident, especially when I received the second threatening letter the following morning.

'As you can imagine, I began to suspect a connection not only between these events but with Gustafo Herrera. I therefore made enquiries of the hotel proprietor. Without alluding to my suspicions, I merely described the man, adding that I had seen him several times and was curious to know who he might be. According to the proprietor, the man was a Mr Kemp, who had rented an empty croft not far away from the hotel where he had been staying for the past three weeks. In other words, his arrival pre-dated my wife's and mine. Apart from these few facts, the proprietor could tell me nothing more about him. It was then that I decided to take the ferry to the mainland and send the telegram to your brother, requesting your assistance, as I knew your reputation as a private consulting agent.'

Rising to his feet, Grice Paterson moved to the window.

'If you would care to join me, gentlemen,' he continued, 'you will be able to see the croft where Kemp is living.'

The window overlooked the side of the hotel, with the sea to the left, and to the right the cliffs where the landscape began gently to fall away to a large, shallow dip in the terrain before rising again to steeper slopes in the far distance. At closer view – in fact, a mere hundred yards away on the very perimeter of the hotel grounds – the tops of some trees were visible, curiously at ground level, extending some distance inland from the edge of the cliff. Apart from these, the scenery was bare except for grass and heather through which a single track wound its tortuous way, alternately disappearing and reappearing as the contours of the land rose and fell. It was empty also of any sign of habitation save for a low, whitewashed cottage in the middle distance about a quarter of a mile away which was standing side on to the track.

'That is where Mr Kemp is staying,' Grice Paterson remarked.

'And those trees?' Holmes enquired, pointing to the feature which had also caught my attention.

'They grow in a glen from which the hotel gets its name, although it is more like a gorge or a ravine,' Grice Paterson explained. 'The steep sides protect the trees from the weather, otherwise they could not survive there. It is a picturesque place with a stream running through it, and eventually emerges at the beach, although I do not recommend that route to the sea. It is very rugged and dangerous in places. The easier way is to use the steps which lead down from the garden.

'If you follow the track in the other direction, towards the croft where Kemp is living, you will cross the glen by a bridge and will have a good view of it, without the trouble of climbing down into it. The track, by the way, is a continuation of the road up to the hotel from Stranhyde.'

'And that white shape down there on the left?' Holmes continued, indicating a pale patch, only partly visible through the shrubbery.

'Oh, that is Miss Gordon's sunshade.'

'Miss Gordon?'

'The young lady with the limp. You may have noticed her at luncheon. At the far side of the terrace there is a path which leads down to the lower terrace, overlooking the glen. Miss Gordon is there most mornings and afternoons, sketching or painting the views. She is a very talented artist. And now gentlemen—'

He broke off as there came a knock upon the door.

'Who is it?' he called out.

'The porter, sir,' came the reply.

With a gesture to us to move out of sight, our client walked across the room and opened the door.

'A parcel for you, sir,' we heard the porter announce.

There was a pause before Grice Paterson responded, but when he spoke his voice was admirably calm and steady.

'Thank you, McPherson. Oh, by the way, when was it delivered?'

'It wasna delivered as such, Mr Grice Paterson. It was found by one o' the maids when she went out into the yard tae fetch in the dry linen fra the washline. It was lying there o' the ground.'

'Who left it?'

'That I canna say, sir, nor when it was placed there. But, as ye may tell for yourself, the paper is damp so it must have been left last nicht or early this morning when the dew was still o' the ground.'

'Thank you, McPherson,' Grice Paterson said in the same steady voice.

We heard the chink of money as coins changed hands, followed by the porter's expression of thanks. Then the door was shut and Grice Paterson came back into the room, carrying a package about eighteen inches square. As he put it down on the table beside the two threatening letters, Holmes and I came forward to inspect it.

It was wrapped in brown paper and addressed in a similar manner to those other two missives in black capital letters. The string which secured the parcel was fastened on top by a double knot which our client was about to untie when Holmes put out a hand to detain him.

'Leave it!' said he. 'It could be useful evidence. A man will invariably tie a knot in the same fashion time and time again without being aware himself of the habit.' Producing a penknife, he cut the string on either side of the knot and, having released it, put both it and the knife into his pocket. Then he stood back to allow Grice Paterson to unwrap the parcel, which he did with nervous alacrity. Off came the brown paper to reveal a cardboard box which, once opened, seemed to contain nothing more sinister than heather. At the sight of it our client's expression turned from anxiety to one of baffled relief. But the relief was short-lived, for when this top layer was removed the true contents of the parcel immediately became apparent.

Lying inside, on a bed of more heather, was the skull of a sheep, bleached white by long exposure to the sun and air which had made the more fragile parts, such as the edges of the eye-sockets and nostrils, so brittle that fragments had crumbled away, giving the impression not just of death but of hideous decay. And that was not the only shocking aspect of this macabre object. Written across the top of the skull in large capitals were the letters 'RIP'.

Grice Paterson, who had started back with an exclamation of horror, began hurriedly to stuff the heather back into the box and rewrap the paper round it before thrusting the parcel into Holmes's hands.

'For God's sake, take it!' cried he. 'I would not for the world have my wife see it. This business has already had a dreadful effect on her nerves. But I think, Mr Holmes, that you may now understand the urgency of this affair.'

'Indeed I do,' Holmes assured him grimly. 'We are dealing here with someone who not only seeks revenge but takes a great deal of perverted pleasure in tormenting his victim, as a cat plays with a mouse.'

'Then what do you advise me to do?' our client exclaimed. 'Should I cut short my visit and return to London? Or should I remain here?'

'Stay here!' Holmes replied without any hesitation. 'If you return to London, you will resolve nothing. Whoever is responsible for these threats could follow you and carry them out there, where it would be even more difficult to protect you. Indeed, like my brother Mycroft, I am surprised that your adversary did not choose London in the first place where he would be less conspicuous than on a small island such as Uffa. But, no doubt, his reason will become clear in time.' Picking up the parcel, he added, 'Watson and I will begin our enquiries immediately. Meanwhile, I advise you to remain in or near the hotel.'

With that warning, Holmes and I took our leave, first making sure that no one was outside in the passage to witness our departure.

Four

We returned to Holmes's room where he placed the parcel inside his wardrobe and then locked the door on it, remarking as he did so, 'I shall get rid of it later. However, for the time being, I had better keep it. Like the knot in the string, it might be useful as evidence. And now, my dear fellow, if you are not too fatigued by the overnight journey, I suggest we explore the ground a little. A walk past the croft where the mysterious Kemp is staying will make an excellent start to our enquiries.'

We left shortly afterwards, setting off down the drive to join the track which led up from Stranhyde and continued on past the back of the hotel, following the route we had already seen from Grice Paterson's bedroom window. It was about a ten-minute walk to the bridge over the glen to which our client had referred, and we paused in the middle to look about us.

Viewing the place from above and at close quarters, I could see why Grice Paterson had described it as a gorge or a ravine, for it was a deep, steep-sided crack which ran in both directions, as if the land had been torn apart by some gigantic cataclysm in the past. Huge, moss-covered rocks lay strewn about, over which a narrow burn or stream tumbled in a roar of water and white spray, swirling into eddies or plunging down in cataracts before continuing its frenzied, headlong race to the sea.

In between these rocks, clumps of ferns were growing as well as trees, mostly birch or pine. They leaned haphazardly at angles, clutching desperately with their roots at the shallow pockets of soil. None of them rose any higher than the lip of the ravine where the bitter, salt-laden winter gales, blowing in from the sea, had stunted their growth.

To our left, between these trees, I again caught a glimpse of Miss Gordon's white sunshade on the lower terrace of the hotel garden. I could understand her desire to paint the scene for it had a wild, haunting beauty even though the green light filtering through the branches gave it a gloomy melancholy air while the ceaseless noise of the tumbling water seemed to stun the very senses. Conversation was impossible and Holmes had to touch my arm and gesture with his other hand to indicate it was time to move on.

Beyond the ravine the track swung towards the sea, gently dipping and rising with the contours of the land. As we crested each of these slopes the croft came into closer view so that, little by little, we were able to make out more details of the place. It was set at right angles to the track, its front facing us, its rear turned to the distant mountains, and was surrounded by a low stone wall which in places had tumbled into ruins.

There were no signs of human beings. Indeed, the whole landscape seemed deserted. We were therefore considerably surprised when, on reaching the top of yet another incline, we saw the figure of a man coming towards us, as if he had at that moment materialised from the ground. However, once the initial shock of his sudden appearance had passed, I realised he must have emerged from the croft in those few moments when we were out of sight of it below the slope.

Although he was wearing neither the long cloak nor the wide-brimmed hat which Grice Paterson had described, merely ordinary tweeds, nevertheless there was no doubt in my mind that the man was none other than the mysterious figure who had appeared on the cliff tops and who, I assumed, was behind the threats to our client's life.

'A fortuitous meeting,' Holmes remarked to me in a murmured aside. 'Now we know he is not in residence, we may break into his cottage and search it at our leisure. Good afternoon!' he continued, raising his voice as the man drew nearer.

Apart from nodding curtly, the man made no other response. During that brief face-to-face encounter before we went on our separate ways, I – and I am sure Holmes, too – had enough time to study him closely.

At first sight, his appearance did not strike me as particularly foreign. His clothes were undoubtedly English in their style and his bearing also had that freedom and confidence of movement which suggested an English country squire used to striding about his estates. But that impression was not borne out by his features, which belonged more to the intelligentsia than the landed gentry. It was a long, dark face, although the impression of darkness was found more in his expression than in the actual colour of his skin. It was austere, harsh even, lacking all humour and of the type the Scots term dour.

We had now drawn level with the croft and Holmes paused to cast a backward glance along the track. The man was no longer in sight, having disappeared briefly from view in that same declivity in the ground from the top of which we had first observed him.

'Quick, Watson!' Holmes said urgently, and, vaulting over the low wall, made for the back of the building where I soon joined him. We waited there for several minutes in what had once been a cobbled yard but which was now overgrown with grass, until the man reappeared in view. Having assured ourselves that he had not once glanced back in our direction, we turned our attention to the cottage – or at least Holmes did so – first trying the back door, which was locked. However, the wooden frame of a small, ill-fitting window beside it soon yielded to the blade of Holmes's penknife and, pushing the casement inwards, he scrambled through the opening, offering me a hand as I hoisted myself in after him.

We found ourselves in a low, dark room, its rough walls whitewashed and its flagstone floor bare except for an old rug lying in front of an open fireplace. A wooden settle, a table and two upright chairs supplied the only furniture. The room was apparently lit by candles for I saw no other means of illumination.

A curtain separated this living area from the sleeping quarter which was little more than an alcove containing a bed and a chest of drawers. Windows back and front looked in one direction towards the distant mountains, in the other to the track along which we had come. It was at the front-facing window that Holmes stationed me to keep watch – while he searched the cottage – in case its occupant might return unexpectedly and find us there. This proved an unnecessary pre-caution for the man calling himself Kemp never turned once, not even to look behind him, but continued on his errand. His figure alternately disappeared and reappeared as the land rose and fell, each time growing smaller and smaller, until he vanished completely at the point where the track passed behind the hotel and descended towards Stranhyde.

The search of the cottage was soon completed for there was so little in the way of furniture to examine. In fact, Kemp seemed to have few possessions apart from clothes which were either stowed away in the drawers or hung from nails in the walls. It was among these garments that Holmes found the evidence which indubitably linked Kemp to the mysterious stranger whom Grice Paterson had seen on the cliffs above the beach. In fact, this confirmation needed no seeking out for it was hanging in plain view from a hook on the back of the door and consisted of a long, dark cloak and a broad-brimmed hat of soft, black felt.

The bottle of ink together with the pen with which he had addressed the threatening messages and the parcel, as well as inscribing the skull with the letters RIP, were also openly displayed on the mantelshelf above the fireplace among a litter of other objects, including a clock, a tea caddy and a bowl containing three eggs.

It was the grate below this mantelshelf which took up much of Holmes's time. A fire had evidently burned there fairly recently for on top of a mound of soft ash were lying larger, fresh-looking flakes of charred paper among which some white fragments remained intact.

Turning my attention momentarily from the window, I saw Holmes kneel down and, with the aid of a pair of tweezers which he took from his pocket, gently lift one of these unburnt scraps which he transferred to his notebook for safe keeping.

Everywhere had now been thoroughly examined, except for a basket standing on the hearth which contained peat and kindling. It was not until Holmes had taken these out and reached his hand inside the basket that he came up with something quite unexpected – a small bundle of cloth wrapped round something hard which, when he laid it down on the floor and unwound its covering, proved to be a handgun.

'A Smith and Wesson!' Holmes exclaimed softly, sitting back on his heels and regarding it with sombre interest. 'So, Watson, we now know how Grice Paterson is supposed to die.'

'What are you going to do, Holmes?' I asked in some alarm. 'Do you intend taking it?'

'Certainly not! That would achieve nothing except to reveal our hand. No. I shall put it back where it was.'

As he spoke he began rewrapping the gun, taking great care to fold the cloth in exactly the same manner in which he had found it.

'But are you not taking an enormous risk with Grice Paterson's life by leaving it there?' I protested.

'He is already under sentence of death. If I remove the gun it will only postpone the danger, not avert it. The only way to achieve that is to lure his enemy into the open and then seize him.'

'How?'

'My dear Watson, at the moment I have not the slightest idea. I am waiting for a flash of inspiration.' Putting the bundle back into the basket, he re-covered it with the wood. Rising to his feet, he added, 'In the meantime, I suggest we leave now, before Kemp returns and finds us here. Besides, I want to look at the place where he appeared on the cliff top above the beach.'

Five

We left by the same way we had come, climbing out through the small rear window into the yard where Holmes paused to smear earth over the place where he had forced open the casement to cover up the marks on the wooden frame. That done, we set off across the open land towards the sea.

Because of the relative flatness of the surrounding terrain, I had forgotten how high this part of the coast was until I reached the edge of the cliff and peered down over it. It was a dizzying sensation for we were higher even than the gulls which swooped and hovered below us, their hoarse, melancholy cries mingling with the constant surge of the sea. The beach seemed small and far away, a narrow crescent of rocks and sand edging a cove, beyond which the restless ocean stretched away to an unseen horizon, lost in the dazzle of sun and water.

But the altitude offered us an excellent view of the general setting. To the left, I could make out the place where the ravine emerged at last at the foot of the cliffs, marked by a dark cleft in the rocks and the silvery flash of the stream which ran across the beach in a series of small rivulets to join the sea. A little further off, the roof and turrets of the hotel were visible on the adjoining headland. To the right, the beach dwindled and disappeared as the cliff closed round it like a huge, defensive wall.

However, it was what lay immediately below us which attracted Holmes's attention. Pointing downwards, he remarked, 'There is the pool where Grice Paterson went swimming.'

The rock pool was at the point where the beach began to narrow and a tumbled mass of huge granite boulders lay piled up close to the shore's edge. At high tide it would be completely covered, but the sea had already begun to recede and it was just possible to make out an irregular stretch of calm water caught between the rocks, its placid surface catching and reflecting the light.

To my alarm, Holmes threw himself down upon the ground and cautiously began to edge himself forward until his head and shoulders were extended beyond the edge of the cliff. I was about to seize him by the ankles, fearful that a rock might detach itself beneath him and send him pitching into the abyss below, when, to my great relief, he wriggled back to a safe distance and stood upright, brushing soil from his hands and knees. Whatever it was he had wanted to examine in such a foolhardy manner remained unexplained, although he seemed satisfied with what he had discovered.

'Time to go, Watson!' said he briskly, and began striding back towards the track, where he turned in the direction of the hotel.

As I hurried to catch up with him, I wondered if we might meet Kemp on his way back from Stranhyde where I assumed he had gone to buy provisions. But we saw no one until we reached the terrace of the hotel where we encountered the lady whom Grice Paterson had referred to as Miss Gordon. She was coming from the direction of the ravine where, no doubt, she had spent the afternoon sketching on the lower terrace for, as well as her stick, she was carrying an artist's satchel in her other hand. She was followed by the porter who was loaded with a folding chair, a large white sunshade and a collapsible easel. As we stood aside, she acknowledged the courtesy with a slight inclination of her head although she did not speak.

I was struck once more by the strange beauty of her features. My admiration was touched also by compassion for her physical handicap which, encountering her now at closer quarters, I could see was congenital rather than the result of an accident. Below the hem of her gown I caught a glimpse of her left shoe, the sole of which was raised as if to compensate for some malformation either in the foot or in the leg.

As we entered the hotel behind her, Holmes murmured, 'Wait here, Watson, there's a good fellow. I shall not be long. There is a small matter I want to look into.'

His manner, though casual, discouraged me from questioning him or even following him as he crossed the hall to the door marked 'Drawing Room'. He disappeared inside, closing the door behind him.

Left to my own devices, I wandered about aimlessly for a few moments and then decided to engage in a little exploration of my own. To the left of the desk was the door marked 'Bar'. Since our arrival, there had not been time to examine it. Tempted by the thought of Holmes and I indulging ourselves in a glass or two of good Scotch malt whisky later in the evening, I pushed open the door and stepped inside.

Although the room was dark-panelled, there were plenty of mirrors and polished brass fittings which gave it a cheerful air, and it was in one of these mirrors, the one behind the bar, that I caught sight of Kemp. He was seated facing the counter, his back towards me, and was therefore not aware of my arrival so that, once I had recovered from the shock of his unexpected presence, I was able to study him for a few moments.

He sat alone with a glass of whisky on the table before him, his expression morose as if he were absorbed in his own dark thoughts. There were other people in the bar, but he seemed untouched by their conversation and laughter, like the brooding ghost of Banquo at Macbeth's feast.

I slipped quietly away before either he or the bartender had noticed me and, returning to the hall, met Holmes as he emerged from the drawing room, having completed whatever mysterious errand he had been engaged on.

'Holmes!' I said urgently, hurrying forward to meet him. 'I have just seen Kemp in the bar, sitting there as large as life!'

His eyebrows shot up in astonished incredulity.

'Are you quite sure it was Kemp?'

'Absolutely certain. What do you suppose he is doing here?'

'I cannot for the life of me imagine. But I suspect it is part of the plot which grows more complex by the hour!'

'Should we not warn Grice Paterson? He could be in danger.'

'He is quite safe as long as he remains in the hotel. But he must be told of this unexpected turn of events. By a stroke of good fortune, I have just spoken to him and his wife in the drawing room and have arranged for us to meet him in his room in a quarter of an hour. Therefore, let us go upstairs, Watson, for I want to spend the time before our conference in thinking over this new twist to the affair and what possible relevance it can have to the case.'

Six

'And so, Grice Paterson,' Holmes concluded, 'I think I can say with every confidence that Kemp is the man who not only sent the parcel and the threatening letters but was also the figure wearing the cloak and the broad-brimmed hat whom you saw on the cliff top.'

The three of us were seated in our client's bedroom, Mrs Grice Paterson having again preferred not to attend our meeting but to remain downstairs in the drawing room. Holmes had just finished giving a brief account for our activities that afternoon, including the evidence he had found in the croft which pointed to Kemp's involvement in the affair, as well as my own sighting of him in the hotel bar.

'However,' Holmes continued, 'I still believe the case is much more complex than might at first appear.'

'Why do you say that?' Grice Paterson asked. 'I would have thought it was all perfectly straightforward. Kemp is Gustafo Herrera who has tracked me down in order to avenge his brother's death.'

'Oh, the motive is clear enough. It is other aspects of the case which concern me. Take Kemp's visit to the hotel this afternoon. He must know you are suspicious of him so why has he chosen to break cover like this and appear in the open? There would seem to be no reason for it and yet I feel his decision is part of a deliberate plan. He is manipulating the situation in some fashion – quite how or why, I do not yet know. But I believe the same purpose lies behind all his actions, even the choice of the island of Uffa as the place for the assassination rather than London, as I have remarked before. And then there is this.'

Taking out his notebook, he removed the fragment of unburnt paper he had retrieved from the grate in Kemp's cottage and laid it down on the table. It was, I saw, a scrap of newspaper, charred along its edges.

Having explained for Grice Paterson's benefit where he had found it, Holmes continued, 'As Dr Watson will affirm, I have made a study of different newspaper types and I can state quite categorically that the print you see here on this fragment is exactly the same as that of the words and individual letters which were used to compose the two threatening messages you received. I can also assure you that both are from *The Times*, an unusual newspaper, do you not agree, to find in the grate of a crofter's cottage?

'However, when we returned to the hotel, I made a point of checking in the drawing room, where I met you, Mr Grice Paterson, and where I also found a copy of *The Times* – a day late, I may add, as it has to be brought over by ferry from the mainland.'

Grice Paterson's eyebrows drew together in a frown.

'Are you suggesting that someone staying in the hotel is in league with Kemp?'

'It is a possibility,' Holmes said coolly. 'On the other hand, our suspect may have retrieved a back copy of the newspaper from the hotel dustbin on one of his night-time forays when he left the letters or the parcel. Alternatively, he may have brought it with him or bought a copy in Stranhyde, although I doubt London newspapers are on sale there. However, on the assumption that Kemp may have an accomplice, what do you know of the other hotel guests?'

'Very little,' Grice Paterson confessed. 'I think we may discount the two family parties staying here. The presence of young children would surely rule them out. Besides, they have stayed here regularly over the past few years. The same objection applies to Miss Gordon, the single lady who is partly crippled. She, too, has been a guest here for the past two summers. Moreover, I would not have thought that a woman, particularly one who is handicapped in that manner, would make a very likely accomplice.

'The four young men are strangers, although I understand they are medical students from Edinburgh university and are keen walkers and rock-climbers. The middle-aged man, who is here with his wife, is a professor of archaeology and is studying the two prehistoric stone circles on the island. Mr Lomax, the other man, who is on his own, I have not seen before either but I understand he is, like me, an amateur ornithologist. He seems a harmless enough fellow.'

'But nevertheless with an excuse to move freely about the place,' Holmes pointed out.

'That is certainly true,' Grice Paterson acceded, 'but the same could be said of Professor Arrowsmith or the medical students. To be frank, Mr Holmes, I am not at all convinced by your theory that Kemp is in league with someone else, certainly not with anyone staying in the hotel.'

'You may be correct, Mr Grice Paterson,' Holmes acknowledged. 'Nevertheless, I am still certain that there are more twists and turns to this plot than we have yet uncovered.' With apparent inconsequentiality, he added, 'When do you and your wife propose leaving?'

'Friday week.'

'In ten days' time,' Holmes said musingly. 'Therefore, if Kemp makes good his threat to kill you, he must act before then. At the moment he holds all the cards and is thus controlling the state of play. I suggest we turn that to our advantage.'

'How?' Grice Paterson enquired.

'By seizing the initiative ourselves. In doing so, we may force him into taking precipitate action which may lead him to make mistakes. I therefore suggest, Mr Grice Paterson, that you inform the proprietor that you intend leaving the day after tomorrow and, at the same time, make sure the other hotel guests know of your decision. If there is an accomplice among them, word will get back to Kemp of your imminent departure. If there is no accomplice, we shall proceed with our plan regardless. By the way, what clothes do you wear when you go down to the beach to bathe?'

'Clothes?' Grice Paterson seemed as perplexed as I at this unexpected question. 'Why, a panama hat, a linen jacket, an ordinary white shirt and a pair of grey flannel trousers.'

'I assume you take a towel with you?'

'Yes. It is a large, striped towel which we brought with us.'

'May I borrow these things?'

'Of course you may but I do not see where all this is leading, Mr Holmes,' Grice Paterson began, and then stopped short. By the sudden change in his expression, from bewilderment to startled awareness, I realised that he, too, like me, had grasped the significance of Holmes's seemingly casual question. 'You are proposing to disguise yourself as me, are you not?' he demanded. 'I cannot allow it, Mr Holmes! It is much too dangerous!'

'Then what alternative do you suggest, my dear sir?' Holmes asked in a tone of sweet reasonableness. 'Either we seize this nettle now and tear it out root and stem or we leave it where it is to go on growing. Do you want to spend the rest of your life under the shadow of Kemp's threats against you? That is no future for any man, Mr Grice Paterson. As for my own safety, you may rest assured that I value my life as much as you do yours and I am not foolish enough to risk it in some dangerous enterprise which could well be fatal. Now, sir, will you give me what I have asked for?'

As Grice Paterson hesitated, the gong for dinner sounded downstairs and, as if its deep, reverberating tones had prompted him to come to a decision, he said, 'Very well, then, Mr Holmes, providing you will give me your word that no harm will come to you.'

'Gladly,' Holmes replied lightly, a smile touching the corners of his lips.

However, it was still with evident reluctance that Grice Paterson found the items of clothing Holmes had requested, and handed them to him together with the towel. He seemed about to add a further protest but my old friend forestalled him.

'I would like you and your wife to return to your bedroom after breakfast tomorrow morning and remain there until I send for you. It is most vital that you are not seen either in the hotel or in its grounds. And,' he added, pausing at the door, 'do please remember to advertise the fact that you intend leaving Uffa on the day after tomorrow.'

Seven

With this parting remark from my old friend, we returned to our own rooms where Holmes hung Grice Paterson's clothes in his wardrobe. Then, after hurriedly changing out of our informal tweeds into more suitable evening attire, we went down for dinner, stopping only briefly on our way to glance in at the bar which we found completely empty of both hotel guests and Kemp's dark, malevolent presence.

We chose the same table at which we had taken lunch, for it gave us a good view of the whole dining room. Because of our late arrival, all the other guests were already seated and, throughout the meal, we had the opportunity to observe them at our leisure.

My attention was particularly drawn to Mr Lomax, the amateur ornithologist, who, out of all the others, seemed the most likely candidate for Kemp's accomplice, if indeed he had one. Watching him, I could understand Grice Paterson's remark as to his seeming harmlessness. He was a small, inoffensive-looking man, wearing gold-rimmed pince-nez, who had a fussy, almost old-maidish air about him.

And then, suddenly becoming aware of my scrutiny, he lifted his eyes to look in my direction. In those few seconds before I hastily transferred my attention elsewhere, his whole demeanour seemed to change, his face sharpening and that mild expression turning to one of suspicion and, I thought, of dislike.

However, by the time the Grice Patersons rose to leave the room, that air of affable politeness was back in place. As our client paused at Lomax's table, the man's features had again assumed their good-natured amiability. I heard Grice Paterson enquire how he had enjoyed his day and if he had had any luck with his ornithological activities, to which Lomax replied that he had indeed, having observed a merlin that afternoon.

'I envy you your good fortune!' Grice Paterson exclaimed heartily. 'I am afraid my own studies will be cut short this year as we have decided to leave the day after tomorrow.'

'That is a great pity,' Lomax replied, both his voice and his features expressing polite regret.

'I intend making the most of the remaining time by taking one last swim tomorrow morning at low tide,' our client concluded, before wishing Lomax good evening and following his wife out of the room.

As far as I could see, none of the guests, not even Lomax, had responded in any positive manner to this last piece of information, although Grice Paterson's voice must have been audible to all of them.

Not long after their departure Holmes and I also left, neither of us any the wiser as to whether or not Lomax was part of the conspiracy, as Holmes remarked once we were out of earshot of the other diners.

I had been hoping that we might retire to the bar but, when I suggested it, Holmes replied, 'Later, my dear fellow. First I want to find the steps which lead down to the beach.'

They lay at the far end of the lawn in front of the hotel and, although steep, the treads were broad and smooth, while a wooden handrail running alongside them made descending or ascending relatively easy. Holmes made no attempt to go down them but, turning away, he lit his pipe and began to stroll through the gardens.

It was a pleasant evening and so calm that the only sound was that of the gentle lapping of the waves against the shore. To the west the sun was already beginning to set, dipping towards the horizon and flooding the sea with golden light so bright that it hurt the eyes to look at it.

Holmes was in a pensive mood which seemed to accord with the serenity of the scene and we sauntered back in silence towards the hotel terrace. Once there, however, he announced with a sudden briskness, as if he had at that very moment come to a decision about some aspect of the case, 'I think a dram or two of good malt whisky is called for, my dear fellow.'

We entered the bar and joined those other guests who had already gathered there, including the four medical students, the two husbands from the family parties and Mr Lomax, who sat alone in a far corner, apparently absorbed in a book, no doubt about birds.

The proximity of these others made private conversation between us impossible and we talked about general subjects. From time to time I saw my old friend's attention wander momentarily towards the solitary figure of Lomax whom he scrutinised with a veiled speculation.

The only reference Holmes made to the case was when we were about to leave. Raising his glass, he remarked, 'Here's to our enterprise, my dear fellow. Let us wish it every success.'

As he spoke, I saw his glance stray again in Lomax's direction.

'I'll drink to that,' I replied, raising my own glass.

I had half expected Holmes to invite me into his room in order that we might discuss the case in private but I was disappointed.

Halting outside his door, he said firmly, 'Goodnight, my old friend. I shall see you tomorrow when, all going to plan, we shall see an end to this affair. By the way, do remember to bring your gun with you.'

'But, Holmes . . .' I began in protest.

There was so much I wanted to ask him. Was he indeed convinced that Lomax might be Kemp's accomplice? To what precise use was he intending to put Grice Paterson's clothes? And, most important of all, how dangerous was his proposed enterprise? For, despite the assurance Holmes had given to Grice Paterson that his life would not be placed in danger, I was not myself totally convinced.

I was not given the opportunity. Before I could say anything more Holmes had entered his room, closing the door resolutely behind him.

Although I was fatigued, both by the journey and by the long walk we had taken that afternoon, I slept only fitfully, my mind going over and over past events and those yet to come.

In the early hours I was disturbed from this shallow slumber by a faint sound somewhere close at hand. Instantly, I was wide awake, convinced that what I had heard was the sound of Holmes's door being shut, but although I strained my ears I could hear nothing more.

Getting out of bed and putting on my dressing-gown, I crept to my own door, opening it as silently as I could. The moon was shining full through the landing window and, by its light, I made my way down the passage to Holmes's room. His door was unlocked and, turning the handle with great care, I stepped inside.

It was obvious at once that his bed was empty. The covers were thrown back and his nightclothes were lying carelessly across the pillow. Going quickly to the window, I parted the curtains to look out, but there was no sign of him. The gardens lay quiet and empty in the bright moonlight and nothing moved except for the restless sea beyond the cliff top, shining silver this time, not gold.

It was pointless to try following him when I had no idea where he had gone or why, although I suspected he was on some mission connected with the case. So, settling down in the armchair by the window, I prepared to await his return.

It was over an hour before I caught the soft creak of a floorboard in the passage outside and then saw, rather than heard, the knob of the door slowly turning. Seconds later Holmes, fully dressed, slipped quietly into the room.

It says much for his iron control that, on catching sight of me, he gave no audible exclamation of surprise, only a quick intake of breath.

'Watson!' he said softly. 'Why are you here? If I disturbed you, my dear fellow, I apologise.'

'I was not properly asleep,' I whispered back, feeling constrained to speak in lowered tones. 'What on earth were you doing at this time of the night?'

'Putting the finishing touches to my plan,' he replied, his eyes glittering with amusement in the moonlight. 'You shall see why tomorrow. And now, Watson, goodnight for the second time.'

I had no intention of being dismissed so easily.

'Holmes,' said I, 'I am not leaving this room until I have the same assurance you gave Grice Paterson. Will you swear to me that you will not put your life in danger?'

He hesitated before replying. Then he said at last, 'There is no certainty in this world of either life or death but, my old friend, I do promise you that I intend coming out of this alive, if that is at all possible.'

And with that I had to be content. Holmes had opened wide the door and there was nothing more I could do except walk past him and return to my own room.

Eight

We left the hotel the next morning at ten o'clock, the time Grice Paterson had told us was the hour he usually went for his early swim. Following Holmes's instructions, I made sure I took my army revolver with me in my pocket.

We waited until Miss Gordon, accompanied by the hotel porter carrying her sketching apparatus, was safely installed on the lower terrace, out of sight of the steps which led down to the beach. As soon as both had disappeared from view, Holmes and I set off at a rapid pace for these very steps, which we quickly descended.

I had no idea what plan my old friend had in mind for he took nothing with him, certainly not Grice Paterson's clothes which he had been so eager to borrow the previous day and which, I had assumed, would play a part in whatever scheme he had devised. However, I hesitated to question him. There was a closed, hard look about his features which I knew from experience meant his thoughts were concentrated on the task in hand and any interruption would be unwelcome.

He broke his silence only when we reached the bottom of the steps.

'Keep close to the cliff, Watson,' he ordered in an abrupt tone. 'We cannot be seen there by anyone who may be watching from the headland.'

'You are quite sure of that, Holmes?' I asked. My own nerves were stretched almost to breaking point and I fancied that we were surrounded by unseen eyes, all of them fixed on Holmes.

'Of course!' he replied testily. 'It was one of the aspects of the terrain I made special note of yesterday when, if you remember, I lay down to look over the edge of the cliff.'

While he was speaking we had reached and passed the opening to the ravine where the stream finally emerged in a series of shallow, freshwater rivulets which flowed across the beach to join the vast salt expanse of the sea. Having crossed them, I assumed we would continue walking to the far end of the cove where the pool was situated. However, to my surprise, Holmes suddenly halted at a wide crevice at the base of the cliff, well above the tideline, into which he thrust his hand and removed a bundle which had been hidden there.

'Keep cave, my dear fellow,' said he. 'It would ruin everything if someone from the hotel decided, on this morning of all others, to take a stroll along the beach.'

I did as I was bade but no one came, and by the time I turned back Holmes had already changed into Grice Paterson's linen jacket, grey flannels and panama.

I have remembered before on Holmes's amazing capacity to take on not only the outward appearance of those individuals he was impersonating but also to assume their entire identities. It was so in this case. His whole bearing had subtly changed. His head was held at a different angle, his shoulders were raised a little and drawn back. Even his spine had stiffened. Apart from his features, everything else about him so closely resembled our client's demeanour that I was tempted for a second to believe it was Grice Paterson himself who had been concealed inside that crevice and not merely his clothes.

'Now, listen, Watson,' Holmes was saying urgently, 'in a moment I shall walk across the beach towards the pool. There is no need for you to be alarmed for my safety at this point. One of the other features I noticed yesterday was the line of fire. It is too oblique for Kemp to risk attempting a shot. He will wait until I am returning up the beach from my swim when I shall present a much easier target.'

'You intend swimming, Holmes?' I asked in much alarm.

'My dear fellow, I am touched by your concern but, believe me, it is not called for. The rocks surrounding the pool provide excellent cover. Besides, I must keep as far as possible to Grice Paterson's routine. If I am seen not to take a swim, our adversary may become suspicious.'

'But won't he think it suspicious that you, or rather Grice Paterson, are there at all?' I protested. 'He knows our client has altered his usual habit of swimming in the morning to later in the day because he is aware of the danger and has, in fact, recently given up bathing entirely.'

'I take your point, Watson. We can only hope that word has got back to Kemp of our client's intention to take one last swim this morning, assuming, of course, that the man has an accomplice at the hotel. Failing that, we must trust that he will conclude that Grice Paterson has reverted to his usual habit of swimming in the morning for the very reason that his afternoon bathe has in its turn become too dangerous. We must also bear in mind that, if he has been informed of Grice Paterson's intention to leave Uffa tomorrow morning, he will be under pressure to act quickly while his quarry still remains on the island. Now, Watson, it is time I made my move.'

'What am I supposed to do?' I asked, loath to stand idly by while my old friend risked his life.

'Nothing, except remain out of sight. When the time for action comes, the signal will be clear enough. Well, wish me luck, Watson,' he added lightly.

Before I had time to reply, he had turned away and was already beginning to walk across the empty beach with the striped bathing towel rolled up under his arm.

It is no exaggeration to state that the next few moments were among the longest I had ever spent as, rigid with apprehension, I watched his lone figure walk those hundred yards or so towards the safety of the rocks. He seemed so dreadfully exposed that, despite his assurances that he would be in no danger, I expected every second to hear the sound of a shot and to see him fall face downwards onto the sand. God knows what his thoughts were, but as he continued on his solitary way there was no sign on his part of any fear or hesitation.

It was only when he reached the rocky outcrop that I realised I had literally been holding my breath. It was a double relief to see him disappear from sight behind one of the larger rocks and to feel at last the air being expelled from my lungs.

For the next half-hour I caught only glimpses of Holmes, although it was possible to deduce what his actions were even if he himself was largely out of sight. His panama was removed, for an unseen hand placed it on top of the boulder and also spread out the striped towel beside it. He must also have discarded his other clothes and entered the pool for not long afterwards I caught glimpses between the rocks of an arm or a head raised momentarily above the water, only to vanish again a second later.

After about twenty minutes, I assumed he must have emerged from the pool for I saw the towel disappear, drawn down by the same unseen hand, and a little later the panama hat was also removed.

My relief was enormous. It was apparent that Holmes had taken his swim, dried himself on the towel and had presumably reassumed Grice Paterson's attire. Nothing untoward had happened so far. If Kemp was indeed watching from the cliff top, he must be waiting for Holmes to leave the shelter of the rocks and begin to walk back across the open beach. Obvious though this should have been, the realisation struck me like a blow from a fist. In my anxiety over the early stages of the plan, I had not considered how Holmes proposed to bring it to a conclusion. How else could he entrap Kemp except by coming out into the open?

It was while I was trying to puzzle out how Holmes intended to solve this terrifying dilemma that a movement above the rocky outcrop caught my attention. Holmes, now fully dressed in Grice Paterson's panama and linen jacket, had appeared in sight, sitting upright with his back against the boulder, his head and shoulders clearly visible. Indeed, as I stood there, aghast at his foolhardiness, I saw his head tilt downwards as his hand was raised to adjust the angle of his hat.

What followed afterwards happened so quickly that I hardly had time to witness it properly, let alone come to terms with the events and their subsequent outcome.

A shot rang out, the report reverberating so loudly against the cliffs that it sounded more like a salvo of gunfire than a single explosion. At almost the same moment the panama was sent spinning away and Holmes disappeared from sight, flung forward by the impact of the bullet. Too late I shouted out a warning which came quite involuntarily. It took longer for me to gain sufficient control of my muscles to start running towards him. I still remember my emotions quite clearly. Above the initial rush of fear and horror, which set my heart and pulses racing so fiercely that I felt almost suffocated by the intensity, a small, cold, logical part of my brain told me that all action was futile. Holmes was dead and there was nothing I could do to save him.

Hardly had I gone two paces, however, when, to my utter astonishment, Holmes appeared above the rocks, waving an arm and shouting, 'Watson! Quick, man! The ravine!'

Nine

Such was Holmes's dominant nature that it never crossed my mind to query this order even for a second. Spinning on my heel, I began to run in the opposite direction, my jubilation at his miraculous escape adding extra swiftness to my feet. At the same time I was aware that my old friend was only a few yards behind me.

We reached the opening to the ravine neck and neck, although Holmes's agility soon set him a pace or two in front of me as he leapt like a stag from rock to rock. There was no time, and indeed no breath, to question him. I was intent only on clambering after him, ducking to avoid low branches or scrabbling for footholds in a crevice between the boulders.

I was deafened, too, by the roar of the stream which raced beside us and which made conversation impossible. It added also to the hazards of the climb for the rocks were slippery with spray. One false step could have sent either of us plunging down to the bottom of the gorge.

I do not know how long we continued this perilous upward scramble. All my concentration was centred on reaching the next rock in safety. But we must have been approaching close to the hotel for, pausing momentarily to draw breath, I caught a glimpse of something pale above me to the right, glimmering in the green shadows cast by the trees. For a second I was puzzled as to what it could be and then I realised it was Miss Gordon's white sunshade set out on the lower terrace of the hotel garden.

At almost the same time I became aware of something else about twenty yards ahead of me to the far left. At first I could not make out what that was either except, unlike the sunshade, it was moving, and moving rapidly, too. But the birches grew too close together and all I could make out was the flicker of some dark shape as it advanced down the opposite slope towards the stream.

'Look to the left, Holmes!' I shouted to draw his attention to it, but he had also noticed it for, like me, he had halted to watch its progress.

The next second it emerged from the trees and, for the first time, I saw it clearly. It was a tall, cloaked figure in a wide-brimmed hat, bounding across the stream from rock to rock like some wild creature escaping from its predators. With one last leap it reached the far side of the burn and began to ascent the other side of the gorge.

We set off after it, Holmes in front, myself a few yards behind him. There was no doubt in my mind that the figure was Kemp and that he was returning from the cliff top after his unsuccessful attempt on Holmes's life – or rather, as he himself must have believed, his successful attempt on Grice Paterson's. But his presence here in the gorge bewildered me. Surely he should have returned to his own cottage? I could see no purpose behind his decision to take this treacherous route which led nowhere except to the hotel.

We had by now reached the steepest part of the ravine and for us, and also for Kemp, the ascent was more precipitous. It was no longer a matter of climbing, more of clawing our way upwards, using whatever small foot- or finger-hold we could find as we hauled ourselves from one great craggy boulder to the next. Our quarry was still somewhere ahead of us, although we caught only intermittent glimpses of him as he clambered in and out of sight behind the rocks and the trees.

Neither of us therefore witnessed exactly what happened. We heard only a sudden, terrifying and terrified scream as a shower of small stones went rattling past about twenty yards in front of us, followed by the dark shape of Kemp's body, rolling and bouncing from rock to rock, like a rag doll hurled downwards by some giant hand.

I was, of course, nearer to the place where Kemp had fallen than Holmes. Even so, he was only a few feet behind me by the time I had lowered myself down the steep incline up which I had so laboriously scrambled only a short time before. Kemp's body had come to rest in a deep crevice between two great boulders and was lying half-concealed in a clump of ferns so that at first I could not see his head properly, only glimpse it between the fronds. From the little I could see, I was convinced that the man must be dead. The face was so battered and covered with blood that the features were unrecognisable, and my medical experience told me no one could have survived those dreadful injuries. I was puzzled, however, by some light-coloured tendrils, also soaked in blood, which, like a pale, unfamiliar weed, seemed to be growing out of the crevice with the ferns and which lay scattered about the corpse.

It was not until Holmes joined me and together, after a great effort, we succeeded in lifting the body to lay it down on a flatter surface that, with a shock of horror and bewilderment, I realised those strands were human hair.

Holmes must have read my thoughts in my expression for he said grimly, 'Yes, Watson, It is not Herrera as you supposed. It is Miss Gordon.'

I could see now that he was correct. As her body had pitched from rock to rock, the broad-brimmed hat must have tumbled off and the hair become loosened from its braided coils to spread across the shoulders, its rich blonde beauty darkened and bedraggled with her own blood.

'She is dead, I assume?' Holmes asked abruptly.

'Yes, Holmes. There is no question of that. You can see from the way the head lies that the neck is broken.'

For a few seconds he stood, stony-faced, in silence, looking down at the body. Then, stooping over it, he felt in the pockets of the cloak.

'There is no sign of Herrera's Smith and Wesson,' he said at last, standing upright. 'It must have dropped from her pocket as she fell. We shall have to look for it later when we return to retrieve the body, but for now there is unfinished business to attend to before we can call an end to this affair.'

I assumed he was referring to Kemp, or rather Herrera, but I hesitated to ask him. His face was fixed, rigid and implacable. Turning away, he set off once more up the ravine with a terrible energy which was almost superhuman in its strength as if, by stretching nerves and muscles to their limit, he was trying to distance himself from Miss Gordon's body and also from whatever bitter thoughts were troubling his mind.

I followed more cautiously, concentrating only on the ascent and ignoring those questions which were crowding in upon me but which I dared not consider in case I, too, lost my footing and plunged headlong.

I came at last to the top where I found, to my surprise, a length of rope dangling from the upper bar of a railing some feet above me. With the help of this and Holmes's outstretched hand, I managed to climb over this last hazard to find myself on a flat expanse of rock which I took to be the lower terrace of the hotel's garden where, as Grice Paterson had told us, Miss Gordon was in the habit of sitting while she sketched or painted the view. Indeed, her folding chair, easel and white sunshade were set out upon it, the latter opened and slotted into a metal support screwed to the side of the chair.

The terrace itself was a natural feature which extended out over the ravine like a large granite balcony and afforded superb views not only of the ravine itself but also across it to the cliffs and the sea beyond. As a safety measure a waist-high wall topped with an iron railing surrounded it on three sides for there was a sheer drop from the edge of the terrace to the ravine below.

I was about to make some comment on the wild, magnificent beauty of the setting when Holmes forestalled me.

'You have your gun, Watson?' he demanded.

'Yes,' I replied, sick at heart for I had already guessed what was to follow.

'Then get it ready,' came the peremptory command. Its brusqueness was tempered by the remark he added half to himself as he turned away. 'And let us pray God you do not need to use it.'

With that, he went striding ahead of me along a narrow path edged with shrubs which led up to the main terrace in front of the hotel. Although I was prepared for the encounter, it still came as a shock when, as we emerged onto this terrace, I saw Kemp strolling along it in the leisurely manner of a man enjoying the fresh air and the view. He had his back to us and was therefore unaware of our arrival until Holmes addressed him.

'Gustafo Herrera!' he called out.

The man spun round to face us, responding involuntarily to his real name and only realising his mistake after a few seconds when it was too late. I saw his look of startled surprise replaced by one of anger and horrified dismay at having acknowledged, in that one unguarded moment, his true identity. 'Who are you? What do you want?' he demanded hoarsely.

All the colour had drained from his face, leaving a ghastly pallor in which the dark eyes seemed to burn with a fierce and desperate life.

'My name is Sherlock Holmes,' my old friend replied crisply. 'My colleague, Dr Watson, and I are here to enquire into the threats against Mr Grice Paterson's life. I have evidence to prove that you and Miss Gordon were conspiring to murder him. Now, sir, if you will be so good as to accompany us into the hotel, I shall be much obliged. Watson, keep him covered, there's a good fellow.'

'Where is Miss Gordon?' Herrera exclaimed, starting forward. 'What have you done with her?'

'I am afraid the lady fell while attempting to climb up the ravine ...' Holmes began in a voice of genuine regret.

He got no further. With a bellow of mingled rage, horror and despair, Gustafo Herrera charged at us and in one great burst of stupendous energy and strength thrust both of us aside as if we were no more substantial than stalks of corn. Holmes was caught off balance and I was knocked to the ground, losing my grip on the revolver which spun away out of my reach. Before I could regain my feet Herrera had snatched it up and had disappeared down the path. Holmes sprinted after him, shouting to me to follow.

By the time we reached the lower terrace Herrera had already crossed it and had leapt up onto the surrounding wall where he sat crouched like the bird of prey from which he and his comrades had taken the name *Los Halcónes*. In his right hand he held my gun, in his left the rope which was still attached to the iron railing.

It was obvious what he intended to do. With the aid of the rope he would lower himself into the ravine from where, no doubt, he hoped to make his escape across the island to Stranhyde where he would either steal a boat or, by threatening a fisherman with the gun, force the man to take him across to the mainland. It was a desperate plan but one which might indeed have succeeded if only because of its audacity and the reckless courage of its perpetrator. Even if it failed, Herrera would not allow himself to be taken easily. He was now armed and, knowing the man's mettle, I was quite certain that his capture would have to be paid for in blood.

Ironically, it was this very gun which was eventually to prove his undoing. As Holmes and I ran forward, Herrera raised the revolver and took aim.

'Keep back or, by God, I will fire!' he shouted, his finger on the trigger.

At the same moment he began to lower himself backwards over the edge of the wall, letting the rope run free through his left hand and using his feet to thrust himself away from the overhang of the rock face. This impetus sent the rope twisting as if it were suddenly imbued with a life and purpose of its own, swinging his body this way and that like a pendulum out of control.

Holmes and I ran to the railing and, as we peered down, I saw Herrera's face turned up towards us as it swayed to and fro several feet below, his eyes wide with terror and his mouth open on a silent scream. Before we could reach out to help him, his right hand, the one holding the gun, clutched wildly at the rope to save himself from falling.

The next instant a single shot rang out and a red hole appeared just below the left side of his jaw. A second later his body went hurtling into the ravine to disappear from sight among the rocks and the tangle of vegetation.

Ten

It was not until two hours later that Holmes had the opportunity to give the Grice Patersons a full account of that morning's dreadful events. In the meantime, the porter had been despatched in the hotel's wagonette to Stranhyde for extra men to help carry the bodies of Herrera and Miss Gordon from the ravine. Both corpses were then placed on trestles in an outhouse to await the arrival of the police from Oban, a messenger having been sent there with a letter from Holmes, explaining the situation. They were not expected to arrive until the following morning.

While waiting for the men from Stranhyde, Holmes, with my help, had searched Miss Gordon's room. We had found certain documents and letters which added new information, such as her real identity, to those facts which Holmes had already deduced.

'She was Señora Elizabeth Herrera, née Rankin, the widow of Julio Herrera,' Holmes began as the four of us sat in our client's room, Mrs Grice Paterson having joined us on this occasion to hear Holmes's account. 'After the execution of her husband, she fled to Mexico and from there travelled to England under the name of Mary Gordon. Her intention was, of course, to avenge her husband's death on you, Mr Grice Paterson, because it was your evidence in court which had proved his guilt.

'Tracking you down last year in London was relatively easy and she could have shot you there, but it meant waiting outside your house for an opportunity and that would have looked suspicious. She also ran the risk of being seen by witnesses who could later testify against her. It was while she was thinking over the problem that she discovered you and your wife spent every August on the island of Uffa.

'I still do not know exactly how she found this out. Perhaps she followed you to Euston and, by bribing the porter who carried your luggage, learned it was labelled with the name and address of this hotel. Or she may have called at your house in your absence and managed to obtain the information from one of the servants.

'It was about this same time, I believe, that she received a letter from her brother-in-law, Gustafo Herrera, telling of his escape from prison and giving his address in New York where he was then living. She wrote to him there, suggesting he come to London.

'His arrival meant, of course, that she now had an accomplice who was as determined as she to avenge Julio Herrera's death. With his help, the proposed murder could now be refined to a more sophisticated and personal killing than a mere shooting down of her intended victim in the street. For, Mr Grice Paterson, she wanted you to know that you were under sentence of death, just as her husband had known, and to have the exquisite pleasure of witnessing your suffering, and your wife's as well. That was impossible in London. But what if the murder took place in or near the Glencastle Hotel on Uffa?

'Consequently, last summer Señora Herrera took a room at the hotel under her assumed name, the purpose being to inspect the island as a possible setting for the crime and to establish herself here as a perfectly harmless spinster who was unfortunately crippled and therefore would not be suspected of playing an active role in your subsequent death. It was during that first visit she learned that the crofter's cottage was to let.'

'I was going to ask how she managed to find that out,' Grice Paterson remarked.

'I questioned the hotel proprietor on that very point,' my old friend replied. 'It was quite simple. It seems Miss Gordon, or rather Señora Herrera, hired the hotel gig one afternoon to drive down to the harbour where she wanted to sketch. A postcard advertising the cottage was pinned up on a noticeboard outside the tavern for all to see.'

'I apologise for interrupting you,' said our client. 'Pray continue, Mr Holmes.'

'I shall be as brief as I can. By the time Señora Herrera left Uffa last summer, she already had in mind a rough outline of how your murder was to be carried out with Gustafo's assistance. He would rent the cottage under the name of Kemp while she would return to the hotel as Miss Gordon and continue her routine of sketching every day from the lower terrace. The sight of her white sunshade would not only dissuade other guests from using the terrace but would convince any casual observer that she remained seated under it, engrossed in her drawing.

'Meanwhile, Gustafo would deliver the threatening letters and the parcel to the hotel at night. It was at this point that she made her first mistake. By giving Gustafo one of the hotel's copies of *The Times* from which to compose the threatening letters, she made me suspect that he might have an accomplice at Glencastle.

'Gustafo had another part to play in the scheme. He was to draw attention to himself by appearing on the cliff top, thereby making himself a prime suspect, but when questioned about the crime he would be able to prove he had an alibi. To do this he had to appear at the hotel several times *before* the murder was committed, thus establishing a pattern of behaviour. It would have looked suspicious if the only occasion he visited the place was at the very time of your death.'

'So that was why Dr Watson saw him in the bar late yesterday afternoon?' Grice Paterson enquired.

'Exactly so. Of course, the plan was that yesterday's visit was to be the first of several. But it aroused my suspicions. It was then I decided to take matters into my own hands. By asking you to announce your imminent departure and your intention of taking a last morning swim at the beach, I forced them to act more quickly than they had anticipated.

'I do not know how Señora Herrera passed this information on to Gustafo, although they must have had some means of communication. Most probably she left messages for him hidden at the lower terrace which he picked up at night. However it was arranged, Gustafo was warned of your decision to leave and in consequence their own plans had to be brought forward.

'I suggest the murder was originally timed to take place next week, after Gustafo had established his habit of visiting the hotel and you yourself, Mr Grice Paterson, having not seen the mysterious stranger on the cliff top for several days or received any more threatening letters, had assumed that the danger was over and it was safe to resume taking your customary swim. Nevertheless, even though the timing had to be altered, they decided to carry out the plan as arranged.

'I am sure you, Mr Grice Paterson, and also Dr Watson, are aware of what that plan entailed. Miss Gordon would settle herself as usual on the lower terrace with her artist's equipment, taking with her in her satchel more suitable footwear to replace the shoes she was wearing, one of which had a raised heel as part of her pretence of being crippled. Having positioned the parasol so that it would hide her movements, she then put on the cloak and hat which Gustafo had hidden in the bushes last night. With the clothing, he had also left a length of rope which she used to lower herself over the railings. By this means, she contrived to descend the steepest part of the gorge without too much difficulty. Having reached the bottom, she then crossed the stream and climbed up the far side, almost certainly with the help of another rope. That can be ascertained later when the police arrive and the ravine can be properly examined. Herrera was, of course, waiting for her at the top to hand over the revolver.

'At this point the two of them parted company, Herrera crossing the ravine by the bridge and continuing on to the hotel where, as I have already learned from the hotel staff, he sat in the drawing room, drinking coffee and reading *The Times*. He then strolled up and down the terrace, thereby establishing his alibi. Witnesses would be prepared to swear that at the time of your murder, Mr Grice Paterson, he was nowhere near the scene of the crime.

'In the meantime, Señora Herrera had crossed the cliff top to that point which directly overlooked the pool where I, acting under your guise, was undressing behind the rocks, her intention being to shoot at the first opportunity I, or rather my alter ego, provided.'

'You are referring to some kind of dummy you set up behind the rocks, are you not?' I enquired.

'Of course, my dear fellow. But as Mr Grice Paterson has not yet seen it, I had better explain,' Holmes replied. 'Last night I crept out of the hotel with one of my shirts and a pillowcase, both of which I stuffed with heather, tying the pillowcase on top of the shirt to serve as a head. I then left the mannikin hidden among the rocks by the pool. After I had taken my swim, I draped your linen jacket round it and placed your panama on its head, propping it up so that the head and shoulders were visible above the rocks. To anyone watching from the cliff top, it would appear that it was you, Mr Grice Paterson. To add to the verisimilitude, I deliberately raised my hand to adjust the panama.'

'But the head moved as well, Holmes!' I interjected. 'How on earth did you create that effect?'

'Oh, that!' Holmes laughed heartily. 'It was exceedingly simple! I had stiffened the head with a piece of driftwood to which I attached two lengths of string – the same string, incidentally, which was tied round the parcel containing the sheep's skull. By gently pulling on the strings, I was able to move the head like that of a marionette.

'I should add that, up to that moment, I was still not certain who would carry out the murder, Miss Gordon or Lomax the ornithologist, both of whom seemed likely candidates. I kept watch through a crevice between the rocks and as soon as the assassin appeared on the cliff top I knew exactly who it must be. The figure was tall; Lomax is short.

'At the same moment it came to me in a flash precisely how Miss Gordon, alias Señora Herrera, was going to carry out her plan and establish her own alibi. She would return through the ravine to the lower terrace where she would divest herself of the cloak and hat, leaving them concealed somewhere for Gustafo to collect later and destroy. She would also untie the rope from the rail and hide that as well. When the porter came to carry her artist's equipment back to the hotel at the agreed time of half past eleven, it would appear that she had been sketching there all morning.

'Meanwhile, you, Mrs Grice Paterson, would have grown increasingly uneasy about your husband's absence and would have raised the alarm. The hotel proprietor would have sent someone to the beach where your husband's body would have been found. But when the police arrived from Oban to question everybody, both Miss Gordon and Mr Kemp, despite the latter's suspicious behaviour, would be ruled out as suspects as both had perfect alibis.'

At this point the hotel proprietor knocked on the door to announce the arrival of the men from Stranhyde. Holmes and I left to help with the melancholy task of retrieving the bodies.

There is little more I wish to add to this account. After the police arrived the next morning and had taken statements from us all, Holmes and I, together with the Grice Patersons, returned to London.

I understand from Mycroft Holmes that the Grice Patersons never went back to Uffa, preferring to spend their holidays on another Scottish island where the scenery is as beautiful but where there is nothing to remind them of their terrible ordeal of that August of 1887 and its tragic consequences.